D0438016

WIT'CH STAR

Also by James Clemens

Wit'ch Fire
Wit'ch Storm
Wit'ch War
Wit'ch Gate

WIT'CH

STAR

James Clemens

WITHDRAWN

BALLANTINE BOOKS | NEW YORK

To Spencer Orey,
for keeping the magic alive in a new generation

A Del Rey® Book
Published by The Ballantine Publishing Group
Copyright © 2002 by Jim Czajkowski

www.delreydigital.com

Library of Congress Cataloging-in-Publication Data is available
upon request from the publisher.

ISBN 0-345-44245-8

Manufactured in the United States of America

First Edition: December 2002

10 9 8 7 6 5 4 3 2 1

ACKNOWLEDGMENTS

Thanks to all the friends and family who made this journey through Alasea possible, especially one group of devoted colleagues: Chris Crowe, Michael Gallowglas, Lee Garrett, Dennis Grayson, Penny Hill (thanks for the pens!), Debbie Nelson, Dave Meek, Jane O'Riva, Chris Smith, Jude and Steve Prey, Carolyn McCray, Caroline Williams, Royale Adams, and Jean Colgrove. Additionally, a special thanks to everyone at Del Rey, past and present, who have made it a joy to tell Elena's story: Steve Saffel, Denise Fitzer, Kuo-Yu Liang, Colleen Lindsay, Kathleen O'Shea, Chris Schluep, and especially Veronica Chapman, who guided me on every step of this journey. And lastly, of course, my dedicated agents, here and abroad, Russ Galen and Danny Baror.

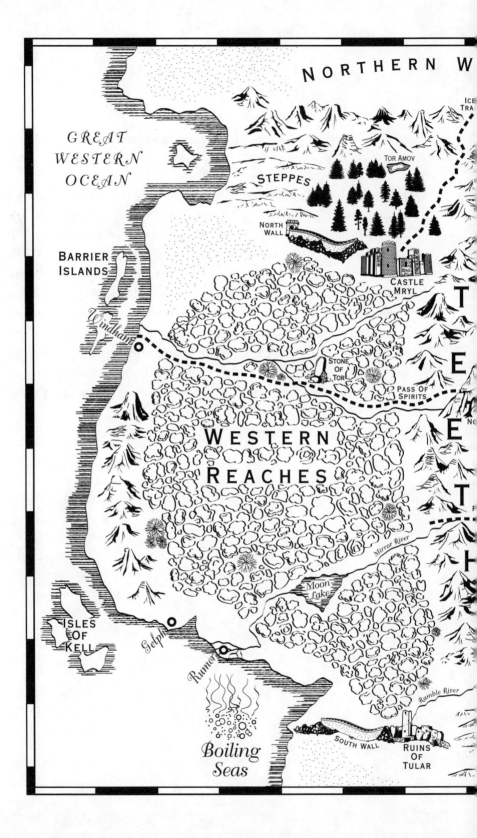

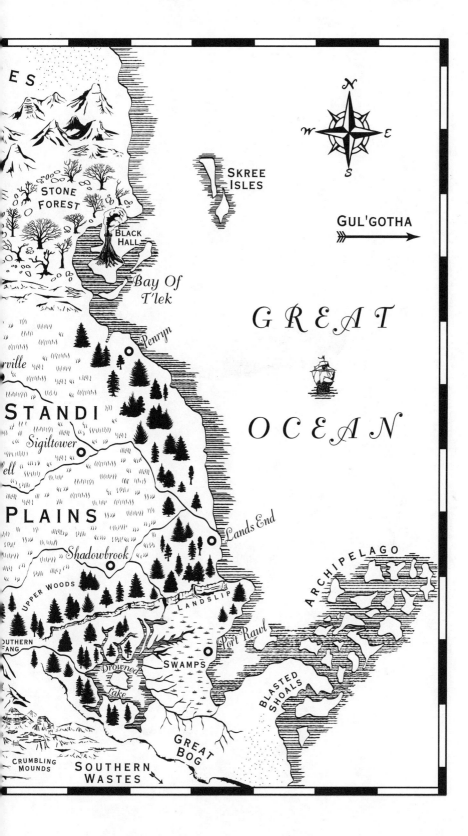

FOREWORD

by
Jir'rob Sordun, D.F.S., M.A.,
Director of University Studies (U.D.B.)

As I prefaced the first book, so for this last book.

No word of warning will be given here; there is no advantage to be gained. In your hands, you hold the last of the Kelvish Scrolls, the final blasphemies of the madman from the Isles of Kell. Either you are prepared to withstand what's to come, or you are not. Either you will gain the crimson sash of graduation, or you will swing at the gallows of Au'tree. So why speak now?

The answer is simple: *Now is the moment for the final truth to be spoken.*

Ahead of each student lies either death or salvation. It is time to cast aside falsehoods and misconceptions for a true understanding of our past . . . and our future. Before you join the inner cabal of Commonwealth scholars, a final revelation must be bared . . . a truth you must come to understand before undertaking this last journey into the mind of a madman.

And what is this truth?

The author is *not* a liar.

Though this may seem contradictory to prior warnings, it is in fact *not* a contradiction. Fundamentally, and in many ways, the author can be construed as a liar—as stated in previous forewords and instructions. But from a *historical* context, the madman speaks the truth. Ancient forbidden texts corroborate and substantiate the histories of the wit'ch named Elena Morin'stal. She existed as a real figure who shaped our world. The stories in the Scrolls are not fantasies, but realities—our *true* past.

But therein lies the danger. The final act of the wit'ch, as you will read, threatens our entire society. Its revelation could bring ruin and madness to all the corridors of the Commonwealth. Thus the Scrolls must be kept hidden from the unschooled masses.

This course of study is to prepare you to be guardians of the Commonwealth. Certain truths are too poisonous for the uninitiated. To protect society as a whole, these truths must be nullified, discredited, and disavowed.

This is the reason you have been trained these past four years to disbelieve what you have been reading and studying. From here, you must walk a fine line between reality and fantasy.

The wit'ch existed. She shaped our world. Here the madman of Kell did not lie.

However, the author remains a liar on a much broader level. The final act of the wit'ch, the physical act, can be believed—but *not* the consequence. Here is the ultimate falsehood, the danger to society that lurks in simple words spoken atop Winter's Eyrie. The words were spoken—but were they indeed the truth?

I put to you that ultimately it does not matter. Truth or lie, the words remain damnable to the Commonwealth. Hence, the entire life of the wit'ch must be repudiated. It is the safest course for all.

Consequently, as you read this last book, you must accept two contradictory truths:

The author is a liar.

The author is not a liar.

A true scholar must learn to walk between these two lines. Only death and ruin lie outside.

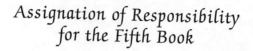

Assignation of Responsibility
for the Fifth Book

This copy is being assigned to you and is your sole responsibility. Its loss, alteration, or destruction will result in severe penalties (as stated in your local ordinances). Any transmission, copying, or even oral reading in the presence of a nonclassmate is strictly forbidden. By signing below and placing your fingerprint, you accept all responsibility and release the university from any damage the text may cause you (or those around you) by its perusal.

_____   _____
Signature   Date

Place inked print of the fifth
finger of your right hand here:

*** WARNING ***

If you should perchance come upon this text outside of proper university channels, please close this book now and alert the proper authorities for safe retrieval. Failure to do so can lead to your immediate arrest and incarceration.

YOU HAVE BEEN WARNED.

WIT'CH STAR

With the passing of the long night

comes magick's last light.

IT IS STRANGE TO DREAM OF DEATH ON A BRIGHT SPRING DAY.

All around the Isles of Kell, life freshens to the warming sun. From the coastal beaches, children's laughter tinkles on the breezes as the days stretch longer. The hills glow with green, and flowers spread soft petals to the touch of new light. Shutters are thrown back, and window boxes are planted. It is a time of rebirth.

But I stare out from my garret at brightness and know that death is a penstroke away. A flourish of ink and I am gone. The promise of the wit'ch to free me from the endless march of seasons has never felt more real. I savor it at as I sit.

On my desk, I have gathered the tools of my trade and have spared no expense in their purchase, shedding my wealth like a snake's skin. The finest parchment from Windham, the smoothest ink procured by the traders in Da'bau, the handsome quills from the snowy egrets that wade through the canal city of Que-quay across the sea.

All is in readiness, awaiting one last tale to tell. Like an alchemist, I will conjure death from ink and parchment.

But I find myself waiting. Dust gathers across the rolled parchment and tiny glass jars of ink. Why? Not because I doubt the promise of the wit'ch or fear death on this spring day. Indeed, at first I thought I merely savored the end, holding it off like an exquisite torture.

But I was wrong. The reason was far simpler.

It came to me this morning as I gazed at a branch outside my garret window, where a small kak'ora had built her feathered nest. The mother bird's plumage is a brilliant black with a bright red breast, as if her throat has been slashed. She spends the day hunting flittering insects or rooting in the dirt between the cobbles on the street below. This leaves her nest mostly empty, exposing her trio of eggs to my hollow gaze.

For several days, I'd studied this tiny clutch, suspecting some mystery to solve in their smooth shells, in the small brown specklings against the blue background. But what?

It dawned on me this morning. Each egg is a symbol of life's endless possibilities. What path lies ahead for these fledglings? They all might die before hatching, suffocating in their own shells. Or one might be caught by a prowling cat as it learns to fly, another might waste of disease or starvation—or return next spring to this same nest to start a new family, starting the cycle all over again. So much potential, so many paths, all nestled in eggs no larger than my thumb.

Life's endless possibilities . . . that is what I discovered this morning.

What does it mean to me? Am I to cast aside my pursuit of death and embrace life again?

No . . . certainly not.

As I stared at those eggs, I realized that it was not potential that makes life worth living, but the discovery of one's own unique path through life—from womb to grave—that brings significance to one's existence.

What I begged of the wit'ch, what she granted to me as both boon and curse—endless life—was a mockery. When all the ages stretch infinitely in front of you, the potential and possibilities in life become endless. When all paths are open to you, you become merely potential—never real. With so many paths, it is easy to lose oneself.

No longer. This morning, staring at those eggs, I knew that I had tired of potential, and wanted only to see my life defined again.

A beginning, a middle, and an *end*.

The sum total of life—and I want it back.

So once again I join ink to paper, conjuring life and worlds through the alchemy of the printed word. Each letter brings me closer to death, closer to bringing meaning back to my life.

Did the wit'ch know this truth even back then? Had she offered me this one last chance to touch grace?

We will see.

Already I drift back to another time, a distant place. Follow me toward the jangle of bells, as one last player steps onto the stage, a latecomer to the festivities. Do you see him? The fellow with the blue skin, all dressed in motley and playing the fool.

Watch him closely . . .

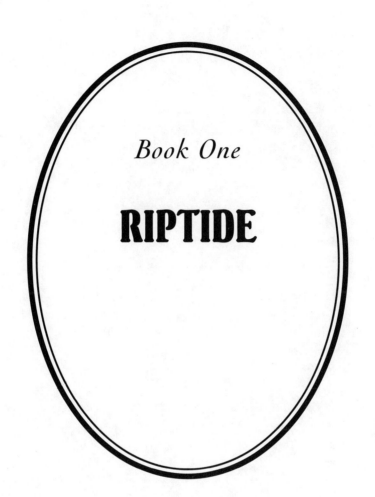

Book One

RIPTIDE

1

Seated on the Rosethorn Throne, Elena studied the riddle before her. The small stranger, dressed in a patchwork of silks and linens, appeared just a boy with his smooth and unlined face—but he was clearly no youngster. His manner was too calm under the gazes of those gathered in the Great Hall. His eyes glinted with sarcastic amusement, bitter and road-worn. And the set of his lips, shadowing a smile, remained both hard and cold.

Elena felt a twinge of unease near the man, despite his illusion of innocence.

The stranger dropped to one knee before her, sweeping off his foppish hat. Scores of bells—tin, silver, gold, and copper, sewn throughout his clothes—jangled brightly.

A taller figure stepped to the tiny man's side—Prince Tylamon Royson, lord of Castle Mryl to the north. The prince-turned-pirate had forgone his usual finery and wore scuffed boots and a salt-scarred black cloak. His cheeks were ruddy, and his sandy hair was unkempt. He had arrived at the island's docks with the rising sun, requesting immediate audience with Elena and the war council.

The prince bowed to one knee, then motioned to the stranger. "May I present Harlequin Quail? He has come far, with news you should hear."

Elena motioned for them both to stand. "Rise, Lord Tyrus. Be welcome." She studied the newcomer as he rose to his feet amid another chorus of jingling. The man had indeed come from afar. His face was oddly complexioned: a paleness that bordered on blue, as if he were forever suffocating. But it was the hue of his eyes that was the most striking—a shining gold, full of a wry slyness.

"I'm sorry for disturbing you so early on this summer morning," Lord Tyrus intoned formally, straightening his disheveled cloak as if noticing for the first time his sorry state.

Er'ril, Elena's liegeman and husband, spoke from his station beside the throne. "What is this urgency, Lord Tyrus? We have no time for fools and jesters."

Elena did not have to glance to the side to know the Standi plainsman wore his usual hard scowl. She had seen it often enough over the last two moons as sour tidings had been flowing into Alasea: supply chains to the island cut off by monsters and strange weather; townships struck by fires and plagues; ill-shaped beasts roaming the countryside.

But the worst tidings struck closer to home.

Elementals, those rare folk tuned to the Land's energy, were succumbing to some dread malaise. The mer'ai were losing their sea sense and their link to their dragons; the elv'in ships could not fly as high or far; and now Nee'lahn reported that the voice of her lute was growing weaker as the tree spirit faded inside. Clearly whatever damage had been inflicted upon the Land by the Weirgates was continuing its onslaught. Elemental magicks waned as if from a bleeding wound.

As a consequence, the press of dwindling time weighed upon them all. If they were to act against the Gul'gotha, it must be soon—before their own forces weakened further, before the gifts of the Land faded completely away. But their armies were spread wide. As matters stood, the campaign against the Dark Lord's stronghold, the volcanic Blackhall, could begin no sooner than next spring. Er'ril said it would take until midwinter to position all their armies; and an assault upon the island then, when the northern seas were beset with savage storms, would give the advantage to Blackhall.

So spring at the earliest, when the winter storms died away.

Elena had begun to doubt whether they'd be ready even then. So much was still unknown. Tol'chuk had yet to return from his own lands; gone these past two moons with Fardale and a handful of others, he sought to question his og're elders about the link between heartstone and ebon'stone. Many of the elv'in scoutships had not returned from reconnaissance over Blackhall. The d'warf army, led by Wennar, had sent crows with news that their forces yet gathered near Penryn. The d'warf captain wanted more time to rally his people. But time was short for all of them.

And now this urgent news from afar.

Lord Tyrus turned to his companion. "Harlequin, tell them what you've learned."

The tiny figure nodded. "I come with tidings both bright and grim." A coin appeared in his hand as if conjured from nothing. With the flick of a wrist, he tossed it high into the air. Torchlight glinted off gold.

Elena's gaze tracked the coin's flight as it danced among the rafters, then fell. She startled back on her throne upon finding the strange man now toe-to-toe before her, leaning in. He had crossed the distance in a heartbeat, silent despite the hundred bells he wore.

Even Er'ril was caught by surprise. With a roar, he swept out his sword and bared it between queen and jester. "What trick is this?"

As answer, the man caught the falling coin in an outstretched palm, winked salaciously at Elena, then backed down the two steps, again jangling with a chorus of bells.

Lord Tyrus spoke up, a cold smile on his face. "Be not fooled by Harlequin's motley appearance. For these past ten winters, he has been my master spy, in service to the Pirate Guild of Port Rawl. There are no better eyes and ears to sneak upon others unaware."

Elena straightened in her seat. "So it would seem."

Er'ril pulled back his sword but did not sheathe it. "Enough tricks. If he comes with information, let's hear it."

"As the iron man asks, so it shall be." Harlequin held up his gold coin to the flash of torchlight. "First the bright news. You've cut the Black Heart a deeper wound than even you suspect by the destruction of his black statues. He's lost his precious d'warf army and is left with only men and monsters to defend his volcanic lair."

Tyrus interrupted. "Harlequin has spent the last half winter scouting the edges of Blackhall. He's prepared charts and logs of the Dark Lord's forces and strengths."

"How did he come by these?" Er'ril grumbled.

Harlequin stared brazenly back. "From under the nose of the Dark Lord's own lieutenant. A brother of yours, is he not?"

Elena glanced to Er'ril and saw the anger in his eye.

"He is *not* my brother," her liegeman said coldly.

Elena spoke into the tension. "You were inside Blackhall itself?"

Harlequin's mask of amusement cracked. Elena spotted a glimpse of something pained and darker beyond. "Aye," he whispered. "I've walked its monstrous halls and shadowed rooms—and pray I never do so again."

Elena leaned forward. "And you mentioned grim news, Master Quail?"

"Grim news indeed." Harlequin lifted his arm and opened the fingers that had clenched around the gold coin. Upon his palm now rested a lump of coal. "If you wish to defeat the Black Heart, it must be done by Midsummer Eve."

Elena frowned. "In one moon's time?"

"Impossible," Er'ril scoffed.

Harlequin fixed Elena with those strange gold eyes. "If you don't stop the Black Beast by the next full moon, you will all be dead."

MERIC RAN THE LENGTH OF THE *STORMWING*. HIS FEET FLEW ACROSS THE FAmiliar planks, hurdling balustrades and leaping decks. His eyes remained fixed to the skies. Through the morning mists, a dark speck was visible high overhead, plummeting gracelessly out of the sky. It was one of the elv'in scoutships, returning from the lands and seas around the volcanic island of Blackhall.

Something was wrong.

Reaching the prow of his own ship, Meric lifted both arms and cast out his powers. A surge of energy billowed through his form and into the sky, racing upward to flow into the empty well that was the other's boat's iron keel. Meric fed his power, but the plummeting ship continued its dive toward the waters around A'loa Glen.

As he fought the inevitable, Meric felt the weight of the other ship upon his own shoulders. He was driven to one knee as the *Stormwing*, drained of its own magickal energies, began to drift lower toward the docks.

Gasping in his exertions, Meric refused to relent. *Mother above, help me!*

He now saw with two sets of eyes: a pair looking up and a pair looking down. Linked between the two ships, he felt the weak beat of the ship's captain, Frelisha—a second cousin to his mother. She was barely alive. She must have drained all her energies to bring the ship even this close to home.

Below, Meric whispered into the wind. "Do not give up, Cousin."

He was heard. Through his magickal connection, the last words of the captain reached him. "We are betrayed!"

With this final utterance, the heartbeat held between Meric's upraised hands fluttered once more, then stopped forever.

"No!" Meric fell to his other knee.

A moment later, a huge shadow shot past the starboard rail. The explosion of wood and blast of water nearby were a distant echo. Meric slumped to his planks, head hanging. As alarm bells clanged along the docks and shouts rose in a chorus of panic, one word whispered from his lips: "Betrayed . . ."

SEATED IN THE GRAND COURTYARD OF THE CASTLE KEEP, NEE'LAHN WATCHED the children pause in their play as bells rang along the docks beyond the stone walls. Her own fingers stopped in midstrum on the strings of her lute.

Something had happened at the docks.

A few steps away, little Rodricko lowered his stick, a pretend sword, and glanced to his mother. His opponent in this playful sparring match—the Dre'rendi child Sheeshon—cocked her head at the noise, her own fake sword forgotten.

Nee'lahn rolled to her knees and swung her lute over a shoulder, bumping the thin trunk of the koa'kona behind her. Leaves shook overhead. The fragile sapling was thin-limbed and top-heavy with summer leaves—not unlike the male child that was its bonded twin.

"Rodricko, come away," Nee'lahn said, reaching out to the boy. Rodricko was all limbs and awkwardness. *Thank the Mother, his initial growth surge is about over.* Both tree and boy would grow into their forms more gradually from here.

"Sheeshon, you too," Nee'lahn added. "Let's see if the kitchens are ready with your porridge."

As Nee'lahn straightened, she dug her bare toes into the rich loam at the base of the tree and took strength from the energy in the soil. She readied herself to enter the stone halls of the castle. Reluctant to leave, she drew the strength of root deep inside her.

Around them, the gardens of the Grand Courtyard were in the full bloom of summer. Tiny white flowers garlanded the ivy-encrusted walls. The dogwoods stood amid cloaks of fallen petals. Red berries dotted the trimmed bushes that lined the crushed white-gravel paths. Most glorious of all were the hundreds of rosebushes, newly planted last fall. They had blossomed into a riot of colors: blushing pinks, dusky purples, honeyed yellows. Even the sea breezes were given color and substance by their sweet fragrances.

But it was more than beauty that held her here, for only in this courtyard were her past, present, and future gathered in one place: the lute that held the heart of her own beloved, the sapling that sprang from the seed of her bonded, and the boy who represented all the hopes of the nyphai people.

Sighing, Nee'lahn tousled the mop of sun-bleached curls atop Rodricko's head and took the boy's hand. So much hope in such a little package.

Sheeshon reached to take Rodricko's other hand, the webbed folds between the Dre'rendi girl's fingers marking her as a link between the seafaring Bloodriders and the ocean-dwelling mer'ai. Rodricko joined hands with her. Over the past moons, the two children, alike in their uniqueness, had become all but inseparable.

"Let's see if the kitchens are ready," Nee'lahn said, turning.

She stepped away, but Rodricko seemed to have taken root in the soil. "Mama, what about the bud song? You promised I could try."

Nee'lahn opened her mouth to object. She was anxious to learn what had arisen at the docks, but already the alarm bells were echoing away.

"You promised," Rodricko repeated.

Nee'lahn frowned, then glanced to the tree. She had promised. It was indeed time he learned his own song, but she was hesitant, reluctant to let Rodricko go.

"I'm old enough. And this night the moon is full!"

Nee'lahn found no way to object. Traditionally among the nyphai, the first full moon of summer was when the young bonded with their new trees, when babe and seed became woman and tree.

"Are you sure you're ready, Rodricko?"

"He's ready," Sheeshon answered, her small eyes surprisingly certain. Nee'lahn had heard the child was rich in sea magicks, an ability to sense beyond the horizons to what's to come. The *rajor maga*, it was termed by the Dre'rendi.

"Please, Mama," Rodricko begged.

The dock bells had gone silent.

"You may try the bud song; then it's off to the kitchens before the cook gets angry."

Rodricko's face brightened like a sun coming through the clouds. He turned to Sheeshon. "Come on. I have to get ready."

Sheeshon, always the more sober child, frowned. "You must hurry, if we have to finish before the kitchen closes."

Nee'lahn nodded. "Go ahead, but don't be disappointed if you fail. Maybe next summer . . ."

Rodricko nodded, though clearly deaf to her words. He crossed to the tree and knelt on limbs nearly as thin as the sapling's branches. Now would be the moment when all the fates would either come together or fall into disarray, for Rodricko was the first male nyphai. Both sapling and boy were unique, the result of the union of Nee'lahn's tree and the twisted Grim wraith Cecelia. Who knew if the ancient rites, songs, and patterns of growth would hold true here?

Nee'lahn held her breath.

Rodricko touched the tree's bark, drawing a fingernail down through the thin outer coating. A droplet of sap flowed, and the sapling's treesong rose up from its deep thrum and quested out for Rodricko. Nee'lahn listened with both ears and heart. The boy was either attuned to the song, or he would be rebuffed. She was not sure which she hoped. A part of her wanted him to fail. She had been given so little time with him, less than a single winter . . .

Rodricko used a rose thorn to prick a finger, drawing blood. He reached his wounded finger toward the flow of sap.

"Sing," she whispered. "Let the tree hear your heart."

He glanced over his shoulder toward her, his eyes shining with his fear. The boy sensed the weight of the moment.

Sing, she willed to him silently.

And he did. His lips parted, and as he exhaled, the sweetest notes flowed forth. His voice was so bright that the sun seemed to grow pale in comparison. The world grew dark around the edges, as if night had come early, but around the sapling, a pool of luminescence grew brighter and brighter.

In response, the sapling's own song swelled, like a flower drawn to the sun. At first tentatively, then more fully, boy and sapling became transfixed in treesong.

At that moment, Nee'lahn knew the boy would succeed. Tears flowed down her cheeks with both relief and loss. There was no turning back. Nee'lahn could feel the surge of elemental magick from boy and tree, one feeding on the other, building until it was impossible to say where one began and the other ended.

Two songs became one.

Nee'lahn found herself on her knees without realizing she had moved. Treesong filled the world. She had never heard such a chorus before.

She craned up at the thin branches; she knew what would come next. Leaves began to shake as if from a strong breeze. Each branch tip throbbed with treesong and elemental energy. And still tree and boy sang in harmony, voices louder, strained, beautiful, expectant.

With nowhere else to go, the magick trapped in the tips of each branch had only one course left to follow.

From the end of each tiny branch, buds pushed from stems, growing from magick and blood: petaled expressions of the treesong brought to existence by the union of boy and sapling.

He—they—had done it.

A gasp escaped from Rodricko, both joy and pain.

Slowly the treesong faded, as if draining down a well, exhausted. The summer sun returned to the courtyard.

Rodricko turned, his small face shining with joy and pride. "I did it, Mama." His voice was now deeper, richer, almost a man's voice. But he was no man. She heard the lilt of magick behind his voice. He was nyphai. He turned back to his tree. "We are now one."

Nee'lahn remained silent, her gaze fixed on the tree. *What have we done?* she thought silently. *Sweet Mother, what have we done?*

Hanging from the tips of each branch were indeed the buds of new union. They would open for the first time this evening with the rising of the summer's first moon. But Rodricko's flowers were not the bright violet of the nyphai, jewels among the greenery. Instead, from each tip hung buds the color of clotted blood, black and bruised—the same night shade as the Grim wraiths.

Nee'lahn covered her face and began to sob.

"Mama," Rodricko spoke at her side, "what's wrong?"

DEEP BELOW THE GRAND COURTYARD, JOACH SLOUCHED ALONG A NARROW tunnel. It had taken him a full moon's time to find this hidden path. Much of the secret tunnel system under the Edifice had fallen to ruin, destroyed during the awakening of Ragnar'k from his stony sleep. Joach remembered that day: his own harrowing escape from Greshym's enthrallment, his flight with Brother Moris, the battle at the heart of the island. Though less than two winters had passed, it now seemed like ages. He was an old man, his youth stolen from him.

Joach rested, leaning heavily upon his stone staff, a length of petrified gray wood impregnated with green crystals. The end of the stave glowed with a sickly aether, lighting his way. It was the only bit of dark magick left in the dread thing.

His fingers tightened on the staff, sensing the feeble trickle of power remaining. He had struck a bad bargain with Greshym for this length of petrified wood. It had cost Joach his youth, leaving him a wrinkled and brittle version of himself. Standing now deep underground, Joach felt the weight of rock overhead press upon his thin shoulders. His heart pounded in his ears. It had taken him all morning to climb the long-hidden stair to reach here.

"Only a little way more," he promised himself.

Fueled by determination, he continued, praying the chamber he sought was still intact. As he reached the tunnel's end, he used the stump of his right wrist to shove aside a tangle of withered roots hanging across the threshold. They crumbled away at his touch.

He lifted his staff forward.

Beyond, a cavernous chamber opened.

Joach wheezed with relief, and limped past the threshold. Overhead, roots and fibrous stragglers hung like swamp moss, yellow and brittle. Rodricko's thin sapling, above, had yet to send its young roots down into this cavernous tomb. Here death still reigned.

Joach found a certain solace in that gloomy realization. Beyond the castle walls, the summer days were too bright, too green, too full of rebirth. He preferred the shadows.

Exhausted, knees complaining, he advanced. The chamber floor was strewn with boulders and the moldering corpses of the dead. Tiny furred and scaled creatures scurried from his staff's sickly light. Joach ignored the scavengers and lifted his staff. Old scars marked the walls, from the swaths of the balefire wielded by Shorkan and Greshym during the battle. They looked like some ancient writing in charcoal.

If only he could understand it . . .

Joach sighed. So much remained closed to him. He had spent the past two moons holed up in the libraries and nooks, poring over texts, scrolls, and manuscripts. If he ever hoped to regain his youth, he needed to understand the magick that had stolen it. But he was a mere apprentice to the Black Arts, far from true understanding. He had only managed to glean one clue: *Ragnar'k*.

Before joining with Kast, the dragon had slumbered in stone at the heart of the island for untold ages, growing rich with the elemental magick of the dream, imbuing the rocks and crystals here with its energies. Any hope of regaining his own youth lay in the mystery of the dreaming magick. Joach had lost his youth in the dream desert—his youth and one other thing.

He closed his eyes, again feeling the flow of blood across his hand, the slightest gasp in his ear. "Kesla," he whispered out to the cavern of the dead. She too had been like Ragnar'k, a creature of dream.

If all his pain arose out of dream landscape, perhaps his cure lay there, too. This frail hope had finally driven him down into the bowels of the island.

He had a plan.

Using his staff as a crutch, Joach limped over bones and around boulders. Though Ragnar'k was long gone, the dragon had slept in this chamber for so long that every stone, every bit of broken crystal, had been imbued with its magick. Joach planned to tap this elemental power.

Like Greshym, Joach was a dreamweaver. But unlike the darkmage, Joach was also a dream *sculptor*, with the ability to craft substance out of dream. If Joach hoped to take on Greshym and steal back his youth, he would need to hone his skill. But to do that, he first needed energy. He needed the power of the dream.

Joach crossed to the center of the half-collapsed chamber and slowly turned in a circle, studying the room. He sensed the abundance of energy here. Satisfied, he shifted his staff to the crook of his stumped right arm and slipped out a dagger. Clenching the hilt between his teeth, he sliced his left palm. As the blood welled, he spat out the dagger and lifted his wounded hand. Squeezing a fist, he dribbled blood onto the stone floor. Drops splattered at his feet.

Ready, Joach let his eyes drift half closed, slipping into the dream state. The dark chamber grew fitfully brighter, as swaths of rock and wall took on the soft luminescence of residual energies—echoes of the dragon's dream.

A smile formed on Joach's thin lips.

Reaching out with the magick in his own blood, he tied the energies to himself, weaving it all together as was his birthright. Once all was secure, Joach grabbed up his staff again with his bloodied left hand. He lifted the weapon and again slowly turned in a circle, drawing the magick into the staff. He turned and turned, dizzying himself, but did not stop until every dreg of magick was siphoned into the length of stony wood, weaving stone and magick together.

As he worked, the staff grew cold to the touch, trembling with pent-up power. The crystals along the staff's length glowed with brilliance, flaring brighter, even as the cavern grew dimmer.

Soon there was nothing but darkness around Joach.

Satisfied, he lowered the staff and leaned upon it, his legs wobbling and weak. He stared at his crutch. The green crystals there gleamed with a sharp radiance. Joach's shoulders shook with relief. He had done it! He had bound the energy to the staff.

All that was left was to bind the staff to *him*, to give him the skill to

wield it to its fullest extent. Dreamweaving alone could not do the binding that he needed. A deeper connection was necessary, and he knew a
way—an old spell, and one that came with a high cost, as did all things
powerful. But what were a few more winters lost, when so many more
had already been stolen from him? Besides, he had been involved in this
same spell before, when it had been cast by Elena and forged upon
Greshym's old staff. So why not once more? Why not cast by his own
hand, and forged upon this new staff, now ripe with dream energies?

To challenge Greshym, he needed a mighty weapon and the skill to use
it. There was only one way to quickly gain such skill.

He must forge the staff into a *blood weapon*.

Joach prepared himself, concentrating on the red dribble trailing down
the staff's surface. It was not a particularly difficult spell, simpler really
than calling forth balefire. It was the cost that gave him pause. He remembered Elena's sudden aging.

But it was too late to look back. Before he could balk, Joach released the
spell in a flow of words and will.

The effect was immediate. He felt something vital rip from him and
pass through his blood into the staff.

Gasping, he fell to his knees. His vision blurred, but he refused to give
himself over to the darkness. He breathed deeply, sucking in air like a
drowning man. Finally his vision cleared. The room slowed its spin.

Joach pulled the staff across his knees, and stared at the hand that
gripped the wood. As with his sister before him, the spell had aged him
instantly. His fingernails had grown out and curled; his skin had crumpled. Had his sacrifice of winters been worth it?

He lifted the staff. The gray wood was now as white as snow. The green
crystals, aglow with dream energies, stood out starkly, like the crimson
streaks flowing from the withered hand that held it. With each thud of his
heart, the streaks flowed farther down the shaft, fusing staff and body,
forging weapon to wielder.

Joach hauled himself to his feet. When Elena had forged Greshym's old
staff, Joach had become a skilled warrior with the weapon. Would the
same hold true here? Had the fusion granted him, as he hoped, the ability
to wield the dream magicks now woven to the staff?

Shaking back the sleeve of his cloak, Joach exposed the stump of his
right arm, his hand lost to the blood lust of Greshym's beast. If Joach
could mend that injury, then perhaps there was hope—not only for himself, but for them all. A mighty war was coming, and Joach did not want
to remain behind with the children and the feeble.

He reached out to the staff. As his severed wrist touched the petrified wood, Joach willed his magick—not weaving this time, but *sculpting*.

From the stump of his wrist, a phantom hand bloomed out in wisps and tendrils. Ghostly fingers stretched and gripped the staff. Joach's legs shook, but he used his blood connection with the staff to draw upon the dream energies. Slowly the spirit hand grew solid, gaining substance from his focus and attention. Fingers that had once been ghostly became whole. Joach felt the grain of the staff's wood, the sharp edges of the crystalline stone.

He lifted the staff with his dream-sculpted hand and held it aloft. Blood continued to feed the staff through his conjured hand.

Dream had indeed become substance!

Power thrilled through him. Dark magick and dream energies, now fused, were his to command! He pictured a girl with eyes the color of twilight, and his lips moved in a silent vow of vengeance. He would find Greshym and make him pay for his theft, make them all pay for what Joach had lost among the sands.

Joach lowered the staff, then wrapped his sliced palm and took the staff back up in his gloved grip, severing the connection between flesh and petrified wood. As the blood drained out of the white wood, its length grew gray again. For now, he would keep his new blood weapon a secret.

Joach raised his right arm and stared at the sculpted hand, formed out of elemental energy. It would not do to let this be seen yet, either. There would be too many questions . . . and besides, it drained his precious energies. He waved the hand through the air and unbound the pattern, and like a snuffed candle, the hand wisped out of existence, back to just dream.

Using his staff as a crutch, Joach headed out of the cavern.

There would come a time to reveal his secret. But for now he would keep the knowledge close to his aching heart, next to the memory of a tawny-haired girl with the softest of lips.

IN HER CHAMBER, ELENA SETTLED INTO A CHAIR BY THE COALS OF THE MORN-ing's fire. The others took seats or stood by the hearth. A trio of servants passed mugs filled with kaffee and set out platters of warm oat biscuits, sliced apples, cheeses, and cubes of spiced pork.

Er'ril took up position, close by her shoulder. If Elena turned her head, her cheek could touch the hand that gripped the back of her chair. But now was not the time to lean into his strength. Elena sat with her back straight, gloved hands folded in her lap. She kept the worry from her face. *One moon's time . . .*

Harlequin Quail waited by the fire, staring into the coals as if reading some meaning in their last glow. He fingered a silver bell on his doublet until the servants departed.

The uproar at the council after the stranger's pronouncement had made it impossible to continue. From the angered shouts and blusters of disbelief, the assembly would be deaf to reason until their shock wore off.

Then alarm bells had distracted the assembly momentarily. Word quickly reached them that an elv'in scoutship had crashed into the seas. Elena had called for a break in the war council.

Er'ril mumbled beside her. "Where is Meric?"

"He'll be here," Elena answered.

As if proving her words true, there was a knock on the door. A departing servant opened the way for the elv'in prince. Meric bowed into the room, taking in the others with a quick flick of his eyes.

The high keel of the Bloodriders sat in the chair across from Elena, his long black braid, peppered with gray, over one shoulder. His son, Hunt, stood at his side, tall and stiff-backed, his hawk tattoo bright in the hearth's glow.

The other chair, closer to the fire, was occupied by Master Edyll of the mer'ai. The slender, white-haired elder held a steaming mug between his webbed fingers.

Meric nodded to each leader; then his gaze settled briefly on the motley-clothed stranger standing with Lord Tyrus.

Cocking one eyebrow, he turned to Elena. "I'm sorry I'm late," he said with stiff courtliness. "It took a while to settle things at the docks."

Elena nodded. "What happened? Word is that a ship crashed."

"A scoutship, returning from the north, captained by a cousin of mine." Though Meric's face was locked in his usual stoic countenance, Elena noted the weary glint to his eyes, the mournful cast to his lips. Another member of his family gone. First his brother lost to the deserts, then his mother, who gave her life to save the last refugees of Meric's home city. With the elv'in folk scattered to the winds, Meric was the one to bear the burden of his people here, the last of royal blood. The word "king" was whispered behind his back, but he refused to take up that mantle. "Not until our people are reunited," he had warned all who pressed him. Now another death.

Elena sighed. "I'm sorry, Meric. This war bleeds all of Alasea."

The high keel grumbled from his seat. "Then perhaps we should take the fight to Blackhall before we are bled dry."

Elena knew the Dre'rendi were anxious to turn the prows of their mighty war fleet toward Blackhall. For now, Elena ignored the challenge in the high keel's words. She continued to address Meric. "What happened to your cousin's ship?"

Meric frowned and stared at his toes. "Sy-wen is investigating the wreckage with Ragnar'k as we speak."

Elena sensed Meric was holding back something that disturbed him. "What's wrong?"

Meric's blue eyes sparked sharply from under his silver bangs. "I spoke to Frelisha as the ship tumbled. My cousin died bringing a warning back to us—word of betrayal."

"Betrayal?" Er'ril asked. Elena felt the plainsman's grip tighten on the back of her chair. "What did she mean?"

Meric shook his head. "She died, saying no more."

Elena glanced to Er'ril. His gray eyes were stormy, but his iron countenance melted enough to offer her a reassuring nod.

Master Edyll spoke from near the hearth. "Your cousin's message suggests there is someone in our confidence whom we must not trust."

Elena's gaze flicked to the bell-draped stranger. She was not the only one. The foreigner kept his back to them, staring at the fires, but Lord Tyrus recognized their suspicion.

"I vouch for Harlequin Quail with my own blood," Tyrus said, straightening.

Master Edyll seemed not to hear the pirate's words. He gazed into the dark depths of his mug. "Two messages from the north in one day. One hinting at a need to act swiftly. The other warning to be cautious and wary of those at our side. It does make one wonder which to believe. Maybe—"

A tinkle of bells interrupted the mer'ai elder. Harlequin Quail spun on a heel to face them all. His pale face had reddened; his gold eyes flashed. "Choices? You have no choices! You either bring your forces against the Black Beast by Midsummer Eve, or all will be lost."

Master Edyll's eyes grew large at his outburst, but the high keel laughed deeply, more thunder than amusement. "I like the fire in this fellow's heart!"

Lord Tyrus stepped beside Harlequin, towering over the smaller man. "Do not judge a man by his appearance. You wound a great man by questioning Harlequin's word. When I first came to Port Rawl and worked my way up the Guild, there was only one man whose word and heart I trusted." Tyrus placed a hand on Harlequin's shoulder. "He risked much to discover what defenses the Dark Lord means to set against you. You may doubt him, a stranger here, a fool dressed in bells, but do you doubt me?"

"I meant no affront," Master Edyll said. "But in this dread time, even the word of one's own brother must be suspect."

"Then we are defeated before we've even begun. If we don't trust those at our sides, what hope is there for victory? Even pirates trust their shipmates."

Elena spoke up. "What of this word of betrayal from Meric's cousin?"

Tyrus glanced to the elv'in. "No offense, Prince Meric, but your cousin's warning means nothing to me." He faced Elena again. "Until we have further elaboration, I refuse to go around eyeing each friend with suspicion."

Meric surprisingly agreed. "When I first stepped onto these shores, I was suspicious of everyone and everything." A shadow of a sad smile touched his features. "But I learned otherwise. I've watched a friend forged into an enemy and seen that same man win his name back."

"Kral." Elena nodded.

Meric bowed his head. "I agree with Lord Tyrus. Until we learn more about my cousin's warning, we should proceed with an open heart. If we lose the trust in each other, then we've lost everything."

Elena found her gaze meeting the golden eyes of the stranger. "Tell us then, Master Quail, what have you learned?"

All eyes focused on the small man. He spoke slowly. "While you've sat here licking your wounds, the Black Beast has been a busy worm in his volcanic lair. Though you thwarted his ambitions by breaking his Weirgates, do not deceive yourself that you've driven him from his goal."

"And what is his goal?" Er'ril asked.

"Ah, now you're thinking with your head, old knight. Ever since the Dark Lord arrived on your shores, boiling up out of the world's crust in his fiery volcano, you've tried to drive him from these lands, an invader who must be vanquished."

"So?" Er'ril scoffed. "What would you have had us do? Welcome him with open arms? Throw him a tea party?"

Harlequin barked with laughter. "That's a party I'd love to be invited to." Harlequin snatched up a mug of kaffee, holding it daintily and bowing. His voice changed to an oily whine. *More sweet crackers, Master Black*

Heart? Another dollop of cream?" He straightened, his eyes full of wry amusement. "Maybe your tea party idea could have ended centuries of bloodshed."

Elena felt Er'ril stiffen beside her. She spoke before he burst out in anger. "Master Quail, please, what are you saying?"

"That you will *never* drive the Black Beast of Gul'gotha from these shores." Harlequin set the mug on the hearth's mantel. "Never."

"Our forces drove him from A'loa Glen," the high keel grumbled.

Harlequin faced the man twice his size. "You drove his lieutenants, simpering half-men with delusions of grandeur—*not* the Black Beast. And still you lost half your peoples."

Elena felt a cold stone settle in her belly. The strange man was right.

"And Blackhall makes this island a mere cork in the bath by comparison." He stared around the room. "Have any of you ever been to Blackhall?"

"I've seen it with scopes from the fringes of the Stone Forest," Er'ril said.

"And we've maps and diagrams and sea charts," Hunt added at his father's side.

"Sea charts?" Harlequin shook his head and glanced to Lord Tyrus as if disbelieving the foolishness he was hearing. He faced them again. "I've walked those halls ... as a jester, as a fool, entertainment for the upper floors of that hollowed-out mountain. There are over five thousand rooms and halls, leagues of corridors with monstrous sights at every turn. So listen to my words. What you, Er'ril of Standi, saw through your scopes ... what you have mapped, Captain Hunt ... it is nothing."

Harlequin waved his foppish hat in the air. "It is a mere cap atop the true Blackhall. As much as you see above the waves, it is three—no, at least *four*—times that again beneath the sea." He stared around at the others. "It is *not* an island you plan to lay siege upon. It is an entire *land* in and of itself, a *country* of twisted men, lumbering creatures, and black magicks. That is what you face."

Silence hung in the room.

Then a single silver bell chimed among the hundreds adorning Harlequin's attire. "I've brought you what help I can." He turned to Hunt. "Better maps, more detailed charts of their defenses. For in such a monstrous place as Blackhall, a tiny man like myself, playing the fool, is easily overlooked. But even I, with all my skill, could only burrow down through the uppermost levels of the foul place, a sparrow scritching at the roof tiles." He glanced around the room again. "Trust these words, if you do no others: You will never win Blackhall."

Elena felt the world grow darker around her.

"Then why have us rush to our doom in a moon's time," Master Edyll asked, "if all that awaits us is defeat?"

Harlequin sighed sadly. "Because sometimes losing a battle is not the worst outcome."

"What is worse?" the high keel asked.

Harlequin stared at the Dre'rendi leader as if the man were a child. "Losing the world."

Voices started up in shock, but Lord Tyrus spoke up from near the hearth. "Listen to what he has to say."

Harlequin seemed unaffected by the others and continued. "For centuries, Alasea has fought to drive the Black Beast from these shores. Your ancient Chyric mages drained the last of their blood magick to attempt this. Armies cast their lives upon these shores until the lands ran red. For five centuries, uprisings were crushed under his black fist. All to what end?"

"To free our lands," Er'ril growled. "To shake off his yoke of oppression."

"But did anyone ever ask why?"

Er'ril opened his mouth to speak, but his brow wrinkled in confusion. "What do you mean, why?" he blurted out.

Harlequin leaned against the hearth's mantel. "Why did the Black Heart come here?"

Er'ril's brow crinkled farther.

"It's taken you five hundred winters to discover the Black Heart is not of Gul'gotha but actually an og're, an ancestor of your friend Tol'chuk."

"What are you getting at?"

"You don't know your enemy; you never have. In Blackhall, you see an island and think you understand it, never guessing the depths that are hidden beneath. The same with the master of that island. You know nothing. Why did this og're leave these lands long ago? Why did he appear among the d'warves? Why did he return with conquering armies and magick? Why has he held these lands for so long? Why did he position the Weirgates at points of elemental power around Alasea?" Harlequin stared hard at everyone, golden eyes aglow. "Why is he here?"

After a moment of stunned silence, Er'ril cleared his throat. "Why?"

Harlequin burst from his position with a jingle and cartwheeled head over heels, landing near and pointing his finger at the plainsman's nose. "Finally! After five centuries, someone asked!"

Er'ril leaned away from the man's finger.

Elena spoke up from her seat. "*Why* is he here?"

Harlequin lowered his arm and shrugged. "Mother above if I know." He stepped back to the hearth, staring into the dying coals. "I just thought *someone* should wonder."

Elena frowned. "I don't understand."

"None of you do. Until that changes, the Black Heart has the upper hand."

Master Edyll straightened in his chair. "Now that we've been chastised for our blindness, perhaps you could tell us about this need for urgent action."

Harlequin glanced back over his shoulder. "Under the full moon of Midsummer Eve, the Black Heart will accomplish what he's been seeking to do these past several centuries. Though breaking the Weirgates slowed him, he has one last Gate, and he means to use it to finish what he started."

Elena thought back on her time spent trapped in the Weir, watching the four Gates suck the energy from the world itself. "He seeks to drain the elemental energy from the Land's heart. But why?"

"Why, why, why . . ." Harlequin turned and pulled his cap on his head. "That is a good question. You're learning, my little bird. Why indeed?" He shrugged and winked at her. "I have no idea. But I do know the answer to another question."

"What's that?"

He waggled a finger. "No, not *what* . . . but *where*."

Elena blinked back her confusion. "Where?"

"*Where* the Dark Lord means to act. It's why I scooted my arse out of those black halls as soon as I could. I know when he means to act—the next full moon—and I know where!"

Er'ril straightened. "Where?"

Harlequin glanced between Er'ril and Elena. "Can't you guess?"

Er'ril dropped his hand to his sword hilt. "Enough questions."

"Said like a true warrior," Harlequin said with a sigh. "It's just that sentiment that got us here. Haven't you been listening? There are never enough questions."

Elena sat very still in her chair. One last Weirgate, the Wyvern ebon'stone statue. She pictured when last she had seen it, crated in the hull of a ship. A freighter bound . . . bound for . . . "Oh, Sweet Mother!" she gasped aloud, suddenly understanding. "The Wyvern Gate is heading to my hometown, to Winterfell!"

Harlequin shook his head sadly. "I fear I have worse news than that.

The Black Heart has not been sitting idle as you've plotted, mapped, and charted away the days."

"What do you mean?" Er'ril said, placing a protective hand on Elena's shoulder.

"I managed a glance at a letter from the field, sent by the Dark Lord's lieutenant, Shorkan." Harlequin spoke amid a jingle of mournful bells. "The Weirgate's not *heading* to Winterfell. It's already there."

2

Sy-wen leaned close to the seadragon's neck as it swept through the deep water in a wide curve, banking on one ebony-scaled wing. Her dark green hair trailed out, matching the color of the kelp forest around them. This close to the island of A'loa Glen, the ocean bed was crowded with coral reefs, waving fronds of anemone, and dense patches of kelp. Schools of darting skipperflicks and luminescent krill parted before the giant dragon. Sy-wen twitched her glassy inner eyelids to sharpen her vision.

On your right, Ragnar'k, she sent to her mount.

I see too, my bonded . . . Hold tight . . .

She felt the flaps of scale securing her to her mount squeeze; then the dragon lunged to the right, almost flipping belly-up to make the sharp turn. Sy-wen felt a surge of joy at the rush of water against her bare skin, the bunched muscle between her legs, the blur of ocean. The feeling echoed to the dragon and back at her, tinged with the beast's own senses: the smell of kelp, the trace of blood in the water from a recent shark kill, the sonorous echo of other dragons out in the deeper waters where the giant Leviathans patrolled.

Sy-wen concentrated on their goal. Ahead, a large cloud of silt clouded the clear waters. The elv'in scoutship, piloted by Meric's cousin, must have struck with considerable force to dredge up such volumes of sand and debris. She silently urged Ragnar'k to circle the area before going in closer.

The dragon glided in a gentle, deepening spiral toward the site. The ship had crashed into a trench, dragged by its iron keel straight to the seabed. All that remained floating atop the waves were a few crates, a broken section of mast, and a scattering of planks. The bulk of the broken ship lay below.

Meric had sent word to the mer'ai, seeking help. Sy-wen had left immediately from her mother's Leviathan, where she and Kast had been visiting. She was not sure what Meric thought she might find, but she could at least search for the body of Meric's cousin, to return her to her family. It was a sorrowful duty, but one she would not shirk.

As Ragnar'k swung around the far side of the silt cloud, the stern of the ship came into view; the current was slowly churning the sandy cloud away. The ship lay on its starboard side. The iron keel, forged by lightning, glinted dully in the deepwater gloom. When the ships flew through the air, their keels glowed a coppery hue of sunset. No longer. Here was just iron, dead and dim.

Ragnar'k tucked in his wings and used the sinuous motions of his body to slither over the ruins. A large gray rockshark, nosing around the ship, sped away as the dragon's shadow passed over it.

Sy-wen ignored the predator, her attention focused on the wreckage. The hull had cracked in half upon impact. The masts had been sheared off, but the sails were still tangled by ropes to the shattered ship, flapping in the current like ghosts. *What happened?* she wondered to herself.

But her thoughts weren't hers alone. *Smells strange,* Ragnar'k whispered. *Bad. We go now.*

No, my sweet giant. We must search.

She felt the hint of his worry, but also his acknowledgment.

I must search closer. Can you bring me to the broken section of hull?

As answer, Ragnar'k wound his body in a tight coil and swam down to the seafloor, beside the ragged crack in the hull. Silt churned as his belly and legs brushed the sandy bottom.

You go now? Ragnar'k asked, sorrow behind his sending.

I must. You know.

I know. My heart will miss you.

Sy-wen checked the pair of air pods and the spears on her back. Satisfied, she slid her feet free of the flaps. *Fear not, my love. You're always in my heart.*

A warm sensation coursed through her, sent by the dragon.

I'll see you soon. She spat out the siphon that let her share the dragon's air reserves and allowed her natural buoyancy to lift her from her seat. As soon as she lost contact with the dragon, the seabed floor burst up in a churn of silt and sand. A dark shadow whirled beneath her, swirling and condensing. Sy-wen kicked and swept her arms to hold herself in place amid the swirling cloud, and waited.

There was another reason Sy-wen had been asked to examine the wreckage. She had her own expert on ships and sailing at her side.

From the cloud below her, Kast suddenly appeared, naked, eyes frantically searching. She dove toward him with a smile. His black hair, unbound from its usual long braid, floated around his face, his dragon tattoo bright on cheek and neck. His eyes met hers. Though she couldn't speak heart to heart to him, the same warm sensation coursed through her. Their sharing was an older magick.

He swam up to her and slid his long arms around her waist, staring deep into her eyes. After so long with her, he was growing as comfortable in the sea as she. She reached to the air pod at her side, but instead, his lips found hers. He kissed her deeply.

After too short a time, he broke off. He still could not hold his breath for as long as a true mer'ai.

Sy-wen passed him an air pod, and he bit off the glued tip of its stem. She watched him inhale two breaths. He motioned that he was fine. She freed the second pod and did the same, then pointed to the cracked hull of the elv'in ship. They had drifted up a few spans and had to dive back down toward the dark interior. Kast kept one hand in hers. In the cold waters, his palm was a warm coal.

Together, they slipped between the yawning jaws of the gaping hull. An elv'in scoutship was not a large ship, less than two dragonlengths. Its bow end was no more than a trio of wardrooms and a small kitchen. The stern end contained a storage hold.

Kast motioned that he would check the forward rooms. She nodded. Before departing the Leviathan, they had broken down the search. Since the body of Meric's cousin had not floated up, perhaps it was still trapped in the wreckage.

Sy-wen reached over a shoulder and freed one of her two short spears. She passed the weapon to Kast, remembering the rockshark prowling around the ship earlier. Then she freed her own spear and shook the two fist-sized glowglobes dangling from its butt end. The trapped algae in the kelp pods burst into green brilliance, bathing the wooden interior ribs of the ship in a sickly light.

Kast followed her example, then lifted his spear in a salute and slid from her side. As planned, he would check the bow section; Sy-wen the stern.

Turning, Sy-wen stared at the tumble of crates and barrels that filled the storage space. Some floated, buoyed and bobbing overhead. Others held contents heavy enough to keep them resting against the tilted deck. She stared deeper into the murky hold. The glow of her spear's globes could not penetrate to the far end.

With a glance over her shoulder, Sy-wen watched Kast's feet disappear through a hatch. Alone, she turned back to the gloomy interior of the ship's storage compartment. Raising her spear ahead of her, she kicked off a strut and glided amid the piled debris. Was there some clue to the fate of the scoutship hidden among these crates? She swam slowly, searching for anything suspicious.

With her spear, Sy-wen bumped aside a floating crate, disturbing a large sea turtle. The ocean denizen eyed her with clear annoyance and paddled awkwardly away.

Sy-wen swam deeper into the hold.

Soon she found herself gliding above a nest of small, oddly shaped barrels. Each was perfectly oval in shape and no larger than a human head: They looked like large eggs. But what was odd was their coloring: a deep ebony—so dark in fact, the eggs seemed to suck the light rather than reflect it. She swam closer, intrigued, and saw forked streaks of silver running through the black, like cracks in a shell.

Sy-wen leaned her face nearer, and suddenly knew what she had found. *Sweet Mother above!* Almost choking in panic, she sprang back, paddling. She used her spear to push away from the crowded deck, but her rising back struck a rib of the boat, holding her above the abomination. As she stared down, her heart sickened, and the cold chill of the ocean penetrated her bones. She spun in a tight circle. The objects were scattered all around. There had to be over a hundred of them.

Her eyes were wide with fear.

They were all made of *ebon'stone*! Ebon'stone eggs!

She backed away from the nest, kicking aside crates that floated along the roof. She swam to the broken section of hull and stared up at the sun shining high above the ocean, a watery blur of brightness. She drew strength from the light, as if its purity could cleanse the sight from her eyes.

Something brushed against her shoulder.

She shouted in fright, spitting out her air pod and gulping a mouthful of seawater. Arms grabbed her and spun her around. She found Kast peering down at her with concern. His face was better than any sun.

He dropped his spear and snatched up her discarded air pod, bringing its stem to her lips. She took it gratefully, blowing the water from her mouth, then sucking in air. Half sobbing, she clasped to him and buried her face into his chest.

He held her until her shaking stopped.

After several breaths, she felt strong enough to push away. She sent him a questioning look. He shook his head. He had been unable to find the captain's body. But he lifted his other arm. A book was clasped in his grip. It looked like the ship's log. She nodded. If the water hadn't damaged it too severely, maybe it held a record of what had happened . . . or where the ship had come upon such a foul load.

Biting her lip, she tugged Kast toward the stern hold. He should see what she had discovered. He retrieved his spear, and together they ventured back into the maze of crates and barrels. She quickly returned to the nest of ebon'stone eggs and pointed.

Kast seemed as confused as she had been at first. He swam down, but she restrained him from getting too near. She lowered her spear's glow-globes closer, then felt him stiffen with recognition. He glanced back at her, shock and fear shining in his dark eyes.

She tried to tug him away, but he reached to her waist and slipped free a small net of woven seaweed, normally used to collect sea-tubers and other edibles. He passed her his spear and the logbook, then unfurled her net. She knew what he meant to do.

She grabbed his wrist, wanting to stop him, but she knew he was right. They must return with one of these dreadful eggs. Others would want to see it, examine it, to attempt to divine the danger here.

Sy-wen met Kast's eyes and urged him caution. He nodded, understanding.

He slid from her side and kicked off to where a lone egg lay apart from the others. Kast lowered the net over it, then scooped it up, careful not to touch its surface.

He waved her to lead the way back out. Clutching the logbook to her chest, she swam swiftly out of the broken ship and into the bright waters beyond.

Sy-wen turned and motioned for Kast to draw nearer. Slipping the spears over her shoulder, she motioned with her hands: a bird in flight. He nodded. They must bring their discoveries as quickly as possible to the castle.

Kast slid up to her. He passed her his burden. She was reluctant to accept it but had no choice. She held the book and the twisted handle of the net in one hand. With the other, she reached to the man she loved. He took her fingers and brought her palm to his lips. The heat of his kiss burned.

He then reached and pulled her close, pressing against her, one leg slipping between hers. He squeezed the fear from her with his strong arms. Gasping slightly, she stared up into his eyes and saw the love there.

At last, before she could balk, she slipped her free hand to his cheek and touched his dragon tattoo. His body arched against her, both pain and pleasure. *I have need of you,* she intoned.

The world burst around her. Sand skirled out in a mad whirl. She spun. Her legs were thrown apart, forced by muscle and magick. Under her, a dragon took shape, wings spread, a roar echoed in mind and ear. She clutched her burdens in an iron grip.

To the castle, Ragnar'k. Quickly.

Dragon thoughts and sensations merged with her own. *As you wish, my bonded.*

Her feet slipped into the warm flaps of scale that drew tight around her, holding her secure. She leaned into his neck. *Go, my sweet giant.*

With a burst of muscle and energy, the dragon lunged up, toward the watery sun. Sy-wen held tight to her burdens, but at the back of her mind, she wondered if all this was best left drowned at the bottom of the ocean.

Then dragon and rider burst from the sea. In the distance, she spotted ships on the water and in the air. Farther out, Leviathans spouted jets of spray as they filled their monstrous reserves. The world awaited her, and the dangers ahead must be faced.

Ragnar'k tilted on a wingtip and banked toward the island and the great edifice of A'loa Glen, the last bastion of freedom in this dark world.

Sy-wen glanced down to her netted cargo, wondering again what horror she was carrying forward from this watery grave. She pictured the dark nest in the broken hold and shuddered.

Whatever evil it represented, it must be stopped.

"WINTERFELL . . ." ELENA WHISPERED.

Er'ril stared at the stricken woman. How he wanted to scoop her into his arms and calm that look of dismay. She seemed to sink in on herself, swamped by memories of a childhood lost too young. Her eyes, usually a bright emerald, had gone distant, as if she had to search far back to remember. He tried to remember the little girl he first saw on the cobbled streets of Winterfell. It seemed like ages ago to him also.

He suddenly found her eyes focused back on him. What did she see? An old man wearing a young man's face? What more did he have to offer her? He had forsaken his own immortality for the woman at his side, placing all his hopes for Alasea's future on her small shoulders. He had a sudden urge to drop to his knees and beg her forgiveness.

Instead, he stood his post: knight, liegeman, protector . . . and in some small way, husband. For the past moons, they had given up denying what was in their hearts. Bound by elv'in law, they were husband and wife. But what hearts could admit, their bodies had yet to yield. He ached for her, but the gulf of years still separated them. She was a child wearing a woman's body. He was an old man disguised in a young man's form. That difference had yet to be resolved with their tender touches, glances, and brief kisses.

"Er'ril," Elena said to him, bringing him back to the dilemma presented by this acerbic clown in motley and bells. "We can't dismiss what Master Quail has told us. It rings with truth. We know the Wyvern Gate was heading to the Winterfell when we discovered it. I can't imagine what that dark og're expects to accomplish with only one Weirgate, but it must be stopped."

Er'ril nodded. "Without doubt. But how?"

"We destroyed the others," Elena said. "We will destroy this one. The Wyvern Gate is the last stake that holds Chi imprisoned. Destroy it, and Chi will be free. The Dark Lord of Blackhall will be powerless."

Er'ril grimaced. "So the spirits have said." But he was not so sure, himself. During the last moon, Elena and Er'ril had shared many discussions with the spirits of the Blood Diary: the shade of Aunt Fila and the spirit-being Cho. Five centuries ago, Cho's brother spirit, Chi, had been trapped within the four Weirgates. With three broken, no one could say for sure why Chi remained trapped in this last Gate. Er'ril doubted that the Wyvern Gate was the sole answer. "We dare not place all our hopes that the spirits are correct in this matter."

Harlequin spoke by the hearth. "Spirits, whores, or fools—what does it matter? I read Shorkan's note to his underlings. By Midsummer Eve, he declared, the battle would be over. The last words in his note I can still quote: 'Lo the Eve, wit'ch and world will be broken upon the Master's pyre.'" Harlequin shrugged and picked at a hangnail. "I don't know. That sounded pretty dire to me."

Meric cleared his throat. "It does seem plainly spoken."

"It could be a trap," Er'ril said, "intended to draw Elena out . . . or to make us act before we're ready."

The high keel's face twisted as if he tasted something sickening. "Or a feint, meant to divide our forces."

No one spoke for a few moments, pondering these possibilities.

"I can't ignore the threat to Winterfell," Elena said. "Trap or not, we must attempt to break that last Gate."

Er'ril sighed, recognizing the glint of her determination. "What of the attack on Blackhall? Do we wait until after the Gate is dealt with?"

Elena glanced to her gloved hands. "We dare not. Before our allies' elemental powers wane further, we'll bring them to bear upon the volcanic stronghold. Perhaps with the Dark Lord's attention focused on his own defense, we'll be able to thwart his ambition in the mountains."

"We?" Er'ril asked.

"If this last Gate holds the key to the Dark Lord's goal, then he's sure to have brought strong forces to protect it—even stronger than when his power was divided among the four Gates. If we are to succeed, my strength will be needed. We'll take one of the elv'in ships; once the Gate is destroyed, we can return and help with the siege upon Blackhall."

"You can use my ship," Meric said. "The *Stormwing* is the swiftest, and my magicks are the strongest of my people. I'll lead you to the mountains and back."

"You'll be needed here to lead your people," Elena said.

Meric waved away her words. "The captain of the Thunderclouds, our warships, can lead as well as I, and he's a better warrior and tactician. If the Wyvern Gate is as important as Lord Tyrus' friend suggests, then my skills are best suited in aiding you."

Before the matter could be discussed further, a loud thud sounded overhead, accompanied by the screech of scraped stone. All eyes glanced upward as a familiar roar echoed down to them.

"Ragnar'k," Master Edyll said from his seat.

Meric stood straighter. "Maybe they bring news of my cousin's ship."

Lord Tyrus moved from his space by the hearth. "I'll see if it is so." The pirate prince hurried through the small tower door, allowing in a gust of ocean breeze.

Voices were heard, and then Tyrus returned, minus his cloak. Kast followed, barefooted and wrapped in the prince's garment, Sy-wen at his side. Both newcomers shivered and bore burdens in hand, faces grim.

"There's hot kaffee by the hearth," Er'ril said.

Kast crossed with Sy-wen, drawn by the hearth's warmth. Both were quickly given steaming mugs and updated on the discussions.

Kast stared over at Meric. "I must add more dire tidings."

"Of course you must," Harlequin said with false brightness.

Meric frowned and sat straighter. "Something about my cousin's ship?"

Kast nodded. "We did not find her body, but we found this." He pulled out a large leather-wrapped tome from under his cloak. "The captain's logbook."

Meric accepted the parcel, resting a palm atop it. "Thank you. I pray it contains some answers."

"Pray hard." Kast nodded to Sy-wen. "The log wasn't all we found."

Sy-wen lifted a large dark object, setting it on the table and carefully removing the seaweed net.

"An egg?" Master Edyll asked.

"What strangeness is this?" the high keel asked.

Er'ril stared in disbelief. He choked, unable to find his voice. He saw similar reactions around the room. "Ebon'stone!" he finally gasped.

"We thought as much," Kast said.

"Why did you bring this here?"

"We thought it best you see this for yourselves." His voice grew more grim as he glanced to Er'ril. "There are over a hundred of the cursed things down in the hold of the sunken ship."

"A hundred . . . ?"

"At least that many," Sy-wen added softly.

Elena pointed. "But what are they? What's their purpose?"

Meric squinted his ice-blue eyes. "More importantly, why did my cousin bring them here?"

"Perhaps forced," Master Edyll offered.

The group gathered in a wary circle around the table.

"Whatever danger it represents," Kast said, "I thought we should be prepared. Figure out what risk this single one poses, then address the nest under the sea."

Er'ril noticed one member of the group, usually quick with his tongue, remained quiet. Harlequin Quail stared at the ebon'stone egg with an unreadable glint in his gold eyes—no wry comment or biting wit this time.

Er'ril shifted from Elena's side, moving around the table as if he were examining the egg from all vantages. As he slipped behind the pirate spy, Er'ril slid his sword silently from his sheath and pressed its tip against the base of the small man's skull. "What do you know of this?"

Harlequin did not flinch.

"What are you doing, plainsman?" Lord Tyrus demanded.

"Stay back," Er'ril warned. "This fellow has been to Blackhall and back, as had the ship captained by Meric's cousin. Perhaps he knows something of this threat."

Harlequin sighed and turned, slowly. He faced Er'ril. The swordtip now rested at the hollow of his throat. "I know nothing of these black stones."

Er'ril narrowed his eyes. "You lie."

"Are we back to that argument again?"

"Er'ril . . . ," Elena said with a note of warning.

"I've lived over five centuries," Er'ril said. "I can tell when a man is hiding something."

"I hide nothing," Harlequin turned back to the table, ignoring the sword. "And I spoke the truth. I've never seen such an egg before." His gaze crossed the table to Elena. "But I've seen its fair twin."

"Explain yourself," Er'ril said.

Harlequin stepped toward the table, arms at his side. "As I said before, when in Blackhall, I saw despicable acts committed—some upon those who deserved it, others upon innocents. It was a labyrinth of torture and slaughter. Screams and wails were constant. You got accustomed to it after a while, like birdsong in the wood. It was simply everywhere."

Harlequin stared at the egg. "Then one day, I came upon a chamber in the deepest level that I could reach. It was a long hall, stretching the full length of the mountain. Alcoves lined both sides. In each stood a pillar of volcanic basalt, atop which rested an egg of perfect symmetry, the same size and shape as this one. But these eggs were not the black of midnight, but the rose of dawn. Each was sculpted out of heartstone."

"Heartstone?" Elena whispered.

Harlequin nodded. "It was beautiful. The hall stretched far, each egg glowing with a brightness that reached to the bone and made one feel whole and pure. It was the first time I cried in that sick place, not tears of horror or pain, but of beauty and joy. In some ways, it was the most dreadful sight—such beauty in that well of darkness."

"Heartstone eggs in Blackhall." Er'ril lowered his sword. "Ebon'stone eggs here. It makes no sense."

Elena's brows knit together. "Maybe it does. When we broke the Gates, ebon'stone was transformed into heartstone. Could this be further evidence of some dark link between the two stones?"

Er'ril's frown deepened.

"Connected or not," Master Edyll interrupted, "to have a hundred of these grotesque things sunk so close to our shores is reason for concern."

"I agree," Sy-wen said. "They surely poison the waters with their mere presence."

Elena nodded. "We'll find some way to haul the wreckage and its cargo away from here. In the meantime, we'll examine the captain's logbook, and see if our castle scholars can discover any information about these eggs."

Elena backed slowly away and returned to her seat. "Time presses, and we dare not waste it on mysteries we can't presently solve. We must concentrate our resources and talents upon the war to come."

Er'ril circled the room to stand beside Elena's chair as she continued. "I would have all the four heads of our various forces meet these next three days." She nodded around the room. "The high keel of the Dre'rendi to represent our fleets upon the seas, and Master Edyll of the mer'ai to coordinate our forces below. Lord Tyrus, as head of the pirate brigade, will continue to organize our scouts and spies. And lastly, Meric, you'll need to alert the leader of the Thunderclouds to meet with these others in order to prepare the elv'in warships."

"I'll do so immediately," Meric answered.

"We also must alert Wennar and the d'warf legions," Er'ril added. "Get him moving his foot soldiers north from Penryn toward the Stone Forests."

Elena nodded. "I'll leave the details to the heads of each army. Er'ril will act as my liaison during these next days. By seven days' time, I want our forces ready to set out for Blackhall."

The high keel pounded a fist on the arm of his chair. "It will be done!"

"What of the danger in the mountains?" Harlequin asked.

"Leave that to me." Elena stared at the egg.

Harlequin glanced to Lord Tyrus, then back to Elena. "I would ask one thing of you for my services—that I be allowed to go with you into the mountains."

As Elena frowned, Er'ril spoke up. "Why?"

Harlequin lifted his arms, jangling. "Do I look a warrior? I am a thief, a pickpocket, a slinker in shadows. I am no good when swords are raised and the drums of war sound. But I would give my talents where they are most needed, and follow the path I've started to its end."

Before Elena could answer, Er'ril placed a hand on her shoulder. "If this mission is attempted, then Elena must be surrounded by those she most trusts. Though she may ignore whispers of betrayal, I will not."

Elena opened her mouth to object, but Er'ril stopped her with a stern glance. "Am I your liegeman?" he asked coldly. "Your protector and counsel? Would you take that from me?"

"Of course not," Elena intoned quietly.

Er'ril recognized the hurt in her eyes. Perhaps he had been too harsh, but Elena sometimes opened her heart too easily. Though she had survived much these past winters, she was still tender deep down, vulnerable. He would protect her. He would be hard when Elena could not. It gave meaning to the centuries he had spent on the roads.

"I don't know you, Master Quail," Er'ril said. "So despite Lord Tyrus' assurance, I won't trust you. And until I do, I won't have you with us. I appreciate your help and the risk you've taken. You'll be well paid in gold."

Harlequin flicked a golden bell, setting it to ringing. "I have enough gold." He turned on a heel and retreated toward the door, moving swiftly.

Lord Tyrus shook his head as the man left. "You don't know the man whose offer you so casually cast aside."

"Exactly," Er'ril said, unbending.

Elena spoke up. "It is near to midday. Perhaps we'd best disperse, and begin our long planning for the war to come."

Master Edyll stood with Sy-wen's help. "I'll attend to the council. They must be near to pulling each other's hair out by now."

The other leaders all began to move toward the doors, already planning amongst themselves.

By the door, Elena saw everyone off. She whispered her confidence to each one, gripping hands and exuding warmth. Er'ril watched her. Her fall of curls, grown out almost to her shoulders, framed a fine-boned face, marking her elv'in heritage. But where the elv'in were all slender limbs, Elena was all graceful curves, like a flower grown from land, rather than a wisp blown by the wind. Er'ril found his breath deepening as he looked upon her.

Soon the room was empty. Elena crossed back to him. Er'ril prepared himself to be scolded for his outburst at Harlequin.

Instead Elena sank against him, resting her cheek against his chest.

"Elena . . . ?"

"Just hold me."

He wrapped her in his arms. It was suddenly not so hard to remember the girl from Winterfell.

"I'm afraid to go home."

He held her tight. "I know."

MERIC CLIMBED DOWN THE LONG, WINDING STAIR IN A HALF DAZE, CLUTCH-
ing the sodden logbook under one arm. Lost in his thoughts about his
cousin and her fate, he barely heard the argument commencing behind
him between Hunt and Lord Tyrus. There was no love lost between the
Dre'rendi and the lord of the pirates. Prior to being brought together
here, both sides had been blood-sworn enemies, two sharks of the southern seas preying on the unsuspecting merchant ships and each other. Old
animosities were hard to set aside.

"Your ships may be swifter," Hunt snarled, "but they break like twigs."

"At least on our ships, we're free men. Not slaves!"

Hunt growled. "It was an ancient oath! A bond of honor . . . something
you freebooters and privateers would never understand."

The end of the stairs appeared ahead. Meric hurried forward to escape
their sparring, and ran headlong into Nee'lahn.

She fell back, eyes wide at finding the tower stairs crowded with men.

Meric reached out to catch her as she tripped backward.

"Prince Meric!" Nee'lahn exclaimed, regaining her footing.

"Papa Hunt!" a small voice shouted. From around the nyphai woman's
cloak, a small figure darted, dark hair waving, as she scooted past.

The large Bloodrider bent to swing the small girl up onto his shoulder.
"Sheeshon, what are you doing here?"

Sheeshon spoke rapidly. "We were in the place with all the flowers. But
Rodricko made more flowers with his singing." Sheeshon pointed to the
boy at Nee'lahn's side. The shy youngster was all but buried in his mother's
cloak, his eyes round. "And I ate a bug," Sheeshon finished proudly.

"You did what?"

"It flew in my mouth," she said with a simple finality, as if this were explanation enough.

The high keel pushed past his son, grumbling about the stairs. Master
Edyll agreed. "Why do they have to build these cursed towers so tall?"

The two elders headed down the corridor. Hunt nodded his thanks to
Nee'lahn and followed his father.

Meric was left with Nee'lahn and Lord Tyrus, who carried the net with
the ebon'stone egg. They were to take the egg and logbook to the scholars
at the libraries.

"Where are you going?" Meric asked Nee'lahn.

"I must speak to Elena."

Meric glanced up the twisting stairs. "This is not the best time. She has enough to ponder at the moment." He turned back and finally recognized the distress in her face, the puffiness in her eyes. "What's wrong?"

The nyphai stared up the steps, clearly undecided. Something had shaken her to her roots. She glanced to her towheaded child. "It . . . it's Rodricko."

Meric studied the boy. "Is he sick? Is something wrong?"

"I'm not sure." Nee'lahn was close to tears. "This morning, Rodricko sang his budding song to his young tree, a step toward union and bonding." Her voice began to crack. "But s-something happened."

Meric stepped closer, putting an arm around her shoulders.

She trembled, and her voice dropped to a whisper. "His tree budded. Rodricko was accepted, but . . . but the new flowers, the new buds, they're dark things. Black as any Grim wraith."

Meric met Lord Tyrus' eyes over the top of the nyphai's head. Both were well familiar with the Grim of the Dire Fell, the twisted spirits of Nee'lahn's sisterhood.

"The buds are foul to look upon." Tears began to flow down her cheeks. "Some dread evil for sure."

"We don't know that," Meric consoled, but he knew the sapling was the last tree of Nee'lahn's people, born from the union of her own tree's spirit and a Grim wraith. Had the touch of the Grim somehow tainted the tree?

Nee'lahn clearly thought so. She gazed up at Meric with wounded eyes. "The buds will bloom for the first time this night, releasing their unique magick. But with the buds bearing the mark of the Grim, I don't know what evil may arise." She covered her face with one hand and pulled the boy tighter to her cloak, half burying him so her words were kept from him. "I dare not let my hopes endanger A'loa Glen. The tree must be cut down."

Meric stiffened at this thought. In many ways, the tree represented all of Alasea's hopes. Planted in the site of the original koa'kona that had once graced the island for centuries, the sapling represented a new beginning, a fresh future.

From one step up, Lord Tyrus voiced an even more significant concern. "But what of Rodricko? What will become of him?"

"The tree accepted his song." Nee'lahn choked back a sob. "He is bonded. If the tree dies, then he dies."

Meric's gaze flicked to the child, cuddled tight to his mother. He had been with Nee'lahn when they discovered the boy. Together, they had fought the Grim and the Dark Lord's minions to bring him safely to the island. Meric's face hardened. "Then I will allow no harm to come to his tree."

Nee'lahn clutched at Meric's arm. "You, more than anyone, should understand. It is surely a sign of the Blight. I would rather Rodricko die than be twisted by whatever sickness taints the tree. You saw what happened to my sisters. I won't see it happen to my son. I would rather take an ax to the tree myself." She broke down into sobs.

Stunned, Meric knelt beside the boy child. Rodricko hid his face in the folds of his mother's cloak. The boy might not understand their whispered words, but he knew his mother's distress. Meric glanced up to Nee'lahn and saw the despair in her eyes. Ever since their time in the north together, the two had grown closer, bonded by their two peoples' shared histories and their own hardships and losses. In many ways, here was a part of his new family, and after losing both mother and brother, Meric would lose no more.

Tyrus whispered behind them. "Perhaps we should consider this when emotions are calmer, heads clearer."

Meric stood, his cloak billowing out around him. "No, there is nothing to decide. No harm will come to the tree if it risks Rodricko." He touched Nee'lahn's cheek, gently. "I will not let you act hastily, striking out from fear of only one possible outcome. Mycelle of the Dro used poison to save elementals from becoming ill'guard. But she destroyed *all* the strands of their possible futures because *one* might lead to corruption. I won't let you follow in her footsteps."

Lord Tyrus spoke up, his voice a trace huskier. "Meric is right. Mycelle would not wish this path for anyone."

Nee'lahn glanced to the pirate prince, then back to Meric. "What are we to do?"

Meric lifted his other hand and rested it atop the young boy's head. "Face the future. Come nightfall, we will see what fate holds for the boy and his tree."

HALF A LAND AWAY, GRESHYM POUNDED THE TABLE IN BEAT WITH THE drummer. "Go for five! Go for five!" he chanted drunkenly with the other patrons of the Moon Lake Inn.

The juggler took up a fifth burning brand, tossing it high into the air, to tumble amid the others. The sweating performer darted around the plank stage set up in the common area of the inn, fighting to keep the flaming brands from hitting the straw-strewn floor. Two fellow performers stood by with buckets of water.

Greshym stared blearily at the show. All around Moon Lake, the Celebration of the First Moon was under way, a circus of minstrels, animal acts, and displays of prowess. This evening the festivities would culminate at the shores of Moon Lake, when the summer's first full moon would light the still waters of the Western Reaches' largest lake. Stories claimed the spirits of the wood would grant wishes to those who bathed in the moonlit waters.

Greshym could not care less for such stories. He had all he needed: a flagon of ale, a full belly, and the energy to enjoy all the passions in life. A barmaid came to fill his empty mug. He grabbed a handful of her plump backside.

She squealed. "Master Dismarum!" she scolded with a wink as she swung away.

He had spent the last few nights in her room. A handful of copper had opened both her door and her legs. The memory of those long nights in her arms dulled his interest in juggling and flaming brands.

Greshym caught his reflection in the grimy mirror above the bar. His hair shone golden in the torchlight of the dingy inn; his eyes sparkled with youth; his back was straight, his shoulders broad. He wagered that it might not have taken even those few coppers to open the barmaid's bed. But he had not been content to wait for her interest to flame into desire, not when the same could be achieved much faster with a bit of coin.

Patience was not a virtue of youth.

Greshym intended to experience all life's many sensations and desires. No longer trapped in a decaying form, he wanted to run his new body through its paces. So now he shoved to his feet, and reached for the staff leaning against the table. He no longer needed it to support himself, only as a focus for his power.

He fingered the length of bone, the straight femur of a wybog, a long-limbed forest stalker. The hollow bone, capped at either end by a plug of dried clay, was filled with the blood of a woodsman's newborn babe. The foundling's life energy, tied by an old spell, had charged his staff.

Turning his back on the stage, Greshym tilted his stave toward the performers. The juggler tripped. Torches went sailing, end over end, past the stage. The waterboys ran out to douse the brands before the strawed floor took the flame.

Greshym smiled as the room glowed brighter behind him. Flames roared up. Gasps and cries arose from both patrons and performers. He bit back a chuckle. It was child's play to change water into oil.

Fires roared across the inn's common room. Screams for aid followed Greshym out the door.

Beyond the inn, the expanse of Moon Lake spread before him, cast in copper by the setting sun. Maples and pines framed the lake and spread to the horizons. Among the trees, scores of gaily colored tents had sprung up like summer flowers over the past few days, in preparation for this night's ceremonies. Folk had traveled here from all over Alasea, anticipating the night when a thousand bathers' wishes would be whispered to the full moon.

Greshym himself had come to Moon Lake a fortnight ago and had remained for the festivities, reveling in all of life's textures. He would use this sacred night for his own ends. He stared out at the hundreds of celebrants walking the streets of the small village and squabbling with tin merchants and spice traders. So much life to explore again.

He sauntered toward the deeper forest beyond the village's edge, all but twirling his bone staff. His legs moved strongly; his lungs drew air in without a whisper of a wheeze. Even walking was a joy.

In such good spirits, Greshym pointed his staff at a man taunting a chained and growling sniffer. The purple-skinned predator suddenly broke through its muzzle and bit off three of its taunter's fingers.

Greshym passed the site as whips snapped, driving the sniffer back from the screaming man. "Better wish for a new set of fingers this night," Greshym mumbled.

Then he was in the woods. He hurried his pace, enjoying the pump of muscle, the freedom in his joints. After being trapped for centuries in that old decrepit form, the wonders and joys of this young body never waned. Youth was so wasted on the young.

Around him, the forest light grew dimmer, shaded more darkly as the trees grew denser and taller.

In the dimness, the smell struck him before the sight: the reek of wet goat and the stench of rent bowels. Greshym entered the clearing to find his servant, Rukh, crouched amid a charnel house. The carcasses of countless forest creatures littered the space. The stump gnome had his muzzle buried in the belly of a doe, growling and tearing contentedly.

"Rukh!" Greshym barked.

The hoofed creature sprang straight as if struck by lightning, squealing piggishly. Its tiny pointed ears trembled. "M-master!"

Greshym stared at the gore strewn around the area. Most of the carcasses were only half eaten—he had not been the only one enjoying the varying tastes offered by this night. "I see you've kept busy while I've been gone."

Rukh dropped back to the ground, cowering. "Good here ... good meat." One hand reached to the doe. Claws ripped off the creature's rear leg. Rukh held out the bloody haunch. "M-master eat ... ?"

Greshym found himself too content to be angry. At least the stump gnome had remained where he had left it. He wasn't sure his spell of compulsion would last so long without renewal. "Clean yourself," Greshym commanded, pointing to a nearby stream. "The villagers will smell you from a league away."

"Yes, Master." The creature loped to the brook and leaped fully into it.

Greshym turned from the splashing and stared back in the direction of the village. This night's festivities were going to be especially memorable. But first a bit of preparation was in order. He wanted nothing to interfere with his plans.

Greshym planted his bone stave into the soft loam of the forest floor. It stood straight. He waved his left hand over the top, his lips moving. A babe's wail flowed out of the staff.

"Hush," Greshym whispered. He reached out with the stump of his right hand. Darkness billowed like oily smoke from the plugged end of the hollow bone. He placed the stump of his wrist within the inky fog, intoning softly, weaving the spell he would use this night.

As he worked, the wailing from his staff suddenly took voice—but it was no babe. "I found you!" The voice echoed out into the darkening woods.

Greshym recognized the familiar rasp. "Shorkan," he hissed, backing a step.

The smoke above his staff coalesced into a man's face, eyes glowing red. Even amid the wisps, the Standi features were clear.

Black lips moved. "So you thought to escape the Master's wrath by hiding in the woods."

"I did escape," Greshym spat back, reading the spell woven behind the smoky features. It was a mere search spell, nothing to fear. "And I will escape again. Before this night is over, I'll have the power to hide from even the Black Heart himself."

"So you believe." There was a pause; then laughter flowed from far away. "Moon Lake, of course."

Scowling, Greshym raised his stump and altered the spell before him, reversing it, tapping into Shorkan's own energies. For a brief moment, he saw through the other mage's eyes. The man was far from here—but not at Blackhall. Relieved, Greshym reached deeper into the spell, then suddenly was slammed with such force that he stumbled backward.

"Do not tread where you're not welcome, Greshym." The spell severed, and the smoky face dissolved.

"The same to you, you bastard," Greshym muttered, but he knew Shorkan was already gone. He quickly cast up wards to prevent another penetration.

Greshym scowled at the staff as if it were to blame. It had been risky casting such a powerful spell, one easy to trace. He squinted off to the east as if he could peer through the mountains of the Teeth. "What are you doing in Winterfell?"

Though his nemesis was beyond the mountains, Greshym felt a trickle of worry wheedle into his confidence. He had sensed a dread certainty in the other mage, an amused lack of concern at what Greshym planned. "And what are you up to?"

With no answer, Greshym reached toward the staff, but he saw that a trace of the search spell still remained. He hesitated. He hated to waste magick. Greshym rewove the spell with the residual energy left behind by Shorkan. He waved his stumped wrist.

Smoke billowed out, then swirled back down. A new face formed, old and wrinkled, framed in scraggled white hair. Greshym reached toward the visage, brushing along a cheek. *Ancient, decayed, dying . . .*

There was little energy left in the spell, but Greshym reached deeper, trying to sense the man behind the fog. "Joach . . . ," he whispered. "How does it feel, my boy, to wear a suit of sagging flesh and creaking bones?"

He divined the other was sleeping, napping away the late afternoon, back at A'loa Glen. Joach's breath was a rasping wheeze, his heartbeat a palsied thud.

Greshym smiled and retreated. He dared not reach farther; the boy—or should he say, *old man*—was still potent in dream magicks. He dared not risk crossing into Joach's dreams.

Once free, Greshym ended the spell and stared down at his own body, straight and hale. He took a deep breath and slowly exhaled.

It was good to be young again . . . young with power!

JOACH WOKE WITH A START, TREMBLING ALL OVER. THE SHEETS OF HIS BEDding were soaked with night sweat and clung to his frail form. The nightmare remained with him, vivid and real. He knew in his heart that it had been no ordinary dream. He felt along the edges of the memory. It did not have the starkness of a Weaving, a dream of portent. It was more like a real event.

"Greshym," he mumbled to the empty room. The sweat on his body quickly chilled, sending shivers along his limbs. He glanced to the windows, where a soft breeze fluttered the draperies. The sun was already setting.

He dragged his feet to the floor with a groan. His exertions this past day and night had exhausted him. Muscles and joints protested each movement. But he knew that only the company of others would shake the cobwebs of the nightmare from his mind.

Joach reached for his staff, but as his palm touched the petrified wood, fiery pain shot up his arm to his heart. He doubled over with agony, gasping. He stared sideways at the staff. Its gray surface drained to pale white. Streaks of his own blood suffused the stony wood, flowing from the hand that still gripped it.

In his distraction, he had forgotten to don his glove, accidentally activating the blood weapon with the touch of his flesh. As the initial pain subsided, Joach dragged himself up. He lifted the staff. It was lighter, easier to manipulate—a boon of the magickal bonding. He also sensed the dream energy in the wood, waiting to be tapped. Like the staff, it seemed part of his body.

Joach pointed the staff and sent out a tendril of magick. A small rose grew from the half-filled washbasin. Joach remembered the last time he had willed such a creation into existence: *the night desert, Sheeshon cradled between Kesla and himself, and a rose built of sand and dream to calm a frightened child.*

Lowering the staff, Joach unbound his magick, and the flower fell back to nothingness. Not even a ripple marked the water of the basin.

Just a dream.

The memory of Kesla settled a dark melancholy over his spirit. Joach cradled the staff in the crook of an arm and removed his palm. He wanted nothing of dreams right now.

With the connection broken, the staff faded from ivory back to dull gray. Joach slipped a glove over his hand and took up the staff again. He crossed to his wooden wardrobe. Done with dreams and nightmares, he wanted the company of real people.

Still, as he dressed, the dregs of his nightmare remained. Joach again saw the darkmage Greshym standing in a forest glade, surrounded by offal and torn bodies. A white staff stood planted before him, topped by a cloud of inky darkness. Then those eyes had turned toward him, gleeful yet full of spite. But the worst terror of the dream was the darkmage's appearance: golden-brown hair, smooth skin, strong arms, straight spine, eyes so very bright. Joach saw his own youth mocking him, so close yet impossible to touch.

Sighing, he settled his cloak in place and crossed to the door, bumping across the stones with his staff. He tightened his gloved fingers on the petrified wood and sensed the magick therein; it helped center his spirit. One day, he would find Greshym and take back what was his.

As Joach reached the door, someone knocked on the other side. Frowning, he opened the door to find a young page. The lad bowed. "Master Joach, your sister bids you join her in the Grand Courtyard."

"Why?"

His question seemed to stymie the youngster, whose eyes grew wide. "Sh-she did not say, sir."

"Fine. Shall I follow you?"

"Yes, sir. Certainly, sir." The lad all but sprang away, like a frightened rabbit.

Joach followed, thumping along. He knew the way to the courtyard.

The page paused at the stairs leading down to the central part of the keep, looking back. Joach read impatience in his stance . . . and the vague glint of fear in his eyes. He knew what the boy saw. Joach had once walked these same halls himself, a young aide to a decrepit figure. But now the roles were reversed.

Joach was no longer the boy.

The page disappeared down the stairs.

Joach was now the ancient one, bitter and full of black thoughts.

"I shall have my day," he vowed to the empty hall.

3

As the last rays of the sun melted into twilight, Elena stood in the Grand Courtyard with the others, studying the koa'kona sapling. It seemed a frail thing, dwarfed by the towering stone walls, towers, and battlements of the castle. But its buds were as black as oil, seeming to drip from the stems that held them. Elena pulled her cloak tighter about her shoulders.

"It draws the heat," Nee'lahn whispered from a few steps to the right. "Like the Grim."

Elena had heard the stories of the wraiths of the Dire Fell, shadowy spirits that could suck the lifeforce from all they touched.

"Hush," Meric said at Nee'lahn's side. "It's just the tidal breezes, nothing more."

Meric nodded to Elena. When the elv'in prince had brought word of the tree's strange budding, Elena had agreed heartily that no harm should come to the tree until its true nature could be discerned, especially as the boy's life hung in the balance.

Not all had agreed. "We risk much to spare a single life," Er'ril had argued. But Elena had refused to act hastily, and Er'ril had bowed to her will. Still, he now stood beside her with an ax in one hand. Two guards stood beyond him, armed with pails of pitch and burning torches. Er'ril was taking no chances that magick alone would win out here if something evil arose.

Elena was also taking no extra risks. She had the Blood Diary in a satchel over her shoulder. This was the first night of the full moon. With its light, the book would open the path to the Void, allowing Elena to call upon the unfathomable powers of the book's spirits. Elena shuddered in the cooling evening. She would call upon this well of magicks only if needed.

"The moon rises," a voice said behind her.

Startled out of her reverie, she turned to find Harlequin Quail standing on the gravel path behind her. Not a single bell of the hundreds he wore had jingled at his approach. He stood with his hands shoved deep into his pockets. His pale bluish skin shone in the torchlight.

"What're you doing here?" Er'ril snapped.

Harlequin shrugged, pulled a pipe from a pocket, and began to light the tamped tobacco. "I heard about the kid and his tree. I came to offer what support I can."

"We have more than enough help," Er'ril said with a scowl.

"Then maybe I just came out for a moonlight stroll." His pipe blew to flame. He shifted slightly, putting his back to the plainsman.

Elena frowned at Er'ril and reached to touch Harlequin's elbow. Earlier, he had left too quickly for her to voice her appreciation for the risks he'd taken to bring his dire news. She could at least acknowledge his concern here. "Thank you," she said.

He nodded, his gold eyes shining, unreadable. Behind him the wide door of the courtyard banged open, and a dark shadow emerged. A flicker of fright flashed through her.

Harlequin glanced over his shoulder. "Your brother, is it not?"

Elena saw the man was correct. She had sent a page to fetch Joach. Of them all, her brother was the one most familiar with the black arts. If there was foulness afoot here, then his guidance could prove useful.

Her brother shambled over, leaning heavily upon the staff.

"Looks like he could be your grandfather," Harlequin mumbled around the stem of his pipe.

Joach had not heard the small man's words. Elena forced her expression to remain bland. Even after so long, the sight of her brother aged and decrepit shook her. "Thank you for coming, Joach." She introduced Harlequin Quail.

Her brother nodded, eyeing the stranger with suspicion. Between Er'ril and Joach, it was hard to say who was more jaded and distrustful.

"So what's wrong, El?" he asked, turning back to her.

She quickly explained. Joach's gaze shifted to the tree, studying it with squinted eyes.

"It was good you sent for me," he said as she finished. "Whatever magick broods in these dark buds, we'd best be wary."

She turned back to the tree. "We've weapons both magickal and not."

Joach took in the axes and pails of pitch. "Good, good." He rubbed his hand along the haft of his staff. She noted the calfskin glove. Since his aging, Joach had been becoming more and more susceptible to the cold.

Nee'lahn stepped forward, Rodricko at her side. "It's time. The first full moon of summer is near to rising."

Elena glanced past the castle walls. Half the moon's full face glowed silver on the horizon. It would not be long. She stripped off her own gloves, exposing the ruby rose of her power. Each hand, from the wrist down, whorled with crimson hues. Elena clenched her fingers and willed the wild magicks in her blood to her hands. Deep inside, a chorus of power rang brighter; she balanced and bent that power to her command. Her right fist glowed brighter with the fire of the rising sun, her left took on the azure hues of the moon itself: wit'ch fire and coldfire.

Reaching to her waist, she slid out the silver-and-ebony dagger, its hilt carved into a rose—her wit'ch dagger. She readied the sharp edge to release the magick inside her, to channel the vast energy of the Void into this world.

But first she nicked the tip of a finger, closed her eyes, and daubed the blood on her lids. A flash of fire flared across her vision with a familiar burn. She opened her eyes and looked upon a new world. All was as it was before, but now the hidden traceries of magick became visible to her spellcast eyes. She noted the silver flicker of elemental fire in Nee'lahn, Meric, even the boy.

But it was the tree that held her attention.

What was once wood and greenery now blazed with inner fire. Channels of power ran up the trunk, branching into its limbs, splitting into stems. Pure elemental energy surged up from the land itself, the magick of root and loam.

She had never imagined such power in the small tree. Each bloom was a torch of magick, burning brighter than any star.

She began to doubt her choice in sparing the tree.

Er'ril sensed her distress. "Are you all right?" he asked.

She nodded, biting back her trepidation. If she voiced her doubts, she suspected Er'ril would call for the tree's immediate destruction. So instead, she simply waved forward.

Nee'lahn knelt by the boy, whispering in his ear. Rodricko nodded his head, his eyes on the tree, as he wriggled out of his boots.

As he struggled, Elena studied him. A strong flame of elemental fire blazed in his chest. But stranger still, Elena recognized the bonds between boy and sapling. Silver filaments connected the tree's vast energy to the flicker inside the child's heart. Elena knew Nee'lahn was right. The two were clearly bonded. If the sapling was destroyed, Rodricko would surely fade.

Free of his boots, the boy straightened.

Glancing to the sky, Nee'lahn leaned back on her heels, her face a mask of worry. The moon continued its climb among the stars. The night was perfectly clear. Only a bit of sea mist feathered the horizons.

"Go, Rodricko," Nee'lahn said, shifting her small lute forward. "Waken your tree."

The boy crossed the open loam, his feet sinking into the soft dirt. Under the branches of the tree, Rodricko lifted his hands to a single closed bud. He did not touch its dark petals but only cupped his tiny palms around it.

The bloom swelled with brightness. Silver moonlight bathed the courtyard.

"Sing," Nee'lahn whispered. "The moon is risen full."

Rodricko craned his neck, his boyish features limned in moonlight and shadow. Though his lips did not move, a sweet sound flowed from him. It sounded like the whistle of wind through heavy branches, a soft sighing of notes, the shushed fall of autumn leaves.

Nee'lahn clutched both her hands to her neck, frightened yet proud.

Elena was sure that whatever chorus she heard herself was but a single note compared to what the nyphai woman could hear. The play of magick in the tree was brilliant. Power quickened in the tree and boy. The silver traceries connecting the two grew more substantial. New filaments arced gracefully from the tree and flowed into the boy.

His singing became louder, fuller, deeper.

"It's happening," Nee'lahn said.

Er'ril stirred beside her, hefting his ax into readiness. Elena did not doubt that Er'ril could cleave the trunk with a single swing.

A flicker of elemental fire drew her attention momentarily to the other side. Joach had shuffled closer for a better look, his bleary eyes squinted. But the staff he leaned upon was a shaft of pure flame, a font of immense elemental energy. She stared at Joach, not understanding. Her brother, an elemental tied to the magick of the dream, also bore the familiar silver flame near his heart. Yet, Elena could see fiery strands linking her brother to the staff. She opened her mouth to voice her surprise.

Nee'lahn interrupted. "The flowers bloom!"

Elena's attention shifted back to the tree; she would question Joach later about this strange play of power.

At the sapling, a miraculous transformation was under way. Elemental fire flared between boy and tree. Rodricko was consumed in this blinding fire. From the lack of response in the others, Elena guessed she was the only one to see the flow of magick here. Even Nee'lahn knelt in the boy's shadow, tense and fearful.

Rodricko continued to sing, cupping the flower. Between his raised palms, the single bud began to peel its petals back, blooming in the moonlight.

Each flower on the tree followed suit, and plumes of elemental energy flowed out of the dark petals, vibrating with the boy's song. Elena could almost hear another voice, singing in harmony. *Treesong,* she realized with amazement.

"The flowers glow," Er'ril murmured at her side.

Elena forced her own vision to see past the flames of silvery energy. The dark blooms were indeed glowing in the night. Black petals had opened to fiery hearts, red as molten rock.

Cries, first low, then louder, rose from the tree. But they weren't screams of pain, but of release and joy.

"What's happening?" Er'ril said, the guards behind him holding the pitch and torches ready.

Using her spellcast sight, Elena watched as bursts of energy shot forth from each bloom, spheres of azure brilliance, sailing up into the air, different than the silvery elemental energy of root and loam. This was something new. And the echoing cries were coming from these shining orbs.

Nee'lahn answered the plainsman's query. "The blooms ... they're casting forth bits of lifeforce. I can hear the song of the living set free."

"I see it, too," Elena said. "Energy being cast toward the full moon." She watched the flow of energy sailing toward the face of the full moon, a river of lifeforce.

"It's from the Grim," Nee'lahn whispered, hushed. Her words were not spoken with horror but with awe. "It's all the lives that my sisterhood consumed, set free at long last." Her voice dropped further. "No wonder Cecelia fought so hard for her son—she must have known. A small way to make peace with the evil sown by the wraiths."

The streaming flow of glowing orbs wound toward the evening skies.

Meric helped Nee'lahn to her feet. The pair drifted closer.

Elena joined them in observing the spectacle, quiet celebrants as the spirits were set free. She watched with two sets of eyes. One saw the tree, blooming and aglow. Another saw the sapling ablaze with energy, twined with Rodricko, while overhead a river of spiritual power sailed skyward.

"The flowers are changing," Er'ril said at her side.

As each bloom cast its last azure energy toward the moon, the blossom's petals softened in color, fading from midnight black to violet—the true color of a koa'kona bloom. Only their hearts remained fiery red, both a reminder of and testimony to the penance done here this night.

With relief, Elena watched the silvery river flow into the night sky, sung skyward by the boy.

Harlequin cut into her wonder, his voice sharp with concern. "The moon—what's wrong with the moon!"

SY-WEN SAT ACROSS THE LIBRARY TABLE FROM BROTHER RYN. THE WHITE-robed monk crouched over the ebon'stone egg, a pair of tiny spectacles perched on the tip of his nose. Still he squinted through a chunk of lens in his hand. "Most strange," he muttered. "Come see, lass."

She moved to his side. The pair had spent the afternoon in the castle's main library, searching the dusty scrolls and rat-nibbled tomes for any mention of such stones, but they had learned little that they did not already know. The stone fed on blood, powering some ancient magick that was poorly understood. It was not elemental energy, but neither was it Chyric, like the Weir.

After their long search, they decided to concentrate their energies on the egg itself. The captain's logbook still rested by the library's hearth, drying. The library's chief caretaker warned against opening the sodden book. "The ink'll smear for sure. She must be dried first, cover to cover, before risking a reading."

Sy-wen glanced to the logbook. It rested on a rack beside the hearth, not so close as to risk burning, but near enough to dry. "The morning at the soonest," the caretaker had warned before leaving. "Perhaps not even then."

That left only the egg itself as a source of information.

As Sy-wen joined Brother Ryn, he rubbed a palm over his shaven head. "There is still too much we don't know about its substance, this black stone. But see," he said, and passed his flat disc of magnifying crystal. He pointed to the egg. "Look here. Closely."

She bent with the crystal before her eyes. "What am I looking for?"

Brother Ryn traced a finger along a vein of silver. He did not touch the stone itself—neither of them dared. During their earlier examinations, they had shifted the loathsome thing with copper tongs from the tools by the hearth. "Notice this line of silver here."

"So?" Sy-wen did not understand the significance. The ebon'stone was jagged with veins of silver that forked across its smooth surface like lightning against a night sky. "It looks like all the others."

"Hmm . . . look closer, lass. From the side, if you will."

She shifted slightly, glancing at the egg from a different angle. Then a gasp of surprise escaped her: This vein was not flush with the stone's surface, as the others were. The silver thread was imbedded slightly deeper. "What is it?"

He leaned nearer. "See how this vein runs in a complete circle around the egg? Other lines jaggedly cross its path, attempting to deceive the eye. But this main line zigzags around the egg's circumference—one unending circle."

She followed his finger. He was right! "What does it mean?"

He straightened, accepting back the glass from her. "I'd say that we're looking at the way to open the egg—the proverbial crack in the shell."

Sy-wen cringed back. "A way to open it?" She could not even imagine what horror might be hidden inside, what sickness could be germinating. She suddenly wished Kast were here. But he had left with Hunt and the high keel, to begin the plans for the coming assault.

Brother Ryn glanced to the book drying by the hearth. "If only we had more information about this cursed thing."

She nodded. "Like a way to destroy it."

The old scholar turned back to the egg. "Or to judge the danger it poses."

"The only way to know that would be to open it—and we dare not do that."

Brother Ryn glanced to her. She read the burning curiosity in his eyes. "We can't face what we don't know."

She bit her lip. There were another hundred of the horrible things near the dock of A'loa Glen. Before they chanced moving the wreck, they had to know what was at risk. "But we don't have a clue on how to unlock the stone."

Brother Ryn voiced it aloud. "The stone feeds on blood. Blood must be the key."

Her attention on the dark stone, she sensed the truth to his words. "But the key to what?"

GRESHYM STOOD UNDER A MAPLE TREE NEAR THE WATER'S EDGE. AHEAD, THE great expanse of Moon Lake stretched to the horizons, a dark mirror reflecting the rising full moon. Already hundreds of celebrants lined the banks, waiting for the moment when the moon would reach its highest point and shine down into the center of the lake.

For as long as Greshym could remember, the ritual of the First Moon had been performed here, a custom that dated back into Alasea's distant past. No one knew for sure how or why this observance had first started. The accounts of the origin were as many as they were varied. But one common thread ran through all the stories: On the first moon of summer, the face of the Mother above would appear in the waters and grant wishes to those who bathed in the lake and were true of heart.

And that was the catch, Greshym thought sourly: *to be true of heart.*

Each celebration, scores of participants declared their wishes granted, beating their chests and dropping to their knees. But Greshym suspected all were lying or deluded. Who would be foolish enough to claim their wish *wasn't* fulfilled, lest their own heart be questioned? So each year, the hordes came with their aching joints, their ailing spouses, their secret loves . . . all to jump in a cold, mossy lake.

"So much foolishness," Greshym mumbled, for only he knew the true secret of the lake. And he meant to have his own wish granted, even if it meant the death of every person here.

Behind him, he heard Rukh stir from his hiding place in a scrabble-berry bush. The stump gnome was growing as impatient as its master.

Tinkling music wafted over the waters as a flotilla of sails drifted past on the calm lake, bearing those few whose purses bulged with gold. Past his spot, one of largest barges floated, decorated with fanciful carvings, silk sails, and lanterns shaped like the moon in all its phases. It seemed only the rich were granted such close communion with the mysterious lady of the lake.

But this was not a night for only those with money. All around the shoreline, torches and colored lanterns brightened the water's edge, light-ing the way for the other celebrants. A few children already splashed in the shallows, too excited to wait. Their calls echoed like sharp bells, ring-ing out with joy and delight. The smells from the hundreds of cooking fires filled the crisp summer night with the aromas of charred meats and fragrant stews.

Greshym straightened, knowing his long wait was almost over. The moon was near its highest point. "Rukh!"

The stump gnome crawled on his belly out of the bush.

They crossed the short distance to their lone stretch of beach. Greshym had assured their privacy with a small repulsion spell attached to this spit of land extending out into the lake.

He used a small dagger to dig out the dried clay that plugged the top of his hollow bone staff. His lips moved in a silent spell. He touched the magick in the newborn's blood, the babe's innocent lifeforce. It was his to command.

Around the lake, a hush fell over the crowd. Somewhere in the distance a baby wailed. Did it sense the blood of its brother?

Greshym held out his staff, pointing the open end of the bone toward the wide lake. Upon the water's surface, the moon's reflection continued to glow, but as the moon reached its highest point, the magick of this night began. The reflected face of the moon began to shine brighter, almost blinding to stare upon. Its glow spread to cover the entire lake, turning dark waters to silver.

A cry rose from the crowd. As one, the celebrants cast themselves into the waters: some naked, some clothed, the young, the old. Some went silently, some with pleas shouted to the skies.

Greshym simply smiled—and spoke the last part of the enchantment.

He lowered the tip of his staff to the lake and spilled the spellcast blood upon the bright waters. The stain spread out from his spit of land. No one noticed the blasphemy to the ceremony. All were too busy with their own heartfelt wishes.

The wash of blood expanded, sweeping toward the center of the lake.

What none of the folk here knew was that the waters of Moon Lake were steeped in the elemental magick of pure light, making it a potent well that filled only this one night when the moon was in the perfect position for the waters to absorb its silvery magick. The lake became a font of immense power, energy from the Void itself. The sense of contentment felt by the bathers was nothing more than the intimate wash of this energy over their bodies, mixing their lifeforces with the energy of the Void.

But with the dawn, the effect would quickly fade. Moon energy could not withstand the burn of the sun. And Greshym would not let this font of energy go to waste, not when he had such powerful enemies.

He touched the tip of his staff to the stain in the waters, speaking the spell to draw the lake's power into the hollow bone. As the staff filled with strength a thousandfold, the stain continued to spread over the lake. It would take most of the night to siphon off all the power here.

Greshym's lips split into a hard smile as he worked.

Off to the left, a group of boisterous bathers failed to notice the dark stain sweeping toward them. As the silver waters turned black around them, song and merriment turned to wails and cries.

Greshym watched as the lifeforces of these folk, submerged in the elemental power of the waters, were ripped from their racked bodies. For the briefest moments, their life energy could be seen trying to escape: Ghosts of azure light skated across the dark surface before being sucked away, drowned in the spellcast waters.

As Greshym continued to draw off this energy, other bathers were caught in the wave of darkness. The stain overtook the moon-lantern barge. A cry of distress arose from the captain of the doomed vessel. His wards, already enjoying the waters, were deaf to his calls. They were consumed by the darkness. Even the boat began to sink, its hull no longer adrift on plain water, but sliding under a sea of dark magick.

Deep laughter flowed from Greshym. He appreciated the hearty sound of his own mirth. With the power here, no one could thwart him.

A sharp cry sounded from far across the lake. "Look to the moon!"

Greshym glanced up to the night skies, and his smile screwed down into a frown. The face of the full moon shone as bright as before, but now a crimson scar marked its center, streaming outward in rivulets.

"The moon bleeds!" someone shouted.

Greshym watched the stain begin to stream down toward the lake.

"What is this magick?" he mumbled. It was no effect of his spell. And if not, then whose? He remembered Shorkan's mirth. "The bastard . . ."

He pulled his staff from the waters, readying himself to either fight or flee.

All around the lake cries echoed, "The moon! The moon!"

"WHAT'S HAPPENING TO THE MOON?" ER'RIL ASKED. HE STEPPED CLOSE TO Elena, watching her frown as she gazed up into the evening sky.

She leaned near. "I don't know. "

Directly overhead, the full moon bled streams of fiery crimson. The trails seemed to flow toward them.

"The corruption seems to be flowing down the stream of spirit energy rising from the tree," Elena said. "Back toward us."

Meric stood with Nee'lahn. She cradled her lute to her chest, face staring upward with horror. Harlequin and Joach joined them, frowning at the night skies.

The only one oblivious to the spectacle above was little Rodricko. He continued to sing to his tree, while the glowing blooms continued to shed their darkness and shine with a pure violet brilliance.

"Is it something the boy is doing?" Er'ril asked. "Should we stop him?"

Nee'lahn heard his question. "No. He must finish the ritual."

"This can't be the boy's fault," Meric said. "Something else is amiss here."

"What?" Er'ril asked.

"I know a way to find out," Elena said, shifting around. She tugged at the satchel over her shoulder. "The Blood Diary."

She pulled the tome from the bag. The gilt rose on its leather cover glowed bright silver, matching the moonlight. She prepared to open the book.

Er'ril reached out, placing a palm atop the shining rose. "The Blood Diary is tied to the moon, and now the moon bleeds. Perhaps we should think before opening the path to the Void."

Elena looked him in the eye. "Whatever evil arises here, it has something to do with the moon. If there are answers, Cho may be the only one to divine them."

Er'ril slowly nodded. "Be careful." Ever since the events in Gul'gotha when Cho had possessed Elena, he had been wary of the book's spirits, fearing that Cho had neither Elena's nor Alasea's best interests at heart. The spirit's single-minded pursuit of Chi, her spiritual twin, overwhelmed any concern for this land or its people.

Elena squeezed Er'ril's hand, silently thanking him for his concern. For a moment, he felt the power coursing under the ruby skin of her palm—energy from Cho. Then the young woman broke contact, turning away.

Elena lifted her book, took a deep breath, and opened the leather cover. Neither of them were ready for the explosion of light that followed. Elena was knocked back, but Er'ril caught her. He managed a glimpse of the book's pages. Instead of white parchment, the book was a window into another existence. Beyond the Blood Diary, stars blazed against an inky darkness. Clouds of radiant mists glided around orbs churning with the energies of the endless Void.

Elena regained her feet. The plume of light from the book sailed high, then arced and landed on the courtyard path beside them. The figure of a woman quickly took shape, sculpted of light and energy. Clothed in glowing moonstone that swirled with energies not of this world, the woman turned her face toward Elena. Burning suns raged behind her eyes. *"What is this desecration?"* Cho cried out.

"We don't know," Er'ril answered, trying to match her stern tone.

"It is why we called you forth," Elena added.

Cho stared up to the skies, then down to the tree. *"A bridge,"* she said, her anger still bright. *"A new spirit bridge has opened!"*

The others in the courtyard gathered near, silent witnesses.

"A spirit bridge?" Er'ril asked.

Elena stepped free of his arms. "Maybe we should speak to Fila," she suggested, referring to her own aunt. Er'ril understood Elena's request: her aunt's ghost was also a bridge between worlds.

Cho glanced once more at the moon, then, without even moving, she seemed to melt. Her shoulders relaxed, and her movement as she turned back to them was more natural. The shine of the Void was gone from her eyes.

"Child," she said warmly, "how do you fare?"

"Aunt Fila . . ." Elena's voice caught in her throat.

Er'ril placed a hand on her shoulder, supporting her. "What's happening to the moon?"

The ghostly figure glanced across the courtyard. "Cho was right. The release of spirits from the tree has formed a temporary link between the Void and this world. It is the same as my spirit, a connection between two planes." She turned back to them. "But the link here is not fixed, the way I am fixed to the magick of the Blood Diary. Once the flow of spirits from the koa'kona ceases, the bridge will end."

"But what about the moon?" Elena asked.

Overhead, the moon had grown almost a solid bloodred, streaming fiery trails toward them.

Aunt Fila frowned and motioned Elena to lift one hand. The ruby hue of her Rose matched the color of the moon. "With the bridge open, energy bleeds from the Void to here."

"But why?" Elena asked. "I don't understand."

"Neither do I. Neither does Cho. It shouldn't be happening. Cho is panicked. It is as if something has rent a huge tear in the fabric of her world. It bleeds into ours now."

"What danger does that pose?" Er'ril asked.

The ghost of Aunt Fila shook her head. "If that energy reaches us, it could burn our world to a cinder, or warp the weave of our own existence." Her gaze flicked to the tree. "The bridge must be severed."

"But it's almost over." Nee'lahn said, stepping forward. "Already the last of the dark blooms brighten."

Er'ril saw she was right. Only a handful of blooms remained dark, shining their fiery hearts skyward. Still, if the fate of the world teetered here . . .

He gripped his ax tighter in his hand.

"Can we block the Void's energy?" Elena asked, clearly seeking an alternative to risking Rodricko.

"Not without knowing why this rupture occurred."

"But if we don't know what's causing it," Elena argued, "who's to say that severing the bridge will stop what's happening?"

Aunt Fila's brows knit together. Elena's question clearly disturbed her. "You may be right. That answer must be discovered first. I must consult Cho." She turned away.

Elena glanced to Er'ril. He took her hand, but he kept his grip on the ax. A few steps away, Meric consoled Nee'lahn. Beyond them, a lone boy sang to his tree. For a moment, in the boy's song, Er'ril felt the cusp of fate. For just this instant—with the tableau of players gathered here, the charged flows of power—Er'ril sensed that this very moment was ordained from the forging of the Blood Diary ages ago.

Where did the future go from here?

Finally, after a long silence, Aunt Fila turned back to them. Her eyes were again aglow with the icy fires of the Void: Cho was back. She turned those empty eyes toward Elena. *"I have read the aether. Energy flows into the Void."* She pointed back to the tree, indicating the flow of spirits, then turned back to the crimson moon. *"But something also draws it back out."*

Elena frowned. "Draws it back out?"

Cho's moonstone face threatened to crack. She motioned with ghostly hands, trying to put into words something that had no words. *"Two flows. One moving in, one out—all at the same place."* Again the flicker of her gaze to the moon. *"Energy churns."* She wrung her hands for emphasis.

"A riptide?" Er'ril asked.

Cho cocked her head, as if listening to something inside her. *"Tides . . . moon . . . riptide. Fila understands. Yes . . . riptides."*

Elena frowned. "But why? If the spiritual energy is going in, what's drawing the Void's energy out?"

Cho's form shimmered, her features blurring. Er'ril had enough experience with the spirit to know when it was angered. *"I know not!"* she cried out. *"But I will!"*

"How?" Elena asked.

Again Cho cocked her head, but this time as if the question made no sense . . . or the answer was too plain to speak. *"I return to the Void."* The moonstone apparition swirled upward.

"Wait!" Elena called out. "What do you mean?"

Cho half turned, shimmering between form and pure energy. *"This desecration risks everything . . . myself, my brother, both our worlds. I must go."*

The spirit swept toward the tree in a swirl of light, a woman-shaped comet. She spiraled up the branches and into the sky above.

"She's floating in the river of spirits," Elena said, staring up.

As Er'ril watched, the glow of Cho stretched toward both the tree and the moon, elongating into a shimmering cord. It seemed to hover there for an interminable time, trembling, threatening to break.

Then with a noise unheard by the ears but that vibrated the hairs on Er'ril's arms, the cord snapped—and Cho was gone.

Silence hung like a heavy fog in the aftermath of the display.

Joach was the first to speak. "The koa'kona is spent."

All eyes turned toward the tree. Er'ril realized the silence from a moment ago had been complete. Rodricko had stopped singing and had slumped to his knees before the tree. Er'ril studied the sapling. Each and every bloom now glowed violet, a spray of brilliant jewels in a sea of dark green. Not a single bloom remained dark.

"It's over," Nee'lahn said, shaking with relief. "All the trapped spirits have been set free."

"But the moon still bleeds," Harlequin said.

Er'ril glanced skyward. The moon indeed remained stained. The tear in the Void was still open. Elena had been right. Severing the bridge had *not* stopped the danger.

Elena suddenly gasped behind him.

He turned to her. She was not staring at the moon like the others, but down to the Blood Diary in her hand. The book hung open in her trembling grip.

"The pages . . ." she mumbled, holding out the tome.

Er'ril stared. Plain white parchment shone in the torchlight.

The Void had vanished from the book.

4

DEEP IN THE CASTLE, KAST HURRIED WITH PRINCE TYRUS. HE HAD BEEN urgently summoned away from his meeting with the Dre'rendi keelchiefs. Sy-wen's note warned that Brother Ryn had discovered something about the ebon'stone egg, and they needed his immediate help. Tyrus had also been at the meeting to coordinate his pirate brigade, but he accompanied Kast now because of the man trailing them both.

"Xin, are you sure?" Tyrus asked again.

The zo'ol tribesman nodded. "I sensed a darkness, a well of sickness. A flicker, like a darkfire candle . . . Then it was gone. But it was no imagining. It was real."

Kast frowned back at the shaman. The small man was bare-chested. A single braid of hair trailed over one shoulder, decorated with feathers and bits of shell. His dark skin glowed ebony in the dim halls, making the pale scar of a rising sun on his brow seem to shine with its own light. Kast knew the jungle shaman could read another's heart; this empathy opened paths to others, even far away.

Tyrus pointed to the stairwell opening ahead. "We must let Elena and Er'ril know of this."

Kast scowled. "I'll see what Sy-wen has discovered and join you in the courtyard. Perhaps the darkness has to do with that tree."

Tyrus turned toward the stairway, waving Xin to follow. Kast prepared to head the other direction toward the castle's libraries, but a cry sounded behind him. He swung around in time to see the zo'ol shaman collapse. Both Tyrus and Kast went to his aid.

"What's wrong?" the pirate prince asked.

Xin panted, his face contorted in pain. "The darkness . . . stronger . . ." He lifted an arm. "It comes from that way."

He pointed not to the stairs, but to the passage Kast had been about to take.

Tyrus met his gaze. "Could it be the egg?"

"It must," Kast said. Fear for Sy-wen fired his blood. He passed the tribesman to the prince. "Tell Elena."

Tyrus nodded.

Xin shook his head, like casting out cobwebs. "It's gone again . . . but . . ."

Kast hesitated. "But what?"

Xin glanced up to the two other men. "It . . . it felt familiar . . ." He shook his head. "I don't know."

"And I don't have time," Kast said sharply, and set off down the corridor. He dared wait no longer. The library was on the other side of the castle, beneath the observatory tower. If Sy-wen was in danger . . .

"Be careful," Tyrus called after him.

He increased his speed, running now. He pounded down the hall, careening around a series of bends, almost knocking down a chambermaid with an armful of folded linen. He had no time for apologies. He leaped a short flight of stairs, all but flying up them as if he already bore his dragon wings. The heavy oaken doors of the library were just ahead.

He reached the doors and pulled on the latch. It resisted. Locked. Panicked with imagined terrors, he pounded a fist on the door. "Sy-wen!"

There was no answer.

He pounded again, searching around for something to batter down the door.

"Kast?" Sy-wen's voice called from beyond the locked library doors. His knees weakened with relief as he heard the lock's bolt slide. Then the door swung open.

Sy-wen stared out at him. "What are you doing pounding—?" Then she must have noticed his panting breath and pale face. "What's wrong?"

Kast pushed into the library, searching intently, breathing hard.

"Has something happened?" Sy-wen asked behind him, closing the door.

Down the aisle between the row after row of stacked shelves, a group of white-robed scholars crowded around a hearthside table. The entire library staff must have been summoned. One of the men glanced back to him and waved—Brother Ryn. Kast exhaled loudly, relieved. Nothing appeared amiss.

Sy-wen touched his shoulder. "Kast, tell me. What is it?"

He shook his head. "I . . . I thought something happened."

Sy-wen frowned, moving next to him and walking him toward the other end of the library. "Why would you think that?"

"Your urgent note . . . something Shaman Xin felt." He pulled Sy-wen closer to him and kissed the top of her head. "I'm just glad you're safe."

She placed an arm around his waist as they reached the scholars.

Brother Ryn waved him toward the table, bumping his colleagues aside to make room for the large Bloodrider. "You must see this. Extraordinary, really." He pushed his glasses back from the tip of his nose.

Kast moved closer, but still it took him half a shocked breath to understand what he saw. Two oval bowls lay on the table. Each was jagged-edged and made of ebon'stone. Not two *bowls*, he realized, but two halves of the same shell. "You opened it!" he gasped out.

"It wasn't hard," Sy-wen said at his shoulder, her arm still around his waist. "It just took a little blood." She pointed toward one of the scholars, a young acolyte from his yellow sash, slumped by the far wall. His white robe was a stained ruin down the front. His throat had been sliced. "Actually more than a *little* blood, before we were through," Sy-wen said.

Kast jerked backward, but the arm at his waist locked around him, impossibly strong. He struggled harder, but other hands grabbed him from behind, clamping like iron. "What . . . ?" he finally managed to gasp out.

Brother Ryn stepped toward Sy-wen. "A dragon that is ours to command. You've done well, my dear."

Sy-wen slipped her arm from around Kast's waist, turning to face him while the others held him tight.

Brother Ryn lifted his hand. He clutched a gelatinous creature in his palm. Tentacles writhed over the man's wrist and forearm. One stretched toward Kast, blind and groping. A suckered mouth at the tip puckered open.

Kast paled.

"Do you recognize this little creature?" Brother Ryn asked.

Kast had indeed heard stories of such monsters. Its ilk had possessed the minds of a shipload of Port Rawl pirates. Elena and her allies had barely escaped alive.

Ryn lifted his prize. "The Master has improved on their form. A new generation."

"We've saved the last one for you," Sy-wen said.

Kast strained to pull away.

"But there are another hundred eggs down under the sea," Brother Ryn said. "Each a vessel for a score of these creatures."

"And we're going to fetch them for our Master," Sy-wen said. "You and I."

"Never," he spat.

"You have no choice, my love." She reached toward Kast's cheek, her voice a mocking whisper. "I have need of you."

GRESHYM STARED AT THE BLEEDING MOON, RIVERS OF CRIMSON FLOWING OUT and down.

Under its sickly glow, cries rose all around the lake. Bathers splashed toward shore. In the trees, torches flared brighter from lakeside camps, and the merry music died away. Sails fled the center of the lake. The waters were being abandoned.

Even Rukh was disturbed by the moon's appearance. The stump gnome groveled and whined, digging troughs in the mud with his hooves and claws.

Greshym raised his bone staff, attempting to discern the danger to himself. Across the lake, the blood spell continued its course across the silver waters, continuing to absorb the moonlight trapped here. Eventually he would need to claim this energy for himself, but right now, he maintained his guard.

In the center of the lake, the reflection of the moon marked the brightest spot in the silver waters. Even this mirrored image bore the bloodred stain.

Holding his breath, Greshym watched the tide of his own dark magick encroach upon the marred reflection. He was not sure what would happen when the two merged. He sensed a vastness of power in those corrupted waters. The elemental properties of Moon Lake had absorbed even the energy of this strange phenomenon.

As his dark spell swept through the silver waters toward the crimson, a ghostly shimmer rose from the lake, an azure mist. Greshym frowned. *What was this?*

The mist swirled for a breath upon unseen winds, then wrapped down upon itself. The figure of a woman took shape at its heart, standing in the center of the moon's reflection, in the heart of the ruby stain. Slowly she spun in place, studying the edges of the lake.

Greshym was not the only one to notice her appearance. "It's the Lady of the Lake!" someone called out. Shouts of surprise followed this cry. Eyes turned toward the miracle. The panic from a moment ago died to

awe and amazement. A hushed moment of expectation settled around
the lake.

Was this truly the Lady of the Lake?

Greshym studied her as the tide of his own magick flowed ever closer
to the crimson waters.

The ghostly woman swung to face in Greshym's direction—and though
the distance was far, he sensed her gaze fall upon him. An arm slowly
raised, pointing, accusing.

Greshym lifted his staff, spinning it once, casting out a shield spell
around both him and Rukh. He was glad he took the precaution: a moment later, his blood-borne spell struck the edge of the ruby stain, igniting
a blinding explosion of energy. A storm of raging power blew outward in
all directions. Greshym cringed with Rukh in the bubble of protection.
He watched trees rip from their roots. A sailboat flew past overhead, tumbling end over end, followed by a surging wall of water twice the height
of the tallest tree.

All this washed over and away from Greshym's island of protection.
He fed more and more of his magick into the shield and gaped at the display. *Such power!* He prayed his magick was strong enough to ride out this
storm.

Through his shield spell, he heard a sound like no other, a howl of
winds that had no place on this world.

As he searched for the source, a profound darkness swept over and past
him. In a single heartbeat, Greshym sensed the world vanish.

His blood iced with terror.

He was in the Void.

ELENA SENSED THE MAGICKAL EXPLOSION A MOMENT BEFORE IT HIT. SHE
tore her eyes from the Blood Diary's blank pages and looked to the moon.
The rivers of crimson corruption suddenly stopped their flows, freezing
in place. She knew this was not a boon, but something worse . . . much
worse.

"Er'ril . . . ," she warned.

"What is it?"

She opened her mouth, but she found no words. She simply pointed to
the skies.

The ruby stain on the silvery moon began to darken, then well upward,
like a bubble rising from impossible depths.

"Run," she whispered.

"Where? From what?" Er'ril grabbed her arm.

Elena yanked free. She shoved the Diary at him and grabbed up her wit'ch dagger. She sliced a deep wound across one palm, then the other. She felt none of the pain, only a growing panic.

Er'ril shoved the Diary into his cloak and reached for her. "Elena . . ."

Ignoring him, she raised both hands. She knew it was already too late. Soundlessly, the dark bubble exploded outward. Through spellcast eyes, she watched in horror as a flare of fiery energy raced toward them, chasing along the echo trail of spiritual energy left behind by the tree's blooming.

"Run!" she screamed.

Before anyone could take a single step, the storm's shock wave struck the courtyard like a great weight of water dropped from above.

Elena cast out the magick from both hands, but the energy from above snuffed through her effort and struck her with the force of storm-swept wave. The world vanished around her. Darkness without end consumed her.

Before a single thought could form, a tiny spark shattered the darkness, scintillating and bursting out in a dense tangle of threads and branches. The web swept over her, through her, around her. Her mind extended along the myriad threads, expanding out. She recognized the connection. She had experienced it before, whenever she had touched her magick at its most intimate depths.

It was the web of life, the infinite connection linking all life around the world. Voices filled her head. Images rushed by in a blur. Foreign desires, sensations, dreams swept through her. She fought to hold herself together, to keep from losing herself in this shining tangle of life.

She failed.

Elena tumbled toward the center of the web, a will-o'-the-wisp in a maelstrom. She had no anchor. As she fell, she sensed a greater presence filling her mind, something that was life, but not life. She suddenly knew she was not alone here. Deep in the tangle of the world's lifeweb, something existed. She felt its attention slowly turn her way. It was immense, immutable, forever. It was the spider of this web, the weaver.

Elena struggled to flee. She knew she could not survive its gaze.

Suddenly hands grabbed her, dragging her up and away. Words formed in her mind: *You must not go there!*

Relief surged. It was Cho, returned.

Then she was flung with the force of a thousand suns.

Pain ripped through her.
You must never go there!

TYRUS REACHED THE DOOR TO THE COURTYARD AS THE THUNDERCLAP HIT. THE explosion knocked him to his knees. The entire castle shook. The thick ironwood door before him shuddered and cracked.

"Sweet Mother!" he gasped. Had lightning struck just beyond the threshold? Shaking his head against the echoing boom, he grabbed for the iron latch to the door, then cried out in pain and surprise. His hand had instantly frozen to the metal, so cold it burned. As he yanked back, he left a good swatch of skin on the handle.

Xin was a step behind him. "Something's wrong."

"I think I got that," Tyrus snapped. He wrapped his ice-burned hand in his cloak and snatched at the latch again, but the door failed to budge. Growling his frustration, he kicked out, popping it open through a layer of ice.

The gardens of the Grand Courtyard beyond looked untouched. There was no sign of lightning strike or any storm in the sky. As Tyrus swung about, looking, the edge of his cloak brushed a rose. The pale pink flower crumpled to shards of crystalline petal.

Tyrus stared at the ruin in shock.

Xin reached to the branch of a flowering dogwood. It snapped off at his touch to tinkle and shatter upon the gravel path.

"All frozen," Tyrus said. Under the light of the full moon, the gardens shone with an unnatural gleam. Every surface was rimed with ice, dead.

Movement drew his eye. A small figure crawled from under the shelter of the tree in the center of the gardens—the boy Rodricko. The lad reached to a purple flower of the koa'kona sapling, almost soothing it. Its petals remained soft, unfrozen. The tree suffused a warm radiance, a glow from its hundreds of open blooms. Except for the boy, the tree was the only living thing here.

Xin spoke behind him. "Where are the others?"

Tyrus shook his head. He had no answer.

The gardens were empty.

KAST WAS THE FIRST TO REACT TO THE SUDDEN BOOM THAT ROCKED THE CAStle. As his captors froze in an instant of confusion, Kast lunged and broke the grips that held him. Brother Ryn, still holding the fistful of gelatinous tentacles, stumbled backward. With a roar, Kast grabbed the edge of the library table and heaved upward, using all the strength of his pain and fury. The heavy oaken desk flew high, knocking aside the gathered brethren and striking the hearth. Coals scattered, and the two pieces of ebon'stone shell clattered across the floor.

Fingers clutched at his sleeve. He swung around. It was Sy-wen. "Kast . . . !" She sounded for the moment like herself.

"Sy-wen?"

She stared up at him, frightened.

Kast smashed a fist into her face. Her nose broke under his knuckles; he snatched her wrist and yanked her over his shoulder.

"Grab him!" Brother Ryn screamed.

Kast spun away with the balance of decades atop a rolling deck. Sy-wen's small form was no burden; he raced toward the library doors. There were too many here to fight, especially with their demon-spawn strength. He would gather other defenders, then return to scour the corruption from these halls.

Reaching the doors, Kast had a sudden thought and shoved with his shoulder at the nearest row of stacked shelves. The tall wooden shelf teetered. It was heavy with texts and scrolled parchments.

His pursuers were almost upon him.

Growling with fury, Kast struck again with his shoulder. Sy-wen groaned, but this time the shelf pitched over with a crack, knocking into the next row, sending its neighbor toppling. Row after row collapsed. Dust billowed, and books and scrolls flew.

Kast bounded out the door, but fled no more than four steps. He dumped Sy-wen to the floor, then grabbed a torch, and a lamp from a table.

Sweeping back to the door, Kast flung the lantern at the first pursuer, striking him in the chest. Glass burst and sprayed the man's white robe with oil. Kast shoved him stiff-armed back into the library and struck the torch to the man's chest. "Sorry, my brother."

The oily robe took the flame in a fiery rush. Kast kicked the screaming man into the toppled stacks of dusty tomes and worm-eaten wood. The ancient tinder was ripe for the flame. The fire quickened with a roar. Kast danced back, flinging his torch deeper into the pile of felled books, then spun back to the door and out.

He slammed the thick door and secured it by imbedding his dagger in the jamb, then tied the latch down with his belt. As he worked, he heard screams and cries from inside. The door shook from someone's pounding. There was no other exit from the library, except up a spiral staircase to the observatory, and a deadly fall awaited anyone who attempted to escape in that direction.

Kast turned from the screams. He would have to go for help to make sure this nest was fully burned out. Hurrying, Kast returned to where he had left Sy-wen.

With the hall torch gone to set the fire, the corridor was dark, the shadows thick—and the floor was empty.

He stared down the dark passage. "Sy-wen . . ."

GRESHYM TRIED TO PIERCE THE DARK VOID AROUND HIM. WHERE WAS HE? For a moment, he spotted a flare of crackling light far away in the blackness, a flash of azure lightning. Then it was gone.

He fed magick into his protection spell, draining the last of the dark energy from his bone staff. Despair settled to the marrow of his bones. Behind him, Rukh continued to whine. Did the creature sense its own doom?

Greshym lowered his staff, resigned. At least he had tasted the wine of youth again, even if only a sip.

Then like a bubble popping, the Void vanished, and the world returned around them. The sudden appearance of light and substance knocked Greshym to his knees. Rukh buried his snouted face in the mud, mewling. Greshym nudged him with an elbow. "Quiet, dog!" But his command held no venom. The sight before him had stolen his voice.

The pair still stood on the same spit of land, but Moon Lake was now empty. The lands around were a watery ruin. A leafless, toppled forest spread as far as the eye could see. A clear moon hung over the devastation, blind and cold to the wreckage.

All around, the night remained silent, hushed. No birdsong, no voices, no cries. Greshym strained for sounds of any other survivors. Nothing.

He searched around—then a glimmer of light caught his eye, and he turned back to the center of the lake. Pools of water still stood in deeper pockets of the sandy bottoms; he thought at first he merely saw moonlight reflecting off a puddle. But the shaft of brilliance grew, like a ray of sunshine piercing between two dark clouds—a spear of moonshine from sky to lake.

"What is that?" he murmured, shielding his eyes against the brilliance.

He sensed the flow of magick pulsing in the heart of the brilliant shaft. He lifted his hollow staff. If he could tap into that energy . . .

He took a step toward the lake. Before he could take a second, the spear of light exploded, shattering out in a storm of shards. The blast sent pieces stabbing into the sandy mud. Ice?

He touched the tip of his staff to it. Moonlit energy answered him—these were frozen pieces of the lake. He drew the small bit of magick into the marrow of his weapon, then stared out at the thousands of chunks of ice and smiled. It wasn't as much magick as he had hoped, but it would do for now.

As he gazed out across the lake, he spotted figures rising from the sand and mud in the center of the empty lake. He took a step back warily. Small sounds of shock and disorientation echoed to him.

"Where are we?" a voice asked weakly.

"I don't know." This was spoken with more strength. It also sounded familiar.

"Impossible," Greshym whispered, ducking low. He used the bit of magick in the staff to heighten his vision and sharpen his ears. The figures covered in muck and filth milled together in the center of the lake. Greshym bit back a snarl. It could not be.

Er'ril waded through the muck to Elena's side. With each step, the sandy mud threatened to pull the boots from his feet. "I don't know where we are, but from the stars, it must be far from A'loa Glen."

Elena lifted her face. She had been studying her pale white hands. The Rose was gone from both. "Yes, but where?"

"Somewhere in the forests of the Western Reaches," Nee'lahn answered.

Er'ril glanced over to the small nyphai woman. Meric and one of the castle guards were helping her stand.

Harlequin Quail remained seated in the muck, his expression exasperated. "The Western Reaches . . . great."

"Are you sure?" Joach asked, as the other guard pulled him to his feet. He leaned on his staff, grimacing at the ankle-deep mud.

Nee'lahn stared out at the ruined forest. "I can hear treesong beyond the horizon." Her fingers absently cleaned the mud from her lute. "But the forest here is dead."

"We can see that," Meric said.

"No, you don't understand." Nee'lahn's voice cracked. "It's not just dead—it's *lifeless*. The Land itself is empty." She turned to the others. "Can't you feel it?"

Er'ril searched the ruined landscape. It did indeed seem unnaturally quiet.

"Even dead trees are a part of the cycle of root and loam," Nee'lahn continued, "giving their decaying energy and magick back to the Land. But this soil is empty. Whatever blasted this region tore the elemental magick from tree and Land alike."

No one spoke. The dark and silent forest took on a more ominous shading.

Harlequin finally broke the quiet, pulling out of the sucking mud with a sour look. "But how did we get here and can we get back?"

"It was Cho," Elena answered. "I sensed her when the magick wave struck the courtyard. We must have been carried along the bridge—from one spell to another."

"What do you mean?" Er'ril asked.

"Cho saw two opposing forces upon this night's full moon." She pointed to where the orb now descended toward the horizon. "A spirit bridge heading up and some force drawing energy down ... down to here, I'd imagine." She stared across the dark landscape. "The explosion sucked us along the backwash—up the trace of the spirit bridge and down to this spot, like so much flotsam in a raging current."

"Not all of us." Meric's voice lowered fearfully as he turned to Nee'lahn. "Rodricko ..."

Nee'lahn shook her head. "Fear not. I was watching him when we were struck by the wave. The limbs of his tree sheltered him. He had finished his song ... joined with the tree. As the tree is rooted to the courtyard, so was the boy."

"And he is safe?" Meric asked with clear relief.

Nee'lahn's face tightened. "I must believe so. I'm sure I would sense otherwise."

Er'ril sighed. "We'd best find shelter, get a fire going, and get out of these damp clothes. Then we'll find a way back home."

Joach stood shivering nearby. "A fire sounds good. Once I'm rested, I can try to reach Xin through my black pearl." He patted his pockets.

Er'ril nodded. He knew Joach and the zo'ol shaman had formed a bond—an exchange of gifts and names. This bond allowed them to communicate over long distances. But could it reach this far? That question would wait until morning. Right now, a secure camp was the priority.

They set off toward the forest, working around muddy pools. Er'ril sent the guards forward to scout and aid survivors. He took inventory of the party's weapons. He had his own sword, as did Meric. Joach had his staff, but did he have the strength to wield it?

Er'ril frowned and slogged up to Elena. She had been talking to Harlequin in whispers. The small man spoke with waving hands and jingling bells. Whatever tale he told brought a smile to Elena's lips. For that small blessing, Er'ril could have hugged the strange fellow.

Instead he motioned Elena aside.

"What is it?" she asked.

He took her hands between his own, and found his breath catch in his throat. It was seldom that Elena was not gifted with the magick of the Rose, so it was rare to hold her hands without gloves. He had forgotten the softness of her skin, the warmth of her palm.

"Er'ril . . . ?"

He met her gaze. "We don't know what dangers await us here. You'd best renew your coldfire while the moon is still risen."

Elena seemed to sag, her smile fading. "Of course." She slipped her hand from his and stepped to the side.

He reached for her, then lowered his arm. There were some paths she walked that he couldn't follow.

Elena raised her left hand to the moon. Her eyes closed slightly as she willed the magick again to her. Er'ril stared only at her face. The moonlight cast her into a figure of silver and darkness. After a moment, he saw her lips tighten and her brows furrow. She lowered her arm, then turned to him, holding out her hand, still pale and white.

"It . . . it didn't work."

Er'ril went to her. "Are you sure? Did you do it right?"

She cast him an exasperated look, then stared up at the sky.

"What could've gone wrong?"

Elena leaned into him. "I don't know. Maybe the moon's magick has been too sorely abused this night. Or maybe it's because Cho has vanished. It's her power that channels into me."

"We'll figure this out," Er'ril assured her. "If it's the moon, then we'll know by sunrise. You can renew your wit'ch fire with the dawn."

Elena's voice grew hushed. "And if it fails then, too?"

Er'ril heard the fear in her voice, but also a small thread of relief. He held her tighter. Like the softness of her skin, he sometimes forgot the heavy burden on her shoulders. He simply wrapped his warmth around her. He was always her liegeman, but in moments like this, he could be her husband, too.

They stood in each other's arms long enough to be left behind by the others in their party.

Finally, Elena reached under his cloak, slipping the Blood Diary from the inner pocket of his garment. She ran her pale fingers over the cover. The gilt rose still bore a slight glow of moonshine. She took a shuddering breath. "If it's *not* the moon, then we must search for Cho. We can't win this war without her power."

Er'ril only nodded.

Elena opened the book. As she stared into the pages, a small cry escaped her. She held out the Diary, and Er'ril saw that once again, the pages opened into a dark world streaked with crimson and azure gases and stars clustered too close together.

The Void had returned.

Elena searched expectantly around her. There was no flash or swirl of light. As they waited, a small frown formed on her lips. She rattled the book slightly, as if to shake the spirits loose from the pages.

She turned to Er'ril, still frowning. "Where is Cho?"

GRESHYM CROUCHED AT THE EDGE OF MOON LAKE, EYES AND EARS SHARP ON those hiking across the marshy grounds. He had heard all. *So the wit'ch has lost her powers?* His mouth twitched with a grin. Shorkan and the Master of Blackhall might forgive his past slights if he handed them the wit'ch. Still, there was much risk. He had but the smallest magick at his command.

Greshym focused on the bent-backed figure hobbling with the aid of the elv'in prince and the nyphai lass. *Joach* . . . That boy reeked of magick, as did the familiar staff he leaned upon.

"If I could regain what was once mine . . . ," he whispered, not entirely sure right now if he meant the length of petrified wood or the boy himself. There was much to ponder, but some initial maneuvering needed to be made quickly. He dared not lose this chance.

He leaned to his side and gave Rukh a few stern commands. The stump gnome groveled, then backed off into the deadfall and vanished. Then Greshym turned his attention back upon the group, carefully planning his next move. With his concentration so focused, he failed to notice the one who spied upon him and approached so silently.

As Greshym crouched, all the hairs on his arms and neck suddenly stood on end. He swung around as light burst behind him, a brilliant torch in the night, illuminating his hiding spot for all to see from leagues away.

He threw an arm up against the glare, crying out.

The flare of brilliance formed the figure of a woman, her face shining with icy rage: the Lady of the Lake.

Her voice boomed and echoed, as deafening as her light was bright. *"You are found! You will be judged!"*

Greshym cringed, lifting his drained staff. He knew it was too feeble a weapon against the one he faced. Strange fires burned in those empty eyes.

Confirmation came from the wit'ch's call in the distance. *"Cho!"*

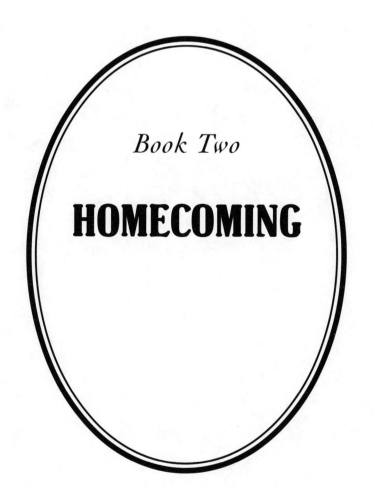

Book Two

HOMECOMING

5

Tol'chuk crouched in the rain like a boulder in the storm, water sluicing over his craggy features. He perched on a granite outcropping, one that gave him a wide view of the valley below and the rising highlands beyond, misted by heavy clouds and sheets of rain. Dawn was breaking, but it was hard to say where night ended and day began: for the past three days, they had seen no sign of moon or sun, just slate-gray skies and feeble glows.

"Such a damp land," a voice said behind him.

He did not have to turn to know Magnam; the d'warf's droll demeanor never changed.

"It be the summer wet season here," Tol'chuk said. "Come midsummer these lands finally dry for a spell, until the winter storms begin."

"Sounds delightful. If I had d'warflings and a nattering wife, I'd bring them here to holiday."

"You could've gone with Wennar and the other d'warves."

Magnam made a rude noise and pulled a pipe from his pocket, waving it dismissively. "I'm no warrior. Camp cook, that's me. I figured a flight to see these homelands of yours was a better idea." Magnam scrambled up the slick rock and stared out at the rain-shrouded highlands. "Yep, some homeland you og'res have."

Tol'chuk glanced over. "At least there be no fireweeds growing every five steps, and no sulfurous pits," he said, referring to the d'warf lands in Gul'gotha, a blasted and festering place. But when he saw the wounded look on Magnam's face, he regretted his bitter words.

Magnam remained quiet for a long time.

Everyone's spirits had been sorely tested, leading to arguments and sullen silences. The flight here had taken much longer than any had expected. The elv'in captain, Jerrick, had tired rapidly, pitted against stormy weather and a growing malaise that sapped his elemental abilities. They were forced to land the scoutship frequently for rest breaks, and it took Jerrick longer to recuperate after each stop—sometimes days at a time. It was only with the help of Mama Freda's tonics that the ship had reached the mountains by the first moon of summer.

Magnam hunched against the wet wind and attempted to light his pipe with a wrapped coal from the fire. He finally gave up and threw the coal over the ridge, sighing loudly. "At least we're finally here." He reached over and patted Tol'chuk on his bent knee. "Welcome home."

Tol'chuk stared across the valley. The great Fang of the North loomed beyond, its upper slopes white from a crust of snow that never melted. Even the thunderclouds could not mask the peak's majesty as it towered over its brethren. Only its sister mountain to the distant south, the Southern Fang, competed for dominance among the chain of peaks.

Squinting his amber eyes, Tol'chuk tried to pierce the mists, to see into his homelands, but failed. Beyond the next valley lay the heart of og're territory. His own people. Why did such a thought strike fear into his heart? One hand reached to his thigh pouch, bulging with his treasure, a chunk of heartstone larger than a goat's skull, the revered and spiritual center of the og're clans. Tol'chuk had succeeded in lifting the curse from the Heart of his people, restoring its full beauty and power. To complete his mission, he must return the jewel to the elders of his tribe, the ancient Triad. So why, after so long a journey, did he want to flee from here?

Magnam seemed to sense his distress. "Homecomings aren't always easy."

Tol'chuk remained quiet for a long moment more. "It be not just coming home that worries me."

"Then what?"

Tol'chuk shook his head. He had left these lands as a murderer, an outcast, the last seed of the foul Oathbreaker. He now returned with a healed crystal, but his own heart had grown heavier. He would have to face the Triad and reveal that not only was he a descendant of the Oathbreaker, but his cursed ancestor still lived. The Oathbreaker was in fact the Dark Lord of these very lands, the one who bore such nefarious names as the *Black Heart* or *Black Beast*, or among the d'warves, the *Nameless One*. It seemed each people had their own curse with which to call his ancestor.

It was this burden he carried in his heart, but he could not shirk his duty. He would trade his shame to learn more about this ancestor and the connection between heartstone and ebon'stone.

"It must be done," he whispered to the Northern Fang.

The snap of a twig announced a newcomer to their early-morning reflections. A sodden mouse of a man stepped from the rain-laden branches. His brown hair lay in drizzled swatches over his face, half hiding his features. He came naked to the granite outcropping, unembarrassed by his lack of clothes. He strode toward them, moving with a certain easy grace. "The sun is up," the man said.

"Fardale?" Magnam asked.

The newcomer nodded. Though he wore the face of Mogweed, this was clearly the brother, Fardale. Once twins in form, the two now shared one body. Mogweed occupied it during the night, Fardale the day. The only advantage to this strange change in their fates was the return of their shape-shifting abilities.

"I'm off to scout the way ahead," Fardale said. His eyes narrowed as he studied the highlands, cocking his head, nose in the air, already scenting the damp gusts.

With a shuddering shake, he fell toward the ground. Reaching out, his arms and legs twisted and bent as if boneless, then settled to a new form, catching his weight. At the same time, naked skin rolled and sprouted a dense growth of dark fur. A growl rose to a wolfish howl. His neck arched back while his lower face stretched to a fanged and snarling snout. Soon Fardale the man was gone, replaced by a giant treewolf, a denizen of the deep wood. Only one feature remained the same between man and beast: a pair of amber eyes, glowing in the drizzling gloom.

Images flashed into Tol'chuk as he met that gaze with his own eyes—a matching set of amber, the heritage from his mother, a *si'lura* changeling like Fardale and Mogweed. Though Tol'chuk could not shape-shift, he could mindspeak with another si'luran. The word pictures of the wolf filled his head: *The open trail, dark at the end . . . a lone wolf traipsing the path, nose to the ground.*

Tol'chuk nodded his understanding.

In a blur of shadow, the wolf vanished into the wood. Once again, Fardale would lead the way, scouting for them.

"He really needs to think variety," Magnam grumbled. "This wolf thing is getting tired. How about a badger?"

Tol'chuk glanced to the d'warf.

"A big, mean badger." Magnam pocketed his unlit pipe. "Yeah, I'd like to see that."

Tol'chuk scowled, dragging himself up. "Do not judge Fardale. The wolf be a form he knows." He glanced to where the shape-shifter had vanished. "I think he draws peace from it."

Magnam shrugged. "I'd feel the same, if I had to share my body with someone else . . . especially that brother of his." The d'warf shook his head.

"Mogweed bears no less a burden."

"I beg to disagree. He doesn't have to hear himself whine night after night."

Tol'chuk climbed off the granite boulder. He had no patience to explain Mogweed's irascible character, even if he could. Instead he pointed back to the woods. "We should help the others break camp."

Together they crossed through the trees. Overhead, pine needles trickled with water. A few paces into the forest, a sharp brightness marked their nighttime campsite. They followed the glow to a rocky overhang, beneath which a small fire still crackled merrily, out of place in the misty gloom of the forest. Magnam joined the remaining members of their small party—the el'vin captain Jerrick, and the elderly blind healer Mama Freda—storing bedrolls and clanking gear into packs.

Most of the supplies had been left in the elv'in scoutship, safely ensconced in an open highland meadow a day's journey from here. It was the closest they dared travel by wind among these now-constant storms. Also Tol'chuk feared how his tribesmen would react to such a strange craft landing in their territory. Og'res had a tendency to attack before asking questions. So for safety's sake, they had left the ship behind as they made the final approach on foot.

Tol'chuk watched them break camp and shook his head. "I still think it be best if you'd all stayed with the ship." He feared bringing even such a small party among his people. Fardale disguised as a wolf was one thing, but bringing a d'warf, a woman, and an elv'in into og're territory risked all their lives.

"Stay behind?" Mama Freda straightened with a small pack containing her herbs and elixirs. "The fate of Alasea may rest on what we discover here. Besides, these highlands are no safer than your homelands."

Tol'chuk couldn't argue that. On the flight here they had seen entire villages razed below, heard rumors from townsfolk of strange beasts prowling the night. As they crossed into the foothills, bands of armed villagers had warned them off from places of pestilence and quarantine. Then one night the ship had crossed high over a burning town. A long army, lit by torches, marched forth from it like a line of fiery ants. Jerrick had spied upon them. "Not men" was all he said as he lowered his spyglass.

After landing, they had decided to travel on together. Few would bother a company with an og're among them.

Jerrick shoveled dirt over their campfire, then dusted his hands. The old elv'in captain looked pale, an effect accentuated by his long white hair. "We're ready."

A tawny-haired creature the size of a small cat clambered out of the branches overhead. Chittering, it shook its wet fur. Its tiny bare face, set in a cowl of fiery fur, scowled. "Bad wet . . . cold to the bones," it griped, mimicking Mogweed's whining tone and words.

"Here, Tikal," Mama Freda said. The gray-haired healer tapped her shoulder. Her pet clambered to the offered perch, then hugged tight. The two were sense-bonded: Mama Freda and the tamrink shared each other's senses, a joining that allowed the blind healer to see through the beast's eyes.

Jerrick shrugged into his gear, then checked Mama Freda's pack, one hand lingering on her shoulder. She leaned her cheek to his fingers, a small gesture of affection. The elderly healer had insisted on accompanying the captain on this long journey. "To help him fight the draining malaise," she had claimed. But from their interactions, it was clear that deeper ties bound them together.

Magnam waddled over with his bundle, patting the small ax on his hip for reassurance. "Let's go see these lands of yours."

Tol'chuk grabbed up the largest pack, heavy with supplies and equipment. With a final scrutiny of their campsite, they set off.

Tol'chuk led the way. By midday, he would be among his own lands. And by nightfall, he'd be within sight of his home caves. He set off through the weeping forest as thunder echoed in the distance, the voice of the mountains calling him home.

Magnam tramped beside him. "You're not alone," he said softly.

Tol'chuk remained silent. He found himself surprisingly comforted by the simple words. Risk or not, he was glad the group had decided to remain together.

Reaching a deer track heading in the right direction, Tol'chuk set off down it. The way descended a steep slope, slick with mud and pine needles. They proceeded slowly, grabbing tree limbs and bushes to keep their footing.

"Where's Fardale?" Jerrick finally grumbled from behind. "Shouldn't he have returned by now to let us know the best path from here?"

Tol'chuk frowned. The wolf usually trotted back to them periodically, alerting them to obstacles or the best way over creeks or rivers, but this morning there had been no sign of Fardale. And it was now near on to midday. The wolf had never been away for so long.

"Probably found a rabbit to chase," Magnam said. "Forgot all about us."

Despite his light manner, Tol'chuk heard the worry in the other's voice. They slowed their pace as they reached the bottom of the vale. A swift brook ran down the center, swollen from the rains. Tol'chuk pointed to an uprooted tree that had fallen across the rushing waters. "We can cross there. Mayhaps Fardale crossed already."

Fording the river they entered a denser forest, darker of needle and shadow. The climb from here was steep, and beyond this last ridge lay the og're lands.

Tol'chuk prayed Fardale had not ventured into those lands on his own. Wolf meat was a delicacy among his people, their warm pelts a valued trading commodity. But it was doubtful many og'res were out in this dreadful weather; most preferred their dry caves and sweltering fires. Still, where was Fardale?

A crackle of lightning split the midday gloom, forking like a net overhead. Thunder immediately followed, rolling down the slope with a roar. It escalated into a howl of anger and challenge.

Tol'chuk froze, well familiar with the call of their companion.

"Fardale . . . ," Mama Freda said. Her tamrink wrapped its tail around the old woman's neck, cringing.

As the thunder rolled away, the howl pitched higher, red with fury.

A new noise accompanied the challenge: coarse bellows, like the grind of boulders.

Magnam glanced to Tol'chuk.

He answered the question in the d'warf's eyes. "Og'res." He stared up the slope. "A hunting pack."

A THOUSAND LEAGUES AWAY, IN THE SWELTERING JUNGLE OF THE SOUTHERN Fang's lower slopes, Jaston heard the cry of an enraged animal. The howl cut through the croaking frogs and the buzz of blood-hungry flies. He froze on the trail, glancing around him. The call had a faraway sound, yet it seemed as close as his own heart. He squinted his eyes, searching. From this ridgeline, the swamplands were visible in the distance, blanketed in familiar mists.

They were the Drowned Lands, his home. He was a swamper—a hunter among the bogs and marshes. He wore gray leather leggings and a matching cloak of kroc'an leather. How he longed to return to his own lands—but he had a mission here.

As he turned back to the Fang, the strange howl rose in pitch, echoing around him. Even the sounds of the jungle died down. And despite the clarity of the call, it still had a faraway feeling to it. Strange. Jaston fingered the scars on the left side of his face, a nervous habit.

"A big doggie got loose," a voice said at his hip.

Jaston glanced down to the small boy and patted his head. "It's just an echo. The Fang plays tricks."

"Is the doggie lost?"

Jaston smiled. "He's fine."

Apparently satisfied, the boy popped his thumb in his mouth. The black-haired lad in simple rough-spun looked no older than five winters, but he was only a fortnight old, a construct of moss, lichen, and swampweed—a golem given life by the swamp wit'ch, Cassa Dar.

Jaston continued up the deer track, shrugging his pack higher on his shoulder. The howling seemed to follow, clinging to him, nipping at his heels. He stopped again. What strangeness was this?

He turned to the boy. "Cassa, can you hear me?"

The boy frowned, then scratched in his ear as if a bug had crawled in there.

"Cassa . . . ?"

The boy spoke again, but with a different voice. "I hear you, my love."

THE SOUND OF HER VOICE WARMED HIM. IF HE CLOSED HIS EYES, HE COULD imagine she was next to him. Even her scent seemed to enter this humid and damp forest: moonblossom, the fragrance sweet and heady. Like the selfsame flower, Cassa Dar was as deadly as she was sweet, a most powerful elemental wit'ch.

"What is it?" Cassa asked, speaking through the boy. The wit'ch had once been a student of the feared Assassins' Guild, sent to Castle Drakk from her d'warf homelands. But an attack by the Dark Lord had fused her to the lands around the stronghold, granting her both longevity and a gift of poisonous magick. And bound to her lands, she had been unable to join Jaston on his journey, forcing them to part. She could only send a bit of her magick as company—her swamp child.

"Do you hear that howl?" he asked.

The boy cocked his head, listening; then one arm raised, palm outward. The child turned in a slow circle. "Treewolf," Cassa said finally.

"Here?" he asked, surprised. Wolves were not native to these lands.

"No." The boy stopped his circle and stared up the slope. "You were right to contact me."

"I don't understand."

The boy glanced to him, but Jaston sensed Cassa Dar's gaze behind those eyes. "It echoes from the Northern Fang."

"That's a thousand leagues away."

The boy nodded. "But you recognize that voice, don't you?"

Jaston didn't understand.

"Listen . . . not just with your ears, but also your heart."

Jaston frowned, but he obeyed the wit'ch he loved. He let his eyelids drift closed. He breathed deeply. The howl wrapped around him, filling his senses.

"He seeks you . . ."

Suddenly Jaston understood. He felt it in his bones. "Fardale," he breathed out. "The shape-shifter . . ." Jaston opened his eyes, now fully recognizing the strange call. He had traveled with the wolf, even saving its life at one point from a tentacled and winged monster.

"It is your past connection that opens this path. Such is the linked magick of these twin peaks."

"The Fangs," he mumbled.

Cassa Dar had explained to him about the two mountains, two fonts of the Land's raw elemental energy. It was a flow of this energy from the Southern Fang that sustained the wit'ch and her swamp. Then a moon ago, she had sensed a sudden thinning of this power, in turn growing weak herself, beyond the general malaise all elementals suffered. This recent weakening was more sudden, sharper. And unlike other elementals, Cassa Dar's life was tied to this energy.

As it waned, so did she.

Jaston could not sit idle. So a fortnight ago he had set out alone to investigate who or what had stanched the flow from the Fang. If possible, he would tear down the magickal dam.

Jaston stared up at the mountain. "Then Fardale must be at the Northern Fang."

The swamp child nodded. "Elena said that the shape-shifter, the og're, and a few others were headed to the homeland of the og'res."

The howl pitched suddenly higher.

"From the sounds of it, they're in trouble," Jaston said. He clutched the swamp child's hand tighter.

"Follow the howl," Cassa said through the boy. "Find the source. We must not lose the connection while it's still open. Only strong emotions keep the peaks linked." The boy headed up the trail, tugging Jaston with him. "Maybe we can open a door at that point."

"Open a door? How?"

"I've lived for centuries in the shadow of the Southern Fang," Cassa explained. "And the libraries of Castle Drakk go even farther back. For ages, folks have believed the mountain haunted. Stories and myths abound. Bodiless voices, ghostly apparitions, disappearances. But the mages of Alasea knew the truth. With strong bonds and dire need, portals can be opened between the two peaks."

"And you know how to do this?"

"No." Cassa Dar's voice grew winded. "I'm heading to the libraries to investigate that answer as we speak, but it's hard for me to maintain this connection while doing both. So take the child to as near the source of the howl as possible. Call for me then."

"Wait! My mission here is to find what weakens the flow of your magick from the Southern Peak."

"The shape-shifter is in more immediate danger than I."

"But—?"

The boy's voice lowered. "And I don't believe it is happenstance that you hear the cry of the wolf."

Jaston frowned. "What do you mean?"

Cassa's voice grew exasperated. "From what I've read of the Fangs, *both* sides of this connection must have a mutual need. You had no way of knowing Fardale was in danger. But you had your own deep need. Perhaps both your desires are somehow mutual. For what you seek, Fardale may hold a clue to that path. You must follow it—not only to save the shape-shifter, but to save me."

Jaston stood stunned.

"Now go, while the connection remains! Find the wolf!"

"I'll try." Jaston turned and listened to the echoing cry. It seemed to be coming from everywhere at once.

Straining, he studied the dense jungle, the midday heat pressing on him like a wet woolen blanket. The sunlight pierced through the canopy of the cloud forest, glowing the woods an emerald green.

Find the wolf! But where to begin looking?

The boy still held his hand. "I want to pet the doggie." He yanked on Jaston's arm.

Jaston followed the driven boy. The creations of the swamp wit'ch had a rudimentary will of their own, but their desires were still Cassa Dar's. The boy's mind translated her whim into his own understanding.

"I like doggies. Doggie scared. I must pet him." The boy set off in a direct path through a curtain of vines.

Jaston allowed himself to trust the youngster's ears. Constructed of magick, perhaps the boy could find the source of the howl.

They tromped up a steep slope, grabbing vines and branches to haul themselves along. The boy scrambled through the underbrush. "Here, doggie, doggie . . . ," he chanted, gasping with the exertion.

They reached a new ridgeline. In the hollow below, a stagnant pond glistened in the bright sunlight. A few frogs leaped from mud banks to plop into the water, sending out ripples.

The boy pointed. "The doggie's thirsty!"

Jaston strained his ears. The howl had turned into growls and warning barks, but the boy had led him true. The calls echoed from this hollow.

"Show me!" Jaston urged.

The boy nodded with youthful exuberance. "I'm gonna pet that doggie." Then he was off, hopping and sliding down into the tiny vale, pulling Jaston in his wake.

In no time, they reached the algae-rimmed pond. Under its placid surface a few fish lazed about. Frogs complained in croaking bellows at their intrusion. The sun shone overhead, bright upon the water.

Jaston's reflection stared back at him, a frown on his face. *What now?* Fardale's voice rose like mist from the pond's surface, then died away.

"Cassa?" Jaston cried out, panicked.

The boy was nearby, searching under bushes for the lost dog. He suddenly straightened as if he were a string puppet. "Jaston," he said, taking on the tones of Cassa Dar. "Blood," she said, sounding exhausted.

"Blood?"

The boy nodded his head. "According to an old text"—Here her words sounded rote, as if she were reading.—" 'thee who are twined might open a path between Fangs by strong need and desire and a measure of blood.' "

"What does that mean?"

"You and Fardale share a bond. You saved the shape-shifter's life, forming spiritual connections between you. That is why his cries reached you. But to open a path to cross bodily will require living substance given to the spell. That substance is your blood."

Jaston stared at the still pond. "But the howling has stopped."

"Try anyway . . . the spell may persist for a short time!"

Frowning, Jaston yanked a dagger from his belt. "How much blood?"

The boy remained silent, but his face screwed tight.

"How much?" he repeated, poising the knife's tip to his forearm.

Cassa shook the child's head. "I don't know. A *measure* . . . That's what the book says."

Jaston sighed. It might be a drop; it might be a bucketful. He dug the knife in firmly. Pain lanced up his arm, but blood streamed down and dribbled across the surface of the pool, spreading a sheen over the crystal waters.

Fish swirled to investigate.

"Nothing's happening," he whispered.

The swamp child knelt at the pond's edge. "This must be the portal. Reflective surfaces have power." The boy turned to Jaston. "But with the howl gone, the spellcast channel must have dissolved. We're too late."

Jaston shoved his arm out farther, refusing to give up. "Maybe it takes more blood." He squeezed a fist, freshening the flow from his wound.

"Jaston, don't waste—"

Somewhere beyond the hollow's ridge, a new yowling suddenly arose. But it was no wolf. Other voices answered this first piercing cry. Screams arose from all around the hollow.

The boy stood. "Sniffers . . . They must have been drawn by the wolf's cries."

Jaston swallowed hard. *And now they've caught the scent of blood.* All hunters were familiar with the giant, purple-skinned predators of the deep forests: all muscle and teeth and hunger, bull sharks of the woods. He listened to the cries: a pack . . . at least eight or nine.

He lowered his arm, forsaking his attempt to aid Fardale. He had his own battle on hand. He drew out his sword with his uninjured arm. The boy moved nearer his side.

The hunting cries of the pack grew to a cacophony. Sniffers used their screams to terrify their prey—and in this case, it was working.

"Jaston, use my poison to whet your blade." The boy took a step back and pulled apart his rough-spun jerkin. "Stab here."

Jaston's brows shot high. "I can't."

"The boy won't feel pain. Remember he's just moss and swampweed."

Jaston still balked.

"He is of my essence," she pleaded. "*Poison and venom.* Use it to taint your sword's touch."

The cries drew closer around him. Somewhere behind him, rustling and the creak of vines warned of hidden encroachment. Jaston moved the tip of the blade to the boy's chest.

The child fingered the sharp edge with unconcerned interest. "Pointy . . . ," the boy mumbled in his own voice.

As Jaston hesitated, staring into those blue and trusting eyes, a growl arose at his shoulder, escalating into a raging howl. Both boy and man glanced down to the pond at their feet. The new call arose from there. It was not a sniffer, but the wolf again.

The pond's glassy surface shimmered; then the curious fish vanished, replaced with an impossible sight: a treewolf crouched, haunches high, snarling.

Fardale!

Beyond the wolf, the threat was clear: a pack of og'res, armed with clubs and lengths of crooked bone. Blood lust gleamed in the monsters' eyes, shining out from the pond.

"Jaston!" the boy suddenly cried in Cassa's voice.

He swung from the pond as a giant creature stalked onto a trail only a leap away. Its skin was the color of a deep bruise. It nose flaps spread wide, inflamed, sucking in the scent of his blood and fear. Black eyes, cold and emotionless, studied him. Fleshy lips rolled slowly back to reveal row after row of ripping teeth.

Rustling arose around him from all sides, followed by cries from other sniffers, whining with hunger. But here stood their leader, full of silent menace—the one granted the kill.

Without a twitch or a cry, the pack leader leaped, springing with a speed that belied its bulk.

Jaston jerked up the tip of his sword. He had no time to poison its edge. Flinching backward with the frightened child clinging to his leg, his foot slipped in the slick pond mud. His sword arm shifted, letting his guard down.

The bulk of the sniffer struck his chest. Razored claws dug into his shoulder. As Jaston tumbled backward into the pond, the pack leader screamed, a wail of triumph and death.

TOL'CHUK REACHED THE TOP OF THE RIDGE FIRST, RACING AHEAD OF THE OTHers. If there was any chance of saving Fardale, he'd have to be quick.

Reaching the top, he searched the highlands beyond for any sign of Fardale. The wolf had gone ominously silent. Had he shifted his shape? Taken flight? Tol'chuk doubted this. Fardale always persisted in his wolfish shape, trusting its form the best.

Tol'chuk held his breath, straining to hear. Though he trusted the shape-shifter's skill and speed, he had also seen og'res hunt. Once on a scent, they were hard to escape and experienced at herding prey into a trap.

And now this silence . . .

"Do you see him?" Magnam bellowed from below.

The d'warf climbed with Mama Freda and Jerrick, working as quickly as possible up the slick trail.

Despairing, Tol'chuk opened his mouth to answer when a savage howl split the highlands. *Fardale!* The cry came from beyond a neighboring hillock. Tol'chuk dared not wait for his friends. He raced along the ridgeline and over the treeless hump of granite, following the call.

The stone was slick from the drizzling rain. On its far side, Tol'chuk lost his footing and slid down the smooth, treacherous rock. A cry of anger and surprise burst from him as he tumbled over a cliff's edge. He flew through the air and splashed into the middle of a creek, swollen from the rains. He sputtered up and saw he had also landed in the midst of a standoff.

A group of six og'res crowded on one side of the creek; Fardale crouched on the other. He was pinned against the hillock's cliffs with no means of escape.

As the og'res gaped, stunned at the sudden intrusion, Tol'chuk clambered out of the stream, backing to Fardale's side. He spoke in the og're tongue. "Leave this wolf to me!" he growled.

One of the og'res lumbered forward. A giant, he knuckled on an arm as thick around as a tree trunk, and he bore a length of log in his free claw. He bared his fangs, yellow and pitted. "Go find your own meat!"

He slammed the log down for emphasis as his hunting companions grunted their agreement.

Tol'chuk didn't know this giant og're, but he recognized the pattern of the scarring on his bulging forearm. Ku'ukla clan—one of the most savage and bestial tribes. It had been a battle between this clan and Tol'chuk's own that had gotten his father killed.

The brute's companions circled tighter, all war-scarred and hardened. Their eyes glowed with blood lust.

"Be gone or die!" their leader warned.

Tol'chuk backed to Fardale and rose to his full height. The group cringed away from the sight of his straightening spine. Tol'chuk had forgotten that particular look of loathing and disgust.

Only the giant kept his position, undaunted, but recognition dawned in his piggish eyes. "He-who-walks-like-a-man," he finally grunted. "Tol'chuk the Banished, son of Len'chuk of the Toktala clan." The og're spat into the creek as if the mention of his name had soured his mouth.

Tol'chuk flinched. He had not thought to be recognized so soon.

The leader's muscles tensed. His shoulders rolled in a clear posture of hatred and challenge, and his voice boomed. "You damn yourself by showing your face again. Your head will adorn our caves!"

With a roar, he advanced into the creek, waving the others to secure the flanks. They closed in from all sides.

Weaponless, Tol'chuk reached for the only means of protection at hand. He clawed open his thigh pouch and pulled out the heartstone. He lifted the stone high.

Six pairs of eyes flicked upward.

"Heartstone!" one of the pack exclaimed.

"The Heart of our people!" Tol'chuk boomed. Once before it had protected him from members of this same clan. He prayed to the Mother above that it would again. "I return it to the Triad. Do not block my path!"

The other og'res hesitated, but the leader advanced. "A trick ... or stolen," he rumbled. But as the giant lunged out of the creek, a new cry shattered the highlands—the piercing wail of another predator. For a breath, everyone froze in confusion and wariness. The giant stood, water sluicing over his scarred form.

Then a tumble of bodies burst forth from the creek.

Tol'chuk leaped back, stunned as a monstrous beast rolled across the far mudbank, landing amid the other og'res. It leaped to its clawed feet, snarling and spitting in blind fury. A sniffer! It ripped into the nearest og're, going for the throat.

But two other figures rolled onto the near side of the creek—a boy and a man. They landed almost at the feet of the giant leader.

The man, bleeding, scrambled backward, yanking the boy clear as a club came smashing down at them, missing by a hair. Splinters flew as the log shattered in half from the force.

The og're roared. "Demons!"

Fardale dashed to defend the newcomers. The man acknowledged the wolf without fear. "Well met, Fardale." They retreated together.

Tol'chuk could not fathom their sudden appearance ... or this recognition. What magick was this?

The child bared his chest to the man. "Quickly ... while the path remains open. I sense it closing already."

To Tol'chuk's horror, the man plunged his sword into the child. With its touch, the boy dissolved into a tangle of wet weed. As the debris fell from the blade, a whisper of a voice followed. "Come back to me ..."

"I will, my love."

Tol'chuk now recognized the swarm of scars twisting one side of the man's face. *Jaston . . . the swamper.* How could this be?

The giant again descended on man and wolf. Tol'chuk shook off his own shock and went to their aid. But Jaston danced lightly under the other's guard and speared the giant's elbow.

The og're bellowed, sweeping backhanded at his attacker with the shattered end of his club. The swamp man went sailing into the air and crashed against the cliff face.

Fardale leaped between them, trying to protect the dazed swamper. Tol'chuk rushed forward, too.

But their help was not needed.

The giant teetered in place for a heartbeat, then toppled back into the creek with a loud splash. From his wounded elbow, his skin darkened and smoked. He did not move again.

"Poison," Jaston explained from where he lay crumpled at the base of the cliff.

Across the creek, the sniffer had finally been dispatched, but two og'res lay dead. The remaining hunters retreated toward the woods. "Drag'nock!" one of them moaned as he fled.

Tol'chuk stared at the dead giant and cringed. *Drag'nock*—he knew that name and despaired. This giant had been the *head* of the entire Ku'ukla clan. Such a death would not go unchallenged. Those who fled would spread the tale; soon the drums of war would echo over the highlands.

Nearby, Fardale crossed to Jaston, nuzzling at the man in warm greeting. The swamper scratched the wolf behind an ear. "Good to see you again, too, Fardale."

Tol'chuk turned to the highlands, clutching the chunk of crystal in his claws. He had come home to return the healed Heart to his people, to offer them hope and peace. Instead he opened the way for war and bloodshed.

Like the Oathbreaker, it seemed his name was to be forever cursed.

6

Mogweed screamed as he was ripped back to awareness. Sharp smells of pine and rain hit his sensitive nose, voices rang sharp and loud; lights stung his eyes like fiery needles; the taste of blood on his tongue gagged him. Mogweed raised his face—*muzzle*—from the belly of a half-chewed rabbit.

He leaped back from the bloody carcass in disgust. The sun's last glimmer shone dully through a gray sky; he shook off the cobwebs of his disorientation. As he stared down at Fardale's dinner, one lip raised in a silent snarl. His brother had known he would be returning to awareness as the sun set. Fardale had purposefully left this little trick, a message and reminder to his twin.

Well, curse you, Brother! This fate is not all my doing!

He opened himself to his shape-shifting gifts, touching that ember in his heart to flame. Bone, muscle, and skin bent to his will. He climbed out of the wolf shape, letting his form slide into its most familiar pattern. The smells grew less acute, the lights dimmer. Voices dipped to reasonable levels.

"It appears Mogweed's returned," Magnam said as he knelt over a tumble of sticks, preparing a fire. "How was your nap?"

It took Mogweed a moment to re-form his voice box, growling wolfishly before finding his proper tongue. "It . . . it's no natural sleep," he finally spat out. He sensed Fardale somewhere deep inside him, taking his place, returning to that dark prison. With nightfall, it was his brother's turn to be locked in a cell without bars, able only to watch what transpired. In that other world, sleep was dreamless. Awakening from that slumber into full awareness was as painful as it was jolting, leaving no true rest.

He searched around him, reorienting himself. The group was setting up a camp in a shallow cave. He frowned. It was scant shelter against the wind and rain.

Mama Freda passed him a set of clothes. "Fardale left these this morning."

Mogweed glanced down at his nakedness, half turning away in embarrassment.

"Nothing I ain't seen," the blind healer said, swinging back to her chores.

As Mogweed climbed shivering into his clothes, Magnam finally got the fire going. Once dressed, Mogweed stepped over and warmed his bare hands before the flames. Though summer was fully upon them, the highland nights were still icy with the touch of winter. The winds never seemed to stop blowing, and brief spats of rain struck like angry slaps. From the rumbles of thunder in the distance, he judged this night would be no different.

His eyes fell upon the newcomer to the group. Jaston stared back at Mogweed from across the fire, his mouth hanging open. His scars glowed bright red in the firelight, and not just from the flame's heat. The swamp man glanced down with a shake of his head. "I . . . I'm sorry. It's just . . . I've never seen a shape-shifter change like that. Mycelle, when we were together, she never . . ." He waved his hand before his face.

Mogweed scowled. He had been traveling for so long with folk familiar with shape-shifting that the man's response grated, but he kept his mouth shut. He owed his life to this swamper's sudden appearance.

"Mycelle . . . ," Jaston continued to blather, "I never saw her change."

Mogweed sighed, tired of the man's squirming, and removed the swamper from his own hook. "She never changed because when you knew her she had settled into the human form, forsaking her shape-shifting nature." His voice dropped to a bitter mumble. "Then she died and was resurrected by that cursed snake that gave her back her si'luran gifts." Mogweed swung away from the fire. For the thousandth time, he wished he had never meddled with her rainbow-striped viper. His attempt to break the curse upon him and his brother had only resulted in an even worse binding.

He slipped past Mama Freda and Jerrick as they laid out bedrolls side by side. They both moved as if they were already half asleep.

Mogweed crossed to the cave's entrance, joining Tol'chuk. The large fellow seldom talked, but his silences and simple companionship were a balm for Mogweed's own frustration and pain. He had not wanted to set out on this journey, preferring the safety of A'loa Glen—but Fardale had volunteered them. And since Mogweed was forced to venture out, he was glad he had the og're at his side.

He kept vigil with Tol'chuk, watching for any marauding hunters. "I thought we were supposed to have reached your home caves by now."

Tol'chuk shrugged.

Mogweed could guess the delay. After the attack on Fardale, the group had proceeded through the mountains warily, moving in a tighter group, cautious. The extra care had slowed their progress so much that Mogweed had eventually dozed off inside Fardale's skull, only waking again when the curse pushed him back into his body, greeting him with a mouthful of raw rabbit.

He was sure Fardale was wolfishly laughing somewhere deep in his head. *Laugh now, Brother,* he thought, *but I swear I'll get the last laugh.*

After a time, Magnam returned with a bit of stew for each of them, steaming in the cold air. Tol'chuk accepted his bowl wordlessly, lost in his own worries.

Mogweed sniffed at his meal, then curled his nose. "Rabbit!"

Magnam chuckled. "Fardale caught two. He likes to share."

Mogweed shoved his bowl back at the d'warf. "I'm not hungry."

"More for me then." Magnam added Mogweed's stew to his own, then handed the dish back to Mogweed. "The kettle is cooling beside the fire."

"So?"

Magnam pointed out into the dark. "There's a stream just yonder. Should be great for cleaning the cookery. Nice and cold, like you like it."

Mogweed opened his mouth, then snapped it shut. What was the use of arguing? Whether he had eaten of this meal or not, he knew his duty. Besides, the chore would give him a way to wile away the lonely nighttime hours. Each evening, he returned to this form only to find the others climbing into their bedrolls, leaving the long night to himself. It left him too much time to think, too much time to curse his present state.

"I'm for bed," the d'warf said, wiping the last of the stew from his bowl with his fingers and tossing the empty dish to Mogweed.

The others soon followed his lead.

Only Tol'chuk remained unmoving, crouched by the entrance, his amber eyes aglow.

Mogweed gathered the cooking utensils in a sack, then grabbed up his own pack. He crossed to the og're. "Where's this creek?"

Tol'chuk pointed. "Beyond that boulder. It runs in a shallow bed."

Mogweed hesitated. With the moon and stars masked by clouds, the night beyond the cave was dark. "Any og'res?" he asked, staring out warily.

"Just half a one," Tol'chuk mumbled, referring to himself.

Mogweed patted his elbow. "You have nothing to be ashamed of," he found himself assuring his large companion. "And neither do I," he added in a whisper to both himself and the wolf inside him. *It wasn't all my fault.*

"I'll watch over you," Tol'chuk said.

Mogweed nodded and set off down the loose escarpment of shale and dirt. He slung the sack of dirty bowls and pots over one shoulder, his own small pack over the other. He shifted muscles in his arms and back to better bear the load, swelling them. The warm flow of tissue reassured him.

Despite his predicament, it was wonderful to use his si'luran abilities again. Full transformations—like the one from wolf to man or back—were taxing, but small adjustments were effortless and fatigued his flesh very little.

As he marched down the short slope, he appreciated the body he wore. It was as comfortable as a worn boot. After wearing this shape for so long, it was like a rut worn in a dirt track—easy to slip into, easy to follow. But with the return of his abilities, small enhancements were now possible. He shivered out a layer of insulating fur over his cold cheeks, sharpened the vision of his eyes so he could see in the dark. *Perhaps this curse is not as bad as it seemed . . .*

Rounding the boulder, he spotted the small creek. It was only a step wide, gurgling down a shallow rock channel. Mogweed shrugged off his packs, dropping the bag of dirty dishes with a clatter, then lowering his own pack carefully. Settling to his haunches, he glanced over a shoulder to make sure the boulder was between him and the og're.

Satisfied, he let his eyelids drift closed and felt for those hidden eyes—Fardale's eyes. Over the many moons since their joining, Mogweed had learned to recognize when his brother was awake inside him by a telltale tingle, that tiny sense of a stranger's eyes on the back of the neck. He felt nothing like that now. Mogweed smiled. As usual, Fardale was fast asleep. After the long hike, his brother must be as tired as the others and not particularly interested in watching Mogweed scrub dirty bowls.

Alone for the moment, Mogweed untied the leather strings of his pack, making sure the carefully tied knot was the same as when he left it. It appeared untouched: No one had rummaged among his private things.

He smiled. With Fardale spending all his time in wolf form, he ignored

Mogweed's pack—as did the others. Its contents were his alone, items collected on his long journey among these lands.

Mogweed sifted through the pack, pushing past his own clothes and then a broken iron chain and collar from a sniffer that Tol'chuk had slain in these same hills so long ago. A tiny goatskin pouch bulged with a few pinches of Elena's red hair. He scrabbled a moldy walnut out of the way. And at last, in the deepest corner of his pack, his fingers reached stone wrapped in linen. He hauled it out.

Sitting back on his heels, he settled the object on a flat rock and pulled away the folded cloth. The ebon'stone bowl sucked in what little light there was behind the sheltering boulder. He checked again behind him, making sure he was not spied upon.

He studied the small treasure. It had once belonged to the spider wit'ch—*Vira'ni*. He ran one finger along the lip of the bowl. Oily to the touch and oddly cold, its surface felt like fever sweat on a dying man.

He bit his lip. Almost every night he stared at the bowl, daring himself to take the next step. And each night he folded the linen back over his secret prize. After the failed attempt to free himself from his twin—the result of which was this strange fusion of forms—Mogweed knew there was only one way to break the curse that joined brother to brother. It would take a stronger magick than even Elena offered, and there was only one source of that magick: the Dark Lord of Gul'gotha, the ancestor of Tol'chuk.

Long ago, in the ancient Keep of Shadowbrook, Mogweed had spoken to the Dark Lord. The monster had spoken through the stone lips of a blackguard, a voice as empty and dead as an open crypt: *For now, stay with those who aid the wit'ch. A time may come when I will ask more of you.*

Mogweed knew that for his curse to be lifted, he would have to face that demon again. And he had learned from the pale twin lordlings of Shadowbrook that the blood of an elemental given to the bowl would call the Black Beast.

He stared at the ebon'stone. Over the past nights, he had feared doing what must be done. *What will be asked of me?* he wondered. He glanced back to the cave. He had traveled far from the side of the wit'ch, the Dark Lord's nemesis. But he knew that his role here with the others was not insignificant. They had entered the og're homelands seeking the answer to the mystery of ebon'stone, the base upon which the Dark Lord built and wielded his power. If that answer was ever discovered, the allies of the wit'ch would gain a marked advantage.

Mogweed shivered. Did he dare play with the power here? Then again, dare he not? Would he be forever doomed to walk in darkness, never seeing the light of day? At the back of his mouth, he still tasted the retch of raw rabbit. Would he be forever yoked to his twin?

Bile burned in his belly. His fingers clenched. This curse must be lifted, no matter what the cost.

Twisting to his pack, he rummaged inside and found a bit of caked and shredded cloth—a bandage that the mountain man, Kral, had worn after being attacked by the d'warves near Castle Mryl. Kral had been an elemental steeped in the magick of the mountains' granite roots. Mogweed had saved the bloody scrap in case he ever risked contacting the Dark Lord. He didn't know if the dried blood would ignite the magick of the bowl, but he was determined for once to try, for time was running short. They were in the heart of og're territory. It was now or never—and *never* was not an option.

With trembling fingers, he dropped the reddish-brown bandage to the bottom of the bowl. He held his breath and waited, watching.

Nothing happened. The bowl continued to suck in the feeble light. The crumpled bit of cloth simply rested in the center.

Mogweed sighed out his trapped breath. "It must take fresh blood," he whispered in frustration. He considered his options. Both Jerrick and Mama Freda bore elemental gifts. But how could he get their blood?

As he pondered his choices, a stench suddenly swelled around him, as if something had died and rotted under his toes. Mogweed tensed, fearing something had crept up on him unaware. He remembered the smell of the og'res through Fardale's nose. They had reeked of wet goats and blood. But this smell was much worse.

He scanned the dark forests across the creek, afraid to move and draw attention to himself. Then motion drew his eye—not from the woods, but from the bowl near his knees.

The bandage in the bowl twisted upon itself like a blind worm. The smell grew stronger around him.

With icy terror lacing his blood, Mogweed watched the brown stain on the cloth drain into the stone of the bowl. In a matter of heartbeats, the white cloth lay pristine against the black ebon'stone, quiet again.

Mogweed swallowed hard. The stench was now overpowering. Gorge rose in his throat. Surely Tol'chuk would smell the corruption and come to investigate.

Fearing discovery, he reached to the linen wrap, meaning to cover the bowl again, but as his fingers neared the ebon'stone, the bit of cloth burst into flame—not with the fiery red of true flame, but with flickers of darkness:

darkfire. The hungry flames ate the light and heat from around the shelter. But as the cloth was consumed, the pyre refused to die away. Flames continued to dance darkly from the hollow of the bowl, reaching high above the rim.

Mogweed snatched his hand away, his fingers frozen from the cold. *What have I done?* Where a moment before he feared discovery, he now wished Tol'chuk would appear and rescue him. Surely the og're noticed something amiss: the smell, the strange bloom of cold . . .

From the flames, a voice crept out like spiders on silk. "So the little mouse roars."

Without turning his head, Mogweed's gaze flicked to the caves, hoping Tol'chuk heard the icy voice of the demon. He was too scared to run, too frightened even to use his shape-shifting gifts. He was once again frozen in this form.

"No one will hear our words. No one will smell the open path—not even the wolf slumbering inside you. You are alone."

He cringed from these words as the cold fog of the voice wrapped around him. His panted breath steamed in the frigid cloud. The nearby creek rimed with ice.

"We taste your heart, shape-shifter. You reek of desire."

Mogweed forced his tongue to speak. "I . . . I want to be free of my brother."

The black flames coiled like snakes. "You ask our help, but do nothing to earn it."

"I will . . . I want . . . anything . . ."

"That will be seen. Do as we ask, when we ask, and we will free you."

Mogweed clenched his cold hands, bringing blood into his fingers. To be separated from his brother . . . to walk again free of Fardale's shadow.

"We will burn the wolf from your heart," the voice whispered, edged with frost. "Your body will be your own."

"Burn the wolf . . . ," he mumbled, not liking the sound of that. "Do you mean kill him?"

"There is only one body crouching here. There can only be *one* master of it."

Mogweed balked. How he longed to be free of Fardale's yoke. In fact, he'd be happy never to see his brother's face again. But to kill him? Could he go that far?

"What would you ask of me?" he finally blurted.

The ice in the air grew even more frigid. "You must destroy the Spirit Gate."

Mogweed frowned, not understanding at first. "What gate is ... ?" Then he remembered: the arch of heartstone under the Fang. It was the magickal portal through which Tol'chuk had been exiled into the world and sent to heal the jeweled Heart of the Og'res. "The Spirit Gate ... How can *I* destroy it?"

The voice grew, filling his head. "It must be shattered with the blood of my last seed!"

Mogweed paled. He meant Tol'chuk!

"And not just a dribble of blood, shape-shifter," the voice finished. "Not like the bit you offered the stone here—but blood squeezed from the seed's very heart. His last blood."

Mogweed shivered, and it had nothing to do with the magick-wrought chill in the air. His own blood pounded in his ears, his heart in his throat.

The flames dancing in the bowl died down as the spell frazzled away. "Slay the og're by the Gate, and you will be free." The voice drifted away. Then a last whisper reached him as the darkfire pyre extinguished: "But fail us, and your screams will echo forever."

Then the woods grew brighter, warmer, the air clean and crisp. It was like awakening from a nightmare. But Mogweed knew this was no figment. He slowly folded the linen wrap back over the ebon'stone bowl, silently wishing he had never touched the cursed thing.

But deeper inside him, a glimmer of hope burned. *To be free ...*

He shoved the bowl into his pack and cinched the leather knot, tying it specially. Once done, he hauled to his feet. His legs were numb, his mind dull with dread. He stumbled around the boulder and stared up at the tiny glow of their campfire. Limned against the brightness was a dark shadow.

Tol'chuk.

Mogweed climbed toward the light, scrabbling up the slight slope. The amber eyes of the og're studied him.

Mogweed could not meet that gaze.

Tol'chuk's face scrunched in confusion. "Where be the bowls?"

He flinched, thinking the og're meant the ebon'stone talisman. Then realized the og're only meant the dirty cookware. Mogweed pointed to the slope. "I left it beside the creek. I'll scrub 'em later. It's too cold right now."

Mogweed tried to slip past the og're to reach the warmth of the fire, but Tol'chuk stopped him.

"Be anything wrong, Mogweed?"

He raised his face to the og're, meeting his concerned gaze, burning under it. "No," he mumbled. "No, nothing's wrong."

Tol'chuk patted his shoulder. In the distance, thunder rolled. "It is a bad night. Stay by the fire."

Mogweed moved past the og're, glad to escape his gaze. Reaching the campfire, he glanced back to the entrance. Tol'chuk sat hunched, staring out into the night, protecting them, watching for any dangers beyond, unaware of the closer threat.

In Mogweed's mind, icy words repeated in his head: *Slay the og're by the Gate, and you will be free.* He faced the fire, turning his back on Tol'chuk.

He had no choice.

7

Tol'chuk marched through the morning drizzle. Overhead the skies were a featureless gray. His companions trailed behind, sodden, slogging, already exhausted. The dreary weather seemed to sap the strength from both leg and heart. They climbed the last switchback to reach a long ridgeline.

He paused at the top. Fardale loped up from where he had been guarding their rear. Ahead the valley was a mix of scraggly trees, bushes, rock, and thorn. Meadow grasses blanketed the rest, trampled into paths. Tol'chuk had forgotten how green the valley was in the spring. Wildflowers brightened patches: yellow honeysuckle, blue irises, red highland poppies. His heart filled with memories.

At the end of the valley, a sheer cliff face blocked the way, a root of the Great Fang itself. A black opening yawned near its base.

"Home." The word was a mumbled sigh.

Fardale growled.

Then Tol'chuk saw them, too. Movement drew his eye. What had appeared to be granite boulders suddenly sprouted limbs and loped away, bleating and raising an alarm. Even through the rain, Tol'chuk smelled the musk of the frightened females. Smaller than their male counterparts, they must have been out grubbing and rooting for tubers and greens. They fled toward the caves, scattering a herd of milk goats.

Tol'chuk led the way down, motioning the others closer. Near the mouth of the tunnel, movement could be seen. Tol'chuk stopped. "Stay together at my side. Do not make any threatening moves."

From the cave, a large group of og'res thundered out—males, the hunters and warriors. They ran at the intruders, knuckling on their arms.

The ground shook as they pounded forward. Most bore clubs or chunks of stone in their claws.

"Let me speak," Tol'chuk whispered to them needlessly.

Magnam stepped to his shoulder. "You're the only one who speaks the language."

Jaston stepped to Tol'chuk's other side. "But will they listen to you?"

Tol'chuk heard the frightened thread in their voices. The others gathered in his shadow as the herd of og'res bore down on them.

Mama Freda's pet tamrink whined on the healer's shoulder. "Big, big, big . . ."

Jerrick took the old healer's hand.

The thunder of the og're charge echoed off the cliff face, sounding like the advance of an army. Tol'chuk stepped forward. He reached into his thigh pouch and pulled out the chunk of heartstone. He raised it high, straightening his back to stand taller.

"I am Tol'chuk, son of Len'chuk of the Toktala clan!" he boomed out in the og're tongue, challenging the thunderous echo with his own voice. "I come at the bidding of the Triad!"

His words seemed to have little impact on the avalanche heading their way. Tol'chuk felt his companions close in behind his back; he kept his position, rock-steady before the onslaught. "Don't move," he murmured in the common tongue to his friends.

The wave of og'res reached them, parting to either side and encircling the group, with weapons at ready. The silence was even more intimidating than the thunder from a moment before.

Tol'chuk found himself facing a scarred boulder of an og're. The ridge bristles spiked along his arched back and almond eyes squinted with menace. Tol'chuk knew this og're—*and he knew Tol'chuk.*

"You slew my son," the og're grumbled, his eyes flaming with fury.

It was Hun'shwa, the father of Fen'shwa, a young thug of an og're that Tol'chuk had accidentally killed on the eve of his *magra* ceremony. When last Tol'chuk had seen this og're, the father had been stricken with grief and despair.

His words now were spoken like a warrior. No grief sounded in his voice; it was shame to openly show sorrow for the dead. But anger rang as clear as a crack of lightning.

"I did," Tol'chuk admitted. He didn't try to explain how he had been defending himself against an ignominious attack by the other. A father did not need to hear those words, and those words did not forgive the act.

"Why should I not kill you all and grind your bones to dust?"

The answer did not come from Tol'chuk, but from the skies overhead. The blanket of perpetual clouds parted, and a dazzling ray of sunshine shone through, illuminating the valley, brightening the green floor, casting a rainbow through the mists to the south.

But all of this paled when compared to the beauty of sunlight striking the raised chunk of heartstone. The Heart ignited with inner fire. A deep warm glow pushed back the morning chill and opened all their eyes to the majesty of life around them. For a moment as the Heart ignited, every living thing shone with its own inner light and force.

Gasps arose from the hardened hunters and warriors. Weapons were lowered. Some fell to their knees.

Tol'chuk stepped forward, keeping the stone in the sunlight. He held it out toward Hun'shwa. It glowed like its name, the true Heart of his people. Even a vengeful father could not deny the truth before him.

"This is why I came back," Tol'chuk said. "To make sure your son and all other spirits of our people could enter the next world. I do the bidding of the Triad. I ask that you allow us to pass."

The older og're stared at the stone. One clawed hand reached toward the brilliant facets. "Fen'shwa . . ." Grief again sounded in his voice.

A few of his fellow hunters and warriors glanced away. *Do not see the grieving.* But Tol'chuk stared at the father. "He has passed beyond."

Hun'shwa held his hand over the stone as if warming his fingers before a fire. "I feel him." Tears rolled down the craggy features. "Fen'shwa . . ."

Tol'chuk remained silent, allowing this father his moment of communion with his son. No one spoke; no one moved.

Finally storm winds closed the gap in the clouds, and the Heart's glow dimmed and faded. A fine drizzle shed from the skies, misting over the valley.

Hun'shwa pulled back his arm; the red fury had died in his eyes. He turned away with a grunt. He had not forgiven Tol'chuk, only acknowledged his right to live. The other og'res followed his lead and swung away.

"Is it safe to go with them?" Jaston asked. His face was white.

Tol'chuk nodded. "We've been accepted. But tread carefully and stay at my side."

"Like a leech," Magnam promised. He and the rest eyed the giants around them nervously, but they crossed the valley unmolested.

Once near the cavern opening, Fardale sniffed the air. Tol'chuk noticed the smell, too. Cooking fires, morning porridges, and the overpowering odor of og'res. The smell brought Tol'chuk back home. He remembered the happy times with his father, and with the few friends who would play with the misshapen og're, the games of toddledarts beside the fire at night. But also came darker memories: being shunned for his half-breed status, the ridicule, the rejection, and worst of all, the day his father's limp body had been carried past him, still bloody from the spear wound. He had never been so alone.

His feet slowed as he neared the dark threshold. The lights of hearths glowed inside, but after the long journey here, Tol'chuk feared taking these last steps.

He felt a touch on his elbow. Magnam whispered up to him while staring straight ahead. "You're not alone," he said, repeating his earlier words.

Tol'chuk glanced around and realized Magnam was right. While out among the lands of Alasea, in a world so much larger than a single cave, he had formed a new family. Taking heart and strength from those at his side, Tol'chuk ended his exile.

He walked forward under the arch of granite.

Once past the entrance, it took him a breath for his eyes to adjust to the gloom of the gigantic cavern. Small fires marked the hearths of each family, bordered by stacked boulders decorated with carved bones. Beyond these home fires, tunnels and smaller caves opened into the family warrens.

Almost every hearth was empty. Tol'chuk was sure the young ones and females were all in their warrens, hiding from these strangers. Only a few bent-backed elders, old hunters, guarded their dens with sharpened logs, eyeing the newcomers with sharp suspicion.

Hun'shwa guided them deeper into the cavern. Tol'chuk spotted his own family caves—dark, cold, and empty. The spark of familial strength he had felt a moment ago dimmed at the sight of a crossed set of deer antlers across the low bouldered gate to the homestead. He knew what the tiny rat skulls dangling from them meant: *cursed.*

Even the neighboring dens were vacant and empty. No one was taking any risks when it came to curses.

Tol'chuk could not blame them. His family traced its roots to the Oathbreaker. Was it any surprise that doom and failure grew out of that accursed lineage?

From a safe distance away, Hun'shwa pointed to the entrance of the warren. "You stay here."

Tol'chuk nodded. He stepped forward and lifted apart the crossed antlers, rattling the old rat skulls. From the corner of his eye, he saw the nearest flank of og'res back away. Tol'chuk ignored them and waved the others through the waist-high gate. "They've given us these caves," he said in the common tongue to his friends. "We can camp here."

"We will bring you wood for your fire," Hun'shwa grumbled as the other og'res dispersed. Once they had cleared away, Hun'shwa approached the stone fence.

Tol'chuk readied himself to be accosted or challenged by the father of Fen'shwa. Instead Hun'shwa reached out and rested a clawed hand on the top stone. Tol'chuk's eyes widened. To touch a cursed homestead was a brave act.

Hun'shwa spoke in a graveled whisper. "Fen'shwa has passed beyond. You've freed his spirit. A father knows these things."

Tol'chuk bowed his head in acknowledgment.

"And though I cannot forgive you for taking my son from me and lessening the joy of my family's hearth, I thank you for bringing us some peace."

Tol'chuk could hear the strain in the other's voice. These were not easy words. Neither were the next.

"Be welcomed home, Tol'chuk, son of Len'chuk." Hun'shwa grunted and swung away, knuckling across the cavern into the gloom.

Tol'chuk watched after him, feeling the first flicker of acceptance. Magnam stepped over to him. "What was that about?"

Tol'chuk shook his head. "Putting ghosts to rest," he mumbled, and turned to help set up camp and bring life back to the cold and empty hearth. It wasn't his blood lineage returned, but it was still family. Maybe this one could lift the curse from the other.

Around the home cave, og'res reappeared from their warrens, returning to stoke fires and stir pots. A pair of females slunk over with an armload of wood that they tossed from beyond the stone fence, fearing to approach any nearer.

As Tol'chuk gathered the scattered branches, he felt a prickle of warning over his skin, a bristling of hair along his arms and neck. Then a deep chiming echoed through the cavern, reverberating off the domed ceiling, vibrating his very bones. Even the hearth fires dimmed, smothered by the sound.

Across the room, all og'res stopped their work.

Mama Freda stood nearby. Tikal ran across from his exploration of a pile of bones and leaped to her shoulder. "What is it?" she asked as the sonorous toning continued.

"It be a call," Tol'chuk whispered.

The noise seemed to rattle the stone under his feet. It was as if someone had struck the granite heart of the mountain with a monstrous crystal hammer.

Mama Freda consoled her pet as it cowered. "A call? From whom? For what?"

"The Triad calls for all the og'res to assemble."

Jaston moved closer with the elv'in captain. "But why?" He stared over the cavern. "Most of you are already here."

"No," Tol'chuk said, "you don't understand. It be a summons for *all* og'res. Every clan, every og're, young or old, male or female."

"Does this happen often?" Mama Freda asked.

Tol'chuk shook his head. "Only once before during my lifetime, when I was a child. It be during the last og're war, when clan fought clan. The Triad called the assembly to broker peace."

"And now?"

"I do not know." He thought upon the conflict with the og'res from the Ku'ukla tribe, the death of their leader. Did the Triad already know?

Slowly the chiming slowed and stopped. Across the chamber, no one moved from the hearths. Low murmurs echoed among a few tribe members.

"Look," Magnam said. "Someone comes." He pointed toward the deepest recesses of the central cave.

A bluish light flickered, outlining a long crack in the back wall, growing brighter as someone approached.

They were not the only ones to notice the intrusion. The low murmurs died away; even the fearful cries of the females were extinguished.

Limned in blue flame, a figure limped from the crack, then another, then one more: three ancient og'res, naked and gnarled. Their eyes glowed, shining green in the darkness.

"The Triad," Tol'chuk breathed.

He watched the skeletal ghosts hobble across the granite floor. Og'res fell to their knees, bowing their heads, hiding their eyes. The trio were the spiritual guardians of the og're clans, the walkers of the dead. They seldom left their own caves and tunnels, but now the trio sidled wordlessly down the central path of the home cave, moving with clear determination.

Tol'chuk remained unbowed as they approached. He had walked the path of the dead to the Spirit Gate at its end. While he respected the Triad, he no longer feared them. He had done his duty, freed the Heart of their people. A spark of fire entered his heart: They had kept so much from him, sending him blind into the world, knowing that he would discover the truth, but not preparing him.

The Triad stopped before the gate to his homestead and spoke, though it was impossible to say which one uttered the words: "You know the truth now."

Tol'chuk's eyes narrowed. The spark in his heart flamed hotter. "You should have told me."

"It is not our way." Words rose like mist from the group. "The Heart of our people had to guide you . . . not just your own."

"And what now? I've rid the heartstone of the Bane. But what of the Oathbreaker?"

The lead og're reached a frail arm toward Tol'chuk. There was no doubt what was asked.

Tol'chuk retrieved the heartstone from his thigh pouch. Even in the feeble flames of the cavern, the jewel sparked with an inner radiance. He held out the stone, and clawed fingers wrapped around it.

"At last." The words were an exhalation of relief. The lead og're turned his back on Tol'chuk and showed the stone to the others. The Triad gathered closer. From among them, the ruby radiance of the Heart flared momentarily brighter. "We've waited so long." This last sounded so tired and forlorn. "Let it be done."

The glow burst out, blinding. The three og'res were shadows in the glare.

Around the cave, exclamations of alarm arose.

"What's happening?" Jaston gasped.

Tol'chuk simply stared, bathed in the edge of the glow himself, awash again with the beauty of all living things, himself included. He stood taller, straighter, unashamed.

Then in a flicker, the light snuffed out. Darkness descended. Tol'chuk felt a hollowness in his heart as the glow left him. Heavy silence again blanketed the cave.

In the feeble shine of firelight, the Triad continued to stand in a cluster around the Heart. From deep in the mountain, the dark chime sounded once more, a single reverberating note, somehow mournful this time. At the threshold to Tol'chuk's homestead, three bodies collapsed to the stone floor with a rattle of bone and limb. The Heart fell amidst the tangle of limbs.

Tol'chuk lunged forward, but he knew the truth before he reached their bodies. *The ancient og'res were dead.*

As he knelt on the stone floor, other og'res rushed forward, including Hun'shwa. He stared across the dead bodies to Tol'chuk, his eyes on fire. "You've slain the Triad!"

CASSA DAR SAT IN THE LIBRARIES OF CASTLE DRAKK. IN HER HEART, SHE sensed the danger to Jaston and the others. Though her magick's reach did not extend all the way to the Northern Fang, there were bonds deeper than elemental magick between her and the swamp man she loved.

Frightened for Jaston, she hunched over the books strewn across the table. With no other eyes to spy on her, she did not bother with the glamor of her magick and simply worked in her true form: a d'warf, wrinkled and bent by centuries of time. She rested one finger on a page in the ancient text she was perusing, a tome that spoke at length on the magickal connection between the two Fangs. A new dread filled her chest and quickened her breath.

Straightening, she waved to one of her swamp children. "Fetch the map from over there!"

The small boy scampered from his post by the table. In a moment he returned, burdened with a long, rolled parchment. She snatched it and quickly unrolled it, spreading all of Alasea before her. She read the passage again from the book and quickly scanned the jotted calculations and noted the paths of power written in the margins.

She sat back and closed her eyes.

Both the Fangs were fonts of the Land's elemental power; from their slopes, veins of power flowed down into Alasea like snowmelt. It was one of these silvery veins that the Dark Lord had sought to sever during his invasion into these very lands. The damage done had caused the sinking of this region, turning plains into swamps and half drowning the island of A'loa Glen.

But it was not the vein that ran down into her lands that concerned her now—but those that ran *between* the peaks. She traced a finger on the map while repeating the words from the book. "Where the northern-flowing veins of the Southern Fang merge with the southern-flowing veins of the northern peak, a twisted knot of power exists, a twining centered between the two mountains." She followed the calculations to the point on the map: *Winter's Eyrie*. She also saw the small town in its shadow. *Winterfell*—the home of the wit'ch.

Deeper than her bonds to Jaston, Cassa Dar was tied to the Land itself. She knew that whatever affliction weakened her came from there. Touching the map she could almost sense the malignancy there.

"Winter's Eyrie . . . ," she whispered.

She pushed from her desk. She had to let the wit'ch know that something foul was afoot. She headed toward the tower-top rookery, to send a crow to A'loa Glen. She prayed word reached someone in time.

As she climbed the stairs, her fears for Jaston grew in her heart. She clenched a fist to her chest. "Be careful, my love."

JASTON STOOD WITH THE OTHERS, CLUSTERED BEHIND TOL'CHUK. THE OG'RE still knelt before the bodies of the elderly trio. The chunk of heartstone nestled among their dead limbs and lifeless forms like a bright egg in a dreadful nest.

Beyond their bodies, a wall of og'res had formed, led by the same one who had challenged them earlier. His words were unintelligible to Jaston, just the grunts and growls of og're speak. But the giant's fury and accusation were clear. Blasted by this tirade, Tol'chuk remained silent, kneeling by the bodies.

Fardale brushed against Jaston's leg. The swamp man felt the tremble as the giant treewolf readied for a fight. Beyond Fardale, Jerrick kept one arm around Mama Freda, while sparks danced among the fingertips on his other hand. Magnam's hand rested on the hilt of his ax. All were ready to defend themselves and their friend.

The angry og're in the lead moved in Tol'chuk's direction, clearly having finally stoked enough fury to risk stepping through the fallen dead. But before he could reach the nest of bodies, the egg at its center flared brighter, warding him away. From the glow, a dark mist spread out.

All backed away, except for Tol'chuk. He simply stared at the display.

The strange fog swirled high, spinning off in three directions, then sweeping back to the stone floor. Each cloud of black mist condensed down, forming the figure of an og're, twisted and skeletal. Even Jaston recognized the Triad. It was as if their shadows had come to life.

Og'res fell to their knees before the sight. Even the leader dropped with a small cry of surprise.

From this misty trio, words flowed, but it was hard to say which shadow spoke. Even more surprising, though the words were clearly og're speak, Jaston understood their meaning.

"We are free at lassst," the shadows intoned, their words echoing as if coming from afar. "For centuries we have held off passing until the Heart was purified, opening the path to the spiritual lands beyond. Now we can shed our weakening bodies. It is time for a new leader to guard the clans. It is time for the *three* to become the *one*."

A misty arm pointed back to Tol'chuk. "Rise and claim the Heart. The burden is now yours."

Tol'chuk's eyes widened. He made a sound of refusal, speaking Og're.

"Half-breed or not, you are og're," the shadowy figures answered dolefully. "Take the Heart and fear not. We will remain in the stone between the two worlds to guide you where we can."

Still Tol'chuk balked, shaking his head.

The words of the ghosts grew sharper. "Do you forsake your duty like your ancestor?"

Tol'chuk's head sprang up.

The words softened. "It is true. The Oathbreaker refused the mantle of guardianship in his time. Will you walk his path or your own?"

Silence again pressed down on the cavern. Then Tol'chuk rose to his feet. Reaching over the bodies, he lifted the jewel from the tangle of limbs. Its glow flared brighter, as if it recognized him.

"The assembly has been summoned for this night," the ghosts echoed. "Go take your place as leader. Dark times lie ahead for our people. Even we can't see down that twisted path. Let the Heart guide you."

The three figures dissolved back to mists and drew into the stone, like smoke up a chimney flue. Words still flowed: "As with your last journey, you know your first step . . . You know where you must go."

Tol'chuk's face tightened.

Jaston saw the understanding in his amber eyes—and the fear.

TOL'CHUK STARED INTO THE CRYSTAL PLANES OF THE HEARTSTONE AS THE LAST of the Triad vanished. Deep in his own heart, he felt familiar hooks take root. This same stone had guided him across Alasea, drawing him along the path to the carved mountain in Gul'gotha. But this time he felt no compulsion, no direction. From here, though he was linked to the Heart, he would need to decide his own path.

The fate of the og're people now rested with him. *Dark times lie ahead.* Tol'chuk did not doubt the final words of the Triad. The Oathbreaker still lived. The Beast would not ignore his people forever, especially while his descendant plotted against him.

Tol'chuk lowered the stone and stared across the Triad's corpses to those kneeling beyond: males and females, the old and the young, the strong and the infirm. They knew nothing of the world beyond their lands, or of the danger on their doorstep.

Tol'chuk stood straighter, no longer hiding his half-breed status. What had once shamed him now seemed insignificant. After the horrors and the acts of bravery he had witnessed on his long journey, by peoples from *all* the lands, such trifles as mixed blood paled to nothing.

As the Triad had stated, he was og're. These were his people. And it was time for him to wake them.

His eyes fell upon Hun'shwa. The leader of the warriors kept his head bowed. "Hun'shwa," Tol'chuk said. "Rise."

The og're obeyed, but would not meet his gaze.

"I'll need three of your hunters to carry our fallen into the Chamber of the Spirits."

The other grunted to those who flanked him; they carefully began clearing the bodies. Hun'shwa addressed Tol'chuk. "What of the Assembly, the summons?"

Tol'chuk frowned; the warrior was right. The other tribes would gather at the Dragon's Skull, unaware of what had occurred here. His own Toktala clan must appear, too. He motioned to Hun'shwa. "Gather our people. We will head out with the setting sun."

Hun'shwa glanced up, eyes flashing. "But the Triad summoned the gathering, and now they are gone. Who will speak?"

Tol'chuk had not considered that far.

Hun'shwa pointed to Tol'chuk and answered his own question. "The elders called you the One. You must lead the Assembly."

Tol'chuk began to object, but he had no argument. It seemed the Triad had not wanted to give Tol'chuk a chance to shirk his duties. This very night, before all the clans, Tol'chuk would need to claim the mantle of spiritual leader.

He tightened his hold on the jeweled stone. "If I must speak, I will need time to prepare."

Tol'chuk watched the elders' bodies being hauled toward the flame-lit crack in the back wall and remembered the last words of the Triad: *You know your first step . . . You know where you must go.* Tol'chuk sighed. Long ago, he had carried the limp form of Fen'shwa through the crack to the Chamber of the Spirits beyond. There he had first faced the Triad and had begun the path that had led full circle back to here.

Holding the stone to his chest, Tol'chuk strode through the cursed gate of his old homestead.

"Where are you going?" Magnam asked behind him.

Tol'chuk pointed toward the bluish flames. He spoke without turning, without stopping. "I must walk the path of the dead."

THROUGH HER PET'S EYES, MAMA FREDA WATCHED THE GIANT STRIDE AWAY. The other og'res fled from his path, a mix of fear and reverence commingled in their musk. Tikal chittered at the smell, his senses more acute than those of a man. Mama Freda waited until their large companion disappeared into the far crack; then, directing Tikal with her own desires, she studied the others.

She suspected they only understood a fraction of what had transpired, while she understood each word. The guttural tongue of these people was not unknown to her—a knowledge she kept to herself. Their language was a mix of gesture, posture, and grunts, requiring both a keen eye and ear. Tikal had both.

"Freda, would you like to rest?" Jerrick asked, offering to guide her to a stone seat by the pile of logs and tinder. The d'warf Magnam began to light a fire. Jaston helped, shaving curls of wood from a branch to catch the flint's spark.

Mama Freda patted the elv'in captain's hand. "I'm fine, Jerrick. Go see if you can dig out some bread and hard cheese. The others must be hungry."

He did not budge. His blue eyes sparked with concern for her. "Freda . . . ?"

"I'm fine," she said more strongly.

She recognized the worry in his hard gaze and sighed. She wished she had never confided in Jerrick about the weakness in her heart. But the pain that had woken her a few nights back had been impossible to hide. She had been forced to admit her secret. Even her herbs could no longer keep the pain at bay, but at least they continued to ease her breathing.

After learning of her ailment, Jerrick had been furious with her for undertaking this journey. But deep inside, Mama Freda knew she had no choice. For countless winters, she had been alone—blind, disfigured, a foreigner among strangers. Only now, so late in her life, had she found someone to share her heart, as Tikal shared her senses. Bonded, one knowing the other. She would not spend her remaining time away from him.

She gave his hand a squeeze of reassurance. "Go help the others."

He nodded and released her. She eyed him as he departed: his white hair tied back, his figure lean and still strong for his age. A smile traced her lips as she turned away. He doted on her like a mother wolf with a lame cub. And for some reason, after so many years as a healer, it felt good to have someone look after her.

She stepped toward the layered stones that marked off Tol'chuk's compound. Fardale guarded the entrance, but Freda aimed farther back, toward a cluster of og'res. She leaned heavily on her cane, appearing feeble, no threat to the og'res beyond the fence line.

The large og're named Hun'shwa stood with a clutch of others, all muscled and scarred. Hun'shwa glanced her way, but dismissed her—not only a female, but a human, and an old, eyeless one at that.

She listened to their talk.

"Do you balk?" one of the others grunted to Hun'shwa. This fellow was the most gnarled og're she had ever seen, like the twisted stump of a tree. He wore a bit of wolfskin over one shoulder in a half cloak.

"Don't press me, Cray'nock," Hun'shwa growled.

"You gave your word to the Ku'ukla clan." The stranger nodded to the flame-lit crack. "That half-breed demon killed my brother." He lifted the edge of his wolfskin to bare the burned scar on his forearm.

Mama Freda saw that the design didn't match the clan markings here.

"I know what I swore to the Ku'ukla," Hun'shwa grumbled angrily.

Cray'nock spat on the stone floor. "Do not be fooled by his magick. He tricks you, weakens your heart with the shade of your son."

Hun'shwa turned to glare at the twisted og're. "Do not mention my son again."

Cray'nock curled his nose, ignoring the threat. "And what of the Triad? Do you truly believe evil was not involved with their deaths?"

Hun'shwa lowered his voice. "Their ghosts—"

The other og're spat again. "Demon trickery. My brother's hunting mates spoke of how he called demons from the sky. What then is a bit of smoke and whispers? More trickery, I say."

Hun'shwa's stony face tightened with doubt.

Cray'nock pressed on. "He killed your son. He murdered Fen'shwa."

Hun'shwa spun with a thunderous growl, but the other og're was already disappearing among his wolfskin-draped brothers.

"Do not speak my son's name!" Hun'shwa rumbled. "I will not warn you again. Do not dare disturb his spirit!"

Cray'nock spoke from among his brethren. "You promised to bring the new Ku'ukla leader the head of that half-breed cur! I ask you again—do you balk?"

Hun'shwa growled. "I will think upon my words."

Cray'nock sneered. "Think quickly, Hun'shwa—or war will come to your caves. The mountains will run red with your clan's blood. This I swear!" He turned away with the others, but not before one final jibe: "And the Ku'ukla clan won't balk!"

As the others left, Hun'shwa was left with a trio of his own warriors. "What will you do?" one of them asked.

Hun'shwa glanced to the crack in the back wall and sighed. "I will make my decision by the time of the Assembly. If the Triad spoke truly, Tol'chuk must be protected."

"And if it was a trick?"

Hun'shwa glowered. "Then I will slay Tol'chuk on the steps of the Dragon." He swung away, waving toward the departing clutch of clansmen. "Watch them."

Mama Freda leaned on her cane, considering the last words of the og're. It was a wise command. She eyed the departing members of the Ku'ukla clan. They did indeed bear watching. Something more was afoot than was plainly evident. Otherwise, why doubt what was witnessed here? The spiritual energies all but touched one's heart—og're or not.

Deep down, Hun'shwa knew the truth. Though he hesitated in betraying his prior promise, she sensed he believed all that had transpired here. But as leader of this tribe, he also had to consider the threat of the Ku'ukla clan.

She studied the hostile group. They, too, had witnessed the miracle of the Triad's passing and a new spiritual leader being chosen, but they denied the truth. Why? Something was hidden here ... something that needed the attention of a closer eye.

She reached to her shoulder and touched Tikal. "Go, follow," she whispered, sending her desire directly into her sense-bonded companion. "Do not be seen."

Tikal shivered, frightened to leave her side. His worries passed to her through their bonds. She stroked the tamrink's fiery mane. "Follow them . . . but stay hidden and quiet."

"Big goat sharp sharp." His eyes grew huge.

"Yes, be careful." She touched Tikal's lips with a finger. "And quiet."

Tikal trembled for a moment more, his eyes on the departing og'res. Then his tail tightened around her neck, embracing. With this short farewell, Tikal bounded from her shoulder and over the fence. He vanished in an instant into the shadows. Mama Freda remained with him, seeing through his eyes as he raced away, staying low, sticking to the darkest corners.

She startled as something touched her.

"The fire's ready," Jerrick said at her shoulder. "Come join us by the warmth."

Mama Freda did not resist this time. She leaned into her lover, letting him guide her. She feigned exhaustion, not blindness. While they walked toward a fire she could not see, her vision ran in shadows toward the cavern entrance. She remained silent about Tikal's mission. The cavern had many ears, and the acoustics were tricky. She would see what she could discover first.

Once near enough, she felt the glow of the fire and used her cane to guide her to a stone seat. Jerrick settled beside her. No one commented on the missing tamrink. It wasn't unusual for Tikal to be off her shoulder and scrounging in dark corners.

She faced the fire, pretending to be basking in its warmth, while deep inside she chased a clutch of og'res out into the drizzling gloom, her eyes sharp, her ears keen to any threat, her nose tasting the musk of those she pursued. Soon Tikal edged close enough for her to hear their grumbled words.

"All is ready?" Cray'nock was asking.

"The traps are set," assured the other.

"Good." Cray'nock glanced back over a shoulder. Tikal dove behind a scrabbleberry bush. The og're sniffed at the air, eyeing the entrance to Toktala home cave. "By nightfall, the entire Fang will be ours."

8

TOL'CHUK WAITED FOR THE LAST OF THE OG'RES TO LEAVE THE CHAMBER OF the Spirits. The laborers draped the last, limp form beside the other two, positioning cold palms down over the eyes of the dead. This was traditionally done to keep the spirits from attempting to reenter the bodies, but Tol'chuk knew such an act was unnecessary here. The Triad had been only too glad to shed the burden of flesh.

With their duty done, the bearers of the dead departed, leaving Tol'chuk alone with the corpses. He stared around the room. He had only been in here twice: during his naming ceremony and again when he had been a bearer of the dead, carrying Fen'shwa's limp body.

Tol'chuk turned in a slow circle. The sacred cavern was oval in shape with a bowled floor, like a bubble in the granite. A dozen torches lit the walls, hissing and flickering with blue flames. Shadows danced along the walls like the ghosts of the departed.

Tol'chuk ignored the display and faced the dark tunnel in the far wall. "The path of the dead," he whispered. It led to the warren of rooms in which the Triad had lived for countless ages. Tol'chuk's grandfather's grandfather had bowed to the trio. Now they were gone. The torch had been passed.

Sighing, Tol'chuk crossed the chamber and unhooked one of the blue-flaming brands, accepting what he must do next: to follow the path of the dead to its end, where his journey first began. Once again he must face the Spirit Gate, the crystal heart of the mountain.

Biting back the fear in his heart, Tol'chuk passed under the arch of the tunnel and into the dark gloom beyond. He attempted to keep his mind empty, his worries at bay. He simply trudged onward, winding down into the silent nether regions of the og're lands.

He was no stranger here, so he was not dismayed when the roof of the passage lowered, forcing him to duck and bow. The air grew bitter with the scent of rock salt and crusted mold. He pressed onward.

Ahead the tunnel branched to the right and left. Which way? Instinctively he knew the answer. Reaching with his free hand, he removed the chunk of heartstone. He held it forward as he neared a pair of corridors and raised the jewel to both paths. It flared brighter when facing the left.

He went that way, trusting the stone to guide him to the Spirit Gate.

After an interminable time and a maze of intersecting passages, Tol'chuk noticed a new glow ahead: not the rose of heartstone, but green like luminescent pond scum.

Moving resolutely, Tol'chuk discovered the source. The tunnels here were covered with eyeless, thumb-long glowworms: floor, walls, and ceiling. They squirmed around and over each other, leaving shiny trails on the bare rock.

Tol'chuk grimaced. He had forgotten about these denizens of the deep cave. He continued onward, crushing them under his bare feet. He remembered Magnam's description of the creatures, how they always appeared whenever veins or deposits of heartstone were mined. Why they migrated here was not known.

Holding the Heart aloft, Tol'chuk continued down the passage. Soon the worms were so plentiful that the torch was no longer necessary. He abandoned the brand at a crossroad and continued with just the stone.

Tol'chuk forged on, his skin shining with sweat and worm slime. Just as he was sure he was lost in this warren of tunnels, the passage suddenly lifted from around his shoulders, opening into a gigantic vault.

Tol'chuk stopped at the entrance, straightening, staring across the space. He held the crystal Heart before him. As if the air were fresher here, the flame in the heartstone fanned brighter, and a brilliance burst out, illuminating every corner of the vaulted room.

Its radiance splashed up against the chamber's far wall and revealed what lay hidden there: an arch of pure heartstone. Its two pillars glinted in the wormlight, each jeweled facet on fire.

Tol'chuk shrank before its majesty, but he moved forward, still holding his stone aloft, shielding his eyes with the other hand.

Bathed in the light, Tol'chuk felt the now-familiar sense of peace and unity with all of life. He stood basking in the radiance for an unknown time.

"Tol'chuk . . ."

He startled in the empty room.

"Tol'chuk, listen to us."

Pulling his thoughts back to the world of worm and rock, he realized the words arose from the heartstone in his clawed grip. Again a dark mist rose from the stone and spread high, drifting toward the Spirit Gate. The cloud settled to a stop, swirling and churning before the massive arch.

"We dare not cross over yet," the shades of the Triad whispered. Tol'chuk heard the longing in their words. "There is something we must show you first."

The mist separated again into three parts. Each sailed to the stone floor and resumed the shape of a bent-backed og're. "Approach the Spirit Gate."

Tol'chuk hesitated. He had traveled through the arch once and was loath to do so again.

The closest shadow turned his way. The greenish glow of eyes stared back at him; Tol'chuk recognized the shine of the worms. Hadn't Magnam mentioned such a phenomenon? He remembered the d'warf's words: *If you hang around the worms long enough, their glow creeps into your own eyes. Some say it lets you see not only this world but into the next . . . into the future.*

Staring at those eyes now, Tol'chuk did not doubt it.

"Come," the figure whispered. For the first time, it sounded as if the words arose from this one individual rather than all three. "It is time you learned the truth."

The other spirits drifted toward the arch, one toward each pillar. As they reached the gate's supports, each ghost disappeared into the stone, vanishing as they had done into the Heart earlier.

Tol'chuk remained alone with the last member of the Triad.

Across the room, a deep droning arose from the arch. As it grew louder, words could be heard—ancient words chanted in a tongue Tol'chuk did not recognize. The intonation traveled up the pillars, and a new sound reverberated outward, as if the original prayer was being echoed by something more ancient than any language. The whole cavern rang with the sound. Tol'chuk's bones seemed to vibrate in tune.

The lone spirit spoke at his shoulder. "It is the Voice of the Fang."

Tol'chuk glanced to the speaker. The misty figure had grown more substantial, seeming to draw strength from the noise itself.

"The Land speaks through the mountain." The spirit pointed again to the arch.

As the droning grew in volume, the wall of granite framed by the heartstone arch began to shimmer in harmony with the Voice. What had once appeared to be a cliff of solid granite now seemed no more than a reflection in a pond that rippled with the droning call.

Even the air grew clearer in the chamber, as if an unfelt wind blew outward from the gate. Tol'chuk breathed deeply, filling his lungs. He felt energy spreading throughout his being. As it reached the hand holding the Heart of the Og'res, the stone flared brighter, vibrating in harmony with the Voice.

Tol'chuk's arm rose of its own bidding, and he felt the now-familiar tug upon his chest. Tol'chuk stepped toward the Spirit Gate, unable to stop himself. A flush of panic iced through him. Was he again doomed to pass through the Gate and be transported elsewhere? He resisted, struggling to control his limbs.

"Do not fight it," the spirit whispered, trailing behind him.

"What's happening?" Tol'chuk squeaked out.

"The Fang calls you. You cannot stop it."

The ghost was correct. Tol'chuk was drawn forward—not under the Gate and beyond like before, but toward one of the two pillars. And with each step, the stone flared brighter, growing into a blinding star in his hand.

Sightless from the glare, Tol'chuk barely registered when he'd stopped. His arm stretched overhead, drawing his spine straighter. He felt the Heart touch the arch, clicking into place; with its touch, he was released from the spell and tumbled backward.

Tol'chuk rubbed his arm. He spotted the Heart resting in a faceted cubby, like a key in a lock. It fit so seamlessly that it would have been impossible to discern if not for the blinding light coming from it.

The ghost spoke. "The stone is the center of the Gate—its *heart*, as much as our own."

The Voice of the Fang suddenly changed in pitch.

"Now watch!" the Triad ghost warned. "Watch as the Gate is made whole."

The shine of the imbedded Heart flowed up into the arch, igniting the larger stone like fire set to oil. The blaze of brilliance swept up into the pillared column, traveling high over the arch, then diving back down the far leg.

As it hit the floor, the glow dimmed—but did not stop!

Tol'chuk gasped.

The star of brilliance could be seen diving down through the floor, shining through the granite like moonlight through a dense fog. The glowing arc passed beneath the arch, then back up into the first pillar, completing an entire circle to rejoin the Heart again.

Tol'chuk gaped at the blazing arch above and the glow of its reflection in the granite below. The unbroken ring reminded him of the mountain people's Citadel: an arch of granite whose reflection in Tor Amon formed a magickal circle. It was the same here.

"Unity," the Triad ghost whispered in a mix of sorrow and joy: "It has been so long since the Heart was hale enough to ignite the Gate fully."

"I don't understand."

The spirit pointed a hand overhead. "The arch you see in the cave is but half of the whole." He shifted his arm toward the floor. "Below lies the other half circle, still buried, completing the Gate."

"A ring of heartstone," Tol'chuk mumbled. "Not just an arch."

The spirit nodded. "With the Heart returned, the way is now open."

"The way to where?"

The ghost again turned those wormglowing eyes toward him. "To the center of all things, the core of the world." The spirit waved an arm toward the Gate. "Behold what lies within the Land's true heart!"

The mirage of rippling granite under the arch suddenly convulsed as if a large boulder had dropped into its center. From either pillar, two sweeping clouds of mist sailed forth—the other spirits returning. The pair joined their brother, and they all watched as the ring of heartstone blazed and the rock in the center rippled and churned. Granite lost form, becoming something else.

Tol'chuk feared what he would see, but he could not tear his eyes away. His breath grew still.

Slowly the churning slowed. The black granite cliff face disappeared. In its place was a sight that dropped Tol'chuk to his knees.

He stared out into a pit of endless darkness, traced with jagged lines of crimson fire. Flares traveled along these veins like fireflies, pulsing and racing. Some seemed to flicker from the ring of heartstone here and travel down those lines. But it wasn't these veins that took the breath from Tol'chuk. Set in the heart of the inky darkness revolved a giant crystal of the purest silver blue, shining like the most perfect diamond in the night.

Tol'chuk could not remove his gaze from its beauty. Though he had no reference by which to judge its size, he knew what he looked upon dwarfed the largest mountain. He was but a mote before its majesty.

"Behold the heart of the world," the Triad intoned together. "The Land's spirit given form. Behold the *Spirit Stone*."

With their words, the shining crystal swelled toward them. Tol'chuk sensed a presence filling the space like pressure under the deepest waters. Unblinking, he stared, feeling complete and whole, even before an energy unfathomable in depth and scope.

And as he watched, he realized the traceries of crimson were in fact veins of heartstone. The webbed net of lines crisscrossed and forked, but all paths led down to the crystal at its center.

The Spirit Stone . . . the true heart of the world.

"She comes," the Triad whispered around him, their voices full of reverence.

Tol'chuk sensed it too, a growing heaviness to the air, a pressure on the ears. Then a figure appeared, stepping forth from the Spirit Gate as if from the stone itself. Limned against the silvery shine, the newcomer was a dark shadow, a living flow of black oil. It was a woman, tall and stately, clothed in a mist of silver tresses that clouded around her, draping over ebony shoulders, obscuring her face, and seeming to wave and sweep as if she moved underwater. The strands roiled and flowed all the way back to the Spirit Stone, blending one to the other.

"Who . . . ? What . . . ?" Tol'chuk stammered.

Drawn to his voice, she stepped forward, turning to him. Her silver tresses washed from her face for a moment. Her features grew to perfect clarity, carved of stone.

Tol'chuk gasped. *"Elena!"*

MAMA FREDA CONTINUED TO WARM HER COLD BONES BY THE FIRE. AT HER side, Jerrick spoke in whispers to Magnam and Jaston, but she listened, instead, with the keen ears of her pet tamrink, her attention on the pack of og'res from the Ku'ukla clan.

It was dizzying to sit so still before a warm fire while another part of her, sharp with senses, raced and sped. Her nose smelled both the sizzle of woodsmoke from the campfire and the goatlike odor of wet og'res.

Mama Freda wrapped her hands over the end of her cane, leaning her chin upon her fingers, while her heart pounded in her ears, fearful for her pet, fearful for them all. From the words of Cray'nock, the Ku'ukla clan planned treachery and bloodshed. She longed to tell the others, but blind as she was here, it was impossible to tell who might eavesdrop. Around her, she heard the scuff of og'res, their grunts, their barked orders. Some were close, keeping an eye on the strangers in their den. For now, she would remain silent until she discovered what trickery the Ku'ukla clan planned.

She focused on Tikal.

By now, the og're pack had crossed the meadow and were well into a patch of rimwood forest nestled in the upper highlands. They were in their own territory, tracing their way back to their home cave and warrens. The group grumbled like low thunder, much of it boasting of the number of heads they would collect during the war to come. But as the rimwood forest of black pines and mountain alder grew denser around them, the party became quieter.

Through Tikal's nose, Mama Freda could smell the edge of fear that now scented their musk. With each step, the scent grew thicker. Her fingers tightened on her cane.

Cray'nock stopped and waved for the others to remain where they were. No one grunted an objection. The gnarled og're straightened his wolfskin cloak nervously, then edged away from the group.

Mama Freda silently urged Tikal to follow this lone og're. The tamrink slipped to the side of the path and circled around the main group. Tikal took to the branches then, scampered high, and ran along the treetops. Here in the dense forest, the canopy was an unbroken road. Her pet's keen eyes never lost sight of Cray'nock as the og're slinked deeper into the dark woods.

Overhead, lightning crackled. A spat of rain pelted down, drumming through the leaves and needles. Tikal slipped lower among the branches, both to avoid the worst of the rain and to keep a watch on the og're as the woods grew denser.

Cray'nock slowed, his gaze darting around him. The sweaty scent of his fear thickened the air.

From a shadowy patch of the deep wood, a voice greeted him, sly and dripping with wickedness. "Have you the head of the one named Tol'chuk?" Mama Freda was surprised to hear the common tongue spoken here, not Og're.

"No, my queen." Cray'nock dropped to his knees, his voice trembling. "The slayer of my brother still lives. He again uses demon trickery, this time to sway the others' hearts."

"What of the pact with the Toktala clan? Their promise?"

Cray'nock bowed his head. "Hun'shwa, their leader, resists. But the Ku'ukla clan is prepared to attack upon your word. We gather near the north woods already."

There followed a long empty silence. Cray'nock trembled among the wet leaves.

"No," the voice suddenly whispered, "we will not attack them in their own caves. I have heard of the summons this night, a gathering at the place called the Dragon's Skull."

Cray'nock nodded. "Yes, my queen."

"That is where we will draw them out. And I will not tolerate any more failures—not from your brother before you, not from you."

"No, my queen."

"I will make sure this time, Cray'nock. Come closer."

The og're climbed to his feet, shuddering, and moved forward, shambling in fear.

Mama Freda urged Tikal to follow. *Who lurks in the woods here?*

As both tamrink and og're moved toward the deepest glade of the wood, Mama Freda made out what looked like snow shining among the branches ahead, as if a small snowstorm had struck this single section of forest. Fluffy mounds of white frosted dark limbs and lay in piles atop shadowy bushes. Even the forest floor was covered with drifts and banks of the snowy whiteness.

What strangeness is this?

Cray'nock crept to the edge of the odd glade, followed by Tikal in the treetops.

Now closer, peering down with the sharp eyes of the tamrink, Mama Freda saw the snow-covered forest was not unoccupied. Thousands of tiny red spiders raced over the white mounds and along thin strands.

Not *snow*, Mama Freda realized with growing horror, *webbing*. The entire glade was enshrouded in silky webs, piled thick and choking everything.

Cray'nock cowered before the giant spider's nest.

From the center of the webbing, something dark stirred. A spiny leg, bloodred in color, pierced out from a dense curtain of netting and cut through the silky mass with ease. Then another appeared . . . and another . . .

What came next, dragged out by those legs, was a horror unlike any Mama Freda had ever imagined—a giant spider, as large as any og're, as dark a red as to be almost black. Its eight legs skittered through the web. Its bulbous shiny abdomen arched up, dripping silk from the spinnarets on its underbelly as it pulled free of its central nest.

But that was not the worst.

Above the engorged abdomen, the torso of a woman stood out starkly. She was as pale as the other half of her was dark. Long blue-black hair hung across her bare breasts, where tiny red spiders raced. She brushed them gently away with her hands, but her attention remained fully on the og're before her.

Cray'nock would not look up into her cold face. "Queen Vira'ni."

Mama Freda jerked by the fire, dropping her cane.

Jerrick spoke at her side. "Freda, are you all right?"

She waved his question away, frozen in fear. She had heard the tale of the spider wit'ch from the others: an ill'guard enemy slain in the woods below the highlands and buried there. But the ill'guard *dead* did not always stay *dead*. As with Rockingham before her, the spider wit'ch had obviously been resurrected and given a new form.

"You will take me to the Dragon's Skull," she whispered, oily and venomous. She pointed to the limbs of the trees around her. "Call your clansmen. We will move my egg sacs there, too."

Cray'nock stared up. Tikal—and Mama Freda—followed his gaze. From the limbs of the trees, scores of heavy silk pods hung, the size of ripe pumpkins. Inside the silky cocoons, dark things churned and vibrated, awaiting release.

The og're trembled at the sight, horror keeping him frozen.

"My children have tasted the blood of this Tol'chuk," Vira'ni continued. "This time we will feast on his body—on the bodies of all who aid him."

"Yes, my queen." Cray'nock climbed to his feet. The spider queen's face lifted as he rose, her eyes piercing. Her gaze swept the silk-shrouded canopy and fixed upon Mama Freda's own.

"We are spied upon!" Vir'ani hissed, pointing in her direction.

"Tikal! Run!" Mama Freda shouted aloud in her panic.

"What's wrong?" Jerrick asked, clutching at her shoulder.

Mama Freda didn't have time to answer. She raced with her tamrink through the trees, struggling to send energy out to him. Then a sharp pain flared in her chest. She gasped.

Her little friend shared her pain. Tikal missed a jump and tumbled wildly. He struck a branch, and a tiny leg snapped. He hit the ground hard, knocking the breath from his chest.

Mama Freda could not breathe herself, but she fought to give the tamrink what strength she could.

Tikal scrambled to his one good leg. In his fright and pain, he chittered, "Tikal, good puppy, run, run."

The fiery agony in Mama Freda's chest burst out into her legs and arms. She barely felt Jerrick cradle her as she fell. Her mind and heart—weak as it was—went out to Tikal. *Run, my little boy, run.*

"Run, run," he echoed aloud in a forest too far away.

The tamrink raced with his injured leg curled against his belly, fleeing on his hands, leaping with his good leg, tail flagging.

Run and hide . . . get away, my little love. By now the pain choked her breathing to a standstill. She could not even gasp.

Tikal fled, flying through the woods—then something snagged his leg, pulling him up short, dropping him to the dirt.

As he struggled to free himself, rolling and jerking, Mama Freda saw what had captured him: a loop of webbing wrapped around his leg. It now drew him back, dragging his panicked body toward the source of the web, the spider queen. Vira'ni lurked down the trail, hunched, legs splayed, a grin of pure venom on her lips.

From under her legs, a wave of tiny red spiders flowed, aiming for little Tikal. Her pet struggled and fought, trying to bite through the constraining web, chewing with his needle teeth.

Tikal!

Suddenly he broke free, rolling back from the sudden release. He turned and bounded away, leaping toward a low-hanging branch. With a flare of relief, Mama Freda felt his fingers latch on.

But the branch was not empty.

Small spiders danced across the bark, across Tikal's fingers, down his thin arm. When they bit, the pain struck Mama Freda, worse than the pain of her own failing heart. The little tamrink fell again, landing amid the wave of spiders.

Mama Freda screamed as he was overrun. "Tikal!"

"Mama, Mama . . ."

Then she felt the beat of his little brave heart clench and stop . . . as did her own.

Deep in a cave, her body arched. Agony lanced through bones and heart.

"What's wrong with her?" Magnam cried out.

"She's dying!" Jerrick said. "Her heart!"

Mama Freda felt darkness close around her, a darkness deeper than any blindness. She struggled to draw one more breath from lungs leaden with approaching death. She gasped out one final warning to her friends, her lover.

"Beware . . . Vira'ni!"

Then the cool balm of darkness erased her pain. As she drifted away from the touch of her lover, feeling his lips press against hers one last time, somewhere in the distant darkness, she heard a tiny piping cry, lost and scared. *Mama, Mama . . .*

Hush, little one, I'm coming.

STUNNED, TOL'CHUK STARED AS THE DARK APPARITION FLOWED OUT OF THE Spirit Gate. "Elena?" he repeated.

The figure focused on him, her dark eyes shining like polished obsidian. Silver tresses continued to billow across her features, moving to unseen currents. Energy crackled along the curls and flowing strands, seeming to sweep out from the Spirit Stone to scintillate over the black skin of the apparition. As she moved from the heartstone arch, the features of her face grew in detail, as if she were arising from the depths of some dark sea.

Tol'chuk recognized his mistake. This figure, while similar in features, was not Elena. The ghostly woman here was much older. Her face was unlined, but the weight of ages marked her eyes and lips, and the silver of her hair was not all magick. Here stood a woman older than centuries.

"Wh-who are you?" he forced out.

The Triad answered his question, their voices full of awe: "The Lady of the Stone. Its guardian and keeper."

The apparition lifted a single dark arm, sweeping back a mist of silver strands. "No," she said, her black lips parting. "No longer." Her words were faint. They also seemed strangely out of sync with the movement of her lips. "I cannot hold back the darkness that comes. My time is past." Her eyes glinted at Tol'chuk. "New guardians are needed."

As Tol'chuk drew back, the Triad stirred in confusion, their figures blurring. "But the Lady of the Stone has been the Gate's eternal guardian."

"No," she repeated again with a shake of her head. "Not eternal . . . just ancient . . . I joined my spirit to the Stone in a time lost to myth and legend."

The Triad murmured, their confusion dissolving their shapes into misty forms. "We don't understand."

"I once went by another name." Her words grew faint. "Your great, great ancestors called me *not* the Lady of the Stone, but a title more cursed in its time: *Tu'la ne la Ra Chayn.*"

Tol'chuk frowned at her last words, for the name was spoken in ancient Og're. But the elders understood, for a wail screeched from the misty figures. "It cannot be!" They fled back from the Gate in horror and shock, shredding apart.

"What's wrong?" Tol'chuk asked, starting up to his feet.

One of the shades sailed past overhead, crying out. *"Tu'la ne la Ra Chayn!"*

"The blasted . . ." another moaned.

"The cursed one!" the third keened.

In their panic, the group had split, no longer united.

Tol'chuk backed a step. "Who?"

The first answered, "She is Tu'la ne la Ra Chayn . . . the Wit'ch of the Spirit Stone!"

Tol'chuk pinched his brows together in confusion. The Triad settled behind him as if for protection.

Before them, the dark woman continued to drift within a sea of silvery strands, ignoring their outburst. She seemed to grow blacker, her misty hair sparking more richly. The anger in her eyes was clear, as was an impossible sadness.

The Triad's words sunk into Tol'chuk. "The Wit'ch of the Spirit Stone," he mumbled, staring at the apparition, frowning. Then realization struck him blind as he again recognized the similarities to Elena. Another wit'ch . . . He stumbled back, choking for a moment, then gasped out the name by which he knew her: "The Wit'ch of Spirit *and* Stone!"

Her eyes remained fixed on Tol'chuk. "The march of time blurs so many meanings and names," she said coldly. "It is strange to have all of your life's successes and defeats boiled down to such a simple phrase, then to have even that misremembered." She sighed. "But you know my true name, don't you, og're?"

He did, seeing in her tireless expression a bit of Elena even here. "Sisa'kofa," he said aloud.

She nodded. "And I know you. The last descendant of Ly'chuk of the Toktala clan."

Tol'chuk frowned in confusion.

"The Oathbreaker," she explained.

Tol'chuk blinked. *Ly'chuk!* That was his ancestor's name, the Oathbreaker's true name. He found his tongue. "I don't understand. How could you be here? Why are you here?"

She waved a ghostly arm. "To answer your first question, I'm not really *here*. My true spirit passed beyond the Spirit Gate ages ago. This form is but an echo, a bit of magick left behind, tied to the energy of the Spirit Stone. As to why? That is a story meant for another's ears, not yours. I left my echo in the Gate, knowing one day the wit'ch who would come after me would be in need of guidance."

"Elena," Tol'chuk said.

The dark figure nodded. "For untold centuries, I've been guardian of the Spirit Stone. From this post, I've guided your people as best I could, but even I could not stop your ancestor's betrayal."

"The Oathbreaker . . ."

"Ly'chuk took the vow of spiritual guardianship and came as a suppli-cant to this very Gate. He was strong in spirit and even stronger in ele-mental gifts."

Tol'chuk jerked with surprise. "The Oathbreaker was an elemental?"

"His gift was the ability to sculpt another person's natural magicks—to take raw talent and refine it."

Her words rang with truth. Tol'chuk remembered all the ill'guard en-countered during their long sojourn. They were examples of this very handiwork, elementals whose gifts were warped to serve the Oathbreaker's need or amusement. "What happened?"

"That even I don't know. One day your ancestor opened the Gate to the Spirit Stone. I felt the magick and came to see Ly'chuk kneeling, crying in pain, his arms raised. As I approached, I felt something tear in the fabric of the world. After that, the Gate slammed shut and remained closed for the next six centuries." She faced the shades of the Triad, "What hap-pened in this chamber that day I do not know."

The og're spirits shifted uncomfortably under her gaze. "We know no more than you," they whispered in unison again. "The Oathbreaker took his vows. But we also sensed the *wrongness*, that rip in the fabric, that you speak of. We rushed here, but we only found the Heart, resting on the floor. When we touched the stone, we knew immediately it was cursed. Tainted, the Heart would no longer fully awaken the Spirit Gate. We were cut off. And in the heartstone, the Bane grew, feeding on our spirits. One of us dreamed that the curse could only be lifted by the last seed of Ly'chuk, the Oathbreaker."

"So we waited . . ." the first elder said, breaking from the others.

"And waited . . ." the second said.

"And waited . . ." the third echoed.

"Until I came," Tol'chuk finished, unable to keep the bitterness from his voice.

A silence settled in the room. So many ages pressed down upon them.

At last, the shadow of Sisa'kofa spoke. "It would seem your burden is not over, og're."

Tol'chuk glanced up. "What do you mean?"

She glanced to the Spirit Gate, her silver hair billowing. "The Land tainted your heartstone with the Bane for a reason: to lock the path to the Spirit Stone. Since that time, I have sensed corruption trying to dig through, have felt the Land's flow of energies being twisted. Something out there hunts for the heart of this world."

"My ancestor," Tol'chuk whispered. "The Oathbreaker."

The shade sighed. "And he grows stronger. Soon he'll break through; my echo of power is no match. But the Spirit Gate opens again." The shade of the wit'ch focused on Tol'chuk. "New champions have arisen, chosen to protect the purity of the world's heart: both you and the new wit'ch."

"Elena."

A nod. "Before my true spirit passed beyond the Gate, I dreamt of her. I saw the dark time ahead. She stood before this same Gate, the blood of friends flowing across the floor ..." The shade of the wit'ch sighed. "I bear a warning meant only for her. It is the reason I am here, a call from the distant past to the present."

"You won't tell us this warning?" Tol'chuk asked, bone-tired of magicks and secrets.

"I cannot. I am an echo of desire and purpose. I have no other path. The young wit'ch must be brought here, and the Spirit Gate must be protected until that time." She stared hard at Tol'chuk. "You must be this guardian."

The Triad whispered again, their eyes aglow with prescient wormlight. "We saw this also. It was why we summoned an assembly at Dragon's Skull." All eyes focused on Tol'chuk. "You must unite the clans. The Gate must be protected!"

Somewhere far away, a howl echoed, traveling down from above.

"Listen," Sisa'kofa said. "Already the darkness closes around us."

Tol'chuk cocked his head, recognizing the cry. *Fardale.*

He began to turn, but the Triad drifted up, wormlit eyes seeking his. "A spirit has been released," they whispered. "One of your companions."

Tol'chuk bolted to his feet. "Who?"

"The old woman," the og're ghosts intoned, keening.

Mama Freda! Tol'chuk swung away, meaning to hurry to his friends' sides.

"Wait!" Sisa'kofa called to him. "Take the Heart! Close the Gate! Above all else, the path to the Spirit Stone must be protected."

Tol'chuk hesitated, then ran to the arch. His clawed fingers grabbed hold of the Heart in its keyhole.

At his side, the spirit of the wit'ch drifted back through the Gate, her

silver tresses sweeping away with her. Over her shoulder, the crystal of the
Spirit Stone shone out from the well of darkness.

"I'll be waiting," the spirit promised. "Waiting for you all."

Tol'chuk felt a sudden chill at these last words, but the wolf howled
again. He had no time for misgivings. He tore the Heart free. The
window upon the world's center vanished, replaced again with a cliff of
granite.

The trio of spirits dissolved and flowed back into the chunk of heartstone. Words trailed. "A darkness comes. Only united will the og're clans
survive."

Tol'chuk shoved the Heart into his thigh pocket. With one last glance
to the heartstone arch, he dashed toward the tunnels. "Then I'll let nothing stop me."

As FARDALE HOWLED HIS GRIEF, JASTON KNELT BY THE HEALER'S BODY. THE
elv'in captain cradled her form, tears flowing down his face. "Why?" he
moaned.

Jaston touched his shoulder in sympathy. He knew no words to ease
this pain. If it had been Cassa Dar on the floor here, he would have been
inconsolable.

Magnam stood over them all. "We've got company." He nodded to the
circle of og'res that had closed around the hearth. They stood a few paces
away, clearly fearful of approaching any closer, but bright menace shone
in their eyes.

Jaston pulled to his feet. "They know something is wrong. Panic may
make them strike out before Tol'chuk can return."

"Where is Lord Boulder?" Magnam said with a scowl. "We could use
someone who can speak the local lingo."

One of the largest og'res pushed through the crowd to approach the
gate to this hearth. Jaston recognized the one Tol'chuk had been talking
to before—Hun'shwa, the clan leader.

The monster knuckled toward the door, shoulders bulled forward.
When he spoke, he rumbled like boulders grinding together, but his
words were in the common tongue, crudely spoken. "What be wrong
here? What be the howling for?" He eyed the wolf.

Fardale had gone quiet, but the giant treewolf kept his post by the gate,
hackles raised.

Jaston stepped forward. "One of our elders has died," he said. "A strain
on her heart."

Hun'shwa narrowed his eyes. "There be much death this day."

A couple og'res grumbled behind their leader, but Hun'shwa waved an arm for them to be silent.

Jaston spoke up, "We ask for a moment of peace to grieve our dead."

The og're knuckled around and grunted for the others to back away. Slowly the group obeyed, but not without many glares and warding gestures toward the cursed homestead. Hun'shwa turned. "You grieve now. Then we take your female to the Chamber of the Spirits."

Jaston nodded and faced the others as the og're left. "I've bought us some time, but I don't know for how long."

Magnam moved closer. The d'warf spoke in low tones. "So who is this Verny that Mama Freda warned us about?"

"Vira'ni." Jaston crossed his arms. "An ill'guard. Elena's group killed her in the rimwood forests not far from here."

"Maybe she did," Magnam said with a scowl. "But for those once touched by the Nameless One, death has no meaning."

"Or maybe her fright was some delusion from the pain and approaching death."

Magnam shook his head. "No, the healer's pet is missing. And I distinctly heard her call out Tikal's name. She saw something—through its eyes—something that froze her heart." The d'warf glanced to Jaston. "What do you know of this Vira'ni?"

"Very little. Something to do with spiders?"

Jerrick cradled Mama Freda's body and spoke through clenched teeth. "I will hunt this demon myself and burn her to ash."

Fardale crossed to the healer, sniffed at her, then circled the fire. As he padded around the flames, he climbed out of his wolf form and back to human. Fur slipped back to bare skin, fangs became teeth, and claws retracted to nails. He rose to stare across the flames at them, panting slightly from the exertion of shifting.

Jaston could still see the wolf in the man: there was the feral set to his lips, the unblinking sternness to his gaze, the stone stillness to his posture. There was no mistaking this man for Mogweed.

"If Vira'ni is near," Fardale said, "we're all in grave danger."

"What do you know of her?" Magnam asked.

Fardale ignored his question and sniffed at the air, raising his face high. "Tol'chuk comes."

A commotion arose from the dark shadows of the deep cave. Og'res grunted in agitation, then parted. Tol'chuk came lumbering through and quickly crossed to the hearth.

"What happened?" His eyes were large, staring down at Mama Freda.

As Magnam explained, Jaston saw the clan leader, Hun'shwa, staring over at their group, as if weighing them. A smaller og're grumbled at his shoulder, but the Hun'shwa growled him away.

"Vira'ni!" Tol'chuk boomed, drawing Jaston's attention around.

Fardale nodded. "Mama Freda died with that name on her lips—a warning. I spied her beast leave the cave near the time you left with your dead elders."

All faces turned to the shape-shifter.

His expression remained stoic. "The healer must have sent him after the og'res wearing the wolfskin cloaks." He all but growled this last bit.

Tol'chuk responded in kind. "Wolfskin!"

Fardale nodded.

Tol'chuk glanced to the eye of the cave. "That could only mean—"

"The Ku'ukla clan," a stern voice said behind them all.

As a group, they all turned. Hun'shwa stood there, head half bowed. "You killed Drag'nock, their leader," he said. "They came with the morning sun and demanded the head of Tol'chuk or their clan would declare war." The eyes of the og're glanced to the floor. "I gave my word that it would be done."

Magnam pulled his ax free. "I'd like to see you try!"

Tol'chuk lifted an arm to calm the d'warf. "And now, Hun'shwa?"

The big og're lifted his eyes. "There be something wrong with the Ku'ukla. After my own fury for my son's death calmed, I could smell it on their skin. They lie as easily as a stream flows." He turned to the cave's entrance. "Your head or not, war will come. The Ku'ukla crave to rule the six clans. The death of Drag'nock will rally them. But . . ." His eyes narrowed.

"But what?" Tol'chuk asked.

Hun'shwa turned to Tol'chuk. "Something else be wrong. Cray'nock be the one who came . . . the last brother of Drag'nock . . . saying their new leader demanded your head."

"His brother?" Tol'chuk asked, his face hardening with suspicion.

"What's the significance?" Jaston asked.

"Cray'nock should be leader after the death of his brother," Tol'chuk explained. "It be our way."

Hun'shwa nodded. "A new leader has arisen. So why didn't he come with his clan's demands? A strange scent clings to the Ku'ukla clan."

"And there be no nose more keen than yours," Tol'chuk said, clearly accepting this statement.

Jaston spoke up. "The Ku'ukla threat . . . and a warning from Mama Freda about the spider wit'ch."

"Darkness closes around us," Tol'chuk whispered, as if repeating someone else's words.

"What do we do?" Magnam asked, still holding his ax.

After a long moment, Tol'chuk turned to them. "Our only hope be to rally the clans this night. United, the og're clans be a force few dare to threaten." He turned to Hun'shwa. "Do I have the support of the Toktala?"

Hun'shwa stared at Tol'chuk, then slowly nodded. "We stand beside you."

"Then prepare the clan. We march for the Dragon's Skull with the setting sun."

Hun'shwa half bowed, then departed.

"What of us?" Magnam asked.

Tol'chuk stared at them, a strange light in his eyes. "You be also my family, my hearth. That makes you og're. And when I speak of uniting the og're clans, I mean *all* og'res."

Jerrick still knelt by the body of the healer. "And Freda? What are we to do with her?"

Tol'chuk's voice grew hard. "She gave her life to bring us warning. She will be honored . . . and *revenged*. This I swear on our new family." Tol'chuk held out a claw toward them all.

Magnam was the first to step up, placing his hand atop Tol'chuk's. Fardale came next, stoic, expressionless, but his eyes glowed stronger as he rested his hand upon the others'.

Jaston felt a stirring in the air, something larger than them all. He moved forward, adding his hand.

Slowly, Jerrick rose to his feet. The elv'in captain stepped to their side. He reached an arm, and with a last glance to his lover, he joined his palm to theirs. Something seemed to spark out at that moment, something that had nothing to do with elv'in wind magick.

Tol'chuk whispered in a low voice. "United."

Thunder boomed in the distance, punctuating his single word.

"A storm is coming," Magnam muttered.

No one disagreed.

9

Cassa Dar stood atop the tower of Castle Drakk. She stared across the Drowned Lands toward the setting sun. Beyond the tower parapets, a wispy sea of swamp mist spread to the horizon. Only the top levels of Castle Drakk rode above the endless expanse, a lone ship in a dead calm.

Distantly, the calls of loons and the mating *cronks* of the deadly kroc'an echoed up from the swamplands below, accompanied by the sweet smell of moss and the heavy odor of decay.

Cassa Dar breathed it all in, drawing strength from her living lands as she readied herself for the spell to come.

A dark shape loomed in the distance—the Southern Fang.

She frowned at the mountain. It was the source of her land's elemental power, but its magick had also snatched the man she loved into danger. Her gaze flicked northward. Every fiber of her body rang with tension.

"Jaston . . ." She sent her heart out toward him, tying a bit of her magick to her love. She held that moment, maintaining the connection for as long as possible.

Satisfied, she swung to the small swamp child standing behind her. He clutched a bulging burlap sack in his arms, hugging it to his chest. The sack was soaking wet, bulging, dribbling swamp water on the stones of the tower.

"Dump the bag here," she directed the lad.

Biting his lip with concentration, the boy undid the rope tie and dumped the contents of his sack. Slops of wet swampweed splashed to the stones. The odor of silty vegetation cloyed up. Small crabs skittered from the pile.

Cassa Dar ignored the tiny scuttling creatures. With the certainty of her elemental magick, she plunged her arm up to the elbow into the sodden mound; her fingers closed around her true quarry.

From the pile, she dragged out the baby king adder. The snake, though just hatched, was as long as the swamp child was tall. Its length, banded in reds and blacks, writhed and curled around her forearm. Its jaws stretched wide, unfolding fangs dripping with oily poison. It hissed sibilantly at her. At this age, its venom was at its most potent, a necessary survival trait in the wilds of the deadly swamp.

"Quiet, little one," she whispered. "There will be time for that later."

With her other hand, she grabbed the adder's tail and unwrapped its length, then drew its body taut, measuring it against the boy's height.

The lad reached for it. "Pretty."

She pulled it from his fingers. "No, child, it's not for you."

Shifting back to the swampweed mound, she planted the snake's tail into the pile and stretched its muscular length straight up. It continued to hiss and bare its venomous fangs.

"Hush, don't waste what you'll need later."

Cassa Dar reached out with the magick stored in her own body. After sending the warning crow to A'loa Glen, she had spent the day steeling herself for this single spell. Taking a deep breath, she emptied her power into the weed and moss, the most basic plants of her magick-drenched lands. Linked, she cast a spell more complex than her usual.

Weeds came alive, crawling up the trapped snake's body like vines up a trellis. Mosses followed, winding and filling in spaces. Cassa Dar concentrated on the form held in her mind, joining her poisonous magick to the venom of the adder. Once the climbing swampweed and mosses grew over the snake's entire length, she freed her hands.

The figure trembled on the stone, roughly approximate to the boy standing nearby. The lad stared at her creation, eyes wide. He had just watched a mirror of his own birth, except for one critical difference: the boy was *only* weed.

Cassa Dar maintained contact with the poisonous asp at the heart of her new golem. She knit and wound one to the other until the two became one.

The spell was not without cost to her. Her legs trembled, and her heart pounded in her ears. Cold sweat covered her from head to toe. She finished her spell with a trembling wave of her hand. Rough lines flowed smooth, and a glamor swept over all.

Upon the stones stood a girl with flowing black hair and pale limbs. Unlike Cassa's boys, she was impossibly slender and lithe, similar to the snake that lurked in her core.

"Pretty," the swamp boy repeated, reaching again.

Cassa Dar knocked away his hand. One final spell was needed. She kept her concentration on the girl. "Wake," she whispered.

Like a butterfly opening its wings for the first time, the child's eyelids fluttered open. Dark eyes stared back from a face as perfect as an ivory doll's. "Mama?" she whispered in a daze.

"Yes, sweetheart. It's time to wake up."

The child stared around her. "Is it time to go?"

Cassa Dar smiled. Her desire had been wed into the creation. "Yes, you mustn't be late."

Cassa Dar felt for the connections between her and the girl. They were as clear as crystal—they had better be when the two were this close. "Go now," she said, leaning back.

The girl stared toward the setting sun, then shifted slightly northward. "You know the way."

The child nodded and strode toward the stone parapets. Her first steps were faltering but grew quickly stronger. She climbed atop the parapets without any fear of the fall.

But then again, she had no need for fear.

From behind her shoulders, wings of weed, glamor, and magick unfolded, spreading wide into the sunlight.

"Go, my sweet," Cassa Dar urged.

The child leaped from the tower. Like her first wobbly steps, her first flight was tumbled and awkward. But in a few beats, she was off and sailing.

Cassa Dar crossed to the tower's edge, watching, leaning on the warm stones. She saw both through her own eyes and her creation. With the bit of poison coiled in her heart, the child carried a bit of the swamp's potency—and as such, a piece of Cassa Dar.

"I pray it is enough," she whispered. She closed her eyes and willed herself to enter the child fully, to touch the venomous energy at the golem's core. Linked still to the flow of elemental power from the Southern Fang, Cassa Dar manipulated the magick and opened a gate. Through the eyes of the flying swamp child, a black hole appeared in the expanse of swamp mist.

She dove her child down toward that magickal portal. The girl swept through the gate and out the far side.

A moment of disorientation coursed through her. Cassa Dar tumbled to the stones of the tower as the swamp child cartwheeled, plummeting downward.

"No!" she gasped, struggling for control. Her connection to her creation was now much fainter. The great distance between them made the child no more than a flickering beacon across a vast, dark lake. It took all her concentration to maintain the contact.

The boy on the tower stepped near her, knowing her need as always. She reached toward him. His hand touched hers. She sucked the magick from his being and ignored the tumble of damp weed and moss that fell at her feet. It was all that was left of the boy, but his bit of power helped focus her.

Far away, the fluttering girl fought her wings open and caught the storm winds ripping up the mountain slopes. She sailed high, spreading Cassa Dar's vision wide. It was much darker here. To the west, a monstrous thunderstorm loomed, with black clouds stacked all the way up the sky. Lightning lanced sharply, while thunder boomed and echoed off the granite cliffs.

Cassa Dar willed the child lower, away from the worst of the storm's winds. Below, a stream ran through a forest of black pine and mountain alders. She knew that stream—she had watched Jaston fight an og're by that streambed.

Back in the swamps, she pressed her forehead to the stones. "I did it," she moaned. She had opened a path back to where her last child had fallen. She sat straighter. This time she could maintain contact with her new creation, a child with a bit of the swamp's poisonous magick at its heart. It was a fragile connection, but so far it held.

She commanded the child to wing toward the slopes of the Northern Fang, into the heart of the storm. She would find Jaston and offer what aid she could. Bonded by love, she sensed the path she must take.

As the child flew, Cassa Dar felt something new, deep in the heart of her creation, another bond. The venomous adder stirred, responding in kind. Trained as an assassin in the art of poison and tied to the miasma of the swamp, Cassa was attuned to all forms of venom.

She opened her senses wider. As she did, ice seeped into her veins, chilling her bones. Not even the heat of the swamp could warm her.

Cassa Dar clenched two fists. Sensitive to the faintest wisps of poison, she knew what she felt. One thought formed in her mind.

Spiders.

TOL'CHUK MARCHED AT THE HEAD OF A COLUMN OF OG'RES. THE STEEP TRAIL climbed in a series of switchbacks up the southern face of the Northern Fang. So far the threatening storm still held off, thundering and booming in the distance. Though the sun had just set, it was already as dark as midnight. Torches lit their way, held by one member of each hearth of the Toktala clan.

Clambering atop a boulder, Tol'chuk watched the line of flames below, spread along the trail. Beyond, the western sky flashed with crackles of lightning.

Jerrick stepped beside his perch. His face was as white as his hair, his eyes lost in grief, but as he turned to the warring skies, he drew strength from the approaching storm.

Magnam climbed up next, holding the torch high. "How much farther to this cursed place?" he grumbled.

Tol'chuk waved vaguely upward. "The entrance be near. Another half league."

Magnam moved past, shaking his head, while Jaston neared with Mogweed. The shape-shifter whined even as he passed. "We should be heading *down*, not up. Or better yet, just stay in those caves and post guards. If there are dangers out here—from that spider wit'ch or enemy og'res—what are we doing so exposed? And another thing . . ."

Jaston just nodded. His expression had glazed over.

Tol'chuk climbed off his rock, joining Hun'shwa as the clan leader lumbered up. The warrior eyed the two men ahead of him.

"Tu'tura," Hun'shwa said with a sneer, nodding to Mogweed, using the og're word for the si'luran shape-shifter. He kept his words in his own tongue. "Those baby stealers are not to be trusted."

Tol'chuk scowled, speaking in og're. "Mogweed might make your ears bleed with his chatter, but he has no intent on our babies. This I swear."

Hun'shwa curled a lip, exposing one fang. "He still smells of treachery."

Tol'chuk did not bother trying to argue. To him, the entire highlands reeked of treachery. The Ku'ukla clan, the spider demoness, the Oathbreaker himself—who knew what other dangers would be faced ahead? He indicated the trail behind him. "Are your hunters ready?"

"They will be."

Tol'chuk nodded. It was forbidden to bring weapons into the Dragon's Skull. Still, they dared not go into the teeth of this storm unprepared. Other plans had been made.

A flicker of light flashed from high up the trail.

"The trackers," Hun'shwa acknowledged. As the clan had marched out at sunset, a pair of trackers had been sent ahead. The og're leader stared at the flickering code. "They've reached the entrance. The way is clear."

Tol'chuk frowned. "And the other clans?"

Hun'shwa remained silent until the flickering died away. "Others already gather. The Sidwo, the W'nod, the Bantu, the Pukta."

"And the Ku'ukla?"

Hun'shwa shook his head. "No sign."

Tol'chuk did not like this. If anything, the Ku'ukla should have arrived first. While there were six different approaches up the Northern Fang to the Skull, one for each clan, the Ku'ukla path was the shortest. Their home caves were within the shadow of the Dragon's Skull.

"What are they planning?" Tol'chuk mumbled.

Hun'shwa shrugged. "We'd best join the gathering. The storm will not hold off forever."

As if agreeing with the og're, a crack of lightning forked overhead, illuminating sky and mountain alike. For a fraction of a breath, the Dragon's Skull was visible overhead. A massive slab of granite jutted like a snout from the southern face of the mountain. Under it, there gaped a wide opening, a tunnel. Framing either side stood two stone pillars, carved into giant fangs, marking the entrance to the Skull.

For untold centuries, the cavern beyond the entrance had been a gathering site for all the clans, a place of neutrality where conflicts could be resolved. It was said that the Skull had once been the true home of all the og're people, their original communal cave. Now it remained a sacred place. None dared defile it with bloodshed.

As the lightning died away, the image persisted in Tol'chuk's eye. Thunder boomed, and a hard, cold rain began to fall, as if the dragon above were roaring and weeping. With a certainty of bone and rock, Tol'chuk knew that blood would flow from the Skull this night.

Hun'shwa dropped back. "I will ready the hunters."

Tol'chuk let him go. He increased his own gait, passing his companions to retake the lead. If there was danger ahead, let him be the first to face it.

As he climbed, he was unable to escape Magnam. The d'warf marched at his shoulder. "I've been thinking," Magnam said as he pulled up his cloak's hood against the rain.

"What about?"

"Once this is over, I'm going to buy myself a little place in the flatlands. Somewhere *dry*, somewhere where the most steps I have to climb is to my porch."

"What about mountains and mining? I thought that be what you d'warves loved?"

Magnam made a rude noise. "Curse that! I'm done with holes and caves. From now on, I want open plains, sprouting fields, and vistas as wide as the world."

Tol'chuk shook his head. "You be a strange d'warf."

"And you're not so typical an og're yourself."

Tol'chuk shrugged. More than anything, during the journey out in the lands of Alasea and back, he had learned one lesson: no one could be judged by their faces alone. There were layers to everyone and everything.

Again light flickered from between the entrance fangs to the Skull. Tol'chuk was not familiar with the hunters' code, but from the frantic way the message was being sent, the urgency was clear.

"What's up with the firefly?" Magnam asked.

Tol'chuk turned to see Hun'shwa rush through the others behind him. Mogweed was knocked on his backside. Jaston and Jerrick flattened against the cliff.

"The Ku'ukla are coming up their western trail, no females or young among them."

Magnam still stood beside Tol'chuk. "What is he saying?" the d'warf asked.

Tol'chuk translated, but Hun'shwa still watched the flickering lights. "There's movement spotted on the eastern path." A long pause. "More Ku'ukla are coming that way."

Atop the slope, other flickers began to shine, blinking from spy tunnels higher up the mountain.

A grumble built up inside Hun'shwa. "Other clans are reporting. The Ku'ukla coming up all the trails!" He continued to stare. "They've stopped a quarter way up!"

Tol'chuk translated for his friends, who gathered around.

"They're surrounding us," Jaston said. "Pinning us down."

A commotion erupted behind their own group, the frantic bleating of females and sharper cries of the young.

"What's going on?" Mogweed squeaked.

"The Ku'ukla be on the lower switchbacks to our own trail," Tol'chuk said, searching around. There was no way down but the clan trails. The rest of the mountain was cliffs and sheer drops.

"Are they going to attack?" Mogweed asked.

"So far they hold their position," Hun'shwa answered, speaking for the first time in the common tongue. His eyes narrowed. "What be they planning? Even without weapons, the other clans could hold the Skull against the Ku'ukla."

"They don't mean to take the Skull," Tol'chuk said. "They mean to keep anyone from leaving."

"Why?"

The answer came from above.

A sharp scream split through the rumbling thunder, followed by a chorus of wails from the score of sentry holes. Tol'chuk froze, as did Hun'shwa. It was difficult to make an og're cry out in pain.

"A trap," Jaston yelled. "We have to retreat."

"We cannot," Hun'shwa grumbled. "We've no weapons against those who hold the lower path. We'd be slaughtered."

"Then what are we to do?" Mogweed asked. The shape-shifter's flesh rippled slightly in his growing panic. His eyes darted around, looking for some way to flee.

Tol'chuk pointed to the upper switchbacks. "Whatever attacks the Skull must be destroyed. We must protect the Spirit Gate."

Mogweed's gaze flicked to him and narrowed. After a moment, the shape-shifter's flesh settled, hardening. He gave a curt nod.

"You wait with the females and the young," Tol'chuk said, pushing forward with Hun'shwa, ignoring the protests from Magnam and Jerrick as he passed. "This is a matter for og're warriors."

"My hunters are ready," Hun'shwa said.

"Then let's flush out our prey."

Half turning, Hun'shwa barked an order, and the cadre of selected warriors bustled forward at their leader's command. Slung around their necks were goat bladders filled with oil. They loped ahead, up the last of the trail, followed by Hun'shwa and Tol'chuk. A second group of hunters trailed them, leaving behind a phalanx of older warriors to guard the remaining clan members.

Ahead the mountain had gone dark. The flashes of signals had died away. A steady rain pummeled the slopes.

"Protect the torches!" Hun'shwa called as he ran. "We must not lose the fire!"

The last switchback appeared, and the entrance to the Dragon's Skull lay ahead. The lead warriors swarmed up toward the granite fangs that flanked the entrance.

"Where are our trackers?" Hun'shwa grumbled, squinting ahead, searching for the og'res he had sent up earlier.

The mountain remained dark. But now it had grown ominously silent. Only thunder rumbled, mournful.

The threshold to the Skull was a slab of granite wide enough to hold all the warriors. The lead group gathered just outside the carved fangs.

There was no sign of their sentries.

Hun'shwa bulled his way forward and stared down the dark throat of the tunnel. He gestured, and a torch was passed to him. He thrust it forward, but the sizzling flame was weak, shining barely past the entrance. He reached to a fellow beside him and grabbed his pair of goat bladders, strung together by a leather cord.

With his torch, he lit one bladder, then the other. Once they were smoldering and red, he winged the pair down the length of the tunnel. They struck the stone floor and burst, spraying the walls with flame. The way ahead was lit.

A few lengths down the tunnel, a body lay sprawled, facedown, feet toward them. Hun'shwa went to investigate, then motioned the others forward.

Tol'chuk reached his side first. The corpse was that of an og're, but its skin lay blackened and bloated as if it had been dead for days.

"One of the trackers," Hun'shwa said. He stared down the flaming passage. A few steps away lay a pair of smaller bodies. From their sizes, the youngsters were probably only a few winters old. They lay in postures of agony, blackened and bloated also. Farther down, other bodies could be seen as bulky shadows. "Ta'lank must have come inside when the screaming started. He only made it a few steps."

One of the hunters near the entrance made a warning noise, and held his torch high, toward the roof. Across the rocky ceiling, silky white drapes hung, blowing with the wet storm gusts.

Tol'chuk reached and pulled down a section. It clung to his claws, sticky and oily. With distaste, he wiped it away. "Spiderwebs," he said without surprise.

"The wit'ch you told us about?" Hun'shwa asked.

"She's here." Tol'chuk stared up at an empty sac of denser webbing that hung limp and flaccid. He imagined whatever had hatched from it had attacked the sentry and the others. Tol'chuk glanced back out the tunnel. "The Ku'ukla must know about Vira'ni. They waited until our clan was on the trail, then closed off any means of escape, driving us up into the deadly web she spun here to catch us."

"What do we do?"

"What we set out to do." Tol'chuk faced back down the tunnel; he knew it wound in a spiral up to the central cavern, with occasional smaller side tunnels leading off to spy holes, sentry posts, and storage spaces. He pointed ahead. "We raze the entire Skull."

"A cleansing fire," Hun'shwa said sternly.

Tol'chuk nodded. He remembered his last encounter with Vira'ni. He still bore the pitted scars from her spiders' bites. In the past, it had taken two fires—ordinary flame and coldfire—to destroy the spider demon's creations. This night it would be no different.

He stared at the oily fires lighting the passage, then squinted at the ruined bodies of the og're children. This night there would be two fires once again: ordinary flame and the *fer'engata*, the *fire of the heart*, the vengeful blood lust of a united og're people.

Tol'chuk strode forward, his eyes flashing with the beginning of his own fury. He saw one of the bloated bodies squirm with something roiling inside. In the past, he had witnessed the poisoned bodies of Vira'ni's prey birthing new horrors; he barked an order to those that followed. "Burn the bodies. Flame everything!"

Hun'shwa quickly joined him. Behind them, the tunnel flared brighter; the ripe smell of charred flesh singed down the tunnel. Hun'shwa swung another corded set of goat bladders, splashing flame farther down the tunnel.

More bodies appeared. One took the flame of the burst bladders, igniting with unnatural speed. A flurry of tiny creatures exploded outward. All aflame, they scurried and fluttered from the burning body like a swarm of fireflies. Tol'chuk crunched through them, followed by the warriors of the Toktala clan.

"So where are the creatures that attacked these others?" Hun'shwa asked.

Tol'chuk had an idea. He wagered every entrance, spy hole, and sentry post of the Skull had been primed with the malignant web sacs of Vira'ni. Once unleashed, the creatures fled inward, killing all in their path.

"Where are they?" Hun'shwa repeated, swatting as a burning scorpion landed on his arm. "Where is this Vira'ni?"

"Where all spiders lurk," Tol'chuk answered, pointing ahead, toward the cavern named the Dragon's Skull. "At the heart of her deadly web."

JASTON HUNKERED UNDER A LIP OF ROCK WITH HIS COMPANIONS. IT OFFERED scant protection against the storm. Rain lashed, cold, stinging like a whip.

The winds had grown, threatening to tear them from the trail. The og'res seemed little bothered by the storm. They crouched on the path like so many tumbled boulders, water sluicing over their craggy features.

The remaining members of the clan, the females and the youngsters, kept apart from the newcomers. Near at hand, a single female suckled a babe and stared round-eyed at them, accusation in her gaze. Whatever curse had befallen the clan had started with the return of Tol'chuk and the arrival of his companions.

Jaston turned from the stare. Down the path, a cadre of hunter-warriors stood guard between their wards and the Ku'ukla clan below. But he also noted the trio of huge og'res closer at hand, keeping near Jaston and the others in case they should prove a danger.

"Whatever Tol'chuk is doing," Magnam said, "he's not exactly furtive." The d'warf stood a step out of the shelter.

Jaston joined him. The entrance to the Dragon's Skull glowed red with flames, as if it were a fire-breathing demon. Winding up from there, each opening in the mountain shone with firelight. Jaston could make out the slight spiral to the pattern, like the winding body of a wyrm—a wyrm with a fire in its belly.

"I hope they have enough oil and fire to reach the chamber," Jaston said.

Magnam squinted through the downpour. "A fire doesn't sound half bad right now." The d'warf continued to stare up, the frustration clear on his face.

Jaston took up sentry with him. "There's little help we can offer Tol'chuk and the others."

"Sometimes, in battle, a *little* help is the difference between victory and defeat."

Jaston glanced over at the d'warf. "I thought you were just a cook?"

"Fine," he growled, "then sometimes a *little* spice is the difference between a great meal and a ruined one."

Jaston sighed. "I don't like being left behind either."

"What do we do if Tol'chuk fails?" Mogweed asked as he huddled deep in the shelter. "Did anyone think of that?"

"Of course," said Magnam, not turning around.

"What?" Mogweed asked, his eyes hopeful of a plan.

Magnam shrugged. "We die."

Mogweed frowned, sinking back.

The elv'in captain placed a hand on the shape-shifter's shoulder. "Fear not. If need be, you can transform into a winged creature and fly from here."

Mogweed stared out into the storm, lancing and forking with spears of lightning, winds howling. From his pale face, it was clear that the prospect of flying into the dark storm did not appeal to the shape-shifter. "Just because I can grow wings, doesn't mean I have a natural ability to fly," he said dully. "It would take time to gain the skill to wing such a fierce storm safely."

"Well, something is managing it," Magnam said. He pointed an arm toward the warring skies.

Jaston glanced to where he pointed, but all he saw was black emptiness, as if the world had vanished beyond the reach of their sizzling torches. Then a crack of lightning flashed, returning the world for a blinding moment. In the skies overhead, a winged creature rode the gusts like a storm-tossed skiff—then darkness swallowed it away.

"What was that?" Jerrick asked. "It's like no bird I've ever seen."

Jaston squinted, waiting for the next bolt of lightning. The elv'in captain was an elemental of the air. If Jerrick couldn't identify the creature . . .

The next crack was farther away, offering just a flicker of light. The shape was gone, vanished from the skies.

"Maybe it's some demon," Mogweed whispered.

Jaston unsheathed his sword. Others slid weapons free, too, except for Jerrick, who lifted a hand crackling with the energy of the storm itself. Og'res might not be allowed to bring weapons to the meeting, but there was no such restriction on man, si'luran, d'warf, or elv'in.

A growl arose from one of the trio of og'res nearby. The baring of weapons and play of magick had drawn their attention.

Lightning again crackled across the night, flaring brighter than the sun. The skies remained empty. Whatever had been spotted earlier had clearly fled.

Then from below the cliff's edge that bordered the trail, a form shot up only a few arm's lengths away. The party tumbled back, retreating under the narrow lip of their temporary shelter. Og'res barked in warning, and grumbled shouts erupted.

The creature alighted on the rain-slick trail. It was a small girl, svelte and thin-limbed. Her wings flapped once, then tucked away behind her. "I have this many fingers," she said, holding up a hand and wiggling her digits.

This provoked a response from an og're warrior. He loped toward the child, fist raised, clearly meaning to smash it to pulp.

Jaston bolted between them. *"No!"* he shouted. Though the word probably meant nothing, the tone and the raised sword spoke clearly.

The og're grumbled, eyes flashing with menace. But he held off for the moment.

Jaston turned to the newcomer. "Cassa?"

The girl stared up at him, crinkling her nose in childish confusion. Then her eyes quickened with intelligence. "Jaston! I found you!"

"Cassa . . . how . . . ?"

"I don't have time for explanations. The ground you stand on reeks of poisons. You must get away, now!"

"I cannot. We're trapped." He quickly related their situation.

As he finished, the child turned to where the spiraling and snaking path of fire led far up the mountain. "It comes from there!" She pointed. "Venom trickles down this peak like a horde of spiders."

Jaston took the child by the wrist.

"Ow!" the girl complained.

"I'm sorry, lass." He spoke rapidly. "Cassa, did you say spiders?"

"That is the poison I scent from that peak."

"Vira'ni," Mogweed cried.

"So the spider wit'ch has spun her web up there," the d'warf said dourly.

"What are we going to do?" Mogweed whined.

Jerrick answered from behind them all, his voice afire with vengeance. "We join Tol'chuk in burning the creature from her nest." Small bolts of energy crackled from his fingers as he pushed past Jaston and the swamp child. "The demoness will pay for Freda's death."

"We can't go up there!" Mogweed yelled. "It would be our deaths!"

Magnam hiked his ax to a shoulder. "I'm going." He stepped forward, heading after Jerrick. "At least we'll be out of the cursed rain and wind. If I'm going to die, I'd rather it be when I'm dry and warm."

Jaston turned to follow them.

"My love," the child said, warning.

"I must. The danger here threatens you as much as it does me."

After a moment, she nodded. "At least keep me with you. It may take poison to fight poison."

Jaston took the girl's hand and glanced back. "Mogweed?"

The shape-shifter looked back at the line of og'res, out to the storm, then up the mountain. He shook his head, then tromped after the others, a scowl on his face. "I hate spiders."

10

THE HEAT HAD GROWN NEAR TO BLISTERING. THE FLAMES BEHIND TOL'CHUK cast his shadow ahead. Flanking him, a pair of og'res tossed a smoldering set of oil-filled bladders down the tunnel's throat; flames burst and the air reeked.

Hun'shwa pushed to his side. "We're almost out of oil."

"How much farther to the Skull?" Tol'chuk asked.

The clan leader squinted. He was covered in soot. Several deep burns marked his skin, blistered and red. "No more than a quarter league."

"Then we protect what we have." Tol'chuk waved back the pair of hunters. "The true fight lies ahead of us."

Hun'shwa nodded.

Tol'chuk marched on, skirting the new flames. Since the last turn in the passage, no more bodies littered the floor. Whatever monsters had been birthed by the spider queen's egg sacs had killed those in the lower levels. Then the victims' screams must have chased any other og'res into the main chamber. The natural response of his people when threatened was to group together. Few menaces could challenge a cornered pack of og'res.

But what had happened to the others? Had they all succumbed like those here, blackened by poison? No one spoke as they continued onward. Dread weighed heavily in everyone's heart.

Hun'shwa shoved the end of a dead torch into the fresh flames and brought it to life. With the sole brand as a light source, they continued down the dark passage. So far they had lost only one of their twenty-odd army. The unfortunate fellow had approached too close to one of the bodies. It had burst before the flame could damage the flock of winged crablike creatures inside. By the time aid reached the hunter, half his face had been consumed, and the beasts were already burrowing into his chest. They were forced to burn him while he still lived. The flames had quickly muffled his screams.

Since then they had proceeded with additional caution.

Tol'chuk refused to let anyone else lead after that. If there were new traps ahead, he wanted to be the first to face them. He walked a step in front of Hun'shwa. The brand the leader held sputtered out, leading to a mumbled curse.

As darkness settled around them, Tol'chuk spotted a weak glow ahead. He hissed for silence. They proceeded more slowly, a short distance toward where a reddish light marked the end of the tunnel, a baleful ruby hole.

Tol'chuk stopped.

"The Dragon's Eye," Hun'shwa mouthed in a hushed whisper. The chamber of the Skull lay beyond the Eye's threshold.

Tol'chuk took a deep breath to steel himself. Hun'shwa placed a hand on his shoulder and gave a short squeeze. In this small gesture, Tol'chuk felt the backing of the entire Toktala clan.

Tol'chuk motioned for the others to hang back, then continued ahead. After a few steps, he found Hun'shwa following. He glanced to his uninvited companion. Hun'shwa ignored his narrowed eyes and nudged him ahead. The larger og're still held the burned-out torch in one hand like a club.

Frowning, Tol'chuk crept forward. They separated to either wall and slid up toward the Eye.

As Tol'chuk approached to within a few steps, a flurry of tiny scraping sounds echoed out to him, like a thousand flint blades rubbing against rock. The sound raised the tiniest hairs of his body.

With a final tightening of his resolve, Tol'chuk moved to the Eye and peered through the threshold. As prepared as he was for any horror, the sight before him stunned him to a stop.

Lit from below, the Dragon's Skull was a cavernous chamber. The Eye opened halfway up one wall. A domed ceiling lay above, cracked in places, allowing rainwater to sluice down in trickling streams, like a hundred waterfalls. Thunder rumbled beyond the mountain, threatening, heavy.

Below the Eye, the bowled floor lay as far down as the roof was high. From the opening of the tunnel, the walls sloped in a series of wide steps or tiers. In a clan-wide gathering, the steps would act as galleries to seat the assembled members.

To his despair, Tol'chuk saw the seats were *not* empty. Thousands of og'res lay slumped upon the tiers, some singly, some in family groups, some in tumbled piles. And strung like Winterfest garland, streams of ropy webbing lay over the still bodies.

Tol'chuk felt his legs weaken, his vision dim. *All the clans . . . his entire people . . .*

"They live," Hun'shwa whispered urgently.

It took Tol'chuk a moment to comprehend. Near at hand, the chest of the closest og're slowly rose and fell while his head lolled, a rope of drool hanging from slack lips.

Tol'chuk peered wider, noticing small movements among the others here. Not dead, he realized with relief, but poisoned or magicked into some unnatural slumber. He straightened near the entrance. As long as they still breathed, there was hope for his people yet.

As he stared, a voice oily and slick rang out from the lowest tier of the stepped cavern. "Tol'chuk! Be welcome!"

Tol'chuk searched, but he knew who called. "Vira'ni . . ."

Down below, the floor was a steamy glowing cauldron. A wide crack split the floor of the chamber, through which molten rock churned and spat tongues of flame. The glow lit the entire cavern.

The Dragon's Throat.

The rainwater streaming from the ceiling ran down the tiers and drizzled into the gullet of the Dragon, raising a continual stream of mist and sweltering steam. Even here at the entrance, the heat challenged that of the flaming passage behind him.

"Come. Don't be shy, my gentle giant."

"Stay hidden," Hun'shwa hissed. Before Tol'chuk could object, Hun'shwa dashed through the Eye and down a few of the tiers. He rose onto his legs, threatening with his makeshift club. "Show yourself, demon!"

A long silence, then cold laughter met his display.

Tol'chuk stepped out. "Get back, Hun'shwa!"

"So it seems you've brought guests. As a host, I'd be remiss not to offer the same courtesy." Tol'chuk spotted movement below: a darker shadow moving through the steam. "Children, don't be bashful. Come and play!"

Again Tol'chuk heard the sounds of knives dragging across rock, skittering and sharp—the same noise had stopped as he had reached the Eye. He searched for the source, but it did not come from the floor below.

He and Hun'shwa craned upward.

What had appeared to be outcroppings of rock dotting the domed roof began to move, scurrying on jointed legs with sharp, armored tips scrabbling and scraping. Each was the size of a large dog. As he stared, Tol'chuk saw others squeeze though the cracks, dragging themselves inside from the mountain's slopes.

"Demonspawn," Hun'shwa growled.

One crawled directly overhead. It appeared a monstrous cross between a crab and a scorpion. But this one had a mouth. Hanging by its rear legs, it clattered at him with its front pincers while baring fangs. Green oil dribbled from its open maw.

Tol'chuk backed from under it. Hun'shwa also retreated.

"Come, my children!" Vira'ni beckoned from below.

Suddenly, from behind them, an og're began to bellow a short way down the tunnel. Tol'chuk knew there were more of these creatures crawling into the passage from the open sentry posts and spy holes, attacking the other hunters from the flanks and rear, driving them forward like the previous attack.

Any retreat was cut off.

Tol'chuk cursed himself for not thinking like a spider. He had never imagined anything could cling to the smooth slopes of the Fang. Now the ceiling crawled with demonspawn, while below he spotted a dark shadow in the steamy mists. This time it did not hide.

"Come, Tol'chuk. Bring the Heart to me and I'll let your slumbering people live. One bauble for so many lives."

A wet gust swept down from the openings above, shivering his hot skin. Thunder rumbled anew as the heart of the storm struck. The wind parted the steam below.

Perched at the edge of the Dragon's Throat was a creature of nightmare: half woman, half spider. The demoness crouched atop eight jointed appendages, her eyes staring directly at Tol'chuk.

Hun'shwa fell back. One of the crab creatures dropped from the ceiling. Responding with the instinct of a true hunter, the og're swung his club and batted the beast backhanded. It flew, mewling, over the tiers and crashed to the stone.

A scream arose from Vira'ni. "No!" Hissing with venom, the demoness spun atop her chitinous legs and grabbed something bundled behind her. Tol'chuk spotted an array of similarly trussed objects.

She swung around, bearing her bundle in one of her pincer-tipped legs. It took a breath for Tol'chuk to recognize the object, wrapped thickly with webbing. Then he spotted an arm waving from the cocoon: a child, an og're child that struggled against its binding.

Vira'ni held it over the molten pit of the Dragon's Throat. "One of your children for one of mine!"

"No!" Tol'chuk cried.

Her eyes met his for a heartbeat—then she dropped the babe. Flailing its arm, the child fell into the crack. As the form struck the molten rock, flames flared up, lipping out of the throat. Then the child was gone.

There had been no cry—only the silent one in Tol'chuk's heart.

Vira'ni whipped around and grabbed two more web-bound children. She held them over the churning pit of molten rock. "I'll only ask one more time, Tol'chuk. Come to me! Bring the Heart!"

"Don't," Hun'shwa warned him. He had retreated to the threshold of the Eye. Behind him, the cries of the hunters deeper down the passage had died down to sporadic howls.

"Go help the others," Tol'chuk ordered his clan leader. "Save as many as you can and leave this place."

"I will not!"

Tol'chuk ripped open his thigh pouch and yanked free the Heart. It burst to a radiant brilliance. "Do as I command!" he shouted.

Hun'shwa staggered backward at his bellow. He hesitated another moment, then seemed to spot the resolve in Tol'chuk's posture. With a final grunt, he fled into the darkness.

Tol'chuk turned back to Vira'ni. He stared at the tumble of bodies around, then at the two dangling children.

"I will not let the innocent die in my name," he mumbled, and met the gaze of the spider queen. He knew in that moment that some battles could never be won. He would not see his entire people sacrificed . . . not even to save the Spirit Gate. It was a burden he was born to bear, the curse of his lineage. Like his forefather, he would forsake his promise. He would give up the Heart to this evil in order to save his tribe.

"Come to me!" she commanded again. So with demonspawn skittering overhead, he climbed toward the steamy floor and the cursed fate that awaited him.

MOGWEED HUNG BACK FROM THE OTHERS . . . BUT NOT TOO FAR BACK. THE passages were hot with smoldering bodies and flaming bits of debris. Most of the bodies appeared to be cratered ruins, as if something had burst out of their chests and bellies.

At first, the group had proceeded quickly. In the fiery wake of the og're hunters, there had been little to slow them. Only a few palm-sized scorpions, limping on broken legs or half burned, scrabbled over the stone.

Then the screams had started, echoing down to them. They proceeded more cautiously. Mogweed had wanted to turn back, but the others overruled him.

Fools, he thought. *And I'm doubly the fool to follow them.* Besides his fear of retreating alone, Mogweed had another concern that kept him with the others: Tol'chuk. The og're was the key to freeing him from the curse of this conjoined body. If the craggy giant was in danger, Mogweed's only hope was to aid in his rescue.

Just ahead of Mogweed, Jerrick moved deftly. The captain, though old, still bore the elv'in gift for speed. Mogweed had to half trot to keep up, but he kept close to the walls, darting past side tunnels, skirting any openings. In the front, Magnam and Jaston led. The strange winged child skipped at the swamper's side, oblivious to the danger.

"Not much farther," Magnam whispered, beginning to slow.

The screams had died down to howls and an occasional bellow of rage. "What's attacking them?" Jaston asked.

The answer crawled out of a hole in the nearby wall. The creature was all armor, spear-tipped tail, and snapping pincers. It skittered out of its hiding place and, before anyone could move, it climbed up the wall on its articulated, spiny legs, going for the advantage of height.

"No you don't, you crawling scab!" Magnam swung out with his ax, moving with speed that belied his bulky shape. He swatted the creature from its perch.

The monster landed on its back, quickly springing up and lashing out with its pincers. The d'warf spun with his ax and cleaved the closest claw. With a mewling howl, it skittered backward.

"Don't like that, do you?" Magnam growled. He struck out with his ax again, nicking its raised tail. The beast spun on him, striking with lightning speed. Fanged jaws stretched wide as it sought flesh to bite.

"Careful," the swamp child warned in Cassa Dar's voice. "It's pure poison."

"Poison it may be, but I'm the cure." Magnam kicked the creature up against the nearest wall, holding it in place with his boot. Its legs scrabbled at him, but he slammed his ax into its midsection with a crack of armor shell. Green ooze flowed from the wound, steaming over Magnam's boot, etching the leather. "I just polished those!" he shouted, and brought the ax down again and again. Soon all that was left was a mash of scale and twitching limbs. Magnam scowled and backed away. He studied his fouled ax head, searching vainly for something to wipe it on, then gave up. The sounds of a similar battle continued farther up the passage. Magnam waved them on. "Let's go!"

Mogweed peeled himself off the wall and followed, eyeing each shadow now with suspicion.

Jaston clapped the d'warf on the shoulder. "That was some damn fancy ax work. And you say you're just a camp cook."

Magnam shrugged. "What cook doesn't know how to prepare crab?"

Jerrick hissed from a short distance ahead. The elv'in captain had sped forward and now crouched at a bend. "Trouble," he said with his usual elv'in stoicism, but energy crackled around the hand he had raised toward them.

They joined him. Beyond the turn, the passage ahead was a battlefield, almost blocked with og're bodies. Farther up the tunnel, a handful of og'res used torches as flaming brands or clubs to hold off more of the crablike creatures. The entire passage crawled with them.

"We can't go that way!" Mogweed whined.

"We can't go back," Jaston said.

The group glanced behind them. Another dozen monsters scrabbled out from neighboring passages or through sentry holes in the wall. A pair fought over the remains of the creature killed by Magnam.

"They must've been drawn by the blood of their own," Magnam noted.

They were surrounded.

Jerrick stood up and moved to the far wall. He had a good view up and down both passages. He lifted his arms, one hand pointed each direction.

"What are you doing?" the swamper asked.

"Clearing the way," he said simply. "I suggest you stay low."

His eyes drifted closed. Energy danced around his fingers, crackling outward, shooting from fingertips in dazzles.

Mogweed ducked to the floor. The others crouched.

The child at Jaston's side pointed at the elv'in. "Sparkly!" Jaston pulled her arm down.

Around them, the air began to smell of lightning, and the power tingled Mogweed's skin. Somewhere beyond the walls, thunder boomed. Mogweed kept half his attention on the elv'in, half on the passages, where the creatures in the lower tunnel were drawn by Jerrick's display and skittered toward them.

"What are you waiting for?" Mogweed mumbled.

Jerrick heard him. "The heart of the storm." The el'vin craned his neck. His white hair plumed out sparking with fire. A nimbus of energy shimmered over his form.

Magnam drove back one of the crab demons with a swipe of his ax. "You're looking impressive, Cap—but these bugs are about to climb up our arses."

"It comes . . . ," Jerrick whispered. His skin grew translucent, but now several of the beasts from *up* the tunnel scuttled toward them. Mogweed gripped his dagger.

A single crab raced toward the elv'in, running up the wall. Mogweed bit his lip, frozen in indecision and fear, as the creature came racing like a moth to a flame. At the last instant, Mogweed leaped forward, dagger raised in defense.

"Down!" Jerrick screamed.

Mogweed was blown back as energy blasted outward, blinding him. He struck the wall and crashed to a heap. He blinked away the dazzle in time to see crackles of lightning flowing out from both arms of the elv'in. The creature that had threatened a heartbeat ago lay on the floor, a smoking cinder, legs curled tight.

Mogweed rolled to watch lightning chase down both corridors, crackling from the elv'in and diving in through the spy holes and sentry windows. This was no wild energy, but a living thing, snapping and forking to strike every one of the foul creatures.

Up the corridors, the og'res saw the destruction and dove to the floor. The deadly barrage swept over them and beyond, leaving them untouched.

Then like the flicker of lightning in a storm, the display vanished. The passage went black as pitch until Mogweed's eyes readjusted. The passage's flames seemed dim and feeble after the living lightning.

"You did it," Magnam said, rising to his feet.

Jerrick still stood in the corridor, but he suddenly slumped limbless to the floor. The swamp man barely caught him before the captain's head struck the floor.

"Captain Jerrick!" Jaston called.

"Drained . . . ," he whispered, his eyes fluttering closed. "Freda . . ."

Jaston held him. The captain's pale skin remained translucent, his breathing shallow.

Mogweed slid to his other side. "Is he going to be all right?"

The swamper frowned. "I don't know. I don't think he struck at the demons with just the heart of the storm. I think he used his own, too."

Mogweed believed him. He doubted even Meric could have displayed such force.

The elv'in captain took one more deep breath, exhaling one last time. "My love . . ."

For a moment, Mogweed thought he heard an answer, the same words whispered again from afar. But maybe it was just an echo. Then Jerrick lay still.

"He's gone," Jaston said.

Magnam joined them. He eyed down the passage, where five or six og'res were climbing to their feet with shock. "I don't see Tol'chuk."

Mogweed saw the d'warf was right. From the group down the passage, a single og're bulled forward—Hun'shwa, the og're leader. He worked through the piled dead toward them and glanced to the limp form of Jerrick. He curled a fist to his forehead, bowing his head in a moment of respect. "He died a warrior. He will be honored and remembered."

"Not if we don't live to tell the tale," Magnam said. "Where's Tol'chuk?"

Hun'shwa lowered his arm. "He went to face the spider wit'ch alone."

"What?" the d'warf gasped. "And you let him?"

If an og're could look chagrined, this one did. "He commanded it."

"And you obeyed?" Magnam rolled his eyes. "What happened?"

Hun'shwa quickly related the tale of Vira'ni and what lay at the tunnel's end.

"More of the creatures." Magnam sighed. He stared around the group, his brow furrowed. "An ax, a sword, a dagger, and an og're's fist against a spider queen and her horde. This is not a recipe for victory."

Mogweed stood, wrapping his arms around his chest. "Then what are we going to do?"

The d'warf focused those hard eyes on him. "There may be a way."

"How?" Jaston asked as he lowered the elv'in captain to the floor.

Magnam did not glance to the swamp man. He continued to stare at Mogweed. "It will depend on this one here."

Mogweed took a step back. "Me?"

TOL'CHUK STRAIGHTENED FROM HIS CROUCH, GLANCING BACK UP TO THE Dragon's Eye, the entrance to the huge cavern. Thunder rumbled away. A moment ago, lightning had burst out of the Eye and lapped into the chamber, like the forked tongue of a snake, then had vanished away.

Unable to fathom this display, he twisted around, clutching the Heart in a fist. His lungs burned, and the scent of brimstone and sulfur filled his senses.

Two steps down and across the pit, Vira'ni still stared toward the Eye, her face transfixed in a horrified expression. Her dark hair lay limp against her pale skin, soaked by the constant steamy mists. From the waist down, her form merged with that of the spider. Its ruby shell glistened and shone, pebbled with beads of condensing water.

Overhead, her demonspawn had frozen in place, becoming again just rocky bumps on the ceiling.

With the wit'ch distracted, Tol'chuk searched quickly for a weapon. All around him lay the sprawled members of the other clans; ropes and mounds of webbing shrouded their still-breathing forms. He saw no weapon among them. No one dared come to this sacred place with a club or bone ax.

He did not know what to do. All he knew was that two of the tribe's children were in danger, dangled over the pit by the wit'ch. He tightened his grip on the Heart. The chunk of heartstone was the key to the Spirit Gate; to give it up threatened the whole world. But right now, his world was nothing more than these two children.

Vira'ni moaned. "My babies!" she cried. "Someone slew my babies." Her limbs shook with her rage. Tossed about, the og're children cried out.

Tol'chuk hurried down the last steps and faced Vira'ni across the crack in the floor. Here the heat was near to unbearable, wafting up from the molten heart of the mountain. A constant hissing roar seemed to flow from the Throat along with the scalding steam.

He lifted the heartstone to draw her attention. In the misty chamber, the Heart shone with its own light. "I have what you want, Vira'ni! What your Master wants! Do not make more children suffer!" He pleaded with his eyes and posture.

Vira'ni narrowed eyes still smoldering with fury. For a long moment, she locked gazes with him.

Tol'chuk feared she would toss these children into the molten cauldron as she had the other. "Please ... I know you be a mother, too. Show mercy."

One eye twitched. "A mother ...," she mumbled.

"*All* mothers fear not only for their own children, but *all* children," Tol'chuk pressed.

Her brow furrowed with confusion, and she gave a nod at his words. She glanced to the og're young in her grip as if surprised to find them there. " Poor, scared things ..." She began to pull back the children.

Then from across the cavern, the familiar flinty scrape of claw on rock sounded. Both Tol'chuk and Vira'ni turned.

Out of the Eye, one of the demonspawn skittered into the chamber. It was badly singed, missing one pincer and two of its eight legs. A mewling escaped its throat. It tried to clamber down toward the demoness that had birthed it, but it mostly fell and rolled, a pathetic sight.

"My little one!" Vira'ni cried, anger rising in her voice. She tossed one of the og're children aside and beckoned with the free claw. "Who hurt you, my sweet?"

Tol'chuk silently cursed the untimely return.

As the loathsome child reached her side and scuttled under her swollen shell of a belly, raw fury flamed her next words. "We will make them pay! For each of my babies harmed, I'll take a score of yours!" She rattled the last child in her grip. "And I'll start with this one!"

A new noise sounded from the Eye, and a band of og'res burst into the room, brandishing torches. To Tol'chuk's surprise, he saw among them the stout figure of Magnam and the wiry form of the swamp man. And from their midst burst some winged creature. It sailed over the room, keeping a distance from the demon-strewn roof. Tol'chuk squinted and realized it was some strange child. What new demon was this?

But Vira'ni seemed equally confused, craning her neck. "It's a little girl."

Tol'chuk frowned. Had the others chased this new creature in here? Words in Og're reached Tol'chuk—from Hun'shwa. "Be ready!"

Tol'chuk glanced to him. Ready for what?

Vira'ni followed the flight of the demon child. Then suddenly her expression shifted to one of shock. Her gaze darted downward. "What's wrong, little—" Then a scream burst from her as her bulbous rear suddenly arched high, as if shoved from below.

What was happening?

Off balance, Vira'ni toppled headfirst into the chasm. Her limbs flew wide as she fought to maintain her balance. The articulated legs caught the rocky edge of the pit, keeping her from a plunge into the molten rock, holding her precariously in place. She screamed in fear, trying to scrabble backward, but something still kept her rear end pushed up, blocking her retreat.

Responding with pure instinct, Tol'chuk lunged forward. He dove around the Throat's edge. Ripping the young one free from her flailing pincers, he tossed the child to safety.

"Are you going to help me?" someone screamed from behind Vira'ni.

Tol'chuk ran back and spotted Mogweed under the spider's belly. He strained against her bulk, pushing up with both arms, while webbing flowed from holes along the backside of the spider, half covering the struggling shape-shifter.

Tol'chuk instantly understood the ruse. The injured demonspawn— had been a disguised Mogweed! The others had distracted Vira'ni long enough for the shape-shifter to get in place and attack.

"Don't just stand there!" Mogweed yelled, spitting webbing from his lips.

Tol'chuk turned and saw Vira'ni trying to sidle sideways off the pit. Tol'chuk shifted to block her. "You and your Master want the Heart!" he bellowed. "Then have it, wit'ch!"

He drew to his full height and swung the stone with all the strength of his arm and shoulder. He struck her in the side of the head and felt bone crack with the impact. Blood sprayed his hand.

Her wailing scream ended as if cut by a blade. Her struggling form jerked; then the strength went out of her limbs, and the wit'ch toppled into the Dragon's Throat.

Tol'chuk dove to the side, dragging the shape-shifter out of harm's way.

From the Throat, a gout of fire roared up as the monstrous bulk struck the molten core. The heat blistered Tol'chuk's back. He sheltered Mogweed under him.

Then it died quickly away.

Tol'chuk rolled around. There was no sign of the demoness.

From the ceiling, clots of oily blackness fell, striking the floor in wet splashes—demonspawn falling back to nothing with their birth mother gone.

Tol'chuk sat where he had fallen. He clapped Mogweed on the shoulder.

The shape-shifter looked haggard, but oddly proud.

The others quickly joined them. Magnam stepped to the edge of the steaming Throat. "I'd like to see the Nameless One try to revive that wit'ch now."

The strange winged creature landed nearby and Jaston went to her side. "Tol'chuk, this is one of Cassa Dar's swamp children."

The child took in the slumbering clans. "Sleep poison," she said in a voice much older than her form. "It will wear off."

Hun'shwa reached out a hand to help Tol'chuk stand. "When they awake, we will have a new leader—a leader of all the clans."

Tol'chuk stared around at the mass of og'res. "What about Cray'nock and the Ku'ukla?"

Hun'shwa barked to one of the other hunters. The og're loped away.

"We'll hold them off until the other clans awake." His voice grew hard. "Then we will make them suffer for the blood here."

Tol'chuk frowned. More fighting between the clans ... It wasn't what the og're tribe needed right now. But he saw no other way. Against the darkness to come, the clans had to be united. If necessary, the Ku'ukla would be forced to bend their knee.

Nearby, one of the other hunters pointed to Tol'chuk. "Kree'nawl!" he said fiercely, beating a fist to his chest.

The chant was carried by the others. "Kree'nawl! Kree'nawl!"

At his side, Mogweed stared as Hun'shwa joined his voice with the others. "What are they saying?" the shape-shifter asked, wobbling a bit, clearly exhausted.

"Wit'ch Slayer," Tol'chuk translated with a frown.

Mogweed scowled. "Wit'ch slayer? Don't let Er'ril hear them call you that."

Tol'chuk clapped him on the shoulder again.

Magnam stepped away from the edge of the Throat. Frowning, the d'warf pointed to Tol'chuk's hand. "Is that the Heart?"

Tol'chuk lifted the stone with which he had slain the wit'ch. "Of course. Why—?" Then he saw it, too. He held the stone higher as the blood drained cold to his feet.

The Heart was black as pitch and streaked with veins of silver.

"It's changed to ebon'stone!" Mogweed gasped.

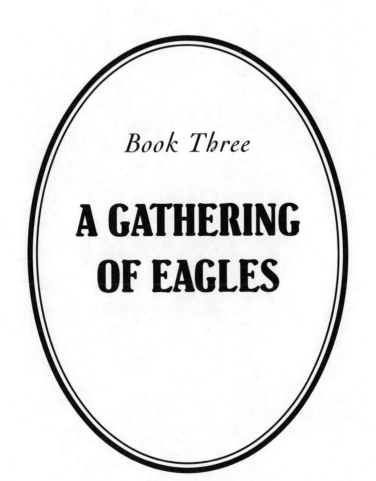

Book Three

A GATHERING
OF EAGLES

11

ELENA WAITED FOR ER'RIL TO FINISH WITH THE HORSE TRADER. THE PAIR HAD been arguing all morning over terms for the necessary mounts and tack.

Her ears long grown deaf to the debate, Elena leaned on the corral's fence and stared toward the bustle of Woodbine, a loggers' and trappers' village carved out of the great forest of the Western Reaches on the Mirror River. From this small hill, she could spy down upon the crowded streets jammed with overflowing carts and refugees, like themselves, from the magickal devastation around Moon Lake.

It had taken Elena's party eight days to reach the township here. Traveling east, they had followed the Mirror River through the ruined forest that had stretched for two leagues beyond the banks of the lake. Hiking through the fallen logs and tangled limbs had been slow. By the second day, they had reached virgin forest and found the trail crowded with others fleeing the devastation. Along the way, Elena had heard many tales of tragedy and woe: destroyed homes, grave injuries, missing family members.

"All because of me," she mumbled as she stood by the corral. The haunted faces of parents, the hollow eyes of children, the tears—all because of a war of magicks. It wore on her strength, leaving her constantly weary and sullen.

She glanced down to her gloved hands and remembered the night they were transported here. She had been unable to touch the moon magick. For just that one night, she had been an ordinary woman with two snow-white hands and an unburdened heart. It had felt so freeing. But come dawn, her powers had returned. First wit'ch fire from the sun, then coldfire from the next night's moon. And once again, she had become the Wit'ch of Spirit and Stone.

Sighing, Elena noted a figure climbing the rutted road up the hill toward the horse barns. He jangled as he walked. She lifted an arm in greeting.

Harlequin Quail acknowledged her with a nod and marched over. His expression was not a happy one.

"What's wrong?" she asked.

Her words drew a small smile from the diminutive man. "Looking at the black side of things these days, aren't we?"

She stared over his shoulder at the crowded streets. "These are black days."

"Perhaps this will cheer you up." He reached a hand toward her, offering a palmful of gold coins.

Elena's eyes widened. Magicked from the castle courtyard without warning, they had arrived here with little resources: a few pieces of silver and a few more of copper. And out here in the wilds, they dared not reveal their true identities, lest they make matters worse. Along the trek here, they had heard tales, stories of their own exploits at A'loa Glen and beyond. But as often as not, the tales cast them as the villains. This far into the wilderness, stories from the distant shores had a way of changing from one mouth to another. So the group kept their silence, especially with the recent devastation to the region. Tempers were high, suspicions even higher, forcing them to scrounge for supplies with the meager coins in hand.

Elena stared now at the fistful of gold. "Where . . . ? How . . . ?"

Harlequin shrugged. "The way I figure, so many of these merchants are scalping these poor folks flooding in here, it was up to someone to lighten their greedy purses."

"You stole it?"

He shrugged again. "I prefer to consider it a secret tax to the cause." The man nodded to Er'ril and the horse trader and stepped toward them. "Let's see if we can shorten this war of wills before someone gets hurt."

Elena noted that Er'ril had indeed grown red-faced. His voice was strained with suppressed fury. "That mare is not worth half the price you ask!"

The plainsman was right. The nag was bow-backed and looked to be at least thirty winters old.

"I've plenty of other folk interested in horses these days," the trader said calmly, nodding to the jammed streets of Woodbine.

Er'ril opened his mouth to argue, but Elena motioned him to step away. Harlequin showed him his bounty. The plainsman's face registered the same shock, then relaxed with relief. He turned to the trader, a pock-faced fellow dressed in leathers with a horsewhip on his hip. "Let me see your finest steeds."

The man blinked in surprise. "I thought you said . . ." He glanced to the nag.

"Your finest," Er'ril repeated.

The trader frowned at him with suspicion. "Don't waste my time, sir. If you don't have the coppers for Millie here, then you'll not have the gold for my best."

Er'ril picked up one of the coins from Harlequin's palm. "Is this gold enough for you?"

The trader eyed the coin, his eyebrows rising. His posture straightened. "Well then, this way, sir!" The man crossed to a gate in a neighboring corral and ushered them through toward a set of barns under the eaves of the forest.

A loud explosion of splintering wood sounded from one of the two barns they were nearing. Er'ril's hand dropped to his sword. Another blast of shattered planking erupted. A pair of men came diving out a small door.

The trader called to them. "What's the matter now?"

One of the men dusted off his leather leggings with a lasso of rope. "We was just tryin' to move the black to another stall."

The other answered, coiling up a length of whip. "The demon came near to crackin' my skull."

The trader glanced back to them. "I'm sorry, folks, for the commotion. I bought a big horse off some trappers a couple days ago; it looked great for log-dredging, but the dang thing is as mean as a kettle is black."

Another crash sounded inside.

The trader shook his head. "I should've known better when they brought the demon in here hobbled in shackles." He loosened his own whip from his belt. "Dang trappers said they found it running wild up north. Must have some blood of those wild Steppe stallions in it or somethin'." He waved his men to accompany him toward the barn. "This'll only take a few moments."

Er'ril frowned at the delay, and Elena understood his consternation. Joach had reached Xin back at A'loa Glen via his black pearl, a magickal link to the zo'ol tribesman. An elv'in scoutship would meet them at the summit of the Pass of Tears in another six days. They did not want to miss the rendezvous.

As the horsemen disappeared into the barn, Elena stepped with Er'ril and Harlequin to one of the fences. Word coming from A'loa Glen was a mix of both bright and dark. Their forces were already en route toward Blackhall. The elv'in warships and the fleet of the Dre'rendi had set sail two days ago, accompanied undersea by the leviathans and dragons of the mer'ai. Farther north, the d'warf army marched overland from Penryn, heading toward the Stone Forest, which lay within the shadow of the volcanic peak. So far all was going well.

But not all of the news was this hopeful. Elena had also heard about Sywen's corruption by something hatched from the ebon'stone egg. The mer'ai woman still remained missing, so Kast had stayed behind at A'loa Glen, protecting the island and searching for his mate.

Pondering Kast's loss now, Elena stared over at Er'ril. She could only imagine the Bloodrider's pain. If she had lost Er'ril . . .

Across the yard, the barn doors crashed open. A large black form flew into the corral, huffing and stamping. It moved with grace and speed, a storm of muscle and steel-shod hooves, followed out by the three horsemen.

One had a lasso around the beast's neck and was being dragged across the rutted dirt. He finally let go and tumbled to a stop. The other two chased the huge horse, their whips snapping in chorus to their screams.

Harlequin stared at the giant beast, his eyes huge. "What a mound of horseflesh. I'd hate to be the one owning that monster."

Er'ril stepped forward and waved to the horse trader. "How much for the black?" he yelled.

The trader ran past, red-faced and panting. "If you can catch him, he's yours for a dang copper!"

"Deal!" Er'ril called back.

"Are you daft, man?" Harlequin gaped at him. "That beast will kill the lot of us."

Er'ril ignored him and whistled sharply. The giant black stallion skidded in its tracks, turning sharply and pawing at the ground. White plumes blew from its nostrils. Its wild eyes focused on the trio by the fence.

Er'ril whistled again.

In response, the horse whinnied loudly and galloped toward them, kicking up dirt. The trader dove out of his way before being trampled.

With a curse, Harlequin leaped away. "Get back, lass!" he called to Elena.

She waved away his concern and stepped to Er'ril's side. The stallion thundered over to them, then stopped with a loud huff. Sweat steamed off its glossy black coat, and one steel-shod hoof dug at the dirt. The horse sniffed at them, then reached a nose toward Elena.

She reached a gloved hand to the stallion and reassured the giant beast with her touch. "It's good to see you again, too, Rorshaf."

The stallion was Kral's war charger. She remembered how the steed had been lost a winter ago, when the mountain man and the others had been attacked near the Stone of Tor up in northern reaches of the forest.

She patted the mighty stallion as it nuzzled her hand. A sad whinny flowed from its chest. She leaned closer, hugging her arms around his neck. For a moment, old memories flooded her: of the endless trail, she atop her gray mare, Mist, and the mountain man leading the way atop his war charger. In some small way, it was like having a piece of Kral returned to them.

She whispered in the stallion's ear. "We miss him, too."

At her side, Er'ril flipped the trader a dull copper coin. "We'll take him!"

MERIC ARGUED WITH THE MERCHANT. "YOU CAN'T EXPECT EIGHT COPPERS FOR that paltry bag of dried peaches. Eight should buy at least four bags."

The merchant pulled up a second bag and placed it beside the first, as if he were doling out satchels of diamonds. "That's the best I can do, friend." He motioned vaguely to the crowds that filled the riverside bazaar.

Meric plunked down the coins and grabbed up his supplies: dried peaches, cranberries, and nuts. With a grumble, he turned to Nee'lahn. "Let's go."

The two of them strode through the jammed bazaar. Hawkers of every sort, from bakers to tailors, called from open-air stalls that lined the wharves. Nearby, a merchant of pots banged his wares for attention, while in the next stall, a butcher waved the flies from the hanging flanks of skinned rabbit.

Deaf and blind to the merchants, Nee'lahn stared at the river. It was all muddy banks, as the river's normal flow went to fill the empty lake so many leagues away. Until the winter rains could refill the waterways, travel by river had been choked off.

Thus they were forced to travel overland. So while Er'ril bargained for horses, Meric and Nee'lahn were hunting up larder and supplies, but it was no easy task. With the hoarding of goods, the flow of displaced folk, and the stagnant traffic, each copper bought less and less.

Meric jingled the handful of coins left in his pocket. So far he had the dried goods, a crate of hardcake, and some cookware. It had even cost a copper to have the supplies delivered to their rooms at the inn. If Er'ril hadn't assigned the castle guards to aid the refugees, they could have helped carry supplies. But then, Meric thought ruefully, they would have to purchase more supplies—and with what coin? Meric sighed, scouting out his next battle. Somewhere in the long bazaar, there was supposed to be a merchant who sold dried and salted meats, but so far, they had not come across his stall.

They pushed through the crowd. About them were faces of fear and worry. Families carried their lives on their backs. Children, normally boisterous and loud in a bazaar, were unusually quiet, holding the hands of their parents.

Nee'lahn sighed, her expression weary and sad as she stared around. "The magickal blast harmed more than just the lake and the surrounding forest. That single wound continues to bleed this region."

"This region and our own purse," Meric added.

"Yes, but we'll surely manage. Can the same be said for many of these folk?" Nee'lahn stared down at a little girl who clutched a tattered doll to her chest. Her eyes were haunted. Her father walked through the stalls with the same eyes, his left arm splinted and slung.

Meric eyed the pair, too, as they disappeared into the crowds. Had the man been injured by the blast? A twinge of guilt cut through his frustration. Though they were not directly to blame, where did their own responsibility for this tragedy begin or end?

Meric motioned Nee'lahn ahead. "Let's finish and get back to the inn."

After a few more spent coins, they made their final purchases. Meric paid out his last two coppers for a wax-sealed comb of honey.

As they turned back to the inn, Nee'lahn leaned closer to Meric. "We're being followed," she whispered.

"What?" He resisted the urge to swing around.

"Pause at the next stall and look over your right shoulder. The fellow with the green cloak and slouched hat."

Meric searched, then spotted the man. He was tall, broad-shouldered, his features hidden in shadow by his hat. Meric was careful not to stare for too long, lest the man know he had been spotted. He glanced to Nee'lahn. "A thief perhaps."

She nodded. "We'd best be wary."

They continued onward. The green-cloaked fellow kept a distance away, but he never left their trail.

Soon they were free of the riverside bazaar and back into the streets. Here the way was less crowded. The lurker had to keep a greater distance.

Meric frowned at the fellow's persistence. He was clearly not an ordinary cutpurse; victims were easier to target in the tumult of the bazaar. So what did this fellow want? Meric touched his own magick, drawing energy from the winds flowing up the river channel. He lowered a hand casually to the sword on his hip and prepared to act with the speed of an elv'in if necessary.

Nee'lahn flicked her eyes to his sword. "Perhaps rather than waiting for an attack, we should spring the trap first."

Meric glanced to her. "Do you have the strength?" The trek through the ruined woods around Moon Lake had taxed the nyphai woman. But once back in healthy forest, she had slowly revived.

She nodded, swinging her lute from her shoulder. "Though this town is cut from the Western Reaches, it is but a ship atop a sea. Under the land here, the forest persists in the flow of roots and the richness of loam."

Meric noticed how she grew more beautiful as she touched her own magick. It was a subtle change: a sharper cast to her violet eyes, a deeper honey to her hair, a richer glow to her skin. "Then let us indeed lay our own snare."

"Follow me," Nee'lahn said, and ducked into a narrow side street. Here there were only a few people on the rutted road. She increased her pace, searching for something.

"What are you—?"

"Here!" she whispered, tugging him toward an alehouse window. Inside, a few patrons sat around plank tables, gripping flagons of mead as if their lives depended on each drop.

"The alley," Nee'lahn whispered. "On my word."

Meric noticed the shadowy space between the alehouse and a neighboring blacksmith. The sound of hammers and the hissing roar of forges echoed to the streets.

"Here he comes," Nee'lahn whispered, nodding to the reflection in the window. "Quickly."

She led him into the alley. They hurried toward a pile of empty barrels stacked near a side door to the alehouse. The yeasty reek of stale hops filled the space.

"We'll wait for him here," she said as Meric shrugged out of his bags and hid their supplies by the barrels. "Be ready with your blade, but let me act first." Nee'lahn slid the cloth covering from her lute. She ran her fingers along the strings and grew even more lovely as her magick swelled inside her. She now shone with an inner warmth and richness that ached his heart. "He comes," she whispered, drawing him back to their plight and pushing him farther into their hiding place.

Between the stacked barrels, Meric and Nee'lahn spied as the lurker stepped to the mouth of the alley. He glanced up and down the street. His very posture was a frown. Slowly he slipped into the shadows between the alehouse and the blacksmith.

Meric felt Nee'lahn tense beside him.

The attacker glanced back to the street. He waved. A second and a third man entered the alley. They were similarly clad in cloaks and slouched hats.

Meric flinched. There wasn't just one thief. He glanced back; the alley ended a few steps behind them at a brick wall. The only other way out was the side door to the alehouse. But even if it was unlocked, it lay on the far side of the barrels.

Nee'lahn squeezed his hand, silently warning him to be ready. Then her hands moved to her lute.

Meric tightened his grip on his sword. There were only three, and the two of them had the advantage of surprise. Then Meric startled as another two cloaked figures entered the alley.

The odds had just worsened, and now Meric wasn't sure who had the advantage of surprise. Yet another figure entered the alley, making it a total of six attackers.

Nee'lahn remained where she stood, calm and shining. Meric was surprised the others in the alley did not spot her beacon.

From his vantage, Meric watched the first lurker edge toward the piled barrels. The fellow waved one of his cohorts to test the alehouse door. The man whisked to obey.

Meric tensed. The banging of hammer on anvil from the neighboring smithy seemed to echo Meric's own heartbeat, thudding loud in his ears. The cloaked figure tested the door. It was indeed locked or barred.

In the alley, all eyes swung to the stack of barrels.

So much for the advantage of surprise.

The hammering continued, seeming much louder. Then one bright note cut through the noise: a single plucked lute string.

Everyone froze in the alley.

Nee'lahn strummed down the remaining strings, building a complex chord that rang through the alley.

The first lurker pointed, but before anyone could move, a tangle of roots shot out of the ground, tangling up like a net. Three men were captured. The remaining three bolted away.

"Run!" Nee'lahn cried. But before they could take two steps, the root-captured figures underwent a strange transformation.

Meric grabbed Nee'lahn and pulled her away.

All three melted down out of their cloaks and slithered snakelike from their root cages, a flow of living flesh. Once beyond the bindings, each formed a different forest creature: a woodland cat, a giant eagle, and a white wolf. The transformed beasts took flight on wings and paws.

But at the mouth of the alley, the wolf stopped. This beast had been the first lurker. Meric now sensed it was a female—a she-wolf. Her pelt shone snow-white in the sunlight of the street. She glanced to them, her eyes burning amber with fury. Then she was gone.

"Shape-shifters," Nee'lahn gasped.

JOACH SAT IN A CHAIR ACROSS FROM GRESHYM. THE INN WINDOW WAS thrown open, allowing the sounds of the town to echo up to their second-floor room: the shouts of merchants, the babble of common folk, and somewhere nearby a lone babe wailed. They were all the sounds of life—and before him, trussed in ropes, sat the very figure of such vitality.

The darkmage smiled at him from an unlined face, his hair a rich brown. His shoulders were square, his back straight. Joach could not remember ever being so hale. Yet he knew he must have once been, for staring him in the face was his *own* youth, stolen by a spell.

Joach leaned on his staff, his cheek resting against the petrified wood. The afternoon heat threatened to lull him into a drowse, but he fought against it. The trek here had worn his joints sore and ached his heart. But worse than the hard leagues was his proximity to Greshym. For the past winter, Joach had plotted revenge, planned ways to reclaim his stolen youth. Now his enemy had been dropped at his feet, bound and impotent.

And he could do nothing about it.

His grip tightened on his staff. He frowned at the Blood Diary resting atop a table in the room, the source of his consternation.

Greshym noted his attention. "Destroy the book and we can have at it, my boy."

Joach straightened in his seat, wincing with pain. "As much as I might wish it, that will never happen. But don't worry. There will come a time when we will settle our old scores." These last words were as much a promise to himself as to the darkmage.

Greshym's smile became bitter. "Then spend your last winters dreaming of youth, because that's all you'll ever have." The darkmage glared over to the Diary.

The magickal tome bound Greshym here much more than the ropes with which Er'ril had secured the man. Cho had cast a spell upon the darkmage in her fury, drawing a bit of his spirit into the Void and tying it there. Thus bound, any magick Greshym collected would be drawn immediately into the Void. The spell effectively stripped the darkmage of his powers.

Unfortunately, it also stymied any of Joach's spells; any magick—dream or dark—cast upon Greshym was simply sucked into the Void, too.

Neither of them could act. It was a stalemate of wills and power.

Days ago, upon capturing Greshym, Er'ril had wanted to slice the mage's throat, but Elena argued against such rash action. They faced a great battle at Blackhall, and any knowledge of the volcanic peak's secret defenses or forces could prove crucial. Also Greshym had intimate experience of the Black Heart and his lieutenant Shorkan, details that could mean the difference between victory and defeat in the days ahead. So the darkmage was allowed to live, a prisoner amongst them.

Greshym sighed. "There is so much I can teach you, Joach, so little you understand of your full potential." These words sounded both tired and oddly honest.

Joach squinted at his adversary. "There's nothing you can teach me that I'd want to learn." But even to his own ears, these words rang hollow.

Greshym shrugged. "You're too raw to your talent to know what you dismiss so readily."

Joach's eye twitched. He knew he was rising to bait but he couldn't help it. "Like what?"

"You're a dream sculptor. Such a one as you hasn't been born in countless generations. If I bore such a gift . . ." His words trailed off. The tip of his tongue moistened his lip. "I could stand against the Black Heart himself."

Again Joach sensed the honesty behind these words. True or not, Greshym believed it. "What do you mean?" he asked.

Greshym's eyes focused back on Joach. "All I will tell you is that the line between dream and reality is not as firmly drawn as most imagine. If you believe in a dream solidly enough, sculpt it with enough of your heart and spirit, it can cross over into reality."

Joach swallowed hard. Had not Shaman Parthus hinted at such a blurring of the line between reality and dream?

Greshym spoke softly. "I know what you want, Joach."

"You know nothing."

Young eyes stared, and a young mouth spoke one word. "Kesla."

Anger filled those spaces inside Joach that were hollow and empty. His voice boiled over with this fury. "Never speak her name again, mage. Elena's wish or not, I'll take a dagger to you."

Greshym shrugged at the threat. "Death is also a blurry line when one is granted life by the Black Heart."

Joach scowled, but he knew he could never kill the mage, not until he regained his youth and learned this hinted secret: a way to make dreams real. He pictured a girl with golden hair and violet eyes, and the weary ache in his heart threatened to overwhelm him.

Oblivious to Joach's pain, Greshym continued, leaning back in his chair, "We are not unalike, my boy."

Joach scoffed.

"Do we not both crave the youth robbed from us? Is this not so?" His voice dropped to a sly level. "Must we always be enemies? Couldn't we share what we both desire?"

Joach frowned. "Share?"

"I give you back half the years stolen, and I keep the other half. Each will be a bit older, but neither will be decrepit."

"Why should I do that?"

"To learn what I might teach you."

Joach ran his fingers down this staff. The ripe dream energies trapped there flowed like his own blood. Over these past winters, he had grown in his power, but he was far from a master. Could Kesla indeed be made real? "What would be the cost for such a lesson?"

"Mere trifles. My freedom, my life."

"So you can betray us again?"

Greshym rolled his eyes. "You place too much importance on your own significance to me. In truth, I had hope never to see the lot of you again."

Joach looked doubtful.

"There is no love lost between Shorkan and myself, as you well know. I've betrayed the Black Heart for my own desires. Do you truly think I want any dealings with them?"

"Why? What is this difference between you and Shorkan? Why is he so unfailing in his allegiance and you so fickle?"

"Ah . . ." Greshym leaned back as much as the ropes would allow. "Before the book was forged, Shorkan was always more . . . well, *dedicated* to his causes. To him, everything in the world was divided along clearly defined lines: black and white, right and wrong. I had a more pragmatic view of life. To me the world was a tad more gray. So when the Blood Diary was forged and the spell attempted to split the good from the bad, it had a harder time with me. I carried many shades of gray, so the division was not as crisp and clear. I suspect it was one reason the spell left me so disfigured: immortal but aging of body."

"So you're saying Shorkan is more loyal because it was easier to draw off all that was good in him, leaving only the black for the Dark Lord."

Greshym sighed. "While I'm still laced with shades of gray."

Joach stared at the figure before him, wondering at this revelation.

"So free me," Greshym continued, "and I'll leave you to your little war. You'll be free to join such a battle, a younger self, ripe with dream magicks the likes of which you've never—dare I say—*dreamed*!"

Joach listened, uncertain. He knew Greshym could never be trusted. But perhaps with enough safeguards in place . . .

The door to the room banged open, startling Joach. He twisted around, earning another painful twinge from his aching back.

Meric burst into the room, out of breath, followed by Nee'lahn. "Are Elena and Er'ril not back yet?"

Greshym frowned and nodded to the room's cot. "They're hiding under the bed."

Meric was so shaken he even glanced there.

"They're still rounding up horses and tack," Joach said. "What's wrong?"

Nee'lahn answered, clearly the calmer of the two. "Si'lura," she said. "We were followed through the market."

"Shape-shifters?" Joach pulled himself to his feet. "Why were they following you?"

Meric found his tongue. "Maybe they were common brigands." He tossed the purchased supplies atop the bed. "Laden as we were, we may have been simple targets."

Greshym spoke from his chair. "Si'lura have little need for dried peaches and kettle pots. They are forest creatures, half wild. I'd suggest you think deeper upon this encounter. I doubt it was chance that they are here."

"I agree," Nee'lahn said to Meric. "That she-wolf seemed more than a mere thief."

His reply was cut off when a commotion erupted from the inn courtyard: shouts and the clatter of hooves, followed by a sharp whinny and a crash of pottery.

A voice cut through the excitement. "Step away!"

Meric hurried to the open window. "It's Er'ril."

"I'll lead the black!" the plainsman yelled. "Stable the others!"

"You'll pay for those pots!" another man cried. Joach recognized the innkeeper's voice.

"This should settle our accounts," Er'ril said.

A short pause. "Gold! Break all the pots you want, good sir!"

Joach and Nee'lahn joined Meric at the window. Below was chaos. Ten horses jostled about in the cramped courtyard, churning up dust and dirt. Most wore saddles and packs. He spotted Harlequin darting toward the kitchen door of the inn, attempting to avoid being trampled. Elena rode a sleek brown mare, while Er'ril led a monstrous black stallion toward the stables.

Meric stiffened beside Nee'lahn. "Isn't that Kral's mount?"

"Rorshaf," Nee'lahn agreed, and frowned. "What strangeness is this?"

"We should help settle the horses," Meric suggested. "And tell about the shape-shifters."

Nee'lahn nodded, and the pair headed out the door.

Joach returned to his chair and his guard duty. The darkmage's eyes followed him.

"This next leg of the journey should prove most interesting," Greshym mumbled. "Shape-shifters . . . strange reunions . . ."

"So?"

"After having lived for so many centuries, I've learned one thing." Greshym's eyes bore into Joach. "Never trust chance encounters."

12

Er'ril rode Rorshaf down the rutted path. Since they had left Woodbine three days ago, the forest road had dwindled to this narrow, crooked trail that followed the Mirror River. All day long, their party had not come across a single fellow traveler. And with the sun setting, the trail stretched empty ahead of them. It seemed the world had shrunk down to just their small group and the endless forest beyond.

Still, empty trail or not, Er'ril maintained his vigilance. Entire armies could lurk in this dark wood and keep themselves hidden. A deep green gloom settled with the waning sunlight. In the distance, nesting birds sang and argued, but otherwise the forest remained silent. The quiet pressed down upon their group. Everyone spoke in hushed whispers. Even the horses seemed to tread softly, their hooves muffled by the carpet of pine needles and thick loam.

With night falling, Er'ril searched for a campsite. He wanted somewhere near the river but high enough to offer an advantage if they were attacked.

As he studied the terrain, Elena shuffled her brown mare forward to join him. He glanced over to her. She wore a green riding cloak over brown leggings and a gray shirt. Her face was worn and tired, but some of the despair in her eyes had faded since leaving the sorry streets of Woodbine. The plight of the many hundreds displaced by the magickal explosion had affected her deeply. But here in the woods, free of the constant reminder, she slowly regained her center, her strength.

"We've had word from A'loa Glen," she said.

Er'ril twisted in his saddle and spotted Joach pocketing the large black pearl that connected him to the zo'ol shaman, Xin, back at the castle. Beyond Joach, the others rode in a line, including Greshym. The darkmage had been lashed to the saddle, his horse tethered to Meric's gelding. Greshym caught his eye. He wore an amused smile and gave a nod in Er'ril's direction. The pair shared a history that extended back centuries.

Er'ril tore his gaze back to Elena. "How fare the preparations for the siege of Blackhall?"

Elena walked her mare beside the larger stallion. "Xin relayed a message from Prince Tyrus. He leads his pirate brigade in advance of the other fleets. They are a fortnight out from the Bay of T'lek."

Er'ril nodded. The icy northern bay surrounded the volcanic eruption that was Blackhall. "They're making good headway."

"He anticipates the assault will be ready to strike with the next moon."

Er'ril grimaced. It frustrated him to be stuck in the Western Reaches during this critical time. For centuries, he had dreamed of bringing the battle for freedom to the shores of Blackhall itself, but now that it was actually happening, he was lost, hundreds of leagues away, whisked away by a miscast spell.

He bit back his anger and drew his thoughts to their own objective. "And what of the threat in Winterfell? Any word of the Wyvern Gate?"

There was a long, pained silence. Elena finally spoke. "No. An envoy was sent from Standi, but they never returned."

A growl built in Er'ril's chest.

Elena continued. "Rumors continue of razed foothill villages and attacks by misshapen beasts at night."

"The sooner we rendezvous with the elv'in ship, the sooner we can discover the answers on our own."

Elena sighed. "The ship has already set out. Barring any unforeseen obstacles, we should both reach the Pass of Tears at the same time."

Er'ril frowned. *Barring any unforeseen obstacles* ... Dare he hope for such a lucky circumstance?

A voice arose on his other side. Harlequin Quail marched his small piebald gelding up from the ranks. "Is that a fire ahead?"

Er'ril stared forward. To the right of the trail, a faint flickering of firelight illuminated the deep gloom, the glow reflecting off the neighboring Mirror River. "A campfire," he said, frowning, angry at himself for letting his attention wander.

"Perhaps they're other travelers?" Elena offered.

Er'ril pulled his stallion to a halt and signaled for the others to follow suit. He could make out shadows moving against the light. There appeared to be more than one in the other party. "I'll go ahead. Everyone else remain here."

Nee'lahn slid from her horse. "I should go with you. If there is a danger in these woods, the forest will protect us." The nyphai woman shone with a stunning vitality. She had clearly drawn considerable magick from the wood during this journey.

Er'ril nodded. Nee'lahn was in her own element here.

She handed Meric her lute. "Keep it safe," she said. Her fingers lingered a moment longer on the elv'in prince's hand; then she turned to Er'ril. "Continue along the path. I'll cross through the forest."

Without waiting for an answer, she headed into the woods, where the trees swallowed her away as if she were a mere figment.

Er'ril nudged Rorshaf and began down the trail.

"Be careful," Elena warned.

"Always," he assured her. He walked his horse at a steady pace. There was no use attempting stealth. He suspected whoever camped here already knew of their presence. In a few moments, he crossed around a crook in the path. The others disappeared behind him. Beyond the bend, the trail continued in a gentle arc toward the river. At its nearest point lay the strangers' campsite.

Er'ril slowed his pace and Rorshaf huffed, sensing his rider's wariness.

This close, Er'ril could make out the shapes by the fire. He was relieved to see they were mere men. *Five*—a manageable number as long as more were not hidden in the woods.

Er'ril kept one eye on the campsite and another on the surrounding forest. There appeared to be no others. Then again, he could not spot Nee'lahn, either.

Er'ril moved his war charger forward. "Ho! What news of the trail?" he called out, a common greeting among travelers.

One shadowy figure stepped to the trail. It was a tall, broad-shouldered man with a coppery beard that draped down his bare chest. He wore a pair of dappled leggings and black boots.

Though he clearly bore no weapons, Er'ril sensed a wary menace in the man's cold, hard stare.

Rorshaf snorted loudly, dancing angrily on his hooves.

The other's eyes shifted from Er'ril to the stallion, then widened with recognition. "Bloody Mother!" the man grunted coarsely, taking a step back. "It's that demon we sold in Woodbine."

Er'ril calmed Rorshaf. He recalled the horse trader's mention of trappers. Were these the men who sold the stallion?

"Mean cuss, that one," the bearded stranger said. "But I see he's taken a shine to you."

Er'ril shrugged, keeping one hand on his upper thigh, his wrist touching his sword's hilt. "He just takes a firm hand."

"That so?" The man's attitude remained gruff, but a bit more respect entered his tone. "He nearly took off one of my men's thumbs when he licked a whip on the monster."

Er'ril frowned. "Not all commands require the crack of a lash to be firm." As he spoke, he noted the others by the fire, staring back at them.

Another of the group stepped to the trail, a slender woman dressed in the same dappled outfit of green and blacks. She, too, had hair that shone in hues of red and copper, shorn to her shoulders. She laid a hand on the larger fellow's arm.

"Excuse my brother's welcome," she said. "These are sour times in the Reaches, and a healthy suspicion is wise in the wilds."

Er'ril shifted his hand a fraction from his sword. "My companions and I mean no threat. We only seek word of the trail ahead."

"There is little we can share, since we travel the same direction as you . . . away from Woodbine." She gestured back to the fire. "But night falls, and we can offer the warmth of our hearth and the hospitality of our camp instead."

Her brother's face had darkened with these words, his brows bunching like storm clouds. But he remained silent—the offer had been made.

Er'ril glanced to the bright fire, then out to the black woods. He sensed no malice in the two before him, only wariness. In this dark forest, a few extra eyes guarding against dangers were as welcome as any fire. "I thank you," he said, bringing his fist to his belly in the common gesture of hospitality accepted. "May the Mother bless your hearths for your generosity."

As he finished, a scream suddenly shattered through the quiet woods, freezing everyone in place for a heartbeat. A sword appeared in Er'ril's fist as the cry died away.

Er'ril searched the forest. It was Nee'lahn. He was sure of it.

Immediately the thunder of hooves sounded on the trail behind them. Er'ril swung around in his saddle and spotted Elena, leading the others swiftly on horseback around the crook in the trail. The scream must have panicked them forward to his aid.

The gruff trapper backed a step. "What betrayal is this?" He pulled his sister toward the trees.

"We mean no harm!" Er'ril called. He feared creating a new enemy at his back. Whatever lay out in the wood had best be faced together. "Fear not from us! It is the woods you must guard against!"

The woman shook out of her brother's grip. Er'ril met her gaze, his eyes pleading as hoofbeats thundered behind him. She turned to the larger man. "I believe him, Gunther. If there is evil afoot, let us join forces."

The man scowled, then nodded. He swung into the woods. "To the fire then, Bryanna!" He shouted to his men. "Arm up!"

The woman called to Er'ril. "Ready your people and join us at the fire." With a swirl of her cloak, she followed her brother.

Er'ril raised his blade. "To me!" he called, as his own companions closed the gap.

Elena was the first to reach his side, her mare's chest heaving. "Nee'lahn . . . ," she said breathlessly.

"I know." He slipped from Rorshaf's saddle. "We'll secure things here, then search for her."

Atop his piebald gelding, Harlequin nodded toward the fire. "And what about this rangy lot? Do you trust them?"

"We have no choice. Besides, I'd rather have these trappers where I can see them." He led the giant war charger toward the fire. "Follow me."

Still mounted, the others walked their horses behind him. Ahead, extra branches were added to the bonfire, driving the blaze higher, while the Mirror River flowed shallow between muddy banks. The rest of the forest remained dark as the sun finally set.

Er'ril tied off his mount near where the trappers' horses were tethered. The others dismounted and did the same.

Meric landed lightly on the ground and stepped to the horse behind him. "What about Greshym?"

Er'ril frowned as the darkmage was loosened and pulled to the ground. Though the man's arms were still bound and Cho's dampening spell remained in place, he dared not leave the mage unguarded. He turned to Joach. "Keep a watch on him."

Joach nodded. He shifted his gray staff under one arm and grabbed Greshym's elbow with the other.

Meric crossed to Er'ril's side. "We must find Nee'lahn," he said anxiously.

"We'll find her," Elena assured him, stepping to join them.

She went to remove her gloves, but Er'ril stopped her with a touch to her arm. "Not yet . . . Use your magick only if necessary."

Elena hesitated, then secured her gloves. She reached to her waist and pulled free her silver dagger.

Harlequin in tow, Er'ril led the group to the campfire. Gunther and Bryanna joined them. The other three trappers, all men, stood with their backs to the fire, watching the woods. All of them bore short swords. Gunther also carried a hand ax in his other fist. Bryanna had a bow in hand and a quiver of fletched arrows over a shoulder.

Gunther eyed their group, his gaze lingering an extra moment on Elena. He then turned a stern eye on Er'ril. "Have you any idea what threatens us?"

Er'ril shook his head. "The scream was one of our companions, a woman. She was in the woods."

Gunther's eyes narrowed with suspicion, but before Er'ril could elaborate, Bryanna gasped. "The forest!"

Er'ril and the others turned their attentions outward. Just beyond the reach of the firelight, eyes glowed back at them, at least a score. Some were low to the ground, others higher in the branches of the trees.

As Er'ril raised his sword, other eyes bloomed, deeper in the forest surrounding them. With each breath, more and more appeared, in all directions, even across the river.

Elena stripped off her gloves. This time Er'ril did not object.

More eyes appeared in every size and shape, extending leagues into the trackless woods. Some glowed through narrow slits, while others were round as saucers. Only one feature was shared by all: *Each pair of eyes glowed amber.*

"Shape-shifters," Meric whispered.

Er'ril stared out at the silent army around them. "What do they want?"

Gunther spoke at Er'ril's shoulder. "We've had dealings with the si'lura before, trading and such. But I've never seen a gathering like this."

"It makes no sense," Bryanna said. "They've never been hostile unless provoked."

Er'ril shared a glance with Meric. Shape-shifters again—but why? What were they after?

"Maybe it's the horse," one of the other trappers mumbled.

Er'ril glanced to the speaker. "What do you mean? What about the stallion?"

Gunther waved away the man's words away with his ax. "That makes no sense."

Er'ril refused to let this strange statement pass. Iron entered his voice. "Explain yourself."

Bryanna answered, speaking rapidly. "We traded a cask of bitterwort spice for the black a few leagues from here. It was said the stallion came from the flooded forest, where the Stone of Tor fell. We figured to fetch a good price in Woodbine—it's a logging town where a stout horse is always in demand."

"Now we know why the black went for so cheap a price," Gunther grumbled into his beard.

"What does this have to do with the si'lura?"

Bryanna glanced to him. "That's who we bought the stallion from."

They all stared out into the dark wood. Hundreds of eyes glowed back at them. What was going on?

DAZED AND BLEEDING FROM A CUT ON HER FOREHEAD, NEE'LAHN STRUGGLED against her bonds. The ropes bound her to the trunk of a large oak. She heard the song of the mighty tree, but gagged with a roll of cloth, she could not join her voice. Without song, she was cut off from the magick all around her.

She watched dark shapes lope, slither, and pad among the trees, indistinct shadows in the gloom. She had been caught by surprise, walking into a trap as she had focused on the flickering flames of the campfire. The treesong of the forest had offered no alarm. But then again, why should the Great Wood be concerned with shape-shifters? The si'lura had been denizens of the deep glade for as long as the forest had lived, as much its caretakers as the nyphai had been for Lok'ai'hera.

Blind and deaf to their presence, she had been attacked from above. Something large had leaped from the branches and clubbed her to the ground. A single cry of surprise was all she had managed before she blacked out. Moments later, she had woken into full night, gagged and bound to the tree.

She relented in her struggle against the ropes, taking deep breaths, pushing back her initial panic. She had friends nearby, and though her tongue was bound by the roll of cloth, she could still touch a fraction of the magick around her. She took another deep breath, letting her eyes drift half closed, and hummed from the core of her spirit. She married her soft notes to the thrum of treesong, merging the two.

Though the contact was weak, she called what she could: the smallest roots of the oak at her back. She felt the richness of the loam as the rootlets wormed to the surface. If she could wind the small limbs into her bonds and loosen a hand—

A growl sounded on her left, full of threat. The hum of power died in her throat as a large white she-wolf stalked from the darker forest and revealed its white pelt and glowing amber eyes. Nee'lahn recognized the shape-shifter who had tracked them through the streets of Woodbine.

The wolf circled the tree once, rumbling a long growl. As it crossed back into sight, its flesh melted and the shape-shifter shimmered from its wolfskin, straightening and rising. A woman's face replaced the wolf's, but the amber eyes still glowed with a feral bit of the wild forest. She stood naked before Nee'lahn, unabashed, shoulders back. A long flow of white hair, straight and fluid, draped to the middle of her back.

"Attempt to free yourself again with your magick, and you'll find your throat torn out before you can take two steps."

Nee'lahn did not doubt the threat. She remained silent and stared back at the si'luran woman.

The shape-shifter's eyes narrowed, studying her. "We have your companions surrounded," she said quietly. "But before we attack, I want to know why you broke your vows to the forest, nyphai."

Nee'lahn's brow crinkled with confusion.

A hand shot out toward her face. Nee'lahn cringed back, but the woman's fingers settled to her gag. "I'll loosen your tongue, but one note of magick from you and it'll be your last."

Knowing that any hope of freedom lay in cooperation, Nee'lahn nodded once in acknowledgment.

With a deft flick of fingers, the gag fell away. Nee'lahn coughed. "Wh-who are you?"

The si'luran's back straightened. "My name is Thorn, prime tracker of the Freshling clan, third daughter of the elder'root. You're to be brought before my father and the Council of Wishnu, to be judged for your atrocities against our forest."

Nee'lahn was taken aback. "What do you mean?"

Thorn snarled. "Nothing happens in the Reaches that is beyond the eyes of the si'lura. We have been watching you, nyphai, since you first were reborn here in our forests."

Nee'lahn could not hide her shock. Over a winter ago, she had used the magick of the great forest to pull her spirit from its resting place inside a black acorn and birth her body anew. She'd had no idea that the si'luran people were aware of her.

"We watched you and your companions last winter, leaving a path of destruction."

"We destroyed nothing. We sought to mend the Northwall and fend off the Grim wraiths who harried the edges of the forest."

"You brought down the Stone of Tor," Thorn spat back. "A place sacred to the si'luran people."

Nee'lahn was stunned. She remembered the crash of the pinnacle of stone. While imprisoned in a wagon headed to Castle Mryl, she had felt the rending of the forest and the resultant flooding as the toppled peak dammed up rivers and streams. A good portion of the Western Reaches had been destroyed that day. "The Grim had to be stopped," she offered weakly.

Thorn's eyes flashed with ire. "The results of your actions were a thousandfold worse than any threat from the Grim."

Nee'lahn remained silent.

"The forest gave you life, and you repaid it with death."

"You don't understand—"

"And now Moon Lake," the shape-shifter continued, ignoring her protest as she stalked back and forth. "Hundreds of my people were slain—but you walked out unscathed. Word spread quickly through the si'lura, one mind speaking to another. We recognized you. Again you walk our forests and leave a wake of devastation." Fiery rage entered her voice. "But no more!"

Nee'lahn listened, stunned at the accusation. But a small part of her understood this one's fury. This was their home. They knew nothing of the greater war beyond the woods. Isolated from the world at large, all the si'lura saw were great swaths of their homeland forests destroyed, and at each instance, the same person had been present.

Nee'lahn stared into the angry eyes of the other and recognized the true face of those caught in the battle of magicks. All these folk saw of the small victories against the Dark Lord was the destruction of their own homes, their own peoples. Here stood the folk who bore the brunt of the larger battle, forgotten and dismissed, never mentioned in tales or songs—those left behind.

Nee'lahn struggled to find words to encompass the pain, some reason to justify the loss of lands and people. But all she came up with were three heartfelt words. "I am sorry."

Thorn stopped in her tracks. Her eyes narrowed as she studied Nee'lahn. It was the suspicion of a wolf staring back at her.

Nee'lahn faced the accusation in the other's gaze. "I am truly sorry for all you lost."

A crinkle marred Thorn's smooth brow. The fire dimmed in her eyes. When next she spoke, it was a plea: "Why?"

Nee'lahn slowly shook her head. She had no answer to why some folks suffered so that others might live freely, why there was always a price in blood that had to be paid. "There is much guilt I and my companions bear. Over these last winters, we've stared too hard at the larger world and grown blind to those nearer at hand. Of that we are guilty. But there is a greater war that threatens not just portions of the Western Reaches, but the *entire* forest. It is a battle for the very heart of the Land."

A shimmer of doubt passed over Thorn's features.

Nee'lahn continued. "The world bleeds, not just here but across many lands. So while I'm sorry for the loss of your people and the wounded forest, I cannot apologize for the war we wage. Though the forest bleeds now, it will heal and grow stronger. But if the darkness claims it, nothing will survive."

Thorn turned away from her words. "You speak from your heart; this I can tell. But the elder'root of the si'lura has called for you and your companions to stand before the Council of Wishnu. His call must be answered."

Nee'lahn sighed. "I will not fight your father's summons. And if I can explain to the others, neither will they." She sensed it was time to face those who had been harmed in this war, to acknowledge their pain and sorrow. After Woodbine, she sensed Elena would agree.

"Then I'll let you speak to your companions. But if any try to flee . . ." A growl of threat flowed from the woman.

Nee'lahn sensed the shaky balance achieved here. These lands belonged to the si'lura. Even with Elena's magick, they would be hard-pressed to escape the forest. This summons to account for their actions here in the Western Reaches would have to be answered.

Thorn turned and loosened the vine ropes that bound the nyphai woman, but did not free her wrists. Nee'lahn stumbled away from the tree. Thorn caught her elbow to help her keep her feet.

Nee'lahn straightened. In the surrounding gloom, the flash of amber eyes flickered though the forest. She sensed the strained anger out there in the woods. It would be a hard wound to soothe.

She turned to Thorn to thank her for this small amount of trust.

The shape-shifter's eyes remained wary, but the fury had dulled. In its wake, something else shone in her eyes: sorrow and loss. Clearly Thorn had lost someone close to her. Nee'lahn suspected it was this pain that had fueled the rage of a few moments ago.

Nee'lahn repeated her earlier words. "I am sorry."

Thorn's gaze hardened. "He should have been with you," she mumbled under her breath as she guided Nee'lahn forward.

Her strange comment mystified Nee'lahn. "Who?"

Thorn's lip edged into a snarl. "Fardale. He was with your party last winter as you traveled north. I tracked him myself."

Nee'lahn glanced to her. The two si'luran brothers had been banished from the forest due to their curse, ostracized by their own people. But she sensed something more personal in Thorn's tones. "You knew Fardale?"

The snarl deepened. "He was my mate."

Nee'lahn tripped over a stone.

Thorn continued speaking through clenched teeth. "But he was cursed after our first union and forced to leave."

Nee'lahn sensed conflicting emotions warring in the si'luran woman: anger, pain, sorrow, and loss. And she now understood why it was Thorn who had hunted them all along. She saw the pained love in the other's eyes. "He still lives," Nee'lahn said softly. "He fights the darkness, as we do here."

Thorn turned away. "It doesn't matter." But from the way her voice cracked, the exact opposite was the truth. It was her next comment, though, that stunned Nee'lahn into silence. "I had just hoped Fardale could meet his son."

ELENA STOOD WITH HER BACK TO THE FIRE. THE FLAMES DANCED SHADOWS among the trees, while hundreds of pairs of amber eyes stared silently upon them.

"We must find Nee'lahn," Meric insisted. His silver hair shimmered, moving to the unseen winds of his magick.

"It is death to go out there now," Er'ril warned. "Let us see how this plays out."

"What are the shape-shifters waiting for?" Harlequin asked. He bore two daggers, flipping them end over end, catching the handles deftly each time. They flashed in the firelight.

The large trapper, Gunther, answered. "They seek to unman us. To make us run in fear."

"We'll not run," Elena said calmly. She clenched a fist, building her magick to a deep crimson glow. Wit'ch fire in her right hand, coldfire in her left. She kept her fingers tight around the rose-carved handle of her silver dagger, ready to bloody her hands and unleash the magick pent inside. The wild chorus sang in her heart as she touched that part of her that was Cho, a being of unfathomable nature.

Bryanna gasped, staring wide-eyed at Elena's hands. "What manner of demon are you?"

Elena glanced to her face. "I am as much a woman as you." She held up her hand. "Like the shape-shifters out there, I simply bear a unique gift."

"Do not listen to her," a voice said coldly behind them. "She's a wit'ch." It was Greshym. The darkmage sat beside the fire, his elbows bound behind him. "She'll kill you all before this night is over."

Joach cracked Greshym a blow to the side of the head with his staff.

Er'ril stepped toward him. "Speak your lies again and I'll remove your tongue."

Bryanna frowned at Elena. "Wit'ch?"

Elena sensed the suspicion growing around her. One of the other trappers touched his forehead with his thumb in a warding against evil.

"I bear magick," she said. "But in my heart, I am a woman like any other. I—"

"So you *are* a wit'ch!" Gunther blustered, his face growing as red as his beard. "A woman who bears magick! You admit it!"

Tensions rose around the fire. Gazes shifted between the si'luran army in the woods and the strife within the camp.

Amidst this strain, Harlequin suddenly laughed loudly, a bright sound accompanied by the jingling of bells. Eyes turned to him. "All of you strapping forest men frightened of this little slip of a woman," the small man scoffed. "So what if Elena has a bit of magick? Don't all women?" He eyed Bryanna up and down. "Something tells me a pretty lass like you has turned a man or two stone hard with nothing more than a smile and a wink. That's what I call *true* magick!" The small man's bells rang with amusement.

Gunther growled at the implication.

"You're not helping, Harlequin," Meric warned.

"I will not suffer a wit'ch in my camp," Gunther grumbled. "I'll throw the lot of you to the shape-shifters."

Bryanna stepped forward. "Enough, Brother."

He opened his mouth again, but a glare from his sister silenced him.

"I sense no evil from her," Bryanna insisted, "only concern for their lost friend." She turned to Elena. "Once this matter with the shape-shifters is finished, I would know more of these powers of yours."

Elena nodded gratefully. "It is a long story."

Bryanna turned to the forest, directing her arrow outward. "Then if we survive this night, I'd like to hear it."

"I give you my word."

One of the trappers who stood nearest the woods suddenly stumbled closer to the fires. "Someone comes!"

Elena turned her full attention back to the forest. The legion of amber eyes remained steady, but the distinct sound of crunching leaves and the shuffle of steps sounded. Sword tips moved in the direction of the noise.

Two dark shapes became distinct from the deeper gloom. One figure bore the amber eyes of the si'lura. The pair stopped just beyond the reach of the firelight.

"Who's there?" Gunther called out, stepping forward. "What do you want?"

A voice called back. "It is I . . . Nee'lahn!"

Meric gasped with relief.

Gunther glanced back to their party. Er'ril nodded his confirmation and moved to join the trapper. Elena followed him.

The two figures in the woods continued forward again. Elena saw with relief that it was indeed their friend. Nee'lahn was paler than usual and a trail of dried blood marred her forehead.

Meric hurried to her side. Nee'lahn allowed herself to be pulled into his embrace. "You're safe." Elena met Nee'lahn's gaze over the elv'in prince's shoulder. Her eyes denied Meric's words.

Firelight limned the second figure, reflecting from her snowy hair. There was a wildness about her that reminded Elena of Fardale. She stood straight and unafraid before so many blades.

"Thorn," Bryanna whispered with shock, naming this shape-shifter.

"You know her?" Elena asked, raising an eyebrow.

The trapper woman nodded. "She sold us the black stallion."

The shape-shifter turned her amber eyes toward them. "The stallion was bait," she said simply, crossing her arms.

"What do you mean?" Elena asked.

Pulling from Meric's arms, Nee'lahn answered. "The si'lura captured Rorshaf after the destruction of the Stone of Tor."

Thorn nodded and spoke coldly. "We searched the stallion's packs for any clue as to why a nyphai and her companions would wreak such havoc to our forests. We discovered nothing of use, but kept the horse in case it was needed again."

"Then the si'lura heard of the devastation around Moon Lake," Nee'lahn explained. "They planted Rorshaf in Woodbine, the closest village to the blasted region. They hoped whoever was to blame for the lake's destruction would end up there and perhaps recognize the horse, linking the two events."

"But in the end, the horse was not needed." Thorn glanced to Nee'lahn. "While spying in the town, I scented someone familiar."

Nee'lahn faced the others. "They hold us to blame for the destruction both here and up north."

"That's ridiculous," Er'ril said.

Elena touched his arm. "These are their lands, Er'ril." She faced Thorn, recognizing the hundreds of eyes watching from the wood. "What would you have of us?"

"The elder'root of our clan has called for you to stand before our council and explain yourselves. His summons will not be disobeyed."

"We don't have time," Er'ril argued. "We've a rendezvous."

Nee'lahn moved closer to them. "Calm yourself, plainsman. The Council of Wishnu meets just two days from here in the direction of the mountains. It would require no more than a single day to plead our case, and with the cooperation of the si'lura, we could make up this extra time."

"But we did nothing wrong," Er'ril said.

Nee'lahn raised one eyebrow. "Didn't we?"

Elena found Thorn's gaze on her. The shape-shifter stood proud, her face unreadable, but in her eyes, a font of sorrow shone.

"We'll go with them," Elena said finally, cutting into the dispute.

Er'ril frowned and motioned her aside. "We know little about these shape-shifters. Over the centuries, they've had little contact with outsiders."

"But they're also a people of Alasea, as much as any man. Their blood has been spilled to protect these lands, willingly or not. They deserve an explanation for the price they've paid and may yet pay again. These are their lands. I will not burn a path through them now for the sake of expediency."

Er'ril stared at her, his storm-gray eyes judging her resolve.

A shadow of a smile came unbidden to her lips as she read the deep lines of Er'ril's brow. He already agreed with her, but the guardian in him feared for her. She reached a hand to smooth those worried creases from the corner of his lips with the caress of her thumb.

He covered her hand with his own. "Elena . . . ," he whispered with a brush of breath.

She stared into his eyes. "You say we don't know these people. But we know Fardale, even Mogweed. At their core, they are a noble and just people."

"Fardale maybe," he grumbled, "but Mogweed is cut from a different cloth."

"I think you just need to look a little deeper into that one's heart. In many ways, he's more sensitive than his brother."

"If you say so . . ." Er'ril sounded little convinced, but he pulled her hand from his cheek and kissed her palm. The warmth of his lips threatened to melt the strength from her legs.

"I do," she said, and reluctantly pulled her hand away, closing her fingers around the warmth of his touch, trying to trap this other magick within her heart.

"So we go with the shape-shifters?" he asked.

She nodded. "It is time we face the path we've left behind us." She glanced to those gathered here, old companions and new. Her eyes found Thorn's. "If we are to forge a future for these lands, we must not neglect our past."

Er'ril circled her with his arm. "But can we survive the present?"

She leaned into him. "We can together."

GRESHYM ROCKED WITH THE MOTION OF THE HORSE, EXHAUSTED AND SADDLE sore. Daybreak neared. They had ridden all night. With the si'luran army as protectors, there was nothing to fear in the dark wood.

They had set out into the nighttime forest, heading off the main trail. Greshym was quickly lost without his magick senses, and from the way Er'ril kept searching the stars and the woods around him, it seemed the plainsman fared no better.

At first, there had been furtive whispers among the party. He heard snatches of familiar stories as Elena related her coming to power to Bryanna. He had listened with half an ear while pretending to drowse. Though he knew most of the story, some startling bits filled in gaps in his own knowledge. One point particularly intrigued him: She mentioned something about the ebon'stone transforming into heartstone.

He pondered this throughout the night. He had never heard of such a property. He sensed a key to power lay in the answer to this mystery.

Eventually, the entire party had grown quiet, too tired to speak. Only the plodding of the horses accompanied their progress. The shape-shifters out in the woods moved with uncanny stealth, lost in the gloom. But the party knew their captors were still out there, for the flash of amber eyes flickered periodically around them from the wood.

Greshym studied the approaching dawn. They were to rest with the rising sun and set out again by midday. The shape-shifter named Thorn had said they'd reach the si'luran gathering place by nightfall.

Greshym felt a noose growing ever tighter around his neck. The forest was thick with si'luran shape-shifters, and with each heavy plod of his horse's hoof, he was one step closer to where Shorkan waited beyond the mountains. He had enemies on all sides.

He reached to the tiny bit of magick remaining in his heart. It was nothing but the smallest drop, not even enough to loosen his bonds to relieve the chafing of the ropes. But it did allow him to sense a familiar heartbeat deep in the woods, a heart that had been bound to him before his magick had been evaporated. He sent a silent message to this other, encouraging his continued allegiance.

Follow, Rukh. Follow and stay hidden.

Through his connection, he felt the tiniest thrill of response.

Greshym sighed. For now, it was all he could do. The stump gnome kept pace with their party, trailing by a full league so as not to be caught. At least Rukh had managed to collect the bone staff Greshym had abandoned in the mud beside Moon Lake. The stave was empty of any magick, but like the stump gnome, it was a tool that could prove useful.

Narrowing his eyes, Greshym studied one other resource here, useless now, but full of possibility.

He watched Joach hanging in his saddle, drowsing, half asleep.

As the day brightened, so did Greshym's hopes. A plan twisted slowly into place in his head. Only two things were necessary: patience . . . and a fair amount of blood.

13

ELENA SOAKED HER FEET IN THE COOL WATERS OF A STREAM, HER BOOTS ON A mossy boulder beside her. She stretched a cramp in her back. They had traveled all the prior night and, after a short rest, a good portion of the day. She leaned back and stared at the sun shining through the branches. A fresh breeze swept along the stream, lifting the muggy air trapped under the dense canopy. Elena drew a deep breath. Summer was indeed upon them, but evening neared; the steaming sun would soon give way to the cool moon.

The crunch of boots drew her attention as Joach limped toward her, a grimace of pain on his face.

Elena scooted to the side and patted a seat. "Come soak. It feels wonderful."

Joach dropped to her side like a puppet whose strings had been cut. "I don't know if I could get my boots off—my ankles have swollen tight inside them." He shoved his feet, boots and all, into the water.

Elena patted her brother's gloved fingers, a small gesture of family. But he didn't seem to notice. He simply stared at the sun-dappled waters, his shoulders slumped with exhaustion.

"I used to ride the orchards all day," he mumbled. "And still come home and run my errands."

"Once this is over, we'll find a way to reverse the spell. I promise," she said.

But he seemed as deaf to her words as to her touch. "I can't stand even looking at him, knowing it's my own youth mocking me."

Elena glanced to Joach's hand. His fingers, once strong from picking apples and weeding the orchard, were now just bone and withered skin under the thin riding glove. But as she listened to her brother, she sensed that more was stolen from Joach than just youth. A good portion of his spirit and heart had vanished, too.

He slipped his hand to the staff across his knees; the foul thing now gave him more solace than his own flesh and blood. She studied the length of petrified gray wood, impregnated with jaundiced bits of crystal. She had put off a certain talk long enough. "Joach," she began, "what have you done to your staff?"

His eyes narrowed as he turned to her. "What do you mean?"

Elena recalled the night of the last full moon, when they had all been transported here. In the courtyard, she had seen Joach's staff aflame with elemental energies. But of more concern were the glowing strands of power that had linked her brother to the weapon. "I see you always wear a glove."

"So? It helps my grip. I have little strength anymore."

She knew Joach well enough to tell when he was lying. "I saw how you were linked to the staff," she said. "It was like when I bonded you to the poi'wood staff aboard the *Pale Stallion*. You've created a blood weapon, tied your spirit to the wood."

He remained silent for several long breaths. When he spoke, it was a strained whisper. "I have lost everything. My magic is all I have left, my only hope. I linked myself to it so I could wield it better."

"Joach . . ." Warning filled her voice. "Er'ril told me how such weapons, forged in blood and spirit, can become living things without conscience or mercy. Blood weapons can grow to corrupt their wielders."

Joach shook his head. "I won't let that happen. I only need the staff long enough to break this curse upon me. After that, I'll burn the foul thing myself." He lifted an arm and shook back his riding cloak to reveal his stumped wrist. "But before that happens, let me show you what it's capable of achieving."

Light shimmered over the end of his arm; then a hand bloomed into existence, appearing out of nothing. Elena stared in shock as he flexed the new fingers. The hand appeared as real as his other. The only difference was this one was smooth and unlined, a conjure of youth.

Joach picked up a rock, then lobbed it downstream. The splash dislodged a few frogs, sending them plopping into the creek. He held up his hand. "It's a dream sculpted into reality."

It took half a breath for Elena to find her voice. "Joach, you shouldn't have risked such dangerous magick."

"I had to." Bitterness lay thick on his tongue. "I've lost too much."

"But forging yourself into a blood weapon is not the answer. Why did you do this? Do you hope to conjure yourself a new body?"

Joach scowled. "That would be mere illusion. I'd still be aged and bent-backed behind the glamor."

"Then why? I said before, we'll find a way to regain your youth. I'm sure—"

"It's not just my youth," he interrupted. Tears misted his eyes. His face tightened as he held back a deeper emotion. He finally spoke in a strained sob. "It's Kesla . . ."

Elena sensed that there were words her brother had put off speaking. She remained silent.

"She was so beautiful."

"I remember."

"But it was more. The way she laughed so brightly. The heat of her touch, as if she always walked under the desert sun. And her eyes . . . They were the violet of a bottomless moonlit oasis."

"You loved her."

A tear rolled down his cheek. "But she was nothing."

Elena frowned at the sudden bitterness of his words.

"Nothing but a figment." He lifted his conjured hand and waved it away, casting it back to dream. He lowered his stump and turned again to his staff. "No more real than my hand."

Elena allowed him a quiet moment, then spoke firmly. "You're wrong. She wasn't mere dream. She lived, like any woman lives."

Joach shook his head, turning away and refusing to hear her.

"Who can say where any of us comes from?" she continued. "When our flesh is born of man and a woman, how does our spirit infuse our bodies? Or do you think we're all just so much clay?"

"Of course not."

"I met Kesla. She was not just sand and dream. She had as much spirit as any of us. And if her spirit was real, then so was she, no matter how she was born."

He sighed, clearly unsure.

Elena reached and grabbed his real hand, placing it between her two palms. "You loved her. Kesla could not have touched your spirit unless she was more than dream, unless she had the true spirit of life."

He pulled his hand away. "But does it matter anymore? She's gone."

Elena spoke softly. "As long as you remember her, her spirit will live through you."

Joach sagged. "How long will that last? With this aged body . . ." He shook his head.

She patted his knee. "We'll find a way through this, together."

He showed no response to her words, sinking again into his private thoughts.

Voices rose in argument nearby. Elena glanced over a shoulder. Er'ril marched with Harlequin toward them. She pulled her feet from the stream and grabbed her boots. Standing, she touched Joach on the shoulder.

He mumbled under his breath. "Go. I'm fine."

She heard the lie behind his words, but time would have to heal his heart. She turned to the others and crossed quickly in their direction, cutting them off. She did not want Joach disturbed. "What's wrong?" she asked.

Er'ril's face was flushed with anger. "Harlequin snuck off and spied upon Thorn and her people." He glared down at the small man. "He was caught."

Harlequin shrugged. "It's hard to sneak up on a people with all the senses of the forest's creatures."

"I warned you against aggravating them." Er'ril clenched a fist.

Harlequin rolled his eyes. "I don't remember bending my knee to you, plainsman. It's my hide, too, that's at risk here; I have the right to protect it as I see fit."

Elena held up a hand. "What happened after you were caught?"

Harlequin cast daggers with his eyes at Er'ril. "Nothing. They sent me back with my tail tucked, that's all."

Er'ril scowled. "Thorn was furious. She was shaking with anger."

"That's the way she always looks," Harlequin mumbled.

"What did she say?"

Er'ril sighed. "Nothing. She just strode back into the wood."

Harlequin shrugged his arms with a jingle of bells. "So no harm done."

"You don't know that," Er'ril spat back. "The si'lura are angry already. Provoking them—"

"I didn't provoke them. I just watched them."

"Enough," Elena declared. "What's done is done. Harlequin, in the future, I'd ask you to respect my liegeman's wishes. He speaks with my authority. And as I recall, you did bend your knee to me."

The small man bowed his head. "Yes, milady."

Er'ril crossed his arms.

Elena turned to him. "And Er'ril, when compared to the destruction of their forest home, I doubt Harlequin's spying will significantly slant their animosity one way or the other. And if he had learned anything of value—"

"He didn't," Er'ril interrupted.

"I never said that," Harlequin said innocently.

Both Elena and Er'ril focused on the man. "You heard something?" Elena asked.

"It wasn't much. They speak so much through their eyes, but Thorn was still in her woman's shape. And a comely shape, she has—that long white hair, the shape of her bare backside. I wouldn't mind—"

"Get on with it," Er'ril shouted.

Harlequin lifted an eyebrow. "What? Am I not allowed to appreciate the shape-shifting artistry of our captor?"

Er'ril glowered, his ruddy face growing darker.

"Please go on," Elena said.

Harlequin straightened the fall of his motley jacket. "As I was saying before being interrupted, Thorn still wore her womanly form. I guess some messages could not be readily exchanged from woman to deer. The antlered fellow needed plainer speech."

"What did she tell him?" Er'ril asked.

"She instructed our cloven-hoofed shape-shifter to run ahead and alert the council to our approach—and to let her father—the elder'root— know that neither Mogweed nor Fardale were with us."

"Mogweed and Fardale?" Er'ril crinkled his brow. "What do they have to do with any of this?"

"That's the strange part. She told her messenger to inform her father that, with the brothers missing, any hope of saving the forest's root was doomed."

Elena crinkled her brow. "Saving the forest's root?" She stared at the tall trees around her. Since they had left the trails, the woods had grown denser, thicker, older. The very air was heavy with the odor of loam and scent of green life. Nothing seemed amiss. And if something had been, Nee'lahn would surely have sensed it.

"What do Fardale and Mogweed have to do with any of this?" Er'ril asked.

Harlequin shrugged. "That's all I learned before being spotted."

"It makes no sense," Elena said.

"Maybe not, but—" Harlequin glanced over a shoulder, then dropped his voice. "—it does suggest that these si'lura have intentions that go be- yond what they speak aloud. Secrets meant only for their own people.

And if those shape-shifting brothers are somehow key to this . . ." Harlequin raised an eyebrow.

Elena frowned. "I don't understand the concern."

Er'ril's face grew grim. "To keep their secret, the si'lura might not let us go."

"They'd imprison us?"

"If we're lucky," Harlequin said. "There are more *permanent* ways of silencing us."

Elena's eyes widened.

Er'ril stared out at the shadowy woods, where a dark army waited. "We'd best tread lightly from here."

TRAILING THE OTHERS, MERIC RODE BESIDE NEE'LAHN THROUGH THE DARK forest. Night had fallen, and the moon had yet to rise. A single torch lit the way under the arched bower, carried by Thorn atop one of the trappers' horses. The forest around them had grown taller, spearing skyward in a tangle of branches. The stars were barely visible.

"I can't believe what I'm seeing," Nee'lahn whispered, drawing him back from the skies. "What an ancient growth of forest. Perhaps as old as all the Western Reaches. Some of these trees are found nowhere else in the world." She pointed to a tree with a trunk that rose in a straight spiral, throwing out branches at regular intervals. "That's a giant gnarl. They were thought to have vanished ages ago, but here one grows."

"I've seen old-growth forests like this before," Bryanna intruded, riding on the other side of Nee'lahn. She glanced behind them, at the empty path. Her voice filled with dread. "They dot the Reaches, but the si'lura guard such places. Trappers know better than to enter these lands. In the past, loggers have attempted to plunder the rich woods, but all who tried were slain by the shape-shifters. It is death to walk these lands."

Meric kept one hand on his reins and another on the hilt of his slender sword, but the cold touch of steel offered no reassurance. The si'lura had not bothered to take any of their weapons—which disturbed him more than if their captors had stripped them all bare.

"This grove here is one of the largest I've ever seen," Bryanna said in hushed tones. "It must stretch a full league in all directions."

"And it stretches even farther under the soil," Nee'lahn said, wonder still shining in her words. "The ancient woodsong here echoes up from depths beyond anything I've heard. It rivals Lok'ai'hera and grows richer with each step. It must reach the core of the world itself."

She was silent for a long moment, then spoke in heartfelt tones. "How I wish Rodricko could see this, hear this song."

Frowning, Meric appreciated none of her wonder. Shadows flowed to either side. Within this dark tide, flashes of amber revealed the continued presence of the army around them.

From up ahead, voices suddenly rose. Meric swung his attention forward. Their guide's torch had stopped at the bottom of a tall, forested hill. Horses and men gathered around the torch; then one broke away, traveling down the line as Harlequin trotted his horse back to them. "We've reached the council site," he said, pointing back to the hill. "Beyond the rise. We're to walk from here."

"Walk?"

Harlequin nodded, his gold eyes shining angrily. "We're to leave our gear with our mounts, including weapons. If anyone is caught with a blade at the council gathering, they will be slain upon the spot."

Meric gripped his sword hilt more tightly.

Harlequin must have noticed his motion. "Thorn says the valley beyond is sacred ground, and none must walk it armed."

Meric scowled and released his grip. He slid from his saddle, bristling with elemental energy. They might take his blade, but he was not going defenseless. He helped Nee'lahn down as the trappers also dismounted. Everyone loosened swords, axes, and bows from their bodies, cinching them to their mounts. Meric lashed his sword to his saddle.

Nearby, Harlequin remained on his horse. "You're also supposed to leave your boots here and walk the hill barefoot."

"What?" Meric asked, shocked by the strange request.

"Like Thorn said . . . sacred ground." Harlequin shrugged. "These are their rules, not mine." He kicked each of his own boots from his feet with deft moves, catching them in each hand, then leaped from his own saddle.

"We should respect their wishes," Nee'lahn said, stepping to a boulder to sit.

Meric grumbled under his breath but obeyed. Still standing, he used the toe of one boot to hold the other's heel. He pulled his foot free and placed it down. As his foot touched the soil, he suddenly felt as if someone had mounted a pack full of stones on his back. His balance teetered. Swinging his arms, he half stumbled, hopping back onto his booted foot. Standing on the one boot, the sudden weight lifted from his shoulders.

"Meric?" Nee'lahn asked, noticing his dance.

"I'm all right. Just dizzy from the long ride, I guess." He placed his foot back down, and the weight suddenly crashed upon his shoulders again. He grunted but kept his balance this time.

With concern on her face, Nee'lahn rose. But as she stood, she gasped and clutched at her chest.

"Nee'lahn!" He stepped to her, struggling under the weight.

She stared up at him, her face stricken. The glow of her skin had faded. Her honey-colored hair had become simple straw, her skin now more ashen than snowy white. It was as if her vitality had been drained away. "I . . . I can't hear woodsong anymore," she cried softly.

Meric sought to combat the extra weight on his shoulders by calling up his elemental magick, but he found the well of wind energy impossible to touch, though he sensed it was still there. He turned to the others around them. They stared at the pair with wrinkled brows.

"What's wrong?" Harlequin asked.

Meric had a suspicion. He lifted his foot from the ground, balancing on his one boot. He lifted an arm, and crackles of energy danced among his fingers. He again felt light on his feet. The power of wind and air was his again.

Then he brought his bare foot back down. As it touched the soil, the energy cascading about his fingers snuffed out, and the weight returned to his shoulders. "The land here . . . it somehow cuts us off from our elemental powers."

Nee'lahn had regained her composure, her eyes widening. "Meric is right."

"No wonder they want us to walk barefoot onto their sacred lands," Harlequin said. "No magick."

"They mean to take all our defenses away," Meric said. He stood on the strange soil. Was this what it felt to walk as an ordinary man? He took a few steps, struggling under the weight.

Nee'lahn joined him, reaching out with a hand. He took it, each seeking solace in another who could understand this plight.

"I've never felt like this," she whispered. "I can feel the vigor of root and loam in my heart, but I can't bring it forth into my blood."

"I know. It's like my magick is locked in a vault, and I've lost the key."

A call arose from up ahead. "We're being summoned," Harlequin said.

Meric spotted the torch borne by Thorn. Their guide had started up the slope. They were on the move again.

With a shudder, he shook out of his other boot. Once barefoot, Meric and Nee'lahn followed, hand in hand.

Reaching the foot of the hill, Meric spied Joach without his staff, half carried between Elena and Er'ril. A step behind them, Gunther climbed with Greshym locked in one of his meaty paws. The darkmage's wrists had been bound behind his back.

Meric began the long climb, struggling under the extra weight. He had never imagined how much his magick had been part of his body. Without it, the pull of the world upon his limbs seemed to have grown tenfold.

Nee'lahn breathed hard, as if trying to draw strength from the air. "I cannot hear even the faintest whisper of treesong. A moment ago, it filled the entire world. How could I be so deaf to it now?"

"It's the land here. It must dampen our elemental abilities, as Cho did to Greshym's magick."

"I've never heard of such an effect."

Meric nodded to the glowing torch. "It seems the si'lura are good at keeping their secrets."

Further talk was silenced by the climb. It took all their efforts to plant one foot in front of the other. Soon they lagged behind the others. The faint light from the torch vanished as Thorn crested the hill and continued over the rise. The woods grew darker around them. Only the moon, shining its gibbous face down upon them, lit their way.

"Only a little farther," Meric muttered. Nee'lahn nodded. Panting and sweating in the cool air, the pair followed the last of their party over the hill. At last, Meric saw what lay beyond.

"Sweet Mother," he exhaled. From the height, he could see leagues ahead. It wasn't a hill they had been climbing, but the lip of a gigantic bowl. Spread before them lay an oval valley, forested with trees that made the giants from before seem like mere twigs. Their branches were decorated with lanterns, as if the stars had fallen from the skies and scattered in the deep forest here. Larger fires also dotted the forest floor, shining up from below.

Nee'lahn gripped Meric's upper arm, fingers digging deep. "It cannot be! The trees . . ."

Meric shook his head. "I don't recognize them."

"How could you?" she mumbled, falling to her knees despite the grip on his arm. "They are the Old Ones."

He knelt beside her and studied the closest specimen. It rose from the valley floor and climbed high above the rim. Its bark was white, like a birch, but each wide leaf was the color of burnt copper, as if autumn had come early to this summer valley.

Nee'lahn glanced at him, tears on her cheek. "The Old Ones come from before even the koa'kona, from before our two peoples walked the world. It is from the Old Ones that all other trees descend." A sob escaped her. "We thought them gone, dead for countless centuries. During the time of the nyphai, all that remained of these ancients were a few isolated stumps, hollow and dead, lost in various deep forests. A grove such as this cannot exist." She implored him with his eyes. "The nyphai would have known!"

Meric stared out at the grove. "Perhaps not if they grew from this loam. As you said yourself, here you are deaf to any treesong. Maybe the Land itself hides this grove."

"But why?" she asked, staring again at the forest.

He shook his head. "The si'lura may know."

Nee'lahn pulled herself to her feet. "I must find out. I must commune with these ancients."

Meric helped her down the slope, trailing in the footprints of the others. Only now did he notice the shapes moving among the fires below. He had thought the number of shape-shifters that had accompanied them was an army, but below was a gathering a hundredfold larger. As he worked down the trail into the ancient valley, he stared at those around him. Animals of every ilk moved through the woods: lumbering bears, fleet deer, loping wolves, slinking woodland cats. Winged creatures swooped and dove: eagles, rocs, giant golden hawks. But these beasts were but a small fraction of the gathering. Most denizens of this grove wore a blended mix of features.

A small boy ran past their trail. Instead of hair, he bore a crown of feathers and trailed a long, furred tail. He paused, staring wide-eyed at the strangers, amber eyes aglow.

"Finch!" a woman called sharply. She stepped from around a noosegill bush. She was slender and tall, her bare skin covered with a sleek pelt of striped black-and-white fur. "Get away from these strangers."

The boy cocked his head like a bird, then glanced to his elder. His eyes flared brighter as he silently communicated.

"Don't argue with me. Get to our fire!" She pointed an arm.

The boy dashed off into the woods, his tail a flag behind him. The woman studied them through narrowed lids, then spun faster than an eye could follow, leaping away after her child.

Meric lost her among the trees and bushes. But around him, a kaleidoscope of shapes and configurations kept them company. Most seemed drawn by curiosity, but other faces lit with enmity and wariness.

Meric increased his pace, closing the distance with their own group, where Bryanna watched the spectacle with her mouth hanging open. "I never imagined there were so many. These must be the si'lura from this entire region, maybe from all the Western Reaches."

Meric studied the spread of fires throughout the valley. The trapper woman could be correct.

Ahead, Elena and Er'ril carried Joach between them, while Harlequin and Gunther flanked the darkmage Greshym. Thorn called for a stop. "Wait here. I must go forward alone to announce your presence." She disappeared ahead.

Elena glanced to Meric and Nee'lahn. "Joach thinks the ground here saps his elemental strength, but he's so exhausted that he's not sure."

"Your brother is correct," Nee'lahn said. "We're cut off from our magick."

"We've entered a nexus." Greshym spoke casually, but Meric sensed a thread of surprise in the other's voice.

"What's a nexus?" Elena asked.

Greshym shrugged.

Gunther shook him. "Answer the lass."

Greshym glanced to his large, bearded companion. "Gunther, being a trapper, I imagine you've a lodestone to find your way through these endless woods. May I see it?"

The man frowned, but his sister nodded to him. With a grumble, he reached into a pocket of his jerkin and pulled out a satchel. He dumped its contents onto his palm: a small bowl and a chunk of cork with an imbedded sliver of lodestone.

"Lodestone is tuned to the world's energy," Greshym explained. "Used with skill, it will point toward true north."

"So?" Gunther said, speaking all their thoughts.

Greshym nodded to the large man's hand. "Go ahead and try."

The big man snarled, but again his sister encouraged him. "Do as he asks, Gunther."

The trapper dropped to one knee, settled the bowl, then removed a leather water flask from his hip. He filled the bowl, then floated the cork atop the water's surface.

Meric leaned closer. The cork and lodestone spun slightly as if trying to center on true north, but instead of settling into position, it continued to spin, faster and faster. It became a blur in the center of the cup, water sloshing from the sides.

"A nexus," Greshym said. "Here the Land's energies are in flux. As with the lodestone, an elemental will be unable to align himself here." He nodded to Meric and Nee'lahn. "You haven't lost your powers. You simply can't tune yourself to the Land's energy."

Meric watched the lodestone spin.

From up ahead, music suddenly welled out into the night. Everyone turned to look. Under the spread of branches, flutes and reeds piped hauntingly, accompanied by the beat of stretched leather and hollow wood. Around them, the babble and murmurs of those gathered in the valley grew hushed, and as the silence grew, the music seemed to swell louder.

Thorn strode toward them, no longer bearing her torch. "The council awaits," she announced, and waved for them to follow.

Gunther packed his lodestone away, and they all marched after their guide. Nee'lahn slipped her hand into Meric's. As they walked, she stared out at the old forest. "A nexus . . . and here stand the Old Ones."

"Do you think it means anything?"

Her eyes squinted, and she shook her head.

Meric sensed she was holding something back, but he also knew better than to press her. She needed time to ponder something in her own heart. So he continued in silence.

With each step, the music quickened around them. Horns joined the flutes, deep and mournful, while the drums continued to pound solemnly. Thorn's pace became more brisk.

Er'ril helped Joach along. "I don't like this. We could be walking into a trap."

"Trap or not," Harlequin said, "it seems we've no choice but to run headlong into it."

Meric glanced behind him. Thousands of amber eyes stared in their direction—not at them, but toward where they marched.

"The forest opens ahead," Nee'lahn said.

Meric swung his attention around. Thorn led the way under an arch of branches. Beyond the threshold, moonlight shone brighter, unimpeded by the usual thick canopy. Bathed in silver, a wide meadow opened, gently sloping down from the ring of forest around them.

Meric studied the open glade.

Before them, a gentle slope of grass descended toward a wide central pool. An island in its center humped from the dark waters, and from this small spit of land, one of the largest Old Ones grew. Its trunk was twice as thick as any of the other giants, its branches a crown of ivory and gold.

The group stared out at the sight, stunned. The hidden musicians had halted their playing at the appearance of their party. A deep silence pressed down upon the valley.

Below, at the foot of the giant tree, the pool's waters were not still. They slowly churned, flowing in a continual swirl around the central island as if stirred from below.

Meric knew what he was seeing.

"The heart of the nexus," Nee'lahn whispered beside him.

ER'RIL HAD LESS INTEREST IN THE POOL AND THE GIANT TREE THAN IN THE ring of folk around the water's edge. A group of twenty men and women draped in simple white cloaks stood guard around the tree's pool. Each wore a garland of coppery leaves in his or her hair.

"The Council of Wishnu," Thorn intoned solemnly. She glanced to their party. "Come."

Under the heavy silence, the group followed Thorn down the slope. Ahead the elders of the si'lura walked the edge of the pool to gather before it. Er'ril kept one eye on them and another on the surrounding forest. Though he spotted not a single pair of amber eyes out in the woods, he sensed the attention and focus of an entire people upon this meeting.

Er'ril passed Joach to Harlequin. Free, he motioned Elena to step ahead with him. It would be up to them to convince this council that the damage to their forest had been done to protect against a greater evil. But as he stared at the hard faces, he found no sympathy there.

Thorn stepped before a broad-shouldered man who towered over his brethren. She dropped to one knee. "Father."

His face warmed ever so slightly. "Rise, Child. This night we will forgo formality."

Thorn climbed to her feet. She turned to the others. "Father, these are the folk you've instructed my hunters to bring before you."

The tall man stared at the assembled group. "I am the elder'root," he said. "I've already been informed of who you are." His eyes settled upon Elena with clear suspicion. "And I've heard about your claims of innocence, of how a greater battle beyond our forest has resulted in the recent bouts of devastation."

Er'ril stepped forward. "What we claim is true."

The man's attention never diverted from Elena. "That will be judged this night."

Beyond him, the waters of the central pool began to churn more vigorously, as if sensing the leader's agitation. Er'ril caught a glimpse of something moving through those dark waters, but when he tried to focus on it, it vanished.

Elena moved to Er'ril's side. She stood straight before the other's hard gaze. "Ask us what you will. We will answer with full honesty. We wish to hide nothing. But first let me assure you that the destruction to your homelands was not out of malice to your people or these lands. At each instance, a greater menace was thwarted."

The leader's eyes flicked toward Greshym. "So we have heard."

"If he's heard so much, why are we here?" Harlequin mumbled behind them.

The small man's whisper did not pass unnoticed. "You are here to prove what you speak," the elder'root said. "And to answer other questions."

Elena spoke again. "We will do all we can to help you understand our cause and purpose."

The leader nodded. "Well spoken, lass. Then tell us what happened to Mogweed and Fardale."

Elena glanced to Er'ril, the question catching her by surprise. Er'ril answered for her. "The twin brothers came to us frozen in their forms, one a wolf, the other a man."

"This I know. It was I who banished them from our forests."

Er'ril nodded. "They told us how they were sent from the forest because they could no longer shape-shift."

The leader neither acknowledged nor denied his words. "And now? What has become of the brothers?"

Er'ril grimaced. "Through the magick of a healing snake's poison, their two bodies have merged, fused into one form. Fardale rules the body during the day, Mogweed at night. But once again they are able to shift like true si'lura."

The leader looked stricken, and the other members of the council began to murmur. Finally, the leader held up an arm, silencing them. "Is what you say the truth?"

Er'ril nodded once, standing straight-backed. "I swear on my very honor."

The elder'root closed his eyes. "Then what we had hoped is lost forever." The leader of the si'lura sighed, his shoulders slumping. "Your war has done more damage to our forest than mere drowned woods and blasted lakes. It has corrupted the hope of our entire people." He turned to face the council. The members' eyes glowed a richer amber as they communicated to one another, conferring, judging.

Thorn stepped to Er'ril's side. "My father had placed too much hope upon Mogweed and Fardale." Her words were bitter. "We've wasted over two winters on the words of a long-dead prophet."

Er'ril faced the huntress. "Maybe it's time you shared what you've kept hidden. Elena bears enough magick that she could have burned her way through your pack of hunters, but she came here because her heart aches for those innocents harmed in our war. She came to make amends, to explain, to hide nothing from your people."

Elena had stepped to his side. Er'ril found his hand in hers. She squeezed his fingers.

He continued, letting his passion shine. "Fardale . . . even Mogweed . . . have proven themselves brave allies for our cause. If there is more we should know, more that could either help them or help us understand what's happened to them, then you owe it to both them and us to explain."

Thorn's expression grew more pained with each word. Finally she could hold her tongue no longer. "Don't you think I want to help them?" she demanded. "Fardale was my mate." She turned away. "But my father had no choice. Only after they had left the forests, only after I was found to be with child, did my father tell me the true reason for the pair's banishment."

"Tell us," Er'ril urged. Elena nodded at his side. Slowly the others gathered around, listening in, but keeping a respectful distance.

Thorn met Elena's gaze, her eyes glimmering with tears. "The story starts in the distant past, when the forests of the Western Reaches were young. It is said that our people were born out of the Land itself, birthed to minister to this great forest." She glanced over to the pool and the giant tree. "Our earliest stories say that the first of our people rose from this very pool. Born of water, our flesh flows, allowing us to share the forms of all the forest's creatures." The huntress stared out at the ring of woods. "This is a sacred place. These are the first trees to grow from these lands."

"The Old Ones," Nee'lahn whispered behind them.

Thorn nodded. "From these trees, all others were born. The entire Western Reaches flowed out from this grove, as did our people. Our two lives are linked."

"Are you saying you're bonded to these trees as the nyphai are to their own?" Elena asked.

Thorn shook her head, glancing to Nee'lahn. "No, our linking is different." Thorn stared back at the pool and the giant white-barked elder.

"Rather than one tree for one individual, our entire people are bonded to that sole tree. We are its children."

A stunned silence spread through the group. "How could that be?" Nee'lahn asked. "You yourself gave birth to Fardale's child."

Thorn sighed. "It is only our *spirits* that are tied to the tree, not our *bodies*. Each new si'lura born is spiritually linked to the tree. It is our Spiritual Root. Without this connection, we'd fade . . . first our ability to shift, then our very lives."

"No wonder the secrecy," Harlequin whispered at Er'ril's shoulder.

Er'ril glanced to the small man, reading the significance behind his narrowed gaze. *Would they be allowed to leave with this intimate knowledge?*

Er'ril swung around with a frown. Once started down this path, there was no going back. "What does this have to do with Fardale and Mogweed?" he grumbled to Thorn.

Thorn nodded. "I'm coming to that, but first I must tell of a threat that arose here five centuries ago."

"That was when Alasea was attacked by the Dark Lord," Er'ril noted.

"We know little of such matters," Thorn said. "But during that time, a great shaking rocked our lands. It lasted three days and nights. Trees toppled, rivers were diverted, and the ground split into chasms."

Er'ril nodded. "I remember those quakes. They occurred as the southern plains of Standi were sunk by the Dark Lord, forming the swamps and bogs of the Drowned Lands."

Thorn narrowed one eye. "You remember the quakes? How could that be?"

Er'ril waved away her query. "Go on. What happened after the ground shook?"

Thorn stared suspiciously a moment, then went on. "Even here in our homeland grove, we lost half our ancient trees."

Nee'lahn groaned. "So many of the Old Ones lost . . ."

"But the true damage was not known for another century." The huntress stared back at the central tree. "The Spirit Root was also somehow sickened by the shaking. The leaders of that time noticed—"

"Thorn," a voice interrupted sternly, cutting through her words.

They turned to find the eyes of the council upon them again. The elder'root stood before them, his face hard. "Thorn, you speak out of turn."

"Father, they have a right to know."

"The secrets of the si'lura—"

"—are going to doom us all," Thorn snapped. "For too long, we've turned our backs to the world beyond our forests. This blindness is as much to blame for the destruction in the Western Reaches as these folks here."

Her father's expression darkened. "That is not for you to decide."

Thorn clamped her lips tight, folding her arms.

The elder'root turned to Er'ril and Elena. "There is a way to judge your words," he said. "An ancient ritual used by the si'lura to divine the truth of your heart."

"And what is this ritual?" Er'ril asked.

The tall man swung an arm toward the central pool. At his signal, the council retreated to the water's edge, circling around the banks of the pool. "The Root must weigh your spirit."

Thorn gasped. "Father, that's unfair! The Spirit Root has not responded in ages."

Her father's eyes flashed. "Again, Daughter, I'll ask you to watch your tongue, or I'll have you taken from my sight."

Thorn's face reddened, but she obeyed.

Er'ril stepped forward. "Tell us what we must do to prove ourselves."

The elder'root stared another moment at his daughter, then turned again to Er'ril. Beyond him, the council had resumed their positions around the pool, but now they had joined arms. A gap in their ranks remained. The spot awaited their leader to complete the circle.

The elder'root spoke to their group. "The Root must judge one of your party. If you speak the truth, the Spirit of the Root will rise and acknowledge you. If you speak with a false heart, you will be shunned."

Elena stepped around Er'ril. "I will take on this task."

"No." He grabbed Elena's arm. "You mustn't risk yourself."

She freed her arm, gently but firmly. "We will honor their custom."

"Then let me be the one to be judged."

Elena turned her back on the council, faced him, and stepped closer. Her voice dropped to an intimate whisper. "Er'ril, I need to do this." Her eyes were pained as she stared up at him.

He reached toward her cheek, wanting to soothe that ache. But he dropped his hand. He recognized the desire in her heart. Elena *wanted* to be judged. The sorrow and tragedy of the past half moon weighed on her, and here was a chance for her to lighten her burden, to gain acknowledgment that their cause was just, that the innocents lost in this battle had died for a true reason.

He took her hand instead. "Elena . . ."

"I'll be careful." She leaned into him. "And I'm not defenseless. My magicks have not been weakened by the nexus. Being blood-borne, my powers are still my own."

He lifted her gloved hand and pressed it against her heart. "Still, remember where lies your greatest strength."

She moved her hand to his chest. "How could I forget?"

Er'ril was overwhelmed by a desire to kiss the woman he loved. It took all his restraint to resist. A tremble passed through his form. His breathing grew deeper.

Elena must have sensed this war of emotions and broke the stalemate. She leaned up and kissed his lips softly, a mere brush of breaths, the touch of skin on skin. She spoke between their lips. "I'll let nothing keep us apart."

Her touch and words broke his control. He crushed her against him, turning a soft kiss into something deeper, a heat that spoke of passions yet unfathomed. But now was not the time to explore those depths. Both of them knew this truth and broke away at the same time. Only their eyes remained upon one another.

Harlequin mumbled, "Maybe a dip in that cool pool will do them both some good."

Elena glanced to the small man, shattering the moment.

"If you're ready," the elder'root said, "the Spirit Root awaits."

Elena nodded, but Er'ril caught her hand one more time. "Take care."

She squeezed his fingers. "I will. I won't forget my promise." She turned and joined the elder'root.

As they walked away, Elena's words echoed in his heart: *I'll let nothing keep us apart.* He prayed it was a promise she could keep.

The group followed, but only Elena was allowed through the ring of council members. Once past them, she stepped to the edge of the pool. She turned to the elder'root as the shape-shifter closed the gap in the circle. "Show me what I must do."

The council leader slipped a cord from around his neck. Hanging from the loop was a long splinter of white wood, polished to a sharp point. He handed it to her. "The *syn*, a sliver of the Spirit Root itself."

Elena accepted the talisman.

"You must pierce a finger and mark the pool with your blood."

"Blood? Why blood?"

"The Root must taste your essence to judge your heart." The elder'root joined hands with his other council members, completing the circle. As he did so, the flesh of his hand melted into his neighbors'.

Er'ril saw this effect spread around the ring. Shape-shifter melted into shape-shifter, forming a ring of flowing flesh, connecting through their arms, encircling the pool and mystical tree.

Elena stared at the sliver of wood. "Perhaps we should choose another."

"The circle is formed and cannot be broken," the Elder'root intoned, his voice deeper, more resonant.

Elena's lips thinned to hard lines. She faced the pool and stripped off a glove. With her back turned, no one seemed to notice the ruby hue to her skin.

Er'ril stepped closer, his own hands clenched into fists.

A voice spoke at his side. Thorn still wore a sour expression. "It is nothing to fear, plainsman. Ever since the quakes five centuries ago, the Root has grown sedate. It has been ages since the Root has stirred from the sacred pool."

Er'ril prayed the huntress was correct. "Then tell me what happened here," he urged. "What happened five centuries ago?"

Thorn glanced to her father as a chanting arose from the circle. She hesitated, then leaned closer. "The Root is the living heart of our people," she said with a nod to the tree. "It has given guidance and foresight to our people for untold centuries. It speaks with the voice and wisdom of the ages. But after the quakes, the Root went silent. It would occasionally stir, but all communion with the elder'root, the one chosen by the Spirit Root to lead our people, ceased. The last time the Root even stirred was to select my father from the council to replace the last leader."

"But what do Mogweed and Fardale have to do with all this?"

Thorn sighed, then spoke. "The last time the Root spoke, on the final day of the quakes, it communed with the elder'root of that age. The Root said that a dark time lay ahead, but that one day, twin brothers would be born amongst us. These twins would be known by their curse and would have to be sent blind into the world. The pair would mark either a new beginning for us or herald our end, depending on whether they ever found a cure."

"And this newest twist of the curse upon the brothers?"

Thorn shook her head. "It bodes the end of our people."

Across the way, the chanting ended, and the elder'root nodded from his position. "The moon nears its highest point. Let us begin."

Elena turned. Within the circle of flowing flesh, she positioned the syn of the si'lura against a ruby finger of her right hand.

"Under this night's moon," the elder'root continued solemnly, "let the Root taste the blood of the accused!"

Elena pierced her finger with the splinter of white wood. The effect was immediate and dazzling. The syn burst into flame, flashing bright, then burned instantly to ash.

A stunned cry arose from the joined council.

Elena held up her empty hands as ash fell between her fingers.

"Blasphemer!" someone cried out from the council ring.

Er'ril started toward her, but a sudden upwelling roiled the pool's waters. "Elena!" he called in warning.

She glanced back to him, her expression confused.

Behind her, the waters suddenly exploded upward. A giant beast shot out of the waters, drenched and slithering skyward. It was a monstrous white worm, draped with tentacles and writhing feelers.

"The Root!" Thorn gasped. "It wakes!"

With her words, Er'ril recognized his initial mistaken impression. The creature of the pool was *not* a worm, but a dripping length of white-barked root, trailing with squirming rootlets and fibers.

The shocked cry of the council turned to one of wonder.

"The Spirit Root has found you worthy!" the Elder'root shouted. "It stirs from its depths at long last!"

Elena had been knocked back by the sudden uprising of the living root. She crouched, swamped by the surge of water. "What am I to do now?" she shouted back to the council members.

"Nothing!" the elder'root said. "The Root acknowledges you! Your heart is judged pure. The trial is over!"

Elena backed away from the pool.

"It's over?" Er'ril mumbled.

The joined council members began to separate, hands re-forming and letting go of one another. As the chain broke, the length of root began to subside back into the pool.

Thorn's voice filled with wonder. "I had never thought to see the Root stir. This is a wondrous night. It gives us all hope."

The elder'root echoed his daughter's sentiment. "Perhaps all's not lost."

Elena turned to face the si'luran leader. She appeared still shaken. Her gaze brushed Er'ril's. She silently nodded that she was fine.

The length of Root had sunk until only a few rootlets waved above the waters. But a sudden swirl closer to the bank caught Er'ril's eye. A tangle of white roots burst from the shallows and grabbed Elena. In a heartbeat, she was jerked from her feet and dragged high into the air.

"Elena!" Er'ril shouted, leaping forward. The elder'root fell back from the attack. Thorn also seemed stunned. He ran past them both.

Trapped in the net of writhing roots, Elena struggled futilely. Her cry reached his ears. "Er'ril!" Then with the speed of a cracking whip, the tangle of roots jerked their captive into the pool and away. A loud splash marked the impact.

Er'ril slipped in the slick mud and slid on his knees to the edge of the pool. Water sloshed the banks, but grew quickly still. The moonlit pool, shaded by the branches of the giant tree, was as black as pitch. Nothing could be seen in its depths.

He shoved up, ready to dive in, but Thorn gripped his arm. "It is death to enter those waters. The pull of the current will drag you down, too."

Er'ril knocked her hand away and faced the waters, searching, desperate, a prayer on his lips. "Elena . . ."

14

Writing in the tangle, Elena held her breath in a strained panic. Her eyes were stretched wide, seeking some means of escape. Darkness enveloped her, and a chill reached down to her bones. The water's pressure grew on her ears as she was dragged ever deeper.

Desperate for escape, she reached to the chorus of wild magicks in her heart and drove them toward her wounded hand. In the darkness, a crimson torch bloomed, blazing bright—her wit'ch fire, bleeding forth from her pricked finger. The mere touch had burned the si'luran talisman to ash. Perhaps it could free her now.

But a part of her balked from such action. She sensed she could burn her way out of this tangle, but if she attacked with her magickal fire, what would be the consequence? She pictured the entire tree falling to ash like the sliver of the syn. If the tree were destroyed, what of the si'lura? Could she risk an entire people? Was her own life worth such a price? She understood her role in prophecies and portents. She knew the fight against the Dark Lord overshadowed all. But here and now, the fate of an entire people hung in the balance.

The pressure continued to build in her ears. Tiny lights began to dance in her vision from the lack of air. If she were to free herself, she would have to act now.

She blazed the torch of her magick brighter. *Don't make me do this . . .*

In the cold depths, nothing answered.

Her chest burned for air.

She closed her eyes and reached out with her wit'ch fire. Faces flashed across her mind's eye: Fardale, Mogweed, even Thorn, the proud huntress standing before her father. She remembered Aunt My, a shape-shifter who had loved her like a daughter. And out amongst the forests, a milling throng yet waited. So many other stories, so many other lives. Was hers so much more important?

Elena curled her outstretched fingers into a fist, snuffing out her magick. There were some costs she wasn't willing to pay. She stopped her struggles and gave in to the chill.

As she relaxed her panic, words quietly sifted into her awareness, spoken with a familiar voice: *Child . . . of blood and stone . . .*

It took her a moment to recall where she had heard those same words before. Her nose filled with the memory of woodsmoke. Her ears remembered the screech of a hunting predator. It was back during the orchard fire, the pyre that had marked the beginning of her long journey. She and Joach had sought shelter in the hollow husk of a great tree. She had given the giant a name: *Old Man.* The night they had sheltered there, she had heard this same voice. She remembered those words: *Child . . . of blood and stone . . . a boon . . . seek my children . . .*

Here it was again. Words filled her head. *Child . . . of blood and stone . . . heed me . . .*

Elena found it hard to concentrate. Her heart pounded in her ears. The dance of lights before her eyes grew more flurried as the lack of air swooned her. Nee'lahn had called these ancient, primitive trees the *Old Ones.* Was that ancient stump, the Old Man, one of these same trees?

Words formed in her head: *Heed me . . . Breathe . . .*

Elena had no choice but to obey. Her strained chest heaved. Water rushed in through her mouth and nose, choking, gagging, sweeping with a cold weight into her chest.

Breathe . . .

And to her surprise, she realized she could. The sense of suffocation dissolved away. She breathed in and out. It was a strange sensation, inhaling and exhaling the cool waters. The tiny sparks of light vanished from her vision.

Breathe the living waters . . .

The tangle of roots fell away, releasing her, a soft glow arose from the smaller roots, a pure white light. She did not need spellcast eyes to recognize the elemental energy here. The glow spread down the rootlets to the main taproot. A blaze of light grew under her, and with it came a deep warmth, driving off the water's chill.

She floated in place. With her lungs heavy with water, her natural buoyancy seemed to be thwarted.

She spoke into the waters, another odd sensation with water moving through her mouth. The words were muffled to her own ears, but she sensed someone listening. "Who are you?"

We are the Guardians, the Old Ones, the Root of the world. You have been found worthy.

Elena's brow crinkled.

You chose that which is greater than one's own self.

Elena slowly understood. She had chosen not to burn the spiritual tree, protecting the fate of a people over her own life. This had been a test, one she had passed. Still, a bit of anger flared inside her.

Her emotions must have been sensed. *You will be tested again, child of blood and stone . . . this we know. Next time it will be far worse.*

Elena felt the truth of these words, and a shiver of fear traced through her. "Why am I here?" she asked. "What do you wish of me?"

Our children . . . the folk of flowing water and flesh . . .

"The si'lura?"

She sensed agreement. *It is time for them to leave the forests. To protect their home, they must now abandon it.*

"Leave? Where will they go?"

To where you take them.

Elena felt a surge of shock. "Where I take them?" She stared down at the glowing mass of roots. "Why me?"

Across the mountains, a dark root worms toward the world's heart. To protect itself, the world pulls its reach back to its core, curling down upon itself.

"I don't understand."

The time of our guardianship is over.

The words grew fainter, the glow below her ebbing. Elena sensed that the Spirit Root must have lain dormant for centuries, storing its last energies for this final burst of communication. Now it was quickly fading.

She who came before you foretold your coming . . . foretold this dark tide . . .

"Who?"

The ancient speaker seemed to have grown deaf to her words. *She waits for you . . . She knew you would come . . .*

The glow of the Root flared brighter. Elena hoped it was a sign of renewed vitality, but the surge quickly faded again. Below her, something stirred, rising from the depths toward her.

She knew you would come . . . A twisting cord of root snaked upward. Something held in its glowing grip was thrust at her; she had no choice but to take it. She stared in horror at what lay in her hands . . . at the rose-carved handle.

Lead our children with this sign . . . The voice was a dwindling whisper. *Take them where they must stand* . . .

"Wh-where is that?" Elena pleaded.

To the Twins . . . the Twins . . . the Twins . . .

With each fading echo, the glow subsided, ebbing away into the waters until only darkness lay around her.

The Spirit Root had died—and with it, so did the magicks in the waters.

At that instant, Elena found it impossible to breathe. Her lungs, a moment ago filled with living water, now held only cold pond water. She choked and gagged; leaden limbs fought the pull of the depths. She craned her neck and spotted the bare glimmer of moonlight, impossibly far away. She struggled, but the face of the moon grew smaller as she was sucked downward.

A blackness that had nothing to do with the depths closed around her.

Er'ril . . . help me . . .

CROUCHED AT THE BANK, ER'RIL STARED INTO THE SACRED POOL, HIS HEART pounding in his ears. The others gathered around him—his own party and the council members.

Earlier, his desperate need to dive in after Elena had diminished as the waters had begun to glow. The shine from the deep had cast the surface of the pool to silver.

"Pure elemental energy," Nee'lahn had whispered.

The elder'root had tears in his eyes. "The Spirit of the Root! I hear the echo of its voice."

Thorn had taken her father's hand in her own. "It's a miracle."

Er'ril had known that Elena was alive—but for how long? With his heart clenched like a fist in his chest, he had watched the waxing and waning of the pool's glow, ready to leap at any moment.

And then the pool had gone dark and quiet.

Er'ril turned to the elder'root. "Do you still hear the voice of the Root?"

The stricken look on the man's face was answer enough. The leader of the si'lura fell to his knees.

Thorn dropped beside him. "Father!"

"What is going on?" Er'ril asked. "What about Elena?"

The elder'root dug his hands into the muddy bank. "It's gone," he whispered.

Er'ril swung back to the pool. "No!" With panic tightening his chest, he dove straight into the depths. The water's chill struck him immediately, but fear fired his blood. He kicked and swept his arms, driving down into the dark.

Elena . . .

He felt a tugging, toward the depths below, and hope surged in his chest. Was it some magick of Elena's? Then the gentle pull became an inescapable drag. It was not her magick, he realized, but the pool's current. He was trapped in the vortex. He fought the tide, but after a frantic moment, he let his resistance go. Elena was down here somewhere. Let the current take him to the bottom—that is, if there *was* a bottom to the endless pool.

As the darkness around him grew complete, he lost sense of his surroundings. Was he traveling up or down now? The only way he could measure was by the growing pressure on his ears. His chest, too, felt the water's weight, as if the pool were squeezing the air from his lungs.

Thorn had been right. It was death to enter these swirling waters. But death was a small price to pay for a chance to reach Elena, if only to hold her one last time.

Er'ril . . . *help me* . . .

At first, he was sure it was his strained mind that had voiced this plea. But his heart could not deny the hope. *Elena!*

From out of the darkness, a glimmer of silver caught his eye from far below, glowing with its own light. The current swirled him down toward the feeble light.

As he neared, he saw the shine came from a rod of silver—clutched in the grip of a dark figure that spun in an eddy of the current, limp and lifeless.

Er'ril kicked his way over to Elena. In the glow, he saw her eyes open but sightless. He swam up to her, pulling her into his arms. At least he would have his last wish before he died. He clutched her hard to his strained chest.

Then he felt it—the beat of her heart against him.

She lived!

He struggled for some way to free them both. He searched, but darkness lay all around them. They were but a mote of light in a raging current. *Elena* . . .

There was no answer this time.

He stared down into her face, then her hands. They shone ruby in the light from the silver object. He saw that it was not a rod, but a sword, shining with its own inner light. Elena's fingers clung instinctively to the magickal blade.

His lungs on fire, Er'ril freed a hand and grabbed the hilt of the sword. If he could not awake Elena, perhaps he could rouse the wit'ch!

He stared into Elena's slack face once more. *Forgive me!*

He drew the sword from between her palms as if unsheathing it from a scabbard. The fine blade sliced through her skin, and a bloom of blood flowed free.

Elena jerked as if struck by lightning.

In his head, a wailing exploded, a chorus of wild lusts and madness.

Er'ril resisted the urge to kick away. Instead he clung to the woman he loved, his arms and legs wrapping tight around her. Blood flowed between them, a mix of ice and fire, while the screams of wild magick howled all around them.

Er'ril squeezed his eyes tight. *Elena, come back to me . . .*

MERIC STOOD WITH THE OTHERS BY THE BANK OF THE POOL.

Nee'lahn spoke at his shoulder. "The waters . . ." She pointed an arm. "They no longer churn."

Meric realized she was right. The swirl of the waters had ceased. The surface of the pool was flat and featureless.

"The nexus has ended," Greshym said. "The world has cut off this channel to its heart."

As if hearing him, a strange howl rose from the pool like a mist. The cry sailed off into the night and away. No one spoke for a long breath.

Then the elder'root lunged up from where he had been kneeling, lost in his grief. He faced the group now, his furious eyes taking them all in. "You all did this! You and that demoness!"

Thorn tried to put a restraining hand on her father, but he shook her away.

Meric met his challenge without flinching. "This is not our doing."

Thorn stepped between them, her stance pure wolf. "What has happened here?"

Meric and the elder'root stared each other down.

Her father answered, froth on his lips. "The Spirit Root is dead! Slain by their demoness!"

"She would not have done that," Meric spat back. "Not even to save her own life!" As much as it trembled his heart, he knew his words to be true.

Thorn must have sensed his passion and held up her arms, urging restraint. "Father, we should give this some thought before—"

A gust of wind swirled into the sacred valley. Leaves tumbled from above, a fall of copper as thick as a heavy snowfall.

The elder'root glanced up. The leaves fell from the branches overhead, cascading down, leaving limbs bare. The pool became covered with a raft of fallen leaves. "There is your answer, Daughter! The Spirit has left us, destroyed by these heathens!"

A great cry rose from the valley's edges. All the ancient trees were shedding their leaves, as if laying their own death shrouds at their rooted feet.

"All the Old Ones," Nee'lahn murmured, "all dying."

"Step aside, Daughter," the elder'root said with thick menace. "Before our people die, I will see the blood of these desecrators darken our soil."

The elder'root hunched where he stood; then with a roar, he burst outward, his cloak shredding as the beast inside him was unleashed. Black fur sprouted; a muzzle of fanged teeth pushed forth with a roar. Hands became heavy paws of razored claws. The huge bear rose on muscled legs and bellowed its rage.

Thorn backed from the display. "Father! No!" She barely dodged a heavy swat meant to knock her aside.

Meric stepped past her "Go, girl. This isn't your fight." He crouched, ready to meet the challenge.

With a howl, the bear leaped at Meric, claws extended to rip flesh from bone. But before the bulk could hit, a wall of brambles shot from the soil, coming between them. The bear hit the thorny barrier while Meric stumbled back.

"Over here!" Nee'lahn called.

Meric risked a glance backward. The others were gathered in a cluster, including the trappers. Nee'lahn stood before them, straight-backed, arms extended, fingers splayed.

"With the nexus gone," Nee'lahn explained, "we have our magick again! Can't you feel it?"

Meric, distracted by the elder'root, had failed to notice that the weight had lifted from his shoulders. He reached to his magick, and his silver hair flared around his shoulders with a nimbus of energy. He was whole again!

Meric backed to join the others as the elder'root tore at the tangle of brambles and briars, bleeding from the thousand thorns. Nee'lahn spread her arms, and the bramble barrier swept out in both directions, circling the party within its thorny ramparts. She continued to feed her power, calling upon her magicks, thickening the bulwarks, growing it taller.

Beyond her defenses, the shape-shifters attacked, taking their lead from the elder'root. All around the valley, si'lura flowed toward the fighting, enraged by the sight of the ancient trees dead and bare. The crunch of foot, paw, and hoof through the fall of leaves sounded everywhere, like the crackle of a deadly forest fire.

Above their heads, shape-shifters took to wing, diving toward the island in the center of the bramble sea. But Meric cast out his own magick and fouled their aim with sudden gusts and impossible currents.

Closer at hand, others tried to burrow through or under the barrier, but Nee'lahn blocked them at every turn.

Slowly turning, back to back, as in some deadly dance, Nee'lahn and Meric fought to hold their ramparts.

IN THE MIDDLE OF THE FRAY, JOACH HUDDLED WITH HARLEQUIN, STARING toward the great dead tree, barren of leaves. "Elena . . ."

Beyond the barrier, the pool was covered with copper leaves. Nothing stirred. There was no sign of Er'ril or Elena.

Over the past moons, Joach had experienced all manners of despair—the loss of his youth, the death of Kesla—but at this moment he knew he'd barely touched the true depths of hopelessness. It was a well without bottom, and he was falling ever deeper. The screams and howls around him muted, colors dulled, bled of their substance.

A sharp cry twitched his eyes to the left. He spotted Bryanna being tugged toward a hole that had opened in the ground. Her bare foot was gripped in the vice of armored pincers.

Her brother, Gunther, leaped to her aid, silent in his purpose and determination. He grabbed the pincers with his fingers, then bulled his shoulders and pried them apart. Something mewled down in the hole.

Bryanna tugged her foot free and rolled away.

"Stand back!" Nee'lahn called from across the way.

Gunther let go of the pincers and hurtled away. At his heels, a tangle of briars swelled from the ground and clogged the hole, growing thicker with every heartbeat.

"There are too many!" Nee'lahn cried out. "They're coming from all sides."

As if to demonstrate this point, something large dove past Joach's shoulder, snatched up one of the trappers, and winged past the brambles. Joach followed its flight. The plucked man struggled, his shoulder impaled by the claws of the giant roc. His weight was too much for the shape-shifter to hold aloft. The trapper was shaken lose. He fell hard to the ground outside the barriers.

"Dimont!" Gunther cried.

But it was already too late—the trapper was set upon by a score of beasts: wolves, sniffers, cats.

"We can't hold out much longer," Meric called.

Joach shook his head. What did it matter? What were they holding out for?

A familiar roar sounded behind him. Joach turned to see a bear rise up on its hind legs. Behind the elder'root, the slope of the valley was covered with si'lura of every shape and size, beasts of every ilk. Though Joach could not communicate in the mindspeak of the shape-shifters, he still read their leader's black thoughts: He meant to slay them all.

"Here they come!" Meric shouted.

With a howl of blood lust, the elder'root led his people in a final charge. But before they could crash against the thorny barrier, a crack of thunder split the valley. The clap of noise froze everyone in place, stopping the charge in midstride. In the center of the leaf-strewn pool, the trunk of the great Spirit Tree had split from crown to root, its two halves tilting apart but not toppling. A heavy mist rose from the shattered wood.

A chill spread outward, as if true winter had come to the summer valley. "Hoarfrost," Nee'lahn whispered, arms lowering slightly.

Past the briars, the shape-shifters began to stir. Growls and hissing rose anew, but more subdued, unsure.

Only Thorn, still wearing her womanly form, stepped closer to the pond and tree. "What does this mean?" she asked. Her words were not shouted, but the sudden quiet made her easy to hear. She faced both sides of the warring field, as if unclear who to blame, who might have answers.

But the answer came from behind her. The leaves floating atop the pond swirled in a tight eddy; then a fist of ice blasted forth, carried high into the air atop a pillar of frozen water.

Thorn danced away as the pond sloshed over the banks, but the water never reached the mud. In midsplash, the waters froze into crystalline sculptures. The entire pond froze over, spreading outward from the pillar. Then the freeze blew outward, turning the mud solid and fissuring its banks, while mists of hoarfrost blanketed the center of the valley. Where these ice fogs brushed the bramble ramparts, leaves curled black and stalks shattered from the cold.

All eyes focused on the fist of ice atop the pillar. Through the crystalline surface, a darker shape was evident.

"Elena . . ." Joach whispered.

As if hearing him, the fist suddenly blew outward in a hail of ripping shards. As the blast cleared, Joach saw Elena and Er'ril. Elena crouched, her left hand planted atop the pillar—the hand of coldfire now pale and empty.

She held her other hand out toward those gathered below. Wit'ch fire danced around her ruby fingers.

Er'ril rose groggily behind her.

Joach stood. "Elena!"

STILL DAZED, HER LUNGS ACHING, ELENA TRIED TO MAKE SENSE OF THE SCENE before her. The moonlit valley was filled with shape-shifters. Close at hand, a ring of briars surrounded her friends. She heard Joach call out, but his voice sounded strangely distant.

Her ears still rang with the pressure of the depths. Her breathing was ragged and loud in her ears. Further, the magick spent in driving her to the surface of the pond had left her feeling hollow and empty.

Moments ago, near to drowning, she had been dragged from oblivion by a chorus of wild magicks surging in her blood. When she found Er'ril clinging to her, she had reacted out of blind instinct, more for Er'ril's safety than her own. Touching her coldfire, she fed her magick into the waters below her, propelling them both to the surface atop a column of ice. Once out of the pond, a bit of her fiery magick had freed them from the icy cocoon.

Now released, Elena reined in her wit'ch fire, extinguishing the dancing flames and driving back the call of wild magicks.

"Are you all right?" she asked Er'ril. Her words were weak and hoarse.

He crawled to his knees. "I am . . . now that you're safe." She drew strength from the iron in his voice.

Below, Thorn stepped nearer. "What happened?" the huntress called up to them.

Elena shifted atop her pillar, standing with care on the slick summit. On his knees, Er'ril helped hold her steady as her legs trembled from the cold. Icicles still hung from her clothes and hair. A violent shiver threatened to topple her from her perch.

"Elena," Thorn repeated, "what happened?"

A bear padded up to the huntress. Elena's eyes widened at the sight of the huge beast. Then with a shake, the bearish features faded to something that was a blend of animal and man: Thorn's father, the elder'root of the si'lura.

A growl of challenge arose from his throat before words slowly formed. "You've killed us all!"

Elena had trouble making sense of these words. She searched for some way down from the pillar. Already the ice was melting in rivulets and runnels.

"Be careful," Er'ril mumbled behind her, teeth chattering. "The si'lura think you destroyed their Spirit Tree."

Elena stopped her search and stared at the pair gathered below. She fought her numb tongue. "Destroy the Root? I would never—"

"Lies!" the elder'root shouted. An echo of growls accompanied him from the others.

Thorn stepped farther forward, as if distancing herself from both her father and his accusation. "Then tell us what happened."

Elena glanced back to the ice-blasted tree, its trunk split in half. She stared out at the bare trees framing the valley. They were all dead. " 'The time of our guardianship is over . . .' " she mumbled, echoing the words of the Root.

"What was that?" Thorn asked.

Elena breathed deeply. "The Root spoke to me," she said, shivering, struggling to make her voice firm. "It said that to protect these forests, you must abandon them."

"Never!" the elder'root exclaimed.

Thorn held a palm toward her father, pleading patience. "Where are we to go?"

"To seek the Twins."

Thorn gasped. "Fardale and Mogweed?"

Elena nodded. A bit of warmth slowly returned to her limbs. "I believe that was what the Old One meant. I sensed a picture of the two brothers."

"These are lies!" the elder'root hissed.

"Father," Thorn argued, "you yourself said the Root communed with Elena. Would it have done so if she had meant it harm? The Root knows a person's heart."

Her words seemed to shake her father. For a moment, the beastly features threatened to overwhelm the man. "The Root was sick . . . Perhaps it didn't know a demon could wear such an innocent face."

"You saw the glow, Father. The Root has not shone with such brilliance in ages. It chose her for this message."

"To leave the forests and seek the cursed Twins?"

Thorn shook her head. "The Root has always guided us. Shall we ignore its last message?"

"How do we know this stranger speaks the truth to us?"

Now it was Thorn's turn to seem unsure. She faced Elena, her eyes pleading for some sign, some proof.

Elena was unsure what to do. Er'ril leaned closer. "Perhaps you should show them this." He half unsheathed a length of silver sword. Elena's eyes widened as she recognized the talisman from the Root. "You were clutching it when I found you."

She nodded and took the weapon in her left hand, pulling it free. She recalled the plea of the Root: *Lead my people with this sign . . .*

Elena fought the shaking of her limbs. She cleared her aching throat and raised her voice for all to hear. "I am charged to lead you from your forests! So the Root has burdened me! As proof, it has given me this!"

She lifted the sword for all to see. Its razored edges were so sharp that it was hard to define the weapon's boundaries. Touched by moonlight, the blade ignited with its own inner shine, blazing bright into the night. Gasps arose throughout the valley.

"It cannot be!" the elder'root exclaimed. He dropped to his knees, while the other shape-shifters milled in confusion.

"Father, what's wrong?"

The elder'root reached blindly toward his daughter. "It is something shared only between the great Root and its chosen. A secret promise sworn by the elder'root of each generation."

"What promise?"

His voice was a whisper, but Elena heard him. "To follow the one foretold in ages past, she who would bear the Sword of the Rose again."

Thorn stared up at Elena and the shining blade. "The Sword of the Rose?"

Elena knew what she held aloft; she had recognized the sword from the moment it was laid in her hands. Back at A'loa Glen, Elena had read every text, rumor, and tale about her ancestor, Sisa'kofa, and she recognized the weapon borne by the ancient wit'ch. It had been described countless times and called by many names: *Demon Blade*, *Spirit Stealer*, *Wit'ch Sword*. By whatever name, the length of shining silver with its rose-carved hilt could not be mistaken.

She raised the sword forged of elemental silver, the same metal that channeled the Land's energy. Even now, she felt the power vibrating within the blade's length.

"The Root is gone," she intoned. "It has returned to the world's heart to offer its strength against a greater threat."

"What are we to do without it?" Thorn asked. "It is our spiritual center. With it gone, we will die."

Elena stared out at the gathered army. "But for now, you live! The fate of your people is not yet decided. I am to lead you beyond these forests, to the Twins. The brothers hold the key to your future."

Angered mutterings rumbled from those gathered below. But the elder'root stood, holding up an arm to draw attention his way. He faced his people. "So it was foretold. So it will be!"

Others made sounds of disagreement, but the elder'root stood fast. He faced the crowd until they grew silent. None challenged openly now, but an undercurrent of doubt persisted.

"We will prevail," the elder'root said plainly. "The Root has guided our people since we rose from the waters of our birth. We will trust its judgment now."

Softer murmurs flowed through the crowd. Elena sensed her duty here was done for now. She knew their leader would eventually sway most to their cause. With the tide turned, the strength ebbed from her limbs. The sword trembled as she lowered it.

Then Er'ril was there. He caught the blade by its pommel, she returned it to his safekeeping. Ever her protector . . .

He slipped it into his empty scabbard.

She swung her attention to the pillar. With her right hand, she cast out tendrils of wit'ch fire and melted a chute down the ice tower. It was steep, but Er'ril wrapped her in his arms, and they slid down the trough of melted ice. At the bottom, Er'ril lifted her, holding her tight. She pressed her cheek against his chest. Despite the soaking and ice, he was so warm.

The elder'root stepped toward them, all signs of the beast gone. The leader's eyes shone with regret. "I'm sorry . . ."

Er'ril brushed past him and headed for the gap in the briars. Once through, he began to order those around him. Elena barely heard, listening instead to the thump of his heart. ". . . horses and tents. And build a large fire . . ."

Elena slipped her hand through Er'ril's shirt, resting her palm against his hot skin. She closed her eyes and sank into his warmth.

For now, this was fire enough.

AS DAWNED NEARED, GRESHYM WATCHED ER'RIL LEAVE ELENA'S TENT AND cross to the fire. From the clear relief on the man's face, the girl must be recovering well from her dunking and the freezing touch of her own magick. A si'luran healer had taken her draughts of steaming herbs, a mix of peppermint and ale-leaf, from the smell of it. Afterward Greshym had overheard the shape-shifter telling the trapper Bryanna that Elena should recover fully in the next day or two.

Still, throughout the long night, Er'ril kept returning to the camp's fire to gather fresh coals to warm her blankets. As the plainsman bent by the fire, Greshym eyed the rose-carved pommel of the sword he bore. It shone bright as a star, even in the feeble firelight.

Shadowsedge . . . That was what Sisa'kofa had called the sword herself, leading to the rumor that it was sharp enough to separate a man from his own shadow.

Greshym's eyes narrowed as he studied the sheathed blade. He could not believe his luck to have the ancient weapon within reach. Such a boon could not be ignored, even if it meant delaying his own plans.

As Er'ril gathered fresh coals into a pan, Greshym let his eyelids drift closed. He sought the familiar heartbeat of his servant. Rukh hid well outside the si'luran valley. Greshym sent a silent message to the stump gnome.

Earlier, Greshym had eavesdropped on a terse conversation between Er'ril and the elder'root. He knew where the group was going next: to the Northern Fang, where Mogweed and Fardale had last been headed.

He bound his orders to Rukh as well as he could, using the last dregs of his magick. The beast would have to set out immediately to reach those same lands in time. *Keep my staff safe,* he urged. He knew Rukh still carried the length of hollow bone. He sensed the gnome's fear of the tool, but the creature would obey. Satisfied, Greshym brought his attention back to where Er'ril returned to Elena's tent, hot coals in hand, oblivious to the dire weapon he carried at his side.

A voice intruded on Greshym's reveries. "What are you plotting?" Joach asked harshly behind him.

Greshym glanced over his shoulder. "So you couldn't sleep, either," he commented, ignoring the boy's question.

Joach settled to a boulder with a sigh. "It's that sword; I saw you studying it. You think to use its magick against us."

Greshym shook his head, smiling broadly. "I wouldn't touch that weapon for all the magick in the Land."

Joach's face tightened with suspicion. "Why's that?"

"You know why." Greshym nodded to the boy's petrified wood staff. When Joach's fingers clenched protectively to the stave, Greshym smiled. *The boy was already lost to it . . . he just didn't know it yet.*

"Why?" Joach repeated.

He might as well be honest—the truth might do him more good than a lie. Greshym glanced back to the tent. "That sword was once wielded by Sisa'kofa, your sister's ancestor."

"I know," Joach said sourly. "Elena told me."

"Of course she did. Once touched, how could she not know it?"

"What do you mean?"

Greshym laughed at the boy's naïveté. "Joach, my young pupil, have you learned nothing? Would you not know your own staff?"

"What does one have to do with the other?"

Greshym rolled his eyes. "My boy, you're not the only one to ever create a blood weapon."

Joach's eyes widened with shock.

Greshym nodded. "Sisa'kofa bled her own essence into that blade. Naturally one wit'ch recognized the touch of another."

"The Sword of the Rose . . . ?"

"It's a blood weapon," Greshym finished. "Created by Sisa'kofa. One of the most powerful and darkest weapons ever forged." Greshym sighed, leaning back. "It will destroy your sister."

ER'RIL PASSED INTO THE TENT. THE CHILL OF THE NIGHT AIR WAS QUICKLY warmed away by the heat of the tent's interior. As he crept carefully over to the pile of blankets and furs, he found Elena's eyes open and staring at him.

"You should sleep," he whispered, slipping the pan of warm coals under the foot of her makeshift bed.

"Can't sleep . . . ," her voice rasped.

He sighed and settled beside her. He felt her forehead. She was still cool to the touch. He glanced to the door.

She must have read his mind. "I have enough coals." A hand wormed out of the nest of blankets and sought his. She stared into his eyes. He knew what she wanted.

"Just this one night . . . ," she said hoarsely. "Hold me."

Er'ril squeezed her fingers, seeking some way to deny what she asked.

There was so much yet to do. But as he stared into her wounded face, he let it go. This night, he would follow his heart.

In the weak glow of the single lamp, he undid his sword belt and dropped it to the floor. She watched his every move as he pulled out of his leathers and slipped free of his leggings. Standing only in his smallclothes, he knelt and pulled back the furs and blankets. Then he slipped out of the last of his garments and slid under the coverings.

He nestled deeper, seeking her out. He pulled her to him, wrapping her in his arms, sharing his warmth.

She settled her head against his bare chest. He lowered his cheek to her hair and breathed in the scent of her. She stirred against him, soft and smooth-skinned. A shiver that had nothing to do with cold passed through him.

She murmured something unintelligible.

"I love you, too," he answered.

SIX DAYS LATER, ELENA STOOD AT THE PROW OF THE *WINDSPRITE*, AN ELV'IN scoutship. With the aid of the si'lura, they had made the journey to the Pass of Tears without mishap. The rendezvous ship had been waiting, moored to the tops of the highland pines.

Elena stared down the slope of the pass all the way back to the forests of the Western Reaches. But it was near at hand, spread along the pass, that the si'luran army was breaking camp for the next leg of the journey.

Craning forward, Elena stared north. Somewhere beyond the horizon lay their destination: the Northern Fang. She would follow the direction of the Spirit Root and lead the si'lura to the twin brothers. With luck, perhaps the other party had succeeded among the og'res.

The scuff of a boot sounded behind her. She turned and found Er'ril standing there, his face dark with worry. "Joach was able to reach Tyrus. His pirate brigade is in the Bay of T'lek that surrounds Blackhall."

"And the main fleet?"

"Three days behind him."

"That's as we planned, isn't it?"

"Yes, but Tyrus has fears for the d'warf armies." Er'ril's brow knit with concern. "In the past three days, they've had no answers to the crows sent to Wennar. Tyrus is heading to the northern coasts to investigate the sudden silence."

"When will we know more?"

"Two days at the least."

Elena nodded, calculating, "We should be almost to the Northern Fang by then." She bit her lip, then asked the question worrying her most. "What about Sy-wen?"

Er'ril frowned. "No word. Kast remains at A'loa Glen, but there has been no sign of her."

Elena slipped an arm around his waist, grateful to have him at her side. He matched her embrace, pulling her to him. The ship's sails snapped overhead as she leaned into him, wishing the moment could stretch forever. After the night in the tent, duty and decorum had kept them mostly apart. Still, after sharing her bed, some dam had broken between them. Er'ril's chance kisses were held longer; his hands sought her out with more passion. And when she looked into his eyes, the hunger there was no longer hidden, only restrained by the moment.

Soon a horn sounded from below, echoing up to the ship. Er'ril sighed. "That would be Thorn. The si'lura are ready to depart."

Elena nodded. "Then we should be under way. Are we all stowed and ready?"

"Yes," Er'ril said, giving her a final squeeze, "even the horses."

Despite the dire news, Elena could not stop a smile from forming as she remembered the struggle to haul Rorshaf aboard ship. The war charger had not been too keen on this mode of travel, but Elena had no intention of leaving the stallion behind.

Er'ril leaned in, teasing. "Rorshaf's never going to forgive you, no matter how many apples you coax him with." He quickly kissed her, then headed toward the stern deck, where Meric and the ship's captain were conferring. Belted to his hip was the ancient sword, the silver rose on the pommel glinting in the morning sunlight.

Shadowsedge.

Joach had told them of Greshym's words, revealing the weapon to be a blood sword. As a test, Elena had bloodied one hand and wielded the weapon. She had indeed felt the dark power stretch into her.

Er'ril had wanted the blade tossed down the nearest deep hole, but Elena had refused. The sword was revered by the si'lura, and it was a talisman left by Sisa'kofa, for her alone. To compromise, Er'ril insisted on keeping the blade at his own side: out of harm's way, but close enough for its use if necessary.

A second horn sounded from below. "Ho!" Meric called. "We're under way!"

The ship lurched as mooring lines were freed and hauled aboard. The sails swelled with winds that were not entirely natural. And then they were off and flying.

A great flurry of wings erupted from the ground. Soon the winds were filled with eagles of every color and feather: snowy, brown, rust, black, gray, and silver. Wings snapped wide and glided the currents and warm uprisings. The growing flock flanked the larger elv'in ship and followed its lead over the mountains.

Elena watched the gathering of eagles in the sky.

"So it begins," a voice said behind her.

She turned and found Harlequin smoking a pipe.

He pointed its glowing stem toward the sky. "Let's just hope this isn't their last flight."

Book Four

BLACK SEAS

15

RISING THROUGH THE SHALLOWS AROUND A'LOA GLEN, KAST CLUNG TO THE mer'ai rider before him. Their mount, a sinuous jade seadragon, flowed toward the docks, maneuvering through the ruins of the half-submerged city. Kast stared around him at the man-made reefs that had once been towers and homes. Schools of skipperflicks darted through windows and doorways. Over the centuries, the sea had reclaimed this territory as its own. The dragon swam over a toppled statue, now festooned with anemone and scuttling crabs.

A graveyard, Kast thought dourly, lost in a black mood. Since Sy-wen's disappearance, the ocean had held none of its charm or mystery. It had become just a cold, unforgiving landscape. He could not even transform into Ragnar'k and travel the seas on his own. Only Sy-wen's touch could ignite the magick and release the dragon inside him.

So he was glad when they finally broke the sea's surface into the late afternoon sunlight. He spat out the end of his air pod and drew a lungful of clean air, shivering in the thin breeze.

The dragon, a slender female, surged under him.

"Ho, Helia," the rider ahead of him whispered, patting his mount's neck with clear affection. The young mer'ai was little more than a boy, just recently bonded to his dragon. In fact, most of the mer'ai left here were the young and the elderly. They were quartered in the single Leviathan remaining in the deeper waters, with Sy-wen's mother, Linora. She and Master Edyll had remained behind until her daughter's fate could be determined. All others had departed days ago with the warships of the Dre'rendi and the elv'in.

Kast squeezed the young rider's upper arm. "Thanks for your help, Ty-lyn. And for Helia's skill."

His words straightened the boy's shoulders with pride. "My dragon was birthed from the best of the bloodlines. You even knew her sire."

Kast frowned, not understanding what the young rider meant. "I did?"

"The jade," the boy insisted.

His words made no sense to Kast, but the boy must have caught his confusion. "Helia is a jade. The dragon's color comes from the *father*, another jade."

As if sensing she was being spoken about, Helia glanced back over a shoulder. Kast's brows pinched. *A jade.* As seadragon and man studied one another, Kast suddenly understood. The similarities in features between daughter and father were plainly evident now that he truly looked. After having spent so much time with the mer'ai, Kast had grown to recognize the subtle differences between the majestic creatures. "A jade male . . . ," he mumbled.

The boy nodded. "One of the best bloodlines."

Kast reached up and ran a finger along the nasal ridge of the sniffing dragon. For a moment, he felt close again to Sy-wen; she had loved this one's brave father with all her heart. *Conch,* the bonded mount of Sy-wen's mother.

Tears blurred his vision.

Ty-lyn glanced past Kast's shoulder. "Here come the others."

Kast turned. From the waters, another six dragons rose. Their riders dragged woven nets, heavy with ebon'stone eggs. At the sight, fury overwhelmed him, drying his tears with the heat.

"That's the last of 'em," the boy commented.

Kast growled in the back of his throat. After seven days, the crashed elv'in scoutship had been scoured of its deadly cargo. Over a hundred eggs were already stored deep in a windowless stone cellar, its single door guarded by a dozen armed guards. Once these last eggs joined the foul clutch, the room would be bricked up, never to be opened. It was the safest course. The cargo could not be left unwatched on the seabed floor, and all attempts to destroy the eggs with fire or hammer had failed.

So it had been necessary to secure the clutch and the tentacled beasts incubating inside. It was a grim duty after so many deaths: the ship's crew, the corrupted scholars, even the priceless library. Now a suffocating rage burned within Kast, a smoldering fury. He seldom slept. He rarely visited the kitchens, and then he shoveled food into his mouth untasted. He sought anything to keep himself busy. While the fleets prepared for the assault on Blackhall, Kast had found plenty to fill his days and nights. But now with the forces gone, Kast kept himself occupied bolstering up the defenses of A'loa Glen, including securing the clutch of ebon'stone eggs.

Earlier this morning, Kast had gone on this last journey to the ship to ensure the matter had been dealt with completely. Even the sands around the crashed ship had been sifted and searched to make sure not a single egg was missed.

As Kast turned to the island, a black despair settled into him. In the past, he had faced demons and monsters, seen friends slain, but what scared him most and threatened to paralyze him now was the empty bed that awaited him. For the thousandth time, he pictured the cold eyes of Sy-wen as she had laughed at his struggles in the library, how her fingers had reached toward him . . . not with love, but with something as cold as the slime at the bottom of the sea.

"Someone waits for us," Ty-lyn said, drawing Kast's attention back to the present.

The dragons and their riders swept toward the docks. One of the figures standing there raised an arm in greeting: Hunt, the high keel's son. Behind him stood a cadre of Bloodriders.

As the dragons drew abreast of the docks, Hunt reached down and offered a hand. Kast took it and allowed himself to be hauled up to the planks. "What's wrong?" he asked, noting the man's pinched brow and hard stance.

"You'd better get dressed," Hunt said, and nodded to the pile of clothes Kast had left at the end of the docks.

Kast dried off with his own shirt, then slipped on the damp garment; he'd let it dry on the walk back to the castle. He pushed into his boots and strapped on his sword belt, then turned his attention back to his fellow Bloodrider.

Hunt was studying the other seadragons. "Is that the last haul?"

Kast nodded. "Eighteen."

Hunt's eyes never left the seas and the dragons. "How soon can these be hauled to the dungeon?"

Kast frowned at the lowering sun. "By dusk at the latest."

Hunt waved to the other Bloodriders. "I've brought men to help make that sooner."

"What's the urgency?"

Hunt didn't answer. His only response was a slight narrowing of his eyes. He refused to speak aloud.

Curling a fist, Kast held back any further questions. Instead he nodded imperceptibly to Hunt, indicating he understood. He swung to Ty-lyn and his mount, Helia, bobbing in the waves. "You and the others are to haul this last clutch to the dungeon cell as quickly as possible. We've additional men to help. Alert the others."

"It will be done!" Ty-lyn struck a fist to his shoulder in salute. "Ho, Helia!" Rider and dragon twisted away.

Kast turned back to Hunt, who was directing his men, speaking in hushed, terse tones. When he finished, the cadre leader nodded, stepping back. "We'll watch with the eyes of a hawk," he said.

"What are they to watch?" Kast asked Hunt. "What's the urgency with these last eggs?"

"Come." Hunt headed down the pier. "There's something I must show you."

Kast kept pace with him. "What is it?" he asked irritably, tired of half answers.

Hunt waited until they were out of earshot of the others. "Two of the eggs are missing."

Kast stumbled to a stop. "What?" Shock raised his voice.

Hunt motioned him to keep quiet and keep moving. "They vanished during the midnight shift last night. I questioned the guards. None admit leaving their posts or sleeping, but this morning the egg count is less by two."

Kast shook his head. "How could that be? A dozen swordsmen couldn't all have so been lax in their duty as to let a thief through."

Hunt glanced to Kast, his face unreadable. "Last night, the shift was composed of all mer'ai."

Kast's brows pinched. It was common for shifts to be entirely elv'in, or Dre'rendi, or mer'ai. But Kast understood the unspoken suspicion behind Hunt's words. *Sy-wen was mer'ai.* Was there some connection to a theft that occurred during a mer'ai shift? It seemed improbable, but Kast now understood the cadre of Bloodriders brought to the dock. *We'll watch with the eyes of a hawk.*

Hunt leaned in closer, his voice lowering another note. "This morning I confirmed the dungeon count myself. And while doing so, I found something else."

"What?"

"Something you should see for yourself." They had reached the end of the docks, and the usual crowds of fisherfolk and shippers closed around them, silencing their talk of traitors and betrayals.

Kast climbed the streets in silence, lost in his thoughts. Part of him, deep in his heart, hoped Sy-wen *had* played a role in this midnight theft—for the past half moon, there had been no sign of the woman he loved. Kast feared she had already struck out for Blackhall, never to be seen again. But if she had stolen the eggs . . . if she was still here . . .

A seed of hope rooted in his spirit.

They reached the castle and passed through the gates and guards. Hunt led the way through the forecourt and down to the dungeons, where two guards stood post with spears and belted swords. Both were Bloodriders; Hunt was taking no chances.

Beyond the guards at the entrance, steps led down to a dark passage that trailed far under the castle. Their footfalls echoed hollowly until they reached an ironbound door. Hunt knocked his knuckles on the oaken frame. A small panel opened, and a scarred face peered out—the mute dungeon keep, Gost. The disfigured man grunted in recognition, the rattle of keys sounded, and the door opened with a scream of rusted hinges. The scarred man waved them in.

"Thank you, Gost," Hunt said.

The dungeon keep nodded. His eyes were red-rimmed; a scrabbled growth of beard marked his chin. Kast knew his story. The heavy-limbed fellow had endured tortures beyond speaking in these very dungeons during the occupation by the Dark Lord's forces, including having his tongue cut out. Fear again shone bright in the man's eyes now: Gost had not been happy to have his warren of cells become a vault for the ebon'stone eggs.

Kast couldn't blame him. Even in this room, one could sense the clutch: a prickling of the tiny hairs over one's body, a thickness to the air that felt oily. From the worn condition of the man, Kast doubted sleep came easy here.

Bowing, Gost led them across the room that doubled as his living space. He used his keys to unlock the far door, the entrance to the main dungeons.

Once through, Kast motioned to the door being locked behind them. "Did Gost notice anything last night when the theft occurred?"

Hunt shook his head. "The keep had let no one through his room since the change of guard just before midnight."

"Then how did the thief get down here?"

"I couldn't say, unless Gost was part of the conspiracy."

"I don't believe he'd side with the Black Heart, not after the suffering he endured here."

"Then maybe he was duped . . . or enthralled."

Kast shook his head as they crossed down the rows of cells. Ahead, at the end of the passage, torches blazed. Men milled, a dozen, all Blood-riders, Hunt's own men.

Hunt nodded to the captain of the guard. "Everything secure, Wrent?"

The man nodded, standing straight, shoulders thrown back. "We've let no one in or out, as you instructed." Kast recognized the man as Hunt's cousin. His warrior's braid reached to his waist, the sign of many success-ful battles. He also bore a scar across his seahawk tattoo, a pale slash as if the hawk's throat had been cut.

Hunt jangled a set of keys from a pocket and stepped to the door. Kast followed along with Wrent. The cell door, a stout construction of fire-hardened oak banded in iron with a small barred window, was doubly locked. It took one of Hunt's keys and one of Wrent's to free the way.

As they unlocked the door, Kast again wondered how anyone could have stolen the two eggs. Even with the aid of the mer'ai on duty last night, how had the thief gotten past Gost? How had the locks been man-aged? It seemed an impossible theft.

Kast could fathom only one explanation. Since Sy-wen's corruption, he had investigated the accounts of the malignant tentacled creatures, from Tok and his experiences aboard Captain Jarplin's ship, to Elena and her "cure" of Brother Flint. One thing seemed clear: Once corrupted with the beasts, there was some malignant connection among those infected, a de-monic link between the creatures that allowed communication. If this was so, then with the Brotherhood of Scholars tainted, Sy-wen would have ac-cess to their knowledge of A'loa Glen and its castle, including its maze of secret passages and tunnels. Could she use this knowledge to slip past the safeguards and steal the eggs? And what other evil could she have achieved already? The thought chilled him.

The creak of hinges drew his attention as Wrent hauled the heavy door open. The prickling sensation swelled, like spiders skittering across bare skin. The others in the hall, all battle-hard men, took a step away.

Hunt grabbed a torch from the wall. "Keep your guard up while the way is unbarred. Don't let anyone near."

Wrent saluted. "It will be done."

Hunt led the way through the door with his torch, and Wrent closed the door behind them. Kast studied the dim room. He had chosen this cell because it was large enough to hold the entire clutch of a hundred eggs and had been carved from the stone of the island itself, solid rock all around. Hunt's torch flickered shadows on the walls.

Eggs lay everywhere in neat stacks, like the nesting grounds of some foul flock. The biggest pile, a pyramid, stood in the room's center, reaching to the ceiling itself. The heap of ebon'stone absorbed the torchlight, casting no reflection. Even the room's scant warmth seemed to be sucked away by the clutch, leaving the air cold. Their breaths blew white with each exhalation.

"The missing eggs were taken from over here." Hunt circled to the far side, where one of the smaller piles was clearly lower than the others.

"And the vanished eggs aren't elsewhere in the room?"

"I counted twice," Hunt said. "And on the second count, I found this." The tall Bloodrider dropped to a knee beside a neighboring pile. He lowered his torch and pointed to the stack's base. Something was lodged there. "I didn't want to disturb it before you saw it yourself."

Kast bent down. It was a scrap of cloth. He reached and fingered the material. His breath caught in his throat. *Sharkskin.* His fingers yanked the material free, held it closer to the torch. "It's Sy-wen's."

"Are you sure?"

Kast could only nod.

Hunt straightened, standing. "I'm sorry, Kast. I know how this must fire your blood. I, too, would be furious."

Kast had to turn away, not to hide his anger, but his joy. His fingers closed over the scrap of sharkskin. She *was* still here!

Hunt offered further words of consolation, but Kast remained deaf to them. He raised the bit of leathery cloth to his nose and breathed in the faint scent of sea salt and the hint of Sy-wen's skin. *My love . . .*

". . . all the mer'ai on duty." Hunt's words slowly intruded. "I'll have them rounded up again."

Kast lowered the scrap and nodded. Hunt led the way back toward the door. As they neared it, they heard the scrape of a sliding bolt. Hunt glanced back to Kast with pinched brows—then the clash of steel sounded from beyond the room. Cries arose.

Both men rushed forward. Hunt yanked on the handle, but the way was locked. "Wrent!"

Kast pushed to the small, barred window. By the dim torchlight, he watched the quick slaughter of five Bloodriders, set upon by their own brothers. Curved daggers sliced throats open, spilling rivers of spurting blood. Bodies were impaled on pikes and swords. In a matter of moments, the dead lay strewn, entrails oozing from deep wounds, blood seeping into wide black pools on the stone.

Wrent's face suddenly appeared at the window, blocking the view. The warrior now wore a wide leer, froth at the corner of his lips.

"Wrent! What have you done?" Hunt tried to reach through the bars, but he could not even get his fists between the iron.

Kast pulled him back with one hand and slid his sword out with the other. "He's corrupted. It's not the mer'ai that were the traitors, but our own men."

Wrent continued to leer.

"Then why did Wrent alert me to the missing eggs?"

Kast stared down at the scrap of sharkskin. "So you'd find this and fetch me here. It's a trap."

As if to confirm this, a large *crack* sounded behind them, as if a stone had been shattered by a hammer. Both men turned to the center pile of eggs.

... *crack* ... *crack* ... *crack* ...

"They're hatching," Kast said.

The pile shook before them. The topmost egg in the pyramid toppled from its perch and bounced to the floor. As it struck and rolled near them, it split open, steaming green into the cold air. Fist-sized globs of gelatinous slime splattered out in all directions, striking the floor and walls with wet slaps.

One struck Hunt's leg, clinging to it. He smacked it away with the butt of his torch and danced back. "Sweet Mother!"

On the floor, the offending glob sprouted tentacles and began to hop, like a sick toad.

"Stand back!" Kast warned.

All around—on floor, ceiling, and walls—the other scattered fists of slime grew wormy appendages and questing tentacles.

Hunt thrust out his torch, ready to defend with his flame. But instead of deterring the creatures, the brand's heat seemed to attract them. Their moist feelers all swung in unison toward the heat, and they rolled and slimed their way forward.

"We have to get out of here," Hunt said as more eggs cracked throughout the cell.

"There's no escape," Kast said calmly, ready with his sword.

Hunt's voice edged toward panic. "Why didn't the guards just slay us? Why lure us here?"

A new voice, full of mirth, intruded behind them. "Because we need a dragon, Brother Hunt."

Kast swung around. At the barred window, the leering face of Wrent had been replaced by another. Kast's heart burst at the sight of those sea-blue eyes and the pale face framed in deep green hair. Despite the danger, Kast felt a surge of relief. "Sy-wen . . ."

AS EVENING NEARED, PRINCE TYRUS LOWERED HIS SPYGLASS AND CALLED down from the *Black Folly*'s crow's nest. He had to grip the edge of the nest to keep from falling headlong to the deck of his ship. "Signal fires to the north!" he yelled to his first mate. "Turn us into the next cove."

He straightened, knowing his order would be obeyed. His legs easily rode the teeter of the ship's central mast as he swayed atop his perch. His face burned from the days of salt and wind. The coast lay a quarter league away. Here in the far north, the shore was an unbroken cliff face topped by storm-burned pines twisted into agonized shapes by the ceaseless winds that swept across the Bay of T'lek.

As sails snapped and the ship edged nearer the coastal cliffs, Tyrus focused his spyglass on the bonfire atop the cliff face. He sought the makers of the signal blaze, praying to see the squat forms of d'warves, but nothing moved. He made out a small village beyond the fire. The hamlet lay in ruins: chimneys toppled, roofs collapsed, walls scorched from old blazes. But despite the abandoned look to the town, a fresh pyre smoked into the darkening skies. It was clearly a signal meant for seafarers, but who had set it and why? Tyrus searched with his spyglass and found no answer.

Tyrus dared not pass by without sending a shore party to investigate. For the past four days, he and his crew had been scouring the coastline for any sign of Wennar and his d'warf party. Every morning he sent out crows, and each evening they returned to the ship with the same messages still attached to their legs, unread, untouched.

"Mother above, where are you?" he muttered as he searched.

The main battle fleet was two days out from these same waters. If need be, the combined fleets would attack the island on their own, but the plan had been for the d'warf army to drive north through the Stone Forest. Then while the fleets attacked from the south, the d'warves would charge over the arch of volcanic stone that connected the island's northern coast to the mainland.

Now the plan was in jeopardy.

Growling his frustration, Tyrus slammed his spyglass closed and pulled open the hatch to the crow's nest. He clambered down the rope ladder.

His first mate, Blyth, met him at the foot of the mast. The shaven-headed pirate was tall and wiry, a whip of a man whose tongue was as sharp as his sword. He wore a cutlass over one shoulder, and a bolo on his other hip. "Is it the d'warf army?"

"Can't say . . . but we have to check it out. It's the first sign of life we've seen in days."

Blyth nodded. "We should watch our arses, though. Something don't strike me right about this place."

Tyrus trusted his first mate's instincts. "How so?"

Blyth pointed to the bonfire. It disappeared around the point as the ship entered the sheltered cove. "Someone goes to all the trouble to set a fire like that, then where are they?"

A call sounded from the prow. "Dockworks ahead!"

Tyrus and Blyth hurried forward and joined the seaman whose duty it was to watch for shoals and reefs. He pointed to the base of the cove's cliffs, and a set of four piers, or what remained of them. Pilings jutted from the waters like broken teeth. Bits of planking clung to some. The damage seemed at least a winter old.

"No one's been fishing out of this hole in a while," Blyth mumbled.

"Drop anchor here," Tyrus ordered. "We'll take a party ashore in one of the longboats. We'll take another three men. That'll leave an even dozen left to guard the ship."

"Aye." Blyth turned to obey, already shouting commands.

Tyrus studied the lay of the land as sails were reefed and the ship slowed. In the shadow of the cove's cliffs, the last of the sun's glow disappeared. Evening had already claimed the small bay. He stared at the stone walls. A heavy mist clung in patches, promising the night to come to be foggy and damp. They'd best make short work of this search; he didn't want the *Black Folly* to be trapped by the icy, blinding fogs of this northern clime.

Tyrus wrapped his cloak tighter around his shoulders as the cold sucked at his warmth. It was hard to believe that midsummer was only a few days away. Here in the far north, winter never truly let go. On their search through T'lek Bay, they had even seen ice floes drifting south, bobbing in the current, flowing down from the Northern Wastes as the ice pack broke apart from the spring thaw. It made traveling these summer seas especially treacherous . . . and the dense fog only added to the danger.

The creak of rope on wheel sounded to the starboard side as the longboat was lowered. It landed with a muffled splash. Rope ladders were tossed over rails.

Blyth appeared at his side. "All set, Captain."

"Who's coming ashore with us?"

"Sticks, Hurl, and Fletch."

Tyrus nodded, watching the trio gather, clapping each other on the shoulders and checking weapons. Sticks was the largest of the pirates, bowlegged, with arms as thick around as any og're's. His frame was not suited to the delicacy of the sword—he preferred the pair of ironwood clubs hooked to his belt, studded with steel.

At his side, Hurl stood with a sharpening stone, honing the edges of his hand axes. Blue-eyed with straw-colored hair, he hailed from these same northern lands. He had seen his family slaughtered by the dog soldiers of the Gul'gotha, leaving him an orphan on the cold, hard streets of Penryn. He bore no love for the denizens of Blackhall.

And, of course, ever at Hurl's side was Fletch. The two were inseparable, one dark, one light, tied by bonds deeper than any brothers'. The black-haired Steppeman knelt on one knee, stringing his bow. He seldom spoke, but there was no better archer than the dark-eyed man.

Blyth had chosen well, picking a party whose skills were diverse and complementary. If trouble arose, Tyrus had little doubt they could handle it.

Satisfied, he crossed to the shore party with Blyth. "Let's load up!"

The group clambered down the ladders to the longboats. Hurl and Fletch took the oars, while Sticks hunched in the stern, manning the rudder. From the bow, Tyrus and Blyth watched the waters ahead for any dangerous shoals or reefs.

Blyth spoke as they crossed into the bay. "You needn't have come, Captain. We could scout these lands on our own."

Tyrus remained silent. His first mate was right.

"And even if it were a captain's duty," Blyth continued more softly, "it sure as the Mother's sweet teat isn't a prince's."

Tyrus grimaced. Blyth had been at his side since he had first stumbled into Port Rawl, full of anger, sorrow, and spite. The bloody planks of the corsairs had suited him fine to vent his bile upon the seas. But now the world again called him to duty. The mantle of Castle Mryl was his to bear, left to him by his father. But deep in his heart, he wondered if he had the strength to be a king's son, his father's son.

"You can't hide forever among us pirates," Blyth mumbled under his breath.

Tyrus sighed. "Leave be."

His first mate and friend shrugged. "For now, Captain . . . for now."

As true night closed in, they maneuvered through the shallows to the remains of the village docks. They tied up to a piling and climbed onto the crumbled end of a stone jetty. A steep stair, carved from the rock of the cliffs, led up toward the village.

Tyrus eyed the climb sourly. Mists had already grown dense as evening fog rolled in from the sea, thickening against the shore. The top of the cliffs could no longer be seen, but the glow from the signal fire lit a patch of fog.

"Let's be done with this business as quickly as possible," Tyrus mumbled.

No one argued.

The climb proved even trickier than expected. Besides the damp from the mists, algae and moss covered each step, as slippery as ice.

"No one's used these stairs in ages," Blyth said.

Tyrus agreed. Any good townsfolk would maintain the steps with salt and moss-killer. The state of the stairs was not a heartening sign.

"Then who set the fire?" Hurl asked.

"That's what I intend to find out," Tyrus said. "That bonfire didn't set itself."

At long last, they reached the top and found a cobbled thoroughfare stretching toward the village, dark and silent. By now, the fog lay like a smothering blanket. They entered the small town cautiously, weapons in hand. Nothing moved but the flickering glow of the fire beyond the village.

The party signaled each other with practiced hand gestures. Tyrus, Blyth, and Sticks took one side of the street. Hurl and Fletch edged along the other side. They moved with care, ears pricked, muscles tense, weapons ready.

Every structure they passed showed signs of damage: shattered windows, storefronts singed with soot, upper stories collapsed into lower. Clearly the town had been laid to waste, but amid all the devastation, something was plainly missing.

"The town's a graveyard," Blyth muttered, "but where are the dead?"

There were no bodies, not a single one, not even the bones of those who had died here.

Tyrus frowned. "Maybe those that survived buried their dead before moving on."

Blyth raised an eyebrow in disbelief. "I'd more believe carrion feeders. At least one winter has passed since whatever befell this hamlet. The woods around here are full of starving wolves."

"You'd see nests of gnawed bones, then."

"Maybe if we searched the buildings, you'd find such things." Blyth shrugged, as if dismissing the subject. The past was the past. What did it matter now?

Tyrus, though, couldn't let it go. What had happened here? Who had set the fire, and why?

They passed the town square, now a ruin. Beyond its edge lay the open cliffs and the bonfire, its flames licking into the foggy night over the shattered rooftops of the last buildings. Even the crackle of its logs echoed out to them. The group closed tighter as they slipped to the edge of town.

There lay a small cliffside park, edged by a flagstone wall. An overgrown garden of roses and holly bushes lined stone paths. There was even a tiny, raftered pavilion, untouched by the destruction. A statue guarded the entrance to the park. It stood unmolested, except for the stain of the bird droppings and the moss hanging from its stony limbs.

Hurl stopped before it, his head quirked to the side. He reached and gently pulled away a few lengths of moss. The features of the granite statue were worn by rain and wind, but a dark glower could still be seen. The figure stood with his arms crossed, clearly guarding, standing post. "The Stone Magus," he mumbled with a trace of worry.

"What's that?" Tyrus asked.

He shook his head and muttered under his breath, then stepped around the statue and studied the park. Other statues dotted the overgrown landscape, some large, some small.

All other eyes were drawn to the park's center, where a blaze as tall as two men threw back the dark and the fog. It was a heartening sight after the gloom of the ravaged village. Even from across the grounds, the warmth of the fire was felt. After a moment of silent study, the party drew toward its light and heat like so many moths.

Still, Tyrus knew better than to let his guard down. His gaze swept the park, the pavilion, the last edges of the town. Nothing moved. Nothing threatened.

Ahead, logs shifted in the fire, popping and cracking like some old man shifting his bones in a chair. The noise filled the hollow silence.

Tyrus signaled his men to fan out to either side. Blyth remained with him, while the others spread across the park and approached the fire from all sides.

As he searched, Tyrus wished he had his ancient family sword, the length of Mrylian steel with the snow panther pommel. But he had left it with Kral, who carried it to his grave, a symbol of a blood oath between Castle Mryl and the mountain man's lost people. Now the prince bore a sword from the armory of A'loa Glen, a fine and ancient blade, but one that seemed crude compared to the craftsmanship of the former. His fingers tightened on the hilt. A true swordsman made do with the weapons at hand, he told himself.

A call drew his attention to where Hurl and Fletch stood before another statue. Fletch waved his bow, indicating they should all gather.

Tyrus marched over.

It was a statue of black granite, an amazing representation of a deer, its head bent to nibble at a rosebush.

Fletch reached toward the stone, but Hurl batted his hand away. He turned to Tyrus. "We have to leave."

Tyrus frowned. "Why?"

Hurl waved an arm. "Look around!" The whites of his eyes shone with growing panic. He crossed swiftly to a statue of a pair of children hiding behind a bush. On a casual glance, it appeared they were playing hide-and-seek, but on closer inspection, the terror on their faces told another story. The two clutched each other in fright.

Tyrus crinkled his brow, glancing to neighboring statues: a man frozen in midrun, a trio of weeping maids, an elder on his knees. "I don't understand," he said.

"They're the villagers!" Hurl cried. "Frozen in stone."

"That's ridiculous," Blyth grumbled.

Hurl continued. "The statue at the entrance—it's the Stone Magus. He's marked this park as his own."

"Why? Who is this Magus?" Tyrus asked.

"We must leave—now!" Hurl began to head away.

Blyth blocked him. "The captain asked you a question, Mate." The threat was clear in his voice.

Hurl still looked ready to bolt, but Fletch appeared at his shoulder and placed a hand on his arm. His touch calmed the man somewhat, but he still trembled.

Tyrus moved nearer. "Tell us of this Magus. I've never heard of such a man."

"You've lived your life on the other side of the Teeth or in Port Rawl, not in the shadows of Blackhall like my people." Hurl's eyes darted at each flickering shadow. "We northerners here have a saying: 'A silent tongue speaks loudly.'"

"Now is no time for silent tongues," Tyrus intoned. "Tell us what you know of the Stone Magus. Is he friend or foe?"

Hurl frowned. "Both, neither—I don't know. I only know pieces of stories. I thought them fireside fancies." He waved an arm around him. "But this, and the statue at the entrance—it's right out of those tales."

"Maybe you'd better tell us these stories."

A final tremor passed through Hurl. He touched his friend's hand, drawing strength and collecting himself; his voice was stronger when next he spoke. "The stories of the Magus stretch far back, to the time when the Stone Forest was green and Blackhall never darkened our shores."

"Was there ever such a time?" Blyth muttered dourly.

"There was," Hurl said. "In the distant past, this northernmost forest was revered by all. It was rich in deer, rabbit, and fox, a spot of green when all the world turned to snow and ice in winter, and a cool bower from the summer's heat. But for all its wonders, there was something unsettling about the dark wood, rumors of strange laughter, of mischief played on those that overnighted, of floating lights to mislead the unsuspecting, even sightings of tiny folk no larger than one's hand—the *fae-nee*, they were called."

Blyth shook his head. "Wives' tales."

Hurl ignored him. "With such stories, none dared make their home in that dark wood except one."

"The Magus," Tyrus guessed.

Hurl nodded, still watching the park. "Deep in the wood, a great healer kept a homestead, a place where even the animals of the forest would go for a touch of his hand. He held the trees of the forest in deep reverence, so he made his home inside a hillside, in a warren of chambers lined by stone, warmed by many hearths, bright from windows that opened right through the hillside. He kept his home there for as far back as any could remember."

Sticks spoke. For such a large man, he had a very soft voice. "And the wee folk didn't bother him in their forest?"

"Ah, there's the rub. For some say the fae-nee were the children of the Magus."

"What?" Blyth blurted.

Hurl ignored the first mate. "In his loneliness, it was said he carved tiny men and women out of the wood of his homeland trees. And with his healing touch and deep love of forest, he brought the figures to life."

"Tiny wood people," Blyth scoffed. "Why are we wasting time with such addled stories? I thought we were looking for who set this fire."

Tyrus frowned and waved for Hurl to continue. "What became of this Magus?"

Hurl rubbed at the stubble on his chin. "Blackhall. That's what became of him. When the volcano erupted off the northern coasts, its ash and heat seared the forests, turning wood to stone. The Magus was never seen again."

"And that's the end of your story?" Blyth threw his arms in the air.

Hurl shook his head. "No. A century later, it begins again. People began to tell tales of someone living in the stone forest. A figure of stone, like the forest, but one that stalked its dead bower with vengeance in its cold heart."

"The *Stone* Magus," Tyrus said.

Hurl nodded. "A sect of worshipers formed, and said they could call upon the Stone Magus to protect a home or village."

"And you think he was called here?"

Hurl stared back at the ruined village shrouded in mist. His voice dropped to a whisper. "Maybe he was. Maybe the Magus could turn flesh to stone with a glance." The man's gaze settled back to the pair of huddled children. "But the stories vary. In many, the appearance of the Magus was as much a curse as a boon, destroying the good with the bad. Many of the tales end with these words: 'Remember and never forget, the Stone Magus' heart has also gone to stone.'"

Tyrus frowned and turned to the fire blazing in the park's center. "Well, Stone Magus or not, someone's been here recently, and I won't leave until I find out more." Tyrus waved back to the fires. "Let's see if we can discover who set this blaze and be done with this place."

"Aye, Captain." Blyth and the others circled through the park and again approached the fire from all directions. Five pairs of eyes studied the empty grounds and took up posts with their backs against the fire. Shadows cast out in all directions.

Blyth frowned. "What now?"

"I guess we've been too subtle in our approach. Maybe something more bold." Tyrus cleared his throat, then filled his lungs. "Ho!" he bellowed out into the misty night. "We mean no harm! We seek news of lost companions! If whoever set this blaze is out there, we ask gently that you show yourselves!"

His pleaded words echoed out over the cliffs, unanswered.

Sticks spoke from the other side of the flames. "Maybe they fled when they saw us coming. After what happened to the village here, they may be shy of strangers."

Tyrus sighed. If Sticks was right, any hope to gain knowledge of the fate of Wennar and his army ended here. But whoever had set the mighty blaze had done so to attract a passing eye: This was no tiny campfire, but a beacon set against the night. So why hide now?

Tyrus widened his stance and studied the park. Had some surviving member of the Magus' sect set this bonfire as a simple act of worship, then moved on? Was their nighttime search so much wasted effort? Or was there something more going on? He glanced back to Hurl. "This Magus, when did—?"

A muffled explosion erupted behind them, followed by a flare from beyond the cliffs. All eyes turned to the sea, where a sheet of fire stretched high into the sky with a roar, then collapsed down on itself.

"The ship!" Tyrus shouted.

They raced to the cliff's edge. Tyrus skidded to a stop and looked down upon an awful sight. The *Black Folly* lay where it had anchored, but flames now consumed it, turning the ship into a bonfire brighter than the one behind them.

"Wh-what happened?" Blyth asked weakly.

The answer was soon revealed in the waters around the ship. Lit by the flames, dark shapes moved through the waters, swimming toward shore with webbed fingers and snaking tails.

Sticks pointed one of his clubs to the cliff face below. "There!"

Climbing toward them were a score of leathery shapes. The beasts scrambled up the slick rock, using clawed hands and feet. Spotted, the hairless creatures revealed their razored teeth. A hiss, like steam from a boiling kettle, rose from the waters and cliffs.

"Sea goblins!" Blyth swore harshly.

Tyrus now understood what had happened to the seaside township— the fate of the villagers, the lack of bodies. He risked a glance behind him and was not surprised to see black forms scuttling out from the ruins: hundreds of goblins. He heard the rattle of their flinty tail spikes, the poisonous weapons of the creatures' females. The blaze here had nothing to do with the Stone Magus or lost d'warves. It was simply a crude lure to attract prey to these shores.

The village, the cliffs, the cove . . . it was a feeding nest for the drak'il, the sea-dwelling race of goblins—and Tyrus had led his men blindly into it.

The pack of drak'il closed in.

"We're trapped," Blyth said.

———

KAST HUDDLED WITH HUNT IN A CORNER OF THE DUNGEON AND SEARCHED for some means of escape, some weapon besides his sword and Hunt's torch. The locked room echoed with the pops and crackles of opening eggs. The entire clutch was hatching. Empty shells clattered to the stone floor, while the green gases from the fractured eggs choked the chamber, reeking of maggoty meat and swooning the two men's senses.

Kast's head swam; his ears rang.

He fought to maintain his vigilance, stomping and spearing any of the tentacled slugs that drew too near. A moment ago, one had managed to slide down his blade and touch his hand. There had been a burn of poison as he shook it away—then his hand had gone numb, forcing him to use his left arm to battle the beasts.

He now understood the fate of his love. Between the noxious gases and the deadening touch of the creatures' tentacles, Sy-wen and Brother Ryn must have been caught by surprise, numbed and poisoned before they could defend themselves, allowing the creatures to root into their skulls and possess their minds.

Hunt plunged his burning torch into more of the creatures, searing them from the ceiling and walls. He limped as he worked, one leg as useless as Kast's right hand. But the slimy creatures continued their relentless approach, flowing from scores of broken eggs.

All around the room, the slugs slimed across the floor, oozed up the walls, and hung from the roof. With each choking breath, their numbers swelled, while Kast's vision grew fuzzy.

So many . . . He sensed their doom, but a more disquieting thought intruded on his despair. In this room, there were enough of the slime creatures to contaminate half the castle's residents. So why feed so many of these slugs to Hunt's flame and his sword? Was it simply to possess the dragon? Or was there something deeper at work?

He stared down at his own sword. He knew one way to thwart the ambush here, a way to stop the enemy from gaining what it so clearly wanted. If he had to take his own life to save Ragnar'k, then so be it.

He gripped his hilt tighter.

"I . . . can't last much . . . longer," Hunt mumbled blearily. The tall Bloodrider wobbled on his one good leg.

Kast offered his shoulder to support, still guarding with his sword.

Sy-wen spoke from the door. "Breathe deep, my love," she mocked. "Soon you'll be back in my arms."

Kast had avoided looking toward the dungeon door. It unnerved him to find the face of the woman he loved staring so blandly at his own destruction. But now he spoke with passion: "Sy-wen, if you hear me, fight the demon! I know your heart! Nothing can withstand its strength!"

At the doorway, Sy-wen's left eye twitched. Her face tightened with lines of strain.

Was he heard? "Sy-wen, please try." His heart ached for her. He sent the last of his strength, falling to one knee.

But it was no use. Like the ocean after a passing storm, Sy-wen's face relaxed, and sibilant laughter, cold and mirthless, flowed from the lips he so longed to kiss. "Such love," the demon said bitterly. "But nothing can resist the Master's command."

At his side, Hunt collapsed with a groan.

Kast tried to haul him up but his numb hand fouled his grip. The Bloodrider fell to the stone floor, and his torch skittered out of reach. Before Kast could help, a score of gelatinous beasts dripped from the ceiling and fell atop Hunt's body. Hunt struggled to rise, but the numbing poison of the many beasts overwhelmed him.

With the torch gone, Kast found himself attacked from all sides. He could not go to his companion's aid. His sword flashed, slicing and skewering.

Hunt lay unmoving. Not even his chest rose and fell, but Kast saw the awareness in the other's eyes. Awake in a dead body. The fear in the man's eyes was as bright as any torch.

One of the poisonous beasts slid up Hunt's cheek, stretching out its tentacles. A tip brushed the edge of his nostril, thinning and slipping inside. The creature oozed forward, its body sliming into a more watery state. Unimpeded, its bulk flowed after its disappearing tentacle.

Kast now understood this new generation's means of access to its victim's skull. Drilling was no longer necessary. Despite his own danger, he lunged to his friend's aid. Hunt's eyes shone with panic and horror . . . and something deeper, a silent plea to end his life now while he was still his own man. Kast dove forward with his sword, unsure how he meant to use it. But as he poised with his sword over his friend, he watched the last of the creature suck away into Hunt's skull.

He was too late. He had no other choice.

He plunged the blade down—but before his sword struck, something landed on the back of his neck, burning with a thousand fires. Kast fell over Hunt, numb from the neck down. His sword clattered from his limp fingers.

On his side, he found he could only move his lips, his eyes. He gasped, struggling to breathe, but a great stone pressed on his chest.

Then the dungeon door swung open. From his vantage, he watched the approach of bare feet, stepping deftly around the tentacled beasts. He knew those ankles and the tiny webs between the delicate toes.

Sy-wen spoke harshly. "Gather the *simaltra*. We'll need as many as possible if we mean to take over both the castle and the Leviathan."

"And the second shipment of eggs?" It was Wrent, the captain of the guard.

"They'll be here by nightfall. So we must have the island secure, communication cut off, and the Leviathan under way by dawn. The new eggs must be seeded among the war fleet before they reach Blackhall."

Kast's mind ran with the plan laid out here. The demons meant to sally forth from A'loa Glen, wearing the faces of trusted friends, and spread their corruption among the fleet. Whether their plan succeeded or not, such an attack would weaken the fleet and sow distrust, just when the fleets needed to be at their most united.

He struggled for some way to raise a warning. But how? Distress must have been evident on his face. Sy-wen knelt beside him. She held one of the simaltra in one hand. "Do not fret, my love." She bent forward.

Kast gasped out one last plea. "Sy-wen . . ."

"Too late for begging, my love."

Despite her words, Kast noted the smallest twitch of her left eye. He prayed to the Mother above that he was heard. He knew it was possible for the possessed to break free for brief moments. The elv'in captain of the befouled scoutship had managed to warn Meric and crash her own ship. Even Sy-wen had done it, back in the library. Now he needed her to do it one more time—for just a fleeting moment.

He met Sy-wen's gaze as she reached out with the beast. He read what he could in her eyes, seeking some answer, some clue to salvation here. There had to be a reason the enemy needed Ragnar'k. He was sure it wasn't just for the dragon's strength. For all this effort, there had to be more purpose here.

Then, as he stared into the eyes of his love, he caught a glimmer of an answer. Shining clear from the demon were two emotions: *fear and relief.*

Understanding bloomed. The dragon frightened them! Something about Ragnar'k threatened their plan.

Kast fought the weight on his chest and drew a large breath. He reached with all the love and strength in his heart and spoke the words he hoped Sy-wen would understand: *"I have need of you!"*

Again the left eye twitched. The hand that bore the tentacled simaltra paused, shaking ever so slightly.

"I need you, Sy-wen . . . ," he pleaded again.

"Kast?" The voice was weak, a whisper on a wind, but it was thunder in his ears.

"Now, my love . . . I need you now!"

Her other hand lifted, reaching haltingly toward him. Then this hand also stopped. Sy-wen knelt, frozen in a silent war, with two hands held out—in one palm, a beast meant to corrupt, and in the other, an offer of salvation.

Kast struggled to move, but his body could not fight the poisons. All he could do was lift his neck, raising his cheek from the stone floor, offering his dragon tattoo. It took every last dreg of his strength. He had no more breath for words, only his eyes, pleading, full of his heart's desire.

But once again, love failed against the chokehold of demonic magick.

Something died in Sy-wen's eyes. The hand bearing the beast again reached foward. A leering smile twitched her lips. Kast leaned away, but his body was an anchor he could not escape. The simaltra touched him. The burning slime of the creature seared his face. He closed his eyes, knowing he had lost.

Sy-wen, I love you. Now and forever.

He waited for the slumber of the green gases to take him away from the horror and loss. But before he could escape, a flame, a thousandfold more intense than the touch of the simaltra, scorched his other cheek. He felt fingers trace his neck, spreading the fire, marking the borders of his dragon tattoo.

A whisper reached him through the pain, a balm that turned agony into ecstasy. "I have need of you . . ."

16

TYRUS AND THE OTHERS RETREATED TO THE BONFIRE. A THICK FOG HAD rolled in from the sea, blanketing the coastal cliffs and shrinking their world to the confines of the small park. Even the village had been swallowed by the mists.

But the real threat could not be so easily wiped away. A continual hiss of hunger and blood lust echoed from all sides. Occasional darker shadows skittered through the fog.

"If this soup grows any thicker," Blyth mumbled, "we won't see the weapons in our own hands."

"Keep steady," Tyrus warned. He raised his sword, judging the sea breeze. "The cover of the fog could prove as much a boon to us as to the goblins."

"How so?" Hurl whispered. "Do you think we can slip away?"

"The drak'il are creatures of the sea. If we can sneak through town and make it to the woods beyond, the beasts might not give chase."

Sticks rubbed his clubs together, the way a man might warm his hands. "If we can't *sneak* through town, then we'll bludgeon our way through."

Beyond the large man, Fletch knelt on one knee, his bow nocked with an arrow that tracked the drak'il as they closed around the park, worrying its edges. "Why don't they come at us?" the Steppeman asked softly.

No one answered for a long breath, until Hurl spoke. "It's the park. They sense the wrongness here. Their noses are sharper than ours."

"Mother above," Blyth snapped, "not more of that prattle about that cursed Stone Magus."

Hurl's face darkened, but Tyrus noted how the man's eyes flicked to the statues of the two frightened children.

"Well, something's keeping them back," Fletch offered.

Blyth could not argue this fact. For the moment, the beasts were indeed delaying their attack. But the hissing grew steadily around them.

Still, their reluctance to attack made Tyrus wonder: if the drak'il were so reluctant to enter the park, why set the false signal fire here? A bonfire set elsewhere would have lured a ship just as easily from the sea.

In the fire behind him, logs shifted with a creaking crackle. Tyrus wondered if his initial suspicion that the goblins had set the fire could be wrong. But if the drak'il hadn't set it, then who did, and why?

As he wondered, the sea breeze died away. The fog settled thicker— the moment Tyrus had been waiting for. "Ready, men," he whispered, tightening his grip on his sword. "On my command, we'll head for the northern wall, run its base, then over the wall and through town. We must keep hidden in the fog for as long as possible. Once discovered, they'll be on us as thick as fleas on a mangy dog's arse."

Heads nodded all around.

Tyrus' gaze fell on their archer. "Time to prove your skill, Master Fletch." He pointed to the south. "Can you strike one of the drak'il over there?"

Fletch swung around. "Aye, Captain. It'll be dead before it strikes the ground."

"No," Tyrus said. "Shoot for a leg or arm. We want the foul thing screeching like a wounded bird."

Fletch nodded and took aim.

"On my word," Tyrus said.

With one of their own wounded, the drak'il would flock to the south, believing their prey were trying to break free there. With the goblins distracted, Tyrus and his men would make their escape in the opposite direction.

"Ready," he whispered. Dark shapes moved along the southern wall. "Now!"

With the skill of his Steppe clansmen, Fletch let loose an arrow. It whistled through the misty air, then struck with a soft thud of flesh. A wheedling cry of pain cut through the steady hiss.

"Go!" Tyrus whispered.

Leading the way, he raced surefooted down a flagstone path, weaving around bushes and statues. The others followed, as silent and fleet of foot as himself. Ahead, the waist-high wall grew clearer out of the mists.

Tyrus reached the wall and ran along its length, bent in a half crouch to limit his exposure. At the northeast corner of the park, he motioned the others over the short wall. He stood guard as Hurl, Fletch, and Blyth scrambled over. Sticks waved him to go next, crouching with his clubs.

Across the park, the squeals from the wounded goblin ended with a gurgled outburst. The drak'il were not kind to their wounded. Silence descended.

Time was running short.

Tyrus turned to the wall as a commotion erupted from the mists: scuffles, a single grunt, a quick squeak. Tyrus swore under his breath.

Blyth's face appeared at the wall. *"Goblin,"* he mouthed apologetically. His eyes were sharp with wary concern.

Off to both sides, hoots and sharp hisses arose. Claws scrabbled on stone, drawing closer. The drak'il were circling back.

Tyrus vaulted the low wall, quickly followed by Sticks. A goblin lay at their feet. Its skull had been cleaved in two. Hurl knelt beside it, wiping his ax clean in a mound of grass.

Crouching, Tyrus pointed to the nearest street of the village. Again he led the way and raced across the scarp of bare dirt and grass. He dove into the shelter of the narrow street and flew down the broken, weedy cobbles. The avenue split and crisscrossed others. Tyrus didn't stop to get his bearings at any forking or crossroads. He trusted his own instincts. Still, with the fog this thick, one deserted street looked like another.

Behind them, the drak'il horde erupted with shrieks and furious yips; their dead brethren must have been discovered. The furious hissing echoed along the streets and added to the confusion of direction. At times, it sounded as if they were running toward the cries, rather than away.

Didn't I pass that burned shell of building already? Tyrus stumbled to a stop, panting silently, and searched around him. Three streets led from here.

Blyth slid beside him. "Captain?" he whispered.

Tyrus shook his head, shrugging his lack of certainty.

Somewhere nearby a slate roof tile crashed on cobblestone, but again the echoes played tricks with the sound. Tyrus searched the neighboring rooftops. Nothing but fog.

Blyth pointed his sword toward one street, motioning them in that direction. But Hurl stepped forward and nodded another way.

The strum of a bowstring sounded, and a goblin crashed to the stones from an upper-story window, an arrow feathering its eye. Fletch straightened from his crouch, drawing another arrow from his quiver.

Sticks waved his club toward all the streets, silently indicating that any way was better than staying where they were.

Tyrus couldn't argue with the giant's logic and took off.

They ran, sticking close to the walls. Streets flew by. Either the village had grown in this beastly fog, or they had indeed made some wrong turns. They should have been out the village and into the woods by now.

At least the screeches of the goblins had grown quieter. But that itself was unnerving. Their pace slowed again, eyes darting toward every dark shadow.

Then with a final few steps, the buildings vanished on either side. It took several more steps until they were sure they had cleared the village.

A gasp of relief escaped Blyth. Tyrus leaped ahead, hope surging. In his exuberance to escape the fog-bound trap, he ran headlong into a dark form that suddenly appeared out the mists. He could not catch his legs in time and fell at the stranger's feet.

He sprang up to discover the lurker was not a living creature, but another statue. He stared up into a familiar face: the worn stone visage of a stern patriarch, standing with his arms crossed—the statue that guarded the entrance to the cliffside park. His heart sank to the bottom of his belly. "We've run full circle," he gasped, turning to the others.

Hurl backed a step. "No!"

Tyrus thought the Northman was simply voicing his despair, but Fletch gasped, his voice full of horror. "There's no bonfire."

Tyrus' eyes widened. Even the fog shouldn't hide the huge blaze, especially so close. He swung around to find the statue reaching for him.

Stone-cold fingers latched onto his neck.

His men, hardened pirates and loyal to their captain, came to his aid with sword and ax. But the fingers continued to tighten, and he was lifted by his neck off the ground like a kitten. His vision darkened. The sword fell from his grip, but he fought and struggled, kicking and digging at the fingers that held him trapped—to no avail.

His airway closed off. His head pounded with each beat of his heart—and still the fingers squeezed. The world vanished into darkness. His legs and arms became as heavy as lead.

But even this assessment was proven wrong in the next heartbeat. "Sweet Mother . . ." Hurl's voice rang in his pounding ears. "He's turning the captain to stone!"

Sy-wen woke to herself, called forth by a dragon's bellow. She blinked as the world of light and sound returned to her. The dark cave of malice in which she had been trapped no longer held her. She was free!

Ragnar'k roared under her as she straddled his neck. He dug his silvered claws into the dungeon floor and fanned his wings, knocking aside piled eggs. Tentacled creatures lurched away from the crush of his claws. Sy-wen felt burning on the bottoms of her feet, sharing the dragon's senses as he squashed the foul things under his claws.

She sobbed aloud, both at the joy at being free and at the heartache that tore her being. She remembered the atrocities she had committed, the innocent blood on her hands. Possessed by the simaltra, she had watched all, experienced all, unable to control her body, while dark tendrils had wormed into her deepest secrets and memories. Her will had been ripped from her, replaced with something as black as the bottom of the deepest sea.

The dragon surged under her. She ducked from the low ceiling, almost crushed against it. Ragnar'k was wild, maddened by a rage unlike any she had felt before. He struck out with blind fury, bellowing, roaring. She felt drowned in his anger and grief, but underneath his seething emotions, she recognized the cause of his rage. Tied to his heart, she saw it was for *herself* the giant grieved.

"Ragnar'k," she whispered. "I'm here. Calm yourself."

The dragon froze in midstrike, one claw raised. *Bonded?*

"Yes, my love. It is I."

He lowered his claw. *I dreamed you lost, swallowed by tentacles.*

"It was not a dream," she whispered, yet unsure what exactly had transpired. Why was she free again? She remembered sensing Kast's need, the pleading of his eyes, the love in his heart. She had stretched all her energies to touch that heart.

Then the explosion of magick ... and she was free. Her will was her own again.

Kast, my love.

A flow of warmth entered her from two hearts, dragon and man.

New tears filled her eyes, but she wiped them away and stared around the room. The dungeon door was wide open, but the men under the simaltra's thrall had vanished. While possessed, she had not been privy to the innermost plots of the Dark Lord's monsters, but she knew they feared Ragnar'k. They had hoped to possess Kast and thus hold the dragon in check. But with Ragnar'k free, they now retreated, withdrawing their dark tentacle from A'loa Glen. It was a small battle won, but a larger war still loomed.

As Sy-wen searched the room, she realized one other was missing.

Hunt was gone.

She recalled the penetration of the high keel's son by the simaltra and despaired. It seemed she had been the only one freed by the dragon's magick.

Closer at hand, the tentacled beasts retreated from the dragon's assault, sliding along walls, floor, and ceiling. Ragnar'k stretched his neck and bellowed, warning them away.

But the effect was more profound.

Under the direct brunt of his roar, the creatures shriveled and dried as if under a searing wind. A large swath of the beasts dropped like dried clots from the stone wall and ceilings, dead.

Sy-wen stared in amazement. In the past, the trumpet of the dragon had been capable of stripping dark magicks from the skal'tum, the winged demons of the Black Heart. A similar magick must be at work here. The black spells of the beasts could not withstand the elemental energy of the dragon's roar.

As the desiccated beasts fell, she sent her silent encouragement to her mount.

Ragnar'k swept the room with his bellows, scorching and charring the horde. He tromped through the cracked eggshells, rooting out any last ones and roaring them into oblivion. She sensed his satisfaction as he sifted through the rest of the room, sniffing and pawing.

"Is that all of them?" she asked, trusting her dragon's keen nose.

Before he could answer, a commotion arose from the doorway. Guardsmen bristled at the threshold with spears. The dungeon keep, Gost, stood among them. He must have fetched the reinforcements when Ragnar'k had begun to bellow.

Sy-wen lifted an arm. "Stand back," she warned. "It might not be safe to enter here yet."

One of the guardsmen pushed forward. She recognized Py-ran, grandson of Master Edyll and lieutenant of the mer'ai forces still here. "Sy-wen?"

"Fear not." She answered the suspicion in his eye. "The magick of Ragnar'k has broken the hold of my demon possessor."

Py-ran's gaze remained narrowed. No one lowered his spear.

She understood their fears. How could she be trusted?

Py-ran spoke. "We ran into a cadre of Bloodriders on the way down here. They attacked us, then fled through a hidden door."

A Dre'rendi called from the cluster of guards, his voice shocked with horror. "One was Wrent, the captain of our guard. Another was the high keel's own son."

Sy-wen groaned. With Hunt's knowledge of the Dre'rendi forces available to the Dark Lord, the danger to the fleet heading toward Black-hall was heightened. The escaped group had to be stopped before it was too late.

"I will loose the magick of the dragon," Sy-wen said. "If you don't believe my word, perhaps you will Kast's."

Sy-wen shifted from her seat, sliding from her perch to the stones. She was careful to keep one hand in contact with the dragon until she was ready. Spears and swords followed her every move.

She ignored them and turned to Ragnar'k. "I must let you go, my great giant."

Bonded . . . you must not leave.

She heard the deep grief in his voice. "I must. I must prove that I'm free of the tentacles."

But, bonded . . . you are not.

She frowned and sent her thoughts silently. *I am my own woman.*

No. The dragon's thoughts were firm. *I smell one knot of tentacles still in this stone cave.*

"Where?" she said aloud.

Ragnar'k swung his nose and sniffed at her hair. *Here . . . inside you. It still lives. It hides where I can't reach it, but it still squirms, waiting.*

Sy-wen sensed the truth of the dragon's words. She wasn't free. Though the magick of Ragnar'k had broken the simaltra's hold on her, freeing her from her prison temporarily, it had failed to destroy the beast. It still lived inside her skull, waiting to claim her again.

Her fingers clutched a ridge of scale. She felt her legs weaken. Without the dragon, the evil inside her would take over again. Horror filled her at the realization that to free Kast, she must lose herself.

"Sy-wen?" Py-ran called from the doorway, clearly wondering at the delay.

She faced her fellow mer'ai. "I . . . I was mistaken," she whispered, her chest hollow with despair. "I'm not free."

Py-ran frowned at her words.

"Bring four of your men. Circle me with spears. I must not escape."

"I don't understand."

Sy-wen shook her head. "When I free the dragon and call back Kast, I will be possessed again."

His face grew pale. "Then don't let go of the dragon."

Sy-wen waved her free arm around the cell. "And imprison all three of us here? Ragnar'k is too large to fit out the dungeon door."

"There must be another way."

Sy-wen leaned her forehead against the dragon. "We must trust Kast to find it."

Stay with me, Ragnar'k urged. *I will dig our way out of this stone cave. My heart is strong, my claws stronger.*

Sy-wen smiled despite the tears. *No one doubts your heart, my giant, but true freedom does not lie that way.*

Ragnar'k remained silent for a long time, but she sensed his understanding and his fear. It resonated with her own terror. She dreaded allowing herself to be trapped, alone again in that dark prison.

Not alone, Ragnar'k whispered in her heart. *You're never alone.*

She again felt the flow of warmth from two hearts. She drew the heat and love around her like a blanket, wrapping it tight. Before her fears could overwhelm her, she stepped back, dropping her hand from the dragon's side.

The world exploded into a whirlwind of black scale. Inner barriers shattered—then she was falling down a well, and cold tentacles unfurled to catch her.

She clutched the blanket of warm love to her heart with all her might.

Save me . . . , she whispered out to the emptiness.

AROUND TYRUS, THE WORLD HARDENED, AS IF THE VERY AIR THICKENED—FIRST to molasses, then to mortar, then to stone. He did not feel his limbs and body solidify into granite. He simply could no longer move. Through eyes that would not blink, he watched the stone statue slam his body down, driving his legs into the soft loam as a man might plant a fence post.

Even time seemed trapped. He watched his men harry the Stone Magus, who without a doubt this creature was. Their voices grew high-pitched; their efforts became frantic blurs. Time sped into the future, leaving Tyrus behind. Helpless, Tyrus watched his men, one after the other, succumb to the same spell. Statues grew around him: Blyth frozen with his sword raised, Sticks crouched with his clubs crossed in futile defense, Fletch frozen with his bow in midpull.

One last battle ensued. A blur that was Hurl fought the demon from his childhood tales. The Stone Magus bore the man's ax chops with no reaction, his face fixed in the same stern glower.

Tyrus watched as a stone hand snapped out with a speed that belied the flow of time and grabbed Hurl by the wrist. The last of his men was about to succumb to the Magus' spell.

He refused to let it happen; he fought the leaden air. If he could only move a finger, he sensed the spell would break. He fed his desire and will into one hand.

Move, damn you . . . move!

Before him, Hurl's flesh and clothes grew the gray of unpolished granite, spreading inward from his struggling limbs. From the vantage in his eddy of time, the transformation seemed but a matter of heartbeats.

Tyrus continued to fight. He had no choice.

Hurl was slammed into the soil, a granite statue of horror and fury. The Stone Magus stared at his collection. His lips moved, and he uttered words of distaste and disgust. He must have been speaking very slowly, because the words were plain and clear. "Pirates . . . scum of the sea . . . you prey upon the carrion left behind by the Dark Lord. I curse your black hearts and leave you here to watch the world pass you forever by."

Tyrus fought all the harder. *We are not your enemy!* he sent silently. *We fight the same cause!*

But he was not heard. The stone figure turned away, moving at what appeared to Tyrus to be normal speed, but from the whip of clouds overhead, his gait must be slow, a creep of stone across the foggy field.

Wait! Tyrus yelled in his mind. He willed his stone limbs to move. A hand, a finger . . . anything. As he strained, his vision blackened with the effort. *Sweet Mother, release me!*

Laughter answered him, so very faint and far away. But it was not the voice of the Mother above. It was a deeper, grumbled sound that rose from the stony ground under him. Words followed, even fainter: *Remember your roots, fool.* The ridicule was blunted by a sense of peace and friendship.

Who . . . ?

Laughter again; this time it sounded more mournful. *We are stone, you and I. One Rock, one Granite. Have you forgotten your oath-brother?*

Tyrus felt his heart thud in his chest with recognition. *Kral!* His mind churned with confusion and shock. *How . . . ?*

I reach you through old allegiances bound in blood and sworn upon Mrylian steel. What is made of stone never truly dies, only slumbers. I heard you calling through the stone, crying for release from your own blood. Thick laughter grumbled. *Such foolishness . . .*

Tyrus felt his anger boil up. *I'm trapped in a statue.*

So? A sigh sounded, like a shifting of slabs of stone deep underground. *You've lived too long among pirates and brigands. Have you forgotten your birthright? You are* Lord Tylamon Royson, *heir and king of Castle Mryl, lord of the Northwall. Granite flows in your veins.*

Tyrus inwardly frowned. *At the Northwall perhaps, but not here.*

Whatever ground you walk, you are still a prince, Kral said with a finality that brooked no argument. *Granite is granite.*

Tyrus searched his heart. Could this be true?

Kral's voice began to fade, slipping back into the rocky roots of the world. *Stone can never hold you prisoner. We are rock, you and I. What more magick do you need?*

No further words followed.

Kral?

There was no answer. But for the briefest flicker, Tyrus sensed something else, a touch of prophecy, the Scrying that was also his family's birthright. Though the mountain man's time had ended in this age, he would be called for one last, great task, in a time yet to come. So Tyrus did not call out to him. He released the giant man to his stony slumber. *Guard my family sword well, man of the mountains. Wield it with honor.*

Tyrus focused back on the present, surprised to see the Stone Magus only steps away, plodding slowly along.

Tyrus concentrated. He abandoned any hope of moving a hand or finger. Instead he drew his energy inside him, to his own heart. He remembered Castle Mryl, his home and love. At the Northwall, he had but to press his palms against the granite and will the living energy in the stone to transform him into stone, allowing him to flow into and through the great wall as if through water.

Granite is granite. The mountain man's words echoed in his heart.

Tyrus centered himself, remembering who he was, what blood ran in his veins. Then he touched the magick in his heart, sending out his desire and will.

Slowly he felt the air around him soften. Stone melted to mortar. His raised arm sank under its own weight.

Tyrus held his heart calm, allowing the world to continue to thaw. His limbs bent from their frozen postures. His lips parted; his chest expanded. He took a cautious step, pulling his feet from the soil. It was like slogging through molasses, but he was moving! And time slipped back to its normal groove, a well-worn rut. The scudding clouds slowed to a gentle roll across the skies.

Tyrus raised his limbs. They were still the dark gray of unpolished stone. The spell remained intact, but he was no longer a fixed statue. He craned his neck and spotted the Stone Magus. With time back to its regular flow, the Magus appeared to be merely a statue in the misty woods. But his limbs were indeed moving with a steady and determined grind as he climbed the rise.

Tyrus sheathed his stone sword and pursued his quarry. He would not leave his shipmates frozen. He would force the monster back, to free his friends. Tyrus climbed the rise, but his pace was only a fraction more hurried than the Magus'. Granite was indeed granite, and though it flowed, it was still heavy. With each step, his feet sank into the leafy muck of the woodland floor. It was like marching through thick snow, but Tyrus plodded onward.

He was within a few lengths of the Magus when his quarry sensed the pursuit. The stern face swung in his direction.

Tyrus gained a small amount of satisfaction from the surprised look that spread like lava over the man's stone face.

"How?" the Magus asked.

Tyrus hauled his way up the slope. "You are not the only one with stone in his blood."

"Demon! Black-heart fiend . . ." The slurs flowed from the cold lips as the Magus faced him. Fingers folded into stone fists.

"I am no demon." Tyrus drew even with him near the top of the rise. "It is not I who turns innocent men into statues and leaves them to die."

Features hardened into a frown. "Innocent? I saw your ship. Pirates. Sea-sharks." A growl rumbled up his rocky throat, and a hint of madness shone from his eyes. "You are no better than the beasts that infest the town."

"You judge us falsely. We meant no harm. We came ashore only to look for lost friends."

He sneered. "This is not your land. You and your lost friends don't belong here. I will protect it as I see fit." With the determination of a boulder rolling down a hill, he turned away.

Tyrus raised a hand to stop him, but it was knocked away with the sound of crashing rocks as the Magus continued to the top of the rise.

"You must lift your spell from my friends," Tyrus called, dragging himself after the Magus. "I will pursue you to *Blackhall* itself, if need be!"

The mention of the Dark Lord's lair had the desired effect. The Magus swung around with a speed that belied his heavy stone limbs. "Never mention that foul place, that blight upon these northern woods."

"You claim to protect these lands. Why then do you thwart the very men who bring war upon that dread island?"

Confusion mixed with suspicion in the other's face.

Tyrus pressed. "It is *you* who do the Black Heart's will here, not I!"

Anger built in the other. "Lies!" he spat.

Tyrus held out his hands. "Stone does not lie. If you are birthed from the Land as its avatar, then you will know truth written in granite."

The Magus stared at his open palms, then slowly placed his own hands atop Tyrus'.

Tyrus looked the other in the eye, granite meeting granite. He prayed the creature's stony madness would clear enough for him to recognize the truth. He spoke boldly. "In ten days' time, four armies will converge on Blackhall, bearing the magick of the Land itself. We will lay down our lives to break into that lair and wrest the wyrm from his black hole."

With each word, the eyes of the Magus grew wider. The ravening glint faded for the moment. "You speak with a true tongue."

Tyrus bit back a sigh of relief.

The Stone Magus lifted away his hands and covered his face. "Will this pain never end?"

Tyrus stepped closer to him. "It is not too late to change what you've wrought. Release the spell that holds my men."

The Magus stumbled a few steps down the far side of the ridge. "I cannot." His words were a choked wail.

Tyrus pursued him. "Why?"

The stone figure glanced over a shoulder. "There is no way to lift the spell. Once cast, it cannot be undone. It is why I return regularly to the village."

Tyrus frowned; then understanding dawned on him. "The stone villagers . . . the bonfire . . ."

"A tragic mistake . . ." Rocky shoulders slumped in grief. "Two winters ago, the village here was attacked by dog soldiers and monsters. I was summoned near the end of the fighting. From the park, I cast out my magick. I was so blinded with rage at the murder and pillaging that I failed to notice my own energy spilling over into the grounds around me. The townsfolk were frozen in place in their own refuge."

The Magus shook his head. "I destroyed the statues of the attackers, buried the dead, and built a fire both to mark the town as my own and to offer light and warmth to those I imprisoned falsely. It is all I can do. The drak'il moved in last winter. As long as the goblins left the park alone, I allowed them to haunt the ruins. They are simpleminded beasts, and their hunger guards the park as much as I do. I did not want the resting place of those poor villagers disturbed."

Tyrus heard the pain in the other's voice. Guilt weighed heavier than granite on this one's heart. "There is no way to lift the curse?"

The other stood in a posture of grief. His silence was answer enough.

Tyrus clenched his stone fingers. What was he to do now? No ship, no men . . .

Overhead, the skies had begun to lighten to the east. Much of the night had disappeared while he had stood frozen, trapped in the time eddy. Now a morning breeze began to shred the blanket of mists. Patches of starlight shone clear.

Tyrus stared out at the valley below him, lost in thought. Across the valley floor, starshine limned an empty stretch of felled forest. From his vantage, it appeared the woods below and across the next rise had been axed and harvested, leaving behind only a landscape of stumps that spread as far as the eye could see.

An entire forest of stumps.

Who would need so much wood?

The winds gusted over the ridge, driving away the fog. With the brighter light, Tyrus recognized the error of his assumption. He stared in horror below.

A voice spoke behind him. "At least I accomplished some good here," the Stone Magus mumbled. "If nothing else, this dread legion of the Dark Lord will harm no others."

Tyrus found himself frozen again, unable to move, a statue like the thousands down below.

At long last, he had found the d'warf army.

17

KAST KNELT BESIDE THE DEAD BOY IN THE NORTH TOWER. GLASSY EYES STARED up at the hallway's raftered ceiling, and a grimace of pain marked the cold lips. A slow seep of blood still flowed from the jagged slice through the boy's throat. The kill had been recent.

Reaching out a hand, Kast closed the boy's eyes. He had not thought his heart could be any heavier this night. "I'm sorry, Ty-lyn," he said, remembering the lad's exuberance, his youthful pride and joy in his dragon, Helia. So much life . . . now gone forever.

Kast surveyed the other mer'ai, slain and strewn about the hall and across the entrance to the tower stairs. *An ambush* . . . The mer'ai group had been returning with the last eggs from the crashed scoutship. They would have had no reason to fear Hunt or the captain of the Bloodrider guard.

And there was no doubt who had attacked and murdered the group here. The handiwork was clearly Dre'rendi—and not a single ebon'stone egg remained.

Kast cursed under his breath. The murders here were his fault. He had delayed too long in the dungeons below, watching as Sy-wen had been bound hand and foot. She had fought, frothing, spouting foul oaths, laughing with mad glee. Heartsore, Kast had been too stunned to act quickly. He had not thought to send an immediate warning and guards to the mer'ai returning from the sea with the last eggs.

He stared down at the result of his shortsightedness. These days, blood was the wage of a single misstep. Kast stood and clenched his fists. No longer. It was time to bring the war to its rightful place.

Hurried steps sounded behind him. He turned to find Py-ran rushing toward him, flanked by three other mer'ai. "We followed their trail," Py-ran said. "They made for the docks."

"All of them?"

"We're fairly certain. We talked to some folk in the streets." The mer'ai warrior's voice lowered. "But there are more bodies at the dock. One of the Dre'rendi wave-chasers was commandeered."

Kast spat out a curse, pounding a fist on his sword hilt. "I want elv'in scoutships in the air and hunting for them immediately."

"I've already spoken to the commander of the elv'in. He's arranging a squad of pursuers."

Kast nodded at the lieutenant's efficiency. But he knew in his heart that there was little chance of finding Hunt and the others. The high keel's son knew the maze of Archipelago's islands better than anyone. They would lose themselves in the mist, and before the moon set, they would be in a new ship, taking one by force if necessary and scuttling the small wave-chaser. By tomorrow they would be gone.

But Kast did not succumb to frustration. It was time to stretch the game to a broader scope. From Sy-wen, he knew the plot of the possessed: to gather more eggs and sow them among the war fleet.

In such knowledge, there was power. Rather than whiling away ener-gies in useless pursuit, it was time to lay a trap for the possessed, to meet them where they were going.

Kast turned to Py-ran. "Send word again to the elv'in commander. I need a ship ready by dawn."

"To hunt the others?"

"No, I'm turning the island and its defenses over to you. Word of this betrayal and the potential danger must reach the fleet. With Xin failing to reach Tyrus this night, our lines of communication are down. I can't risk such important information to the vagaries of a crow's flight. I mean to take a ship myself to the fleet and set up defenses against the possessed."

The shock of his words darkened the other's face. "But A'loa Glen . . . ?"

"I have full confidence in your abilities to hold the walls here, Lieutenant."

"But—?"

Kast clapped the fellow on the shoulder, but he barely saw Py-ran standing before him any longer. His eyes were already staring through the walls and over the ramparts. In his heart, he knew the last assault had been waged in the dungeons here. The true battle had rolled over and past them, heading north, heading for Blackhall.

"They attacked here because they fear Ragnar'k," he mumbled, recalling the hate in Sy-wen's mad eyes. "But I will teach them the true meaning of fear."

Py-ran backed a step with a half bow. "I will alert the commander immediately."

Kast slowly unclenched a fist. He glanced to the ruin in the hall, his eyes settling on the pale face of a boy. Blood pooled around Ty-lyn. He remembered the youngster's laugh, his bright smile, his simple, proud love of his jade dragon. Somewhere, echoing out over the black seas, a lone dragon wailed a mournful piping. It sang to the sorrow and pain in his own chest.

He turned away as his vision blurred; he wiped his eyes. There was only one answer for the bloodshed here: *to make sure it never happened again.*

He strode down the hall.

Dawn could not come soon enough.

TYRUS STOOD AMONG THE RANKS OF STONE D'WARVES. THE STARS IN THE EASTern skies faded with the beginning of the new day's light. In that strange twixt between night and morning, everything took on a silvery cast, as if this army of d'warves only waited for the morning light to wake them from this unnatural slumber.

Tyrus moved slowly down the ranks. He felt the granite eyes of the soldiers on him. He remembered what it was like to have the world harden around you, holding you trapped. He stared out at the row upon row, rank upon rank: foot soldier, ax-lord, lieutenant, and captain.

Somewhere in this vast army, Wennar, their commander, stood in this valley or upon the ridge. Tyrus sought to find him, to offer what consolations he could, to promise that this war upon the d'warves' old slavemaster would not end in this field of stone and granite.

"I did not know," a quiet voice said behind him.

Tyrus closed his eyes. He had yet to find his way to forgiveness here.

"When last I heard of the d'warves," the Stone Magus said, "they were the underlings of the Dark Lord, his hands and legs upon our lands. I thought only to protect."

Tyrus turned to look upon the worn visage. "You were once a healer, if the stories I've heard are correct." The prince waved his arm over the graveyard of living stone. "Do you see what your blind rage has wrought? It has taken life and twisted it most foully. How are your actions any more righteous than the Black Heart himself?"

"I didn't know."

Tyrus would not let this excuse stand. "Ignorance is the deadliest poison. The power you were granted was a responsibility placed in your hands. It was not for you to vent your own hurt upon this world. With power comes responsibility."

The figure bent under the weight of his words. "I didn't ask for this power." The Magus straightened, holding out his stone hands. "I can't feel anything. Not the wind on my face, not the rain. Not the brush of a hand on a cheek, not the softness of a child's skin. Anything I touch turns to stone."

Tyrus recognized a bottomless well of pain in the other's eyes—and a madness that was barely kept in check.

"Free me . . . ," the man pleaded.

As Tyrus stared at the Magus, understanding came to him. It was not rage at the Dark Lord that fueled his rage, but simple loneliness. The Magus had lived all his life in these northern woods, a hermit dwelling in a hillside. But as isolated as he was, he had never been fully alone; the world could still touch him in all its myriad and intimate ways.

But with the transformation, that had all changed.

The Magus was as much trapped in stone as any other here. Locked away from the world, he had lost contact with it. He had forgotten what it meant to live and breathe. Tyrus remembered Hurl's warning: *Remember and never forget, the Stone Magus' heart has also gone to stone.* Those words were more prophetic than any imagined.

Tyrus might not be able to forgive, but he could pity. He stared at the statue with its arms raised in pleading. "We'll find a way to free them," he said, and motioned with his own granite arm. "The d'warves, my men, and the villagers."

"It can't be done," the Magus said, his limbs lowering in defeat.

Tyrus stared out at the army as the eastern skies grew brighter. To the north, hills appeared from the darkness. Bare, skeletal trees covered their slopes. It was the edge of the Stone Forest, the onetime home of the sad figure standing beside him.

"Tell me of the coming of Blackhall," Tyrus said.

The Magus covered his face. "It was too awful a time. I don't want to touch those memories again."

"You must," Tyrus said more harshly. He confronted the man, pulling one hand away from his face. "If there's any hope to reverse your magick, I must know how your powers came to be."

The Magus shook his head. "It was too dark a time to look upon."

Tyrus shoved down his other arm. "Then look on this!" he shouted, and motioned to the stone army. "Thousands imprisoned by your hand, trapped in stone like you. Can you hear them crying for release? Can you feel their eyes begging?"

"No . . . no . . ." The Magus fell to his knees. He rocked in place. "I didn't know."

"Now you do! And you owe them more than a bonfire at night and weepy words of sorrow. If the cost is to face your past, then you must pay it."

The Magus continued to rock. His heavy knees furrowed the soil. Tyrus prayed he had not pushed the creature too far, driven him back into ravening madness.

Then slowly words tumbled from his stone lips. "I was gathering herbs from a woodland glen, anise and hawksbreath." He lifted his hands to his nose. "I can still smell them on my fingers."

Tyrus moved a step closer, though he feared touching the man, lest he draw him from these ancient memories.

"Then a great roar, like a thousand thunderstorms crashing together split the quiet. The ground shook, heaving up in great swells then falling again, as if the land itself had become a stormy sea. I was thrown down and clung to the soil with my fists, praying to the Mother above and the Land below. I thought my prayers answered when the quaking slowed and stopped. I rose and fled back to my hillside home. When I got there, I found all the windows shattered, my great oak door cracked in half. I went inside to see what was left of my home and belongings . . . Then . . ."

The rocking of the Magus became more frantic; a wail rose from his throat, boiling out as if from the turmoil inside the stone man.

"It is over," Tyrus murmured. "You're safe here."

The figure seemed deaf, but after a moment, words keened through the cries. "A wind . . . a hot, searing, foul wind came screaming from the sea. It blasted every leaf from every tree. Saplings were uprooted. Older trees cracked and tumbled end over end. I fled and cowered in the root cellar, and still I could not escape the burn of the winds. It was impossible to breathe." The Magus clutched at his throat as he rocked, gasping, choking.

"Calm yourself," Tyrus urged. "The wind is gone, lost in the past."

The Magus shook his head. "It's never gone. I can still hear its howl in my ears. It is the scream of the damned." His voice rose and took on a fevered edge.

Tyrus reached for the distressed man, but the Magus stopped rocking. His eyes were wide open, but Tyrus knew he was not seeing the world around him.

"Day became night as the wind screamed away. I fled my home, but the world was gone. A smoke that glowed with sick energies covered the skies and lands. Ash fell like rain. And far to the east, the skies glowed an angry red—the face of all that was evil in the world. I could not meet that gaze, so I dove back into my home. But there was no escape."

Slowly the rocking started again. "The air sickened. The land shook. Wicked cries echoed down to me. I covered my head, but still they found me." A new note entered his voice with these last words; it sounded like joy.

"Who found you?"

"My little ones . . . the fae-nee."

Tyrus remembered Hurl's story of the tiny carvings brought to life by the healer. Was it true? Or was this madness?

The Magus continued. "I had thought them surely destroyed, but they found me curled in my cellar. I went to greet them, but they were frightened. They fled . . . all but the first of the fae-nee that I created—Raal, a northern word for *king*." The last was said with thick bitterness. "He forced me to look upon myself."

"Look upon yourself?"

"He made me turn and see the form buried in ash at my feet."

Tyrus frowned in confusion.

"Raal wiped away the ash and revealed the stone figure upon the floor of the root cellar. He made me stare at it." As the Magus spoke, fingers rose and gently probed chin, cheekbones, and line of nose. "I hardly recognized my own face."

Tyrus' eyes widened.

"But there was no denying what lay on the cellar's floor: my corpse. I was dead and hadn't even known it. My spirit must have become lost in that volcanic fog, unable to escape to the Mother above. But Raal, curse him, made me face my own death."

"What happened after that?"

"Raal called the other fae-nee to him. They circled both the body and my spirit and gave back what I had granted them." A wail rose again. "I didn't ask for it."

"What did they give you?"

"Life," the Stone Mage cried. "The life I had breathed into them, they returned to me a hundredfold."

Tyrus weighed this claim. He had heard of elementals that could animate nonliving objects, some for days. But if the madman here was to be believed, he had imbued these creations of his, these *fae-nee*, with independent life.

"I was forced back into my body. And as such magick could enliven wood, so it did to stone. I rose from that cellar floor, alive again, but trapped in a shell of hard ash."

"And your ability to change others into stone?"

The Magus shook his head. "I don't know. It was wrong to cast a spell while there was so much corruption in the air. The fae-nee must have been affected by the black magick in that foul ash or the loathsome energies wafting through the blanket of glowing fog. But when I rose, I quickly discovered all I touched turned to stone. Over time, I learned it was a curse I could cast out from my body." The Magus again covered his face. "But the cost . . . it was too high."

"What cost?"

The Magus lowered his hands and glared at Tyrus. "Haven't you been listening?" Madness laced his words. "The fae-nee gave me back what I gave them—their life! I woke to find nothing but whittled pieces of wood in the cellar. My children were gone!" The Magus clenched one fist. "Except for Raal. He still lived. He left me in the woods and said that when Blackhall sank again, I would be free to rest."

"And what became of this Raal?"

The Magus gestured to the barren northern hills. "He's in the Stone Forest, curse his eyes. Rebuilding his brethren."

"The fae-nee?"

"The spell did not only affect me," the Magus said. "The warping of that magick changed Raal, too. He can now chisel petrified wood from the Stone Forest and grant it life, adding to his brethren, becoming a true king as I named him. But his children are not sweet and innocent. I've seen them. Though their flesh is as pale as the wood from which they came, there is something dark about them. I can't even stand to look—"

Tyrus cut him off. "You said their *flesh* is pale?"

The Magus turned from the hills to look at him. "You still aren't listening! It was the warp of magick. I can change the living into stone. Raal can change stone into the living."

Tyrus sensed the balance of forces here, a warp and weave of fearsome energies. He studied the hills stubbled with skeletal trees. The first rays of the sun glinted off the crystalline branches of the petrified forest. Deeper in the woods, mists moved through the trees, swirling like disembodied spirits.

Did an answer lay out there? Could Raal reverse what the Magus had wrought? And if he could, would he do so?

He turned to the Magus. "I want to meet this Raal."

The stone figure glanced to him as if he were the mad one. "The fae-nee don't tolerate strangers. As I said, they've grown dark of heart. I haven't seen Raal in over two centuries."

"Then it's high time for a family reunion," Tyrus said. "Let's go pay your kin a visit."

"No," the Stone Magus said. "They'll kill you."

Tyrus patted the granite that made up his chest. "I'd like to see them try." He faced the Stone Forest. "Take me to this king of the fae-nee."

It WAS GOOD TO FEEL THE ROLLING PLANKS OF A DECK UNDERFOOT, EVEN IF the ship flew leagues above the true sea. Kast closed his eyes and felt the wind whipping through his hair, tugging at his cloak, shoving against his chest. Among the Dre'rendi, it was said the wind had teeth. This morning Kast could feel its bite.

He kept one hand on the bow deck's rail as the *Ravenswing* swept northward. They had favorable weather: a fierce southeaster blew out from the Blasted Shoals. Kast felt the energy in the air, a mix of lightning and sea salt. The elv'in captain, Lisla, was adding her own magick to fill the sails and steady the course. The plan was to reach the fleet in three days' time, and it would take every bit of the captain's talent to achieve this end.

They had left at dawn: a crew of elv'in warriors, a squad of Blood-riders, and Master Edyll of the mer'ai. They also bore one prisoner, trussed and locked in a small stateroom: Sy-wen. Kast could not leave her behind. In the war to come, Ragnar'k could be important, and she was the only one who could unlock the dragon inside him.

But there was another reason he hauled Sy-wen along on this journey: *hope.* Somewhere locked inside the evil was the one he loved. He gripped the rail, digging in his fingernails. He would find a way to free her or die trying.

A hatch slammed open behind him, caught by the fierce winds and thrown wide as the small zo'ol tribesman climbed to the deck. Having lived among pirates, Xin was experienced with walking the deck of a storm-swept ship. He hurried toward Kast, not bothering with the safety ropes, bent against the wind. Shaven-headed, the tribesman's single braid of hair was a flag behind him.

"I've reached Lord Tyrus!" he said breathlessly as he took a place beside Kast. The pale scar of an eye on his forehead seemed to glow with joy. "He lives!"

"What news does he bear? How fares the fleet?"

Xin held up a hand. "I made only a flicker of contact. His sending is muffled, as if he speaks with his mouth covered. All I could understand was something about the d'warves. But he lives!"

"Is he with the fleet?"

The tribesman frowned. "No, I think he is alone."

"Alone?"

Xin shrugged. "I will rest and try again later."

Kast nodded, relieved. "I'll need you to pass word to Joach."

Xin fingered the shark tooth pendant around his neck. He used the talisman to communicate with Elena's group. "I spoke with Joach before we departed. He knows we're en route north."

"And their group?"

"They expect to reach the og're lands in another day or two. Travel is slowed by the waning elemental energies. Even my contact with the others weakens."

Kast sighed. It was hard coordinating so many fronts with just messenger crows and a single shaman with the ability to farspeak. Now even his skills faltered. How he wished Xin could communicate with more than just Joach and Tyrus.

Xin spoke, sensing his frustration. "Such is the way of the wizen," he explained, holding up his arms. "Two hands, right and left—those are the two ways a man may greet another. That is the limit of my magick."

Kast patted the tribesman on the shoulder. "I know, Xin. And if wishes were coppers, we'd all be rich men."

"I will do my best to reach Tyrus. But there is something else . . ."

Kast heard the hesitation in the other. "What is it?"

He glanced away. "The one who holds your heart . . . She is in danger."

"I know. The tentacled creature—"

"No, it is more. My abilities to farspeak are tied to my deeper gift—to read another's heart, not just his thoughts. The mind is less trustworthy than the heart."

"And what have you sensed?"

"The creature nests in your love's skull, coiled and holding her will trapped. But it is her heart that worries me. She loses hope. She knows that she can only be free if you are gone. In this, she despairs."

"I will find a way to break this curse," he said fiercely.

Xin placed a palm on Kast's chest. "Your heart is an open book. I know your determination—and so does Sy-wen. Her fear above all else is that you will do something rash, something that will harm yourself, so she might be free."

Kast glanced out over the rail. He remembered his promise a moment ago: to find a way to free her or die trying. He did not deny Xin's words.

"She feels the same," Xin said again, clearly reading what his heart held close. "She would rather die than see you come to harm. Corrupted as she is, she cannot see a way to hope. There is where the true danger to her lies."

Frustrated and powerless, Kast felt tears well.

"Though her cell is deep in the ship's hold, she remains a beacon to a wizen like myself. The creature's madness is like kerosene thrown on fire; it shines like a blaze in the night. But at its heart rests a bastion of goodness and love. It has glowed as fierce as the fiery madness around it. But now . . ." His voice trailed off.

Kast spoke the words he knew to be true. He too had felt it. "It fades."

"She allows herself to be consumed, like tinder in a blaze."

Kast took a shuddering breath and asked the question that terrified him. "Is there a way to stop it?"

Xin did not answer. Kast turned to him. The tribesman met his gaze. There was an answer in those eyes.

"I must go to her," Kast said.

"You are both one heart. In that there is strength."

Since the incident in the dungeon, he had avoided any contact with Sy-wen, fearing it would unman him when he most needed to be strong.

"There is a storm unlike any other on the horizon," Xin continued. "If you mean to face it, you'll need all your heart."

Kast glanced again to the sweep of sea and clouds. He took a deep breath, drawing strength from the salty winds, steeling himself for his meeting with Sy-wen.

Xin touched him on the arm. "I go to my cabin. If I learn anything new, I'll alert you immediately."

"Thank you," he mumbled as the tribesman departed. Once alone, Kast sought the dragon inside him. With each transformation, the line between the two thinned. He could sense Ragnar'k brooding. "She'll need both of us," he whispered to the dragon. "It will take both our hearts to bolster hers."

A roar echoed through his being. Their wills were one.

Kast strode the planks to the middeck ladder. He clambered down and headed toward the stern hatch. Overhead, elv'in sailors hung from the rigging, calling to one another. The mainsail snapped angrily as an adjustment was made. The winds howled in protest. The ship bucked as if riding a wave crest, then sped faster. The captain plied her skies with the skill of the best seafarer, always seeking the best line, calculating, adapting.

Unlatching the stern hatch, Kast left the deck and the ship to her captain. He climbed down the stairs to the passageway below. It smelled musty after the free winds above, and foreign. The timbers used to build the elv'in ship came from lands other than Alasea. The resins were too sharp to the nose, discomfiting. And everywhere the air seemed to resonate with a whine just beyond the reach of ears, vibrations that tingled the smallest hairs. As much as the ship might appear like any other seafaring vessel, it was not.

Kast crossed down another deck. Down here lay the crews' quarters and storage rooms. But one cabin had been converted into a makeshift prisoner cell.

At the end of the passage, two Bloodrider guards flanked the door—Garnek and Narn. They drew straighter at the sight of Kast. He crossed toward them, feeling the hum of the elemental-wrought iron keel under his feet.

Garnek stepped forward as he approached. "Do you need assistance, sir?"

"I came to see Sy-wen."

"Yes, sir." He turned to Narn and nodded. The way was quickly unlocked, and the newly installed bar removed.

Kast passed between them, and Narn stepped to follow, a hand on his sword. "No," Kast said. "I would visit her alone."

"Sir, your own rules say none may visit the prisoner by themselves. A guard must be present."

Kast paused in the doorway and glanced over his shoulder.

Narn's eyes widened a fraction at the expression he found on the other's face. "Of course, sir," he mumbled, backing a step. "We'll stand guard outside."

Kast entered, then waited for the door to be locked and bolted behind him. A single oil lantern hung from a hook in a rafter. Set to the lowest flame, its meager light created more shadows than it vanquished.

Girding himself with a deep breath, he crossed to the room's lone bed. Straw ticking covered the hard wood, and atop the bunk lay the girl he loved, each limb tied to one of the posts.

Kast did not bother to turn the flame higher in the lantern. What the dim light revealed already threatened to break his will.

Sy-wen had been stripped naked, the easier to keep her clean. A blanket had been tossed over her, but her thrashings had dislodged it. It lay crumpled on the floor beside the bed.

He bent and picked it up. Her eyes tracked his every movement, like some shark eyeing its prey, waiting to strike. Her hair lay like a tangle of seaweed on the pillow.

He shook out the wool blanket and swept it over her form.

This kindness earned sharp laughter. "Join me, lover," she rasped. Her lips were bloody, and froth flecked her chin. "There's always room for another. Loosen these ropes and I'll show you pleasures like you've never experienced before from this wench."

Kast tried to close his ears to these words. "Sy-wen," he said, speaking not to the thing on the bed, but to the mer'ai woman buried deep inside. He reached to touch her cheek, but the creature flung herself at him, snapping at his fingers like a starving cur.

He pulled back his hand and sat on the edge of the bed. "Sy-wen, I know you can hear me. You must not lose hope—not for your freedom, not for us." But his own words sounded hollow. How could he recharge her confidence when his own ebbed to such a low tide?

Laughter bubbled from the bed, mirthless and cold.

Kast closed his eyes, his shoulders trembling with grief. It was wrong to come here. It was too hard. But deep inside him, a dragon roared. The simple, raw love of a beast for its bonded welled through him. He basked in its glow and discovered something that had never occurred to him.

Love did not have to be hard. It was a simple thing, uncomplicated, pure, and glorious. No matter the trappings, hardships, and entanglements, at its core, love was simply warmth, two hearts fueling one another, stoking a flame together.

Kast shoved aside all thoughts of tentacled creatures, great wars, and black magick. He listened to Ragnar'k roar, and deep inside him, he echoed this call of love, a chorus of two hearts. He found blind strength and stood.

Crossing to the lantern, he twisted the flame brighter. He would not hide in shadows any longer. He turned back to the bunk.

Sy-wen still sneered at him with disdain, but now he recognized the shine of her eyes, the fullness of her lower lip, the soft tones of her skin. But it wasn't just her physicality; he saw her spirit, the heart that had stolen his. There was nothing so dark that it could dim that light.

He sank back to the bed.

Somewhere far away he heard the laughter and the slurs and curses.

But it fell on deaf ears. It was only mud on a diamond; he could easily wipe it away.

"Sy-wen," he whispered, "I love you."

He loosened the rope that bound her right wrist and drew her hand to his cheek. He ignored her attempts to break free; his fingers were iron on her wrist. He pulled her palm to his cheek, careful to avoid his dragon tattoo on the other. Nails dug at his skin, but they were worn and dull. He felt nothing.

"Sy-wen," he murmured.

Slowly the fingers relaxed on his face. Her cold palm grew warm as it rested against his skin. He felt his love returned to him from afar, stoked from another's heart.

"We are not lost to one another, not even now." His voice was a breath, nothing more. "Nothing of any importance has been taken from us." He pressed her palm more firmly to him. "This is all that matters. Us, together—that is a purity nothing can corrupt."

The heat bloomed on his skin. Faint words reached him from the bed. ". . . love you . . ."

Kast squeezed the fingers and drew them to his lips. He kissed her palm long and with a passion that melted away everything but his love. Time stretched forever. The moment became written on their spirits, to last them through the hardships to come.

Sy-wen . . .

Finally, a commotion at the door drew him away. Shouts erupted, followed by a small girl's scream.

Kast sat up straight. A clawed hand swiped at his eyes, but his grip did not fail him. He forced Sy-wen's arm down and re-bound the wrist to the bedpost.

He risked a touch to her cheek, but beyond the door, the childish cries of a small girl continued, accompanied by the furious anger of a young boy. Scowling, Kast crossed to the door and pounded on the oaken frame. "Unbar the way."

A latch clanged, and wood scraped as the door was yanked open.

Beyond the threshold, the two Dre'rendi guards faced a pair of elv'in sailors. The thin-limbed newcomers each held a child by the upper arm.

He stared in shock at the pair of youngsters.

The girl spotted him, too. "Uncle Kast!"

"Sheeshon?" Kast stepped toward her. "What are you doing here?" He had left the child in the care of Mader Geel, her nanny, back at the island.

"We snuck aboard," Sheeshon said. "I hid in an apple barrel. He hid in a box." She pointed to the other child, and Kast recognized Rodricko, Nee'lahn's boy. His eyes were stretched wide, and his lower lip trembled as he fought back tears.

One of the elv'in sailors spoke. "Captain Lisla sensed them in the hold. She sent us to root through for stowaways."

Kast waved for the two sailors to release the children. He knelt by Sheeshon and pulled the boy to his side, tucking him under an arm. "Why did you sneak onto the ship?"

Sheeshon stared over his shoulder. Her eyes crinkled, and an arm pointed. "Aunt Sy-wen . . . is she sick?"

Kast glanced behind him. The cabin door was still open. Frowning, he motioned for Narn to close and lock the door, then turned back to the young girl. "She's fine, little one. She needs to rest."

Sheeshon nodded sagely. "She's got worms in her head."

Kast was taken aback by her words. He knew Sheeshon bore her grandfather's gift of the rajor maga, an ability to see beyond horizons, but at times like this, it chilled him to see such insight mixed with childish simplicity. He pinched her chin and drew her attention to him. "Sheeshon, why are you here?"

Her voice shrunk to a whispered secret. "Hunt needs me."

Kast sighed. Back at the castle, he had tried to explain to her that Hunt was simply away. He should have known that such lies would not be believed by someone with her abilities, especially when she was bonded to Hunt by ancient magicks.

"We're trying to find him," Kast said. "But you shouldn't have left Mader Geel. She'll be scared for you."

"I had to come. Hunt needs me."

"And what about Rodricko?" Kast asked.

"He had to come, too. He didn't want to, but I swore that I'd scrimshaw him a pony if he didn't cry."

"And I didn't cry!" Rodricko burst out.

"Well, you were gonna."

Kast shook his head. Both children looked exhausted, red-eyed, and limp of limb. He gathered them under his arms and turned to the guards and sailors. "I'll take them to my cabin. Send a crow back to A'loa Glen with the news of the children. If I know Mader Geel, she'll have the entire castle torn apart stone by stone looking for the girl."

One of the elv'in stepped forward. "Captain Lisla said she is prepared to head back to the island at your word."

Kast nodded. He hated the delay in backtracking, but he had no choice "Have her tack around as soon as the winds are favorable."

"No!" Sheeshon said. "We don't want to go back."

"Hush, child. Rodricko can't leave his tree for very long. He is nyphai. He must go back."

"No, he doesn't! I showed him how." She glared at the boy. "Show Uncle Kast."

Rodricko shook his head. "I don't want to."

Kast hiked the boy higher. "What is Sheeshon talking about?"

"Show him!" Sheeshon demanded.

Kast leaned his forehead against the boy's. "It'll be our secret. You and me. Bloodrider brothers."

Rodricko's eyes widened. He stammered, then reached in his jacket and pulled out a twig upon which hung a heavy flower. It was rumpled, but clearly one of the koa'kona blooms. "Sheeshon says that I got to prick my finger and put blood on the broken end of the stem. It'll keep the flower fresh, and I'll feel good."

"Have you tried this already?"

Rodricko nodded. "I used a rose thorn."

"He yipped like a puppy when you step on its tail," Sheeshon added.

"I did not!'

Kast frowned at the girl. "Sheeshon, where did you get this idea?"

She squirmed, biting her lips. She would not meet his eyes.

"Sheeshon . . ." He kept his tone stern.

She leaned closer, pressing her cheek to his. "Papa told me in a dream. He showed me."

Kast knew she meant her grandfather, Pinorr, the shaman of the Dre'rendi. He had died during the War of the Isles. Could the child be right? Would Rodricko be safe as long as he watered the twig in his own blood?

"Papa says Rodricko is different. He comes from bloodsuckers."

Kast startled. Sheeshon knew nothing about Rodricko's heritage, that his roots traced back to the Grim wraiths. He turned to the boy. At half a day out from the island and the tree the boy should be ailing, fading, and weak. But besides appearing tired, Rodricko was pink of cheek and full of nervous energy. He did not seem to be suffering in any way.

"What should I tell the captain?" the elv'in asked.

Kast considered the situation. Dare he put faith in Sheeshon's dream? A boy's life hung on this hook. But so much also depended on a swift rendezvous with the fleet.

"Sir?"

Kast straightened and stepped away with the children in his arms. "Stay the northerly course for now."

Sheeshon clapped, then hugged him around the neck. "We're going to find Hunt!"

"Yes, we are." Kast headed to his stateroom at the other end of the passageway.

As they reached the door, Sheeshon whispered in his ear. "When I'm growed up, I'm gonna marry him."

He lowered her to the floor. "Hunt is too old for you."

Sheeshon giggled. "Not Hunt, silly." She pointed a small finger toward Rodricko, then pressed the same finger to her lips, indicating secrecy.

Kast tousled her hair. He hoped that girlish fancy came to pass. As such, a part of him still balked at his decision to continue with the voyage. He was leading the children into a realm of danger beyond the darkest contemplation.

He opened the door and guided Sheeshon ahead of him, then followed with the younger boy in his arms. Rodricko was already dozing off.

Sheeshon clambered onto the bed, and he settled the boy beside her. Rodricko crawled to the pillow and fell into its embrace.

"You both rest," Kast ordered. "I don't want either one of you even stepping off this bed." He turned to go, but the girl reached out and touched his arm. "Uncle Kast, Papa told me to tell you something."

Gooseflesh prickled the skin on his arm. "Your papa . . . from another dream?"

"No, the same dream as the one about Rodricko." Sheeshon yawned, a jawbreaker that would not stop.

Kast had to restrain himself against reaching out and shaking the girl. "What did he say?" His voice was strained.

Sheeshon curled into a tired ball. "Papa says you have to kill the dragon."

"Kill Ragnar'k?" His words were not so much a question as simple shock.

But Sheeshon answered it anyway, stifling another yawn, " 'Cause the dragon will eat the world."

18

THE SUMMER SUN OFFERED NO WARMTH IN THE COLD, WINTRY WOODS. TYRUS marched over soil as hard and flinty as the trees themselves, while gray ash puffed up with each step. He grumbled under his breath, while the Magus trod ahead of him, slogging up a wake of clogging soot, moving no faster than a man might crawl.

"How much farther?" Tyrus asked.

The Magus pointed vaguely ahead. "Still another league."

"And you're sure Raal will be there?"

"With Raal, I can never be certain. He has become as wild as his creations."

Tyrus studied the woods to right and left. Though the trees were leafless, the forest remained gloomy from the fog-shaded sun. Still, green life poked through here and there: twisted and stunted bushes bearing more thorns than leaves, scraggly grasses, a few gnarled saplings. And with the greenery came all sorts of small life: beetles, snails, snakes, voles, and scrawny rabbits. He even spotted one deer.

But conspicuously absent were any sign of the fae-nee, the tiny inhabitants of the dead forest. Throughout the trek yesterday and this morning, he had sought some evidence of the creatures: tiny footprints in the ash, distant voices, movement. But it was as if he and the Magus were the only ones who moved through the woods.

Only during the night had he caught flickers of motion from deep in the wood, but they could easily have been ordinary woodland creatures. Still, Tyrus sensed that little was ordinary that moved through this forest at night.

The only other creature he had spotted in the woods was something large that had lumbered past along a hill's ridge in the distance. It was like nothing Tyrus had ever seen. It was gray-skinned—or perhaps just ash-covered like himself—and moved on all fours. Its head was like a bull, but with a drape of tentacles hanging above its wide mouth. It marched along, gathering anything green from the forest floor with its tentacles and feeding its gullet.

Tyrus had given it a wide berth. Even granite could break if trampled under the bulk of such a gigantic creature.

But besides this lone beast, the woods appeared empty of life. It lay dead silent—no birdsong, not even a whisper of insects. Each step they took sounded loud and abrasive.

Tyrus was glad to have company on this journey, even the taciturn Magus. The Stone Forest was not a landscape to walk alone. It was a place of madness, where empty hills and vales drained one's spirit, and loneliness was compounded.

Finally, the Magus broke the stony silence. "We near my old home." His face swung like a plant seeking sunlight. "I would see it before we pass into the deeper wood."

"Is that wise?" Tyrus asked. He feared that his companion might become mired in old memories and grief at the sight of his former homestead. "Perhaps we should go directly to Raal."

"No," the Magus droned, swinging in a westerly direction. "I would see my home again."

Tyrus had no choice but to follow. The Magus led the way up a long slope and through a section of trees that grew more densely together. As Tyrus followed, he noted strange pocks on the tree trunks they passed. They appeared at first natural, but as more and more became apparent, he realized they were nooks and cubbies cut or chiseled from the trees.

He paused to examine one of these holes. It was about two handspans tall and one wide, crudely hacked.

The Magus noticed his attention. "Raw material from which the fae-nee were born." He spoke as he marched up the hill. "I would take a chunk of wood from a tree and sit with it until it spoke to me."

Tyrus closed the distance between them. "Spoke to you?"

"Each piece would eventually reveal its form to me, whether it be a man or woman, a child, an animal." He shrugged. "Then I'd chip away the wood to free what was hidden inside."

"Then you'd give it life," Tyrus said.

The Magus' voice dropped to a sad whisper. "My mother . . . She was always ailing, but she always had a smile for her only child. She taught me our family gift."

An elemental lineage, Tyrus thought, passed from one generation to another. And now it's passed to fae-nee creations.

"But Raal . . ." Bitterness lay thick on the Magus' tongue. "He's stolen my mother's gift and fouled it."

Tyrus sighed. He only hoped the little creature still bore this gift—then he might be able to free the d'warf army and his companions back at the village. It was a thin hope that drove the prince forward into this bleak wood.

The Magus reached the summit of the hill and gazed down. Tyrus joined him.

Below lay a small vale, set in stone—a glimpse from the time of Blackhall's creation. A small section of forest had been cleared away. Stone fences marked boundaries of what must once have been a garden. There was even a tiny stone outbuilding, roofless now, its thatch long fallen away. It must have been a pen or small barn. The far slope of the vale was cleared of trees, an empty expanse of ash and rock. Open holes dotted the slope, some still glinting with shards of glass, like the icy teeth of some subterranean monster: windows into the Magus' home. A larger hole, surrounded by slabs of broken rock, must be the entrance.

At the foot of the hill, a thin stream moved with a sluggish gurgle, its waters a sickly green. The place reeked of ash and brimstone.

"Home . . . ," the Magus moaned, a sound full of heartbreak. Still, he started down the slope, determined to dredge up old pains.

Tyrus followed. He had no choice—he had opened this wound back among the field of d'warf statues and would have to see it through. They forded the small stream, not bothering with the broken remains of a narrow bridge. Both men were made of stone; even this sickly water could not taint them.

Once across, the Magus led the way to the entrance. "I've not been back here since I first fled in horror from the root cellar."

"Five centuries?"

The Magus nodded and bent to enter his old home. "I would go alone from here."

Tyrus thought to object. Whatever the fellow found in there would likely send him into a pit of depression from which he might never climb free. But there was no use in arguing. Once set rolling, a boulder could not be easily stopped.

The Magus climbed over the tumble of rocks and disappeared inside. Tyrus noted that the slabs of rock here were petrified wood, too—what was left of the door, once stout oak, was now broken stone.

Tyrus stepped back from the threshold with distaste. A thin wind howled through the spindly branches of the surrounding trees—they appeared like bony fingers scratching at the smoky, soot-filled skies. This was the domain of the Dark Lord, a small peek into the world he would create.

Despair settled like ice around the prince's granite heart.

He turned from the skies. Off to the left, a bit of color drew his eye. It stood out against the ash-gray of the landscape: a small dandyflower, a weed growing from between two slabs of the entryway door. It was a sickly specimen: a bit of green, a feeble curl of yellow petals no larger than a thumbnail. But it pushed from the rock and brightened the world for its short life.

Tyrus smiled. He had never seen anything more beautiful. The sight fired a fierce determination in his heart.

Even here life fought against the Dark Lord's corruption. With renewed hope, Tyrus faced the dread forest and skies.

Then a scream burst behind him, echoing up from the bowels of the underground home, ripe with pain, horror, and outrage.

Tyrus swung around, sweeping out his sword, a sliver of polished granite. "Magus!"

The wail fled into the woods, fading away.

"Magus!" he bellowed again. "Answer me!" He held his breath, but there was no answer. The silence pressed down on his ears, squeezing his throat. Even the winds had quieted, as if shocked by the scream.

He faced the dark threshold to the subterranean abode. After another long moment, he took a single step toward the entrance. He had no idea what lay below, but he also knew he had no choice but to go see. The Magus was the only one who knew where Raal hid in the Stone Forest. If there was to be any hope for the others, Tyrus would have to brave the darkness below.

Gripping his sword hilt tighter, the prince picked his way over the rocky rubble and ducked through the entrance. The hall beyond was murky, and the passages extending out were even darker. He had no torch. But the Magus had found his way down without light. Hopefully the broken windows would offer some illumination.

With his sword held before him, he moved toward the passage he had seen the Magus take. The darkness closed around him immediately. He crept one step at a time, sweeping out with his sword, seeking obstacles. Slowly he shuffled down the hall. His eyes quickly grew strained. His ears sought any sound that might lead him to his quarry.

The hall ended at a cross passage. Tyrus paused. To the left, the way seemed fractionally brighter. A window must light that direction. But which way did the Magus go—toward the light or away? Tyrus scrunched his brows. He had an inkling of where his companion would head. The Magus had come back here to face his past, back to his roots, back to where he was born into this stone-cold world—*the cellar to this haunted home.*

Tyrus sensed the best course was to the right; the floor seemed to slope slightly downward that way. Taking a deep breath, he headed into the darkness. He was rewarded soon thereafter by discovering a set of stairs on the left. As he stood on the top stair, he heard a slight tinkle from a bit of rock bouncing down the steps. Someone had passed recently this way, loosening what had been untouched for ages.

Had the Magus braved the dark stair? Maybe the scream was from a fall. Could the Magus have hit his stone head and blacked out?

No, the scream had been full of anger and horror. Tyrus took a step down the well. Then another. The way was narrow and steep, stair edges crumbling underfoot—a tricky climb even with light. In darkness, it was pure treachery. His eyes sought any light.

More pebbles tumbled, dislodged by his own feet. The narrow stairway spiraled, tight and confining. As he rounded another turn, he began to make out his sword arm, a darker shadow cutting through the gloom. Light! There was light seeping from down below!

His pace increased. With each step, details emerged: the stone walls, the worn steps, the turn of the stairwell. The light took on a richer cast, a reddish glow. Fire.

Who could have set a flame down here? He reached the end of the stairs and stopped. A short passage stretched to an open doorway. Lights flickered up ahead, clearly a fire or torch.

With the tumble of stones from the stairs and his own echoing footsteps, there was no need to pretend secrecy. "Magus!" he called out. "Are you all right?"

There was a long hollow silence—then a whisper of laughter.

"Magus?"

The laughter swelled, full of depths that spoke of madness and malice. It echoed up the stairway.

But as Tyrus stood on the step, he knew he was mistaken. The sniggering behind him was *not* echoes. A pebble bounced down from above. The stairway behind him was no longer empty.

A voice, brittle enough to shatter glass, called out from the cellar room. "Come, Prince of Pirates, join us where it all began."

There was no doubt who spoke ahead. It wasn't the Magus, but his creation—*Raal.*

Tyrus moved forward. He had come to meet this creature; he wouldn't balk now. And from the sounds behind him, he doubted he would be allowed to leave.

Crossing to the doorway, he stepped into the cellar. The room was shallow but wide; a single torch was jammed into a hole in one wall. Its light revealed old, crumbled shelves, and sacks of burlap huddled in the corner. Ash and dust covered all.

In the center of the cellar stood the Stone Magus, his back to Tyrus. He seemed frozen in place, a true statue again.

Laughter crackled from beyond the figure. "Welcome, Prince of Granite!"

Tyrus edged around the walls, circling the frozen Magus to get a clear view of Raal, his adversary here.

As he crept around, he found the space in front of the Magus empty. Tyrus frowned. Had Raal circled in step with him, keeping the statue always between them, staying hidden?

Tyrus suspected a trap and stopped, sword ready. "Who speaks?" he said. "Show yourself."

"You know who I am!" the other said gleefully. The Stone Magus turned his head and stared at Tyrus. Laughter flowed from his flinty lips. "I'm Raal, lord and king of the fae-nee!"

KAST LEANED OVER THE RAIL OF THE *RAVENSWING* AND STUDIED THE STRANGE sea passing under the keel of the ship. As a Bloodrider, he had sailed many treacherous waters: the maze of the Archipelago, the squall-ridden Blasted Shoals, the haunted channels of Kree-kree, the fog-bound shores of the Breshen Jungle. But he had never seen anything like these northern waters that surrounded Blackhall.

It was an ocean of ice and fire.

Throughout the Bay of T'lek, mountains of ice rode the waves like blue-humped seabeasts. Other areas of the sea roiled with steam, boiling like a kettle atop a flame. Steam and fog misted into a storm on the sea's surface. The currents of the bay were as tangled as any knotted rope. Its seabed was a trap of volcanic reefs and jagged atolls that seemed to appear and disappear at whim.

Nothing was constant about this sea. Not the winds, not the weather.

Master Edyll stood beside him, a companion in this vigil. The silver-haired elder of the mer'ai shook his head with resignation. "These waters will be a difficult field from which to wage a war."

Kast didn't bother with false cheer. He kept his face grim.

"We should reach the fleet by dawn," the elder said.

"If the captain can manage these temperamental winds."

"She's a strong lass. She'll manage."

Kast nodded at this. Over the past two days, he had learned to respect the lithe captain of the *Ravenswing*. Lisla ran a tight ship, kept all in order, and seemed tireless despite the malaise that affected her powers. The elv'in craft had swept over the oceans like a leaf in a storm. She had three skilled windblowers, elementals to conjure winds, on hand day and night. They shuffled one man out to rest a quarter of the day. Otherwise, the pair on duty were ceaseless in the aid of their captain.

Kast glanced back to where Lisla stood by the rudder of her ship. Her coppery hair billowed with winds as she manned her post. Her skin was as pale as the scudding clouds overheard. And though the blue of her eyes was as sharp as when they first took flight two days back, he was not sure she had slept.

He admired her. The trip would normally have taken five to six days; she had cut the time in half. With such folk at their side, Kast could almost foresee victory in the war ahead.

"I spoke to Xin earlier," Edyll continued. "He still can't clearly reach Lord Tyrus. The prince lives, but the details are scant."

Kast heard the concern in the mer'ai elder's voice. He also noticed the way his companion rubbed at the fleshy web between his thumb and forefinger. "What worries you about this? It is probably just due to the waning elemental energies."

"No, Xin spoke to Joach this morning. He says Joach sounded crisp and hale, though that distance is even greater than to Lord Tyrus."

Kast's brow crinkled. "So you think the prince is in trouble?"

"And what of the d'warf army? Where have they gone? Lord Tyrus goes in search of them along the coast, and now he's mysteriously out of communication. I don't like it. The Dark Lord has already attacked A'loa Glen with that sick clutch of evil, and he now threatens to seed the fleet with the eggs. Who's to say what evil he aims toward our land armies?"

Edyll pointed an arm over the rail toward the roiling sea of ice and fire and continued. "It is not the condition of the battlefield that concerns me, but the state of our own forces. The full moon is due in another five days, and we are far from ready for a full-scale assault."

"War never picks a convenient time," Kast said. "You must simply grab your sword and either defend or attack."

The older man shook his head and mumbled, "Spoken like a true Bloodrider."

Kast sighed. "We will win this war."

"Why do you think that?"

He turned to the misty seas and the northern horizons. "Because we must. There is no future without victory."

A long silence stretched; then Edyll spoke softly. "And no hope for Sy-wen?"

Kast gripped the rail, his head bowed. "I love my niece," the elder said. "But the battle ahead is larger than any one individual. Hard sacrifices will need to be made. Remember that you are the Dragonkin reborn."

Kast scowled, but his hand rose to touch the tattoo of a black dragon on his cheek and neck. He recalled the picture of the forefather of both their peoples: Dre'rendi and mer'ai. The figure in the ancient painting had been riding a white dragon and bore the same dark tattoo. The past had come full circle back to the present, like the curled dragon on his cheek, its tail touching its nose.

"The Dragonkin made difficult choices during his time, and I suspect you'll face decisions even harder."

Kast remained silent. A question already weighed heavy on his heart, something he had discussed with no others. Sheeshon's words echoed in his heart: *Papa says you have to kill the dragon.*

"You'll have to put the good of the world above your own heart," Master Edyll finished. "Can you do this?"

Kast clenched a fist atop the rail. "It seems I must."

Edyll nodded. "You are truly the Dragonkin reborn." He patted him on the shoulder, then headed for the shelter of the lower decks.

Kast remained on deck, alone, his thoughts lost to the winds. He remembered the painting of his forefather on his great white seadragon. What would the Dragonkin have done if faced with the same dilemma? Could he have slain his own mount? Was he that hard? Could anyone be that hard?

Over the winters of their union, the walls between dragon and man had worn thinner. Kast knew the dragon's heart as certainly as his own.

There was a wildness to Ragnar'k, but also a well of loyalty and love for Sy-wen that was as bottomless as his own. In this love, the man and dragon were bonded in ways more intimate than any rider and his mount. He had no idea how to slay Ragnar'k, and if he knew, would he have the heart?

Words echoed with warning in his head: *The dragon will eat the world.* Sheeshon's gift of the rajor maga was unquestioned, but she was only a child. Could she have misinterpreted the meaning of her prophetic dreams? Dare he place such important decisions into her hands?

And then there was Sy-wen to consider. Only the magick of Ragnar'k could break the spell of the tentacled beast in her head. If he killed the dragon, would he be slaying all hope for her freedom?

Kast stood under the snapping sails as the *Ravenswing* swung slightly to port, ever chasing the swifter winds. He raced toward a fate that even prophecy could not penetrate. But as he stood there, he trusted his heart. He could not dismiss the certainty he had seen in Sheeshon's eyes. He had sensed the truth the moment it had been spoken. He remained facing north, letting the cold winds wipe the tears from his cheek.

Ragnar'k must die.

A tremble passed over his form, terror and despair. At first, he thought it was just the emotions of his decision, but the sense of menace grew around him like the clutching arms of a demon. Then a scream arose from below, echoing through the planks.

"Sy-wen!"

Other voices rose in panic from the rigging and deck. The ship's flight faltered as the captain seemed to lose her bearings.

Kast spun and found Sheeshon behind him. She held up a bit of half-carved ivory. His hands took it out of reflex. It was a crude boat with sails and a prominent keel, but there was something sinister about it. Coarse faces had been carved into its sides, twisted into malignant or terrified visages.

"A bone boat," Sheeshon said.

Sy-wen's scream died away, and the trembling terror passed. As the boat steadied, Kast collected himself. "Scrimshaw," he agreed with the child. "Bone ivory." He passed the boat back to the child.

But Sheeshon seemed disinterested in her carving. "Not that!" she said. She pointed down to the seas. "Over there."

Kast glanced to where she pointed. Against the dark blue seas, the ship below was the white of something dredged from the bottom of the blackest sea. But it raced with a speed that had nothing to do with winds and currents. It was as if the oceans themselves rejected the sick craft and sought to expel it from the waters, sending it flying northward.

Frowning, Kast grabbed a spyglass from his hip and sought a better view. It took him half a moment to find it. Once he did, every hair on his arms and neck rose with a pebbling gooseflesh. He knew he was staring at the source of his terror from a moment ago. It was not winds that filled those sails, but fear and horror. The craft must have passed near enough for them to feel its wake.

He stared at the monstrous construction. Its prow was a skeleton, its bony arms outstretched to the skies in supplication or pain. Its sides were not planks of wood, but fused bones and skulls. Even its stitched sails seemed too leathery for cloth. *Skin* came to mind at the sight, accentuated by the dripping gore that seemed to flow along the rigging, like blood through a corpse's veins.

"A bone boat," Kast mumbled.

Sheeshon pointed. "Hunt's down there! Let's go see what he's doing!"

Tyrus faced the Stone Magus in the dusty cellar. "Raal?"

The figure swung to face him fully. Stone eyes narrowed, and lips pulled into a wicked sneer of amusement. "Welcome to the heart of my kingdom." He half bowed, mocking. "One lord of stone to another."

"I don't understand."

The statue straightened, running a palm over his form as if smoothing rumpled clothing. "We share this prison of stone. Magus and king. Man and fae-nee."

Shock slowed. "You're one person!"

"Two spirits, one body."

Tyrus' thoughts turned to Fardale and Mogweed. The twins were similarly afflicted. "The magick . . ."

"It not only warped. It also wove. During the spell where the Magus' spirit was sewn back into his stone corpse, I was woven into the mix like yeast into a bread's flour."

"Then why did you wait until now to reveal yourself?"

"It was not my choice." A familiar bitterness soured his words. "The Magus only lets me out when he sinks so deep into his well of blackness that I can slide past him to the surface."

"And can I speak to the Magus now? Can he hear me?"

"Not unless I allow it! I control the body." Laughter flowed after this.

"And I won't allow it." He covered his ears with his stone palms. "Let the sleeper sleep!"

Tyrus watched this display with a furrowed brow. The relationship, though similar to Mogweed and Fardale's plight, was clearly different—and something struck him as wrong. This new speaker still sounded at the edges like the Magus. Was it just the limits in range of a stone throat, or was it something more sinister? And Raal had called him by name a moment ago, knowing him as prince and pirate. This spirit would not know that, unless it shared the Magus' ears and mind.

Subtle mannerisms struck him: the way the eyes shifted to the left just before he spoke, the way one hand's fingers would curl and uncurl while speaking. These characteristics of the Stone Magus persisted in Raal. Were the two truly different? Were they two spirits sharing one body, or had one spirit split into two minds?

"Come. It's been forever and a day since I met any of my children. Let us see how they've fared in my absence." Raal clumped his stone form back to the door. He paused only to grab up the torch from the wall.

Tyrus had no choice but to follow. Raal led the way to the spiraling stairway. He thrust his torch forward and called up the steps. "Children of the fae-nee, come to your king! Come greet our poor castle's guest!"

From beyond the reach of the firelight, laughter answered this summons. A pebble rolled down the steps, then another.

"They come," Raal whispered, his smile stretching. "My children . . ."

Tyrus heard an echo of the Magus' pain behind the excitement, but his own attention focused on the stairway. The first of the fae-nee crept shyly into the firelight.

Tyrus gawked.

The first creature was no taller than two handspans, hairless and gray of skin. It walked on two legs like a man, but the joints bent backward, more like a bird. Its head was taken up by its two eyes, black and moist. The mouth underneath was a lipless slit.

Others clambered after this one: some spindly with heads too large for their bodies, others squat with toady faces, some walked upright, others on all fours. There was even one pair joined by a single arm. But no matter the shapes, they all bore the same large black eyes, full of dark mischief.

Raal knelt to greet his offspring. They came to him like rats swarming over a corpse, climbing his stone arms, perching on his shoulder or head. Laughter flowed from Raal, echoed by his children, piping sharply from hundreds of tiny throats.

Tyrus backed away, fearing their touch.

Raal straightened and stood in the sea of pale gray flesh. "Their father is home."

Tyrus frowned as more fae-nee clambered into the bowels of this dark dwelling. "You made all of them?"

"With my own hands, my own magick."

It must have been centuries of work. One of the fae-nee crept near to Tyrus. It moved as if it were boneless. It had only one eye and stretched its neck to sniff at him, curious but wary of this granite stranger. It slipped to his leg. Then moving faster than the eye could follow, it raced up his limb to his waist.

Tyrus winced as claws dug into his granite flesh. From its perch, it continued to sniff at his form, clearly confused. Tyrus grabbed it, pulling it free. It hissed and snapped at his fingers, biting deep into the granite of his thumb. Pain welled. It seemed his granite flesh was not impervious to the fae-nee. Birthed from the poisonous petrified wood, stone could harm stone.

He tossed the creature back among its brethren, where it was lost in the shuffle of flesh and limbs. Tyrus pressed his wounded thumb to his chest. A single drop of blood fell to the floor. Another fae-nee sniffed at the splatter, then lapped it up.

Blood feeders.

Tyrus backed another step. Of the hundreds here, no two were alike. The roil of flesh was like the ravings of a madman given form and substance.

Tyrus quailed at the enormity of the task before him. How could he convince the Magus or Raal to help him? Hope of a cure for the d'warf army faded—but he knew he could not give up without trying. Perhaps if he better understood the magick at work here . . . "Raal," he called out.

The stone figure focused back to him.

"I would see how you make one of your fae-nee."

Raal waved a hand dismissively, knocking loose one of his creations. It fell squalling among the others. He ignored it. "I have enough children to care for."

"So how would one more be a burden? Or can't you bring another into existence?"

Raal's eyes narrowed. "You doubt me . . ." A vein of menace laced his words.

Tyrus held his breath, sensing the moment could go either way. The hundreds of pairs of eyes swung upon him like a murder of crows eyeing a worm. At a word from their king, he could be torn limb from limb, a feast of blood for this foul brotherhood. But something shone in Raal's expression, hidden under the menace: loneliness and fear.

Understanding dawned. How long had it been since anyone had conversed with the Magus or Raal? The pack at his feet were clearly mindless, creations of madness given life. They were feeble company.

"Come above," Raal finally said. "I'll show you what I can do." He stalked through the fae-nee at his feet. They ran from his legs and up the stairs ahead of him.

Tyrus followed, leery of the stragglers, those fae-nee that moved more slowly, shambling or crawling. His thumb still ached from the bite. As he climbed, he kept his sword between him and these last fae-nee. A small creature that looked like a six-legged spider scrabbled ahead of him. He sidestepped its clumsy progress and followed Raal with his torch.

They reached the top of the stairs and wound their way to a chamber with a large cold hearth. A broken window let in wan sunlight. Raal slipped his torch into a wall slot and waved Tyrus inside.

The fae-nee swarmed ahead at their master's signal and climbed over chairs, tables, and benches. Pottery on a shelf fell with a loud crash, startling Tyrus. Other fae-nee ran through the hearth, leaving tiny footprints of ash.

Raal scowled but entered with Tyrus. "They're excited to have visitors."

"So I see."

A wood rat was ferreted out by the horde. It ran across the stone floor, but it was set upon by the fae-nee. They tore it apart before it could cross half the room. Its squeal was brief as it disappeared under their many claws and teeth.

Raal crossed to a bench on the far wall. Metal tools were spread on the tabletop and hung on pegs on the walls. Tyrus, following, recognized woodworking chisels, awls, and knifes. Chunks of petrified wood in various stages of sculpting rested on the bench.

Raal reached to one of these. "I was working on this before the Magus last took command of the body." He collected a chunk of stone chiseled into the likeness of a dog. A vague snarl marked its lips.

Grabbing a sharp-pointed awl, Raal set to work on the piece. He dug and scraped, changed tools, flipped his handiwork one way, then another. Tyrus let him work, fearful of disturbing his concentration.

Seen through the open window, the sun was setting into gloomy twilight, as one statue worked on another.

Tyrus used the time to plan a strategy. If Raal could indeed change stone to flesh, then he must convince him to break the spell on the d'warves. But what coin could he offer this madman?

He had no clear answer when Raal finished. "That will do," he said. "It is hard to hear the voice in the wood after it's stone."

Tyrus remembered similar words from the Magus, how the wood spoke to him, telling him what it wanted to be. Tyrus stared at the wolflike carving. If the wood itself told him to sculpt this, then the tree must have been mad. The dog had horns on its head; its hind legs looked like a bird's, ending in claws.

"You can breathe life into this?" he asked, suddenly unsure he wanted Raal to do so.

"Yes." Raal studied his handiwork. "It only takes a bit of concentration."

Tyrus stepped around for a better view. He saw that most of the other fae-nee also were fixed on the new statue.

"And a little blood," Raal mumbled. He grabbed up one of the fae-nee nearby and stabbed it with the awl he had been using.

It screamed like a wounded bird, but Raal lifted it and spattered its blood over his new statue. Where each drop touched, stone melted into gray flesh. The transformation spread like thawing ice over the sculpture's entire surface. In a short moment, the wolfish creature appeared flesh.

Raal tossed aside the wounded fae-nee. It scrambled away, licking at its wounded side. On the bench, the wolf stood unmoving, as still as any statue, only carved of gray flesh.

Leaning forward, Raal blew across the form, starting at the back end and working forward. Where his breath touched, the flesh seemed to ripple, coming alive. Legs bent, its tiny chest heaved, its neck craned. Then, as Raal straightened from his labors, wide black eyes opened to stare anew at the world.

"Welcome, little one. Welcome to this dark world." Laughter followed, echoed by the other fae-nee.

Tyrus gaped as the creature tested its legs, throwing its head around, trying to skewer anything nearby with its tiny horns. It bounded off the table to join the others. Several gathered around the newcomer, sniffing and pawing at it.

Raal swung around. "That is how my children are born. Blood and breath."

Tyrus remained speechless. *Blood to melt stone to flesh . . . breath for life.* Was that the answer? Could the blood of the fae-nee break the spell that held the others trapped in stone? And since the others already had life, would they even need Raal's breath?

He stared at the mass of cavorting creatures. How much blood would it take?

There was only one way to find out.

He crossed to the bench. The wounded fae-nee had left a trail of blood atop the table. It was black but also seemed to glow a sickly green, like the stream that ran past the house. Tyrus leaned forward, placing his granite palm atop a tiny pool of the brackish blood.

With its touch, a shock trembled up his arm. His legs weakened, and a gasp flew out of his lips. He stumbled back, raising his hand before his face. His granite palm was now pale flesh. As he stared, the transformation raced up his arm with a warm tingling. The heat warmed the stone. Clothing and skin bloomed with color and life.

Raal stared at him in shock.

Tyrus gasped again as the spell dissolved from him, spreading over his torso and down his legs. He watched his other arm come to life, starting at the shoulder and sweeping down to his hand and up the length of his sword. In moments, bright steel reflected in the firelight.

He straightened and moved his limbs. He felt lighter, more spry.

"The Magus' spell . . . you broke it!" A cry escaped Raal's throat. It was pure madness, a mix of horror and delight, an impossible sound. Turning to the bench, he smeared some of the blood on his own stone flesh. He held his finger out toward Tyrus: the finger remained gray stone. "Why doesn't it work for me?" he screamed, sounding distinctly like the Magus. "Why is this a key to your prison and not mine?"

Tyrus backed from this tirade.

The fae-nee, sensing the distress of their master, churned and grew more agitated. Wails piped from their throats, too, an echo of their creator. Several were staring his way. Their black eyes glowed with suspicion . . . and something more dire. *Blood lust.* Tyrus was no longer stone. They must smell his flesh. He remembered the fate of the wood rat. If they set upon him, how far would he get before being brought down?

The wolf creature stalked out of the pack, nose in the air, gray lips pulling back to reveal gray teeth.

"Why can't I break free?" Raal wailed.

Tyrus knew he was doomed unless he could gain the support of the fae-nee king. "The magick that created you must have been more complex.

As you said yourself, the energies of your creation were warped by the foul birth throes of Blackhall. The blood of the fae-nee must not be strong enough to break the spell."

Raal screamed in despair. The fae-nee surged toward Tyrus, sensing the source of their master's distress.

Tyrus held the sword before him. The wolf creature leaped, but he kicked it away. "There might be a way!" he cried. "A way to set you free!"

The wailing cut off with his words, and screams faded from the fae-nee. A heavy silence settled into the room. The horde held back.

The stone figure was a statue, bent under the weight of centuries of loneliness and madness. "How?"

Tyrus spoke slowly. "If there is a way, I need both Raal and the Magus listening. It took both of you to create your stone prison. It'll take both to free you."

The figure remained frozen for a breath, then nodded. "We're listening."

Tyrus gulped. He had no clear answer; he had sought only to delay the inevitable by dangling the possibility of hope. Now he had to think quickly. For the moment, sanity was needed: He could not risk Raal's wild ravings, nor the Magus' immovable depression. They were two extremes. He needed a middle ground between the cold stone of the Magus and the raging fire that was Raal.

As he thought this, connections clicked in his own head. He blinked in shock. *Of course!* A plan began to form.

He faced the figure before him with renewed determination. "The Magus can turn flesh to stone. Raal can breathe life into stone. Opposite magicks!"

Again a slow nod.

"What if you both cast your spell at the same time?"

His words crinkled the other's brow. "Would one not simply negate the other?" This sounded like the Magus, leaden with hopelessness.

"Not if you cast it upon yourselves!"

"Impossible!" This fiery retort was clearly Raal again. "What good would that do?"

Tyrus pressed on. They were not two spirits in one body, but one mind divided, one magick divided. If he could bring those parts together—even for a moment . . . "What would it hurt to try?" he answered back.

Silence pressed. Then lips moved. "What do we do?" the Magus asked dourly.

"This is a fool's errand," came next from the same mouth, sharp and impatient. The fae-nee shifted nervously, chittering and scrapping amongst themselves, as divided as their master.

After a moment, Tyrus explained. "At the same moment, I want the Magus to cast a spell of stone upon yourself, while Raal wills the stone of your current form back to flesh." He paused, then stressed the most important part. "It must be done at the same time . . . on my signal!"

The statue stared back, doubt and menace clear in the expression. "We will do it."

Tyrus lifted his arm. Despite his own uncertain conviction, he tried to instill confidence with his words. "On my count from five, I will drop my hand and point. Both must act together."

There was no response, just a narrowed stare.

"*Five . . . four . . .*" He prayed that by working together, with two halves of one mind trying to cast opposite spells, that a break in the stalemate would be achieved. "*. . . three . . . two . . .*" But what would be the result? He feared there was as much chance of making things worse as better. But he had no choice. "*. . . one . . .*"

He pointed his hand at the statue.

For a moment, nothing changed. The stone figure stood dead still.

Then a tremble began at the fingers and toes, a palsy that spread up the arms and legs and struck the torso with a shock like a bolt of lightning. The body spasmed, rocking. The head was thrown back. The mouth stretched open in a silent scream.

The fae-nee fled from the display, retreating to the walls. They couldn't leave, but they didn't want to stay.

Tyrus suspected a similar war going on in the stone figure before him, locked in a posture of pure agony and torment.

A gasp escaped the throat. "Run . . . Tyrus, run . . ."

For the first time, he knew he was hearing the true voice of the man who had once lived here: the healer. Whirling about, he dashed to the door and fled blindly through the dark halls.

A scream burst behind him; then the ground shook. An acrid wafting of sulfur flew up from behind him. And still, he ran . . .

Tyrus spotted the exit ahead, a square of gloom set in a world of shadow. He raced to it and dove out into the open air. He didn't stop. Some instinct, a quivering of tiny hairs on his body, made him fly down the last of the slope. He reached the sickly stream and leaped with all the strength in his legs.

As he flew, he glanced behind him and saw a horrifying sight. A gray wave of petrifaction spread out from the slope, changing grass to stone, bush to granite. It spread out in all directions.

Then Tyrus hit the opposite bank of the stream. He took the brunt on his shoulder and rolled. Crying out in panic, he flung himself up and away, sure the magick would overwhelm him in a heartbeat.

But it didn't.

He turned and saw that the explosion of petrifying magick had halted at the stream, dying away.

Panting, he stared without blinking. The convulsion of energies had subsided. Beyond the stagnant green stream, the landscape was a sculpture of stone. He had not expected such a backwash of magick.

He cupped his mouth and called across the stream. "Magus! Raal!"

There was no answer. Chewing his lip, he debated his choices here. Nothing now blocked him from leaving. The spell was gone from his body; he was flesh and blood again. But what of the others? What of the d'warf army?

He grabbed up a handful of muddy reeds from the bank and tossed them over the stream. They landed on the stone soil, but remained green. Whatever magick had been spent here, it had ended.

Using some stepping stones in the brook, Tyrus crossed the waters and carefully tested the flinty soil himself. Nothing happened. Satisfied, he crept back to the shattered doorway. He called again, but still there was no answer. He listened for any telltale scrape or patter of feet. Were the fae-nee still about?

Not a single sound echoed out to him. He balked at what he had to do, but he gathered his resolve. The sun was almost gone, and he'd rather discover what lay within while there was at least some daylight. He reentered the home.

Straining his senses, he retraced his steps to the hearth room. Stopping outside, he saw that the torch had blown out. The only light came from the broken window.

He slid forward, creeping on his toes. Tyrus found himself trembling, worn from the panic and terror of the last half day. He stepped into the room.

What he found there stunned him. The fae-nee were still there, but now they were all stone again, frozen in place like some macabre tableau.

But the stone figure was gone. In its place, curled on the floor, was a man, as much flesh and blood as himself. He was blond like any Northerner, with a shadow of beard. A young man.

Tyrus hurried forward. To his surprise, he found the fellow still breathing. He knelt and touched his shoulder. "Magus?"

The man's eyes were open, but he didn't seem to see. His lips moved and slowly sounds emerged. "I . . . I killed them."

Tyrus glanced to the stone figures. "Maybe it's best."

"No, not these stillborn monsters. Before . . ." The eyes closed with unspoken pain. "I was dying, suffocating in ash and smoke. I panicked . . . called my children to me . . ." There was a long silence, then a whisper. "They came because they were scared, frightened like any child seeking the consolation of a father. Blind to their love and trust, I ripped the very life from them in my fear . . . in my fight for life. The last was poor Raal. He saw me devour the others to keep myself alive, and still he didn't leave. He came into my arms without protest. He leaned his cheek against mine. And I stole the life from him."

Tyrus now understood what had ripped the man's mind in two: guilt.

"And for what?" the figure finished. "To be entombed in ash and walk the world. To turn all I touched to cold stone like my heart. It was too much." His shoulders shook, but no tears flowed.

"Do not blame yourself. It was a monstrous time. The birth of Blackhall in your own domain would fray any man's heart."

A hand reached up and grasped his fingers. No words of thanks were uttered, but they were understood. The two of them remained like this for several breaths.

Then the light-haired man spoke again, faintly. "It is time to follow the path I was meant to journey long ago. And as I die, so do my spells." His lips stopped moving. "But first . . ." Tyrus felt a jolt through his hand as the man's life left him. ". . . a gift."

He stared down at the pale face, still and quiet, but no longer a statue. In death, the Magus had found his way back to life.

Tyrus stood. With a sad shake of his head, he departed this tomb and sought the last sunshine left in the day.

Standing in the doorway, he watched the stony landscape melt back to grass, dirt, and scrabbly bushes. The Magus' spell was indeed unraveling. As he stared at the hopeful sight, he prayed the same was true elsewhere. With the Magus gone, would his friends and the frozen d'warf army be freed?

There was only one way to find out.

Tyrus stepped through the rubble of an oaken door. As he did so, he spotted the small dandyflower growing amid the debris. Like the grass, it had also faded from stone back to green leaves and yellow petals. Tyrus reached down, plucking it free.

As he did so, the stem grew black, then the leaves, then the petals. In a heartbeat, he held only a granite replica of the flower. His eyes widened with horror.

Shocked, he dropped the flower. It shattered at his toes.

Only then did he remember the last words of the Magus.

But first . . . a gift.

SY-WEN SWEPT THROUGH THE FOGGY NIGHT ATOP RAGNAR'K. SHE CLOSED HER eyes to savor the freedom of the open sky. Earlier, she had been dragged from belowdecks spitting and cursing, still possessed by the wickedness in her skull. But as before, Kast had called her forth enough to release the dragon.

Atop her mount, united by the bonded magick, she was her own self again. And Master Edyll had told her about the malignant boat they followed—the ship of bone.

The possessed, led by Hunt, raced the foul creation toward the fleet, intending to seed their evil among the ships. They had to be stopped.

She and Ragnar'k were to scout the ship and prepare a plan of attack, while the *Ravenswing* kept high among the clouds, awaiting her signal to dive down and attack. Both Bloodrider and elv'in warriors readied for the assault.

Ragnar'k banked on a wingtip and swept seaward.

Sy-wen opened her eyes. Below she spotted the pale ship sweeping through the waves. Distantly she swore she heard screams carried on the winds. It was the wake of fear left by the ship, a palpable evil. Muffled by the magick of her dragon, it was dulled and blunted. Still, a small tremble passed over her skin.

Bad ship, Ragnar'k grumbled, sensing her heart.

Sy-wen didn't argue. The foul craft, its crew, its cargo—all of it had to be destroyed before it reached the fleet. But she had friends aboard the ship, as innocent as she herself. She pictured Hunt, his broad, easy smile, his love and concern for Sheeshon.

A twinge of guilt traced through her. Why was she allowed to live while the others were sentenced to a watery grave?

The dragon swept over the boat and circled back. No alarm was raised. The ebony scales of Ragnar'k blended with the dark night. Sy-wen studied the empty deck. There was not even a steersman. It was ominous to see a ship in full sail without a single sailor on deck—especially in these treacherous seas.

Around the ship, mountains of ice rode the currents, while other sections of the sea boiled and spat with searing steam. To sail such waters blindly was to invite certain death. But still the ship sped on, leaving a wake of screams.

Spied upon this close, the leathery sails were clearly skin, stretched and stitched with sinew. The rigging appeared damp with blood and gore. The skeleton at the prow held up bony arms toward the skies, pleading. The skull's mouth was frozen open in a silent wail.

Sy-wen felt bile rising in her throat at the sight of it. It seemed mad to board such a craft, but they must. This den of evil had to be destroyed.

"Circle back to the *Ravenswing*," she whispered, sending her desire through her thoughts as much as her words. "We'll attack when the moon is fully risen."

Ragnar'k beat his wings to spiral back up toward the waiting ship. Movement below drew her attention. She focused back on the dread craft, where a hatch opened and someone stepped to the deck, face raised, searching.

Hide, she urged her mount.

Ragnar'k swept into one of the steamy fog banks, vanishing inside. All sign of the ship was lost below. The world itself vanished in a cloud of warm haze. Water beaded her skin, smelling of brimstone.

Sy-wen shivered despite the warmth and prayed they hadn't been spotted. For that brief moment, as the sentinel below had raised his face to the skies, she had recognized Hunt.

Catching an updraft, Ragnar'k flew high and cleared the fog bank. Starlight and moonlight shone brighter. The dragon's wings glistened with jeweled droplets. With a final shudder, she left the terror of the ghost ship behind and turned her face to the open skies.

Half a league away, she spotted the *Ravenswing*, its iron keel ruddy in the night. She directed Ragnar'k back home. They dared not wait any longer before waging their assault. Whether Hunt had spotted them or not, he was clearly wary.

Ragnar'k swept over to the elv'in ship, drawing abreast. He swept along as Sy-wen called to the ship's captain and pointed toward the seas below. "Now! As we planned, but we must go now!"

Captain Lisla acknowledged her with a wave. Other elv'in stood behind her, along with a tight group of Bloodriders. All were armed.

The captain yelled to her crew. Foresails were reefed, and lines were hauled with practiced precision. Lisla stood midship, her figure limned in energy. She cast her arms skyward, then swept them apart and down.

The *Ravenswing*, an extension of her body and spirit, bucked up, then dove steeply toward the fog-shrouded ocean. Its keel shone brighter as it dropped away.

Ragnar'k tucked his wings and followed, dropping like a stone from the skies. Sy-wen leaned against the dragon's hot neck, her feet clamped tight in the flaps on either side. Wind ripped at her, threatening to tear her from her perch. Despite the danger, delight surged through her. In her heart, a dragon roared a matching pleasure. The sensations blurred, and it became impossible to tell where dragon ended and rider began.

Ragnar'k passed the diving ship, and the pair broke through the clouds, the ocean spreading before them. Blue ice glinted against the black sea. Plumes of steam rose like ghostly towers of some lost city. And amid the wild ocean, a single ship scudded over the waves.

Go! she urged. *Do not let them escape.*

Never, my bonded . . . never!

Behind the sending of the dragon, she felt the heart of another. She touched that smaller heart and felt a pride and fierceness that matched a hundred dragons. Sy-wen smiled into the winds. Whatever came of this night, for this moment they were all together.

Sy-wen sensed the *Ravenswing* sweeping in behind her. She did not slow or glance over a shoulder. It was now or never.

Ragnar'k dove toward the pale ship. Whether screams still filled its sail, Sy-wen could not say. Winds howled around her, blanketing her. The sails of the other ship swelled as the dragon swooped down; its bone deck grew wide.

It was not empty.

As she had feared, Hunt had roused the ship. But it was too late to turn back.

"Take them down!" she shouted into the wind.

Ragnar'k was an arrow pointed at the center of the deck. Sy-wen ducked lower. The dragon's scales were a hearth burning under her. At the last moment, his wings shot out, cupping the wind. Clawed legs swung forward to land.

Men on deck fled from the onslaught, lest they be crushed.

Ragnar'k roared as he smote the deck, scattering all from his path. Claws dug into the bony planks. Sy-wen was thrown forward by the impact, but she was held fast by her mount. She crouched up as one wing lashed out and snapped the bone of the foremast, toppling it seaward.

As the possessed fled the dragon, she glanced back and saw the *Ravenswing* sweep over the boat. Ropes dropped from hatches in the bow and stern. Ladders unfurled, thrown over the rails.

From the hatches, elv'in dropped headfirst down the ropes with one leg twisted in the lengths as support. They looked to be plunging to their deaths, but at the last moment they slowed, then flipped to land catlike on the deck, swords ready.

Following them down the ladders, the Bloodriders clambered and slid with equal alacrity. They leaped to the deck, bellowing war cries, armed with axes and swords.

Then the two forces met. The possessed fought like wild beasts. Once Dre'rendi themselves, they were skilled fighters; now, directed by the creatures inside them, they used tooth and nail as readily as their blades.

Screams rose all around. Sails snapped as if in a tempest.

By the stern, a line of archers dropped to their knees and shot flaming arrows skyward, peppering the underside the *Ravenswing*. Fires ignited, but buckets of water were cast upon the small blazes before they could spread.

Around the dragon, the fighting grew fierce. Sy-wen sat in the eye of the storm. The dragon's wings protected her, while Ragnar'k snatched any of the enemy who came too near. Their broken bodies were tossed overboard.

Across the deck, blood washed over bone.

From her perch, Sy-wen was the only one to notice the transformation. The bloody bones of the deck rippled. Leathery flesh grew as if fed by the blood and gore. Gasping, she realized the fight was feeding the foul creation, bringing it from bone to life.

She yelled across the deck. "Beware! The ship comes alive!"

But the sounds of battle muffled her warning. She watched an elv'in step on a patch of transformed deck. Under his feet, a maw opened, lined by sharp teeth. Caught by surprise, he fell into the waiting jaws, arms flailing. As he slid down, the teeth clamped shut, biting through his chest with a crunch of bone. He didn't even have time to scream. Few noted his fate.

The others must be warned! she cried to her dragon. Already the spread of flesh swept over the decks.

Be ready! Ragnar'k answered.

The dragon's chest swelled under her; then he stretched his neck and roared with all his might. The cry split the sounds of battle.

Sy-wen did not wait. In the moment of stunned silence that followed, she screamed to be heard. "Beware the ship! It comes to life under you!"

Several of the combatants stared down at the decks. Others retreated from the flow of flesh.

Then the fighting resumed. The tides of battle turned against them. The possessed fought with renewed vigor, aided now by the ship itself. Jagged mouths appeared everywhere, snaking out with fleshy tongues to drag attackers to their doom.

A horn sounded from above, the call to retreat.

Men leaped to ropes and ladders. The possessed attempted to follow but were kicked off or cut free. The *Ravenswing* lurched away.

Ragnar'k spread his wings and leaped skyward to follow. But the blood-fed ship was not ready to let them escape. The transformation swept up the mast, changing bone into a clawed limb.

Without momentum or the speed to escape, Ragnar'k was snatched from the skies, gripped by a hind leg. Sy-wen was jarred from her seat and flung sideways. But before she could fall to the monstrous deck below, her left leg was wrenched, twisting her knee savagely. Crying out, she hung by one ankle from the dragon, her foot still locked in one flap.

Ragnar'k snaked his neck around and bit into the clawed grip that held him. Bone broke. Spouts of black blood ran down the mast, but still the claw held, dragging them back to the deck.

Then a bloom of flame exploded from the ship below, shooting high into the sky.

Sy-wen was baffled by the fire until she saw a pair of barrels topple past her. They struck the deck and burst with fiery blasts. She craned up and saw the *Ravenswing* above them. More barrels were being shoved out hatches to bombard the monstrous ship.

Attacked anew, the claw weakened enough for Ragnar'k to break free. But the dragon was off-kilter, too close to the deck. He fell before he could get his wings out to catch himself. He struck the deck hard, managing at the last moment to roll and swing Sy-wen above him to keep from crushing her under his own weight.

Bonded!

"I'm safe," she gasped out, swinging to resume her seat. Then an arrow struck her shoulder. The impact more than the pain surprised her. She sprawled across the dragon's neck.

Ragnar'k, sharing her senses, roared in fury.

Sy-wen turned to see Hunt toss aside his bow and leap atop the dragon's back, his sword raised above his head.

She tried to raise an arm in defense, but pain from the arrow dimmed her vision. The sword plunged toward her.

Then Hunt was torn from the dragon's back, flung upward. His sword went flying as Ragnar'k shook the Bloodrider gripped in his jaws.

No! Sy-wen sent, sensing the murderous intent of her mount. *To the* Ravenswing.

Muscle surged under her, then they were aloft. She watched more barrels strike the ship, exploding with flame. It burned from prow to stern, igniting the marrow of the bone ship.

Ragnar'k banked away as the ship sank under the waves. The last she saw of the monstrous thing was its living mast clawing at the skies before it, too, sank away.

She closed her eyes, blacking out. When she opened her eyes, she was back on the *Ravenswing*. Men and elv'in bustled around her.

She pushed up, but a familiar voice warned her, "Lie still, my dear." It was Master Edyll. "We've taken the arrow out, but a healer's gone to fetch more dragon's blood."

She nodded weakly. The blood of a dragon could heal any wound—except for the evil inside her. She lay stretched atop the warm dragon. *Ragnar'k . . .*

I'm here, my bonded . . . I'm safe.

She sighed. Across the deck, she saw Hunt pinned to the deck, a Bloodrider on each limb. His upper torso had been stripped and an arc of bite wounds marked his flesh. An elv'in healer attempted to minister to his injuries, but he thrashed and fought, howling and snapping like a wild dog.

I carried him to the ship, Ragnar'k explained, sensing her confusion. *As you wanted.*

She remembered her last order when the dragon had attacked Hunt. She had only meant for the dragon to drop the Bloodrider and escape, but Ragnar'k must have divined her heart, known the affection she had for the large man.

From atop the dragon, she watched Hunt struggle and howl. Soon she would be doing the same. Without the dragon's magick, the demon would overwhelm her again, turning her into a raving beast. Tears welled at this thought—and with her vision blurred, she was a moment too late in noticing the danger to another. She shoved up despite the pain in her shoulder. "Sheeshon! No!"

The tiny girl had broken through the milling warriors and dropped beside the pinned Hunt. She reached to her bonded Bloodrider. "I have need of you." Her fingers touched Hunt's tattoo, and his body convulsed with the magickal connection. The reaction was so violent and sudden that the guards holding the man were knocked aside.

Sy-wen fought to go to her aid, but the dragon held her ankles, refusing to let her go.

Hunt grabbed up the small girl.

"No!" Sy-wen moaned.

But instead of any harm, Hunt curled his limbs around Sheeshon protectively. A sob escaped the large man's throat as he kissed the top of her head.

Pikes and swords surrounded the pair. Master Edyll pushed forward. "Master Hunt . . . ?"

"I'm myself," he gasped. "Sheeshon's touch—it broke the creature's hold."

Sheeshon nodded, her small hands hugging tight. "But he still has worms in his head."

Master Edyll glanced between Hunt and Sy-wen. "Like Sy-wen's bond to her dragon. As long as Sheeshon ignites the magickal bond and stays in contact—"

"He'll be free," Sy-wen mumbled to herself. It cheered her to see the two together—it fueled her hope that one day the same might be true for her and Kast.

A healer appeared at her side with a small cask of dragon's blood. "We should see to your injuries," he said.

She nodded, but she knew there were no salves to heal her deepest wounds. Instead, she watched Hunt and Sheeshon as the healer worked on her shoulder. For the moment, she forgot her despair.

One day, my love . . . One day I'll hold you in my arms again.

BELOWDECKS ABOARD THE *DRAGONSHEART*, KAST LEANED OVER A TABLE COVered with sea charts and maps. The high keel and his portly advisor, Bilatus, stood on the other side of the table. Three days had passed since the sinking of the bone ship, and in another two days, they would lead the fleets to Blackhall.

Shaman Bilatus straightened with a groan. "Perhaps we could plan better strategies if our eyes weren't crossing with exhaustion." He ran a hand over his balding pate and shrugged his blue robes higher on his shoulder.

The high keel matched the shaman's tired expression, but he just stared harder at the scrolls and outlines. Kast understood his determination: the man had seen what had become of his son. Kast and the high keel shared this personal torment: to see a loved one suffer and be unable to help.

"The attacks grow bolder upon us," the high keel grumbled. "The mer'ai had to fend off another assault by a kraken this morning."

"I heard," Kast said. "And the elv'in were harried by patrols of skal'tum last night."

The high keel slammed a fist on the table. "We should strike now! Why this cursed waiting?"

"You know why," Kast answered. "Tyrus leads the d'warves through the Stone Forest. They aren't in position to attack the north entrance of the mountain."

"Let them join the fighting when they can! What's to stop us from striking at the south?"

Kast sighed. It was an old argument; the broader plan had already been laid out. There were only two ways into Blackhall. As the sun rose two days from now, the d'warves would attack over the land bridge from the north while the Dre'rendi and mer'ai assaulted the southern seaport and the elv'in warships gave support from the air to both parties.

The finer details were still fluid and under discussion by various fleets. Day and night, crows flew between ships on the sea and in the air. Messenger riders swept through the ocean depths atop their dragons with final orders or suggestions. The complete plan was coming together. Now was not the time to rush.

As the high keel grumbled, Kast glanced to Bilatus. The shaman placed a hand on the old man's shoulder. "You need to rest."

The high keel shook out of his grip. "Leave me be!"

Kast cracked a kink in his back. "Well, I need some fresh air," he said. "We'll come back to this at moonrise."

"I could use something from the galley," the high keel conceded grudgingly.

"I'll join you down there," Kast said. "I'm going to walk the deck first."

The other pair nodded. Together they left the room and went their separate ways.

Kast climbed atop the deck and breathed in the night air. It smelled of salt and sulfur. The cold winds turned steamy for a breath as a stray breeze gusted from another direction. These were strange seas indeed.

He crossed to the starboard rail. The dark sea was filled with sails all around. Overhead, elv'in ships hovered or floated over the masts, great black thunderheads aglow with ruddy fires. In the distance, Kast could make out the piping of dragons. Closer by, a lute was playing softly, while somewhere else, a seaman sang to the night of some missing love.

Kast leaned on the rail. It would all be over soon. He shook his head. All this planning was for naught. The true war would be fought on another field far from here.

Whatever final evil the Dark Lord expected to visit on this world, its heart was not to be found among these strange seas. Their efforts here were no more than a feint, a distraction against the true attack.

Kast didn't even dare glance to the east, toward the distant mountains and the small town of Winterfell. That was not his battle.

Instead he focused on the north, where the horizons glowed a fiery red, where a dark shadow loomed, waiting.

A shadow named Blackhall.

Book Five

WINTER'S EYRIE

19

TOL'CHUK SAT BEFORE THE FIRE AT HIS FAMILY'S HEARTH. DAWN WAS A SHORT way off; the others were still rolled into blankets around the floor.

He gazed into the flames, content with these quiet moments before the true day started. Across the cavern, a calm silence filled the space. No shouts, no challenges, no demands on his time.

But that would change as soon as the sun rose. As the new spiritual leader of the tribes, the clans were his responsibility. It was a weight as heavy as the stone in his thigh pouch. His fingers settled to the goatskin satchel.

The Heart remained corrupted, transformed into ebon'stone by the blood of the ill'guard Vira'ni. He feared bringing the stone near the Spirit Gate in the core of the mountain, lest its corruption spread into the heart-stone arch. Thus he dared not open the Gate and consult Sisa'kofa for guidance. Days passed, while the last words of Sisa'kofa still echoed in his chest: *The Spirit Gate must be protected . . . You must be this guardian.*

But what was he to do from here? He had united the clans, rooted out the treachery of the Ku'ukla. But the tribes grew impatient. Og'res were not known for their cooperation nor for their easy temperament. Skirmishes broke out daily among the gathered og'res.

Some direction was needed, and all eyes turned to him. But what was he to do? Where did they go from here?

The sound of running feet drew his attention to Mogweed. The shape-shifter raced across the cavern toward the hearth. He had taken to night-time sojourns, getting braver each evening, venturing farther from the warmth of the hearth.

From his pale face, it looked as if something had frightened or excited him. "A ship!" he blurted, gasping.

Tol'chuk stood, frowning.

Mogweed waved an arm toward the brightening entrance to the cavern. "An *elv'in* ship! Coming from the south!"

His shouts roused the others. Blankets were thrown back. Magnam rolled to his feet. "Is it Jerrick's scoutship?" the d'warf asked, rubbing at one eye. "The one we hid?"

"No, it's larger! Someone comes! Maybe they mean to rescue us!"

Jaston sat up, half cradling the small swamp child in his arms. Her wings stretched as she woke. "It must be from A'loa Glen. Maybe they received the crow sent from Cassa Dar."

Tol'chuk hoped so. Through the swamp child, they had communicated all that had occurred here to Cassa Dar, and she had sent a crow to A'loa Glen with the information. But so far there had been no response.

Magnam scowled. "I doubt a ship could reach here so quickly from the island. It's been only a handful of days."

"But it *is* an elv'in ship!" Mogweed all but danced. "Come see! The og'res camped outside are already rousing—the sight has them spooked."

Tol'chuk grabbed a cloak and waved Mogweed forward. They'd best hurry. A flying ship could set the whole encamped valley into a panic.

Mogweed rushed toward the entrance with the others trailing. But as he reached the threshold, his feet suddenly went out from under him, sending him sprawling with a howl to the stone floor.

Tol'chuk reached a clawed hand to help him up, but the man shoved to his feet on his own. He straightened and ran a hand through his hair, then turned a baffled face toward Tol'chuk. "What's happening?"

Tol'chuk sighed and nodded to Magnam. "Tell Fardale about the ship." He pushed past the dazed shape-shifter and stared at the sun rising to the east. Dawn. The twins had traded places again.

Beyond the cavern entrance, the valley floor was aglow with hundreds of campfires. The meadow grasses were beaten to mud by the many og'res assembled here, as if a rain of boulders had fallen from the slopes of the Northern Fang. Already sounds of alarm were spreading throughout the valley. Og'res stood and pointed toward the southern skies. Females bleated nervously.

Tol'chuk stared across the valley. Night still ruled the skies to the west, but the uppermost cliffs of the Fang were already bathed in sunlight. As he searched the skies, he spotted the ship sailing from the south. Still in darkness, its iron keel glowed with ruddy magick, while lamps in the rigging lit the billowing sails. Then the ship hoved around the flank of a cliff and crested into sunlight. It burst into dawn with a shimmer of sailcloth and the gentle warmth of its dark wood.

Cries grew louder among the og'res.

Hun'shwa appeared from among the mass and loped over to the group gathered at the entrance to the Toktala cavern. "What new demon attacks?" he asked in Og're. The war leader of the tribes bore a club in his free hand, knuckling on his other. He was ready to fight.

"I believe they be friends," Tol'chuk answered in the common tongue. "Allies."

Hun'shwa glanced doubtfully to the ship sweeping toward the valley.

"Find the head of each clan," Tol'chuk said. "Spread word that the ship must not be attacked."

Hun'shwa nodded with a grunt. "It will be done." Then he loped down the slope, bellowing for the clan heads to gather.

Jaston stepped forward with the winged swamp child at his knee. The girl sucked a thumb and stared wide-eyed at the sky. "Pretty," she mumbled around her thumb.

"I'll send the swamp child up to the ship," Jaston said. "Cassa Dar can let them know where we are, what the condition is down here."

Tol'chuk nodded, but one eye narrowed as he watched the ship. As the elv'in craft flew closer, a great flock of birds followed, swooping and diving in its wake, as if blown up from the rimwood forests in the lower valleys. With each breath, more and more appeared, filling the skies.

"What's with all the birds?" Magnam asked on his other side, voicing Tol'chuk's own concern.

As answer, Fardale shoved through them, knocking into Jaston. He craned up, his face frozen in disbelief. "Si'lura!" he gasped.

Tol'chuk moved alongside him. "What be you saying?"

Fardale swept a hand across the sky. "The eagles and hawks . . . they're all my people!"

Tol'chuk frowned at the dark flock building up behind the handsome ship. *A shape-shifter army?* Either it was an invasion from the Western Reaches, or more forces than the og're legions had been swept here by the tides of fate. Tol'chuk wished he had risked unlocking the Spirit Gate and consulting Sisa'kofa. "Send the swamp child," he ordered Jaston. "Let's find out who comes with such an army."

"Look!" Magnam called out.

All eyes focused back to the ship. A bloom of fire suddenly flared over the ship's prow. It blazed high into the sky, shooting above the masts.

Og'res fled from the ship's shadow, panicked by the display. Hun'shwa could be heard bellowing for calm.

In the sky, the ball of fire coalesced into a giant rose, petals of fire opening to the dawn. More gasps and shouts echoed over the valley.

The group at the cavern entrance had gone mute, mouths hanging open. They all knew the sigil blazing in the skies.

"It be Elena!" Tol'chuk finally said, his voice full of shock.

"How could she be here?" Magnam asked.

Tol'chuk gaped up at the ship, the fiery rose, the gathered army. A cold dread entered his heart. He sensed many paths gathered here this day, paths foretold in prophecies as old as these same mountains. But from this day forward, no magick could divine the road ahead. They stood poised on a cusp of fate, darkness all around, and only one light to lead them from here.

Tol'chuk stared up at the blazing rose of wit'ch fire and prayed Elena was strong enough to bear such a burden.

ER'RIL LOWERED THE SPYGLASS. ELENA STOOD BESIDE HIM, HER RIGHT HAND extended toward the skies. He watched as she deftly tied off her magick and slipped a calfskin glove over her ruby hand, now a touch paler after the magickal display.

He stepped to her side. "I've spotted Tol'chuk and Mogweed by the cavern entrance," he said.

"So they're still here . . . good." Her eyes still shone with the song of her wild magicks.

"I also saw Jaston with them."

Her brow crinkled. "The swamper? Are you sure?" The confusion dimmed the glow of magick in her face, and Er'ril was glad for it. Warmth reentered her features.

"It's hard to mistake that scarred face," he assured her, taking her arm. The others lined the rails to either side, but he didn't care who saw; he was long past hiding his affection for Elena. "I watched Jaston kneeling beside some strange child. It takes wing toward us as I speak."

"A winged child?" She searched the skies until she spotted the small figure in flight. "Could it be one of Cassa Dar's creations?"

Er'ril shrugged. "It seems we'll all have stories to share."

Together, they gazed out at the valley below, lit with morning fires and covered with the rocky shapes of hundreds of og'res.

"It'll be good to see Tol'chuk and everyone else again," Elena murmured.

Er'ril heard the trace of regret in her voice. He kissed the top of her head. The last days here aboard the *Windsprite* had been calm and restful: no threats, no monsters, no dark magicks, only the sun, the wind, and the skies. But now the signs of the war showed clearly on the earth below: burned homesteads, skeletal remains of towns, and bands of strange beasts roaming the forest.

Er'ril suddenly understood the elv'in nature a little better. Above, in the open skies, the world seemed a simpler and brighter place.

"We could always just keep flying," he whispered in her ear.

She slipped her arms around him. "Don't tempt me."

How he wished it were that easy. But he knew there were no words to sway Elena from her true course. So he allowed her this small illusion of this possibility of escape. "The winged child comes," he noted.

He felt her sigh. "Then it's time to return to the world," she whispered into his chest.

Er'ril lifted her face and wiped the tears from her eyes before anyone else saw them. "We'll face it together."

BY MIDDAY, ELENA WAS BONE-TIRED AS SHE CALLED THE WAR COUNCIL TO OR-der. The tensions between the shape-shifters and the ogres remained thick. Both sides had long histories of isolation and mistrust. How could she forge them into a single army, when she doubted she had the strength for even this meeting? Earlier, the reunions between Elena's group and Tol'chuk's had been joyous but still heavy with sorrow.

Jerrick, Mama Freda, and little Tikal . . . all dead.

She sat, her eyes still puffy from unshed tears. After she heard the story of Vira'ni reborn and the treachery here, a hopelessness had dragged on her spirit, and she had seen the stricken look on Er'ril's face. He had once loved Vira'ni—and now this abomination had been unleashed upon the mountains and had taken the lives of their friends. *Did the evil in this world never die?*

She reached a hand to Er'ril. He squeezed her fingers. Everyone was gathered. It was time to begin.

She stood and stared around the chamber as torches of blue flame danced shadows on the walls. Tol'chuk had named this place the Chamber of the Spirits, a sacred cavern to the og're tribes. To one side of the

central fire, the five heads of the og're clans had gathered with their lieutenants. Across from them sat the elder'root and his cadre of fellow shape-
shifters. Between them were the members of her own party.

All eyes were upon her.

Elena spoke firmly. "Three nights from now, when the moon waxes
full, the world will end." She stared around at the mix of faces and races.
"*All* our worlds. Not just the forests of the Western Reaches, not just the
mountains of the Fang, not just the islands of the coast nor the plains beyond. *All our worlds will end.*"

She let her words soak into the crowd.

"You know this to be true?" Hun'shwa, the war leader of the united
clans, asked.

Elena glanced to Harlequin Quail, then back to Hun'shwa. "We have
word from a trusted source. But on our journey here, we have seen the
fires burning among the foothill villages. We have seen the camps gathering in the highlands below your peak."

Tol'chuk spoke from his bouldered seat. "Even the Triad spoke of this
danger before passing on."

Hun'shwa nodded. Grumbles passed among the other og'res.

"What are we to do?" the elder'root asked. He wore a white robe and
no other adornment, setting aside his crown of leaves for this meeting.

Elena waved Er'ril to stand.

Dressed in black finery, he was an imposing figure. His black hair had
been pulled back into a severe braid. His cheeks still glowed from the
blade he had used to shave his stubble.

A thrill passed through her at the sight of him. On the trip here, they
had come to share, if not their bodies, at least their bed. Under the blankets, away from eyes and responsibilities, they had spent quiet moments
sharing the warmth of each other's touches, exploring boundaries that
neither were ready to cross yet.

Er'ril spoke to the gathered heads, drawing her back to the moment.
"A great evil has been brought into these highlands, a statue of foul black
stone sculpted into the likeness of a wyvern. It is the heart of the darkness
that threatens our world. In the next two days, we will send scouts by air
and on the ground. We must hunt out where it has been hidden—for
when the sun rises in two days' time, we will bring both our armies down
upon its lair and destroy it."

"This will stop the evil?" Hun'shwa asked.

Elena sighed as Er'ril glanced to her. She remembered the demoness
Vira'ni. "Evil will always survive," she said plainly.

Concerned murmurs rose from the gathering.

"But our efforts will protect the world for now," she finished. "It is all one can do in life—fight evil where it is found."

"Where will it be found?" the elder'root asked. "The foothills are vast. A search for a single statue could consume hundreds of days, not just two."

"We know roughly where the statue was going," she said. "To Winter-fell . . . the place where I grew up."

Stunned silence met this revelation.

But the next to speak surprised even Elena. "I know more exactly where such an evil might lie." The words came from the strange child at Jaston's side—one of the swamp wit'ch's golems, a winged girl of perfect beauty. But the voice that spoke was ancient and came from much farther than the boundaries of this room: It was Cassa Dar. "When I studied the texts to send Jaston from one Fang to the other, I came upon a treatise that spoke of the confluence of elemental energies between the two Fangs. If the Weirgate is positioned anywhere, I wager it will be there."

"And where is that?" Elena asked.

"If my calculations are correct, at a place named Winter's Eyrie."

Elena gasped. Er'ril tensed beside her. The place had a long and bloody history. It was where her Uncle Bol had set up his cabin and met his death. In Er'ril's time, it was where the Chyric mages had their school—until it was sacked by the Gul'gothal armies and destroyed. And in the caverns under the Eyrie, Elena and Er'ril had discovered the living crystal statue of the boy, De'nal, pierced through the heart by Er'ril's own sword. So much tragedy had grown out of that one spot . . . Could it be true? Could they have come full circle back to where all their journeys had started?

"Winter's Eyrie . . ."

"It'll be a place to start looking," Er'ril whispered.

An icy dread shivered Elena's spine. The Eyrie was fraught with awful memories: the dark tunnels, the hiss of goblins, the fight with the mul'-gothra in the open field. It was on those empty highlands she had come to accept her power.

"And if the statue be there," one of the clan leaders said gruffly, "who will lead the armies in two days' time?" The og're stared with suspicion toward the elder'root and his shape-shifters.

Elena tried to answer this question. "Each army will have its own leader. Hun'shwa for the og'res. The elder'root for the si'lura."

This was met with murmurs of agreement, but Er'ril placed a restraining hand on her elbow. "No!" he said boldly.

Angry eyes turned in his direction. Elena's brow crinkled.

"Er'ril . . . ?" She had hoped to settle the matter without strife, but she saw the hard look in his eyes and remained quiet.

"An army divided is twice as likely to be vanquished," he declared. "Any hope for victory will require the full cooperation of both sides. I've fought many campaigns against the Dark Lord's forces. Alasea was lost the first time because our lands were fractured, our peoples too concerned with their own lands rather than the greater cause. I will not see that happen here, not on a battlefield where the fate of the world teeters. We will be one army! That we will settle right now!"

Elena's eyes widened. She had not seen such fire in him in a long time, as if he was coming awake after a prolonged slumber. Having been cast aside as her guardian, stripped of his immortality, and given the token badge of her liegeman, he had lately grown more dour and ill at ease. But here he had clearly found his footing again, coming alive as when she first met him.

"We will choose a leader here! Now!"

In the tense moment that followed, an og're spoke from near the back wall, bold in his anonymity. "Who will that be? You? A man?"

An eruption of angry outbursts followed. Er'ril simply stood before the onslaught, a boulder in a stormy sea. He waited until the tide ebbed. "No," he said. "My place is beside Elena."

She thought to object; he would make an excellent commander. But he backed a step and glanced to her, a ghost of a smile on his lips, and for the first time, she saw satisfaction in his eyes rather than simple responsibility. This was where he wanted to be, not where he *had* to be.

"Then who?" the speaker called from the back wall.

Er'ril shrugged. "That is for you all to decide."

New arguments ensued.

"Er'ril," Elena whispered out of the side of her mouth, "is this wise? We don't want to start a war in this very room."

"Patience, my love. They will choose the right one."

"Why?"

"Because they know I'm right. They will choose, but like all leaders, they must be allowed to bluster a bit."

"Are you sure?"

He squeezed her hand. "It's worked many a time on you."

She glanced to him, not sure if she should be shocked or amused.

Before she could decide, a voice bellowed through the raging debate.

"There be a clear choice!" Hun'shwa bulled forward. He swung his thick arm and pointed. "I say Tol'chuk!"

A moment of quiet followed his outburst, but faces screwed into expressions of doubt, even among the og'res. Tol'chuk looked the most shocked of all.

"He be already our spiritual leader," Hun'shwa said to the heads of his own clans. "But he also showed his bravery in the battle against Vira'ni. He saved our families' lives!"

A murmur of agreement passed through the og'res.

Hun'shwa turned to the si'lura. "In his veins runs the blood of your own people. If we join og're army to shape-shifter, then the best leader be of both bloods!"

Elena opened her mouth to agree, but Er'ril squeezed her hand. "Not yet," he whispered.

The elder'root conferred with his own people, then faced Hun'shwa. "We do not know this og're. We can't place the trust of—"

"Trust?" Fardale stepped forward, still wearing Mogweed's face. He had been standing tensely with Thorn, the daughter of the elder'root. With the urgency and press of the two armies coming together, the pair had little time together, and from their half-angry postures, there was still much unspoken between them. "If it is his trustworthiness you question," Fardale continued as he strode up to Tol'chuk, "then doubt my own heart. I know this fellow. You will find none more fierce in his loyalty in all the lands. Loyal not just to his og're clans nor his si'luran friends, but to all who are good of heart and who care for the fate of our peoples."

The elder'root remained expressionless.

Thorn spoke at his side. "Father, the Root sent us to the twins. Perhaps we should heed Fardale in this matter."

A long sigh escaped the elder'root. "So be it."

Only one person remained unconvinced. Tol'chuk stood up. "I'm no war leader."

Er'ril slipped from Elena's side and placed a hand on his shoulder. "That's what makes you the best choice. You'll take counsel from both sides without prejudice. That's the most important feature of a leader, to surround himself with wise counsel and heed their words."

Tol'chuk stared at the plainsman as if he were mad, but he remained silent. Even he knew a leader was needed to unite the two armies, even if only as a figurehead.

Magnam rolled his eyes. "First, spiritual leader, now the head of two armies. What next, The Nameless One's throne?" His wide grin blunted his words.

Elena stared as Er'ril clapped Tol'chuk on the shoulder a final time and turned back to her. "You knew they would choose Tol'chuk," she said as he stepped to her side.

He shrugged. "I've been doing this a long time."

Behind Er'ril's shoulder, Tol'chuk was swamped by the other leaders. Elena felt sorry for their friend. "Will he be all right?"

"He'll manage. We all will."

Jaston brought the swamp child over to them. "I suppose Tol'chuk will be occupied for a time."

"No doubt," Er'ril agreed.

Jaston shifted closer. "Then I'd best be the one to tell you this. Tol'chuk had wanted to wait until after the council to speak to you alone, but we shouldn't wait any longer."

"Speak to us about what?" she asked.

Jaston pulled the pair a few steps away and lowered his voice. "It's about Sisa'kofa."

Er'ril jerked in surprise. "What?" His hand fell to the rose pommel of the sword at his belt, Sisa'kofa's own sword.

Jaston's next words made no sense, but they still shivered Elena's skin. "The wit'ch waits for you down below."

JOACH SAT IN THE MIDDAY SUMMER SUN, HIS NOSE CRINKLING AT THE SMELL of the og're camp in the valley below. The heat felt good on his aching bones. After the days of cold travel aboard the *Windsprite*, he had not thought his limbs would ever thaw.

Seated near the cavern, he heard a commotion behind him.

"The council must be breaking up," Greshym said. The darkmage sat a few paces away, basking, too. His skin had been bronzed by the wind and the sun aboard the elv'in ship. His hair shone with copper and brown. He all but glowed with his stolen youth. Beyond him stood a pair of shapeshifters with spears and slung bows, guarding the mage. Greshym ignored them. "Why didn't you attend?"

Joach heard the silky smoothness in the other's voice, sly and full of artifice, but he answered anyway. "It's a *war* council. Look at this body. Do you think I'll be leading the assault into the foothills?"

Greshym shrugged. "A dream sculptor of your skill is not without resources. Have you practiced the magick I taught you?"

Sighing, Joach fingered the length of gray petrified wood. Despite his initial misgivings on the journey here, he had taken to trying the spells gleaned from the darkmage. They had indeed refined his sculpting ability. One spell had even strengthened his ties to the staff, weaving blood and stone more intimately for better control.

"Show me," Greshym said. "Show me what you've learned."

Joach glanced to the pair of shape-shifters, but their attention was elsewhere. With his magick stripped by Cho's spell, Greshym posed little danger.

Happy to demonstrate his skill, Joach shook off his glove and shifted his staff. As his flesh touched the stony wood, he felt the familiar tug on his heart. He watched veins of crimson flow into the length, his blood feeding the staff. In a matter of heartbeats, the gray wood had lightened to white. Exhilaration trembled through his body, a sense of the power at his fingertips. He had barely delved the surface of the dream magicks stored in the staff. He pointed its butt end toward the ground, and his lips moved in a silent spell. From the end of the staff, dribbles of blood seeped into the trampled mud at his feet, his own blood running through the stone, a trick of the spell Greshym had taught him.

Following the drops of blood, Joach sent his spirit slipping out into the hazy landscape between reality and dream. Atop the mud, a simple rose grew out of the dreaming, pushing into this existence. But it was no sandy construction. Its leaves were a summer green, its petals as crimson as his heart's blood, its thorns as real as the staff he held.

The darkmage pursed his lips. "Not bad. You're learning."

"It's perfect," Joach said, trembling with the flow of blood between his flesh and the staff, suddenly cold again. The sun seemed to have been bled of its warmth.

Greshym leaned closer, studying it, then leaned back. "But there is no life in it. It might as well be a painting."

He frowned at the criticism. "So?"

"We both know why you practice so hard, Joach, why you sit with me eking bits of arcane magick from my lore." Greshym waved a hand dismissively over the sculpted rose. "This will never do if you want to bring Kesla back from the sands."

Joach swallowed, hardly breathing. "Then how? How do I bring life out of nothingness?"

Greshym shook his head. "You take and take from me, my aged boy, but you never give." His voice lowered to a hushed whisper. "You are one step from piercing the final veil between true life and the mere appearance of life."

Joach was no fool. He knew the darkmage had been passing on these stray bits of magick in the hopes of earning his eventual freedom. But there was only one spell he wanted to know, this last one: how to bring life into his creations. Yet each time he spoke with Greshym, he reached this same stubborn wall of resistance.

"Let me show you," the darkmage said with an exasperated sigh. He reached a finger toward the rose.

Joach growled a warning, lifting his staff to ward him back.

Greshym paused, finger hovering. "Fear not. You know I have no magick. I don't even have the ability to steal magick from you or your staff. That cursed spell and book keep me dampened."

Joach pulled back his staff. "Then show me what you intend to show me, and be done with it."

Greshym touched a single petal, then straightened, dusting his fingers.

Joach frowned. There seemed to be no change in the rose. "So?"

The darkmage waved to the plant. "Look closer."

Joach leaned in, cocking his head. His spine sent pangs of protest as he bent over. "I don't—" Then he saw it, at the corners of the leaves, brown curls, edges of decay that hadn't been there a moment ago. But Greshym had no magick to alter his sculpting.

"It lives now," Greshym said as if reading his thoughts. "It bows to time like all things. Nothing in life is perfect. With life comes all its imperfection."

"Impossible . . ."

Greshym knelt forward, and before Joach could cry out, he yanked the rose from the mud and tossed it at Joach.

The attack roused the shape-shifter guards. Spears suddenly bristled, and Greshym was driven back to his seat.

"Look!" the darkmage spat. "Do you doubt your own eyes?"

Joach waved the guards away as he slipped his glove back on, breaking the blood spell on his weapon. The petrified wood went gray again. He lifted the muddy rose from his lap; the fragrance filled his senses. He shook the clods of dirt from the other end. Roots! The rose had roots!

His hands began to shake. He had not sculpted roots. Why would such a creation need roots when he himself was the source of its growth? He stared toward Greshym, stunned. "How . . . ?"

The darkmage folded his arms. "You take and take."

Joach held the rose tenderly. Greshym had no magick—how could he have done this? Joach cradled the flower as if it were Kesla herself. *Life . . . He brought it to life . . .* He stared over at the darkmage. He could not hide the anguish and hope in his expression.

"I can teach you," Greshym said. "And I can grant you half your youth back. I'll keep half; you get half. Equal and fair."

"I don't care about the stolen winters," he gasped. "Just the spell."

Greshym cocked his head. "My boy, if you want to bring Kesla back, you'll need *both*."

Joach frowned.

"Life takes life, Joach. It is not born out of nothing."

"What do you mean?"

Greshym nodded to the rose. "That flower cost me thirty-four days of my life. And if you want to bring Kesla back, it'll take more than days . . . it'll take a good chunk of your own life." Greshym eyed Joach up and down. "Life which you can't afford to give up in your current state."

Joach found himself growing breathless, as if the air were suddenly too thin. "What will it cost me for this knowledge?"

"Nothing, my boy. All I ask is my freedom, and I'll be on my way. I won't even ask you to destroy your sister's precious book."

He could not hide his surprise.

"You drive a hard bargain, Joach. I realize that you can't or won't betray your sister. So be it. All I want is my freedom."

"How can I trust you?"

Greshym shrugged. "With the book still bound, I'll have no magick, not until I'm well away from its reach . . . at least five leagues, I believe. So if you let me go and I haven't kept my end of the bargain, then there is nothing stopping you from catching me again. I can't be more fair than that."

"What of the war? Your knowledge . . . ?"

The darkmage rolled his eyes. "You know these highlands better than I. I've told you all I know already."

Joach searched for a trick. "For your freedom, you'll give me the secret of life and half my years back."

Greshym nodded.

Joach could not bring himself to make this pact. He stood, still holding the rose. "I'll need to think on it."

"Don't think too long, my boy. Once this final war starts, I expect the iron plainsman of Standi will find me more a risk than a boon to the cause. If you wait too long, you might find both your youth and my secrets spilled upon the ground at the point of his sharp sword."

Joach knew these words to be true. If he was to make this bargain with Greshym, it would have to be in the next day.

He slipped the rose into a pocket of his cloak. "I will give you my answer by nightfall."

GRESHYM WATCHED THE BOY STALK OFF. HE HAD NOTED THE CARE WITH which the boy treated the rose. All Joach's hopes for his love were wrapped in that little flower.

You've already given me your answer, Joach.

He leaned against the cliff wall. The midday sun heated his face as he closed his eyes. He searched out with his mind, but if Rukh was out there with his bone staff, the gnome was still too far away to be felt.

You'd better be out there, my dogged friend. If my plan is to succeed, I'll need that staff.

He sighed. He would keep his bargain with Joach—give him half his youth back and teach him the trick to bring life into his art. But he wasn't going to leave. Freedom or not, he needed one other item.

Shadowsedge.

There was no more powerful talisman in all the world. Even the Dark Lord himself could not withstand the magick of that sword. Sisa'kofa had chosen wisely to hide her weapon in the energy-dampening nexus of the Western Reaches. Otherwise, the Black Heart would have smelled such a tool from across the world and hunted it down.

But now it was within his own reach! And he was not leaving without it.

Greshym soaked in the sun, content that this was his last day of captivity. He again pictured Joach pocketing his precious rose.

You're mine again, boy, and this time, you'll dance your way to your own doom. Whether you want to learn it or not, I'll enlighten you on the most powerful black magick of them all: the corrupting power of love.

ER'RIL STOOD BEFORE TOL'CHUK UNABLE TO BELIEVE WHAT HE WAS SEEING. *Impossible,* he thought. The og're held the Heart of his people—there was no mistaking its shape and size. But it had gone black with corruption, lined by streaks of silver.

"It's ebon'stone!" Elena gasped.

Tol'chuk kept his back to the cavern, hunched over the stone. Almost all the war council members had abandoned the Chamber of the Spirits. Even Hun'shwa and the elder'root had left to discuss how best to scout the highlands around Winter's Eyrie. Jaston had gone with them, offering the use of the winged swamp child to aid in surveillance. The only ones left were members of their immediate party: Nee'lahn, Meric, Harlequin Quail, Fardale, Thorn, and the d'warf Magnam. They clustered around the og're.

Still, Tol'chuk kept his voice low. "The blood of Vira'ni corrupted the stone. I dare not risk opening the Spirit Gate. The taint of the stone might spread." Tol'chuk had already explained about the ring of heartstone at the core of the Northern Fang and the spirit found bound to it: *Sisa'kofa.*

"None but a handful know of the Heart's corruption," Tol'chuk finished.

Elena stepped forward and studied the stone, careful not to touch it. "If it changed once, there must be a way to change it back."

Nee'lahn joined her. "The blood of an ill'guard transformed it. Maybe that is a clue."

Meric nodded. "Tainted elemental blood corrupted the stone . . ."

Nee'lahn straightened. "Then mayhaps pure elemental blood could purify it!"

Er'ril narrowed his eyes. *Could the answer be that simple?*

"I'll try," Meric said.

"I don't know," Elena warned. "Ill'guard are created by ebon'stone. Its touch might harm you. Remember the ebon'stone Weirgates were capable of sucking the spirit from right out of your body."

"But this is much smaller," Meric said, growing excited. "Besides, I don't have to touch it. I can just drizzle blood over it."

"It's worth trying," Nee'lahn added quietly.

Er'ril turned to Elena. "What do you think?"

Elena sighed. "Here is a heart of a mystery. Ebon'stone and heartstone. If we can discover the answer, it may help us in the war to come. We still have another Weirgate to destroy to free Chi." She faced Meric. "Perhaps it is worth the risk."

The elv'in prince nodded and slipped a dagger from his belt.

Tol'chuk carefully laid the chunk of ebon'stone on the cavern floor and backed away. Biting his lip, Meric took his place before the Heart. He lifted his eyes to Elena, who nodded. Then he glanced to Nee'lahn. The nyphai stood with both fists clutched to her chest.

Meric grabbed the blade of his dagger, squeezing. The only sign of the pain was a slight squinting of his eyes. Blood flowed from his closed fist. He lifted it over the Heart and bathed the black stone with his own blood.

The droplets struck the crystal and simply disappeared, sucked away into oblivion.

Meric frowned and tightened his fist, increasing the flow. "Maybe it takes more," he mumbled between clenched teeth.

They all waited. Blood streamed into the stone, while some drops splattered on the stone floor. But the ebon'stone remained as black as ever. Only the silver veins in the stone seemed to glow as the foulness fed on Meric's blood.

"Stop!" Elena said. "It's clearly not working."

Meric did not argue; the truth of her words was plain. Nee'lahn crossed to his side with a strip of linen from her own shirt. She helped wrap his hand.

Harlequin Quail shook his head. "Any other bloody ideas?"

Magnam grunted. The d'warf had stood with his arms crossed the entire time. His eyes flicked between Tol'chuk and the stone. "Maybe we're looking at this wrong. We're not thinking large enough."

"What do you mean?" Meric asked, his voice bitter with his defeat.

Magnam unfolded his arms and began to pace. "I'm not sure. But I think you were on the right path. Ebon'stone is heartstone tainted by the touch of an ill'guard's blood. But what is an ill'guard?"

"A corrupted elemental," Er'ril snapped. "What are you getting at?"

"Let me talk it out. Ebon'stone is to heartstone as an ill'guard is to an elemental." Magnam continued to stalk. "So what is an elemental?"

"A person gifted with a bit of the Land's magick," Nee'lahn answered, straightening at Meric's side.

"And what about heartstone itself?" Magnam continued. "Old Mad Mimbly said it's the Land's own blood."

"I don't see your point," Er'ril said.

Meric answered. "Elementals bear the gift of the Land's magick. Heartstone is the Land's blood. The corruption of an elemental is not a corruption of his blood; it's a corruption of the Land's magick inside him!"

"So?"

"It's not *my* blood that can purify the stone! It's the Land's blood!"

"Which is heartstone," Elena cried, her eyes going wide. "Are you saying heartstone can cure ebon'stone?"

The d'warf shrugged. "According to Mad Mimbly, heartstone was essential to staving off the darkness that was to follow. We d'warves thought him addled, but maybe instead he was speaking the plainest truth." Magnam turned to Tol'chuk. "And we saw Lord Boulder here demonstrate this very truth—when he freed you from the Manticore Weirgate, shattering you free with the chunk of rock at our feet."

"And the Weirgate changed into heartstone!" Elena said.

"But it be the magick in the Heart that freed her," Tol'chuk said. "Be this not so?"

Magnam shook his head. "That's what we all thought. But now I wonder otherwise. In Gul'gotha, the Heart was empty of your people's spirits. Did you not yourself declare the stone dead, just plain crystal? There was no extra magick in the Heart. It was simply heartstone, the Land's own blood . . . but that was apparently magick enough."

A stunned silence followed. If Magnam was right, the answer lay before them.

"Could this be true?" Elena asked, hushed.

"I remember something else," Tol'chuk mumbled as he lifted the Heart from the floor. "In the cellars below Shadowbrook, the ill'guard Torwren feared the Heart. He fled from it. I thought he feared the magick in the stone, but maybe he merely feared the stone itself."

Er'ril spoke into the silence that followed. "We all know how to find out if this cure will work or not."

Their eyes left the ebon'stone Heart and focused on him.

"We test it," he declared. "We see if the ring of heartstone can purify the Heart."

Tol'chuk glanced to the tunnel. "If it fails, we risk the entire Gate."

"I say we must attempt it," Er'ril said firmly. "If it's proven true, then we'll have a real means of thwarting the Black Heart."

Elena stepped to Tol'chuk's side. She touched his elbow. "I agree. And I think you sense the truth of Magnam's words."

After a reluctant pause, Tol'chuk nodded, then turned to lead the way. "I will take you all to the Gate, but I pray we be correct."

Elena met Er'ril's gaze. He could read the worry in her eyes. It was a significant risk.

Meric and Nee'lahn followed Tol'chuk, with the others in tow. Er'ril followed with Elena. As they neared the tunnel, her hand slipped into his. Her fingers trembled. "Are you all right?" he asked.

"Could this have been the answer all along?" she mumbled. "If heartstone could purify ebon'stone, could it have been used to cure the ill'guard, too—Vira'ni and Kral, and so many others? If we had only known . . ."

He squeezed her fingers. "It's certain doom to stare behind you and wonder at the paths you didn't take. There is only one path anyone needs to walk, and that's straight ahead of them."

From a few steps ahead, Harlequin glanced back to them. He must have heard their words. "This is our only path? Great. I heard what Tol'chuk calls this passage."

"What?" Elena asked.

Harlequin nodded to the tunnel ahead. "The Path of the Dead."

"Oh . . ." Elena's footsteps faltered.

Er'ril pulled her more snugly against his side. "It's just a name, not an omen." Still, like her, he knew what lay at the end of this tunnel. Either they would corrupt the Gate or open it—*but which outcome was worse?*

Both Elena and Er'ril had heard Tol'chuk's story earlier. They knew what awaited them beyond the ring of heartstone at the core of the world. But neither of them wished to speak that name aloud.

Sisa'kofa.

20

FROM THE DARK CELL OF HIS IMPRISONMENT, MOGWEED STARED OUT THROUGH Fardale's eyes. All day long he had watched and listened . . .

And now they were headed to the Spirit Gate!

Now he studied the path they followed. He had tried these past many days to convince Tol'chuk to show him the arch of heartstone, but the og're had refused, too wary of letting the chunk of ebon'stone near the Gate. Now, at long last, they were going there, but he was trapped in Fardale's head, unable to act.

He cursed his luck.

At hand was the key to unlock his prison. He recalled the message from the Dark Lord, echoing out from the ebon'stone bowl: *You must destroy the Spirit Gate . . . It must be shattered with the blood of my last seed!* Mogweed stared past Meric and Nee'lahn. Tol'chuk strode with a torch raised before him, lighting the way.

It was Tol'chuk's blood that could free Mogweed. All he had to do was slay the og're at the Gate—then the Dark Lord would break the curse upon him. Of course, there was one more price to be paid for his freedom.

We will burn the wolf from your heart . . .

That was the final cost—Fardale's life. According to the Dark Lord, only one could survive the breaking of the curse. One body, one spirit.

But could he take that step, too? The dilemma had weighed upon him these last days. Suddenly he was not so displeased with his current imprisonment. Chained up in Fardale's skull, the choice was taken from him. For now, he would simply spy, and plot his victory for a later time, when his heart was not so conflicted.

Content in this realization, Mogweed allowed his attention to focus back to the world beyond Fardale's eyes—even though his brother spent most of his time casting sidelong glances to his snowy-tressed companion.

Thorn, the daughter of the elder'root, moved with easy grace down the tunnel. Mogweed could sense the wolfish lusts of his brother, the slight widening of his nostrils as he took in her scent, the thudding of his heart and drum of his blood.

Thorn, a wolf herself at heart, sensed Fardale's attention. She slowed her pace to match his. Her eyes glowed with something unspoken. Then words filled his head, reaching both their minds. *I must speak to you . . . I must tell you something . . .*

Mogweed became lost in the mix of her emotions: fear, anger, shame, heartache, and a trace of the lust that matched Fardale's own.

"What is it?" Fardale asked aloud, his words clipped and short. His brother's anger clearly blinded him to the depth of Thorn's emotions.

Mogweed smiled at the two former lovers, unable to speak their hearts. He enjoyed their torment. Fardale still anguished over his exile from the Western Reaches, by edict of Thorn's own father. Fardale had begged her to come with him, but she had turned her back on him, refusing.

Thorn caught the edge of Fardale's anger, and it plainly flared her own. Her eyes grew brighter in the dark tunnel. She continued to mindspeak. *There is something I should have said before. You deserve to know.*

Fardale remained silent. Anger bolted his tongue, while heartache kept him from reaching out with his inner thoughts.

Thorn continued. *There was a reason I did not go with you from the forest.* She suddenly glanced away and spoke aloud. "I wanted to . . . I truly did . . . but you left me no choice."

"I?" Fardale's outburst drew Meric's attention. The elv'in glanced back. Fardale lowered his voice. "I begged you on my knee. I would have done anything to keep from leaving your side. How did I leave you no choice?"

Fury rose in the glow of Thorn's eyes . . . and a fierce pride. "You left me with child."

Mogweed flinched in surprise—and whether it was his own shock or Fardale's, the pair tripped in the tunnel, catching up against one wall. Fardale straightened. He met Thorn's gaze fully. *A child?* he sent.

She nodded, keeping their eyes locked. An image formed: *A wild babe running through the woods, his head covered by a crown of feathers, flagging a furred tail behind him.* Thorn spoke aloud. "I named him Finch. He's back in the forest, with the other children and the infirm."

"I have a son . . ."

Fardale's shock was no less than Mogweed's. *A son . . . from the union the night they were cursed!*

But Fardale's surprise tilted and fell into a well of anger. "Why didn't you tell me?"

"I didn't know . . . not until after my father passed judgment upon you." She turned from the hurt on Fardale's face. "Then it was too late. You had to leave the forest. I knew if I told you of the child that you'd refuse to go. And I could not go with you . . . not with a growing belly and soon a child to care for." She glanced back to Fardale. Her eyes shone with shame.

Fardale finally recognized her pain. "And you were scared," he mumbled. "For yourself and your child . . ."

"And you," she added in a whisper. "I knew you couldn't stay, or you'd be lost to the wolf, settled into a wild beast with no memory of your heritage. But how it ached my heart to see you leave while knowing your baby was in my womb . . . especially when I could not say a word."

Fardale went to her. Mogweed sensed their two hearts seeking each other. Images fluttered between them, too fast for the mind to follow, but not the heart, a lifetime of joys and sorrows shared in a moment. This was the greatest gift of the si'lura: to commune so intimately, through thoughts, memories, emotions.

Mogweed floated above these deeper sendings. He could not reach that far into his brother's spirit. But still he sensed their thoughts, a barest flicker of a richer flame.

Mogweed found he had been jealous of his brother before—but never as much as now. He retreated from their union, not to give them privacy, but from shame and a nameless pain that welled through him. He turned his back upon the fire of their passion and sought the oblivion of cool darkness.

And as the walls of his cell closed around him, Mogweed stoked fire inside. He knew there was only one true way to escape this prison. No matter what the price in blood . . . *I must break free.*

ELENA SENSED THE TUNNEL'S END.

With each step deeper underground, a pressure built, pushing upon her ears and chest, making breathing increasingly difficult. It was as if she were again sinking into the bottomless pool around the Root of the world.

Er'ril would occasionally comment on something, but his words were muffled by the growing weight. A bubble of isolation surrounded her. She felt a distancing from everyone and everything. Even the brightness of the torch held by Tol'chuk grew muted and dull.

None of the others seemed affected. They continued to talk as if nothing were the matter.

Soon the tunnel walls began to gleam with thousands of glowworms. "We be near," Tol'chuk called back.

But Elena already knew this. The pressure had started to level out. Her eyes ached, her heart thudded, but she continued on.

"Are you all right?" Er'ril asked. His words sounded far away.

Elena nodded. "It's the magick here. The air is heavy with it."

"You look pale."

"I'm fine." And she was. She sensed no malignancy, simply the presence of something vastly larger than herself. But a part of her still cowered before the enormity of it.

Er'ril squeezed her fingers, but even this gesture was dulled. Nothing could hold off the magick here . . . not even love.

Tol'chuk marched on, and at last the tunnel opened into a great chamber. The others followed him into the room. Er'ril and Elena were the last to enter.

All eyes were already fixed on the far wall. An arch of fiery brilliance climbed to impossible heights within the echoing chamber.

"The Spirit Gate," Tol'chuk said needlessly.

"With that much heartstone," Harlequin Quail muttered, "we could simply buy off the Dark Lord."

Elena stared in awe. According to Tol'chuk, what they beheld was only part of the whole. The arch here was but half of a solid ring of heartstone.

Magnam stepped beside Harlequin. "If the Dark Lord ever got hold of this much heartstone, I fear the depths of the evil he might perform. Can you imagine an arch of this size transformed into ebon'stone? It would make the four Weirgates seem like a whore's glass baubles."

The d'warf's words roused worried expressions on everyone's features, especially Tol'chuk's.

The og're faced the Spirit Gate. One clawed hand covered his thigh pouch, as if he were trying to hide it from the arch of heartstone. "Perhaps we should think longer on this choice."

"No." Elena moved to Tol'chuk's side. "I can sense the magick here— that bit of ebon'stone cannot threaten its might. It would take something the size of a Weirgate to challenge it."

She recognized the doubtful glint in Tol'chuk's eyes. She touched his arm, willing him to trust her.

Slowly he nodded. With a worried frown, he stepped toward one leg of the arch, fingering the ties to the pouch and tugging it open. With his head half turned, Tol'chuk was the last to see what he unleashed.

Inky jets of darkness plumed from the opened pouch, shooting high over Tol'chuk's shoulder.

Elena gasped. Er'ril gripped her shoulder, pulling her back.

"Mother above!" Magnam exclaimed.

Seeing their reactions, Tol'chuk spun around. He stared up at the black cloud hovering under the arch. "It be the Triad!" he cried out. "I thought them gone when the stone turned black."

Apparently this was not so.

As Elena watched, jagged forks of silvery brightness crackled through the roiling darkness, like lightning in a storm cloud. But this was no ordinary storm cloud. Rather it appeared more a mist of ebon'stone. And laughter, as black as the mists from which it issued, flowed out the churning darkness.

"Get back!" Er'ril shouted to Tol'chuk. He waved for the others to retreat to the tunnel.

Tol'chuk crouched under the cloud. "But the Triad . . ."

"They've been twisted like the Heart!" Nee'lahn called to him as Meric drew her back with the others. "Like my sisters, the Grim wraiths!"

Only Tol'chuk did not move. "But the Gate! I cannot abandon it!"

Words of dark amusement flowed from the cloud. "And we wouldn't let you." The mists split into three shredded bits of darkness. Two fled to either leg of the arch, with the last sailing high to the pinnacle. Separate now, they appeared vaguely og're in shape.

"No!" Tol'chuk cried, straightening. "I won't let you harm the Gate!"

"It be not we who mean to harm it!" The words seemed to rise from all three shadows. Jagged crackles of lightning shot forth from the spirits guarding the legs of the arch. The bolts of silver lanced out and snared Tol'chuk by the arms.

Tethered between the two, he was torn off his feet and yanked forward. Crying out, Tol'chuk fought, but his arms were stretched to the point of dislocation. In a heartbeat, he was pinned under the arch, hanging in midair between the two legs

Er'ril ran forward, yanking free his sword. The wit'ch sword gleamed like an icicle, its elemental steel blade singing out of its sheath.

Elena ripped off her gloves and grabbed the dagger at her waist. With deft slices, she cut each palm and called forth her magick. Flames ignited over both hands: wit'ch fire and coldfire.

She sensed Meric and Nee'lahn flanking her. The others returned with them. None of them would abandon Tol'chuk to the wraiths.

From the peak of the arch, the third shadow cast more bolts of silver, warding them back. The jagged spears struck with the might of true steel. Er'ril dodged a bolt, rolling to the side. Bits of rock blasted from the stone floor where he had been standing.

Other spears aimed for their group.

They scattered. The hammer blows echoed throughout the cavern.

"Back to the tunnel!" Er'ril shouted from behind an outcropping of stone. "I'll go for Tol'chuk!"

Elena picked herself up from the floor. "Do as he says."

Meric met her eyes, defiant, angry. Similar expressions flashed among the others. Even Magnam, with no magick of his own, shook his head. The d'warf had taken a blow to the shoulder. Blood flowed down his arm and still, he didn't budge.

"Help Tol'chuk!" Nee'lahn urged. "We'll offer what aid we can!"

The next barrage of lightning lashed out. Elena cast a shield of coldfire before her, blocking the energy. Still the bolt was strong enough to knock her back. She tried to take another step, but more strikes bombarded her, one after the other, pounding her back.

From the corner of her eye, she saw Fardale and Thorn drop to all fours, shifting into two wolves, one dark, one snowy. They raced across the floor in a zigzagging pattern, passing in front of her while bolts chased after them.

With the momentary distraction, Elena fought her way forward. She spotted Er'ril behind the outcropping, pinned down in the center of the room. Blasts struck his shelter, shattering chunks of rock, eroding his hiding space away.

On the far side of the chamber, Meric moved with the unnatural speed of his people, impossible to catch, while Nee'lahn crouched behind a boulder with Magnam, binding his wound. There was no sign of Harlequin Quail. The master spy had fled.

Elena turned her attention forward. It was a stalemate; neither group was strong enough to break the other. Elena feared using her full power against the wraiths that hovered in front of the heartstone arch. Even if her magicks could harm pure spirit, the backlash might harm the Spirit

Gate. If the ring of heartstone were shattered, so would be all hope of learning whatever Sisa'kofa knew. It was too important to risk a direct attack.

Around her, the chamber echoed with lightning blasts, making it difficult to think. Elena kept up her shield as she slowly worked forward, trying to reach Er'ril.

But what then? How did you defeat an enemy that had no substance?

Off to the side, Thorn was suddenly tossed in the air as she caught the edge of a blast. She struck the stone and rolled back to flee on three legs, leaving bloody footprints behind, her snowy flank singed black. Fardale raced around her, keeping the bolts away.

The stalemate was beginning to fray—and not in their favor.

Elena moved ahead as an explosive strike rocked the cavern, blinding her for a heartbeat. All three spirits had struck the outcropping behind which Er'ril hid. Rock dust plumed up. As it wafted away, Elena spotted Er'ril sprawled under a tumble of rock, not moving.

She raced forward. Her anger and fear melded her magick into a shield around her. "Er'ril!"

His legs were pinned under rock. Blood seeped from a scalp wound and from one ear, but a groan answered her. He still lived! One hand scrabbled blindly on the stone. She saw his hand was attempting to reach the rose sword, still trying to fight.

His effort fired her. She snatched up Shadowsedge.

"No . . . ," he mumbled weakly.

But as her bloody palm gripped the hilt, a jolt tore through her body. She was on her feet before she knew it. Magick fed into the blade and ignited its length into pure flame.

Lightning struck toward her from three directions. But unbidden, her sword parried each bolt, driving it aside or absorbing its energy into her own magick. She was not knocked back this time. She danced across the cavern floor, feinting and parrying the multiple attacks, one against three.

Around the chamber, the attacks on the others faded. The wraiths needed all their attention to hold her back.

And still Elena danced. Her feet moved with a skill not her own, her arm flashing with magick uncalled. A corner of her mind recognized this control: She had once fought her aunt Mycelle with a blade whetted in her own magickal blood. She remembered the surety of steel melded to her flesh. But that experience paled when compared to what she felt now.

Shadowsedge had been forged of elemental steel, fused with the blood of Sisa'kofa, her ancestor. Elena had not only joined steel to herself, but to the skill of an ancient wit'ch.

Lightning danced around her in a blinding display. Blocked by her blows, bolts struck walls and ceiling. Rock tumbled from above. The others retreated to the walls. Even they knew the fight was now between her and the three wraiths.

A smile grew on her lips.

Closer at hand, words reached her from behind. "Elena . . ." It was Er'ril, groggy. "The sword . . . a blood weapon." His voice grew stronger. "It is only steel. You must control it."

She dismissed his warnings. She was in perfect control. With a flick of her wrist, she parried a bolt back toward the wielder. The lethal force struck the granite wall under the arch, exploding the stone.

Was that not proof of her control?

Her smile stretched, exposing her teeth. Magick sang in her blood, steel in her ears. She backhanded another bolt, driving it to strike the wall again. With each breath, her skill grew.

A cry of pain sounded from ahead, a pebble in a raging sea.

"Elena!" It was Er'ril again. "Look at what you do!" he yelled at her.

Elena shook off his words. She knew what she was doing.

"Look with your heart! Do not forget the woman inside you!"

As his words sank into her heart, she remembered a moment from long ago, but not far from here. She had stood atop a mountain pass in virgin snow. She had joined a ruby hand to a pale one, joining wit'ch to woman. She had accepted her power at that moment, recognized the weight of her responsibility. But she had also recognized that which she *refused* to lose: her heart, her humanity, her ability to love.

"Er'ril . . ."

"Trust your heart . . . not cold steel . . ."

A veil slowly lifted from her eyes. Lightning struck at her feet, jolting her back, stumbling her away. She cried out as the world came back into focus. The perfect blend of magick and steel shattered around her.

Across the chamber, Tol'chuk still hung between the two legs of the arch. But to either side of him, the smooth wall was deeply pitted where her parried bolts had struck. She had come within an arm's length of killing the og're, her friend.

More lightning chased her. She fought it with the blade, but now she did not release herself fully to the sword. She sought a balance somewhere in between—and her skill ebbed. Blows again jolted her, threaten-

ing to tear the sword from her grip. The surety of victory faded. Elena
sensed that only by releasing herself fully to the sword would she have
the skill to bring the fight forward to the Gate, but if she did that, she
risked losing herself and those around her. Steel did not care about love,
only victory.

Movement by the Gate drew her attention. A small hand waved at her.
It came from near a pile of rubble at the base of the wall, under Tol'chuk's
feet. A figure rose from hiding—Harlequin Quail!

The spy held a dagger in his teeth and motioned with his hands. Elena
frowned, then understanding dawned. Her eyes grew wide.

Of course . . .

She risked a glance behind her. "I need everyone who can still move to
be ready on my word!" Elena turned back and parried another bolt
toward the ceiling.

Sounds of affirmation echoed out to her.

She locked gazes with Harlequin Quail. She prayed his plan was
sound. *"Now!* Rush the Gate!"

Elena burst through a flurry of lightning strikes. To either side, the others raced forward: Meric with his unnatural speed, Fardale, Magnam,
even Thorn raced on her three good legs.

Lightning shattered out in all directions at this last drive toward the
Spirit Gate, but their efforts were a feint.

Under Tol'chuk, the short man dressed in motley and bells leaped with
an unnatural silence. Moving with a grace that defied bone and muscle, he
grabbed Tol'chuk's ankle with one hand, pulled himself up, and used his
dagger to slice the pouch hanging from the og're's thigh.

Harlequin then dropped and landed in a crouch, both hands held out.
The ebon'stone Heart tumbled out the bottom of the pouch and into his
waiting palms.

With his prize in hand, he raced from under Tol'chuk and aimed
toward one of the pillared legs of heartstone. Only then did one of the
wraiths notice the man under their misty noses. A bolt of lightning lashed
out at him.

Harlequin dove forward with a jangle of bells, somersaulted twice, and
was at the arch. Without pause he flew up the granite wall like a spider.
Another bolt struck at him, but he was already leaping toward the arch.
With the Heart held out before him, he slammed its dark shape into the
gap where it fit with perfection.

A scream erupted from the trio of wraiths.

Harlequin leaped aside.

Brightness flared along the arch, exploding with such brilliance that all were driven back. The wraiths were burned from their perches, blasted into wailing fragments.

Tol'chuk, no longer restrained, dropped to the stone floor. He landed in a half crouch, swinging to face the Gate

Elena retreated to Er'ril's side. He reached to her, blood dripping down his face. She dropped the sword and took his hand. The pressure she had felt in the tunnels grew to an enormity that threatened to drown her. Wincing, she leaned near him. "Are you all right?"

He grimaced. "I've felt better."

Worried, Elena turned to the arch. The wall, framed in glowing heart-stone, began to shimmer. Granite dissolved into illusion. The Gate was opening. The flow of ruby light trailed down under the stone floor and around again, marking the buried ring of heartstone.

When the brilliance reached the chunk of blackened stone at its heart, the ruby glow swelled over the darkness and overwhelmed it, wiping it away. With this release, the entire ring blossomed with a light that pierced flesh and bone.

For a moment, Elena felt a linking similar to that with the blood sword, a melding of her spirit to the energy here. But instead of being limited to the length of a steel blade, her essence sailed forth in all directions. The boundaries were vast, farther than her mind could fathom. In that instant, she knew to what she was blood-bonded.

The world . . . all the lands, all the peoples . . .

For the barest moment, she sensed all life. In the past, she had experienced hints of this interconnectivity, a vast web of all living things—but never more than at this moment. The beauty and symmetry grew into a harmony that was both complex and simple. It was a chorus without music, a perfect crystalline matrix of silver life force.

Her magick sang with her ecstasy.

Then, like a snuffed candle, it was taken from her. The cavern snapped back into focus. The pressure popped away into oblivion, gone. A sob escaped her clenched throat.

"Elena . . . ?" Fingers squeezed her hand.

She squeezed back, not ready for words.

Against the far wall, the ring of heartstone had opened. Beyond the threshold lay a well of darkness streaked with fissures of forking and crisscrossing veins of crimson fire. Bursts of brilliance raced along and disappeared, almost too quickly for the eye to follow, like shooting stars across a night sky. But this display was but a backdrop for the true marvel at the heart of the well.

In the center, slowly spinning, was a crystal the color of a clear morning sky. The stone seemed to swell toward the Gate, growing to fill the ring of heartstone.

The Spirit Stone . . .

The glow bathed the group huddled before its immensity. Elena again felt the connection to all living things. She sensed the beauty of her own lifeforce, of all those in the room, a shine of silvery energy. In Meric and Nee'lahn, she also recognized the flame of their elemental fire, a tiny spark of brighter magick.

In that moment, Elena realized a startling thing. They were the same: the lifeforce in all things and the silver energy of an elemental's fire. She gaped at the stone. The same was true before her. The crystal was an amalgam of lifeforce and elemental silver. It was both! And with this realization came another. She had seen such a crystal once before.

She was not the only to make this connection. *"De'nal,"* Er'ril whispered in awe and sorrow.

Elena knew he was right. The boy had been sculpted of the same crystal as here: lifeforce and elemental silver, fused into a brilliant crystalline form. There was something important about this connection. Elena could almost grasp it.

Then from the heart of the stone, a droplet of darkness appeared. It rose toward them, tangled in a cloud of silver strands. Tol'chuk backed toward Er'ril and Elena. "The Wit'ch of the Spirit Stone."

Readying herself, Elena gave Er'ril's hand a final squeeze. Then she stood and stepped forward.

From the Gate, a dark figure of carved ebony rose like a swimmer from the depths of a silver sea. The silver strands wafted apart, moving to currents unseen. The figure floated free, stepping out of the Gate and hovering at its threshold.

It was a woman, cloaked only in a cloud of silvery strands. Elena saw that these filaments were the figure's own tresses, floating in wisps around her face, sweeping over her shoulders and about her form, flowing all the way back to the heart of the Spirit Stone.

In turn, the energy of the crystal swept out in bright flares of magick along these strands and sparked over her dark skin, defining her shape, as if continually sculpting her out of the darkness of the Gate's well.

But Elena barely noted any of this. Her eyes were fixed on the woman's face, smiling down upon her. It was her own face! Maybe a bit older. Only the eyes were truly someone else's, ripe with ancient knowledge and magick.

"Sisa'kofa," she greeted her.

The woman nodded. "Elena . . . at long last." Her voice seemed slightly out of time with the movement of her lips.

Elena was too stunned to speak, but the figure smiled so warmly that her frozen tongue melted. "I . . . I have so many questions."

"So do we all in life," Sisa'kofa answered, "but I'm afraid I can only offer the guidance left to me by my predecessor. I am only the shadow of the one you name Sisa'kofa, bound to the stone to pass on one last message. What I've learned during my guardianship here, I've already told the seed of Ly'chuk."

Elena nodded. Tol'chuk had already related the history of the Dark Lord, of his ancestor's betrayal that had started in this very room and earned him the name Oathbreaker. "What else must I know?" she asked. "What message do you bear?"

"I've come to tell you that you fight the wrong enemy," the shadow of the witch said. "You have all along."

"But the Dark Lord seeks to blacken the very heart of the Land. You've said as much yourself," she blurted out.

Sisa'kofa nodded. "It is so."

"Then how is the Dark Lord not our enemy?"

The sea of glowing strands stirred. "You do not listen. He may be an enemy, but he is the wrong enemy. Let the others you've gathered to your side face Ly'chuk and his darkness. You must ready yourself for the true danger to the world."

"And what is that?"

The figure wafted through the air, stretching from the Gate to hover before her. One dark hand rose and brushed her cheek, a sensation that was both ice and fire on her skin. "Not what, but *who*," she whispered.

"Who?" Elena echoed.

The wit'ch leaned near to her ear. There was no breath, but the answer still reached her. "You."

Elena stumbled back in shock. "Me?"

The spirit drifted forward, following. "There is a dark tide coming, foreseen for ages past, by seers from many lands. All the threads of prophecy wrap around a single spirit—not Ly'chuk, but you, Elena Morin'stal, descendant of wit'ches and elv'in blood. You will hold the threads to the world's fate."

"What must I do?"

"You will face a choice, a cusp of prophecy. Your choosing will either damn or save all. That is where the true danger lies."

"How?" Elena straightened, a flame of anger burning through her shock. "Even at the cost of my own life, I will certainly choose to save the world."

The wit'ch smiled darkly. "There is the heart of the danger of which I speak, the reason I've locked a part of my spirit in stone all these ages. I have come to tell you that your choice—either way—will doom all."

Elena stared at her tormentor, then spoke weakly. "Then what must I do?"

Sisa'kofa shook her head, stirring up the silvery nest around her figure. "I can't answer that. All the fates whirl into the dark tide that is to come. None can see what lies beyond."

"But . . ."

The dark figure leaned close. "Look to your heart. Look to the friends you love. Find your own path out of the darkness—a path that none but you will see."

"How?"

The wit'ch reached forward again with an ebony-sculpted hand and touched a finger to her chest, a touch of ice and fire. "The answer is here already. You must find it . . . or you will certainly doom the world."

ER'RIL LAY IN A STUPOR OF PAIN. EVERY MOVEMENT GROUND THE CRUSHED bones of his trapped legs in fiery agony. Still, when he saw Elena stumble away from the wit'ch with despair etched into every feature, he tried to drag himself from the tumble of rocks.

Elena crumpled to her knees on the stone floor, as if crushed under the weight of the spirit's words.

"Elena!" he cried—but she seemed deaf to him. He reached toward her, but she was too far away.

What did the wit'ch say to her?

While they had conversed, he could see their lips moving, but no words reached him or the others. Some magick muffled their speech.

Then the silence shattered away. The wit'ch spoke to Elena, but now all could hear. "What I have told you, you must keep to your heart alone. None here have heard our words."

Elena stared up, her face a mask of fear. "How can I keep silent about this?"

Sisa'kofa knelt, reaching a hand to Elena's tears as they started to flow. "Because you must. You know this in your own heart. You will weaken their resolve when they most need to be strong. This message is for you alone. It is a challenge you must face."

"But how am I . . . ?" Elena glanced to the others. Her gaze settled on Er'ril. "How . . . ?" she whispered, tears flowing.

The wit'ch followed Elena's gaze. Er'ril found himself staring into dark, ageless eyes. They seemed to ask something of him—but what?

As he tried to decipher the meaning, Sisa'kofa spoke to Elena. "The *hows* of the world, I don't know. Only the certainty of the outcome."

Elena covered her face, weeping. Sisa'kofa continued to stare at Er'ril, silently willing something from him.

Er'ril, trapped and broken under rock, did the only thing he could. "Elena," he said softly.

She heard him this time and lowered her hands.

"I love you," he said, meeting her eyes. "Whatever grief you bear, I will always be at your side."

"Er'ril," she sobbed, her heart breaking before him. "You don't know—"

"I do *know*," he cut her off. "I love you . . . and nothing else matters."

"But—"

"I love you, and you love me. Is this not true?"

She nodded, sobbing. Er'ril had never wanted to take her in his arms more than at this moment. But he could not. He could only reach her with his words, comfort her with his heart.

"I will always love you," he said. "Bound on my word, I am your liege-man. Bound with elv'in blood, I am your husband. But it is my heart and spirit that bind me truly to you. You are my life, and nothing will ever change this. Not now, not ever."

Elena took a deep, shuddering breath. "Er'ril . . ." Her voice was still pained, but it had retreated from the pit of despair and agony of a moment ago.

The wit'ch rose from beside Elena. "My duty is finished. I must be set free."

Elena wiped her eyes. "How?"

Sisa'kofa pointed to the sword abandoned on the floor. "Shadows-edge . . . it is a blade made to cut through magick, to break the strongest spells. You must take it and sever my connections to the world's heart."

Elena stared at the sword as if it were a poisonous snake.

"Do this, and I will grant you a final boon."

Elena glanced questioningly to the wit'ch, but no answer was given. The wit'ch simply motioned to the sword.

Elena took up the sword and shoved to her feet. She crossed behind the figure, to where the flow of silver strands streamed back toward the world's heart. Elena raised the sword.

Er'ril heard a whisper from the wit'ch. "At long last . . . ," she murmured, closing her eyes.

Elena brought down the sword. As it cleaved through the silvery tangle, a bright light burst throughout the room, blinding them all for a scintillating heartbeat.

Then the world returned.

Elena stood a few paces away, still holding the sword in both her hands. The wit'ch was gone. Beyond her, the Gate remained open. The Spirit Stone still shone in the heart of the world, but now it retreated back, growing smaller until it winked away, taking its dark well. Ordinary granite filled the space.

Tol'chuk cried out.

It was only then that Er'ril realized that the arch of heartstone was gone! The entire Spirit Gate had vanished!

Elena stared up at the empty wall, exhausted. "Like the Spirit Root of the Western Reaches," she mumbled. "The Land is pulling back. Only the shadow of the wit'ch was holding this gateway open. With Sisa'kofa gone, the Land readies itself for the final battle."

"But the Gate," Tol'chuk said. "It is the heart of our clans."

"No," Elena answered. "As long as the Land thrives, your clans will always have a heart. It exists for all lands, for all peoples. None can claim it as their sole property."

She turned around. Her eyes fell upon Er'ril with a confused frown.

He could not fathom her expression until Meric stepped to his shoulder. "I think you can get up off the floor," the elv'in prince said.

Er'ril looked behind him. The pile of rock had disappeared. He rolled to his feet, inspecting his limbs. There was no pain, no broken bones. Not even his clothes were torn. He glanced to the others. No one else was injured.

"All our wounds are healed!" he said, stunned.

"The final boon," Elena said with a spark of bright relief. She crossed to his side and dropped her sword. She clasped him to her. "Er'ril!"

He wrapped his arms around her. "Hush."

She shuddered against him.

"I love you," he whispered, but as he stared at the blank wall, a part of him prayed it would be enough. A fear grew in him.

What did the wit'ch tell her?

21

CASSA DAR LAY STRETCHED ON HER BED IN THE UPPERMOST TOWER CHAMBER of Castle Drakk. Her eyes stared up at the raftered ceiling, but her sight was far from the swamps of her home.

Instead, she sailed over the wooded highland countryside, looking through the eyes of her swamp child. The connection was tenuous—the distances were vast, and her powers weakened as the flow of elemental energies continued their slow ebb. It was only the strength of the poison in the winged child that kept her link intact. The infant king adder at the heart of her magickal construction of moss and weed remained strong, rich in venoms.

Still, it was hard to breach the distances. It taxed her. Her castle children dragged up plates of dried fruits and boiled fish, but she could only pick at their offerings. She had remained bedridden, too exhausted to move from the room.

But she knew the importance of her mission.

Just after midday, she had taken wing along with six si'luran scouts. The shape-shifters had been assigned to scout the trails that their forces would take tomorrow. The plan was to head out just after sunrise and reach the highlands below the Fang by nightfall. From there, they would set upon Winter's Eyrie by the following dawn.

For that to happen, their armies would need to move swiftly, with a clear path and a clearer goal. They must fall upon their enemy like a torrent of snowmelt from the heights.

But where was the enemy? What did they face?

That was her mission.

Half a world from her castle home, Cassa Dar sailed over treetops. The sun was near to setting. She banked on a warm uprising, circling higher. She was almost to her goal and dared not be spotted.

Below, the world was a sea of green. Highland forests stretched to the horizons north and south, fringing the peaks of the Teeth. But to the east, a great swath of devastation marred the beauty, as if the green sea washed up against a stripped and blackened island.

Smoke rose in columns from the green forest, marking the ruins of hamlets and farms. She had swept over one such site a short time ago: a homestead, recently razed. Embers still glowed through the pall of smoke, revealing a charnel house of horrors. Livestock had been brutally slaughtered, the remains strewn everywhere. From the air, she had spotted a cow sprawled in offal and blood, torn in half. Nor had the owners of the farm escaped the slaughter. Eight heads were piked among the ruins, women and children, an entire family, even their pet dog.

Since then, she had avoided those sites, focusing on the blackened forest ahead. From that island of death amid the green sea, a plume of black smoke sailed high into the air. It was not the smolder of the other smaller pyres—whatever cast out such smoke continued to burn fierce and deep. She knew she had no choice but to scout out what lay ahead.

Satisfied with her height, she sailed toward the black sigil in the summer sky. From the ground, she would appear no more than a speck, impossible to spot. A part of her quailed at approaching any nearer, but she flew onward, cresting higher, banking in a wide curve toward the island of dead trees.

Once she was within half a league, she could make out a wide valley stretched between the upper highlands and the lower foothills. From the organized rows of trees below, it must have once been a mighty orchard, sectioned into family farms and centered on a modestly sized township.

"Sweet Mother . . . ," Cassa Dar whispered in her chamber room. Though she had never been here, she knew this valley. Elena had described it in detail, from the small mill by the stream to the wide pond by the town's edge. It was the girl's own home, Winterfell.

Cassa remained at the edges of the valley.

Like the homestead she had passed earlier, the town was a burned-out husk. Brick buildings had been scorched. Some walls still stood; others had been razed to the ground. Cassa Dar banked away, aiming for the well of dark smoke at the north end of the valley.

Below, the orchard had fared no better than the town. Not only had all the trees been denuded of leaves, but even their branches were missing. All that remained were dead trunks, stripped and bare—a valley of wooden spikes awaiting bodies to be spitted. It was a disheartening sight; she could only imagine what such a discovery would do to Elena. This had been her home.

"Poor child . . ."

She swung her gaze from the devastation below to the column of smoke at the north end of the valley, the region named Winter's Eyrie. The destruction of the lower valley rose up toward it, a path of sorrow and pain.

She dared not get too close. Though the township and orchards seemed empty of any living thing, whatever flagged the fire below would surely be wary of prying eyes. Still, she had been sent to search for the last Weirgate. While this was surely suspicious, she could not return with just her grave misgivings. She needed proof upon which to target their armies.

So Cassa Dar urged her swamp child to higher elevations. She would have to get as close as possible without being spotted.

Ahead, the plume of smoke grew, filling the world with its foulness. On the journey from the mountains, the entire highlands had reeked of soot and woodsmoke, but here the winds were foul, smelling of burned flesh, scorched blood, and the tang of something twisted and unnatural.

As Cassa Dar climbed higher over the valley, she spotted the source of the smoke. A great pit lay blasted into the land. She swung closer. The hole, circular in shape, had to be two leagues across. From what she could see of the edges of the monstrous pit, the hole seemed to descend in giant stairsteps, huge tiers gouged from the land, dropping one after another into the ground.

Whatever the purpose of the pit, its construction was still under way. From the smoke, fires would suddenly flare, shooting high into the sky. Echoes of pounding and muffled explosions rose from within the column of smoke, sounding impossibly far away.

How deep is this pit?

Cassa Dar edged around the periphery of the dark construction. The outer circles of the pit were as empty as the orchard valley, but screams rose on the winds, amid howls and the clanging of steel. She sensed movement deep below: a churning of the smoke, darker shapes lumbering through the pall, limned in the flashes of fire.

The hole was clearly not empty.

She braved a closer pass, determined it would be her last. She would report what she discovered here and leave the decisions to the war council.

As she swept nearer, searching the heart of the smoky pit, she sensed a presence swell before her. Towering ahead, the column of darkness took on a new form: It sprouted black wings, and a neck stretched forth out of the darkness. Fiery eyes opened above a smoky beak. A dark malignancy searched out.

Cassa Dar knew better than to tarry. She dove away, sensing that to be spotted by that presence would be certain doom. She fell back into the desolate orchard valley, dropping among the bare trunks, skirting and winging with the momentum of her dive.

Trunks flashed past.

She dodged right and left, then rolled into the cover of a streambed. She flew just above the sludgy, muddy waters, keeping the banks of the stream between her and the smoky searcher. At any moment, she expected a monstrous black claw to snatch her away. Even hundreds of leagues away, she knew she was not safe from the evil. If caught, both child and creator would be destroyed.

Fueled by fear and aided by the innate skill of her creation, she winged down the stream, sweeping at impossible speeds, a prayer on her lips.

Then the stream emptied into a millpond, and the banks fell away. Exposed, Cassa Dar rolled and searched behind her. She was surprised at how far she had traveled. The smoky shape was only a smudge on the horizon.

Watching from a distance, she saw the spread of black wings fold back into the cloud. The beaked visage dissolved into smoke. The last to vanish were the fiery eyes. They searched a moment longer—then they were gone.

Cassa Dar shook with relief. She had come near to awakening the beast at the heart of the monstrous black pit.

Thankful to escape its attention, she urged the swamp child out of the valley and away. The sun was disappearing into the mountains to the west. She chased after it, ready to return to her friends, to Jaston.

She glanced once more behind her. The black smudge stood out against the darkening sky. She had found what she had come seeking. There was no doubt what beast had risen from the smoke: the black wings, the sharp beak, the fiery eyes. It had been the shadow of the Wyvern, the last Weirgate. It must surely lie at the heart of the pit.

With a heavy heart, Cassa Dar fled the devastation. In two days' time, she would return—she and all the others.

They had no choice.

A shudder of dread passed through the swamp child, and far away in her castle tower, Cassa Dar made a quiet plea. "Mother above, have mercy on us all."

"HAVE YOU MADE YOUR DECISION, BOY?"

Leaning on his staff, Joach frowned down at Greshym. He clenched his gloved fingers, resisting the urge to smash that satisfied smirk from the darkmage's face. Greshym had knowledge he needed.

The darkmage sat in a pile of moldy straw in his makeshift cell, a small cave at the end of a blind tunnel off the main og're cavern. His arms had been tied behind him and his legs bound. There were two guards, og'res armed with clubs, posted at the end of the tunnel—the only exit.

"The sun has set," Greshym pressed. "What is your decision?"

Joach crouched, his old knees cracking. He supported himself with his stone staff. "Let's be clear—if I free you, you'll teach me how to imbue true life into my creations, and return the winters of my youth that you stole from me."

"Half the winters. *Half,*" Greshym corrected. "That was the deal."

"And once you're free, you'll leave here."

"Do you think I want to stay? To be recaptured?"

Joach narrowed his eyes. Could he trust the darkmage? Surely not, but he could not risk losing this one chance. All day long, he had stared at the dream-sculpted rose, smelled its petals, fingered its green leaves. As the sun set, he had planted the flower in the meadow outside the caves, offering fresh loam to its new roots. He had stood guard over it as the sun disappeared. It truly lived. For such magick, he would risk anything.

As he crouched, he pictured a girl with twilight eyes and skin as warm as the desert sands. Anything—he would risk anything to touch her again, to watch her smile under moonlight.

Greshym's eyes glinted in the torchlight filtering from the tunnel beyond the cave. A vague smile marked his lips, but also a trace of sadness.

Joach lowered his voice. "First tell me how you brought life into the flower without any magick. Do this and I will slice your bonds."

"And after that?"

"I'll get you past the guards. Once away, you'll return my years, then be gone from these mountains."

Greshym nodded. "I'll need a horse."

Joach thought for a moment, then sighed. "Agreed."

Greshym rolled up onto his knees. "Then let us begin our last dance. To understand what I did to the rose, you must first understand about lifeforces, the flow of energies that separates the living from the dead." The darkmage stared across at him. "All lifeforce is the same energy, but it is made unique by each individual's spirit. A spirit will imbue this energy with its pattern. Sculpting it, if you like, into something unique."

"What does this have to do with the rose?"

"I'm getting to that, my boy. Though you have the face of an old man, you have the patience of a brash youngster."

"Go on," Joach urged, irritated by the darkmage's jovial chiding.

Greshym sighed. "As you know, I stole a large font of your lifeforce. It aged you, making me younger."

Anger flared in Joach, but he bit his tongue to keep the mage talking.

"I had to rip it from you, and it is not an easy thing to do . . . for life energy, once patterned, is immutable. It can't change. The lifeforce that keeps me young is still patterned after you."

"It is still me?" Joach trembled with the horror of this thought.

"And it wants to return to you, like a stream wants to flow down a mountainside. You are its most natural vessel, but I keep it dammed inside of me by the force of my will, nothing more. For it to flow back to you would only take a touch of my hand and the release of my will."

"It's that simple?" Joach could not keep the shock out of his voice.

"Indeed."

"And the rose?"

"You created it with your own sculpting. It is as much a part of you as your arm or your leg. To bring it to life, I had only to touch its petals and will the energy I hold to flow into it—energy patterned to you, patterned the same as the rose. Once the empty cup was full, I stanched the flow and broke contact. But the rose now lived."

Joach sat back, stunned. "So anything I dream sculpt, I can bring to true life by pouring my own energy into it, simply willing it to live."

The darkmage nodded. "Some of the strongest magicks are the simplest."

Joach closed his eyes. A tremble passed over his limbs. If it were true, he could bring Kesla back to life! But could he trust Greshym's word? He wanted proof first himself. He positioned his staff over his knees.

"What are you doing?" Greshym asked.

"Testing your word." Joach shook back the sleeve of his cloak and exposed the stump of his wrist. He had lost the hand to this one's gnomish dog. He passed the stump over the length of his petrified stave, calling forth the magicks inside, calling forth the sculpture of the hand stored in his staff. Hand and fingers bloomed into existence, unlined by age, as smooth as when he was young. And though he could move the fingers, even grab objects with the strength of ten men, it was cold and unfeeling, as if he wore a glove of ice over the new hand. Though Joach could grant it the illusion of life, it was still dead.

Joach stared over at Greshym. "To bring something I sculpted to life, all I have to do is will it?"

The darkmage nodded, gaping at his creation. Joach noticed Greshym's eyes flick to his own scarred wrist with clear desire—the darkmage had also lost a hand, centuries ago. "If I had your gifts . . ." he mumbled.

"What must I do?" Joach asked.

Greshym studied the hand. "You must let some of your life energy flow into the new sculpture. To do this, you must merely wish it so. Patterned after you, the energy will fill the void."

Joach stared at the dream hand. *Will it to live? Could it be that simple?* He closed his eyes and pictured himself whole, hale of flesh and bone. He imagined a river flowing through his blood, spreading out from his heart in all directions: down his legs, out his arms, trailing to his fingers and toes. He waited for something to happen—but nothing did. "It didn't work!" he blurted.

"Didn't it?" Greshym asked.

Joach held up his sculpted hand. Only now did he see the corded lines, the bluish veins, the paper-thin skin. It had aged. He compared it to his left hand. They were the same. "I don't understand." He flexed the newly created fingers, and the aged joints ached.

"You've brought the dream to life—true life. It must match the age of your energy. You are old, so it is old."

Joach ran his new hand over his staff. He felt the rough grain and the sharp green crystals imbedded in it. This hand was real! Closing his eyes, his thoughts turned to the one hope in his heart.

Kesla . . .

Greshym must have read his desire. "You've done well here. But to bring something as complex as an entire person to life will take a signifi-cant chunk of your own energy—energy that you don't have to spare."

Joach opened his eyes. "But you'll return half of what you stole if I free you."

The darkmage nodded. "That is the deal." A vague smile again marked Greshym's lips.

Joach knew that there was something yet unspoken, a trick yet to be played, but he would deal with the consequences when they arose. He could not move forward from here without the darkmage's cooperation.

Cradling his staff under one arm, he pulled a dagger from his cloak.

"You had best keep your word, Greshym, or I'll use this same dagger to slice your throat." He leaned forward and cut the man's ropes.

Greshym rubbed his wrists and stretched his arms. "What of the guards?"

Joach waved him aside, then pointed his staff at the spot where Greshym had sat. He unleashed one of the two spells he had prepared before coming here. It had cost him blood and would cost him again much of his stored magick, but the price of his own youth was worth it.

Dream magick plumed from the end of his staff. Upon the stone, a figure took form, sculpted from the energies and drawn into this world. It was an exact replica of the darkmage, bound again in ropes.

Joach took a certain amount of satisfaction from Greshym's shocked expression. "You've more talent than I suspected," Greshym mumbled. "Remarkable."

The replica lay limp and blue-faced. There was no life in the creation, and there never would be.

"They'll believe you dead," Joach said. "You can leave with no searchers on your trail."

Greshym frowned. "Not if they see me walking around like this."

Joach's eyes narrowed. "They won't." He swung his staff at the darkmage's heart.

Greshym backed a step from the threat, but Joach cast out his second spell. Dream magicks swirled. Joach was careful not to let this magick contact the mage, lest the Blood Diary's spell suck it away. Instead he created a shell around Greshym and summoned an illusion to mask his form. The darkmage now appeared to be an elv'in sailor, with coppery hair and pale skin. The magick would not withstand much scrutiny, and any stray hand would pass through the shell, revealing the artifice. But it would suffice for now.

Greshym spoke through the illusion. "Well done."

"Be warned, I can sweep away the magick at any time and call guards if you betray your word."

Greshym nodded, as did his illusory counterpart. "Then let us end this matter."

Joach thumped to the cave entrance and called down the tunnel. "Guards! Come quickly! Something is wrong with the prisoner!"

A shuffle sounded—then one of the og're guards lumbered down to them.

Joach pointed his staff toward the corner of the cell, where the dream-sculpted body lay crumpled. "Dead," he said in the common tongue, speaking simply for the og're to understand. "The man is dead."

The og're leaned into the cell. His nostrils sniffed. "Dead," he said thickly.

Joach nodded. "Send a runner to the flying ship. Let them know."

A grunt answered him. The og're was only too happy to leave; death unsettled the large creatures. With a final wide-eyed stare at the body, the guard knuckled away down the passage.

Joach waved for Greshym to follow. The guards had seen him enter with an elv'in at his side, but then it had been only the illusion sculpted briefly into existence to fool them—an empty shell that was now occupied by the darkmage.

Once out of the passage, the og're guard bellowed to a smaller clansman in his native tongue. With a grumbled assent, the younger og're took off at a loping run toward the cavern's exit.

Joach hobbled past the pair of guards and led Greshym toward the open fields. Starlight shone silver over the highland meadows, while the mountains were dark giants leaning over them. Closer at hand, cook fires of the encamped og're army dotted the fields, and in the near woods, the glow from the si'luran forces. Though the moon was already risen, both camps still were roused and busy. It was easy to slip past unnoticed.

Joach nodded ahead. "I'll take you as far as the corral. Then I expect to have my winters returned to me. If there is any trickery or I'm threatened in any manner, the spell will dissolve. You will be exposed."

"Fair enough," Greshym whispered.

Joach kept a step behind the darkmage, ready for any final deceit, but Greshym just marched toward the crude stockade where a few horses were penned. In a separate stanchion stood Ror'shaf, the mountain man's former steed. The war charger tossed his mane and nickered at their approach. Its nostrils flared, and it pawed one steel-shod hoof in the mud, clearly not liking what it sensed here.

"I'll choose a mount other than that black monster," Greshym said. "It wouldn't do to escape only to break my neck on the first trail."

Joach stepped to the stockade gate. "First, your final payment for your freedom."

The darkmage sighed. "So be it." He turned to Joach. "It will just take a touch—like the rose, earlier."

Joach held out his new hand.

Greshym placed his palm atop Joach's. "Be ready . . . It may be jolting."

Joach braced, but the sensation was nothing for which he could have prepared himself—nor would he have wanted to. A warm wash of pleasure flooded into his palm and up his arm. It welled out in shuddering waves, as if fueled by a beating heart. Filling his legs, it swamped up his torso and over his head. There was a momentary sense of drowning; then his vision, blurred by the event, sharpened again. Greshym pulled his hand away. Joach stared at the darkmage, looking through the illusion of the elv'in to the man hiding inside. Greshym had aged from a young man to someone in his midwinters. His brown hair had gone to balding at the corners and appeared more drab than its coppery hues earlier. But still Greshym was far from an old man.

"How do you feel, boy?" Greshym asked sourly. He was slightly unsteady on his feet. What had wonderfully filled Joach had clearly drained the darkmage.

Joach lifted his arms, amazed at the strength he found there. He straightened the aged crook from his back and lifted one hand to feel his face. It was smooth, the skin clinging instead of sagging. A laugh tumbled from his lips, bold again, not raspy. He took a deep breath, appreciating the swell of his chest. "I'm young again."

"Younger," Greshym said. "You look a man of thirty winters."

Joach didn't care. Compared to a moment before, he felt as young as a newborn babe. Laughter again rose unbidden.

"Am I free to go now?" Greshym asked.

Joach thought of betraying the man and dragging him back to his cell; but Greshym had kept his word, and so would he. "Go, begone from here. None will look for you."

Greshym unhitched the corral gate and fetched one of the horses, a roan gelding. It was unsaddled, but the darkmage grabbed a bridle and reins from a hook and deftly fitted the bit. "What of your new form? Won't the others be suspicious?"

"It's why I created the dead golem of your form to leave behind. Not only will it keep anyone from looking for you, it supplies a reason for my returned age."

Greshym used a rung of the stockade to hoist himself bareback atop his mount. He walked the horse out of the corral.

"I see. You'll claim some of your stolen life automatically returned to you with my death. How convenient."

Joach shrugged. "Do not come back."

"Fear not in that. I believe I've overstayed my welcome as it is."

Greshym glanced back over at Joach. "Oh, one other thing—Enjoy your youth while you can."

"What do you mean?" Joach felt a trickle of dread cut through his joy.

"If you wish to bring Kesla back, it'll take everything I just gave you."

Joach clenched a fist. "What—?"

Greshym held up his one hand. "I am a man of my word. I've given all I said I would. You'll be able to bring her back; then you'll return to the age you were a moment ago—an old, bent-backed graybeard. But Kesla will live."

Joach relaxed his hand. As much as it galled him, he knew the darkmage was right. As long as he could bring Kesla back from her sandy grave, what did it matter? To give up these years in trade for her life was a small price.

Greshym sighed. "I truly hate to see you so miserable. For your help, I'll grant you a final bit of knowledge for free. There is a way you can have both: Kesla and your youth."

"How?" Joach stepped closer.

"Think, boy. Why did I pursue your sister so ardently?"

Joach frowned.

"The book! The Blood Diary! It grants Elena immortality, a font of lifeforces without end. You must merely destroy the book and absorb those energies yourself. You'll have more than enough to both grant Kesla her life and maintain your youthful vigor." Greshym turned and legged his horse on. "You've grown, my boy! Don't stop when you're halfway to everything you dream!"

Joach watched him ride off. He didn't know whether to thank him or curse him. Instead, he simply turned and walked back to camp. He had much to ponder, but as he did so, he appreciated the length of his stride, the sureness of his step, and the strength of his joints.

He had indeed much to ponder.

From the edge of a copse, Mogweed watched Elena's brother stride away from the horse corral. What had he just witnessed? He kept crouched until the elv'in on the horse had vanished into the rimwood forest to the west. Then he rose and stared back toward the og're caves.

What magick was this? The elv'in had touched Joach, and the man had grown younger before his eyes, his back straightening, the winters falling from his features like leaves from a tree. Even his hair had darkened from a silver-gray to a rich auburn, a match to his sister.

Mogweed frowned. Perhaps it was some illusion. Elena's brother was skilled in dream magicks, though he never suspected the man of such skill. Even Joach's stride as he left the corral was sure and firm. Could mere illusion quicken an ancient's step?

He shook his head; it was no concern of his. He had come here with the rising moon, but he had not yet built up the steel in his veins to do what had to be done. He dared wait no longer. Mogweed slipped back into the darker shadows under the trees.

In the center of the glade, his pack still lay where he had left it. The ebon'stone bowl rested atop a small rock. He trembled in the chill of the thin night air. He had failed to destroy the Spirit Gate, but so had the demonic spirits of the Triad.

Mogweed closed his eyes. After the battle, exhausted, he had fallen into that restless slumber inside Fardale's skull, only to awaken with the setting sun. He found himself lying with Thorn, his arms around her naked form. She had been asleep as he slipped away. It seemed she and his brother had not only made peace with their shared pasts, but they had also renewed their former passion. He had crept from the furs with distaste. He remembered the depths of their union, mind to mind, in the tunnels; he was glad he had slept as their bodies mirrored the same union.

With his arms wrapped tight around his chest, Mogweed stared down at the ebon'stone bowl. If he ever hoped to be free of Fardale, he would have to brave the darkness cupped in the bowl of black stone. He knelt. From a pocket, he removed a soiled bandage. Nee'lahn had used it to bind a cut on her forearm, a wound from the Spirit Gate battle. With the miraculous healing afterward, she had had no further need for it. Mogweed had watched through Fardale's eyes as she disposed of it. Upon awakening, he had fetched it from the refuse. Her elemental blood should awaken the bowl's magick.

Still, he hesitated. He closed his eyes. He had no prickling sense of someone staring at the back of his neck. *Good.* Fardale still slept, clearly sated after his rutting with his wolf-mate.

Dream while you still can, Brother. Now it's my turn for a tryst in the dark.

He dropped the bandage into the bowl, then sat back on his heels. As he waited, he felt the chill of the night creep through his cloak. He shivered. Then slowly the air grew frigid as an icy tomb. A stench of rotting entrails and festering wounds filled the space, and a dark mist rose up with the howls of the damned.

Mogweed scuffled a step away as his bowels clenched and bile rose in his throat.

A voice as dark as the stone bowl and as cold as the blackest pit rose from the mists. "You call again, little mouse, you who have failed us."

"I . . . I . . ." Mogweed fought his frozen tongue. "There was nothing I could do."

Tendrils of dark mist sailed out from the bowl. Mogweed scrabbled away, but the arms of mist sailed out and around him, circling him. He cowered in the center, knowing that even a glancing touch of that black fog would suck the life from his bones.

"I will teach you the price of failure."

Mogweed crouched tighter. Things stirred in the mists, creatures darker than the blackest fogs. He squeezed his eyes closed—the sight of these lurkers would surely drive him mad. Yet he could not escape their gibbering cries. The sounds ate at the wall of sanity around his mind.

"Stop," he shouted. "I have information to pay for my failings!"

The hoary voice cut through the beasts in the mists. "Speak now, or lose all!"

Mogweed opened one eye. The mists held back, but he was still co-cooned in the dread fog, held at its hollow heart. "I . . . know when the wit'ch will attack . . . I know their forces . . . their numbers . . ."

Iced laughter met his offer of betrayal. "Little mouse, don't you think we know all that happens in those mountains? We wait for her even now—a trap from which none will escape." Laughter again, and the gibbering rose as the mists stirred anew.

Mogweed knew he was a breath away from being blown out like a candle. "Ly'chuk!" he called out in desperation, using the Dark Lord's real name.

The thread of amusement that had been fading into the ebon'stone bowl abruptly cut off. The voice boomed back at him, sounding as if it came from all around. "Never speak that name!" A lash of mist whipped out and struck his cheek.

Pain exploded across his face, as if his skin had been flailed from the bone and acid poured in the wound. With a cry of agony, Mogweed fell on his side. He clutched his wounded face. He found no injury. He was un-damaged, but the pain persisted, fading too slowly.

Mogweed fought to speak. "Th-they know all about you, not just your true name."

"It matters not." But for the first time, Mogweed heard a trace of doubt in the demon's voice. Mogweed pushed up from the mud. He himself lived in a world of fear, hesitancy, and doubt. This was his own territory; he knew its terrain better than any, how such qualms could be fanned.

"They know all about ebon'stone and heartstone," he lied. "The wit'ch in the Gate revealed all. They know what you did at the Gate on the eve of your oath taking."

Silence met these words. Mogweed sat straighter. He knew the power of secrets exposed, even if they were only suspected. Since a child, Mogweed had held his heart closed and tight, his inner thoughts his own. He knew how it felt when such hidden trappings were exposed for all to see—whether you were king, demon, or simple man.

He pressed his advantage. "For bringing you such critical information, I simply ask a boon." He bowed his head. "Forgive my past failings and allow me to serve you. I will be your eyes and ears among the others. I know their strengths and weaknesses ... as they now know yours," he added, plying his trade with deft skill. "Let me show you their hearts. That is all I ask in trade for my freedom from this crowded prison of flesh."

The silence stretched, but Mogweed knew he wasn't alone. Finally, the voice returned, laced with hoarfrost and ice. "Then prove your words. Tell me where the heart of the wit'ch is most weak."

Mogweed thought quickly. He needed a convincing answer. And though he'd rather trade in lies, he knew he would now have to barter in a bit of the truth. "She is weakest where all women are most tender," he said after a moment. "To damage her the most foully, seek not to harm her directly. There is a spot where she can be shattered with an easier touch." He held his breath, pausing.

"What?" the voice asked acidly.

"Do we have a pact?" Mogweed pressed. "My secrets for my freedom?"

"First a taste of your ware, mouse. Answer my question; then we will barter. What is this weak spot in the wit'ch?"

Mogweed hesitated for a breath more—not for show this time, but in concern for the line he was about to cross.

"Speak or die now! What is her weakness?"

He bowed his head. "Er'ril ... the Standi plainsman. He is all that stands between her and defeat. Destroy him and you'll wound the wit'ch beyond healing." Mogweed felt something black settle in his chest—not from the Dark Lord, but of his own making. He knew that he had crossed a line from which he could never return.

"My lieutenant's brother ... ," the voice hissed from the mists.

Mogweed frowned, then remembered that the demon-mage Shorkan had once been the plainsman's brother. "That is a taste of the knowledge I can bring you," he continued. "Proof that eyes and ears close to the wit'ch can be of advantage."

The mists parted around him, drifting back into the well of the ebon'stone bowl. The voice spoke again. "You've given us something worth pondering. For that, you will be allowed another day of life. But for your freedom of the flesh, a higher price will need to be paid."

Mogweed silently cursed. "What?" he spoke aloud. "Anything."

"You must not only be our eyes and ears . . . but also our *hands*."

Mogweed's brow crinkled. "How so?"

As answer, from out of the darkness over the bowl, something black entered this world. Mogweed stared at it with horror. A single black orb rested in the basin, an egg in a most foul nest. It was the size of a doubled fist. Veins of silver forked over the orb's polished surface. Ebon'stone.

Mogweed knew what lay in the bowl. He had heard the stories of the ebon'stone eggs seeded at A'loa Glen, of the sick clutch that had hatched in the dungeons of the castle, of the contamination of Sy-wen and Hunt. Here was a smaller brother of the others.

"What do you want me to do with this?" he asked the empty night.

Words rose from the bowl, muffled now by the egg. "Take this seed and plant it where we tell you."

Mogweed suspected, from its tiny size, that this egg contained only a single one of the tentacled beasts. Or maybe it contained something even more foul. He shivered at the mere sight of it. Who was this meant for? When last he had communicated with the demon in the bowl, Tol'chuk's life had been the price for Mogweed's freedom. Would it be again? "Where do you want it planted?"

The answer rose from the bowl.

Mogweed gasped, cringing back. The answer chilled him to the marrow of his bones. He wished now it had been Tol'chuk. "Why?" he asked. "It makes no sense."

"It is not your need to know why, little mouse, but to scurry and do our bidding. Only then will you find your way to freedom."

Mogweed balked—but he had no choice. He nodded. "It will be done."

"Fail a second time, and your torment will know no end."

Mogweed fingered the trace of a burn on his cheek. He knew such threats were not idle. He had barely escaped with his life this night. But he had won another chance to shatter the shackles that bound him to his brother. He would not fail this time. He dared not.

As he crouched, a great weight lifted from his shoulders, and warmth filled the void left behind. Mogweed stared at the bowl. The Dark Lord was gone. The doorway between their worlds had closed again.

Sighing with relief, he sagged before the ebon'stone nest. What was asked of him would not be easy, but it had to be accomplished. If he ever wished to be free of his brother, he would simply have to harden his heart against the fears rooted there.

With care, he collected both bowl and egg into his pack, burying them among his personal items. With a final breath to steady himself, he stood and left the tiny copse of woods.

Once free of the trees, he heard raised voices echoing from the entrance of the og're cavern. He strode quickly, ready for the warmth of the caves and the brightness of the hearth fires. As he neared the yawning opening, he saw Elena and Er'ril, along with most of their companions, gathered just inside.

Meric spotted Mogweed and waved him over. Frowning, Mogweed obeyed. They were all gathered around Joach. Sounds of amazement rose from the crowd.

"You look five decades younger," Harlequin muttered, walking in a circle around the boy.

Joach smiled. "And I feel even younger than that."

Mogweed put on a mask of surprise. He had already witnessed the transformation. But for now, he kept up a pretense of shock.

Er'ril wore a scowl. "And Greshym's death brought this boon upon you?"

Joach shrugged. "I can only suppose so." The boy pointed to a bier that bore the slack body of the darkmage, guarded by two og'res. "I can't imagine the two are not related. My youth, his death."

Mogweed stepped to the corpse's side, gaping in shock. The darkmage's face was blue, eyes glassy and blind. *No, this can't be . . .* He turned to the others. "When did he die?"

Elena answered. "He was discovered by Joach just a short time ago. There was no mark on his body." Her eyes flicked toward Joach. "It seems his heart simply gave out."

"Like he had a heart," Magnam mumbled at her side.

But Mogweed caught the suspicious glance shared by Elena and Er'ril. They suspected foul play here, perpetrated by Elena's own brother—murder for the sake of youth.

"You'd best cut the body into bits," Harlequin said. "Bury the parts in separate unmarked graves. From the stories, the dead of the Dark Lord don't always stay dead."

Er'ril nodded. "With the dawn's light, it will be done."

Joach stood among the others: hale of limb, straight of back, his face unlined. He met Mogweed's eyes for a moment, then glanced away. But in that tiny moment, Mogweed sensed something in the other's eyes: something dread unspoken.

Mogweed remembered the exchange by the horse corral. The elv'in sailor had touched Joach, transforming the bent-backed elder into the young man before him now. Then the sailor had ridden off, not toward the elv'in ship, but into the woods.

Mogweed studied Joach. It seemed there was more afoot here than was spoken. Before he could ponder it further, a heavy hand fell on his shoulder, startling him. He turned to find Tol'chuk beside him.

"Strange night," the og're mumbled.

Mogweed bobbed his head, not trusting his voice. Tol'chuk didn't know half how strange this night truly had been. The pack he carried hung hard on his shoulder, and his duty even harder on his heart. *What am I to do now? Why hadn't the Dark Lord known of his minion's death?*

Tol'chuk gave his shoulder a squeeze, then stepped away. "The fires be stoked by the hearth. The furs should be warm. Go and rest yourself."

Mogweed was tempted, but all thoughts of rest were driven away by the sight of the bier. With Greshym dead, how was he to finish his assignment? It was not the og're for whom the egg had been intended—but Greshym. Why the Dark Lord sought to possess one of his own made no sense. Perhaps the egg contained a means of escape for the mage? He shook his head. Once again, due to no blame of his own, Mogweed had failed the Black Beast. He had come too late.

What do I do now? He dared not contact the Dark Lord again this night. It would surely mean his death.

A burst of laughter from Joach drew his attention. The boy was full of mirth, his voice loud with youth and vigor. Mogweed studied the lad, a master of dream and illusion.

He again pictured the elv'in touching Joach, transforming him, then riding off. Where had the elv'in gone? And why? It made no sense.

Mogweed glanced to the cold corpse, then out to the night beyond the cavern entrance. His mind ran along strange paths. *A master of illusion . . .* He turned again at a bark of laughter from the boy. His eyes narrowed.

What have you done, Joach?

The boy's eyes swung toward Mogweed. But before anything could be said, a commotion erupted near the entrance to the cavern. A trundling of og'res burst into the cave, armed with clubs—sentries. They grumbled in their native tongue.

Tol'chuk bouldered through the others and spoke to the guards. "They've spotted the winged child," he reported.

"Cassa!" Jaston exclaimed. "Is she all right?"

The other si'luran scouts had returned at sunset. Only the swamp child had remained out searching the lower hills. Earlier, when Mogweed had slipped from Thorn's furs and left the caves, Jaston had been pacing a rut in the stone floor.

Tol'chuk nodded. "Fear not. She comes."

They all followed the trio of sentries out into the open meadows. Mogweed searched the night skies. It seemed impossible to spot anything in the gloom; even the moon had set. But from his experience with Tol'chuk, he knew an og're could see in the dark.

One of the sentries pointed his club. After a short time, Mogweed spotted a small flitter against the starlight. He watched the shape grow and sweep toward them.

Jaston stepped to Mogweed's side. "It's her!" the swamper exclaimed with joy. Mogweed caught the glint of unshed tears in the man's eyes; he scowled and crossed his arms.

The child flew over the meadow and down toward the gathered group. From the tumbled flight and dogged beat of her wings, she was clearly exhausted. She landed in the grass, her face ashen against her dark hair.

Jaston hurried forward. "Cassa!"

The child lifted a hand of restraint. The voice from the figure was faint, thready with spent energies. "I . . . I have found the last Weirgate!"

22

ELENA AWOKE IN HER CABIN ABOARD THE *WINDSPRITE*, SURPRISED BY THE knocking on the door and doubly surprised that she had fallen asleep. Light streamed through the thin window. She rubbed her eyes. It must be well past midday. Why had Er'ril let her sleep for so long?

Of course, she knew the answer. After Joach's miraculous rejuvenation and the arrival of Cassa Dar's swamp child, the remainder of the night had been lost to discussions and final plans. She'd had no sleep. Only after the armies had rallied and were under way with the rising sun had Er'ril managed to herd her to her cabin for a short rest.

The knock sounded again. "Mistress Elena."

She threw off the blanket. She was still in her clothes from last night. "Yes?" she answered.

"Master Er'ril requests you join him in the galley."

Elena rolled to her feet and slipped into her boots. "I'll be there momentarily." She crossed to a washbasin and gilded mirror. She fixed her hair back with a sweep of her fingers and a silver pin. She met her own eyes in the mirror, seeking some sign of the strength she would need in the next days. But all she saw was a girl with shadows under her eyes and lines of worry etched at their edges.

Sisa'kofa's words still echoed to her from the core of the world: *Elena Morin'stal, descendant of wit'ches and elv'in blood ... You will hold the threads to the world's fate.*

Elena shivered. How could that be? How could she hold the world in her hands? She lifted her two ruby palms. It was scant magick for what would be asked of her.

She sighed. Ever since picking that apple in her family orchard, she had begun a long road that led full circle back where she started. She had learned much about herself, about the hearts of men and women. She had made good friends and lost many. There had to be some purpose in walking this long road, but what? It couldn't just be power and magickal skill. Sisa'kofa had said that she had best look to her own heart and those around her. Elena sensed that an answer lay hidden somewhere in the steps she had taken to get here—an answer she would need to discover too soon.

She stared into the eyes of the mirror. All she saw was a stranger. "What do you know?" she whispered.

The stranger remained silent and unhappy.

The knock sounded again.

Elena closed her eyes, breaking her reverie. Er'ril was right; she had needed the sleep.

Steeling herself, she crossed to the door and opened it. Her escort was a young elv'in lad. He bowed from the waist. She waved him on, and he led her briskly down a crisscross of corridors and up a short stair to the foredeck galley, now a makeshift war room.

Elena entered and found the various leaders of the armies at hand, and many of her companions. They all stood from the table as she approached. The elder'root was dressed in a loose white robe, easy to shed when he shifted into the golden eagle form he wore when rallying his folk. At his side, Tol'chuk stood with Joach. Elena smiled at her brother, still unaccustomed to the man she now saw.

On the other side of the table, Jaston stood with Cassa Dar's child in his arms. The little girl was sucking her thumb, clearly still exhausted. Meric and Nee'lahn stood hand in hand, while beyond them, leaning against the walls, stood Magnam and Harlequin Quail, along with Fardale and Thorn.

Er'ril motioned Elena to an empty seat by the table. "We thought now would be a good time for last strategies," he said. "The sun will soon set, and we want to be in our positions by nightfall for tomorrow's assault on the valley."

"How far out are we?" Elena asked, seating herself.

"My lead scouts have reached the edges of the burned swath," the elder'root answered. "They relay reports even now."

"The rest of the armies?"

"The *Ravenswing* keeps pace with the og're forces," Tol'chuk said. "We expect to be camped at the valley's edge by midnight."

Er'ril pointed to a map on the table. "We drew this up according to

Cassa Dar's report. We'll position the og'res along the western edge of the valley." He pointed with his finger. "At dawn, Hun'shwa's forces will encircle the dredged pit. Once entrenched, the si'luran armies will lead an initial assault from the air, driving as far into the pit as possible, dropping to the ground, and shifting into beasts to hold the next line. In turn, the og'res will charge to bolster their positions and move the lines forward."

"Then the si'luran forces will take wing again," the elder'root said. "And move the fight another step deeper."

Er'ril nodded. "We'll have the two armies leapfrog each other, step by step, down into the pit."

Elena stared at the oval scrawl on the map, shaded in with coal. She studied the rest of the terrain in silence. This was her home. Though crudely drawn, she knew its hills and valleys, its streams and ponds. They were etched on her heart.

"What do you think, Elena?" Er'ril asked.

She nodded silently. Her husband's eyes shone with the fervor of a true knight on the eve of battle. His cheeks glowed ruddy. He was in his own element this day.

But stratagems of war were not *her* calling. "What of us?" she asked, swallowing back a knot in her throat.

Er'ril pinched his brow. "Once the attack is well under way, we'll fly in aboard the *Ravenswing*, getting as low as we can over the center of the pit. Once there, we'll send down Cassa Dar's child to survey the area. If it's clear, we rope down into its heart. Surely that's where the last Weirgate must lie."

"Who else will join us in this last assault?"

Er'ril straightened. "Besides myself, those with the strongest magick to support you—Joach, Meric, and Nee'lahn."

Joach gripped his staff. She saw the pride in her brother's face. After being so long crippled, he was strong and hale, able to protect his sister again. But beneath this fire, she recognized a dark edge to his bearing, a hardness that had not been there before. Last night, she had discussed with Er'ril the possibility that Joach had slain Greshym to regain his youth. Er'ril had agreed with her suspicions, but ultimately, he was more relieved than concerned: Whether at Joach's hand or not, Greshym was gone. Now, seeing the darkness behind Joach's eyes, Elena was not so sure they had escaped the darkmage's evil.

She shifted her attention to Meric and Nee'lahn. The pair had been among her first allies. And where Joach had grown darker, they now shone brighter. She saw how they clasped to each other, always touching. It seemed the long road here had softened, rather than hardened, their hearts. Elena took joy in this. She nodded to them in thanks—both for all they had done in the past and for this last sacrifice.

Er'ril spoke, drawing back her attention. "But we may need more than magick to reach the Wyvern Gate. So a few others will join us in this assault."

"Two shape-shifters," the elder'root said from across the table. "My daughter Thorn and her betrothed, Fardale."

Elena's eyebrows rose as Fardale bowed to her. Though he bore Mog-weed's face, there was still a wolfish carriage to the man, a sense of the wild wood.

"Long ago, I ventured from these forests at your side," Fardale said stiffly. "I've watched you grow from a girl to a woman, from a wit'ch to a queen. And though we could share no words, I've known your heart all along. I will not leave your side now. I can't. Your scent is in my blood. You are my pack." He pressed a fist to his chest in an oath bonding.

"Thank you," Elena mumbled, fighting tears.

"We'll also take a strength of arm," Er'ril added. "Tol'chuk and the d'warf Magnam."

Tol'chuk nodded. "Like Fardale, I could also be nowhere else." His eyes glowed warmly toward her. And though he could not speak mind to mind like a shape-shifter, she heard the love and determination behind his words.

Magnam crossed his arms beside the og're, amusement in his eyes. "And where Lord Boulder goes, I must follow."

"I've also won a place among this illustrious party," Harlequin Quail said with a shrug. "It seems saving all your lives back at the Spirit Gate has softened the plainsman's iron stubbornness."

Er'ril sighed. "His speed and cleverness could prove useful."

Elena surveyed the room. Sisa'kofa had said to look to her friends during the darkest moments ahead. At least they wouldn't be far from her side.

She gathered her courage, bolstered by those around her. "The plan seems sound. What of the assault on Blackhall?"

Joach spoke up. "I've coordinated with Xin back at the *Dragonsheart.* They'll attack the same morning."

"All is ready," she noted.

"As best we can manage," Er'ril said.

Elena stared again at the map. By this time tomorrow, half the world would be at war. Tomorrow, she would lead these, her closest friends and allies, to their doom.

"If this meets with your approval," Er'ril said, "we can send everyone off to spread the word and begin preparations."

Without taking her eyes from the crude map, she nodded. "So be it."

The group broke apart; only Er'ril remained in the galley with her. He poured a mug of steaming tea, brought it to the table, and shoved the hot mug between her cold fingers. "What's wrong?" he asked softly.

"What's wrong?" She waved a hand over the map. "What's right?"

Er'ril grabbed her hand. "Look at me," he said, sitting beside her.

She finally did.

In his eyes, the ruddy glow of his captainship had died down to a simple somberness. He spoke from his heart. "Tomorrow many will die. That is war. But for now we live."

"But—"

"Hush." He brought up her trapped hand and kissed her palm. "For now we live."

The warmth of his lips were a balm on the ache in her chest. She closed her eyes and allowed it to spread through her. Too soon, he pulled away but remained cupping her hand, holding the warmth of his kiss. "I saw your face when you studied the map," he said quietly, touching the heart of her pain with his words. "You recognized where the pit had been dug."

Tears rose. She had been fighting them since she had first viewed the dreadful map. She moved her free hand and touched the charcoal-shaded pit. "Uncle Bol . . ."

Er'ril squeezed her hand. "It was where his cabin once stood. And before that, where the mages of my time had their school."

Elena finally found her voice. "Cassa Dar mentioned a confluence of energies?"

Er'ril nodded. "A knot of power, stronger than any of the Land's pulse points. The Dark Lord means to place the Wyvern Gate at this vital artery of the Land, to corrupt the world once and for all."

"And Uncle Bol placed his cabin atop there."

"Maybe he knew—whether consciously or not . . ."

Elena pinched her brow, remembering a long time ago. "Uncle Bol mentioned something about the caverns under his cabin. He had said he thought the mages built their school there because they sensed the flow of power."

"And De'nal. He fled down into those same caverns. Crystallizing his spirit, waiting for us, maintained by the energies there."

Elena sighed. "So we end this where it began."

Er'ril gathered up her other hand. "And likewise, where we started this road together. We'll end it the same."

She mustered a grateful smile, remembering Sisa'kofa's words. The spirit of the ancient wit'ch had been right. The words spoken before the Gate could not be shared . . . not even with Er'ril. Instead, Elena allowed him the delusion that they were headed into this last fight hand in hand. Clearly he needed to believe this as much as she did, and she would not take that from him. But in the end, she would stand alone, the fate of the world in her hands. She allowed Er'ril to clench those same hands now, the hands of a wit'ch, the hands of a woman.

Hold them while you still can, she thought silently. *Eventually you'll have to let go.*

As the sun set, Meric stood with Nee'lahn atop the bow deck of the *Windsprite.* He closed his eyes and reveled in the winds and the tingle of magick threading through the ship. He longed to reach to the iron keel below; its energies glowed at the edge of his mind's eye. But this was not his ship. The captain, a second cousin on his father's side, was doing an able job of manning the craft and keeping pace with the armies below. His own assistance was not needed.

Instead he cast his senses out, freely plying the winds and gusts. He delved outward, brushing a stray breeze as another might sweep back the locks of hair from a brow. As he did so, he felt the distant thunder beyond the horizon.

A storm rolled toward them from the sea, building and piling clouds of warm and cold air. Moisture, still scented by the sea, filled the skies. The vibrations of forked lightning chased through his senses, and farther yet, winds built like waves, ready to crash upon these highland heights.

Before dawn, the skies would be as much at war as the Land itself. He would alert Er'ril and the others, but the matter could wait for the moment. He opened his eyes. As yet, the skies were clear. Only a few wisps of high clouds, rosy streaks against the bruised purple skies, marred the day's gloaming. The sun set behind them. To the east, purple skies were already dark. A few stars shone.

Nee'lahn stirred beside him. "We near the burned trees."

Meric drew a deep breath. The air smelled of woodsmoke, but no more than a moment ago. In the foothills below, the og'res marched through healthy woods and meadowed glades. For such large creatures, they loped at surprising speeds, boulders rolling downhill from the mountaintop.

He searched wider afield, toward the dark horizon, but he saw nothing but green life. "I don't see the blackened orchard."

Nee'lahn sagged near the rail. "I feel it." Her hand rose to her brow, then settled between her breasts. "It aches worse than any blight. Around me now, the woodsong sings, bright as a highland spring, but ahead and approaching ever closer, I can hear a dreadful discordance—not the silence of my blighted home, but a deep cry of torture." Her hands rose to cover her ears.

Meric leaned his hip against the rail and pulled her into his arms. "Let it go," he whispered to her. "The lament you hear will be the last sad song. I promise you. We will prevail."

She leaned against him. "I pray it will be so . . . but . . ."

He did not need any special magick to hear the thoughts unspoken. "Rodricko is safe," he assured her. "Kast will keep Sheeshon and Rodricko aboard the *Dragonsheart*, out of harm's way."

Nee'lahn made a small sound of negation. "With the dawn, no place will be safe."

He gently kissed her honeyed hair. She smelled of rose petals and orange blossoms. "Your son will be protected."

A murmur, unintelligible to most, but he understood and corrected his words. "*Our* son." With the sun's rise earlier this day, they had made vows to one another, witnessed only by the open skies and the forests below. Who knew if they'd have a chance later? It seemed foolish to hold one's tongue and not speak what was in one's heart. It was in these same forests that the two had first met, ancient enemies with bitter blood between them. But at the end of this long road of hardship and loss, it seemed the past was not so important as the present. His hand sought hers. Fingers entwined, matching their hearts.

"The darkness nears," she whispered.

Meric swung his gaze again to the dark horizon. Just at the edge of the world, green forest tumbled into blackness. A column of smoke rose into the sky, a deeper ink than the twilight murk. He had no ability to hear woodsong, but the plight of the fouled land ahead still screamed in his ears.

He had an urge to call the winds around him, to steal the ship from his cousin and wheel them away. It was death to go into that land, a blasted terrain of hollow defeat. But instead, he clutched Nee'lahn tighter.

Distantly, the storm beyond the horizon thundered in his ears, thudding deep in his chest and echoing in his bones. He was a lightning rod, vibrating to the forces coming together here.

Nee'lahn must have sensed it, too. She lifted her head and stared eastward with him. The line of green hills ended at the blackened forest. It spread as far as the eye could see. "It is the end of the world."

ER'RIL HAD TRIED TO STOP ELENA FROM COMING TOPSIDE, BUT FROM THE STEEL in her eyes, he had known it was futile. But now, seeing her stricken face in the moonlight, he wished he had chained her belowdecks.

She stood at the rail, staring out toward the devastation that had once been her home. The orchards were stripped to fire-hardened spears aimed at the sky. The air reeked of smoke and ash.

With night fallen, the ruined hills shone in spots with the ruddy glow of buried coals. Embers still smoldered; the glow reminded Er'ril of the fires found in the peat bogs below the Northern Steppes. Journeyers had to be cautious of these hotbeds. A careless foot could lead to a fiery doom. But the terrain here, Er'ril suspected, was even more dangerous. There was no telling what dire magicks lay lurking beneath the smoky, smoldering landscape.

For caution's sake, the *Windsprite* kept its distance from the ruined valleys. Below, in forests still green, the og're forces were gathering, setting up the short night's camp. The si'luran army settled also to their own nighttime roosts, some remaining in winged forms, others reverting to whatever felt most comfortable: bears, wolves, forest cats, or a blend in between.

Over the valley, the moon hung heavy and bright, one night from its midsummer fullness—when the world would balance on the success or failure of their actions.

Thunder rumbled like the drums of war. A storm rolled in from the distant coast. According to Meric, the first raindrops would be felt late this night; by morning, they'd be caught in the teeth of the storm. Sloggy footing for an assault, but the storm would be just as hard on the enemy. And under the cover of thunder and rain, perhaps they could get even closer to the pit before having to engage the Dark Lord's armies, whatever they might be.

Er'ril frowned. That's what troubled him most about the sight before him and the long road here. They had encountered no sign of the enemy.

He was not so naïve as to believe that whatever lay out in the pit was not aware of their encroachment. So why no harrying, no gnashing at their flanks? Were the entrenched forces so sure of their own might? It made Er'ril more nervous than if they had to fight for every step.

Across the blasted landscape, the pit was a void, its edges clouded with smoke and dark mists. But at its heart, an infernal glow shone forth, swelling and subsiding like some monstrous forge, breathing in and out. It was a numbing sight, one that drained the spirit to look upon it.

Slowly the others had drifted belowdecks. The plans for the morrow were set, guards and sentinels posted for the night in case the enemy attacked, and after the long journey, all sought whatever comforts they needed on this last night. Some had gone to pray, others to seek the company of friends and lovers, others still to solitary contemplation of the morning. With the dawn, the horns would sound and this last battle for the Weirgate would be under way.

Er'ril stood his post beside Elena. Joach stood on her other side. He seemed no less shocked to discover the fate of their valley home. Though the death of Greshym had rejuvenated the boy, he now leaned on his staff, weighted down by his own heavy heart.

Across the skies, the stars slowly disappeared as clouds rolled across them, the front edges of the storm. Small flickers of lightning danced the fringes. Soon the moon would be gone, and night would claim the valley and wipe the dreadful view away. As Er'ril watched Elena sink into a pit of despair as deep as the one in her homelands, he wished the storm to hurry toward them, to hide the horror from her eyes.

Joach shifted his feet and shrugged his cloak tighter to his shoulders. "It grows cold. Perhaps we should go below." He glanced to Er'ril over the top of Elena's head. Joach motioned with his chin, encouraging Er'ril to help him, then guided Elena back from the rail.

She moved woodenly.

As a gust of wind blew across the deck, Er'ril felt the first drops of rain splatter his cheek, cold and biting. He took Elena's other arm. "We should rest while we can," he muttered.

Together, Joach and Er'ril led her to the foredeck hatch.

Stepping ahead, Joach opened the door and motioned them through. He mumbled to Er'ril as they passed. "Take care of my sister."

"With all my heart," he answered back, breathless with worry.

Joach remained at the doorway. "I'm going to check with Tol'chuk and make sure the og're clans have gathered before I seek my bed."

Er'ril nodded and led Elena to their cabin. She had yet to speak a word. She seemed again the little girl he had once rescued from these very lands—just as mute, just as worn of heart.

Inside, coals shone brightly in the small hearth, and the warmth melted away the chill almost immediately. Er'ril guided Elena to the bed, then bent to help remove her boots.

"I can manage," she finally said, and shook the stubborn boot off. Her voice was not nearly as lost as he would have expected. She fought the other boot to join its twin. It thumped to the floor, followed by a long sigh.

"Are you all right?" Er'ril asked, still on one knee.

She nodded slowly, but her lower lip trembled.

He read her expression and did not press her. Instead, he stood and kicked off his own boots. "We should catch what sleep we can," he said softly.

She stripped out of her calfskin jacket, while he shrugged out of his cloak. Slowly they shed their outer trappings until both stood only in their undergarments. Elena unbound the sash around her waist to let her linen shift fall loose, draping from shoulders to midthigh.

Er'ril rolled back the furs and heavy woolen blanket. He turned to invite her into the bed first, but he found her eyes upon him. Before he could utter a word, she gently pushed him to the bed. She slid her hands under the edge of his own shirt, her palms warm on his still-cold skin. She slid her fingers up his chest, drawing his shirt up with it.

He reached and trapped her hands halfway up. "Elena . . ." They had not slept bare-skinned together since the night of her near freezing in the si'luran glade.

She freed her hands from his grip with a stolid determination and continued to remove his shirt, drawing it over his head and tossing it aside.

He stared into her eyes and saw her need. She stood back and loosened the ties to her own shift from around her neck. The drape of linen fell, shivering down from her shoulders to pile at her ankles. She stepped out, naked, a woman of startling beauty in the light of the hearth. The glow bathed her skin like a flow of liquid light, casting all into warm hues, from the curve of her neck, to the swell of her breasts, to the fullness of her hips.

She came to him in all her womanliness, and he found no breath for words. He made a sound half between drowning and desire.

Standing before him, she let her hands touch him again: his cheek, his neck, down an arm. She drew his own hand and placed his palm on her belly.

He finally found his voice. "Elena, we mustn't . . . not like this . . . not now . . ."

Thunder rumbled from the skies beyond, reminding of the war to come. Its roar trembled through the ship.

Elena slid beside him on the bed. "Why?" she whispered, ignoring his words.

"With dawn, the battle begins. We should—"

She drew the furs over them, drawing him down to the pillows and nest of blankets. Her skin on his own melted his reason. "Why?" she repeated in his ear.

"The war—"

"No," she interrupted again, her lips brushing the tender skin below his ear. "The reason in your heart."

Er'ril closed his eyes as a shudder of desire swept from his toes to the core of his being. He fought to speak without a moan. "I don't know what you mean."

She shifted to stare him in the eye. Flecks of gold swam in her emerald eyes. "You know," she said huskily. "I know. It's been unspoken between us too long."

He was overly conscious of her breast on his arm, but he did know. "I . . . I'm an old man . . . too old." It came out with a relieved rush. "I've lived for over five centuries."

Elena sighed. "And I'm too young."

He opened his eyes and found his voice again. "Despite your womanly body, you're still just a girl of fifteen winters." He could not keep the shame out of his voice.

She stared sadly at him. "Fifteen winters? Perhaps. But in these past winters, it's not only *magick* that has aged me into this womanly body. On this journey, I've slain both enemies and those I've loved. I've led armies to victory and to ruin. I've entered the very heart of darkness and survived death itself. And along this road, I've learned . . ." Tears filled her eyes. "I learned to love . . . *you*."

"Elena . . ." He pulled her into his arms, wrapping her tight to him.

"What does the count of winters matter?" she whispered. "My heart is far older than even the handful of winters that the spell has aged me." Another shuddering sob. A fist thumped his chest, in both irritation and hopelessness. "And you . . . you hardened your heart against the world from the time you were scarcely older than I am now. Your immortality didn't just freeze your age . . . it froze your heart."

Er'ril lay with her and could find no argument for her words. Ever since the Blood Diary had been forged in the inn at Winterfell, he had walked the world one step away from all others. Over the centuries, he had marched thousands of roads and fought countless battles in unnamed fields, but only in the brief time he had spent with Vira'ni had he ever let his heart thaw from the ice of immortality. And even after that short respite, he had let it harden again.

He shifted, lifting Elena's face between his palms. He studied the woman in his arms. Were they truly so far apart in age? In her eyes, he finally saw the truth. The depth of sadness, the age of the woman who stared back at him . . .

"Er'ril—"

"Hush." He rolled to his side, pulling her slightly under him. He now stared down at the woman he loved—the woman he *wanted* to love. For the first time since lying with her, he allowed his desire to break free. It was a fire that burned through his heart and limbs. He gasped, surprised by the intensity of his feelings.

He bent down and kissed her, his will taken from him. Now it was her turn to gasp, lips crushed, breaths shared. Their arms tightened into iron, fingers struggling to hold even tighter.

Thunder cracked somewhere far overhead, while a gust of rain pattered against the wooden sides of the boat, sounding like an arrow barrage. The boat rocked and lurched in the sudden surge of storm winds.

But neither of them acknowledged it, locked in each other's arms, locked in each other's heart.

Er'ril broke finally from the kiss, moving his lips to her neck, to her breast. She arched to meet him, crying out.

"Elena . . . ," he moaned in chorus with her. He lifted his eyes for a moment to meet hers. He rode the crest of a wave from which he was about to tumble. Their gazes met. He sought one last time for a warding signal, some sign to hold off. But all he saw in her eyes was the same shared passion, a fire that melted the boundaries between them.

No words were needed at this moment, but Elena whispered them anyway. "Don't save me . . . just love me."

"Always . . . ," he answered, falling into her. "Always and forever."

FROM A PROMONTORY A LEAGUE AWAY, GRESHYM SAT ATOP HIS ROAN GELDING and stared up at the storm-tossed boat. He studied his target.

The iron keel of the *Windsprite* was a streak of fire in the night. Lightning briefly illuminated the reefed sails and rain-swept masts. The ship bobbed and skipped like a cork riding the winds of the storm. He could just make out the azure brightness of a figure at the stern deck—the captain, he supposed, struggling to ride out the storm. The others must all be below, waiting out the wild weather, waiting for the dawn.

He smiled as a gust parted the limbs of the oak under which he stood and drenched him with water. He shifted the staff in his hands and dried his clothes and body with a small spell, casting out a shield of magick to insulate himself from the storm's cold and dampness.

It was good to have his power returned to him. He glanced to the beast cowering in the lee of his horse, rain sluicing from the stump gnome's gray skin, its peaked ears flat against its skull. Rukh trembled. The gnome's ribs showed along its leathery side, and it moved with a slight limp. The beast had been hard-pressed to cross the forest and meet its master as instructed.

After being freed by Joach, Greshym had fled west beyond the reach of the book's spell—almost five leagues. He had known when he crossed beyond Cho's tether. It was as if something burst inside him, and he knew he was free, his magick available to him again.

Unleashed, it was not hard to discover Rukh's location and meet the gnome. He was relieved that the beast still had his staff. While it was just a hollow length of bone, he would have wasted precious time fashioning a new one. He reclaimed it gratefully and fueled it with simple energies—a woodsman and his family had proven a surprisingly rich source of power. With Rukh's help, he had fed all their hearts' blood into the hollow bone's marrow. The youngest child, a lad of only three winters, even bore a small spark of elemental fire. Enlivened by this surprising fuel, his staff had ripened with magicks. Afterward, Rukh had fed on the meat off the woodsman's bones, the gnome's first decent meal in ages.

Both of them renewed, they had set off back east again in pursuit of Shadowsedge, the wit'ch sword. Greshym had used a bit of magick to make his steed's hooves fly through the woods. He raced back over the pass to close the distance to the marching armies, following their trail, keeping himself cloaked in magick. By nightfall, he was within sight of the ship.

And as he suspected, his magick remained his own. Once broken, Cho's dampening spell had not renewed itself. It would take a fresh spell to bind him again to the book—something he would not let happen. "I'll have my sword," he promised the night.

His plan was simple. During the confusion of the battle tomorrow, he would simply use a black portal to reach the ship, snatch the sword, and be off before anyone was aware. He dared not risk such a venture this night. On this eve of battle, everyone was at their most alert. No, he would be cautious, patient. He would not lose this one chance to gain Shadowsedge for himself. With the blade, there was no one who could stand before him—not Shorkan, not even the Dark Lord himself.

Greshym licked his lips. With the sword's ability to shatter any spell, nothing could touch him. After five centuries, he would finally be free!

A bolt of lightning crackled across the breadth of the sky from one horizon to another. The entire world appeared out of the darkness, limned in silver, frozen in time.

The *Windsprite* hung in the night, a glowing lantern.

Greshym narrowed his eyes. Tuned to all things magickal, he sensed some profound shift in the world, as if a nexus of power had been torn wide. He held his breath, overwhelmed.

Then the lightning flashed away, taking the world with it, leaving only an endless rumble of thunder. The forest around him seemed darker than a moment before.

Despite his insulating spell, Greshym shivered. Something had changed in that moment . . . *but what?*

He turned his steed and fled deeper into the rimwood forest.

No, this was not a night to tread where he was not wanted. Tomorrow would be soon enough.

As dawn neared, Elena lay in the rumple of furs and blankets, listening to the wail of winds and tumult of thunder. In the tiny hearth, the fire had burned down to scant coals, leaving the room dark. Er'ril remained curled at her side, spent, sleeping now as dawn drew nearer.

She could not sleep. Instead, she nestled against the man she loved. His skin kept her warm, his breath on her cheek calmed her, and the beat of his heart echoed between them. She wished this moment to last forever, though she knew that the world would claim them both again.

She stared into the darkness, appreciating the warm ache in the pit of her belly, remembering, trying to understand all that had happened.

As they had joined this stormy night, Er'ril had moved slowly, despite his raging passion. Her virginal blood had been spilled with a brief sharp pain, her cries captured between Er'ril's lips. Then he had moved with a rhythm that she slowly rode to match, first hesitantly, then with a rising passion of her own. The moment seemed endless, ageless, a wave that welled through her, then out in a cry of release and joy, an impossible blend of pain and pleasure. Er'ril met her cry with his own, thunder in her ears.

At that exact moment, a crack of lightning had shattered the world. Blinding light pierced through the small window, a lance of brilliance that cast everything in silver. Elena's eyes had been closed at that moment, but somehow she saw everything in that burst of light: Er'ril poised over her, his face frozen in silver, his mouth open in a grimace of surprise and joy, his brow bunched with the same impossible mix of sensation.

And in that moment of brilliance, the world had shattered away around her. For a heartbeat, she was again lost in the silvery web of all living things. Her mind and body blew outward as she gasped in Er'ril's arms. She heard a thousand voices, experienced all the sensations that the world entertained, saw sights from a million facets—too many to comprehend, but each as clear as a crystal bell. And in the center of the endless web, she sensed an immense presence turn slowly toward her. Cho had once warned her to stay away from this immensity. But now, riding on the waves of her own passion, she was both blown outward and drawn inward at the same time.

There seemed no escape.

Then the lightning across the sky shattered away, dying in an explosion of thunder that shook the very keel of the ship. Elena fell back into her body, back into her bed, back into Er'ril's arms.

As Er'ril was released, too, he fell atop her, kissing her back to reality, Elena had been too stunned to speak of the moment. Tears flowed down her cheeks. She had been a breath away from being lost, destroyed in the very moment of their shared love.

Er'ril mistook her tears, kissing her as any lover might. "I love you," he had whispered in her ear.

But the thousand voices of the web still echoed in her head, drowning out his words. She pulled him down to her. "Hold me," she had whispered. "Don't let go of me."

He did just that, encircling her with his arms, wrapping her in his strong legs. She lay with him, breathing in the musky scent of his cooling skin, bathed in his breaths as they receded into a light slumber.

Now, alone with her thoughts and worries, she closed her eyes against the approach of morning as the ship rocked under her. Long ago, her journey had been heralded by the blood of her first menstra. She sensed now, with the shedding of her virginal blood, that the end was near. The circle complete. *First bleed to first blood . . .*

Elena lay in Er'ril's arms. With limbs tangled, the heat of their bodies blurred where one began and the other ended. Still, Elena had never felt more alone. The end of all neared, and according to Sisa'kofa, she would face it alone. But what would be the ultimate fate?

From blood to blood . . . where will it all end?

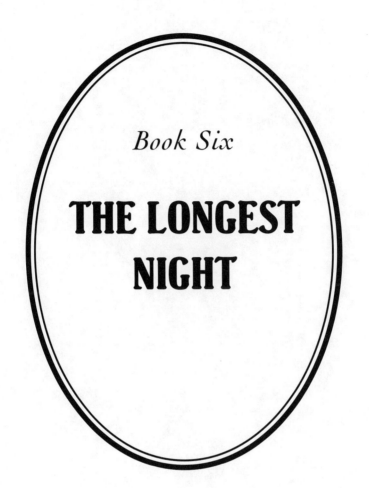

Book Six

THE LONGEST NIGHT

23

Kast waited for Sy-wen to be dragged up from her cell below. From the deck of the *Dragonsheart*, he watched the gray hint of dawn glow to the east. Here in this strange sea of ice and fire, mists hung over the waters, while the sky remained a slate of dark clouds, a roil of smoke and storm. It was near impossible to tell night from day.

But despite the darkness, day was upon them.

Horns sounded in the distance, a call to arms. Sails snapped overhead. The gathered fleets were under way, headed toward Blackhall: the elv'in in the air, the Dre'rendi atop the sea, and the mer'ai below. The last great war was about to begin.

A scuffle sounded behind him. A hatch battered open. He turned to see Sy-wen carried between two Bloodriders, bound wrist and ankle. She kicked and spat and spouted curses. A crazed thing, she was dragged before him. While the larger war loomed, he faced his own first battle.

"We'll eat your hearts!" she screamed at the guards. But when her eyes met his, she went quiet. A slow smile formed on her lips, cold and foul.

"Sy-wen," he said, ignoring the evil before him. "It is time to wake Ragnar'k."

She stared at him with eyes ablaze in madness. Since nearing the shadow of Blackhall, her ravings had worsened. She had scratched gouges in her own face, now scabbed and raw. Her lips were chewed bloody.

"Sy-wen . . ." His heart ached to see her hurt. He nodded to the men.

They unbound her wrists, and one of the guards forced her hand to Kast's cheek. Her fingers were cold on his dragon tattoo, and nails dug at his skin. "She is lost!" A wail rose in her throat. "She is mine!"

Kast ignored the lie. He would know if Sy-wen was truly gone. Two hearts beat in his chest: dragon and man, both bound to the mer'ai woman. He stared into the mad-bright eyes. "Sy-wen, come to me."

Laughter pealed across the deck.

"Come to me . . . one more time."

With the proximity to Blackhall, the tentacled simaltra had rooted deeper into her skull, but Kast needed Sy-wen to break free for only a moment. She had but to take control for a heartbeat and desire the transformation.

He closed his eyes and brought his hand up. He pushed aside the guard's fingers, replacing the man's hand with his own. He leaned his cheek against her palm, fingers lacing with hers. "Sy-wen, my love, my heart . . ." He was not ashamed to display such affection in front of the guards. He was beyond feigning the usual Dre'rendi stoicism. "One last time . . ."

Crawling fingers suddenly relaxed into his own. He felt a gentle warmth infuse the palm. "Stand back," he warned the guards.

Suddenly released, Sy-wen fell into his arms. Her voice was a kitten newly born, a feeble mewl. "Kast . . ."

He opened his eyes and saw the woman he loved. He leaned to kiss her, but the magick ignited between them, driving them apart as a larger heart overtook his and swallowed him away. He tumbled into darkness, where his sensations blurred with those of the dragon.

But he kept a secret in his heart, the words spoken to him by Sheeshon. *The dragon must die.* That was his burden alone. He knew this was truly Sy-wen's last flight. Once she returned to the *Dragonsheart* and released Kast from the dragon, he knew what he had to do. There was no way he could kill Ragnar'k—or rather, only *one* way.

In the coming siege upon the southern piers of the island, he would make sure his spilled blood did the most good. He would use his body and life to forge a path to the volcanic lair of the Dark Lord. Only by dying nobly in battle could he justify slaying Ragnar'k. As he died, so would the dragon inside.

His only regret was that he would be taking the one magick that freed Sy-wen from her dark prison. But in his heart, he knew she was near to being lost already; the monster in her skull swelled inexorably stronger. As he could not escape the fate of Ragnar'k, neither could she escape her own skull.

He sank into the darkness that was the dragon, resolute in his decision. *This day I die.*

Sy-wen leaned atop her dragon. Her shoulders shook with silent sobs. *Free,* her heart sang—but deeper inside, she despaired for Kast. For a glimmering moment she had touched him, felt his cheek on her palm, seen him leaning to kiss her—then in a whirlwind of scale and wing, he was gone, stolen away by an ancient spell. She could not balance the despair of his loss with the joy of her release. Her heart was a storm, her body convulsing with sobs.

Bonded, Ragnar'k sent gently to her, *he is not lost to you. He is here with us.*

Sy-wen patted her giant. They shared sensations, but the dragon could not reach the depths of her heart, nor understand the simple need of a woman for the touch of her lover. A caress could mean more than a thousand words, and a kiss was a chorus without end.

But all this was denied her. The pain was almost worse than the prison of her skull.

She lifted her face to the dark morning. Mists clung to the seas, masking all but the closest ships. Horns sounded over the waters. She took a deep breath. She knew her duty this day: to fly to the foul sandy shores of Blackhall and scout the defenses there. She would do her duty, then return to her prison, waiting to be summoned again if needed.

A voice called to her. She turned to find Master Edyll moving briskly toward her despite his cane. A pair of children trailed behind him: Sheeshon and Rodricko. "Sy-wen!" Master Edyll huffed in the icy morning. "A request!"

She smiled at the elder, both mentor and grandfather to her.

As he drew near, his brows knit together. "Child, are you all right?"

She wiped away the last of her tears. "You should be down below. We head into black seas."

He frowned. "No place is safe this dread day. And I have a request while you're out with the dragon." Sheeshon came around his right side, the smaller Rodricko on his left. He patted Sheeshon on the head. "The children have heard of your flight and begged—or rather nagged with some urgency—that I take them to you."

Sy-wen lifted an eyebrow. "What do they want?"

"Mayhaps they should tell you themselves." Master Edyll guided Sheeshon ahead and rested his hands on her small shoulders. "Go on. Tell her."

Sheeshon's eyes were as wide as saucers as the dragon swung its head around to stare at the trio.

This child rode with us before, Ragnar'k sent to her. He sniffed noisily, which earned a squeak from Sheeshon. Rodricko backed farther into Master Edyll's cloak.

"Fear not, little one," Sy-wen said. "He won't hurt you. What did you want to tell me?"

Sheeshon's eyes never left the giant black dragon's. "I . . . we . . . Roddie and I . . . we want you to take something to that volcano place."

She frowned. "I'm not sure I can do that."

Master Edyll interrupted. "Listen to the child first," he urged her. He plucked Rodricko from the folds of his cloak and pushed the lad forward. Rodricko clutched a tiny sprig with a single flower in his small fingers. Sy-wen had heard the tale of the boy, how this thin stalk was his link to his tree back at the island. It was all that sustained him away from his bonded sapling.

As Rodricko joined her, Sheeshon straightened, clearly biting back her own fear in front of the boy. "We want you to take Roddie's flower to the volcano."

Rodricko did not seem so keen on this plan. He clutched the twig tight to his chest.

Sy-wen narrowed her eyes and glanced over the children to Master Edyll. "But Rodricko needs the flower's magick. It keeps him alive."

The answer came not from the elder, but from Sheeshon. "Roddie doesn't need the flower now!" she said, waving her hands in childish frustration. "He bloodied his finger already. He won't get sick until later."

"Calm yourself," Master Edyll warned the girl.

Sheeshon took a long breath, then let out a sigh. "The flower's got to be put in the smoke. Papa says so."

"I don't want to give her my flower," Rodricko mumbled.

Sheeshon swung on the boy. "You have to. We have to help Hunt."

Rodricko scowled, but his lower lip trembled, near tears. "I still don't want to give her my flower. It's mine, not yours or hers. It's mine only."

Sy-wen stared over the bickering children. "Master Edyll, I really must be going."

He nodded, pulling the squabbling children apart. "I know. But I think we should heed the girl. Sheeshon is rich in sea magicks, able to see what's to come. Her dreams told her to bring Rodricko here, that somehow it will help Hunt."

"I don't see how . . ."

"I don't either. But the child is bonded to the high keel's son. Her abilities could be attuned to his fate. And since you're heading to the island anyway—" He shrugged. "The risk is slight."

Despite her doubts, Sy-wen allowed a glimmer of hope to root in her own heart. If there was a way to help Hunt, could it help her, too? She nodded slowly. "What am I supposed to do with the flower?"

Sheeshon set her lips in a serious line. "You have to wave the flower in the stinky smoke coming out of the ground. Like this!" She flapped an arm in the air.

Sy-wen glanced northward toward where a dull glow marked the volcanic peak. "Is that all?"

"That's what my papa told me."

Sy-wen turned back with a frown. "Your papa?"

Master Edyll dismissed her question with a shake of his head. "Her dreams." He knelt beside Rodricko and spoke to the boy. "Will you let Sy-wen take your flower to the island?"

Rodricko shoved his lip out in a pout. "It's my flower . . ."

He patted the boy's cheek. "Of course. She'll bring it back very soon. I promise."

Sheeshon punched the boy in the arm. "Give it up, Roddie. Quit being such a baby!"

He riled up. "I'm not a baby!" He shoved the twig at the mer'ai elder. Master Edyll took it from his trembling fingers. "See!" Rodricko shouted back at Sheeshon. "I'm no baby!"

The two glared at each other.

Master Edyll stepped carefully around the edge of the dragon's folded wing to reach Sy-wen. He held out the small flowered stem. "Be careful."

As Ragnar'k watched, she took the broken branch, examining its heavy flower. The purple petals were folded over a fiery heart. She sensed no magick from it. Her eyes met Master Edyll's. He must have read the doubt there.

He shrugged. "I know. It seems foolish. They're just children. It could simply be some fantasy of Sheeshon's. But still . . ." He glanced back to the two children.

"What?"

Master Edyll turned back to her. "Sheeshon knew you were going to the island this morning. How many know of this mission of yours?"

"Maybe she overheard someone speaking out of turn."

Master Edyll cocked one eyebrow. "On a Bloodrider ship?" He sighed. "I don't know. Perhaps you're right. But it seems worth the risk."

She nodded. "It is." She tucked the woody stem into the waist of her trousers. "If there is any chance of helping Hunt—" And herself, she added silently. "—then it's worth attempting."

Master Edyll backed away. "Be careful."

Sy-wen took a deep breath. "I will." She patted her dragon's neck. "And I don't go alone."

The elder gathered the children and herded them back out of the way.

Can we go? Ragnar'k asked irritably, snuffing at the gusty winds. She read the longing in his heart to fly free after being trapped inside Kast for so long.

Fly, my heart, fly.

The dragon's joy sang through her as his legs sprang upward, driving them over the ship's rail. Once clear, wings snapped wide and caught the morning winds.

Ragnar'k sailed skyward. Below, the sea was a mix of roiling steam and ice floes surrounded by cold fogs. Ragnar'k circled one of the boiling pools, taking advantage of the rising warm air. The pair swept up in a tight spiral.

From her vantage, Sy-wen spied upon the hundreds of sails flowing northward, gliding through the morning mists like the fins of pale sharks. Overhead, the glowing keels of the elv'in fleet shone around her, small suns in the fog. The captain of the nearest ship spotted them and waved.

She acknowledged him with a salute of her own. Then they were banking away, heading northward themselves. Ragnar'k climbed above the roll of fog. The gray morning turned a shade brighter, but the slate of clouds still dampened the sun to a meager glow.

Bad mountain, Ragnar'k sent in a rumble.

Sy-wen stared ahead. Above the fog bank, the vistas stretched wide in all directions—but to the north, the world ended at a monstrous peak of black rock. It rose out of the mists, stretching toward the cloud banks, belching smoke from its central cone in a roiling column. Vents in its side also spewed black smoke, smaller snakes hissing at the fringes. Red fires blazed across the black cliffs and slopes. Some were from natural fissures and lava tubes exposing the molten heart of the foul mountain. Others glowed from the torchlight within tunneled openings: windows, balconies, and sentry posts. It was said that the chambers within the hollowed-out mountain numbered in the thousands.

Yet despite its menace and horrible history, there was an undeniable majesty to the peak, with its smoke-shrouded cliffs. Even the edges of the cone were broken into towers and crenellated battlements. From the fractured shapes, it was difficult to judge what was created naturally and what was carved by dark magick and monstrous claws.

Sy-wen glided northward, heralded by drums and horn, into the heat that shimmered off the peak. It was not the clean heat of the Archipelago's sun, but the sick swelter of a fever. Even the air reeked—not just of brimstone, but of something more foul, meat left to rot. Her stomach lurched. Below, the blanket of mists and ice fog began to break apart. The seas below appeared again: dark waters, flat and still. As she flew, she soon distanced herself from the last of the ships, leaving the fleet behind her.

Keep high, she warned her mount, now that they ventured alone into the heart of the enemy's territory. Ragnar'k swept up the steamy air, gliding, barely shifting his wings, keeping his movements to a minimum to draw less attention. But the seas below remained empty, not a single ship in sight.

Where were the Dark Lord's forces?

The pair swept onward, crossing the ring of shoals that encircled the island. The tall jagged ridge of reefs was named the Crown of Blackhall. The reef surrounded the peak, a full league from its black sand shores, an impenetrable sea wall as high as the castle walls of A'loa Glen. The jagged ramparts were only open through one narrow break in the rocky shoals. Beyond the ridge, a giant lagoon surrounded the island.

There was only one way to spy what lay within—and that was the reason for this mission. The elv'in ships were too slow to risk such close surveillance. It was up to her and Ragnar'k to scout it out.

The pair swept over the Crown and peered down into the lagoon. Sy-wen frowned. It lay as empty as the seas beyond. An elaborate set of docks jutted into the lagoon from the southern slopes, with a hundred piers and jetties; it took a constant run of ships and supplies to feed and outfit a city of this size. But the dockworks lay abandoned. Not a single ship, not even a skiff, was tied to the piers. Not a soul moved.

Despite the heat from the peak, a chill shivered over Sy-wen's skin.

Beyond the docks, a small township skirted the peak's slope, servicing the deckhands and sailors of the supply ships. Though many found it profitable to do business here, a great number feared to set foot within Blackhall proper. So inns, brothels, trading shops, and other enterprises sprouted like barnacles along the rocky shore between the docks and the Southern Gate. But even here the tangle of streets and alleyways was deserted.

Where was everyone?

Since the allies had cut supply lines to the island as soon as they entered these waters, many ships should have been trapped here. The township should have been full of people.

Beyond the crude town, the Southern Gate yawned above the dockworks: a fissure that went a quarter of the way up the mountainside. It was dark. No glow from the vents, lava tubes, or windows broke the gloom under the gate. No bars or obstructions closed off the passage into the heart of Blackhall. It was open, waiting for them.

Can you get closer? she urged the dragon.

Bonded, I would be away from here.

"As would I, my giant. But we must discover a hint of what ambush awaits the fleet." And Sy-wen had no doubt that a trap was set here. Blackhall was a woman lying with her legs spread wide. But what disease was she carrying? Where was the hidden dagger?

I will try to fly closer, Ragnar'k said, his usual bravado gone. His tension flowed into her.

The dragon tilted on a wingtip and dropped in a plummeting dive toward the dockworks and the open gate beyond. He did not slow as the winds howled past Sy-wen's ears. Ragnar'k clearly wanted to make a fast pass, nothing more. He also maintained the momentum of his fall, ready to use its power to speed a quick escape if necessary.

They skimmed over the scrabble of portside buildings and swept toward the Southern Gate. The fissure into the heart of Blackhall lay dark, towering over them. It had to be a quarter league wide at its base, scaling four times that in height.

As they swept toward the opening, a low droning reached through the wind's howl, drumming deep into her chest. It came from beyond the arched threshold, flowing forth in shivering waves.

Ragnar'k began to bank away, buffeted by the sound.

No, she sent him. *A little closer.*

He obeyed, and they flew into the teeth of the droning. It battered at them like a physical wind. Sy-wen's head soon ached from the sound, and other sounds grew muffled.

But deeper inside her skull, something stirred. Strange sensations bloomed. For a fleeting moment, she smelled kelpweed flowers; then flashes of color swam across her vision; then she heard singing, an old lullaby from her mother, even as she felt a familiar stroke across her breast, Kast's touch.

She gasped as the panoply of sensations rode through her. She knew the source of her inner storm—it came from the lurker in her skull, writhing with the droning from without.

My bonded . . . ? The dragon's flight faltered.

Steady, she sent her mount. She would not let the simaltra distract her from her goal. She strained to see what lay beyond the gloom of the gate, but the darkness was complete. She knew that she dared go no closer. But as she began to order Ragnar'k away, that darkness rippled. At first she thought it a trick of her eyes, but she was not sure. She concentrated, trying to pierce the shroud. If she could only see beyond . . .

Bonded! Beware! The dragon's vision swept over her own, sharpening and crystallizing her eyesight.

Then she saw it, too, and terror clutched her heart. *Away!* she screamed to her mount.

The dragon needed no further prodding. Ragnar'k swept upward in a tight spiral. As he spun toward the distant heights, the pressure fell from her shoulders. Sy-wen glanced back toward the opening, staring with her newly opened eyes. The lurker did not hide *within* the darkness under the gate—it *was* the darkness. She watched the blackness ripple again. It was smooth-skinned, filling the monstrous gate from base to pinnacle, a slick of oil poured into the hole, jamming it tight.

As they fled, she sensed the creature staring back at her, ancient and malignant and aware.

"Hurry," she gasped into the wind.

Then they were past the fissure and flying over volcanic black stone. Sy-wen clutched her dragon. She appreciated her mount's solidness after seeing what filled the gate below. The fleet had to be warned.

Back to the ship!

Ragnar'k banked on a wingtip and swept down the southeastern slopes of the peak, keeping away from the southern port and the sentinel looming over it. Sy-wen found she could breathe again. She hugged tight to her dragon as he glided past smoking cracks and glowing fissures.

Only then did she remember her other duty. She straightened and slipped Rodricko's flowered twig from her waistband. She had promised to wave it within the smoke coming off the peak. Sy-wen considered abandoning this goal, but she spotted a tumble of boulders near the base of the slope, where smoke plumed up in a spiraling font. It was in their direct path.

Ragnar'k, aim for the smoke ahead. She sent her desire to him.

He grumbled his assent, following her silent directions. His neck flaps tightened to her ankles as he flipped sideways. He glided at an angle, intending to brush near the dark column. Sy-wen stretched her arm as far as it would reach—they dared not enter the sick smoke itself. Not only might it scorch with flaming ash, but there was no telling what dread magicks rode that dark current.

Sy-wen thrust the twig near the spouting smoke. Wind whipped her hair. She felt the heat given off by the dark gases, but she kept her arm out. Only a glancing brush, she promised herself; then they'd be away.

Her private thought was acknowledged by the dragon. With infinite skill, Ragnar'k brought them near the smoke—close enough for her to reach with her fingers, but out of the column itself.

She held the flower as they banked past the plume. Her hand disappeared into the smoke. The heat struck her immediately—as if she had shoved her fist into a roaring hearth. But worst of all, the burn raged up her arm and exploded inside her head, taking her sight with it.

Blind now, she felt the dragon lurch beneath her. They tumbled through the air. Gasping, she curled over her wounded hand.

Then they struck the ground—hard.

Jarred by the impact, Sy-wen flew through the air until her shoulder struck something coarse yet yielding. She tumbled to a skidding stop. Her sight slowly returned to her. She pushed to her knees. *Sand . . . black sand . . .*

She lifted her head, but nausea swept through her. She lurched forward as her stomach clenched violently. Bile splattered from her mouth and nose. She stayed hunched for an impossibly long time as her entire body became a tightened fist. The flow of gore streamed out of her. She tasted blood on the back of her tongue, but still her body remained clamped. She teetered above a pit of blackness.

Then at last she was released. Like a bowstring pulled too far and snapped, she fell, gasping and choking, to the sand. It took her several breaths to get her vision back. First, it was like staring through the single lens of a spyglass. The world had shrunk to a narrow tunnel. All she saw was a dark strand of sand, the lap of water, scuttling crabs. Dragging up to an elbow, she blinked, and slowly the view widened.

She spotted Ragnar'k a short way down the beach, sprawled half in the shallows of the lagoon. "Ragnar'k!" she called in a hoarse wheeze.

He lay limp in the green waters, not moving, not breathing.

Dead, her heart rang out. She felt it in her gut and knew it to be true As if sensing her grief, the ground shook under her feet, an ominous rumble.

She forced herself to her knees. "Ragnar'k!" Her cry echoed over the empty stretch of beach and up the unforgiving slopes of Blackhall.

She was alone.

As THE SUN'S FIRST GLOW BRIGHTENED THE MORNING, TYRUS STOOD WITH HIS men and the d'warf general atop a granite cliff head. Below them, the Stone Forest tumbled down to the sea as if seeking to drown itself in the gray-green waters. But stretching out from this coast in a single arched span was a volcanic causeway that connected island to forest. It was their goal, a road straight to the Northern Gate.

Through a spyglass, Tyrus searched the volcanic peak. It had been the silent giant in their midst since they entered the Stone Forest, glowing through the night with balefire and spouts of molten rock. Now they faced the jaws of the giant, open and waiting for them.

The Northern Gate was a monstrous cavern opening, a pocked wound in the side of the mountain, darker than the black stone that framed it. The arch of stone—the Black Road, as it was named—leaned out toward them like a foul tongue.

He lowered his spyglass, his brows pinched. Why were the road and gate unguarded? What trap awaited them?

Tyrus glanced back to the d'warf army, three thousand strong. Covered in ash from head to toe, the columns and lines of d'warves still appeared to be stone. But small movements belied this rocky appearance: the shift of a shield, fingers curling on a sword hilt, the glint of narrowed eyes.

A voice drew his attention forward. "There is no way to assault Blackhall by surprise," Wennar said. "If they don't know we're here already, they will as soon as we hit the Black Road."

Blyth ran a hand over his bald pate. "We'll be exposed on that long road all the way to the island."

"We have no choice," Tyrus mumbled. "Xin has sent word—the fleet moves even now toward the southern piers. We must divide Blackhall's attention. It is our only hope."

Wennar grunted his agreement.

"Ready your forces," Tyrus commanded. "We'll do as we practiced."

Wennar nodded, but Tyrus read the fear in his eyes. "I pray the gift you were granted will be enough," the d'warf said.

It'll have to be, Tyrus thought to himself. He studied the spread of d'warf soldiers. All knew their duties, knew the death they faced, knew that their lives would soon be in his hands. He stared down at his gloved fingers. He prayed they were strong enough to hold so much. How much simpler to be a pirate, where your men knew they'd die bloody and soon. Today so many lives, the lives of good men with families and futures, depended on him. Could he be the prince they needed?

Wennar sounded his horn, and the march began. Ash choked up from the shuffle of a thousand boots. The d'warf army split around the cliff head, like a river around a boulder, and descended the slopes toward the Black Road. With a wave, Wennar descended into the flow, joining his lieutenants, calling out last orders.

Hurl stepped to Tyrus' side, staring out at the stream of armored d'warves. "The Magus would have been proud," the Northerner mumbled.

"Just pray that granite is strong enough to resist what will be thrown at us this day." Tyrus turned to the others. Fletch was already mounted on his small horse, a brown mare to match his bronzed skin. Two quivers of arrows were crossed on his back.

Blyth brought up two more horses. They were all mares, stocky but small. *Hill horses,* Hurl had named them, buying them from a wary-eyed farmer before entering the Stone Forest.

Tyrus climbed into his saddle, as did Blyth and Hurl. Only Sticks remained on his feet. The hill horses, though stocky, were too small to bear the giant's form—if he sat astride them, his feet would drag the ground. Instead, he would keep up as best he could on foot.

Tyrus studied his fellow pirates atop the cliff. He weighed them with his eyes. They remained steady, survivors of many sea battles. "Into the teeth of darkness we now go," he said to them stiffly. "I would think no one a coward to turn back now."

They stared back at him. Finally, Blyth laughed. Hurl rolled his eyes and slapped Fletch's knee. Fletch flashed a rare grin. Together they turned their horses toward Blackhall.

Sticks followed after them.

Blyth walked his horse beside Tyrus'. "Captain, we're pirates. We've walked the dark path since we were suckling babes." He waved toward Blackhall. "We wouldn't miss the chance to join this fight for all the gold in Port Rawl."

Tyrus found a grim smile rise to his own face. Perhaps he had been wrong earlier. Maybe this was a day for pirates, not princes.

And that was fine by him.

Together, the five of them trundled down the hill in the middle of the d'warf brigade. Already the forefront of the d'warf army had reached the edge of the Black Road. They stopped, awaiting the final command. The other d'warves closed ranks behind them.

Wennar appeared out of the throng. "At your word, Lord Tyrus."

Standing in his stirrups, Tyrus stared down the length of the black span to the peak beyond. This close, it seemed the world itself ended at that wall of volcanic stone. Spouts of smoke snaked up from cracks and fissures, joining the monstrous plume from the cone, blackening the sky.

Tyrus took a steadying breath. "Let it begin."

At his side, Wennar lifted a horn and sounded a sharp note.

With scarcely a pause, the d'warf army mounted the road. The archway was barely wide enough for more than two wagons to pass. Below, the waters were jagged with spears of rock and broken shoals. Death awaited a misstep along the thin span.

In rows of four, the d'warves marched forward, moving swiftly. Column after column followed. Off to the sides, a cadre of other d'warves, armed with spyglasses, watched the waters, the skies, and the peak beyond for any response to their approach. They held horns that curled to their armored shoulders, ready to sound the alarm.

Wennar stood at the edge of the road, nodding to his fellow soldiers, calling out good-natured gibes, patting an occasional d'warf on the shoulder. And still the columns flowed down from the Stone Forest. Not a single soldier broke the steady tread. Slaves for centuries, they were determined at long last to bring their pain and suffering to the door of their former master.

On they marched, four abreast, a flow of armor.

Tyrus shifted in his saddle, the hairs on his neck prickling. Time stretched as the sun, cloaked in slate-gray clouds, climbed the sky. Soldier after soldier streamed past, unwavering. The front of the army was near to halfway across the arch when a sharp, brittle note shattered the tread of the army.

A horn . . . then another horn . . . and another.

Tyrus swung around, sighing out the breath he had been holding all morning. From the peak, a pale mist rose from a thousand cubbies and windows and holes. He yanked out his spyglass and quickly focused on the threat.

Through the glass, he watched the rise of pale shapes, winged aloft. They were easy to pick out against the black stone: bony wings and clawed appendages. Even from this distance, their forms promised venom and death.

Tyrus lowered his glass and counted the pale army banking down to defend the Black Road: hundreds, if not thousands.

"Skal'tum," Wennar said.

Tyrus knew that with the sun covered by heavy clouds, the creatures would be protected by their dark magicks, impervious to normal weapons. Still, he had anticipated such a scenario. The d'warf weapons had been tainted with skal'tum blood, collected after the War of the Isles. Such treatment would allow their blades to pierce the beasts' dark protections.

One thing was not known, nor tested fully.

He glanced to the men around him. He got the nods he wanted.

Tyrus kicked forward, breaking into the column of d'warves. The army had frozen at the sound of the first horn. Across the volcanic span, the d'warves on the road had taken up their assigned positions.

Of the four in each row, the outer pair of d'warves faced the empty air, each shoulder to shoulder with his neighbor, spears thrust up and out, shields raised overhead and back, touching the raised shield of his partner on the far side. Under this archway of raised shields, the inner pairs of d'warves crouched, ready to act.

Tyrus slid off his horse, peeling back his gloves with his teeth. He spat them on the ground, then crossed to the nearest d'warf, who headed the column of shield men on the road's right side. He saw the fear in the d'warf soldier, a young fellow, new to his armor.

Without flinching, Tyrus met his eyes, trying to instill faith, though the youngster trembled a notch, his raised spear jittering.

Tyrus lifted his right hand and brought it to the d'warf's exposed wrist. From their past trials, skin-to-skin contact worked best, though it wasn't necessary.

Wennar spoke at his shoulder. "The skal'tum come!"

Tyrus glanced skyward as the flock dove toward the Black Road and the waiting army. Shrieking cries echoed off the water, singing the promise of a bloody death.

With a steadying sigh, Tyrus gripped the young d'warf's wrist. He closed his eyes and touched the granite inside him, unfettering the magick granted to him by the Magus. It was easy to cast, harder to keep in check, and almost impossible to call back.

Now he let it go.

The petrifying magick welled out and into the d'warf in his grip. He watched the man's wrist go to dark granite, then rush over the rest of his body, turning flesh, armor, and weapons into stone. The magick did not stop there, but spread to his neighbor, who stood shoulder to shoulder, and continued down the line of d'warves, one after the other, turning the entire line to stone—a solid wall of granite. He fed more and more of his magick into the line, swelling it with petrifying energy.

With nowhere else to go, the magick leaped across the raised shields to flow down the other side, petrifying the column of d'warves posted on the left side, too.

"Hurry!" Wennar warned.

Tyrus fed a last bolt of energy, prayed it was enough, and broke contact. He fell back gasping, weak in the knees. Before him lay a long tunnel of granite, a passage composed of living statues. Within the tunnel, the remaining d'warves huddled.

"Here they come!" Wennar shouted.

Stumbling back, Tyrus watched as the skal'tum struck the road, screaming a dreadful cry. But they struck only stone. Many impaled themselves on the festoon of granite spears, crying out and writhing in agony. The more cautious were still blocked by the packed stone soldiers, unable to reach those shielded inside the passage. Claws raked and screams echoed, but the tunnel held.

From within, the huddled d'warves leaped up and jabbed spears at the skal'tum, poking between their stone brothers. Shrieks of blood lust turned to cries of surprise and pain. With careful aim, others shot arrows between the cracks in the shields, striking with cold efficiency, plucking skal'tum from the skies like a rabble of crows.

Sticks appeared with Tyrus' horse. "We should hurry; the trick will not last long!" The giant offered a hand to Tyrus.

He almost reached to take his friend's hand, then saw the black tint to his own fingers. "No!" he said hoarsely—he dared not be touched yet. The petrifying magick was still ripe in him. Clenching his lips, he concentrated and choked back the magick. Stone slowly—too slowly—turned to flesh. It took all his will and constant vigilance to keep the magick in check; it was as much a curse as a boon.

With the magick secured for the moment, he mounted.

Wennar lifted a horn, and a piercing blast burst through the morning, sounding the next stage of the assault. He glanced up to Tyrus and his men. "May the Mother protect you!"

"And you and yours," Tyrus replied ritually.

With the alarm raised, the d'warves inside the passage abandoned their attacks on the skal'tum and raced forward toward Blackhall, running under the shields of their brothers. They moved with surprising speed.

Tyrus kicked his horse after them, leading his men down the living tunnel. "Keep your heads down and your arms close to you!" he commanded as they entered the stone passage. "I'll be sending more petrifying magick into the tunnel, and you won't know when, so don't let your mares brush the shield wall."

"And risk being a statue again?" Blyth said. "Not likely. There's only one part of my body I want turned to hard stone, and that's only when I'm back in one of Port Rawl's brothels."

The quip earned a guffaw from Sticks, who kept pace behind the horses, his head ducked from the arch of raised shields. Wennar led the remaining d'warf army into the passage after them.

Another horn sounded from far ahead. Tyrus sighed with relief. It was the signal he had been waiting for.

He reached a hand out and touched the wall on the right, casting a fresh jolt of energy into the granite. His senses raced with his magick down the line to the end of the tunnel. There, as the horn blast indicated, new guards had joined their brothers, taking up their posts, shoulder to shoulder. The new magick swept over them and petrified the newcomers, extending the reach of the tunnel a few spans closer to the dread mountain.

Tyrus also felt the sick touch of the unfortunate skal'tum who happened to be perched or touching the magick-wrought passage. They, too, were petrified into granite, caught in the spell. A few became a part of the tunnel, grotesque statuary. Others, wings now stone, fell to shatter on the rocky shoals below.

Tyrus broke contact, a tight smile on his lips. Time shrank to a shining moment of the present as he raced on, careful to keep his hands clear of his mount.

Cries reached him—both beast and d'warf. Claws scrabbled at him from cracks in the tunnel. But he pulled his sword and hacked at any that drew too near. His steel blade went to stone at some point, but he could not say when. Poisoned blood, green and noxious, steamed along its length.

And still they raced down the tunnel, chased by screams. His horse sweated under him, whinnying with fear. It sidestepped bodies, soldiers poisoned black by the venomous claws of monsters, and fled onward. There was no retreat.

Then distantly another horn sounded, and Tyrus reached out again with his magick. Black fingers brushed stone. Petrifying energy lanced out. Bit by bit, the living tunnel snaked down the Black Road's span, its creep relentless.

Still, Tyrus was not so fooled by their success as to be emboldened. They fled straight toward the looming mountain of dread evils: Blackhall.

A part of him knew they faced their own doom, but he could not help smiling, showing his teeth. He was a pirate after all.

SY-WEN STUMBLED ACROSS THE SANDY BEACH TOWARD THE PRONE FORM OF her dragon. Tears flowed. "Ragnar'k!" she called futilely, knowing the dragon was gone—and with him, the man she loved. Her bare feet were cut by the glass-sharp rocks. She ignored the pain, barely felt the burn of salt in the wounds as she splashed through the shallows.

"Ragnar'k!" she cried again, her heart bursting.

Then a miracle—a single claw responded. Then his head lolled in the shallows as he tried to shift . . .

Her heart surged. *Still alive!*

Sy-wen stumbled to him, splashing into the deeper waters. The cold of the sea snapped her somewhat back to herself. She stopped with an arm raised toward the dragon as a horrible understanding dawned. She was not touching him . . . yet he remained a dragon!

She fought against a rising panic. Then she remembered when a similar strange circumstance had occurred before. Shortly before the War of the Isles, Ragnar'k had been struck by lightning in a fierce storm and horribly wounded. Until cured, he had remained in dragon form, even when she wasn't touching him.

Surely the same was happening now.

Ragnar'k lifted his head, wobbly on its long neck. Dark eyes stared down at her.

Sy-wen . . . ?

The name filled her head, a familiar touch, but it was not Ragnar'k. "Kast!" She rushed to the dragon's side. "What happened?"

As her palm touched the heated scales, the world blew out in a whirl of wing and smoke. In a matter of heartbeats, Kast stood before her in the shallows, her palm on his tattoo.

He stood naked, looking down on her, his face wide with surprise. "Sy-wen, what—?"

Startled, she pulled her hand down. As her fingers left his skin, the magick flared again. She fell into the waters, buffeted back by magick as the dragon reappeared, crouched before her, chest heaving, wings wide in shock.

Sy-wen's brow bunched. What was happening?

The dragon's head swung toward her.

"Kast?" she asked tentatively.

Yes, it's me, the answer came to her.

She reached toward the steaming snout. "Where's Ragnar'k? Was he injured by the fall from the sky?"

The dragon shook his head in a very human way. *No. I don't sense him within me at all.*

"Are you sure? Maybe he was knocked out."

Sy-wen. The voice was Kast's usual stern firmness. *I've lived with the dragon inside me for over two winters. He is not here. He is gone.*

Sy-wen covered her mouth. "How?"

Touch me, he commanded, extending his neck.

She swallowed back her panic and reached her hand again to the opalescent black scales. She closed her eyes, but still she felt the rush of magick, a flushing from crown to toe.

"Sy-wen?"

She opened her eyes. Kast stood before her again, her palm on his cheek. He grabbed her hand before she could take it away. "Hold tight," he warned. "I think the mer'ai spell has somehow reversed itself. Now your touch calls me *out* of the dragon rather than sending me in it. Don't let go."

She moved to lean against him. She had no problem with this last command. She never wanted to let him go.

"What happened?" he asked.

In his arms, she told the story of their flight, the empty dockworks, and the lurker in the gate. "We were on our way back to the ship."

"Is that all?"

Sy-wen shook her head. "No. Sheeshon's flower . . ." She glanced to the beach. In the black sand, the purple-and-crimson blossom lay in the sand where she had fallen. "Rodricko's flower. Sheeshon had a dream that it had to be bathed in the smoke off the mountain."

"Why?" Kast frowned.

"I don't know—something to do with helping Hunt. Master Edyll believed it important, maybe prophecy. And since we were headed here anyway . . ." She covered her face with a hand. "We shouldn't have attempted it." She explained about the dragon's last flight, the burn of the smoke, the tumble from the sky.

Kast walked with her out of the shallows, hand in hand like any two lovers strolling a beach. He plucked the flower from the black sand.

Sy-wen expected to find the flower a singed ruin, but the purple petals had peeled back to its fiery heart. The flower now glowed like a coal from a fresh fire. "It's bloomed," she said, surprised.

Kast seemed less shocked. His eyes were on her own, his brow wrinkled.

"What's wrong?" she asked.

"You . . . You're not possessed."

She blinked, and then his words sank to her heart. In her panic over Ragnar'k, she had failed to notice the end of the simaltra's possession. She touched her forehead in wonder. She was still herself. She searched inside her mind for the malignant presence of the tentacled beast. Where before it had been a palpable darkness behind her eyes, icy and cold, now she felt nothing. *How could that be?* She stared up into her lover's suspicious eyes. "It's gone. I don't feel it inside me."

Her words did little to dismiss the doubt in Kast's gaze.

"I remember the pain from the smoke. We both tumbled. When I hit, I felt so dreadfully sick." She crossed to the soiled section of the sand, drawing Kast with her. Amid the blood and bile, an oily skin lay like a wrinkled snake's shedding. Kast used the end of the branch to fish it out. He plopped it down and teased out the tentacles.

It was the simaltra . . . or what was left of it.

"I truly am free," she cried. A joyous tide surged in her heart. *Free!* She stared up at Kast as he rose to his feet. Her relief and happiness must have been plain, too bright to doubt any longer.

He swung her into his arms, hugging the breath from her. "You're mine again," he mumbled into her hair. His body shuddered against hers as he allowed himself to believe.

After a moment, Sy-wen pulled away enough to speak. "But what of Ragnar'k?"

Kast stared back at the smoky column. "I'm not sure, but Sheeshon warned me of something—she said I'd have to slay Ragnar'k, that he would eventually pose a risk to the world."

Sy-wen jolted with his words, almost breaking from his arms. "Why would she say that?"

"I don't know. She didn't either." Kast studied the smoky trail in the sky. "The magick from the mountain's heart must be able to suck a foreign essence from a body. It drew the simaltra from you, leaving only the skin that you later expelled. It must also have drawn Ragnar'k out of me, leaving only the dragon's skin behind. But the spell tattooed into my flesh somehow keeps his skin alive, allowing the transformation to continue."

"But without the dragon inside . . ."

"It's just an empty skin," Kast finished, kicking sand over the slimy tentacles.

"Not empty," she argued, reaching to his cheek. "It still has a heart . . . your heart."

He sighed and faced the rising curl of smoke. "Ragnar'k rose from the stone heart of A'loa Glen in a smoky cloud. Now smoke draws him away, perhaps to the very heart of Blackhall."

She heard the worry in his voice. "You fear he'll be twisted by the magick here?"

"Ragnar'k is a spirit of pure elemental magick, the clay from which the Dark Lord sculpts his ill'guard creations. I fear what the fiend could do with the dragon's energy." He circled Sy-wen with his arms again. "Back at A'loa Glen, the whole purpose in seeding the ebon'stone eggs had been to capture Ragnar'k. And now we've delivered him to the very doorstep of the Dark Lord."

Sy-wen mumbled into his chest. "Then we've traded my freedom for the dragon's."

Kast tightened his arms. "Don't speak that way. It is the Mother's blessing that you are free. There was no trade."

Sy-wen leaned against Kast's chest, the joy in her heart soured. "Either way," she finally mumbled, "we must return to the *Dragonsheart* to let them know of the trap and of what has befallen us here—and to return Rodricko's flower before he falls ill from its absence."

He nodded and stepped back. "Then I must fly us home."

Sy-wen shook her head, catching his hand. "No. I can't ride back with you."

Kast's brows pinched.

"You forget, my touch will pull you back into a man," she explained. "You have to go without me."

"And leave you here?"

"I'll hide," she promised. "The news you bear is too important. And Rodricko will need his flower. I'll stay here until you return."

Kast glanced around, clearly searching for another answer. He found none. His eyes settled back to hers, unsure.

"You must," she said simply, putting all her courage in her voice.

"But I'll still be a dragon when I reach the ship."

"You'll find a way to pass on the message. Carve the planks with your claw if you must."

"I only just got you back," he whispered.

She lifted his hand and kissed it. "Deliver the warning. Let the fleet prepare to battle the beast in the gate. While they do that, you return here with Hunt so we can free him. I'll be safe. Now that I'm free, I'll never be enslaved again."

Kast's eyes were still narrowed with worry, but he nodded.

"You'd best hurry." She began to pull away, but he drew her back into an iron embrace.

"I'll not miss this chance," he whispered, then bent and kissed her.

Sy-wen sighed between his lips. It had been too long. She melted into his warm lips, tasting the salt and his breath. Her heart ached and in this moment, she could not hide her own fear. In this kiss, she drew what strength she could from the steel in his arms, the firmness of his lips, the coarse stubble of his cheek. She drew all she could from him.

But it could not last forever. With tears in her eyes, she broke their embrace, pushing him away. "Go ..." *Before I never let you go,* she added from her heart.

He stepped back, arms outstretched, only their fingers touching. His face was flushed, balanced between duty and love.

"Go," she repeated.

"Be safe," he commanded.

She nodded, not trusting her voice any longer.

His fingers dropped from hers. Magick blasted outward, kicking up a small eddy of sand. A moment later, the dragon reappeared on the strand of beach, silver claws dug deep into the black sand. Sy-wen stepped forward and retrieved Rodricko's flower. She placed it before the dragon.

"Fly swiftly," she whispered.

Kast stared at her through a dragon's eyes as tears flowed down her face. Then he gently collected the flower between his teeth and spread his wings. *I'll return soon.* The silent promise filled her heart and mind. Then with a bounding leap, he flung his body into the air. His flight was not as smooth as when Ragnar'k controlled the dragon, but apparently the blending of the two over the past winters had given Kast some ability. After a slight bumbling, he was off, flying over the jagged Crown to the seas beyond the shoals.

She watched him, a fist clutched to her heart.

Under her feet, the ground shook again, this time more violently. The smooth waters of the lagoon rippled. Sy-wen turned from the skies to examine the peak behind her. Gouts of smoke belched from the fissures, and fires spouted from the distant cone with a horrendous roar.

Sy-wen had never felt so alone. She looked to the dwindling form of the dragon, watching until he disappeared, then sank to her knees in the black sand.

She had thought herself free, but now she shrank from the enormity of the black cone and molten fires. She stared toward the misty horizons.

Keep your promise, my love. Return to me soon.

24

ELENA CLUTCHED THE RAILS OF THE *WINDSPRITE* AS STORM WINDS BUFFETED the ship. The deck pitched under her, rolling a wider view of the landscape below. Columns of og'res trudged through the mud and deadfall of the blasted orchards, advancing in a solid line toward the pit. Steam rose, drifting up from the deep coal fires buried in the debris. Neither the fierceness of the past night's storm nor the morning's steady downpour could drown these last reminders of the orchard's fiery destruction.

"They're making good progress," Er'ril said at her side.

"So far," Elena agreed. "But the day has just begun." She huddled within her eelskin cloak, rain slicking off her. One hand settled to the rose-carved pommel of her blood sword, seeking the reassurance of its elemental steel. Since the battle at the Spirit Gate, she kept the sword belted at her side—a dull ache, a constant reminder of her responsibilities.

Below, birds of every shape swept through the rain, keeping pace with the giants on the ground. Only a few scouts of the si'luran army delved deeper toward the pit.

Elena studied their goal.

The excavation had gone strangely quiet during the night. The continual column of smoke had been extinguished or been swamped by the rain. Only a deep mist hung over the pit, like steam on a mug of hot kaffee. It lay thick, obscuring all, stirring in a slow eddy. The sight was more ominous than the furious smoking of yesterday.

The ship rolled again, pulling her vision back toward the skies. The clouds remained low, heavy with rain. Day was upon them, but it was impossible to say exactly where true night ended and morning began. The world had become a continual twilight.

"We should keep belowdecks," Er'ril urged her. "We've sentinels in the crow's nest. At the first sign of trouble, the horns will sound."

Then they should be sounding already, she thought. *The very air reeks of trouble.* But she allowed herself to be guided back toward the deck hatch.

When it opened, she found Joach standing there. She startled back for half a heartbeat before recognizing him. He waved them out of the rain with his staff. "We've assembled all the gear in the ship's stern hold," he said. "Packs with extra ropes, climbing tackle, torches, oil pots. Everyone's seen to their personal weapons and needs. We're ready for the descent into the pit."

Er'ril nodded, shaking out his cloak. "I'd like to inspect it myself." He turned to Elena. "Why don't you and your brother warm yourselves in the galley? I'll be right back."

Joach backed out of the way for Er'ril to pass, then stared strangely at Elena. "El . . . you and Er'ril . . ."

Elena turned her back on her brother, a flush rising to her cheeks. Did he know about last night? Was it so obvious? Did it show on her face? She and Er'ril had made love again just before dawn, one last moment alone to touch, and to heal any last wounds between them.

Joach continued. "You love him, don't you, El?

She kept her back to her brother. "Of course I do."

He touched her shoulder. "Then you can understand how I feel—how I felt—about Kesla." He sighed loudly.

Elena swung back to her brother, realizing his line of inquiry was heading in a different direction than she had thought. She fought back her blush. "I know how much you loved her."

He frowned at her words. "There was something I wanted to talk to you about." He glanced to his toes, a boyish gesture coming from the middle-aged figure.

Elena reached to his hand. "What is it?" She was glad that Joach was finally willing to talk about the pain in his heart. Maybe his rejuvenation after the death of Greshym had healed more than just his aged body.

Still, Joach hesitated.

"Would you rather talk about this in my cabin? We'd have more privacy."

He nodded, clearly relieved.

She led him down the crisscross of corridors to her room. Once at her door, she slipped off her glove and pricked her finger on a sliver of wood. She cast a tendril of wit'ch fire into the lock to melt the frozen metal.

Er'ril had suggested the added precaution to protect the talisman locked inside: the Blood Diary. Now she deftly melted the tumblers free and pushed the door wide for Joach to enter.

Elena cast a glance around the room. The furs and blankets were spread evenly. No evidence of the past night's lovemaking was apparent, but to Elena's senses, the room remained heady with the musky scent of their spent passions. She glanced to Joach, but he seemed oblivious.

Her brother crossed to the small hearth and jostled the coals brighter. As he warmed the room, she slipped out of her wet cloak and hung it on a wall peg. She reached to the oil lamp that swung from a rafter and twisted its wick brighter.

She turned to find her brother standing before the small oaken desk. Atop it lay the Blood Diary, its gilt rose showing the barest glimmer, heralding the coming midsummer moon.

Joach studied the book, hard lines marking his forehead. "According to the elv'in captain, the moon will rise early. It'll be in the skies even before the sun has fully set."

Elena hadn't needed to be told this. With the magick ripe in her, she was tuned to the swelling moon. She knew its movements as well as the beat of her own heart.

"The moon and sun together," Joach mumbled. "Do you remember what Father used to call that?"

Elena smiled. "A fool's moon." She sighed. "A moon too foolish to know the sun hasn't set."

Joach turned from the desk, leaning on his staff. "And look where we head now under a rising fool's moon." A tired grin shadowed his lips. "Who are the true fools?"

Elena unhooked her sword and settled to the bed. She rested the sheathed blade across her knees. Joach took a small stool, sitting with his staff across his own knees. She stared at him, searching back through their lives. How had they come to this room, burdened with the magick each bore?

A silence followed, the only sound the constant patter of rain on the deck above their heads. Finally Elena spoke. "You mentioned Kesla."

Joach's eyes flicked to the Blood Diary. He nodded. "I think I've discovered a way to bring her back."

Elena could not hide the shock in her voice. "Back from the dead?"

Joach visibly swallowed. "She was dream made flesh. Could such truly die?" He lifted his eyes to hers. Pain shone brightly. "My abilities have grown. I think I can sculpt her back into this world. But . . ."

"But should you?" Elena asked softly. "To draw a spirit back to a body, that smacks of the darkest magick. Remember Rockingham, even Vira'ni. The dead should be allowed to die. It is the Mother's final kindness."

"What of Nee'lahn? She died and came back."

Elena shook her head. "She is nyphai. She didn't truly die, only the husk of a body she wore. Her spirit remained here, wrapped in the magick of her woodsong."

"But is Kesla any different? She was born out of the Land's magick. Who's to say her spirit has passed on to the Mother?"

Elena frowned. Joach could be right, but in her heart, Elena feared so dark a path. "What you ask . . . ," she mumbled, shaking her head.

Fire entered his voice. "I never said I was asking."

Elena met his eyes. His pain had flamed into something bitter: His fingers had tightened on his staff. "Joach—"

"What if it was Er'ril?" he blurted angrily.

Elena opened her mouth. Her first impulse was to deny she'd follow his path. But sitting on this bed, where a short time ago they had shared themselves—heart, spirit, and body—she could not say for sure what her own decision would be. "How . . . why do you even think you could accomplish this?"

Joach held out both hands. "I've already done it. I showed you how I could create a solid illusion of my missing hand, but it was a dead, unfeeling creation." He squeezed a fist. "But look! Now it lives. It's fully a part of me again."

"You said that the hand returned with your youth . . . after Greshym died."

He waved her question away with his new hand. "It was more complicated, hard to explain. All that matters is that with Greshym gone, I could do what I couldn't before."

Elena sensed hidden meaning behind her brother's words. "A hand is not a person," she simply said. "A hand does not possess a unique spirit."

"It can be done," Joach insisted. "I have the knowledge, the ability. I . . . I only need one other thing."

"What's that?"

His eyes again drifted to the book on the table. "More life energy. The spell to bring true life to a dream-sculpted creation requires more energy than I have right now."

"How much more?" she asked, standing up. Leaving the sword on the bed, she stepped toward the desk, beginning to understand.

"A lifetime's worth," Joach mumbled. He nodded to the Blood Diary. "Immortality is locked between its covers, the infinite energy of the Void."

"I know this all too well." Elena picked up the book. First it had granted Er'ril immortality to serve as its guardian and keeper. Then its power had passed to her. It did not stop death, but its font of energy could hold off the passing of winters and heal injuries more quickly.

"It would take only a small fraction of that energy to fuel the spell needed to bring Kesla back. Please, Elena . . . Kesla gave her life to break the Basilisk Gate that threatened our lands. We owe it to her to try and bring her back."

Elena felt herself swaying to Joach's cause. Dare she trust her brother's heart in this matter? Could she deny him this attempt? Still, she glanced to Joach's new hand, to the face that was both familiar and strange, and doubt weighed her heart.

Finally, she sighed, putting off such matters for now. "We dare not attempt any spells that might weaken the book before the coming war. I can't risk the world's fate on the possibility of one woman's resurrection."

Joach nodded gratefully. He clearly took her words as agreement, rather than just a postponement. "Of course. I didn't mean we do this now. I must conserve my own magick for the battle to come."

She started to correct Joach's assessment, then thought better of it. She'd leave that discussion until later. It would also give her more time to consider her brother's request.

Joach stood. "Thank you, El . . . I knew you'd understand."

She simply nodded, averting her eyes.

Joach crossed back to the door. "I should see to the final preparations. Harlequin Quail wanted to discuss something about using illusions to confound our enemies."

"If anyone knows a way to sneak us under the guard of the Dark Lord, it would be Harlequin," Elena agreed, holding the door for him.

Joach turned back to her as he slipped away. "Thanks again, El."

She smiled at him, seeing for a moment the simple, honest boy she had left in the orchards. But beneath that something darker stirred. His grip on his foul staff was tight as he thumped away.

She closed the door and leaned back against it, the Blood Diary still clutched to her chest. The gilt rose on its binding glowed with the growing magick of the moon.

Stepping from the door, she flipped open the cover. Blank pages stared back at her. She laid a palm on the parchment, smooth and clean. There was no evidence of the gateway that would open again with the moon's rise. She wished Aunt Fila were here with her now. Joach had awakened old family memories. She closed the book and returned to the cabin's bed. She smoothed a blanket. Even more than Aunt Fila, she wished her mother was here. If only for a few moments . . .

"Mama, what am I to do?" she whispered to the empty room.

For answer, a piercing horn echoed through the ship. She swung around. The sentinels in the crow's nest! Distantly a more muffled horn answered the first, this time from the ground, from the blasted orchard.

It begins!

She ran to the door and tore it open. She was startled to find Joach blocking her way. He must have returned for her when the alarm was raised. "Joach! We must—"

Further words were knocked from her as he struck her straight-armed in the chest. She stumbled backward, caught off balance. She fell back on the bed as Joach pushed into the room after her.

"Joach, what are you—"

Then the illusion fell from the figure as he slammed the door behind him. Red hair faded to brown, features melted from the warm familiarity of her brother to another familiar face—but one far from warm.

Elena could not catch her breath from the shock and disbelief. It was impossible. She had seen his body hacked apart and buried. His name choked from her throat. "Greshym!"

She snatched for her wit'ch dagger, but before her fingers could touch its hilt, a magickal force ripped forth from the darkmage. Elena was thrown to the wall, pinned in place, spread-eagled against the slightly curved planks. She could not move.

Greshym stepped toward her, kicking through the jumble of furs and blankets. "It's no use struggling."

Despite his words, she fought the invisible bonds. Her hands pounded with energy, aglow with magick—coldfire in one, wit'ch fire in the other—but with no blade to release the blood magick, she was kept from her power, at the mercy of this creature.

Greshym leaned near to her. "Now where is the blood sword?"

WITH THE FIRST HORN BLAST, ER'RIL LEAPED TO ONE OF THE UNDERSIDE hatches of the *Windsprite*, while others in the hold scattered to various portholes and hatches. Er'ril dropped beside a coil of rope attached to a complex block-and-tackle pulley system overhead—the conveyance used to haul supplies. He leaned out to stare at the landscape below.

Rain swept in waves, obscuring the view, but clearly something had the og'res roiled. Another horn blast echoed up from the muddy orchard.

He could not see what threatened. All he could make out was columns of og'res breaking down into bouldered lines. Others bounded about, shouting orders that didn't reach this high.

What was going on? He needed a better vantage. Just as he pushed up, a large shape burst up through the hatch, shooting into the hold with a flourish of wings and a gust of wet air. Er'ril rolled away, his sword in his hand as he regained his feet.

But no defense was necessary. The shape, still in flight, spun through the hollow space and landed in a wary pose. The creature was a blend of avian and human features: a crown of feathers, naked legs, arms that trailed long pinions, and a narrow, pinched face. Amber eyes glowed in the dim hold.

Fardale and Thorn appeared at Er'ril's side. "It's one of our scouts!"

Er'ril sheathed his sword. "What is happening?"

The si'luran glanced around the room, panting. "Under attack. From the ground itself. Lying in wait—an ambush." The bird-man locked eyes with Thorn. "The elder'root sends word." His eyes glowed at Thorn for a long silent moment.

She nodded, as Fardale clutched her elbow. Clearly he had caught the silent message, too.

His duty done, the scout dove back out the hatch. Er'ril caught the glimpse of feathers sprouting as the shape-shifter dropped away, becoming a terror-hawk again.

"What did he tell you?" Er'ril asked Thorn.

She turned to him, paler than a moment before. "My father and his army are going even now to join the battle below."

Er'ril clenched a fist. "I must see what they face." He swung up the stairs to the open deck above. When he shouldered open the door, he found the storm growing fiercer; spats of stinging rain pelted the rolling deck. He dragged the hood of his cloak over his head and hunched into the foul weather. He spotted Tol'chuk and Magnam already stationed by a rail, leaning over to peer below.

He hurried over as another hatch banged open in the wind. He turned, expecting to see Elena, but it was Meric and Nee'lahn. "What's happening?" Meric cried into the gale.

Er'ril shook his head. Tol'chuk glanced to them as the entire party assembled at the rail. His brow was furrowed deeply.

Er'ril stared below, his fingers scrabbling for his spyglass.

Through the curtains of rain, he watched carnage, as strange beasts burrowed up from dead branches and muddy leaves.

Yanking his spyglass free of his belt, Er'ril focused down, drawn into the heart of the battle. He watched a black creature unfold from the tangle of roots of an upturned tree. It was all articulated limbs, some cross between a praying mantis and an ant, but it stood as tall as a man. The monster sprang on an og're, wrapping its legs around its victim. Razored mandibles tore at neck and face as both combatants fell, rolling, in the mud.

Elsewhere, monstrous slugs, the size of fallen logs, oozed from subterranean burrows. Their oily skin hissed with poison in the rains. Wormy appendages shot out, burning flesh to bone with a touch. Er'ril watched one of the monstrosities roll over an injured og're, melting straight through the flesh of the fellow's legs.

Bellows echoed up from below, while thunder rumbled over the horizon. It was a slaughterhouse. Er'ril lowered his spyglass, sickened both from the death and his own impotence.

Despite the odds, the og'res slogged forward through the trap, paying in blood for every step. Er'ril gripped the rail almost desperately, willing them his own strength.

"They'll never make it alone," Tol'chuk said at his side.

Er'ril understood. The edge of the pit was still a full league away.

"They're not alone," Fardale said fiercely. He pointed toward the skies.

Against the clouds, the si'luran army massed, a dark flock. Turning in unison, the winged army dove toward the fighting. They fell with all the might of their momentum, striking out with claws and beaks.

Er'ril lifted his spyglass again, his heart thundering in his ears. One golden eagle fell upon the og're still writhing with the black insectoid creature. The bird struck with such speed, Er'ril could barely mark the passage. Only when the chitinous head dropped from the eagle's claws did Er'ril understand. The og're, bloody-faced and roaring, shook off the decapitated monster.

From the skies, death rained upon the hidden lurkers. Slowly the tide of the battle turned. The og'res surged forward, clubs beating a path forward. Working together, the two armies rolled toward the waiting pit.

Er'ril lowered his glass and stared at the hole blasted in the highlands.

He knew this was only the first skirmish. Whatever else lay ahead remained shrouded in the swirling smoky fog.

He glanced down the rail. Tol'chuk stood with Magnam. Meric with Nee'lahn. Fardale and Thorn. All wore matching expressions of tired horror.

From a hatch, Joach and Harlequin appeared, Jaston and the swamp child behind them. Joach waved to Er'ril. "We may have worked out a plan—"

Er'ril cut him off. "Where's your sister?" He had left Elena with her brother. He had thought he was still with her.

Joach scanned the rainy deck. "I . . . I thought she'd be up here. Last I saw, she was in her cabin."

Er'ril's heart climbed into his throat. The horns should have drawn her topside. Cursing his lapse in attention, he shoved past Joach and the others.

Joach was caught up in his wake. "She seemed to want some time alone . . ."

Er'ril was deaf to his words. He burst through the forward hatch, leaping the stairs.

Joach ran after him. "What's wrong?"

Er'ril didn't answer. He raced into the belly of the ship. He had put too much trust in the open air around them, their isolation. He had foolishly let his guard down, trusting Joach to watch after his sister for a moment. But a moment was all it took to lose everything.

He pounded down the length of the ship, praying he wasn't too late. He spotted their cabin door at the end of the hall. Nothing seemed amiss.

Joach yelled, racing after him. "What are you—?"

Ahead, the explosion blasted the door off its hinges, blowing it down the hall. Er'ril was tossed backward, colliding into Joach. The flying door struck them with the force of a hammer, clipping Er'ril on the side of the head as it tumbled past. All sound went silent, his vision skittered, and time paused for a frozen instant.

Then Er'ril slammed into the planks, hitting his head again. He fought against the tide, but the world slipped away . . . into darkness.

ELENA BLINKED THROUGH TEARS AFTER THE MAGICKAL EXPLOSION. SHE WAS still pinned against the wall, helpless. Her head ached; her heart pounded in her throat. Her hands were twin suns of pent energies.

Greshym stood before her, his cloak billowing with energies, staff held

before him like a king's scepter. He had lost all composure, anger and
frustration turning him wild. "Where is the blood sword? Tell me, or I'll
rip this ship apart and pick through the ruins myself!"

The darkmage had the power to back his threat—she only had to look
at the ruin of the doorway to know this. But she remained silent. Since
capturing her, he had battered at her will with horrible figments, whispered promises, but he dared not risk physical harm against her. If he
were to bloody her hands, the magick would be hers again.

It was a standoff.

Elena carefully kept her eyes away from the furs at the darkmage's feet.
His initial attack had thrown the bedding to a jumble at the foot of the
bed. The wit'ch sword lay hidden in the pile. Clearly Greshym believed
the sword more artfully protected—not lying in plain sight.

She kept her eyes fixed on Greshym.

The darkmage's patience had worn thin. He must know his time was
running short.

A voice startled them both. "Greshym!"

The darkmage swung around. Joach stood in the splintered doorway,
his staff raised before him.

"Joach! Get back!"

Her brother ignored her. "You swore you'd not return!"

Greshym shrugged, but kept his staff raised. "I only collect one last
item. Then I'll be on my way."

"Shadowsedge," Joach said, his eyes narrowing.

"It would destroy your sister anyway. I'll find a better use for it."

Elena hung from the wall. Shock coursed through her despite the terror of the moment. Joach plainly was not surprised to find Greshym alive.
From her brother's words, some pact had been made between them. But
why? Just to regain some of his life? Elena stared at Joach's resurrected
hand. No, it had been something more important than his own life. *Kesla.*

She closed her eyes for an awful moment. She had not realized the
depths of her brother's despair.

Greshym spoke. "And I must say, my boy, your timing here could not
have been more opportune."

Elena opened her eyes, sensing a well of power building in the room.

"I had no leverage with which to pry your sister's secret." Greshym
lashed out with his staff, more swiftly than a striking snake. "But with
you here . . ."

A whirl of oily darkness opened behind her brother.

"Joach!" Elena yelled.

Before she could finish her cry, a horrid beast leaped from the darkness and snatched at her brother. It was gray-skinned, muzzled, with peaked ears, and its hands ended in ripping claws. Bone-crushing arms ending in vicious claws grabbed Joach, ripping through his clothes to dig into flesh. His staff tumbled to the floor, rolling out of reach.

The beast lowered its muzzle to Joach's throat, lips curled in a snarl, razored teeth glinting. He snuffled hungrily, piggish eyes bright with blood lust.

"Rukh likes you," Greshym said as her brother struggled. "I think he remembers the taste of your old hand." Joach's struggles became more frantic as the darkmage turned to Elena. "Now perhaps we can negotiate: Shadowsedge, for your brother's life."

Elena stared at the slavering beast.

"And don't expect any further interruptions," the darkmage added. "I've sealed the end of this corridor."

Elena's eyes drifted toward the floor, toward the rumple of blankets and furs. She had no choice. "The sword—"

Then movement caught her eye. Joach's staff was rising from the floor behind Greshym, a shadow building under it. Her brows pinched.

Greshym sensed the danger a moment too late. He swung, but the staff lunged over his head as the shadow burst upward. The darkmage was caught by the neck, choked across the throat by the stone staff. His own bone stave clattered to the floor as he grabbed for his neck. Behind the darkmage, the shadow continued to take shape, as if folding out from another space.

It was Joach!

Greshym's mouth opened in dismay, even as her brother continued to throttle the mage. "I warned you never to return." Joach slammed a boot atop the fallen staff, shattering the length of bone. Blood flowed from the shards, steaming across the planks. A howl rose—and Greshym groaned to match.

Joach glanced to the beast who was holding his facsimile. With a wave of his hand, the image dissolved to sand—then even that vanished.

The goblin startled back to cower against the wall, eyes darting.

"Free my sister," Joach hissed.

Greshym lifted his hand as a scrape of wood sounded by the doorway. All eyes swung around.

Er'ril stood, leaning against the ruined frame, sword in hand. Blood dribbled down his forehead. "Elena . . ."

The moment's distraction was all it took. Greshym slammed his elbow into Joach's rib cage. At the same time, obeying some silent command, the beast leaped at Er'ril with a roar.

Elena fought her bonds, but she could not even move her fingers.

Before her, Joach coughed, the air knocked from his chest. He stumbled back, releasing the darkmage. Greshym leaped free, crouching amid the remains of his shattered staff. He opened his palm over the bloody remnants, and the bone shards reassembled in a flash of magick. His staff snapped back to his fingers.

Joach lifted his own staff, but the darkmage was quicker. Magick blasted out. Her brother was thrown across the cabin to strike the stone hearth—pinned against the wall as surely as Elena.

By the doorway, Er'ril was a whirl of steel. He skewered the darkmage's creature again and again. Then with a final spin, he sliced his sword across the beast's throat. Blood spurted to the ceiling as the creature fell dead to the floor.

Er'ril stalked into the room, the front of his cloak dripping with gore.

Greshym spoke from the corner where he crouched by Joach, his bone staff pointing toward the plainsman. "Even after five centuries, you've not lost your stroke. Now drop your sword and kick it over here."

"No!" Joach spat, seething.

Greshym shoved his stumped wrist toward Joach, whose trapped body convulsed, back arching from the wall despite the restraints. A scream burst from his lips, along with a gout of blood.

"Joach!" Elena cried out.

"Do as I say," Greshym hissed at Er'ril, "or I'll make the girl suffer, too."

After a tense pause, Er'ril dropped his weapon, pushing it away.

Greshym lowered his stumped arm. Joach collapsed, sagging back to the wall, blood dribbling from his lips.

"Joach . . . ?" Elena moaned.

"He'll live with nothing worse than an ache in his belly," Greshym said. "But that can change. It's up to you." He nodded to Er'ril. "And it seems one more life has been added to the pot. You are a hard bargainer, my dear. Now I'm forced to offer *two* lives for the ancient sword."

"Don't do it," Er'ril quickly blurted.

Greshym ignored the plainsman. His eyes stayed on Elena, while his staff remained pointed at Er'ril. "Have you ever seen skin stripped from a body in one tear? It's a bit tricky, but I've had practice. You just pick the one: Er'ril or Joach. Husband or brother." Greshym swung his staff back and forth. "I don't care which."

Elena knew they were defeated. She nodded to the blankets. "The sword is right there, under the furs."

Greshym's eyes widened as he stared to his toes. "It was there all along?" He glanced to Er'ril and shook his head. "I could see her making such an error, but you? You should know better. You hold a talisman strong enough to defeat the Black Heart, and you leave it lying about like kitchen cutlery?" He crossed to the bedding and kicked through it. He was satisfied with a distinct *clank*. "I expected complicated wards that only Elena could unlock."

Er'ril glowered at the darkmage.

Warily, Greshym tucked his staff under his arm and fished through the furs. He straightened with the rose-pommel hilt in hand. He shook off the sheath to reveal the icy length of elemental steel. "Shadowsedge . . ." Greshym said with awe, suppressing a relieved laugh. "Mine at last!"

He dropped his bone staff and kicked it aside. The simple action was enough to tell Elena how awful a weapon the blade must be.

She met Er'ril's eyes. He was staring at her hands. He clearly understood her powers were pent up, unavailable. His eyes returned to hers. "Remember your family's bathing chamber," he whispered. "When you burned it down . . ."

Elena frowned. She had told Er'ril that story long ago. She had barely bloomed to her Rose, just after her first menstra. While soaking in a cooling tub, she had willed the waters to warm, but with no control of her magick, she had come near to boiling herself alive. But what did that have to do with now? She had no access to her powers. She wasn't bloodied . . .

Then her eyes grew wide. Her hands hadn't been bloodied *then*, either. Afterward, thinking back on it, she had figured the release had to do with the bleeding from her first menstra. The flow of blood from the core of her womanhood must have allowed the magick to stream out into the bathwater.

She stared at Er'ril. *From first bleed to first blood . . .*

He knew she still seeped from their first night together. Blood again— from the heart of her womanhood. Could this be a way?

She listened to the magick raging inside her, the pure energy, fresh from the Void. She willed it to flow from her ruby hands, back to her heart. As she did so, the glow faded from her fingers.

Greshym turned to them, holding the sword before him. "As bargained,

I will spare the lives of those you love, but there is another here to whom I owe a debt."

Er'ril stepped between the mage and Elena. "I'll not let you harm her."

Greshym laughed. "Always the knight, Er'ril." The darkmage swung to the desk. "But I intend your woman no harm. I'd prefer she waste her life attacking the Black Heart. To that end, we are united in purpose." He pointed the sword to the Blood Diary. "It is Cho. I mean to make her pay for making me dance like her little puppet." He glanced over his shoulder. "Now you shall understand the full power of the sword—to break spells, to unbind what is bound."

Joach realized his intent the same moment as Elena. "No!" he gasped out, spitting blood.

Greshym eyed him, lowering the sword slightly. "Some dreams are better left dead."

Joach struggled, eyes wild. "I'll make you pay!" The gray stone staff rattled on the planks, but he failed to move it more than a handspan.

Greshym eyed his efforts, lifting one brow. "You are strong, my boy. What I could have done with you, given the time." He shook his head sadly and turned back to the Blood Diary.

Elena did not waste her brother's efforts. In the moment of distraction, she reached to the core of her being and touched the chorus of power there. As the darkmage stepped toward the desk, she lashed out with her magick. Wild energies lanced burning from the heart of her womanhood.

Greshym sensed the release of unstoppable power and lunged forward. The magick blasted through the planks at his heels, missing him by the breadth of a hair.

Splintered wood shattered up. Raw magick crashed through the ship and out the belly, leaving a hole clear through to the ground far below. The backwash cindered Elena's bonds. She fell limply from the wall.

Er'ril was immediately at her side.

Across the ragged hole, the darkmage teetered, the back of his cloak singed. He caught his balance and turned, the sword held before him. "Clever girl," he growled at her. "But you'll never get a second chance. The sword will protect me from even your magick."

Elena knew this to be right. She had wielded the sword herself. It would protect its bearer. "Leave with the sword then," she said, standing. "But I'll not let you harm the Blood Diary."

Greshym frowned at the book on the desk; the smoldering hole lay between him and the Diary. "This is not over, girl. That I promise!"

He stepped forward, ready to leap through the hole and away with his prize. Elena felt the dance of magick in the air.

A blur of movement caught her eye. Er'ril dove from her side, leaping and rolling. As he tumbled, he pulled a dagger from his boot and flung it with all the accuracy of an experienced juggler. The blade struck the mage's wrist, skewering it.

Greshym's sword arm was thrown back. Shadowsedge tumbled from his limp fingers, to clatter harmlessly against the hearth.

The darkmage was not so lucky. Twisted off balance, he began his own slow tumble through the hole. A wail of disbelief shrieked from his throat. With his staff abandoned, stripped of the sword, he had no magick to stop his fall.

Down he went, screaming.

Er'ril knelt at the hole's edge. Elena joined him.

The darkmage's body cartwheeled end over end, arms and legs flailing. Far below, he struck one of the stripped orchard trees. The sharp, broken top pierced his chest. He slid, spiked through the gut, to the midpoint of the tree, then hung there, unmoving.

Joach slid down the wall as death released the binding spell.

Elena remembered Aunt Mycelle's warning long ago about putting too much faith in magick alone. Here was the proof. Shadowsedge, one of the most potent talismans ever crafted against magick, had failed against something as simple as an ordinary Standish dagger.

Er'ril touched Elena's shoulder, drawing her back, but Joach stepped to her other side. His chest heaved. His face was pale with fury. In his hands, he held Greshym's bone staff.

"Not yet," he said in a half moan. His lips continued to move, but no further words were heard.

Elena felt a chill waft out from her brother. "Joach . . . no. It's over."

He ignored her. His lips were blue from the cold coming off him. He lifted the staff and pointed it down. With a final silent utterance, he jabbed it toward the bloody tree below.

A jet of black flame spat from the staff's end: balefire. It ripped through the dark morning, drawing shadows to it as it struck the bloodied tree. Flaming sap and bark blasted out, sailing far into the fields. The balefire burned down to the impaled body and burst with a surge of black flames. A scream of the damned wafted upon its fires for an endless moment, then faded away, leaving only a smoky ruin, flames dancing atop a smoldering stump.

"This time he's truly dead," Joach mumbled. The bone staff crumbled to ash in his fingertips, raining down through the hole. Joach turned his back and strode stiffly toward the door. Without another word, he was gone.

Elena found herself unable to move. She was glad Greshym was gone, the monster who had slain her parents and tormented her brother. But a strange sense of defeat washed through her. She stared from the smoldering stump to the doorway. Who had truly won here?

Er'ril collected a blanket from the floor. He covered her singed clothes. Through the hole, the bright sounds of horns rose to them, reminding them of the other war raging below.

Er'ril drew her up, held her close until her shaking subsided.

After a long moment, she found her voice. "If you hadn't remembered about the blood—" she began, glancing up to him.

"Shush," he whispered. "Do you think my taking your maidenhood was something I'd forget so soon?"

She stared into his eyes and saw a trace of guilt mixed with pained responsibility. She touched his cheek. "If you hadn't . . . we could easily have lost everything this morning."

He simply hugged her tighter. But the horns continued to sound below; the world would not wait forever. Finally, he stepped from her side and retrieved Shadowsedge from the corner, slipping it into his empty sheath.

He met her gaze. "Greshym's appearance—it had something to do with Joach, didn't it?"

Elena nodded. "He did it for Kesla—some way of resurrecting her, a magick or spell that Greshym must have traded for his freedom."

Er'ril glanced toward the doorway. "Once one starts down that dark road . . . Can we still trust him?"

Elena stared toward the empty doorway, wondering at this question, frightened that she even had a doubt. Her words were a whisper. "I don't know."

IT WAS WELL PAST MIDDAY, AND JOACH COULD STILL TASTE THE BITTER alchemy of dragon blood on the back of his tongue. The elixir had healed the ache in his belly from Greshym's attack, but it did little to mend his bruised heart.

He stood at the prow of the *Windsprite*. Rain soaked his hair and ran in rivulets down his neck and back. He didn't bother shivering. The core of his being was colder than the downpour. He lifted his face to the dark skies. It was midday, but it still seemed twilight.

Would this gloom never end?

Gripping his staff, he swung his gaze below. In the battle to come, he would prove himself as best he could. He would not fail.

But despite his determination, Elena's eyes still haunted him. She had said all the right things after the battle belowdecks: how she understood his need, how she forgave him, how he was still her brother. But he had seen something different in her eyes. She no longer held him as close in her heart. And he knew that this was one wound that even dragon blood would never heal.

He closed his eyes on this pain and instead focused on another frustration: Greshym was dead. Joach had made sure of it, striking out with blind fury, casting the balefire that roasted the darkmage's body to ash. But he found little satisfaction in the act . . . in fact, the opposite was true. Without doubt, he hated Greshym with all his heart. The mage had stolen everything from him: parents, his youth, the woman he loved . . . now even the deep bond with his sister. But he understood that an important key to his own identity had been lost forever this morning.

What I could have done with you . . .

These last words of Greshym's ate at him. With the darkmage's demise, so died any hope of understanding the depths and breadth of his own magick. Joach shook his head. While his heart remained bruised, a core of anger grew into a hot ember.

Perhaps Elena had acted too hastily. If she had just waited—

"Are you ready?" Harlequin interrupted his thoughts.

Joach opened his eyes back to the world.

Below, the two armies—og're and si'luran—awaited the final assault on the pit. They had forged ahead through the long morning to within a stone's throw of the crater's rim. There the armies had lain entrenched through the day's middle, tending the wounded and readying for the last surge into the pit.

The landscape below had gone ominously silent. Only the rumble of thunder rolled over the blasted valley. The entire world held its breath.

"Joach?" Harlequin asked again.

Half turning, Joach glanced across the deck. Everyone was assembled, packs in place, weapons sheathed and strapped. He met Elena's gaze. She nodded with reassurance toward him. She stood in black boots and a dark cloak, a match to the knight beside her. Joach caught the glint of the rose pommel at her hip: Shadowsedge. She also carried the Blood Diary inside her cloak, ready for the rising moon.

Joach met her gaze, reading the edge of doubt behind her encouragement. He would not fail. "Sound the charge," he directed the spy.

Harlequin Quail waved to Tol'chuk. The og're, standing at the starboard rail, lifted a curled ram's horn to his lips.

"Let it begin," Joach whispered to himself.

The horn blared across the valley, and a roar answered from below.

The og're army lumbered in a wall of clubs and muscle toward the shrouded pit. Behind them, a sail of wings rose in a dark cloud as the si'lura took to the sky.

"Now," Harlequin said needlessly at his side. The plan had been the small man's, but it was up to Joach to execute it.

Joach fed his blood into his staff. Gray stone turned pale. Green crystals flared along its length. Joach lifted his staff and tapped it on the planks of the ship.

Distantly, he heard Harlequin yell to the *Windsprite*'s captain. The ship slipped forward under his feet. Exclamations of wonder rose from those gathered behind him. He didn't have to turn to know what they saw.

As the elv'in ship surged forward, a twin was left in its place. To the eyes below, it would seem the *Windsprite* never left its position in the skies. The ship sailing forward was masked in cloud and illusion, the spell like the one he had used to catch Greshym by surprise earlier—a diversion, a mock-up to trick the eye. Joach prayed the end result would be more successful this time.

The ship flew onward, riding over the two armies. Then from up ahead, a legion of monsters burst from the mists, leaping and winging forth to meet the assault. Screams carried on the winds. Howls and shivering sounds of madness rose like steam.

But the ship flew above it all, ignored and unseen.

In moments, the battle vanished under the keel, taking the world with it. The landscape became a sea of mists, whirling in a churning eddy. The ship's captain aimed for the eye of the whirlpool, drifting over the pit and down, as if caught in the vortex.

"Everyone below!" Er'ril called. "To the ropes and pulleys!"

Joach stared down a moment longer. Though he knew the ship was cloaked in illusion, he sensed something immense staring back up at them, an abyss of darkness from which there would be no escape. It seemed to call to him. He found himself leaning over the rail, mesmerized by the churning mists.

"Joach?" Harlequin said at his side, touching his elbow. "It's time."

With the man's touch, Joach tore his gaze free—but he could not so easily escape the sense of doom. He shivered and pulled his cloak tighter.

"Are you all right?" the short man in bells asked.

Joach nodded. "I'm fine." On this foul and endless journey, what was one more lie?

25

KAST PREPARED TO LAUNCH FROM THE *DRAGONSHEART* AS AN ARGUMENT played out at his side. Hunt stood on the deck, tugging little Sheeshon toward the dragon. "I won't go without Roddie!" she yelled.

Hunt dropped to one knee. "We must. It's dangerous enough to bring even you."

Beyond the pair, Hunt's father, the high keel, stood with his meaty hands on Rodricko's small shoulders. Beside them, Xin stood with the portly Shaman Bilatus.

It had taken the entire morning to relate the danger of the oily creature lurking in the Southern Gate. Strategies had been rethought. Crows were sent like arrows between ships on the sea and in the air.

Kast was the center of all the flurry. The loss of the dragon was a serious blow, for while Kast could still wing through the air in this form, he was not a gifted flyer. It had taken all his concentration to reach the ship, landing in a tumble across the deck. Despite appearances, he was not Ragnar'k.

After he finally got his message delivered—aided by the considerable skill of Xin to read the secrets in another's heart—plans were quickly altered. A cadre of elv'in Thunderclouds would proceed in advance of the surface fleet. They would lance the creature with bolts from their keels and try to draw it into the open. Then Dre'rendi forces would attack from the sea with catapults. Under this cover, the mer'ai and their dragons would rush the seawall, slipping through the jagged Crown of Blackhall to the lagoon beyond. If the creature tried to flee into the waters, the dragons would be waiting to battle the beast. And once under siege, the monster would be attacked from all sides until victory was achieved.

A trumpet sounded crisply across the morning.

Kast raised his head. The six Thunderclouds were already swelling their sails to sweep forward. Unbidden, a growl escaped his throat. His heart ached with worry for Sy-wen, alone on those black shores. Silver claws dug gouges in the planks. He had spent too long here already. Every beat of his giant heart was another moment that Sy-wen was in danger.

A childish scream drew his attention back to the closer battle.

"Sheeshon, stop fighting me." Hunt's face was as red as his crimson shirt. Kast noted how wasted the high keel's son appeared. His black cloak hung loosely from his rolled shoulders. His cheekbones stuck out more prominently. While possessed, the creature inside Hunt sought to harm its host: refusing to eat, vomiting, digging gouges from his face, tearing hair. But with Sheeshon in hand, Hunt was his own man again, tall, proud, his hair braided in a neat warrior's knot.

Still, Kast's senses, sharpened by the dragon form he wore, smelled the trace of Hunt's fear. It terrified the man to know what he became without the child. Thus, he clung to Sheeshon now. The child had to come with them to the island. For Hunt to be freed by the volcanic smoke, he would have to travel with Kast—and Sheeshon had to accompany them to keep Hunt under control.

But the battle continued.

"Roddie *must* come!" Sheeshon screamed into the overcast day. The child refused to go anywhere without her friend, even to the blasted island.

Rodricko did not share her sentiment. He sank back into the high keel's shadow, eyes wide with fear. He clutched the flowered stem to his chest. The flower lay bloomed under the boy's chin, casting a fiery glow from the heart of its purple petals.

Kast had had enough of this delay. He remembered the fear in Sy-wen. It was a dagger in his heart. *Enough!* The fire in his chest burst out in a roar that tumbled everyone back from his flanks.

Sheeshon's face drained of color. Hunt shielded her under him, as if fearing Kast would attack. Rodricko ducked between the high keel's legs and hid in his cloak.

Only Xin seemed unaffected by his outburst, a broad smile on his small face. "The dragon has lost patience. He bellows his agony for the woman he loves. It is written with fire on his heart."

Again Kast appreciated the tribesman's talent.

Shaman Bilatus wiped his brow, paler than a moment ago. He addressed Hunt. "You cannot fight this child all the way to the island. Kast will have enough to do getting you both safely there. If the child will be calmer with Rodricko along, then so be it."

Kast grunted agreement, tossing his head.

"We'd be putting the boy to needless risk," the high keel argued, standing taller to protect the child.

Bilatus motioned toward Blackhall. "We all stand in the shadow of that cursed peak. The boy is already at risk."

The high keel narrowed his eyes, hardly convinced. Bilatus stepped nearer his leader. "Sheeshon gave us the key to unlock your son's imprisonment. If she hadn't insisted the boy's flower be bathed in the island's smoke—"

His words were waved away by the high keel. "I'm indebted to the girl."

"And you also owe the seven gods of the sea your thanks. The child is blessed with the rajor maga. She hears their whispers from over the horizon. They speak through her."

The high keel's lips hardened to thin lines.

"We should listen to her now," Bilatus said firmly.

The high keel expelled a large breath. "Let it be done then." He unfolded the boy from his sea cloak, then patted him on the shoulder. "Go with Sheeshon and Hunt."

Rodricko didn't move, a statue with large round eyes.

The high keel dropped to one knee. "You are Dre'rendi, are you not? A Bloodrider."

Slowly the boy's head nodded.

"Then you must make your heart as brave as a boulder in an angry surf. That is our way. Can you do this for your high keel?"

Rodricko's eyes brimmed with tears, but he made a small sound of agreement.

"That's a good boy." He turned Rodricko around and passed him to Hunt. The high keel stared hard at his son. "Take care of the children."

"With my own life," Hunt promised. He scooped Rodricko into one arm.

Sheeshon followed willingly, all the fight replaced with excitement. "We get to ride a dragon!" She puffed her tiny chest out. "Course, I rode one before."

In short order, they were mounted on Kast's back. He snugged the flaps around Hunt's ankles to hold him in place. In turn, the big man held the two children clasped between his own legs, arms around them.

"Safe journey!" Bilatus called.

Kast stretched his wings and readied his legs to leap skyward. But a door crashed open nearby. "Wait!" Master Edyll climbed out, a pack in his arms. "Wait . . . Take this with you!"

"What is it?" Hunt asked as the elder limped forward.

He panted, his expression pained. "For Sy-wen."

The high keel frowned as Hunt took the pack, but Master Edyll was as impatient as Kast. "Go!" the elder said, backing away. "Go!"

Kast bunched his legs under him. Hunt hunched over the children. With a burst of legs and sweep of wings, they shoved from the ship into the empty air.

Kast spread his wings, letting the instincts and reflexes of the dragon's body do most of the flying. The wings caught the winds, banking away from the ship. He felt the pressure of his wards atop his back and was careful to balance them as he caught a warm uprising from a boiling section of sea. Though his heart cried to rush to the black beaches and Sy-wen, he kept his pace even.

Sheeshon whooped with excitement, while Rodricko's cries were more moans of worry. "Open your eyes!" Sheeshon yelled into the winds.

"No!" Rodricko answered.

The black mountain covered the horizon ahead of them, and slowly—too slowly—grew to fill more and more of the sky. The plan was for them to sweep onto the beach and have Hunt climb to one of the smoking spouts. Once Hunt was exposed and hopefully cured, he would remain with the children and Sy-wen in hiding. Kast would keep guard from the air while overseeing the assault upon the beast in the gate.

When the mer'ai forces were through the opening in the rocky Crown, a rescue force would be sent to collect Sy-wen, Hunt, and the children. Kast would then turn his full attention upon the battle.

According to Xin, Tyrus had already reached the Northern Gate with the d'warf army. The goal was to join their two forces inside the mountain. A rallying point had been coordinated using the maps provided by Harlequin Quail.

After Sy-wen and the others were safely away, Kast would attempt to penetrate the cavernous gate. If the monster lurking there could be lured away, he would sweep through the gate's threshold, to scout out what lay ahead for their forces.

That was the plan. But Kast had been in hundreds of campaigns and sea battles while sailing the Blasted Shoals with the Dre'rendi: He knew that few plans unfolded without mishap. So he flew with a heavy heart, weighted down by worries.

Overhead, the cadre of Thunderclouds swept forward, iron keels glowing brightly in the gloom of the day. Already spats of lightning ran in shivering tangles over their lengths as the ships' captains fed energy into the magick-wrought iron, readying for the attack. The six ships sailed in a tight formation, an arrow aimed toward the gate.

Kast banked out of their shadows, heading slightly westward, toward where he had left Sy-wen. He slowly increased his pace, and soon they were sweeping over the shoals and gliding low over the lagoon. Ahead, the black sand beach stretched empty.

His heart thundered in his ears. Where was Sy-wen? As he frantically scanned the rocks and sand, he both prayed and feared he had the wrong section of beach. Surely she would have spotted their approach and come out of hiding.

As he reached the beach, he cupped back his wings and extended his legs to land in a running stop in the loose sand. But he barely noted his safe landfall. Instead, roar of frustration bellowed from his throat.

Then Hunt's words cut through the hammer of his heart. "She's over there!"

Kast scrambled around, casting up a plume of sand with his claws. Far down the beach, he spotted a lithe figure leaping down some rocks. *Sy-wen!* Relief flooded through him. He must have overshot his target. He cursed the island for its monotonous shoreline, but his relief made him drunk with joy.

Down the strand, Sy-wen struck the sand running and raced toward them. As she flew, she moved to the wet sands where the waters lapped the beach, seeking firmer footing.

Only then did Kast spot her pursuers.

They looked like four boulders tumbling behind her, craggy and massive. They leaped after her atop massive hind legs, bounding like malignant toads. The one in the lead yowled, revealing a maw that split its head from one side to the other. Daggered fangs lined the mouth.

Kast shrugged the riders from his shoulders. Hunt, already half off, was knocked to his knees in the sand, still clutching a child under each arm.

Free of his burden, Kast leaped forward, closing the distance to Sy-wen in a single bound. He trumpeted his fury at the beasts.

The creatures slowed warily, allowing Sy-wen to race to him.

Get to Hunt! he bellowed at her.

Without a word of argument, she raced under one of his wings, ducking low, lest her touch turn him back into a man. *Careful, my love,* she sent as she passed.

Care was not something on his mind. He was ruled by the dragon instincts rising to the surface. Rage fueled his blood. His vision sharpened upon his prey.

As if noticing the attention, the first of the beasts struck, leaping toward the dragon's long neck, mouth gaping, teeth glinting. Clearly the creatures had never tangled with the likes of a dragon. Kast snatched the toadish beast in midair, clamping hard, fangs piercing deep. Bones splintered. Kast shook the creature, hearing another satisfying crack, then tossed the limp form into the lagoon.

The next two attacked in unison. One went for his throat, the other his belly.

Kast knocked the first aside with a blow from his wing. The other was crushed under silver claws, driven into the sands as Kast spun all his bulk atop the one foot. The beast who had been knocked aside bounded back stubbornly, only to meet Kast's jaws. He bit through the creature's neck, leaving its headless body to scrabble blindly before falling quivering to the sands.

"Kast!" Sy-wen screamed behind him.

He whipped around to find the fourth and final creature had slipped past him during his battle, splashing through the shallows to go after easier prey.

Hunt stood down the beach, sheltering the two children and Sy-wen. He had a sword in one hand and Sheeshon's tiny palm in the other. They dared not break hold of one another.

The beast leaped toward the trio. Hunt tried to retreat from it, but his feet tangled with Sheeshon. They both fell.

Rodricko was left a step ahead of them, frozen in terror. Sy-wen, knocked to her knees herself, reached to snag the boy from the beast's path, but the monster was already in the air, driving down upon the ashen boy.

With a high scream on his lips, the lad thrust his only weapon toward the monster: his fiery flower.

"Roddie!" Sheeshon yelled in terror.

Kast bounded down the strand, but he knew he'd be too late.

The massive beast landed atop the boy.

"Roddie!"

But instead of being crushed, the boy remained standing, wrapped inside the beast who was now no more than a smoke-sculpted version of itself. Then even these features wafted away into a vague cloud.

Inside the smoke puff, Rodricko's flower shone with a fierce fire, petals peeled back from its heart. Then the smoke seemed to draw into its blaze, sucked into the flower's heart—and Rodricko stood unharmed in the sand, holding the flower.

Sy-wen pulled him into her arms. "Rodricko, are you all right?"

Kast stalked to them as Hunt and Sheeshon gained their feet. He watched for other attackers.

Sy-wen spoke. "The flower's magick saved him."

Kast grumbled deep in his chest. *Or perhaps it was the boy himself. His bloodline is shared with that of his mother, a Grim wraith.*

Sy-wen nodded. "The magick of the island's twisted smoke must have quickened the dread parts of his bloodline; it draws the essence from a living being."

As the smoke drew Ragnar'k from me.

"And the simaltra's essence from me."

Kast surveyed the beach, as wary of the magick seeping like fever sweat from the mountain as of any lurking beasts.

A crack of distant thunder suddenly split the quiet. The ground shook under their feet, and thunder pealed again.

Kast swung his neck eastward. Flares of brilliance crackled from around the shoulder of the mountain.

"What's happening?" Sy-wen asked.

The elv'in ships are attacking the beast in the gate. The battle begins.

Hunt explained their plan as the thunder rumbled on, but Kast kept his focus on the landscape around them.

"If they're attacking," Sy-wen said, "we'd best get Hunt to one of the smoke chutes. There's a seepage just up the beach. I discovered it while searching the shoreline."

You were supposed to stay hidden, Kast scolded, now understanding how the creatures had found her.

Sy-wen frowned at him, then led the way.

He rumbled a heavy sigh. Sy-wen was never one to follow instructions. But he could not complain—if she had not disobeyed her own mother, the two would never have met.

Sy-wen marched around an outcropping to where a small crevice spewed a thin column of ash and smoke.

As Kast stood guard, Hunt shoved a hand into the smoke. The effect was immediate. A gasp shuddered up from his heels, shaking his frame. Sheeshon, who still held his hand, was thrown back.

Hunt dropped to his hands and knees, moaning. Then for an endless span, he spewed his belly into the sands. Blood trailed from his lips. And still he remained hunched, heaving, covered in sweat, shaking, while the children clung to Sy-wen.

Finally, Hunt sat back on his heels, wiping his face on his forearm.

"Hunt?" Sy-wen asked tentatively.

He simply nodded. Sheeshon broke out of Sy-wen's arms and rushed to Hunt. "The worms are gone!"

Are we sure? Kast silently asked Sy-wen.

I think we should trust Sheeshon. She would know. Sy-wen faced him, her eyes shining with warmth. *As you knew with me.*

Kast stared into her eyes. How he longed for her touch, to be transformed back into a man, to hold her in his arms. The same desire shone in Sy-wen's eyes. But the dangers here were too great. The dragon was needed as guardian over them all. They dared not risk it.

Finally, Hunt rose—wobbly, but he regained his footing quickly.

The distant pounding of thunder was now almost constant. With the others safe, an anxiety to find out what was happening grew in Kast, stoked by the tremble in the ground below and the rumbles from the skies above.

The dragons should be here soon to take you all to safety, Kast told his wards.

"Hunt and the children, maybe," Sy-wen answered, her back to him. She swung around, holding the bag sent from Master Edyll. She pulled out a long, shimmering garment. "It's a sharkskin bodysuit," she explained, "used by my people for deepwater diving. With the gloves and hood, it covers the entire body." In addition, she pulled out a long belt, fastened with numerous small starfishlike creatures. He recognized them as stunners, tiny paralyzing weapons used by the mer'ai.

Kast was bewildered as Sy-wen quickly slithered into the skintight suit.

She stretched into one of the gloves. "Master Edyll knew I wouldn't want to leave you." She touched his nose with her gloved fingers.

He flinched back, expecting the explosion of magick, but nothing happened. He remained a dragon.

"With the suit, I can ride atop you."

There is no need, he argued. *I can still be a dragon without you.*

She simply frowned at him again. "I'm going." She yanked on her other glove. "And dragon or not, I'd like to see you stop me."

Though a part of him wanted to argue further, deeper down he was relieved. After being separated half the day, he was loath to part from her
again.

Before any further words could be exchanged, Hunt pointed to the lagoon. "Dragons!"

A pair of jade seadragons surged through the shallows, rising with
noisy exhalations of breath. The riders spat out breathing tubes. "Hurry!"
one called. "The path through the Crown grows more heated with every
passing moment."

"What's happening?" Hunt called, splashing forward.

The rider shook his head. "No time. We must be off."

Kast's heightened senses registered their fear. Eyes kept glancing eastward. Their apprehension flowed into him.

Hunt gathered up Sheeshon and Rodricko and aimed for one of the
dragons. But Sheeshon wiggled free. "No, wait!" She dropped to the shallow water, then reached back up to Rodricko. She grabbed his flowered
branch, seemingly oblivious to the fact that a moment ago the tiny object
had slain a beast a hundred times larger than she.

She lifted the branch, studying it, then lifted back a petal to reveal a
small bud sheltered under the larger main flower. She fingered it deli-
cately. No larger than a thumb, its purple leaves were tightly closed.

Kast frowned inwardly. The bud had not been there earlier; Kast was
sure of it. He had carried the stem himself. It must have budded during
the play of magick earlier. He feared for the girl touching it and sounded
a grumbled warning.

He was ignored. Sheeshon pinched the bud between her fingers and
simply tore it free.

"Hey!" Rodricko yelled at her. "That's mine!"

Sheeshon sneered at him. "You don't need two flowers, Roddie! You're
just being a grubby hog."

"I am not a grubby hog!"

Sheeshon stalked over to Sy-wen. "Here." She placed the closed bud in
Sy-wen's gloved hand.

"What do you want me to do with it?" Sy-wen asked.

Sheeshon shrugged. "It's yours. Rodricko needs to learn to share.
Mader Geel said so."

"She did not!" Rodricko blasted back at her. "You're the grubby hog!"

Hunt collected back his charges as the two continued to argue. He
passed Rodricko to one of the riders and climbed behind the other with

Sheeshon. The riders showed their wards how to use the air pods. Hunt lifted an arm in farewell, and the two dragons receded into the deeper waters and vanished away.

Sy-wen crossed to Kast, tucking the petaled bud in a pocket. "It is time we were off, too."

Again he longed for a moment to hold her in his arms, but thunder still echoed, and new noises intruded: the crash of boulders and horns of wars. The catapults aboard the Dre'rendi ships were engaging—but what did they face?

Sy-wen climbed atop Kast, settling her legs around the base of his neck. He felt the warmth of her skin through her thin suit, through his thick scale. "Are you ready?" she whispered.

A rumble built in his chest.

"Then fly, my dragon, fly."

He bunched his legs and obeyed, winging upward with a burst of muscle and speed. Through their bond—dragon and rider—he sensed the flush of her exhilaration. She leaned closer, her warmth melting her into his heart, her sensations blurring with his own.

Their two bodies became one. *Was this what it was like for Ragnar'k?* No wonder the dragon loved her so.

Kast wound on a rising thermal, spiraling up from the beach. The world spread before them.

To the east, he spotted five of the Thunderclouds. As he watched, a burst of lightning crackled down from one of the ships' keels to strike below, but he was not yet high enough to see the target. A shoulder of the mountain still blocked his view to the dockworks.

Off to the south, the Dre'rendi fleet lay outside the rocky Crown. War machines snapped with sharp thunking twangs, casting rocks and flaming barrels of pitch over the shoals to the shadowed shores. Other smaller ships darted through the gap in the broken Crown to take up positions in the lagoon, aided by a surge of dragons at the lead.

What are they fighting? Sy-wen asked, echoing his own thoughts.

He climbed higher, gliding up over the shoulder. Then the beseiged southern port came into view.

The lurker in the gate had indeed been driven out of hiding and into the open. Sy-wen gasped.

The oily darkness flowed and rolled over the ramshackle township, pouring through the streets, a living pool of blackness. It spread out in a thousand streams, feeding along the dockworks and piers, rippling into the lagoon's murky waters. Half its bulk had already spread along the shore and into the lagoon.

And still it oozed outward and along the shores.

"What is it?" Sy-wen asked.

The answer came soon enough. With a rippling convulsion along its bulk, an army appeared out of the darkness: men, beasts, and monsters. They shed their darkness, stepping forth, birthed out of the oily beast. Only thin tethers of blackness remained, attaching each soldier to its master.

From the lagoon, hundreds of ships suddenly rose from the watery depths, tangled in masses of black snakes. Dead men rose from the algae-covered decks, trailing black umbilici, slaves to their master.

"An army of the dead," Sy-wen mumbled, horrified.

Then, worst of all, from the midst of the shrouded township, another ship lifted from its wet grave, its hull caved in, its keel cracked. Kast recognized the missing Thundercloud. It rose now, not upon the elemental glow of its keel, but upon a twisted pillar of oily darkness. Upon its decks, too, sailors slowly stood: elv'in trailing black tethers, slaves now.

"How can we defeat a legion that's already dead?"

On the shores, a flow of creatures poured out of the black womb of the oily creature, all of Blackhall, slaves to the darkness: one army, one purpose.

And still the flows of damnation rolled forth from the gate.

Sy-wen spoke his own heart. "We're doomed."

"HURRY, MEN!" TYRUS YELLED AS HE RACED HIS MARE OVER THE LAST OF THE Black Road, risking a glance behind him.

The tunnel of d'warf statues wound back across the volcanic span. Fletch, Hurl, and Blyth followed on their frothing, wild-eyed mounts, chased in turn by Sticks on foot. Beyond the giant pirate, the remainder of the d'warf legions kept steady pace. Despite the bloody run and carnage, the soldiers had not lost a step. Watching them this day, Tyrus understood how the d'warf armies had been so critical to the Dark Lord's conquest of the lands of Alasea. They were a tide of muscle, steel, and determination, impossible to turn aside.

Riding past the last of the stone d'warves, Tyrus burst from the granite passage and galloped the last stretch of open stone that lay before the Northern Gate. Just past the threshold, a solid iron gate blocked the way into the mountain, lowered earlier as it grew clear to the hidden gatekeepers that the d'warf army would span the Black Road.

As Tyrus rode toward the iron gate, skal'tum screamed, sensing their prey escaping, but they were kept back by d'warf archers positioned with crossbows in the shadow of the gate.

Free of the tunnel, Fletch added his own arrows to the bolts, taking out a skal'tum overhead. It tumbled to the rocky shoals below.

Galloping under the deadly volley, Tyrus reached the massive iron door and slid from his saddle. While he might ignore his exhaustion, his body could not. He fell to his knees, then his hands. Sweat streamed from his face.

His hill horse nickered and ran in tight circles to the side.

The world swam around him for a moment. Hands grabbed him and hauled him up. He glanced to right and left: Sticks and Blyth. "I'm fine," he mumbled. "My legs are just horse sore."

"Sure they are," Blyth said snidely. "Though your hands might be black as stone, your face is pale as my bare arse."

Tyrus smiled sickly. "Thanks for that comparison. As if this day wasn't horrible enough."

Sticks stood over him. "We're safe for the moment. Rest and gather yourself."

Tyrus looked beyond the giant. Hurl and Fletch had joined the d'warf archers in keeping the remaining skal'tum at bay. More and more of the d'warf legions poured from the tunnel to aid in the defense before the gate.

Wennar lumbered up to them. The older d'warf leader looked hardly winded. But his eyes marked the terror of the crossing, and his bright armor was stained with scorch marks from the dripping gore of the skal'tum. "What now?" he asked, glaring up at the solid wall of iron. "We've won here, but to what end? This gate is thicker through than the reach of my arm."

Tyrus nodded. "We have to get through. The other half of the Alasean army already wages war on the Southern Gate."

Wennar slammed a steel-gloved fist on the door in frustration. The clang echoed back to them.

Blyth shook his head. "Why didn't I think of that? We'll just knock and ask politely to be allowed inside. I'm sure they'll oblige."

Wennar frowned at the first mate, while the screeches of monsters wailed behind them. "We can't hold this post forever."

Tyrus stared dully at the iron wall, too tired to come up with an answer.

Sticks nodded toward the gate. "Captain, can you change iron to granite as easily as you've done with flesh?"

"I . . . I don't know," he answered truthfully. "But even if I could, I don't have the reserves for something this size."

His words did not seem to faze the giant. Sticks turned to Wennar. "D'warves are the best miners in the world."

The d'warf general swelled his chest. "I defy any to say otherwise."

"And you've hammers here? And pikes?"

Wennar nodded.

"Bring them to us."

Wennar glanced to Tyrus with a frown.

Understanding grew in Tyrus. He nodded to the d'warf leader. "Do as he says."

Wennar turned, bellowing orders in the d'warvish tongue.

With a sigh, Tyrus swung back to the door. "I still don't know if I have enough reserve."

"Could you draw back some magick from the d'warves who are already stone?" Sticks asked.

"Not after they were brave enough to face the petrifying magick a second time. For now, they're safer as stone. If we survive this, I'll bring them back."

Sticks simply grunted. With no other answer, Tyrus lifted his hands, still black from the backwash of his spell casting. He placed dark palms on gray iron. Closing his eyes, he pushed his energies into the iron. Slipping into that otherworldly state, he willed metal to stone.

Sounds muted; even his heart seemed to slow. But he felt petrifying force pumping out of him with each faltering beat. Before long, he knew that if he cast much more, his heart would slow to a stop, becoming stone, too.

Strangely, he found he didn't care. A part of him quailed at this lack of concern, but he could not muster a challenge to the obstinate disinterest of true granite. Or maybe the torpor was simply his own heart, and the endless doubts that settled with the same weight as stone. It was all too much. He could not do this. He was not his father's son.

Then he was suddenly ripped out of this stony lassitude. The world snapped back to him with screams, bellows, clash of steel—and pain. His arms burned with a deep fire. A moan escaped his lips, flying away like a frightened bird.

His vision focused back on Sticks, dragging him back from the iron gate. "That's enough, Captain!" the giant yelled.

Tyrus found his voice. "Did I . . . did it . . . ?"

"Look for yourself," Blyth said, standing back out of his way.

The gray iron was marred by a swath of black stone wide and high enough to ride a horse through. Already, Wennar's d'warves set to work at shattering through the stone.

Tyrus stared up at the wall of iron. They would be entering Blackhall. He had done it.

"Your arms, Captain."

Tyrus saw that from his elbows on down, he was solid granite, black and unpolished. But with the painful tingle of blood reentering a sleeping limb, his own blood drove off the magick. Slowly stone turned back to flesh.

Blyth was at his side now, giving the d'warves room to swing their hammers. "You were stone all the way to your shoulders—even your neck."

"We were afraid we'd lose you," Sticks added.

Tyrus remembered his slowing heart, his lack of will to fight the torpor of true stone. He knew how close he had been to losing himself. But instead, he mumbled, "It's nothing."

Behind him, the clang of steel exploded into a crash of rock. He swung around. The window of stone in the wall of iron had been shattered. Working quickly, the d'warves cleared the debris as the last stubborn chunks of granite shattered from the iron frame under skilled hammer blows.

Wennar sounded the horn, signaling his lieutenants to be ready to march. Tyrus and his men remounted their steeds. Tyrus kicked his horse forward. If there was a trap laid beyond, let him face it with his magick.

He ducked slightly to pass through the hole in the gate. He held his breath, not knowing what to expect, sword in one hand, the other on his reins.

He was not prepared for what he saw.

He straightened as he passed through the gate. The others followed, gasping as they clopped slowly into the main hall of the Dark Lord's lair.

Blyth voiced his own sentiments. "It's . . . it's beautiful."

His first mate's description hardly encompassed the wonders before them. The hall was as high as the gate itself, extending forever forward, but not in a stark straight course. It meandered invitingly into the distance.

From Harlequin Quail's maps, this one hall tunneled through the entire mountain, connecting the two gates and widening in the middle into a chamber described as "very, very large."

Tyrus gaped around him. He could not imagine anything larger. It was like riding into a glass-blown work of art. There was not a single corner or sharp edge anywhere. Everything was curves of polished black glass. Spiraled columns curled from floor to ceiling. Tiers and balconies, festooned in delicate glass flowers and winding garlands, rose along both walls. And throughout the hall, torches blazed, prisming into colors beyond description, turning black-glass flowers into shining bouquets. A short way down the hall, twin glass sculptures erupted from the floor. One shone with a thousand colors of azure, while its twin reflected only crimsons and reds, a fire to the other's ice. Everywhere there were such wonders of light and glass.

Tyrus stared all around, not daring to blink lest he miss something.

Sticks finally spoke, breaking the charm of the hall upon them. "No one's here."

A part of Tyrus had registered the same. Their steps were the only noise echoing down the brilliant hall. The oddity drew him back to the duty at hand.

He swung around. Through the hole in the gate, the d'warf army marched into the hall. Wennar, ever practical, was assigning guards to the position and ordering others to find the iron gate's mechanism and disable it—with the gate kept closed, it would be easy to defend the small window and guard their backs.

After a few final instructions, they were under way again. Tyrus led the party.

"Where is everyone?" Blyth asked, walking his horse beside Tyrus.

"I don't know." The beauty of the place slowly dimmed from his eyes. He recognized shops that he would see in any village: cobblers, bakers, tailors. And while their windows were full of goods, the shops were empty of both owners and patrons.

It was a beautiful graveyard.

Tensions built with each clopping step of his mount. His eyes strained, trying to discern a trap. The colors grew garish. The constant reflection went from tiresome to addling. But there was no sign of the living.

Tyrus pondered this mystery. It was as if the mountain was hollow, a shell around an empty egg. This comparison raised a shudder: another stone egg. But what would this one hatch?

According to Xin, their two forces should rendezvous at the large chamber in the middle of the concourse. Once united, they would strike downward, into the crèche of the Dark Lord himself.

Tyrus tried to reach Xin through his silver coin, but the magicks of this cursed place confounded his attempts. They were on their own until their forces joined.

As they marched, the winding hall stretched on ahead of them. They clopped across glass bridges over chasms that reflected molten fires far below. They passed gardens of statuary, like parks inside the mountain. A league passed under their hooves, then another. The passage became a blur of light and glass. Where was this central chamber?

The few voices that had been speaking or raised in quiet song had long since died away. They trudged onward.

But when they finally reached the rallying chamber, they were well into it before they realized it. The walls to either side had slowly pulled away, like arms opening. The roof arched higher, until it was as if they were no longer in a hall. Walls and roof were gone; they marched across a moonless, starless plain.

Torches had been posted and planted throughout the floor, a flaming forest that spread out in all directions.

Tyrus called a halt to allow the bulk of the d'warf army to join them in the chamber. The legion traveling with them numbered in the hundreds, but they failed to cover more than the smallest section of the entire floor.

"Over there," Hurl said from his saddle, pointing an arm.

Tyrus followed his direction. The forest of torches blazed brighter there. He unhooked the spyglass from his saddle horn. Through the glass, the blaze grew larger, more distinct. It was a massive fire pit, perhaps the center of the chamber itself.

He lowered the spyglass and frowned. "Let's make for the blaze," he said, hanging in his saddle, exhausted.

So they set out again across the vast chamber, moving as a single force, no longer restricted by walls. The distances were deceiving. They marched and marched, but the fire pit never seemed to grow any closer.

"It's like sailing toward a mountainous coastline," Blyth said. "It's farther than it seems at first glance."

Still, Tyrus refused to relent, and his persistence slowly bore fruit. The fire pit grew from a bright glow to a full blaze. The flames came from a hole in the floor. It gaped large enough to drop a small castle into its fiery depths. The heat kept them from getting too near, but at least the fires would mark their position well.

Satisfied, Tyrus called for them to make camp. He climbed from his horse and fished through his cloak's pockets for his silver coin. He should try to reach Xin . . .

Fletch appeared at his side. "The fire smokes," the Steppeman said in his thick accent.

Tyrus noted the worry in his voice and glanced up. "The fire smokes. Most do."

"Not this one," Fletch said. "Not until just now."

Frowning, Tyrus rounded his horse's flank. The fire pit was shooting vast gouts of black fumes from the lapping flames.

"Alert the others," he ordered Fletch.

As the alarm was raised, Tyrus stared up at the smoke chugging from the fire. There was no hole above the pit, no way for the smoke to escape the mountain. The cloud of fumes grew thicker, a storm cloud building above them all.

Rumbles of unease sounded around him.

Slowly the cloud unfurled wide, smoky wings and snaked out a long, vaporous neck.

Rumbles grew to shouts. Tyrus remained silent, staring. Though the shape was vague, more shadow than substance, he knew what was taking shape before him. He had heard the story from Xin already.

The name formed on his lips as crimson eyes, full of fury and malice, opened in the cloud.

"Ragnar'k."

WITH A GASP, SY-WEN JERKED UPRIGHT IN HER DRAGON'S SADDLE AS A RIP tore open inside her and something pushed through the gap. It felt like the touch of the simaltra, dark and oily, but with something familiar about the touch—something that reached to her heart.

Sy-wen, Kast sent to her, *are you all right?*

Winds rushed past, blowing back her hood and unfurling her damp hair. Screams rose from the war below, but she ignored them all and searched deeper inside her, touching the awakening darkness, opening a connection she thought gone. *Ragnar'k?*

What about him? Kast asked, reading her thoughts. He banked away from the fighting, sensing her distress.

Can't you feel him? she asked. *He's awakened.*

I don't feel anything, but he was bonded to you, not me.

"I feel his rage, smell the smoke," she said.

Where is he?

"Blackhall ..." She knew this with certainty. Letting her eyelids drift closed, she cast out her senses along this new path. Images appeared, flickering. She caught glimpses of a cavern, flames, and figures in the dark.

A man stepped forward, sword in one hand. The other hand was raised in clear threat, fingers blackened and unnatural. As he faced the dragon, Sy-wen recognized his rusty blond hair; his mustache; his sea cloak, now stained and torn. "Tyrus," she mumbled.

The pirate prince? Kast asked, intruding.

"He and the d'warves face the shadow of Ragnar'k."

What of the dragon?

The bond between Sy-wen and Ragnar'k grew stronger with her attention. She read her dragon's heart and despaired. It roiled with dark lusts and raving madness. There was no denying the reality. "He's gone over," she whispered into the wind. "He's ill'guard to the Dark Lord." With this realization, her heart broke. *Oh, my sweet giant ...*

Her anguish was felt and answered from afar. *Bonded ... come to me ... join with me.* The thoughts came from Ragnar'k, but they felt more like the simaltra. Black, oily, full of the promise of pain. There was no love, only ancient bonds of blood and death. *Come share the taste of raw meat torn from bone, listen to the wails as my fangs rip the entrails from soft bellies ... Come join with me, my bonded.*

She pulled her mind away, but she could not sever the connection. Now awakened, the dragon was linked to her.

Ragnar'k sensed her retreat. Dragon laughter followed after her. *We'll always be one.*

Sy-wen opened her eyes. Her cheeks ran with tears. Not even the winds could dry them swiftly enough.

Sy-wen? It was Kast again. His sending was a warmth to melt the ice from her veins, but shivering, she knew Ragnar'k was right. She was again chained to a demon.

"We have to stop him," she moaned.

Ragnar'k? How?

She could hardly think, her heart torn. The ancient bonds between dragon and rider, once formed, wound down to the bones of each. The loss of a dragon would often drive its rider into a despair from which there was no end. To lose your bonded was to lose yourself. But Sy-wen knew she had no choice. "Ragnar'k must be slain," she said aloud, needing to hear the words from her own lips.

She pulled up her sharkskin hood, resolved to do what no rider had ever done in the history of the mer'ai. She would slay her bonded.

Kast banked over the battle below.

As the world tilted on a wingtip, the war appeared below in all its carnage. The army of the dead, controlled by the black beast, engaged the forces of the mer'ai, the Dre'rendi, and the elv'in. It was a battle they could not win. As each ship, dragon, or warrior was slain, the monster would flow over the newly dead, enslaving them. With each death, the Dark Lord's force grew.

Their only defense proved to be fire.

As the battle had waged, it grew clear that flames could burn the oily tethers connecting the dead to their master; once severed, the puppets fell limp and lifeless. Now volleys of flaming arrows sailed through the gloom, while barrels of flaming pitch were cast from catapults in fiery arcs to explode amidst the flowing creature.

Still, the monster remained a tide of darkness, seeming without end. Where one section burned, another flowed forth.

It was a stalemate between living and dead. But the standoff could not last forever. Eventually the barrels of pitch would run out, the supply of arrows would dwindle—and the black beast would roll over them all.

"We can't wait for the others to break through," Sy-wen said. "Ragnar'k moves even now upon Tyrus and the d'warves."

What would you have us do?

"The fleets have lured the monster from the gate. With the way open, I say we chance a flight through the entrance."

Alone?

"We must try. We are of no use in this fight, but we can be vital to defending Tyrus and the others."

Kast remained silent, but Sy-wen knew he would agree. He was at heart a warrior, a Bloodrider. *We must be swift,* he finally said.

"As the wind," she echoed back to him.

Preparing himself, Kast rode a rising warm draft to gain height. Soon they were well above the fighting, near the low clouds. The slopes of black stone steamed from inner fires. *Are you ready?* he sent to her.

"Go," she whispered, leaning closer to his neck. "Just go."

Tilting forward, Kast tucked in his wings. Dragon and rider became a dark arrow pointed at the heart of Blackhall. They fell toward the fighting, gaining speed. Winds screamed past her covered ears. She vaguely sensed the ankle flaps tightening, keeping her seated in place.

The world swelled under them. The dockworks were a flaming ruin. The township ran with rivers of black flesh. Everywhere, the clash of steel divided the living from the dead. The winds reeked of burning flesh, mixed with the rotting stench of the beast itself and the sulfurous brimstone of the volcanic mountain. Sy-wen held her breath, a prayer trapped in her chest.

Then as they flew over the bulk of the dread beast, Sy-wen again felt the buzz in her skull, an echo of the simaltra that threatened to fill the empty spaces left by the tentacled creature from the egg. Sy-wen gasped at the intrusion. She was a lock that the evil here was attempting to pick.

Sy-wen?

Through their bond, she sensed Kast felt none of this. So why her, and not him? Then a thought arose ... an answer that grew to certainty in her heart. Her blood ran cold. She stared again at the beast, studying its snaking tethers, its mastery of puppetry. She now knew what she was seeing. She knew why the Dark Lord had been so desperate to enslave Ragnar'k.

"No ..." she moaned as they plummeted toward the monstrosity here.

Sy-wen? Kast's flight began to bobble, to lose focus. His worry for her was causing him to falter.

"Don't stop! Make for the gate!" She instilled her words with fire.

Kast obeyed. His wings sprang out, catching their fall and turning it into a steep sweep toward the open gate, flying over the rippling darkness below. The monster noted their passage and undulated more vigorously under them.

Sy-wen's head ached, her vision narrowed to the yawning gate before them. Beyond the threshold, fiery light glowed back at them. Torches perhaps?

Kast pulled up to pass just under the arch. Sy-wen's body pressed into the dragon under her. Below, the sea of oily flesh surged and eddied. Ahead, a tangle of tentacles shot skyward, attempting to block their passage.

Sy-wen knew that to brush that black flesh was to be enslaved. *Fly,* she urged her love. *Fly like the true dragon of my heart.*

Kast put all his love into the artistry of his flight. As they came upon the tangle, he swung atop one wingtip, then the other, wending through the grasping tentacles. He swerved and dodged through the threat, at one point rolling through the air in a spiral.

The beast might sense her, but it was blind to the dragon, unable to match its speed or careening flight. In triumph they broke past the beast and shot through the gate.

The hall beyond was huge, cavernous as the gate itself. It was a chute of melted glass lit with a thousand torches. But beyond the gate, the hall was deserted. Sy-wen sensed that the Dark Lord had emptied the entire island to man the monster back at the gate and to fuel the last of his arcane acts. Nothing lived here now but the Black Heart's dread purpose. All subterfuge at governing had fallen away, burned up in this final cause.

But to what end? What did the Dark Lord plan under the first full moon of midsummer?

Kast flew down the hall, maneuvering over bridges or under catwalks with fine movements of his wings' edges.

Back at the gate, Kast sent to her, *you knew something, something you were afraid to speak.*

"The creature . . . I know what it is."

What?

"A giant simaltra. A monstrous version of the smaller ones that possessed Hunt and me. I recognized its touch, the way it ate at my will. I think that's one reason the Dark Lord wanted Ragnar'k out of the way. The dragon's roar, ripe with magicks, could damage the creature, as it did the smaller ones back in the dungeon."

Once captured, Kast added after a stunned moment, *the dragon's magick could be used against us, too.*

"As is being done right now. Ragnar'k challenges Lord Tyrus and the others. I don't think the prince or the others have the magick to fight a demon dragon made of smoke."

Will we fare any better? Kast asked.

She remained silent as they winged down the long, dark hall, as if down the throat of some dark Leviathan that sought to swallow the world.

"We may not have magick," Sy-wen finally said, "but we have something more potent."

What's that?

She narrowed her eyes. "We have each other—and the bonds that tie all three of us together."

Can those bonds withstand the magick of the Dark Lord?

Sy-wen stared down the long hall, unsure. Her voice was faint. "Pray that they will, my love. Pray they will."

26

ER'RIL RODE DOWN THROUGH THE MISTS IN A ROPE SLING. THE WORLD HAD vanished around them. The edges of the pit were half a league away, impossible to discern through the swirling fog. Only their party was visible, clustered together on the ropes lowered from the belly of the *Windsprite*.

Elena swung at his side, wrapped in her cloak, near enough for him to reach out and touch. They had been dropping for an endless time; was there any bottom to this pit?

Even sounds failed to reach them. As they had dropped away from the ship, the echoes of battle—screeches, bellows, roars, and cries—had faded along with the world. The mists seemed to wipe everything away.

Er'ril studied the others, spread around him like so many ripe fruits on a vine. No one spoke. The mists were strangely warm, dampening skin and clothes to an oily sheen. They reeked of sulfur and burned blood.

Er'ril glanced upward. The ship had vanished, lost in the cursed fog. Earlier, the *Windsprite* had dropped to the level of the mists. From the stern hold, ropes and pulleys lowered the party through the belly hatches. They had dropped away unseen—Joach's magick had worked its illusion.

Elena's brother swung nearby, clutching his staff. The length of gray petrified wood shone as pale as new snow, though streaked through with veins of crimson, Joach's own blood.

Around him, the others watched the mists, packs in place, ready for an attack. Weapons glinted in the gloom. Tol'chuk bore a hammer, as did Magnam. Harlequin Quail twiddled a dagger in his fingers, looking almost bored. Jaston, Fardale, and Thorn all bore short swords. Meric and Nee'lahn, hanging side by side, remained weaponless, bearing only the magick inside them.

"The moon rises," Elena whispered beside him. Though her words were no more than a breathless utterance, all heard. Sounds swirled strangely within this unnatural cloud.

Er'ril swung to face her. She opened her cloak enough to reveal where the Blood Diary was tucked. The top of the gilt rose poked above the pocket's edge, glowing as bright as a star.

Frowning, Er'ril glanced upward again. "But the sun still shines," he mumbled.

She nodded, closing her cloak. "A fool's moon." She huddled back to herself. "I dare not open the book until there is solid footing."

He nodded. The magick of Cho's release could alert whatever lurkers hid in the mists below. It was best to wait to consult the spirit of the book until they were safer. Hanging on ropes, they felt exposed, regardless of the thick mists that hid them.

Jaston spoke from the side, sheathing his sword. "Cassa returns." Off to the left, a small winged shape appeared, spiraling up from below. She flapped and glided up to Jaston, settling into the swamper's arms. She was clearly exhausted, her tiny face pale, her wings trembling.

"Cassa?" Jaston whispered, drawing a damp strand from the child's face.

"My connection is thread thin," the child said in a voice far older than her small frame. "I don't know how much longer I can maintain this hold."

"What have you seen?" Er'ril asked.

The child's eyes flicked to him. "The mists end in another forty spans or so, opening into clear air. I dared not stay for very long."

"What did you see?" Elena asked. All eyes were on Jaston and the child, but Er'ril kept a watch around them.

"The mists swirl about the height of a castle tower above the bottom of the pit. Empty rock lies below, but it appears natural, not dug with tools. I spotted stalagmites and outcroppings that seem to have been there for ages."

Er'ril spoke. "They must have dug down and broken into the cavern system under the ancient school of the Chyric mages."

"Where the rock'goblins lived," Elena mumbled.

"I saw no goblins," Cassa said faintly. "There was nothing moving down below."

"Nothing's there?" Er'ril asked. He frowned deeply. Could all of this have been for nothing, a trick to lure Elena away from the true battle at Blackhall? Er'ril's eyes settled with suspicion on the small form of Harlequin Quail, but the man wore a frown that matched his own.

The swamp child spoke again. "The pit lay empty, but I spied a tunnel leaving the space. It glowed fiercely with a most strange light."

Er'ril crinkled his brow. So something *was* down there. "We'll proceed cautiously. We all must be alert."

Mumbles of assent answered him, but Harlequin quipped, "And here I was planning on going in blindfolded."

Er'ril ignored the man. As they continued to drop, winding down through the mists, even the gloomy glow above faded away. They traveled through darkness for an endless stretch, until slowly a silvery shine lit the mists under them. "Be ready," he whispered to the others, as a freshening breeze washed across his damp skin.

Then they were dropping into open air. Below appeared a cavern floor, littered with broken pillars of rock, boulders, and jagged stalagmites. Just at the edges, Er'ril could make out the lowermost step of the excavation here. They had reached the bottom.

And as Cassa Dar had described, the floor remained empty. But Er'ril did not relax his guard: There were plenty of places for creatures to hide. And directly ahead, a tunnel cast out a silvery sheen almost too bright to look upon. It was a constant, substantial light that drew stark shadows across the cavern floor.

Er'ril pointed to a pile of boulders. "We should—"

His rope sling jerked, almost tumbling him from his seat. He clutched at the rope with his free hand. The others were similarly bobbled; Elena swung against him. He grabbed for her, but she jostled away.

"What's happening?" Jaston called out. His swamp child, startled by the swaying, now winged around him in panicked circles.

"Something's attacking our ropes!" Magnam answered.

As if confirming his words, they all began plummeting toward the stone floor, not as fast as if their ropes had been sliced, but much more quickly than their slow descent a moment ago. And with each breath, they fell faster and faster.

"Watch the rocks!" Er'ril yelled as the floor flew up toward them.

Like so many crashing boulders, they struck the floor. Cries arose from among the party. Er'ril took the brunt of his landfall with his legs, then rolled to his shoulder, dispersing the momentum of his landing. He was on his feet in his next breath. He spotted Elena a few steps away. Blood dribbled from her hairline. He rushed to her. "Are you all right?"

She nodded. "Just a scrape. I'm fine." She wiped at the blood and stared around the boulder-littered floor. "The others . . ."

Meric ran up with Nee'lahn. Both seemed unharmed.

"Everyone back!" the elv'in called, his frantic eyes on the mists above. The ropes continued to snake out of the sky, whistling downward. "The ropes weren't cut! The ship—the *Windsprite*—it falls!"

Er'ril gaped upward as Meric's words struck him. Then he grabbed Elena by the arm. "Hurry!" he cried. "Make for the walls!"

They all fled through the forest of stony pillars and jumbled rocks. From above came the ominous sound of splintering wood and the snap of sails in a gale. It grew to fill the pit.

And still they ran. Thorn and Fardale had slipped into half-wolf form, bounding away. Er'ril saw Joach helping Jaston; the swamper limped on one leg, his face gone greenish. Past them, Tol'chuk loped with Magnam at his side.

A crash echoed, sounding directly overhead.

"Seek cover!" Er'ril shouted.

He whirled Elena behind a boulder, sliding to his knees, pulling her under him. He covered his head just as he caught a glimpse of the broken bulk of the ship crashing out of the mists, sails ripped and flapping like the arms of a plummeting man.

He ducked as the explosion of wood on stone blasted across the pit. Timber and debris shattered out, striking the walls with splintered impacts. Just past their boulder, a huge wooden pulley wheel bounced and rolled by. It smashed against the wall, shattering to tinder.

As the echoes of the crash died away, Er'ril jerked to his feet, peering past the boulder. In the center of the pit, the blasted ruins of the proud windship lay half hidden in a plume of silt and rock dust. Small fires already licked greedily at the broken timbers, ignited from shattered barrels of oil. The iron keel was a twisted arm protruding from the broken field.

The others rose from hiding places, faces pale with shock. They slowly gathered, picking their way across the debris, shaken and bruised. Meric looked especially stricken.

"If any of us survive this," Er'ril mumbled, stepping to his side, "we'll bury the crew with honors."

"If there be any bodies here," Tol'chuk said. The og're stepped forward, dragging the upper torso of a monster, one wing still attached to a shoulder. The beast's bald head, peaked ears, and fanged muzzle were well known to all.

"Skal'tum," Elena said.

Joach blanched, Jaston still leaning on his shoulder. "My illusion must have failed."

Elena shook her head. "It lasted long enough to get us here."

"Or *trap* us here," Harlequin Quail said. He stared at the ruins. "We can't say we exactly dropped in unannounced."

Confirming this, screams echoed through the mists from above.

Er'ril stepped forward. "To the tunnel! Now!" He led them off.

As they quickly marched, Jaston pointed upward. "Cassa Dar has gone to scout the tunnel ahead, to see what lies at its end."

Er'ril spotted the small winged child gliding toward the entrance.

As Jaston hobbled to the side, Elena mumbled, "We already know what lies at the end, don't we?"

Er'ril saw the same recognition in Meric, Fardale, and Tol'chuk. There was no forgetting this tunnel.

"We've come full circle," Meric said in hushed tones. "All of us again, missing only the mountain man this time."

Er'ril nodded. Of the original gathering, only Kral was absent, his war charger left behind at the og're encampment. Er'ril stared ahead. Long ago, at the end of this tunnel, the group had discovered the crystal statue of De'nal, the boy-mage who had been one of the three to give their lives to the forging of the Blood Diary. That statue was gone, its Chyric essence given up to ignite the book's magick. Now, Er'ril sensed with icy certainty that a new statue lay beyond this tunnel—not of crystal, but of black stone laced with forked veins of silver.

An ebon'stone statue . . . the last Weirgate.

"Full circle," Er'ril repeated as they reached the threshold to the tunnel, all of them limned in the silvery light. Elena's hand found his. They had walked this path together once before, a girl-child and her knight. Now they would face it together again, joined by more than just oaths and prophecy.

Elena's fingers squeezed his. He felt the love in the small gesture.

Down the tunnel, a winged shape disappeared into the glare.

Er'ril stepped to follow. "It's time to end this."

AS THEY STARTED DOWN THE PASSAGE, MOGWEED SAT WITHIN HIS DARK prison, staring out with Fardale. With everyone distracted by the descent into the pit and the fall of the windship, no one noticed the strange twist of circumstances.

Fardale marched with Thorn, their senses focused outward. They kept their bodies fluid, ready to transform at a moment's notice. And with Fardale's attention on the tunnel, even he failed to note the change in their condition.

Mogweed grinned darkly. No walls confined him now. He could control the body the pair wore. To confirm this, he carefully shifted Fardale's foot to trip on a loose piece of shale. His brother, ever agile, kept his balance and continued on, none the wiser.

I am free! Mogweed realized, barely containing his glee.

On this strange day, when the full moon and the sun shared the same sky, the walls between the two brothers had fallen. It was neither true night, nor true day. Both sun and moon ruled the skies, as the two brothers did this one form.

But only one brother was aware of the change. And as Mogweed had learned long ago, there was much power in secrets.

He settled into his cell. He would wait until the time was right, and watch for a moment when one last betrayal could win his true freedom.

I will be free of you yet, Brother.

CASSA DAR LAY IN HER BED IN CASTLE DRAKK, A SHADOW OF HER FORMER self. Maintaining the connection to her creation far to the north had taxed her body and spirit. Her skin sagged, her color had paled, and even her breathing was a ragged rasp. But worst of all, she felt her ties to her own lands fraying. Her well of elemental powers was running dry.

Day and night, children came to her chamber, feeding her, bringing water and wine. But there was no balm for the ebb of her spiritual energy. She was spread too thin, stretched across half the world.

She closed her eyes and drifted between the boggy damp of her castle tower and the steamy warmth of the shrouded pit. She knew she risked her life in this endeavor, but the entire world was in peril. She would not simply wait for the end here in her isolated castle. She had spent centuries hiding in her swamps, pretending she had a full life with all the creatures of her lands. It was only after finding Jaston that she had remembered the world beyond her bogs and marshes. And once awakened, she knew she could hide no longer. The Dark Lord had enslaved her people and consigned her to this lonely tower. If this was the final battle with the fiend, then—risk or not—she would act with all her will and substance.

In her castle chamber, she lay as weak as a babe atop her blankets. But far to the north, she felt the wind in her wings, the flow of currents through her hair, the strength of young muscle and the certainty of firm bone. She glided down a tunnel shimmering with silver light.

She knew this light. It bathed her, and for the first time since entering the misty pit, her connection to her swamp child grew stronger rather than weaker. The glow was the shine of pure elemental energy, untainted. The swamp child flew through the light like a fish through a bright stream.

Through her connection to the child, this energy flowed back to Cassa Dar. She sighed in her chamber as the well inside her slowly filled. She had never felt such purity. Tears rolled down her cheeks. She knew where she headed; she had read of it in her texts. Ahead lay the confluence of elemental flows, a mixing of channels draining from both the Northern and Southern Fangs. It could be nothing else.

She was drawn toward the light like a moth to flame. Her essence ran out along her connection to join more fully with her swamp child. Without hesitation, she shot out the passage and into a vast chamber beyond. The roof arched high overhead, while the floor was a great bowl under her. It was a spherical chamber, dug from the heart of the granite highlands. Below her, the basin of the bowl churned with a whirlpool of silver, two shades of brilliance swirling toward the center, stark against the black granite. The pattern reminded her of the whorl of mists atop the pit here, a slow eddy spiraling downward.

She wafted out over the glowing basin, a quarter league across. On the far side, she could discern dark openings, other tunnels and passages. She also noted that the edges of the silver pool were fringed with bleached bones, like so much driftwood on a seashore. They were piled high, but the thickest patches were washed up near the tunnel entrance.

But her attention drifted from this foulness and focused back on the pool. It was empty—except for a dark figure in the exact center—a black well into which the swirl of silver drained.

Cassa Dar arced away from it, sensing the danger. Even from this distance, she could make out the black wings, spread wide, and the cowled head lifted in menace. Without a doubt, it was the Wyvern Weirgate, the last of the foul sculptures. She banked back toward the tunnel to report her discoveries when movement caught her eye.

She spiraled back around, hovering. A figure labored near the statue. He searched about with casual indifference, bending on a knee here, leaning to inspect something there. His movements suggested he was unaware of her. She narrowed her eyes, focusing her vision.

Maybe it was the clean well of power swelling inside her, but she dared glide a bit farther over the swirling bowl for a closer look.

It was a mistake.

From her vantage high over the floor, she saw the trap a moment too late, and like a fly in a spider's web, she was caught. With her attention on the whorls of silver and the danger at its center, she had failed to note a matching swirl of darkness across the bow of the roof, a dark reflection of the one below.

From this black eddy, tendrils of power lashed out and down, snatching her in midair. The more she struggled, the tighter the cords wrapped. She was dragged toward the roof, caught as firmly as an ant in molasses. She stared toward the dark whorl before her. The center, positioned directly over the Wyvern Weirgate, was a dark hole in the ceiling, leading to where she didn't know.

Then she spotted the slight dribble of water trickling out of the hole and falling toward the Weirgate below. The hole must extend all the way to the surface. But why? To what purpose? Could she escape by that route?

She looked down as she swirled higher in an ever-tightening circle. The figure by the statue had stopped its inspection and stared up at her. Closer now, she made out the scarred ruin of the man's face. A stubble of black hair grew out from the roiled flesh. He smiled up at her, his eyes burned sockets. He bore a staff, a length of pure ebon'stone. Cassa Dar had heard of Shorkan's burning as he fled an Entrapment ring. With certainty, here stood the architect of the trap that had snared her, a trap meant to snare the others who followed.

As if to confirm this, he lifted his staff and stirred it through the air. Her trapped form spun faster toward the malignant center of the whorl, where damnation surely lay.

She knew she should withdraw her connection to the child, sever it before she herself was caught, too. But if she broke that thin tether, then she could not warn Jaston and the others of the trap set to snare them.

That wasn't an option.

So she did the only other thing she could. She poured more of herself into her creation. Shorkan thought he had caught himself a small child of middling talents. She meant to see how he dealt with a full wit'ch.

From her bed, she cast out her essence, leaving only the thinnest thread to follow back. She flowed in a heartbeat into her creation, filling it with her poisonous magicks. The dark tendrils that held her sizzled and frayed from contact with the venom oozing from her.

Down below, the smile on the darkmage's face dimmed to wary confusion. He pointed his staff at her, and the tendrils of darkness thrashed, renewing their assault.

She ignored the cords and continued to pour herself into her vessel. The child grew among the writhing black snakes, maturing from child to woman in a matter of breaths. The childish trace of consciousness faded, replaced with her own.

Mama, the child called to her as she faded. Cassa touched her essence. *I love you, my sweetness. Now sleep.*

Then the child was gone.

Below, Shorkan hissed, his words easily reaching her. "Wit'ch! You'll never escape with mere elemental trickery!"

Cassa Dar stared down, a bare span from the whorl's center. She smiled calmly, done with running, done with hiding. "Who said I was escaping, mage?"

She opened her mouth and vomited the poison from her belly. It was not only her childish form that had matured, but the creature inside her. The swamp child, now woman, was nothing but a skin. The reptile inside was her true connection here.

Cassa Dar fell out of the trap. Shedding from her skin, she dropped in her true form. The king adder, grown to its full length, writhed through the air to land in a tangle about the darkmage.

Shorkan screamed as she wrapped tight coils around him, writhing up to face the scarred visage. A forked tongue hissed from her lips. She opened her jaws, unhinging fangs as long as a dragon's. Poison flowed from the venom sacs at the base of the snake's skull—and from the core of her being.

She knew she was no match for the darkmage, but she could still strike and do damage. She hissed, spitting poison into his face, then struck as he dodged the spray. Her fangs sank deep into his neck, pumping all the poison she could before he lashed out at her.

Latched to the demon, she felt the venom knock him to his knees, but what would have killed an ordinary man in less than a heartbeat, he survived. She heard a spell tumble from his lips.

Her coils suddenly ignited with a searing fire. Dark flames flared out from the mage—balefire. She knew her death was but a moment away. But still she drained her poison into his being. She heard him gasp, fall to his hands.

As the snake form incinerated, she smiled a venomous grin and fled away—but not down the thread that led to her body back at Castle Drakk. She knew she'd never make it there. That bridge was burned behind her. Instead, she fled to the only place her heart knew well.

A heart that beat in rhythm to her own.

JASTON FELL TO HIS KNEES IN THE TUNNEL. HE KNEW THE MOMENT SHE passed beyond. "Cassa . . ."

The others rushed to his side, but he was blind to them, deaf to them. Her essence filled all his senses. The scent of moonblossom swelled around him. The taste of her lips appeared on his tongue, the brush of her hand on his cheek. "Cassa, what have you done?"

What had to be . . . She bathed him in all she was, holding him nearer than she ever could in life. *But fear not. Hold me in your heart; remember our time. I'll always be no more than a breath away.*

"No," he moaned.

Now go. You all must hurry. Images filled his head: a trap untangled, a wounded demon, weakened for only the moment. *Fight for the world, my love. It is too beautiful to pass into darkness.*

"Cassa, wait . . ."

Her breath was a kiss on his neck. *I love you. I always will.*

Then, like a brush of wind, she vanished. He held a fist against his chest, sobbing, wondering if his heart could continue to beat. But it did . . .

He lifted his head and faced the others. "She's gone."

ER'RIL KNELT OVER JASTON AS THE INJURED MAN EXPLAINED WHAT HE HAD learned. "If Cassa Dar has indeed wounded Shorkan, then we must hurry." he said. "Now may be our only chance. We cannot let her sacrifice be in vain."

Harlequin spoke from near the back of the group. "I'd say we have no choice." He faced the other way down the tunnel. From the direction of the pit, screams still echoed to them, but now the scrabble of claws on rocks sounded, too. If the skal'tum legions were headed down the tunnel, the only way was forward.

"Hurry!" Er'ril ordered.

Nee'lahn and Meric moved to Jaston's side. "You go ahead. Let us slow the monsters."

"Just the three of you?" Elena asked.

The two elementals shone in the silvery light, faces bright. Nee'lahn glanced to Meric, who wore a sly smile. "We'll be enough. Now go. See to the Wyvern and its protector."

Er'ril nodded and started down the hall. "Tol'chuk, take the lead with Magnam and Harlequin, but don't leave the tunnel until we're all together."

Tol'chuk grunted his assent and headed out at a faster clip.

Er'ril turned to Elena. "The Blood Diary—maybe we should keep it closed until we've destroyed the Wyvern Gate."

He read the understanding in her face. Cho had been growing wilder lately, especially when near her lost brother, Chi. If the Wyvern Gate lay ahead, then so did Chi. From Elena's narrowed gaze, she clearly remembered what had happened when the group had confronted the Manticore Gate. Cho had possessed Elena, taking her over and almost killing her in the process.

Er'ril could not risk a repeat of that event. Until this last gate was broken and Chi was free, he did not trust the spirit of the book. It put its own needs and desires above all else, even Elena's safety. And in the battle to come, he had enough to contend with.

Elena patted her cloak. "I'll only open it once the last gate is broken." As she spoke, her other hand closed over the rose hilt of her blood sword. She had enough magick at her command already.

Er'ril glanced behind them. The shape-shifters flanked Joach. Elena's brother clutched his staff, its length already white with the touch of his bare fingers.

Er'ril frowned. Brother and sister ... both bore blood weapons. He prayed they were strong enough to control such talismans.

Joach met his gaze unflinching, but the smallest blush of shame colored his cheeks. The two had shared few words since the second demise of Greshym, the trust between them wounded.

A hiss drew his attention back around. Tol'chuk waved them forward; the others had reached the tunnel exit. Magnam and Harlequin crouched by some rubble, haloed by the silver light.

Er'ril hurried to join them. Beyond the exit, an impossibly vast chamber opened. The floor was a wide basin of silver, while across the roof flowed a similar whorl, this one black as ink, a shadow of the one below.

"The Wyvern Gate," Tol'chuk said, pointing a thick arm toward the center of the silver pool.

Though a distance away, the black shape of the ebon'stone bird could not be mistaken. At the statue's feet, a figure cloaked in black lay facedown on the floor, stark against the silver.

"Shorkan." Er'ril stood and started into the chamber. To reach the brilliant lake, he had to cross a shore of granite, piled with yellowed bones. "Elena, keep behind us. I don't know if Shorkan is feigning his collapse or is truly wounded."

He didn't get any acknowledgment, so he glanced behind him. Elena stood frozen at the tunnel's exit. Her gaze was not on the Wyvern Gate, nor on the collapsed darkmage, but on the bones underfoot.

"Elena," he tried again.

Her only reaction was a widening of her eyes. "The bones . . . They're goblin bones."

Er'ril finally noticed the piled limbs and skulls. From the tiny size and pugged muzzles and fangs, Elena was clearly right. "Rock'goblins."

"The ones I slew."

He crossed back and took her arm, walking her through the graveyard of bones. "We must move forward," he said, pulling her away from those painful memories.

Once past the boneyard, Elena shuddered, shaking off the shock. They stood at the edge of the bright lake.

"Elemental silver," Joach said, "like the river beneath the Southwall of the Wastes. The energy here is tremendous."

Er'ril stepped onto the silver cautiously. "The Dark Lord's minions must have scoured through the granite, exposing the source. Here is where they mean to tap into the heart of the world and corrupt it."

"Unless we can stop them," Elena said with returning vigor.

Er'ril nodded. "Everyone stay alert. We don't know how effective Cassa Dar's poison was on the mage."

Fardale and Thorn melted in their cloaks, becoming a blend of wolf and man. "We'll run forward. If the monster is feigning his weakness, let us be the ones to discover it. We can move the quickest to escape any hidden trap."

Er'ril waved them on. Before he could lower his arm, the pair of shapeshifters were already off. They raced across the silver lake, short swords in hand, but prepared to shift fully into beasts if necessary.

"Let's go!" Er'ril said and followed at a fast clip. He made sure Elena stayed behind their phalanx of weapons.

Harlequin hung back with Er'ril, to stand on Elena's other side, a pair of daggers in hand. The small man's eyes, narrowed with worry, were on the roof.

Er'ril glanced up as they crossed the silver lake, passing under the dark reflection. Though he bore no magick himself, he sensed the enmity pulsing from that darkness.

"If the gate is already here," Elena said, "why have they not already tainted the confluence? What are they waiting for?"

"The moon," Harlequin answered, pointing toward the roof. "There's a hole up there, right above the statue. You can see the light."

Er'ril frowned. Now brought to his attention, he could indeed see a feeble glow in the center of the dark whorl. The storm above must be breaking, the cloud cover opening.

Elena spoke, her voice anxious. "They're waiting for the full moon to shine down upon the Weirgate—but why?"

"There's power in moonlight ... power from the Void," Harlequin said. "Remember our trip from the castle to the Western Reaches? They must need that power to fuel their corruption."

Joach glanced back to them. "Fardale's reached Shorkan." He pointed his staff.

"Hang back a moment," Er'ril warned. His party was halfway between the shore and the statue. Across the way, Fardale edged closer to the prone mage, while Thorn loped in a wary circle around Shorkan and the statue. The Wyvern Gate loomed over all, a dark sentinel of black wing, beak, and claw.

"Let's see what they discover."

MOGWEED TREMBLED IN HIS CELL, CURSING HIS BROTHER'S BRAVERY. HE HAD no desire to face the demon mage alone. Fardale edged closer to the sprawled figure, growling deep in his throat—half man, half wolf—ready to sprint away at a moment's notice. A long black staff rested an arm's length from the scarred hand of the monster; his scowled face was turned away.

Fardale stepped nearer, while Thorn circled around. The pair approached the mage from opposite sides.

Mogweed cringed in the darkness. He knew he could break into control of this body whenever he wanted. With Fardale distracted, it would be simple. But what would he do then? There was nowhere to run.

He fought against his rising panic. *Think,* he screamed to himself. *There must be a way to escape!*

Then it was too late. On the silver floor, the black staff slid with a snap into the mage's hand. With a surge, the darkmage flew to his feet with a howl of rage.

A trap!

Fardale scrambled back. "Run!" he yelled to Thorn, twisting around to do the same.

But before he could even turn, the darkmage thrust up his staff. Tendrils of darkness lashed from above, snaring both wolves. Fardale was jerked off his feet and reeled into the air. Mogweed sensed their certain doom.

Across the silver lake, the others stumbled back as cords sought them, too.

Shorkan held his staff toward the roof. His cowl had fallen back, revealing a swath of ropy scars and burned-out sockets. As his lips moved, he wobbled on his feet. His staff trembled. It seemed his collapse had not been entirely feigned.

As the darkmage fought for control, the snaking cords of darkness spasmed. Flowing like warmed oil, Fardale melted from cloak and pack, out of their grip. *Thorn!* he sent to his mate. *Do as I do!*

Mogweed held his breath as Fardale streamed to the floor and formed a wolf, like wax poured into a mold. The body they wore screamed in protest, sorely used. There were limits to their transforming abilities; their flesh could only ply so much before needing to rest.

Beyond Shorkan's shoulder, Thorn clearly struggled. She had escaped the snare of darkness but had to fight her gelled body into a snowy wolf. She was clearly exhausted, too.

Shorkan turned to her, his staff lowering.

No! Fardale cried, leaping forward. He struck the mage and knocked him to a knee, then rolled up, ready to defend his mate.

The fur on Fardale's shoulder sizzled from contact with the malignant demon. The burn seared into Mogweed. He cried out in his silent prison.

Fardale crouched before the darkmage, hackles raised, teeth bared. *Thorn! Run to the others!*

The attack had given his mate time to finish her shift. She stood, a snowy wolf on a frozen silver lake. Then in a flash of fur, she was gone, flying away. *Hurry, Fardale!* she cast back at him.

Mogweed willed the same, but his brother refused to risk his mate again. He stood his ground, allowing her time to escape.

The mage regained his feet, staff swinging.

Fardale! Run! Mogweed screamed internally. He reached for control of the body. If his brother wouldn't flee, he would!

As he sprang from his cell, a searing blast of darkfire shot over his shoulder from behind. Fardale ducked as the spray of black flames struck the mage square in the chest and threw him against the ebon'stone statue. Shorkan spun his staff and broke the lance of darkfire.

Joach stood a hundred steps away, his staff pointed at the mage. Shorkan gained his feet, but with his attention focused on the boy, the snaking tendrils were in disarray. From the roof, the cloaks and packs of the shape-shifters tumbled to the floor, no longer held.

The rest of their party flanked Joach. Only Elena held back, protected. Thorn reached the others, spinning on her haunches to rejoin the attack.

"You'll never win, Shorkan!" Er'ril called to him. "We've more than enough magick to withstand you!"

Shorkan laughed. "That will be seen, Brother! But either way, you are too late. The moon is risen. Your time here is at an end."

He stamped his staff on the silver floor. All around the edges of the lake, bones jittered and clattered. "It is time to pay in blood for your own misdeeds!" Shorkan called out, lifting his staff high. "To face your own transgressions!"

From the piles, impossible constructions of bone formed. They clambered up as if they had merely been asleep, sprawled and sunning themselves on the shore. Now they arose and scuttled onto the lake, some small and quick, like crabs. Others towered twice the size of an og're, all thick-boned, bearing clubs topped by skulls. Still others ran on all fours like dogs, but with maws full of tiny shattered bones.

The legion converged on the group, encircling the smaller party. Er'ril shouted orders as the monsters closed in.

Shorkan laughed again. He spun his staff toward the roof, readying to attack from above, too. The party would be assaulted from all sides.

Fardale gathered himself. Clearly the wolf had been forgotten during the exchange or was perhaps considered to be no threat. Either way, Fardale meant to prove otherwise. Mogweed couldn't allow that. It was sure death.

As Fardale leaped, so did Mogweed—out from his cell and into the body. His brother was caught by surprise and tumbled back into the empty cell. Mogweed counted on Fardale to believe it was the natural transition from day to night; the sun had to be near to setting anyway. It would take him a few moments to realize the lack of walls to his cell. By that time, Mogweed intended to be away.

But the transition was neither smooth nor unnoticed. Fardale had already begun his lunge. His legs, interrupted in midleap, went out from under him before Mogweed gained control. His frantic motions drew an eye.

Shorkan turned to him. Mogweed backpedaled away but tripped on his own abandoned cloak and pack. A sneer stretched the pale lips of the mage.

"It's time a dog was beaten soundly by its master."

THE WORLD WAS ALL BONES. ELENA CROUCHED AS THE MONSTROUS CON-structions lumbered and skittered around them. Tol'chuk struck his hammer at a beast, shattering through its shoulder, but the broken bones re-formed, flying back into position.

Joach sprayed out jets of balefire, turning all in his path to ash. But from the ash, bone re-formed and shook back into monster and beast.

Their own party, however, did not fare as well. Magnam bled from a shoulder wound, pierced through by a sharpened shard. Harlequin Quail limped on his left leg. Thorn raced through the towering beasts, yanking out bones, snagging and toppling creatures. One of her ears was torn and bleeding.

Er'ril fell back to her side. "Force alone will not win our way through here. We'll need your magick."

They had been holding her in reserve. Now she straightened, palms bloody with coldfire and wit'ch fire. She had seen the result of Joach's balefire, so she kept her right fist closed and opened her left. With a skill born from winters of bloodshed, she cast out twines of coldfire, careful of her companions.

"Everyone down!" Er'ril yelled to the others.

They obeyed, dropping to hands and knees, even bellies.

Elena sent out a wash of coldfire over them, all around her, freezing the bones of the creatures to the marrow. The damp air iced around them, frosting all. The lumbering monsters slowed and stopped their attack.

"Well done, Elena." Er'ril said.

Harlequin Quail lifted his head, staring around him. "Yes, very good. We've built our own prison of ice and bone."

Elena saw that they were indeed encased in a pen of bone.

"We can shatter a path to the gate," Er'ril said and motioned Tol'chuk up with his hammer.

Elena kept her flow of magick trickling to the bone army; she did not want them awakening. But linked to the monstrosities, she sensed a presence, thoughts that fed back through her connection into her heart. Frowning, she focused her attention inward.

Words formed in her head, whispers in an ancient tongue, but understood by her heart: *Lightbringer, stealer of spirits*. She knew who spoke.

"Mother above . . . not again . . ."

THE WHISPERS CONTINUED TO FEED INTO HER. A HANDFUL OF VOICES GREW to hundreds—the spirits of the rock'goblins, those slain at her hand. Drawn to her magick, they had burned to death in her light. Their spirits were still here! They had never passed beyond.

All along, she had thought her crime upon these simple folk to be over and done, a tragedy of the past. She gaped at this army. It had never ended! They were trapped and tormented, and now foully used by the darkmage, their spirits twisted back to their own bones.

Shorkan's earlier words echoed in her heart. *It is time to pay in blood for your own misdeeds . . . face your own trangressions.*

The crash of a hammer sounded on her left. Inside her, it was answered by a howl of pain. Not one voice, but many. Even the squeals of young ones, bleating cries for help.

"They feel it," she moaned, falling to her knees.

Er'ril heard her, saw her fall.

Another hammer blow set up more cries. They filled the hollow ache in her own heart.

Er'ril clutched her. "What's wrong?"

"We're killing them all over again."

She stared up into his face. "Stop Tol'chuk. It has to stop!"

"Why?"

"Do it!" she cried fiercely, tears springing to her eyes. "If you love me, stop him now!"

Er'ril stared for a breath longer, his face worried, but he leaped away.

Elena cut off her magick, hugging her arms around her, rocking. "No more . . . ," she muttered.

Around them, the bone prison remained, but frozen limbs began to creak and pop, fighting through her fading magick.

"What do you want us to do?" Er'ril asked as the bone army began to reawaken.

Elena shook her head. "I don't know."

SHORKAN STEPPED NEARER TO MOGWEED. "YOU SHALL BE THE FIRST AMONG your companions to suffer."

Mogweed tried to scramble away, but his feet remained tangled in his cloak, his pack under one knee. He struggled to pull his tired flesh from wolf back to man, but it resisted. He fought harder. His only hope lay in freeing his tongue. He had to tell the demon that they served the same master, but his tired flesh was sluggish to obey.

The staff lowered toward him.

He sensed Fardale urging him. *Fight!* his brother seemed to yell.

But Mogweed was no warrior. His mind spun, settling instead on another way of convincing the mage. With his limbs half shifted, he grabbed his pack and ripped it open. His crude hand pawed into its contents, digging deep to the small ebon'stone egg given to him by the Dark Lord. It was meant for Greshym, now twice dead. Surely the egg contained some dark magick, a tool to have helped the mage escape their captivity. Mogweed lifted his prize, struggling to speak.

Shorkan's scarred features widened with shock.

Mogweed fought his dull flesh. He gurgled out words. "For you!" He rolled the egg toward the mage. Surely this would prove his loyalty.

The response was not what he expected. Shorkan howled, backing away, the length of his black staff ignited into black flames. "No!" But the prior attacks had weakened the demon. Now it was his turn to stumble.

The egg reached the mage's toes. As it bumped against Shorkan, the egg hatched with a boom, exploding as if thunder itself had been trapped inside the stone shell. The silver lake shattered like thin ice under the darkmage's feet. Cracks skittered from his heels. The ground shook.

Mogweed cowered back as realization dawned: The egg had not been meant as a boon, but as a doom.

Trails of smoke shot up from the egg, wrapping over the demon. Where they touched, flesh and clothes turned to dark crystal. The mage continued a stumbling retreat, but his legs were already hardened. He fell with a crash, and still the smoke pursued him.

The fire in his ebon'stone staff died as his scarred fingers turned to dark crystal. A scream rose from the demon, ending in a tinkling cry. Then after another breath, even this ended.

Mogweed pushed to his feet—still half man, half wolf. Sprawled before him on the silver lake was a statue made of dark crystal. Though he couldn't read Fardale's thoughts, he sensed the confusion, the shock, and also the silent question. *What have you done, Brother?*

Mogweed shook his head. He had no answer. He stared up at the looming Weirgate and slowly backed away. Inside he sensed his brother's quiet suspicions. *Were you betraying us or saving us?*

ER'RIL LIFTED HIS SWORD AS THE BONE ARMY CREAKED FROM ITS FROZEN prison, lumbering toward them again. The others backed to his side. Despite Elena's protests, he meant to fight. He would not let her fall.

A huge bone beast clambered from among its icy brethren. It towered twice Er'ril's height and bore a sickle of broken bone in each clawed hand. It stalked forward.

Elena reached for Er'ril's cloak. "They're not demonic, just victims of the darkmage."

He ignored her. He knew that Shorkan must have set this trap, knowing it would undermine Elena when she most needed to be strong. But he would not let Shorkan win. Er'ril had borne guilt that stretched centuries. For Elena, he would bear even more. Er'ril stepped forward to meet the giant.

"No . . . ," Elena moaned.

As if it heard her, the bone monster froze. A tremble passed through its frame. Then like a house of tumbling cards, it fell apart, clattering down. Bones bounced across the silver floor. The two sickles shattered as they struck.

All around, the army fell apart, collapsing into bony ruins.

Er'ril stood amid the chaos.

"What happened?" Tol'chuk asked.

Elena rose to her feet. "The spell that bound them. It . . . it's gone!"

Er'ril looked beyond the boneyard. What new trick was this? He searched out his brother. Under the gaze of the Wyvern Gate, he saw Fardale collapsed to his knees. Before him lay the darkmage, unmoving on the silver lake.

"Something's happened," Magnam said.

Narrowing his eyes, Er'ril waved them forward. They pushed and kicked through the piled bones; then Er'ril led the way across the lake, sword in hand. Elena followed, her eyes still haunted.

As they neared the Weirgate, the fate of his brother became clear. The darkmage's body had turned to pure crystal, black as sin and hard as ice. Er'ril felt his own body growing numb, but he forced his limbs forward. He stared down at the face of an enemy, the face of a brother he had once loved. He read the lines of torture in the ravaged countenance. Er'ril suspected the agony wasn't all the pain of this crystallization. In those lines, he read the anguish of his brother's true heart.

"Shorkan," he whispered.

"He's gone to crystal," Elena said. "Like De'nal."

"Can he thaw?" Magnam asked ominously, fingering his hammer. "Like the bone monsters?"

"Never," Er'ril said harshly, shuddering at this thought. *Never again.* He glanced to the d'warf. "Give me your weapon."

Magnam hesitated, then did as he asked.

Er'ril hefted the hammer to his shoulder and frowned down at the crystal form of his brother. He remembered all the horrors done in his brother's name. "If you're like De'nal," he said coldly, "a spirit composed of crystal, then you can hear me. I can't deny that part of you was once my brother. But a part does not make a whole. Where De'nal was brightness

and light, you are darkness and corruption. And long ago, I promised to
see your corruption gone from this world."

Before his sorrow weakened him further, he swung the sledge down
with both arms. The crystal shattered into a million pieces, bouncing and
skittering in all directions. "And I keep my promises."

Afterward, Er'ril dropped the hammer and turned away. Tears rose to
his eyes. He wiped them away roughly. Why should he shed a tear for the
demon here?

Elena answered him, as if reading his heart. "Though he was evil,
he was still the last of your brother in this world. You are right to
mourn."

Er'ril shook his head, clearing his throat. He allowed his Standish iron
to harden him. "I'll mourn my brother once this is over." He swung
around to the shape-shifter. "Tell me how this happened."

MOGWEED STARED UP AT THE PLAINSMAN. HOW HE WANTED TO RUN, TO FLEE
his disgrace, but he could not. Those storm-gray eyes bore down on him,
pinning him in place. But he was too shocked to answer, to construct a
clever lie.

Tell them, Fardale seemed to howl inside him.

Tol'chuk stepped to his other side, clapping him on the shoulder. "Fardale, how did you save us?"

Mogweed startled with this question, his eyes wide. *Fardale?* He bit
back a laugh. Of course—they all still thought him his brother. This realization shook him out of his shock.

"I . . . Fardale . . . I didn't do anything." Lies again flowed freely from
his warming tongue. "It must have been the silver lake. It cracked under
the mage, and he . . . he transformed." Mogweed kept his eyes averted
from Thorn. She would know the lie.

Inside, he felt his brother's outrage. Mogweed didn't know how long
his subterfuge would last—hopefully long enough for him to escape before they all learned the truth of his betrayal.

Harlequin Quail pointed toward the roof. "Whether luck or fate, time
runs short. The moon rises already to reach the hole."

Mogweed craned his neck. Through a small hole in the rocky ceiling, a
pale violet sky shone. A corner of the moon peeked past one edge.

"Perhaps whatever magick Shorkan planned here ended with him,"
Magnam said, wrapping his injured shoulder.

Elena slid her sword from her sheath. "I won't trust that until the Weirgate is gone."

Mogweed kept his eyes on the hole above. From the color of the skies, the sun was near to setting. Once it was gone, Fardale would be trapped until the morning. He'd have time to think of a strategy, perhaps escape. He bent to reach for his cloak when he felt his hand spasm, twitching on its own.

No! Not on its own! His arm rose and clenched a fist he hadn't formed of his own will. Fardale knew! Like himself, he had discovered the new freedom.

Mogweed ground his teeth. *I won't give up, Brother!* Still bent, hiding his struggle from the others, he fought his fingers open. *Sunset is so near . . . I only have to hold out a little longer.*

Mogweed tried to straighten, but his body locked. He couldn't move. With both wills fighting for control, neither could win. *I won't give up control!*

"Fardale, what's wrong?" Elena asked behind him.

She must have noted his trembling form, but he dared not give up the struggle, even to speak. The sun would set at any moment. He could almost feel its descent.

"Fardale?"

He heard her step closer, but even a moment's lapse in his will and—

Mogweed's body suddenly jerked free. The abrupt release sent him wheeling up and backward with a shout on his lips, a cry of joy. *Free!*

Then he felt a lance of fire jab through him. Only then did he hear the shouted warning. "Fardale, *no!*"

He stared down. A sword blade protruded from his chest, impossibly bright. His blood welled thickly. He fell to his knees.

"He jumped back," Elena said, aghast. "I couldn't get the blade out of the way!"

Mogweed tried to cough out the heaviness in his chest. Invisible steel bands seemed to have wrapped his ribs, squeezing painfully.

Thorn suddenly appeared in front of him. " Fardale, no . . ."

Mogweed managed a shake of his head. He met the eyes of his brother's mate. *It is not Fardale. The sun has set.* He now knew why he was so suddenly released, caught off guard, off balance.

"Oh, Mogweed . . ." Thorn said, glancing to the others. "It's Mogweed again." She turned back to him, taking his hand. Tears welled in her eyes—she knew both brothers would die from the one sword stroke.

He felt himself slipping already.

Thorn must have noted this, too. Her words became hurried. "Tell him, tell him . . ." Her amber eyes glowed.

He could have turned away, but he didn't. Fardale was still inside him. What did it matter any longer? Let him hear the last words of love from his mate. He kept his eyes locked on Thorn's, taking it all in as his breath grew ragged. Someone grabbed his shoulders and helped him sit.

Through their gazes, Mogweed took in all the love between the two. Flashes of images, scents, memories, small whispers of forgiveness. It was a light almost too bright to look upon. But even such brilliance began to fade as his vision darkened and his body grew colder.

The line between the brothers grew less distinct again. But this time, there was no fight. Mogweed faced Fardale, twins, naked to one another.

I'm sorry, Brother. It was hard to say who even spoke those words.

Then darkness descended over them both . . . and they were gone.

Sobbing, Elena knelt atop the silver lake, her face covered by her hands. "How? After all they've been through . . ."

Er'ril helped lower Mogweed's body to the ground. The sword was still impaled through the middle of his chest. Blood ran in a wide pool around his body. Er'ril turned to Elena, taking her in his arms.

"Why?" she moaned.

"I don't know," he said. "But I don't believe the fault here was solely due to chance. The blade is a blood sword. Such weapons are known to harm too easily and too often. Their tainted steel always seeks blood and death."

His words did little to console her. It was *her* hand that had wielded the blade. She had turned her attention away for the barest moment . . . Then Mogweed had flown backward as if intent upon skewering himself.

Thorn knelt on the other side of the prone body, weeping.

Harlequin spoke from a few steps away. "The moon is almost full risen. If we are to act against the gate, we'd best hurry."

Er'ril helped her stand. "I'll get your sword."

Elena shook free, wiping her eyes. "No, I'll do it." She swallowed hard and stepped toward the body. The rose-pommel hilt ran red with the shape-shifters' blood. Thorn turned away, unable to watch. Elena closed her hand over the hilt, and the sword sang free with ease, as easily as it had slain her friends. As the tip pulled clear, the body seemed to melt under it, as if the blade were all that had held the body together. The form dissolved into a rusty-colored flow. It spread across the silver floor, parting around Thorn's knees. She backed in horror. The two flows drew in on themselves, welling up into bulky mounds that sculpted into two figures curled on the floor. The shapes grew more distinct and familiar: one a dark wolf, one a man.

"Mogweed and Fardale," Er'ril said. "They're finally free."

Tol'chuk shook his head sadly.

Thorn dropped down beside her mate, reaching a hand to his face. With her touch, the wolf suddenly inhaled deeply, then startled up, as if disturbed from sleep. Everyone jumped back, even Thorn.

The shape-shifter spoke tentatively to the wolf as it gained its feet, wobbling slightly. "F-Fardale?"

The wolf lifted its head. Amber eyes glowed toward the si'luran woman. Then Thorn's eyes widened, too. She let out a sob of joy and wrapped her arms around the wolf's neck.

"I guess that'd be a yes," Harlequin commented.

To the side, Mogweed pushed up, rubbing his eyes. "Wh-what happened?" he asked.

"You be alive!" Tol'chuk said, scooping him to his feet.

Mogweed stared down at his limbs, clearly as surprised as any of them. He fingered his naked chest. "I'm healed. How?"

Er'ril pointed to the sword in Elena's stunned fingers. "Shadowsedge was made to break spells. I'd wager its piercing shattered whatever held you together."

"The Spirit Root said we were to take the sword and seek you out," Thorn recalled.

Mogweed stared over at his brother. "So it was the sword all along? We could've been freed anytime."

Elena stared around at the confluence. She remembered the trapped rock'goblin spirits. "I suspect such a miracle could only occur here. You had to die, but your spirits couldn't pass beyond. The confluence held you safe until you were unbound."

Mogweed stared over to his brother. "Either way, we're wolf and man again." He lifted his arm, and a flare of fur sprouted along its length. "But truly bound no longer."

Fardale shifted from wolf to something half man so he could clutch Thorn in his arms. Then he faced his brother. "Mogweed . . ."

Mogweed sighed heavily, then bowed his head and mumbled, "I know . . ."

Fardale crossed to him and hugged him. "You've freed us."

Elena noted the shocked look on the other's face.

Fardale straightened, still resting a hand on Mogweed's shoulder. "Thank you, Brother."

The shock on Mogweed's face persisted. Elena smiled. She suspected the small man had received little praise in his life, always living in the shadow of his brother.

"The moon," Harlequin reminded them.

Elena turned to face the Wyvern Gate. The black bird sat hunched on its ebon'stone claws, ruby eyes staring from its cowl of feathers, its wings outspread as if ready to leap.

It was their last obstacle.

Er'ril placed a hand on her shoulder. "If the sword could break the twins, let's hope it can break the gate."

Elena nodded. If they succeeded, Chi would be free, and the Dark Lord would be stripped of his well of dark magick. She allowed herself a moment of hope—a strange sensation after the winters of despair.

"Let's do it," she said. Even if she lost the blade, she wouldn't shed any tears. She remembered the ease with which the blade had slipped into Mogweed's back. After this night, she was done with the blood sword.

Together, they approached the statue cautiously, but it remained stone. Elena slid one hand, then the other, down the length of the sword's razored edge. Blood flowed freely.

She glanced back to the others; then, setting her lips, she turned. Above the statue, almost all of the moon's fullness filled the hole. They had not a moment more to spare. Stepping closer, she gripped the hilt with both bloodied hands. Immediately she felt the connection to the steel, the surge of confidence, the keen understanding of magick.

"When you're ready," Er'ril said.

She smiled and drove the blade into the sculpted chest of the bird.

Her arms were ready for the blade to clang on stone or shatter against it, but the blade sank into the ebon'stone as if it were mere smoke. But the effect was immediate. The stone bird awoke with a scream, its neck arching up as its wings snapped wide.

"Elena," Er'ril warned.

She drove the sword all the way to its hilt.

Connected to the sword, she felt the Weir beyond the gate, that immensity of madness. But she held tight. Through her bond, she felt the sword's elemental substance bleed into the Weir, its magick sucked into the bottomless well.

Shadowsedge was gone, but Elena continued to hold its hilt pressed to the breast of the stone bird. This sword was not only steel; it was also her own blood, a flow rich in magick—but not *elemental* magick. The Weir did not want her energy. Her magick came from Cho, the Weir from Chi. The two twin but contrary magicks fought each other explosively.

Elena held tight. The elemental steel had pierced the stone, allowing her blood access to the Weir beyond. She felt the build-up of opposite forces within the heart of the bird. It was this fiery fight that tortured the stone wyvern. The bird continued to scream. It beat its wings, but it could not take to the air. It had to await the moon and remain connected to the confluence of silver. Still it tried to shake her free, lifting her off her feet.

"Elena!" Er'ril screamed. From the corner of her eye, she saw him knocked aside by a blow from a stone wing, sliding across the silver floor.

Still, she held tight with both fists to the hilt, hanging from the rose pommel. She would not fail. She fed more and more of her own blood through the hilt and into the Weir. The bird writhed with agony. She glanced up to its ruby eyes, on fire now. Its beaked maw dove at her, ready to rip her away.

But Tol'chuk was there. Heaving with both shoulders, he swung his huge hammer across the side of the bird's head with a clang. The impossibly hard ebon'stone remained intact, but the wyvern's beak was knocked aside.

"Hurry, Elena," Harlequin called out. "The moon comes!"

With the others protecting her, Elena held fast and pumped volumes of magick and blood into the monster. Within the heart of the bird, a fierce tension of forces built to impossible dimensions. She kept her focus, willing her fingers to hold. But from the loss of blood, she had begun to weaken. Her hands were also paling from ruby red to a pale pink. She could not last much longer.

The wyvern fought harder yet. Now it was Tol'chuk's turn to be batted aside like a fly by a horsetail. Unprotected now, she knew she had only one option.

With a final thrust, she emptied the last of her magick into the heart of the stone, giving everything in her. The bird wailed, neck stretched toward the roof. Above, Elena spotted the full face of the moon staring back at her. Was she too late? Silvery light bathed down upon them.

Her fingers began to fail. She pushed a final flow of blood into the monster before falling free. But as her last finger slipped away, she felt the tidal force inside the bird cross some threshold. She understood the two opposite energies—from Cho and Chi—could no longer be contained within the one vessel.

"Back!" she yelled hoarsely, spent.

The blast shattered out, tossing Elena away. The others were buffeted as well, scattered in all directions. She felt the sting of stone striking her body like icy sleet in a windstorm.

She was flung back to the boneyard, rolling among the old remains. Then the blast subsided.

She rolled to her hands and knees, numb and bleeding. Her hands were pale and white, her magick gone. She would have to renew in the spear of moonlight across the room.

But before she could even stand, Meric and Nee'lahn tumbled into the room from the tunnel. Meric had his hands raised. Winds screamed out from him, whirling the small bones around their feet. Then from the tunnel, clinging to stone with claws, skal'tum climbed out, crawling up the walls like so many roaches.

Nee'lahn turned for the first time into the chamber. Her eyes widened with horror.

Elena followed her gaze, swinging around. Her companions were climbing to their feet, bloody from the flying shards. The shatter of stone spread in a circular blast out from the center of the confluence. All that remained of the wyvern was a cloud of ebon'stone dust, aglow in the moonlight. Even the silver floor was gouged by the blast.

The final Weirgate was broken!

Then around her, the goblin bones began to stir, shaking and rattling, then beginning to slide and build on one another. Elena hurriedly gained her feet and stumbled out of the boneyard, while Meric and Nee'lahn ran through the shivering bones to join her.

"There were too many." Nee'lahn gasped. "Jaston . . ." She shook her head with a sob. "He gave his life to buy us time to escape."

Elena's heart ached for the poor man, but her attention remained on the situation at hand. The bone army was awakening again. The skal'tum were still attacking. Why? The Weirgate was gone . . .

Er'ril ran to her side, bleeding from a deep gash on his forehead. "We must get away. There are tunnels on the far side. At least there we'd be better sheltered."

Behind them, the skal'tum began to scream. The plume of dust ahead obscured the view, but she remembered the tunnel openings on the far side. "I must renew," she said, pointing to the pool of moonlight in the room's center.

But as she stepped forward, something shifted within the fading cloud of rock dust. Skal'tum screeched, and bones clattered behind her, but she froze, her eyes fixed forward. Er'ril noted her attention and swung back to the blasted section of floor.

Bathed in moonlight, something stirred within the dust, a figure rising from the debris. Arms lifted, stretching, and legs unbent. From the heart of the Weirgate, a creature was born.

The others gathered to them. The skal'tum held back. In the center of the room stood a huge black figure. Bathed in bright moonlight, the form was clearly made of ebon'stone.

But its eyes were fiery pits.

Elena recognized what type of creature this was. She had been chased through the swamplands by a blackguard, a spirit armored in melted ebon'-stone. But this one wore familiar features—a dark mirror of Tol'chuk.

No one spoke. All knew who stood before them: Ly'chuk, the Oath-breaker, the Black Beast of Gul'gotha.

His words shook the room. "I am born anew."

27

TYRUS RALLIED HIS MEN, FIGHTING TO BE HEARD OVER THE ROAR OF THE dragon, the screams of the dying, and the crackle of the flames from the fire pit.

A bellow drew the prince's attention back to the arch of the dark volcanic room. The dragon swooped higher after its last attack, one of their hill horses in its maw. With a toss of its neck, Ragnar'k flung the bleeding corpse into a phalanx of d'warf archers. They had been trying to wound the dragon with their arrows, but the bolts passed harmlessly through its shape. How did one kill a dragon made of smoke?

He had already tried his petrifying magick to no avail. All he earned was a gash across his back as he rolled from a claw. It made no sense. Though the dragon was mere smoke, its talons and fangs bore enough substance to rip and tear.

Tyrus rounded his own mount among his men. Fletch rode double with Hurl; the Steppeman had come close to joining his mount in the dragon's teeth. Only a last-minute roll from the saddle had saved him.

"What now?" Blyth asked.

"There it goes again," Sticks mumbled from Tyrus' other side. He pointed one of his clubs.

Overhead, the smoke dragon wafted high into the dark chamber, disappearing into the gloom overhead. It was its usual ruse—using the shadows to hide itself, then springing out of darkness to maim and kill.

"Watch for its eyes!" Wennar bellowed from a short distance away.

That was the only warning of an attack. Against the darkness, the dragon's eyes glowed with crimson fire. It was the last sight many of the d'warves saw before meeting a bloody death. So far the men on horses fared better, able to escape Ragnar'k if they were quick enough.

"Our only recourse is retreat," Blyth continued. "We can't win here."

Tyrus remained silent. Winning wasn't the game; they needed to harry the Dark Lord and his forces. Their blood was spent to buy time. "Lead Sticks and the others back to the Black Road."

"And the d'warves?"

Wennar shouted. "Keep your backs to the fire! Use its light!"

"I think he intends to stay."

"And you?" Hurl asked from behind Fletch.

Tyrus rested his sword across his knees.

"It's suicide to stay, Captain," Blyth pressed.

He sighed. "We all die sometime."

His first mate frowned at him. "Spoken like a true pirate, sir. But even a pirate knows when the odds be against him, and when to tack to calmer waters."

Tyrus glanced to his friend. He opened his mouth to object when Blyth's eyes widened. Reflected in his mate's panicked eyes, crimson fire glowed at him.

Tyrus leaped from his saddle at the same time as Blyth. "Down!" he screamed. He hit the stone floor and dodged underneath his own horse. Beyond its hooves, he spotted Sticks' legs. Then suddenly the giant's boots vanished upward, leaving behind a bellow of outrage.

Rolling from under the horse, Tyrus crouched with his sword. He spotted Sticks struggling in the air, his shoulder clutched in one of the dragon's claws. Ragnar'k roared with glee, winging high into the air. The dragon circled with its prey.

Sticks had one of his clubs and batted at his captor, but the length of ironwood merely passed through smoke. The dragon could not be harmed.

Across the floor, archers knelt ready with arrows notched, but none dared shoot with the man in danger.

Ragnar'k carried his struggling prize over the fire pit, still bellowing. Then the claws released the giant. He was dropped toward the flames, arms wheeling, a scream on his lips.

Tyrus could only stare in horror. Then the *twang* of a bowstring sounded from near his ear. He glanced quickly and spotted Fletch fitting another arrow. He turned back. As usual with Fletch, a second arrow wasn't necessary. The first had shot Sticks through the eye, killing him instantly. The giant was limp when his form struck the searing flames.

Tyrus clenched a fist, his fingers going black. "Mount up," he ordered his men. "I want you all away. Now!"

Blyth climbed into his saddle, but he simply sat his horse. "We're pirates, Captain. Since when were we any good at obeying orders?"

Hurl reached out and pulled Fletch into the saddle. "Truly, sir. We'd be craven pirates if we obeyed all our captain's orders."

Tyrus looked them over. "As you said, it's sure death to stay."

Blyth shrugged. "Life's only too short if you haven't lived."

Shaking his head, Tyrus grabbed the pommel of his own saddle and hauled himself up. "And we have lived," he mumbled.

"Aye, Captain."

"Then let's hunt us some dragon!"

SY-WEN CLUNG TO KAST, NOT JUST WITH HER FINGERS BUT WITH ALL HER being. She kept her focus on the man she loved as they flew down the glassy corridor. If her concentration wavered, sensations and lusts from Ragnar'k grew stronger.

She had experienced the dragon's first few kills. The taste of blood had filled her mouth, savage delight had raced through her veins, and the screams of the dying had echoed through her. These thoughts and sensations still threatened to unhinge her, but Kast's presence was an anchor amid the tumult.

Hang on, he urged her now. *We have only a short way to go.*

She closed her eyes, sinking into the simpler, cleaner senses of the dragon she rode. The whisper of wind, the pull of wing, the gentle ache of muscles, the steady thud of a giant heart. She sheltered there.

But like thunder over a horizon, cries and screams still reached her from the other dragon. She wanted to wrap her arms around her head, to clamp the horrors away, but she needed her grip to keep her seat atop Kast as he flashed under spans, around columns, and over gardens of statuary.

As she crouched in her seat, the screams grew louder. Only after a few moments did she realize it wasn't the phantom sense from Ragnar'k, but something she was hearing with her own ears.

We're nearing the central chamber, Kast said.

Sy-wen took a deep breath. *You know what to do?* she asked.

I'll be ready. But what about you?

She heard the concern and took a deep, shuddering breath. Her part was no easier than Kast's. She straightened in her seat and opened herself to Ragnar'k. *Bonded,* she sent to him, *I've come to join you.*

The connection between dragon and rider flared with her focus. *My bonded!* Ragnar'k answered her. The raw sensations of the other dragon swamped over her.

Her fingers clenched. She bit back a gasp of horror. If she hadn't once been possessed by the simaltra, the purely vile thoughts might have overwhelmed her. But she had met such darkness before. She would not let it rule her again.

Come join in the flow of blood!

Sy-wen spotted the end of the tunnel; they were almost to the chamber. She wormed through the madness and spoke to Ragnar'k. *I am already with you.*

His glee filled her head, as she knew it would. Despite his corruption, Ragnar'k was still tied to her by bonds more ancient than any magick. He could not refuse to join with her.

Kast flew them into the huge room. A forest of torches spiked the floor, spreading across the vast cavern. From their height, she could spot a pattern to the torches' positions, a swirl that centered on a giant fire pit in what must be the room's center.

"There," she whispered to Kast. "Aim for the central fire. That's where I last saw Tyrus."

And the prince still lives?

"Yes. Ragnar'k seems fixed on him. He must smell the magick on the man."

Then we must hurry. Kast swept high over the field of torches. *Where is Ragnar'k?*

Sy-wen frowned, unsure. She knew he was in here, but his presence seemed to fill the cavern. It was hard to say where he was precisely, and in the gloom, the smoke of his body was impossible to discern.

As she searched, she spotted the remains of the d'warf army near the pit. Men on horseback wheeled among the d'warves—Tyrus and the others.

She did not need to point them out to Kast; he had keener eyes than hers. "Watch for Ragnar'k."

Then it was as if a cloud passed under them, obscuring their view of the d'warves. Shouts and bellows erupted, and d'warves scattered from under the cloud.

Ragnar'k, Kast said.

"Go to him," Sy-wen whispered. A shiver trembled through her. They risked all in this next venture.

The connection with Ragnar'k flared. *A gift,* he sent, *bloody meat on bone!*

He was attacking again, showing off his prowess. In that small way, he was the Ragnar'k she knew—prideful, boastful. But it had to stop—she didn't know if she could survive the bloodshed when so near Ragnar'k.

Kast sensed her urgency. He tucked his wings and aimed for the misty cloud. Sy-wen leaned close to her love. His body was a steaming hearth after the long flight here.

They dove together, dropping like a boulder from the distant roof. The smoky cloud grew before them. She sensed a startled reaction from Ragnar'k. So focused on his kill, he had failed to realize they were so near.

Then they were shooting through the cloud. Sy-wen felt a scintillation over her skin. *Bonded!* she sent. *Join us!* They shot out from the smoky pall and into clear air.

D'warves fled from Kast's passage. A handful of arrows even spat at him. But Sy-wen heard a familiar bellow.

"Archers down!" It was Wennar.

They flew past the d'warves and near the fire pit. Flames danced high above the edge. The heat drove them to bank aside. Kast tilted on a wing, arcing around.

Sy-wen spotted the misty cloud flowing in their wake. There was nothing a dragon liked better than a chase—and ill'guard or not, Ragnar'k was still a dragon. She felt glee surging in his heart.

But there was one thing a dragon liked better than a hunt.

Bonded! Ragnar'k moaned.

She read his desire. Once bonded, a dragon was never whole without its rider on its back. *Prove your blood, my bonded,* she sent back to him. *Catch us . . . join with us. Let me ride you again!*

Ragnar'k, unfettered by his dark forging, was a creature enslaved to his lusts. He could not refuse a chase, nor resist joining so he could be ridden by his bonded.

Here he comes, Kast said.

"Be ready," she answered. "Keep close to the floor." She risked a glance behind her. A smoky reflection of a dragon followed them, like a monstrous living shadow with eyes of flame. Her blood iced at the sight.

I'm coming for you, Ragnar'k promised.

She tore her gaze around, leaning closer to Kast. "Now," she whispered to his scales. "Let it be now."

Kast silently acknowledged her, slowing and drifting down. He glided over the tops of the torches, blowing out their flames with the winds of his passage, leaving behind a trail of darkness.

Then the darkness caught up with them, sweeping around and into them. The three—Kast, Sy-wen, and Ragnar'k—had been a triumvirate since the beginning of the journey, tangled together by magick, love, and ancient bonds. As the shadow of Ragnar'k fell about them, they became so once again.

Sy-wen fought the intimate touch of the twisted creature. Kast fared no better. Sharing his senses, she felt Ragnar'k fill the body he once wore, blending again with Kast.

Under assault, Kast swung back toward the fires and the threatened soldiers. Through the tumult of madness, a single thought touched her heart. *Now.*

She dared not hesitate, lest Ragnar'k suspect their treachery. Sy-wen ripped off a glove with her teeth as Kast winged near the pit, wings scooping air, slowing, claws out to land. Men, horses, and d'warves fled from their path.

With the scrape of nail on rock, Sy-wen gripped the scales of the dragon under her. With the touch of her bare fingers, the world vanished into a whirlwind of fang, claw, scale, and wing.

Then she was rolling across the stone floor, wrapped in the arms of the man she loved. They tumbled for another breath; then she found Kast atop her, staring down at her. Both were bruised and sore, but he leaned and kissed her deeply.

Sy-wen sank into his heat and lips, relieved. The quiet in her mind after the ravings of Ragnar'k was a balm on her heart. "Kast . . . ," she whispered between his lips. "I have you back."

He responded to her words with passion, holding her tighter. He reached to her bare hand, entwining his fingers, squeezing harder and harder until passion turned to pain. His mouth covered her gasp. Then teeth found her lips, biting, drawing blood.

"Kast!" she cried.

He pulled back, her blood on his lips. His eyes opened, and crimson flames glowed back at her. "Bonded," he hissed. "You are mine!"

TYRUS RACED FROM FAR ACROSS THE CHAMBER, USING HIS REINS TO WHIP HIS mount across the floor. It dodged right and left around the torch poles. Moments ago, he had watched the two dragons merge—flesh and smoke. Then the transformation had flared.

Tyrus had instantly understood what the mer'ai woman had attempted: to merge the spirit dragon back into its own body, then trap it with her magick inside Kast.

Sy-wen screamed, echoing across the room.

Something had clearly gone wrong.

Kast pinned the struggling woman to the stone, but she got a hand free and raked him across the face. He merely laughed.

Tyrus kicked his horse, urging it to close the hundred paces between them.

But he was not the only one in motion. From around the edge of the fire pit, Blyth thundered on his own mount. He was closer. He raced to the struggling pair, leaning out of his saddle. With one hand, Blyth snatched the warrior braid of the Bloodrider.

"Get off her, you oaf!" his first mate bellowed as he rode past.

Kast was torn from his perch and flung aside.

"No!" Sy-wen screamed, lunging to keep one hand clutched to her mate. But a dark explosion blasted outward. Sy-wen was tossed back; even Blyth was unsaddled by the eruption as man became dragon again. The black-scaled beast crouched on the stone, stark against the backdrop of towering flames. Silver claws gouged the glassy floor. It stretched its neck and roared, trumpeting its rage to the roof.

Blyth crab-crawled back to Sy-wen. Both lay in the monster's shadow. His first mate's mount was gone.

Ragnar'k lowered its muzzle toward them. Its eyes matched the flames behind it, bright and hungry.

Blyth yanked out his sword, gaining his feet, shoving Sy-wen behind him, ready to shield her.

Damn fool! Tyrus cursed. It was the wrong time for his first mate to develop a chivalrous streak. He whipped his horse, but he was still too far away.

Then off to the left, a flanking cadre of d'warves appeared, led by Wennar. They dropped to one knee in unison, bows in hand. Arrows flew in a deadly arc, pelting the dragon. Most bounced off the hard scales, but a handful struck deep, tailed feathers quivering.

Ragnar'k jolted up, wings sweeping out, roaring again with rage.

The d'warves held their posts, fresh arrows nocked. Wennar yelled. "Again!"

The barrage flew—but this time, the dragon was ready. A wing struck out, knocking aside the arrows. They fell with a scatter.

Ragnar'k swung his neck, bringing his muzzle back toward Blyth and Sy-wen. The dragon roared, revealing long fangs. Blyth braced himself.

Tyrus was almost to them, coming up on the dragon's wounded left side. He yelled to draw its attention. *"Yahhh!"*

A wing snapped, meant to smash him from his saddle. But Tyrus was already gone. He sprang to a crouch in his saddle, then leaped away, flying through the air, over the wide wing, hands outstretched. He willed the last of his magickal reserves to his fingers. They went black instantly, fed by his panic.

A scream rose from beyond the bulk of the dragon.

Then Tyrus landed atop Ragnar'k. He drove his fingers under the thick scales to the tender flesh beneath and unleashed his magick. He felt scale harden, trapping his fingers. This proved lucky: Ragnar'k bucked as flesh turn to stone. He tried to throw Tyrus off, but the pirate prince was melded to the beast. Flung about, he fed his magick in a fierce rush, emptying his heart. Again he felt the dull disinterest in his own mortality.

Senses ebbed. He heard a roar of alarm, and distantly he felt the dragon's fight die away, fading like himself. Granite flowed outward through wings, down a long neck, into clawed feet. Then with a final push, all was stone.

Both dragon and rider, trapped for eternity.

Tyrus was aware of his heart. Its beat faltered from a solid rhythm to a quivering bag of writhing snakes. He allowed himself to fall toward darkness. It was over.

He slipped away from cold stone to something warmer. Then a light grew around him, bathing him, wrapping him. He felt something touch his lips. It took him a moment to realize it was a kiss.

He knew who held him now. He had only tasted those lips once, but it was enough. The stone of his heart melted into joy. A name formed on his lips. *Mycelle . . .*

He was not answered. He was still too far off, he sensed.

Mycelle, I'm coming to you.

The warm light resisted him, holding him back. *No, my love, you must stay.*

His heart broke. *I have no reason. You were always my light.*

And I always will be . . . But now it is not your time.

I wish it, he said with as much command as he could muster.

A sternness grew. *You wish to die like a pirate . . . but what I ask of you is much harder.* There was a long silence. *Rather than die like a pirate, you must live like a prince. You are needed. For me, live like a prince.*

Tyrus sought words to argue, but deep inside him, he understood her truth. He held onto her a moment longer, wrapped in her light, taking some of it into his heart. Then he let her go.

Promise me . . . , he whispered.

You know I already have. And then nothingness. He was alone.

With the bit of warmth and light held to him, he melted the stone around his heart. The fist of muscle in his chest beat weakly . . . once, twice, and again, stronger, marking the time until they would be reunited again.

Stone melted to flesh. He felt himself slip from atop the granite dragon, but arms were already there, catching him. Vision swirled back, but the world had darkened since last he saw. He looked right and left. Fletch and Hurl held him upright. Beyond them, the flames were gone from the fire pit.

"The fire died along with the dragon," Hurl explained, reading his confused expression.

He took deep breaths, working the stone from the corners of his being.

The dragon filled the world on one side, a granite sculpture of perfect form. It sat on its haunches, wings tucked, neck curled to bring its muzzle close to the floor. Tyrus was close enough to feel the heat steaming off it. It was like standing by a giant coal, fresh from the hearth.

"Blyth," Hurl began, drawing his attention back. "He . . ." The Northman shook his head.

Tyrus then remembered: *the dragon, his first mate, and Sy-wen.* Fear brought his legs under him. He glanced to Fletch, but the Steppeman wouldn't meet his gaze. "Take me to him," he ordered.

Together, they circled a group of d'warves gaping at the stone dragon, to where Wennar knelt over Blyth. Blood pooled under them both. Sy-wen knelt at the edge, face buried in her arms, sobbing.

Tyrus hurried forward, sure Blyth was already gone. But he found the man alive. Wennar had a thick wad of cloth pressed to the first mate's side. Only then did Tyrus notice Blyth's left arm was gone, clear to the shoulder.

Wennar spoke as Tyrus sank to his knees. "The dragon bit the limb clean off."

Blyth struggled to speak and ended up coughing a gout of blood instead.

Tyrus took his hand. "I should've been faster," he muttered. "I'm sorry."

Blyth shook his head. "Pirates live short lives. Shorter than princes."

Tyrus frowned. "I'm no prince—"

"Don't say that again," Blyth blurted fiercely, ending in a racking cough. He gasped and caught his breath. "I knew you were always a prince. It's high time *you* saw it."

Tyrus did not know how to respond.

"Don't mourn me." His first mate's fingers clenched on his as a spasm of pain lanced through the man. He grimaced. "I got to ride to battle with a prince . . . and call him friend." Despite the pain, pride filled the other's voice.

Tyrus smiled sadly. "Who said you were my friend?"

Blyth smiled back, a pirate's smile, but also a man's. He gave Tyrus' fingers a final squeeze. Then the light faded from his eyes, his smile dimmed, and he was gone.

After a long moment, Tyrus sighed and stood. "Be at peace, my friend." Mycelle's words came back to him. *For me, live like a prince.* He made a promise. For her, for Blyth, he would try his best.

SY-WEN STILL KNELT AS THE PIRATE'S BLOOD SEEPED TO HER KNEES. SHE had seen Ragnar'k lunge and snap Blyth up, lifting him off his feet, then throwing him down.

But worst of all, the dragon's savage delight had washed into her, and it had felt like her own. Her heart had beat harder, surging with lusts, as the man was dropped bloody to her feet. A gift.

She covered her face, sobbing. Then she had watched the dragon petrify into granite. Still tied to Ragnar'k, she had heard him fading away, falling down a well without bottom, dragging Kast with him to a stony grave.

She rocked in place, unable to fathom the tragedy. She had lost everything.

Then Lord Tyrus touched her shoulder. "I'm sorry, Sy-wen." he said. "Kast saved us all. The dragon would've consumed all in its path."

She nodded. "I know." She stared up at the dragon, not knowing whether to curse or mourn Ragnar'k. His great muzzle lay almost on the floor, as if he were just reclining toward slumber. His eyes stared at her, no longer afire, just plain granite. She knew the giant had been sorely used, but she had yet to find her way to forgive him. Her grief was too raw.

Wennar spoke from a few steps away. "What do you make of this?" The d'warf general stood at the edge of the hole. "The fire pit's gone cold. The rock's not even warm."

Tyrus stood. "I think the flames and the demon dragon were connected, some volcanic magick." He nodded to the stone giant and held out a palm. "Feel how he still burns like a coal. The fires must have been drawn into him. The heat is fading, though—cooling as the granite sets."

Wennar eyed the dragon, then waved them over. "Come see this."

Tyrus reached to help Sy-wen up, but she shook her head. She did not have the strength to care. Though she lived, her heart was as much stone as the dragon and man she loved. "Leave me be," she moaned.

He tugged her to her feet. Anger flared. She had to restrain herself from striking him, but he pulled her around to face him. "You live," he said fiercely. "Kast and Ragnar'k gave their lives so you might live—so we all might live. You must keep moving."

A sob escaped her. "How? How is that possible?"

"It's not. Such grief is beyond anyone to bear. For now, just survive. Move one foot in front of the other."

She began to protest, but Tyrus took her by the shoulders and walked her toward the pit. Her legs were leaden from her grief. She felt truly of stone.

Wennar looked upon her with concern. She shook out of Tyrus' embrace. She would stand on her own.

"What did you want us to see?" Tyrus asked.

Wennar nodded to the pit. "If the flames and the dragon were one, then both must have been posted here for a reason—a guard dog at the gates, so to speak."

Sy-wen glanced down the hole. Far below, molten rock glowed ruddily.

"Do you see those steps?" Wennar said, sweeping his ax toward the walls of the pit.

She glanced to the sides, her eyes widening. Along the inside of the pit, a spiraling staircase wound down into the depths.

Wennar spoke. "If a demon as fierce as the dragon was set to guard this path, then it must be important."

Tyrus nodded. "It must lead into the heart of the mountain itself."

"Perhaps to the lair of the Dark Lord." Wennar gripped his ax in both meaty fists.

Sy-wen's grief flamed into anger. Her hand fell to her belt, to the line of stunners fastened there. If she had to live, then here she found a reason to act: *revenge.* "We must descend," she said. She looked to Tyrus and Wennar. Their faces were hard, their eyes flinty.

"How could we not?" Tyrus said. "It cost us much blood to open this gate. We won't let those deaths go to waste."

Wennar quickly organized his forces, leaving some behind to tend the wounded. Sy-wen walked back to the dragon. It crouched, steaming slightly in the damp air.

Tyrus kept near her shoulder. She sensed the sliver of guilt in the prince. "Maybe once this is over," he said softly, "I can try freeing the dragon."

Sy-wen took a long moment. How she wanted to latch onto this one hope. But she had seen the flames glowing from their eyes. Ragnar'k was too strong. And even if they could bring him back to flesh, Ragnar'k was an ill'guard. It would be near to impossible to reverse the corruption. And how many more deaths would it take for even the attempt?

"No," she said, her voice cracking. "Ragnar'k arose from stone; let him return to his stony slumber. That's where he belongs."

"But Kast . . . he doesn't belong in there."

Sy-wen crossed to stand near the muzzle of the giant. She reached out with a hand. Was her love in there? Did he sense her? The heat from the granite was rapidly fading. She touched the scaled cheek of the dragon. It remained warm, as if he were still alive. As she drew her hand back, a burn suddenly flamed her fingers. She yanked her arm back, startled.

"What's wrong?" Tyrus asked.

She leaned closer, examining the dragon. From both his wide nostrils, thin streams of steam wafted out, hard to discern against the black granite. She had accidentally scalded her fingers. She shook her head and straightened. "It's just the last traces of the volcanic heat, steaming away."

Tyrus nodded. "We should ready ourselves for the descent."

Sy-wen turned to go, shaking her stinging fingers. She had scalded the same hand when she bathed Rodricko's flower in the smoke of the volcanic crevice. That one act had ultimately led to this tragedy, but it had also unlocked the gate here. She glanced back to the dragon. All because of a child's prophecy—Sheeshon's dream had led them all here.

She pictured the young girl's face, so bright with hope in this dark time. Even her simple love for the boy Rodricko was a beacon of the future, of lives to come. She touched the pocket of her sharkskin suit, where she still carried the bud from the boy's bloom. She pulled the flower free. Its purple petals were still closed in a tight bud. She wondered when it would open; it had taken the volcanic smoke from the crevice to fully bloom Rodricko's flower . . .

It had taken smoke! She whirled around.

Tyrus noted her sudden movement. "Sy-wen . . . ?"

She remembered the prince's own words. *Kast . . . he doesn't belong in there.* She strode back to the dragon. Was she too late?

"What are you doing?" Tyrus asked.

"Trusting in a child's gift," she answered. She thrust the bud into the smoky flow of steam from the dragon's nostrils. Sy-wen ignored the burn. With the touch of petal to smoke, Sy-wen felt a jolt of energy rock through her. She gasped.

In her fingers, the bud bloomed, petals curling back, revealing a fiery heart.

Tyrus stood behind her. "What is this you attempt?"

Sy-wen trembled, suddenly less sure. She slowly pulled the flower from the stream, stepping back. As she withdrew, the smoke seemed to follow her, drawn to the bloom. She continued to retreat. Fingers of smoke clutched the bloom along with her, flowing back into a misty arm.

Tears flowed down her cheeks. Afraid to speak, she stepped back farther. With each step, she drew a figure from the smoke. She went slowly, allowing time for the form to take shape. But the stream from the dragon's nostrils was rapidly diminishing. She sensed that if she didn't pull the figure free before the smoke ceased, all would be lost. In her fear and hope, she stumbled.

The fragile figure dispersed, shaken by her bobbled arm.

"Careful," Tyrus said at her back, now supporting her shoulder.

She held the flower steady, and the form grew sharper again. Tyrus walked her back, holding her. Before them, the clear shape of a man took form. She could not mistake the shadow. "Kast," she moaned.

"A little farther," Tyrus urged. "Hurry. The dragon goes cold."

Sy-wen took another step, and suddenly the figure coalesced into perfect symmetry—a sculpture of Kast in smoke. Together they clutched the single bud between them. Sy-wen could not stop her legs from trembling. The beautiful sight was blurred by tears. "My love . . ."

He remained silent, a shadow.

She knew what she had to do. With her free hand, she reached to his smoky cheek. "I have need of you." She poured all her love into those few words.

Magick ignited between them, but instead of calling forth a dragon, smoke turned to flesh under her touch. It spread out from her fingers, bringing substance and life out of nothingness. In moments, Kast stood before her, pale but whole.

"Sy-wen," he mumbled, almost in disbelief.

She lowered her fingers, barely noting that his dragon tattoo was once again a plain seahawk. Ragnar'k was gone. She hugged the man who held her heart. "Don't ever leave me."

"Never again." Her touch clearly assured him all was real. He wrapped her in his arms, lifting her high. They kissed, melting one into the other. They were only two now, but that was enough for anyone.

KAST FOLLOWED TYRUS DOWN THE WINDING STAIRS. HIS HAND REMAINED firmly in Sy-wen's. The steps were wide enough for four to walk abreast, but the heat and the sheer drop to the molten rock far below kept them walking in pairs, sticking close to the walls of the pit.

Ahead, Tyrus consulted in quiet tones with Wennar. Behind them marched a pair of pirates, one bright, the other dark, a North Coaster and a Steppeman. They had outfitted Kast with rough-fitting gear and a long sword. "Was my father's," Hurl had said with a wink. "Or someone's father, at least."

Beyond them stretched a long line of d'warf soldiers, fifty strong, winding back toward the distant rim of the pit.

Craning his neck, Kast could make out the stone form of Ragnar'k. During his time with the dragon, the border between them had burned away. He could remember the monster's ravings as if they were his own. Still, Kast had also been able to sense the dragon's true heart. For brief moments, he recognized the brightness under siege—the torment and the struggle. And now Ragnar'k was stone, frozen forever.

He turned away with a sigh. He remembered Sy-wen's words as they set off down the stairs, tears in her eyes: *We found Ragnar'k sleeping in stone. Perhaps it was his fate to return.*

Kast took a deep breath, praying the dragon found peace.

Tyrus spoke from below, drawing him out of his thoughts. "A tunnel," he called, pointing down.

Kast stepped nearer the lip. Heat seared his face as he searched the place where Tyrus pointed. Below, after another three turns around the pit, the stairs seemed to end at the mouth of a tunnel. He pulled back, sweat hot on his brow. So there was indeed an end to this stair. They had all feared it would simply wind down into the molten rock.

With a goal in sight, they increased their pace. The heat grew more intense with each step. The air seared the lungs, while the smell of sulfurous brimstone gagged the throat. They were all gasping and sweating as they made the final turn. Their march became a rush toward the tunnel— anything to escape the choking depths of the pit.

Kast supported Sy-wen under one arm. As a mer'ai, a creature of the cool sea, she wilted like kelp on a blistering beach. He hurried her toward the shelter of the tunnel, pressing Tyrus and Wennar onward. By the time they reached the tunnel's mouth, he was carrying Sy-wen, her toes dragging across the stone.

They all tumbled into the dark depths of the passage, moving forward half blindly to make room for the others behind them. Vaguely Kast could make out Wennar struggling to free an oiled brand from his pack. Tyrus was already striking his flint, casting sparks in the gloom.

Still they moved into the darkness, miraculously cool after the intense heat. Sy-wen gasped, able to get her legs under her, though they still trembled.

Kast held her.

Light flared as the torch took the spark. Wennar lifted his brand high and marched on so the entire d'warf legion could push into the coolness.

Kast stared ahead. The tunnel seemed to stretch forever, a slightly curving, bored-out passage.

"A lava flow tube," Wennar said. "I've seen its like before." He continued deeper.

They followed, gaining strength from the cool interior. Even the air seemed less clogged with sulfurs and noxious fumes, almost freshening, though the tunnel headed downward, spiraling tighter, deeper under the mountain. By now they had to be below the level of the sea. This thought did not give him any comfort.

As they continued down the passage, Kast caught the wink of reflection ahead. Tyrus noted it, too. "Something sparks brightly."

They marched forward, drawing closer. The reflected torchlight came from small cubbies, the size of ripe pumpkins, dug out of the walls. Inside were shallow stone basins, and each held a single small orb of red crystal.

"Heartstone," Sy-wen said with amazement. As they stared, a drop fell from the roof of the cubby and struck the stone before them, giving off a tiny chime.

"Blood," Kast said in horror.

Sy-wen leaned closer, then shook her head. "No, not blood. At least not blood like we know it. It's liquid heartstone." She reached to the stone.

"Sy-wen . . . no!"

She touched the seemingly bloody orb, then showed her finger. "These orbs are chunks of heartstone formed from the drips of the Land's own blood."

Tyrus spoke a few steps away, "No, they're not orbs." He pointed into the cubby before him.

Kast joined him. In this cubby, the orb had grown large enough that a certain shape was clear: oval, pointed more at the top where the drips fell atop it, wider at the base, taking the bowled shape of the basin. The shape was unmistakable.

"Eggs," Sy-wen said, covering her mouth.

Kast nodded. "Harlequin Quail said he saw a hall full of such eggs. Here is where they must be formed, awaiting the Dark Lord's touch to fill them with corruption and transform heartstone into ebon'stone."

"But why hide this tunnel so diligently, guard it with the dragon?" Tyrus asked.

Kast pondered this question, glancing down the length of tunnel and its hundreds of cubbies. He turned to Wennar. "I need your men to gather all their weapons . . . everything . . . hammers, swords, axes, even arrowheads."

"Why?" the d'warf general asked.

From farther down the tunnel, one of the d'warf scouts came running back. "There's light ahead! The tunnel ends in another half league!"

Wennar turned to Kast, eyes questioning what to do.

Kast told him. And after a moment of arguing, Wennar grumbled about the needless delay but ordered his men to obey, stretching them along the length of the passages, positioning them before each cubby.

"Why are you doing this?" Sy-wen asked.

"Because it's always been about heartstone."

Once they were finished, Kast led them down the passage, which wound tighter and tighter. The cubbies disappeared, and plain rock covered the walls again. Soon a strong light appeared ahead, shining silver, down the tunnel.

Kast held everyone back while he crept ahead on his own. *What lies beyond?* He took a deep breath, readied himself, then shoved forward.

Standing stark in the light, sword in hand, he stared out into the chamber beyond. His eyes shot wide, and he bit back a gasp. *Sweet Mother!*

28

ELENA KNELT IN THE EYE OF A TEMPEST AS SAVAGE WAR RAGED AROUND HER. The bone army had risen again, battled back by Tol'chuk and Magnam, while Joach spun his staff, casting forth fonts of balefire.

"Hurry, Elena," Er'ril urged. He crouched over her, sword at the ready. Harlequin guarded her other side, daggers glinting.

From the corner of an eye, she saw Thorn, in wolf form, snatched by dark tendrils writhing down from above. But Fardale leaped upward, sword in hand, a howl on his lips. He cut her free with a double-fisted swipe. They tumbled to the silver floor, where Mogweed helped them up, glancing warily around.

Behind her, she felt the backwash of Meric's winds. The elv'in battered any skal'tum who tried to take wing, driving each back against the wall. Once there, Nee'lahn tangled legs and wings in a fist of roots, trapping them to the wall. Here on the lake of pure elemental energy, their powers remained strong.

But despite their best efforts, the group was near to being overwhelmed. They could not maintain this defense for long. In the center of the room, the blackguard figure of Ly'chuk loomed—and they had no hope of defeating the Dark Lord. They were unprepared for such a battle. He should not have been here. He was supposed to have been half a world away in the volcanic crèches of Blackhall.

Elena's mind spun with terror. Their only hope now was to retreat to the tunnels and regroup. But to achieve even that, they needed her magick. And the Dark Lord stood square in the single spear of moonlight in the room.

Another way was needed.

Her pale hands shook as she struggled the Blood Diary from out of her cloak and placed the tome on the shiny floor. Its gilt rose shone with blinding radiance, reflecting the brightness of the midsummer full moon.

"We haven't much time," Er'ril urged her again.

Taking a deep breath, she flung open the book. The pages inside vanished, opening a window into a night sky of dense stars and billowing radiant gases: *the Void.* From this otherworldly landscape, a river of brilliance shot forth, pouring onto this world. A form took shape, hovering before her.

Er'ril helped Elena to her feet.

Moonstone sculpted into a woman, wispy with swirls of light. She was as bright as the Dark Lord was black. Eyes glanced to Elena, glowing with the same starlight as the Void.

"Cho," Elena said.

The figure barely noted her, turning to survey the room. All fell quiet before her gaze. The bone army froze in place; the writhing roof slowed its tangle; the screams of the skal'tum went quiet.

In the silence that followed, a single word chimed. *"Chi."*

The section of the bone army that stood between Cho and the center of the room crumbled and clattered to the floor. The dark figure of ebon'stone waited, staring back at the moonstone entity.

"You!" Cho cried, drifting forward a step. *"You hold Chi!"*

Elena waved for Er'ril to grab the Diary. She followed in the wake of the spirit.

The Dark Lord answered her, mocking and dark. "Chi is mine, for all time."

Elena glanced to Er'ril with concern. Chi was still trapped; they had been too late in breaking the Wyvern Gate. With horror, she realized the Dark Lord was not just a blackguard, but also a *Weirgate* himself. How could they hope to defeat such an enemy?

Under the monster's ebon'stone feet, the silver lake had gone black. The corruption of the confluence was already under way. While they fought to survive, the Black Beast had begun his assault upon the world's heart.

"I will not allow it!" Cho cried with anguish. *"Free Chi!"*

"You hold no sway here," he said darkly. "Fight me and see what I can do!" His eyes flared.

Cho suddenly screamed. *"No!"* She flew back to Elena and Er'ril, hands covering her face. *"Stop it!"* She sank to her knees on the silver floor.

"What's wrong?" Elena asked.

"Chi screams ... The darkness tears at him ..."

"Torture," Er'ril whispered. "He's torturing Chi."

The flare of brightness in the ebon'stone figure dimmed again. "You're too late anyway." His eyes dismissed the weeping figure. "You're all too late." He stalked forward. Where he stepped on the silver lake, the floor went black. Trails of darkness snaked out from each footprint. "I will have my justice on the Land!"

Er'ril stepped forward. "By corrupting it?"

The Black Beast focused on Er'ril. "No, by *destroying* it. I will tear the living heart from the world and crush it in my stone fist."

Elena had caught the signal from Er'ril as he had stepped out. He had motioned to Cho, indicating Elena should renew her magick. She crouched down beside the spirit.

"I need your power," she whispered, thrusting her hands toward Cho.

The spirit studied her pale fingers and shook her head. *"No."*

Elena's brow furrowed. She pushed her hands into the wispy figure, willing the magick to flow into her—but nothing happened. Her fingers remained pale.

The next words from the spirit were warmer. "Only Cho can grant you her power."

Elena glanced up. The eyes that stared at her now were plain, empty of the Void. "Aunt Fila."

A small nod. "Cho refuses. She sees the flows of power here better than you. Ebon'stone and the swirl of energy here hold her brother trapped. There is no hope of freeing him, and any attempt to fight means torturing Chi. I've heard his cries, echoing through Cho to me." Her face grew grim. "It is unfathomable the pain he feels. Cho cannot add to it. And I don't blame her."

Elena clenched two fists inside the misty shape. "But unless we stop him, the demon means to destroy the world. I must have her power."

"Would you rip it from her, like the Dark Lord has done to Chi?"

Elena dropped her arms. "So we are defeated?"

Aunt Fila glanced past her, to the side. "The future is never set. Sometimes paths open that none could foretell. "

Elena craned around. She saw Tol'chuk push forward past Er'ril. The og're stared across the silver lake to his dark twin. "Why?" he said simply.

"Watch," Aunt Fila whispered at Elena's side. "Sometimes fate can be changed with a single word."

———

TOL'CHUK FACED HIS OG'RE ANCESTOR. *"WHY?"* HE REPEATED. "WHY DO YOU do this?" He studied the dark sculpture of himself, even raising a hand to his own face. The likeness was remarkable, but upon closer inspection, he could see small differences. The ebon'stone figure stood slightly shorter, but broader of shoulder. Legs and arms were thicker, more like a true og're's. But like Tol'chuk, his ebon'stone counterpart stood straight-backed instead of knuckling on an arm.

The fiery eyes focused on him. "My last seed," he said with a rumble of anger.

Tol'chuk furrowed his brow. His mixed blood—og're and si'luran—made it impossible for him to father offspring. The direct line to Ly'chuk would end upon Tol'chuk's death.

The two faced each other from a span of twenty steps and a spread of centuries, an og're of flesh, an og're of ebon'stone. Despite the risk, Tol'chuk had to know more. Here stood the source of his cursed lineage. He could not help but wonder how much of this monster was in himself. Were their similarities deeper than just features? He had to know, so he started at the beginning. "Why did you break your oath to the Land?"

Ly'chuk spat, eyes flaring. "The Land deserves no oath." In those fiery eyes, Tol'chuk saw only disdain. "I see what you're searching for. We two are more alike than you know, He-who-walks-like-a-man." This last was spoken mockingly.

"How so?"

"Can you not guess?"

Tol'chuk frowned, but the answer came from behind him. Magnam, ever his shadow, spoke. "Each of you is only half an og're."

Startled, Tol'chuk suddenly recognized the truth of Magnam's words: the straight spine and other subtle differences. "You be half si'luran, like myself?"

"No," Magnam said, stepping closer. "He's half *d'warf*."

Tol'chuk's eyes widened.

"On my father's side," the stone figure answered coldly. "A d'warf trader. He abused an og're female of the Toktala clan and left her with her belly swelling. Like you, I was born a half-breed among clans where bloodlines were everything. It was only my elemental skills that won me honor and respect: my ability to read, bolster, and refine another's talents."

"That gift came from the Land," Magnam reminded. "A Land you seek to destroy."

Ly'chuk's eyes flared crimson. "The Land gives no *gifts*," he said fiercely. "Everything comes with a price that must be paid."

Tol'chuk heard the ancient pain in the other's voice. "Why do you say that?"

Ly'chuk glanced back to the others. During this short truce, no one moved, each fixed on this tale. Ly'chuk faced Tol'chuk again. "Like you, I was barren of seed—another curse of my father's lechery."

Tol'chuk frowned. Ly'chuk could not have been barren, or Tol'chuk couldn't have been born from his lineage. His confused expression was read by his dark ancestor.

"Yes, I found a way to thwart this curse. I found a healer with elemental skills and used my talents to enhance hers. She was able to heal my loins, to enliven my seed. But even this came at a high cost. The healer's abilities were too crude. She burned up with the effort, destroying the Land's gift in her, enfeebling her mind."

"So you raped her talent," Tol'chuk said. "In order that you might sire children."

"Like father, like son," Magnam said under his breath.

The Dark Lord swung toward the d'warf, clenching a fist. Magnam was lifted from the floor by invisible bonds, strangling by the throat. "I was nothing like my father," Ly'chuk roared. "Mine was an accident."

"Let him go!" Tol'chuk boomed, matching his ancestor's tone.

Ly'chuk glared, then flung Magnam away. The d'warf skidded back to the edge of the bone army. Fardale and Thorn went to his aid.

Once it was clear his d'warf friend lived, Tol'chuk focused back to Ly'chuk. "What happened after this accident?"

"Nothing. I lived happily and well among the Toktala clan for a full winter. I fathered a child. But the morning of his birth, I went to the Spirit Gate, to pray for my child, to prepare myself for the oaths to the Land. But . . ." He fell silent, fist tightening. The stained floor under his feet grew darker, fissures spreading out from his heels and toes. His next words were as black as the stone that made up his figure. *"But the Land knew."*

He went silent for a breath. "The Land is a cruel master—far more cruel than I have ever been." A black arm pointed at Nee'lahn and Meric. "You know. You have both felt its wrath. The Blight upon your trees and people was the Land's doing, was it not?"

Meric answered. "The nyphai had been trying to change the natural order, to spread their trees over all the lands. The Land acted in its own defense."

"By destroying all, and mercilessly twisting the nyphai. Is that a reasonable response? How many others have suffered at the hands of the Grim wraiths since then?" His voice rose heatedly. "It is a curse that continued to punish the innocent, to torment the afflicted."

Ly'chuk stared hard at Nee'lahn. Small flames lipped from his dark sockets. She lowered her face.

"She knows I speak the truth." He waved an arm dismissively. "The Land doles its magick, but it is not a gift. It is tyranny. Dare step from the boundaries the Land has set, and you will be beaten down, punished not once, but for all time. As long as the Land exists, we are not allowed to rule our own lives." His breath heaved in and out. "I mean to end this tyranny, to free the world by crushing the Spirit Stone and destroying its elemental heart."

Gasps arose, but Tol'chuk remained silent.

Ly'chuk continued, deaf to their responses, lost in his anger. "You may judge my acts evil, but they are a small price for a larger victory. Many have died, so all could have a future. After this night, the rest of history will be unfettered. The peoples of the world will be free of the magickal yoke of the Land."

Tol'chuk finally spoke. "But what did the Land do to you?"

Ly'chuk panted at his edge of madness. "What did the Land do to me? Like the Grim, the Land took my talent and twisted it foully. It took my skill at honing an elemental's gift and maligned it. I knew from that moment on that all I touched would twist to darkness. What the Land did to me, I was doomed to do unto others. I would corrupt all the elementals I touched."

"Forging ill'guard of them," Tol'chuk said.

A scowl formed. Ly'chuk must have heard the accusation in his voice. "And why not? I was the first of the ill'guard, forged by the Land itself. All the evil that flowed from me started there first."

Tol'chuk began to fathom the depths of derangement here. Centuries of rage, humiliation, torment, and perhaps underneath it, even guilt. But mostly his ancestor dismissed his own culpability. Ly'chuk couched his revenge and outrage in an armor of noble cause.

"I fought the Land that day. I tried to attack the elemental heart, to turn its black magick back on itself. But I was too weak. I was battered and torn, but I made it through the Spirit Gate. And there the Land faced its own mistake." A bitter laugh followed. "I bled into the Gate. Ill'guard blood! My blood tainted all it touched."

Tol'chuk understood. He had seen the same happen to the Heart of his people when Vira'ni's blood had bathed the stone.

"Around my broken body, the blood of the Land twisted and hardened into ebon'stone, encasing me, entombing me. I became a black tumor inside the body of the Land. Before my corruption could spread further, the Land was forced to expel me, somewhere far from the Spirit Gate."

"Gul'gotha."

A nod. "Back to my father's roots, the d'warf homeland. Once there, I reached from my tomb and found d'warf miners with elemental abilities. I drew them to me, bound them to me, and had them dig me free. Then I set about to build my army, to enslave my father's people. I forged a legion of ill'guard, to turn the Land's gift against itself. I constructed vessels of intense power, four statues built from the very stone of my tomb. Manticore, Wyvern, Basilisk, and Griffin. And then as I was about to return to Alasea, a boon came from afar, a spirit of immense energy."

"Chi," Tol'chuk muttered.

"The spirit became curious of Gul'gotha. It drew too near and was captured within the Gates, enslaved as surely as any ill'guard. This Weir of power opened all manner of dread magicks. There were no bounds. My first act upon receiving this boon was to reach into the Land and rip a hole in its crust, sculpting Blackhall from the molten rock of its bowels. It was my foothold back to these lands. From there, I searched for a means to again reach the Land's heart, to crush the Spirit Stone. But the Land had grown wary in its age. It knew how to use its elemental puppets to thwart me. So over the centuries I learned my enemies' weaknesses, those spots where the elemental flows from the Spirit Stone rose close to the surface. I sought to twist the Land as it had twisted me."

"And now this last assault," Tol'chuk said.

"You did me a favor destroying the other Weirgates. It concentrated Chi into one statue, an unstable situation, and with *instability*, there is *possibility*. I saw the potential to use this full moon to bring me here from Blackhall. To use the energy of the Void to link one to the other, to overlap them." He pointed to Elena. "The wit'ch used this same trick to portal to Moon Lake in the Western Reaches."

Tol'chuk nodded with sudden understanding. *No wonder* ... "And once you reached here ... ?" he asked aloud.

"I joined with Chi in the last Weirgate, fusing our two forms."

"And now you mean to use both your powers to attack the Spirit Stone through the elemental lake here."

"At long last, I will have my victory."

Tol'chuk faced the tormented creature before him. He knew in that moment that though they shared the same face, their hearts were as different as night and day. He spoke calmly. "I won't allow it."

Icy laughter flowed. "You have no choice. None can harm me." A dark menace entered his voice. "And more importantly, none *dare* harm me. There are worse fates than a world ruled by a Dark Lord."

Tol'chuk stepped back and lifted an arm, signaling the pair of figures who had crept into the room behind the Dark Lord's shoulder. Tol'chuk's distraction had allowed the pair to prepare unobserved.

"I will be victorious," Ly'chuk sneered.

A *twang* of bowstring punctuated his declaration. Then from the center of his chest an arrow bloomed, skewering from behind, piercing fully through the stone figure.

Both Tol'chuk and Ly'chuk stared down at the arrowhead. It was encrusted with heartstone.

Ly'chuk lifted his fiery gaze to Tol'chuk. "No!"

From around the edges of the hole, ebon'stone changed to heartstone. Like the Heart of the og'res before, a touch of heartstone purified ebon'stone.

"Now!" Kast yelled from the other side of the room. A line of d'warves raced into the chamber.

The Dark Lord yanked forth the arrow. Heartstone changed back to ebon'stone. "I won't be defeated that easily. I am living ebon'stone, not a mere chunk of rock."

Tol'chuk scuttled backward.

"I will herald the new age of Alasea," Ly'chuk boomed, "with all your blood!"

Suddenly the war that had paused began anew. Bone armies re-formed, black tendrils writhed, and skal'tum screamed riotously.

A towering creature of bone swiped at Tol'chuk, slicing a ribbon of pain across his chest. He swung his hammer, shattering through the midsection of the creature, toppling it over. From the ruins, a new creature arose, smaller but quicker, with claws made of sharpened shards. He beat again and again, while other monsters closed in.

He glanced around at the chaos. The d'warf army joined the fray, attacking the room with weapons that glinted with heartstone.

Ly'chuk raged behind him. "You have no hope!"

KAST WAVED THE LAST OF THE D'WARVES FROM THE PASSAGE. IN THE CHAMBER, the army had split into two forces. Wennar already led one group along the south wall, aiming to aid Elena's party. Kast now followed the tail of the other group with Sy-wen, Tyrus, Fletch, and Hurl.

His column looped around the other side of the room. Archers from both sides peppered arrows at the stone figure in the room's center. Kast knew this must be the Black Beast of Gul'gotha. The monster knocked many bolts aside with slaps of his hand and blasts of searing balefire, but many others struck home, like the first arrow from Fletch. Even now, despite the additional weight of the heartstone-encrusted tips, the pirate's aim remained flawless.

And while their strikes had failed to bring down the demon, they kept him off balance for the moment, kept him from turning his magick and attention against them. Kast was glad he had taken the time to have their forces anoint their blades, arrowheads, and axes in the dripping heartstone found in the cubbies, layering a sheen of crystal upon their weapons.

Sy-wen noted the same. "How did you know?"

Kast shook his head. "I simply knew." The Dark Lord had protected that passage with the dragon; he must have had reason to fear the treasure it hid. But Kast knew he wasn't being entirely truthful. As he had stared at the dripping cubbies, he had sensed a familiar tingle ... of Ragnar'k. Whether it was some knowledge shared while merged with his demonic twin, or some last prophetic sending from the dreaming dragon, Kast had felt a need to coat the weapons.

As he ran, he wished the dragon's gifts were strong enough to tell him what to do now. Kast studied his adversary. He could only imagine the power at hand. Perhaps the Dark Lord wasn't accustomed yet to his new status as both blackguard and Weirgate. If so, they dared not give him a chance to gain his footing.

Kast's mind still quailed at the amount of magick it must have taken to fuse Blackhall with this cavern here in Winter's Eyrie. Was this one of the reasons they weren't all burned to bone by now?

Or was there another reason?

Under the monster, the silver floor was stained black, and the darkness was spreading. Kast gaped at the corruption. Were their efforts even a concern to this monster? Or merely a nuisance, like flies on a horse?

But then again, even flies could sting.

Kast gripped his sword tighter. He remembered all that had been done to him and those he loved, all the good lives spent to bring them to this moment. He would not give in to despair, not even when he gasped his last breath.

Across the cavern, the Black Beast howled. "Do you feel it? The Land succumbs!"

WITH THE SOUNDS OF BONES BREAKING AROUND HIM, MERIC SHOVED BOTH
hands overhead, driving a blast of wind into a diving skal'tum. The beast
tried to bank away, but Meric was quicker. The creature was struck in the
chest and driven clear to the ceiling.

At his shoulder, Nee'lahn hummed, desperately but firmly. She waved
an arm, and a nest of roots tangled forth from the high stone and snagged
the demon.

"Another," she warned, pointing left.

Reaching out, Meric drew wind from the blustery night, still wet from
the storms, and swept it toward their new foe. The skal'tum bobbled—then
the winds suddenly died, extinguished like a snuffed candle.

Nee'lahn gasped. "The woodsong ... it's gone!" From the walls and
ceilings, roots suddenly drooped. Skal'tum dropped from their wooden
cages, enraged.

Dark laughter flowed to them. "The Land is almost mine!"

Meric realized what had happened. "He's cut us off from the flow of
elemental magick!" A despair settled to his heart, he sensed their doom.
He had come to these forests to return a king to his people. And now all
was lost: both royal families sundered, his people scattered to the winds or
dying in the clouds in this last great war. And to what end?

He reached a hand out. Fingers entwined into his own. He found comfort there. Come what may, he would not face this night alone.

Overhead, the flock of skal'tum gathered, ready to drop upon their
group.

Around them, the others were faring no better.

JOACH SPUN HIS STAFF, CASTING FORTH FONTS OF BALEFIRE, TURNING BONE TO
ash. But his dark magick was a beacon to the twining snakes of darkness.
He had cast illusions of himself to confound the grasping tendrils, but
suddenly all his dream-sculpted twins vanished, along with his elemental
magick. He had only a bit left, stored in his staff, but he held it in reserve.

With his illusions gone, he was alone, exposed.

A bone dog leaped at him, taking advantage of his startled state. It dove
for his throat, but this demonic creature was beat out by its own ally.

A thick band of darkness dropped a noose around Joach's neck and
yanked him upward, choking. The bone dog shot under his heels and
away, to meet a crushing death under the hammer of Magnam.

Gasping, Joach brought his staff up and cast a stream of balefire at the constricting rope of darkness, but the black energies only seemed to strengthen the noose. His vision tightened to a small knot. He could not breathe at all.

His body swung around in time to see an ax flying toward his face. If he'd had breath, he would have screamed. The ax cleaved just over his head, all but parting his hair, and suddenly he was falling. He struck the floor hard, and rolled away just before a bony behemoth stomped him.

Magnam shoved a sword into his free hand. "Here, plain steel will serve you better."

Joach nodded, taking the weapon. "Thank you."

Magnam grinned, swinging around in time to take a sickle of bone through the chest. The d'warf was lifted high, impaled, his blood flowing down the white bone of the blade.

Joach stared in horror as Magnam was thrown lifeless through the air. Joach lifted the sword as the same bloody creature turned toward him.

How many more would die?

MOGWEED HID IN A CLUSTER OF BOULDERS SHELTERED AGAINST ONE WALL. HE was no fighter. He crouched with a dagger in one hand and a short sword in the other. Nothing could get at him here. To enter the cramped space, he'd had to flow his flesh and squeeze through a gap too small to allow in any real threat. He watched the battle from his shelter.

Thorn raced past in her wolf form, chased by a pair of bone creatures. Mogweed had no real concern. He had watched her ploy a few times. As she leaped a certain boulder, Fardale would pop up with two short swords in hand and cleave the monster's legs off. The limbless beasts would crash to the stone and shatter. Then the trap would be set again.

But this time Fardale wasn't waiting. Thorn landed and spun around, searching for her partner. The moment's distraction was all it took. The two bone beasts struck her full broadside. Razored claws tore deep gashes. Then she was down, under them both.

Before Mogweed knew what he was doing, he was running across the floor, bounding over rubble. He bore his sword and dagger and shifted into a half-wolf form for more speed. He leaped the boulder and struck the two beasts in a tackle, driving them from Thorn's side. He rolled to his feet and hacked and slashed.

Panic and fear turned him wild. Bone shattered all around him. Soon he was just fighting empty air. Gasping, he fell back to Thorn. She lay on her side, blood pooled under her, still in wolf form. Her breathing was wet.

Mogweed glanced up, searching for help. Motion drew his eye from overhead. A skal'tum dove toward him, wings tucked, claws outstretched, mouth open in a silent snarl. Mogweed could not move, frozen in place by terror.

Then just before the monster struck, a huge dark shape leaped over Mogweed's head and struck the skal'tum, tumbling away with it. Mogweed cried out, gaining his feet, ready to flee.

The skal'tum and his adversary struck the rubble of boulders. A gnashing, snarling fight ensued. Mogweed spotted dark fur in flashes behind the beating wings. *Fardale!*

Blades in hand, Mogweed leaped toward the pair. But before he even took a second step, the skal'tum was peppered with arrows. The d'warves had finally reached them.

The skal'tum screeched and fluttered up, trying to escape, but a well-thrown ax, shining ruby, split its skull and sent it wheeling back to crash against the wall.

Mogweed ignored it and ran to his brother's side. "Fardale!" He skidded to his knees. Bloody claw marks raked his brother's shoulder. Poison sizzled from the wound.

Like himself, Fardale was in his half-wolf form. "Thorn . . . ?" His voice was harsh with a pain that had nothing to do with the deep wound.

Mogweed simply shook his head.

"I . . . I was chased away by another skal'tum. I couldn't get back in time." Fardale clutched his arm. "I saw what you did . . . what you attempted . . ."

Mogweed rocked in place, choked on tears. "Why?" he croaked out.

Fardale met his gaze, amber eyes glowing. *You are my brother.*

His silent words made no sense to him. Fardale had sacrificed himself to save him. His heart clenched too tight. *Why?* he repeated.

A wolfish sigh escaped Fardale. His sending grew fainter. *Like it or not, we are one. Whether you see it in yourself or not, we are twins.*

Mogweed shook his head. Around them, the fighting grew more fierce as the d'warves smashed into the monsters with their ruby weapons.

There is much in you that you have yet to discover.

"Fardale . . ."

Care for my son . . . your son . . .

"He is not my son." His voice cracked. What did Fardale think he could give a child?

His brother tightened his hold on his arm. *Promise me.*

"I . . . I don't . . . I can't . . ."

Fardale stared into his eyes, too weak now to speak, even to send. But in those eyes, Mogweed saw everything . . . maybe everything he could be.

With tears flowing, he nodded.

His brother's fingers slipped from his arm. He was gone.

Mogweed rolled from his side and half crawled back to Thorn, expecting her to have already passed. But as he neared her, he saw her chest move weakly.

She must have sensed his presence. A moan escaped her, full of hope.

He sidled up to her, coming into sight.

Her eyes glowed. *Fardale . . .*

Mogweed began to object, then realized in his half-wolf form that he was indeed his brother's twin.

You live. He sensed her relief across the fading bond.

He stared into her eyes.

Our son . . .

Mogweed took a deep breath. "I'll take good care of him. He'll live a long and happy life. I promise this."

She sighed, content. He leaned to her and pressed his cheek to hers, one wolf saying good-bye to another.

A scuff sounded as Tol'chuk rushed up. He stared among them, his eyes suddenly crinkling, unsure.

Mogweed stood. For most of his life, he had been the master of lies. While others had skills of magick or blade, his only talent was a well-turned tongue. For this one last time, he would tell one great lie. He met the og're's gaze. "Mogweed's dead."

Tol'chuk covered his face. "Fardale, I be so sorry." He then turned away. "But we must hurry. We are far from finished here."

He nodded and glanced back to the pair of bodies. A moment ago, he had wondered what he could give Fardale's son. He now had his answer. He could give him back his father.

ELENA HAD FAILED. CHO WOULD NOT HELP IN THE BATTLE AGAINST THE DARK Lord; she hid somewhere, mourning, leaving only Aunt Fila here to offer guidance.

Around them, the fighting raged. There seemed no end to this war, no way to win. The bone army simply re-formed. The tendrils from the sky regenerated when sliced. And the skal'tum continued to seep into the chamber from the tunnel that led to the pit.

At least they had the help of the d'warf army—but it was only more fodder for the monsters.

She stared around at her companions on this long journey. They were far fewer than when they first entered the pit.

Er'ril met her eyes. "Are you ready to attempt this?"

She nodded and stood. He reached a hand to hers, but she drew back. His eyes widened with understanding. She examined her fingers and palms. They were no longer pale, but whorled in dark crimson. It wasn't her Rose. Cho still refused to let her renew, even in the moonlight.

It was simply blood—but the Dark Lord didn't know that. She remembered something Mycelle had once told her. *Sometimes the strongest magick is the strength in one's heart.* She took courage from these words and glanced through the fighting to the ebon'stone figure. "Let's go."

An escort of d'warf ax soldiers forged a path toward the center of the room. Underneath, the floor went from silver to black as they neared their quarry. Beside her marched Tol'chuk, with Aunt Fila trailing a few paces behind, amid wisps of moonlight.

"That's as close as we dare," Er'ril said.

She nodded. The escort of guards parted before her.

She faced Ly'chuk from ten steps away. The stone figure looked scarcely worn; his ebon'stone carapace healed as fast as it was damaged. And now he had developed a new defense: Any weapon, heartstone or otherwise, melted to slag before it could touch his ebon'stone surface. He was impossible to harm. He no longer even paid attention to the war around him.

His focus instead was downward. Where he stood, the floor was darker than black, a color that was the void of light. It was as if he floated in empty air. Elena suspected that once the corruption here was complete, the darkness would open a portal to the heart of the world.

That must not happen.

She and Tol'chuk stepped out across the dark floor. Around them, d'warf armies held ready as skirmishes raged around the cavern.

Ly'chuk frowned at the pair. "A parley, is it? Seeking a truce?"

Elena held up both hands, revealing her ruby fingers and palms. She spoke boldly. "I offer you one last chance to forsake this purpose!"

The black frown deepened, then relaxed as laughter flowed.

"You should listen to her," Tol'chuk intoned.

He began to turn away, a whale ignoring a minnow.

"I will show you what I can do!" Elena said.

He glanced back, one black eyebrow rising.

She waved her hands before her and hummed under her breath. Aunt Fila floated through her and up her arms to hover over her fingertips. She danced atop there and wailed a death cry.

With the figure's attention focused on her aunt, Harlequin flew through the air, tossed from behind her by two of Tyrus' pirates. The small man somersaulted through the apparition with a tinkle of bells. Two daggers with ruby blades flew from his fingers and impaled themselves into the stone figure's startled, fiery eyes.

Ly'chuk screamed, holding his head.

From behind, Wennar flung an ax with both arms. It flew end over end and struck the figure clean in the back. Distracted by the frontal assault, Ly'chuk's attention had wavered enough for the thick blade to penetrate his guard.

As the ax fell away, Sy-wen was already there, running fleet-footed past the back of the stone figure. Something tiny flew from her fingertips. It spun through the air and shot into the cleaved crack before the ebon'stone could heal. A *stunner*, she had called it. The small starfishlike crustacean bore a painful stinger with the strength to stun a giant rockshark.

Ly'chuk trembled on his legs, then let out a ghastly scream, falling to his knees.

"Now!" Er'ril yelled.

Archers from all around the chamber let fly a barrage of arrows, ruby streaks through the air. The impacts sounded like the strike of crystal chimes. Feathers festooned the figure: head, limbs, torso.

Before Ly'chuk could rally against so many different assaults, his entire form turned to bright heartstone.

Tol'chuk had already leaped from Elena's side with the first *twang* of bowstring. He rushed now at the figure with his hammer raised high. Ebon'stone might resist ordinary weapons, but heartstone was like any gem, easily cut with ordinary hammer and chisel.

Tol'chuk's slammed his sledge toward the heartstone figure.

Elena sensed movement overhead. Aunt Fila swirled down, eyes bright with stars and empty spaces. *"No!"* Cho wailed.

The hammer struck home with a shattering crystalline note.

The noise became a physical wave, exploding outward, taking all light and sound with it. Elena felt a tug; then a strangely familiar burning sensation spread all over her body.

She blinked; then her vision returned. She stood alone on the floor of the chamber. Everyone and everything was shoved back to the walls, even ceilings. She turned to see d'warves, men, monsters, bones, all pinned to the stone, impossibly held in place. What was holding them?

A tingling passed over her. She stared down at herself. She was naked. Her body, her limbs ... all glowed ruby red, whorling in darker tides of crimson. Cho had fused with her again, as when she floated inside the Weir.

Elena's eyes widened with horror. She felt the familiar pressure on her ears. She *was* in the Weir again, inside a well of Chi's spiritual energy. She didn't know whether to be glad or worried.

She stared toward where the Dark Lord had once stood.

Amid a scatter of ruby shards lay a pale, naked figure, more skeleton than anything. Ly'chuk—or what was left of him. Then a slow horror filled her. She spun in a circle. The silver floor—the entire confluence—had gone black.

As she gasped, the pressure suddenly popped in her ears. Cries reached her from all around as folk tumbled to the floor. Bones rained down. She crouched, half hiding her nakedness, still ruby from head to toe.

Folk picked themselves up, bewildered, searching out weapons. But they weren't needed.

The bone army, smashed against the walls as Chi burst from his broken vessel, remained just scattered skulls and broken shards. The magick was gone, as was the dark whorl across the roof. Skal'tum took wing, flying toward the tunnel openings.

Er'ril appeared at her side. He held a cloak, but he didn't seem to know if it was safe to approach her. She ran a hand through her hair, relieved that she still had hair. It was burned shorter, but still present.

Suddenly a cool sensation swept over her, chilling her and raising gooseflesh. Mists wafted from her body and formed the azure figure of Cho again. Elena stared back down at herself as Er'ril rushed forward. Her skin was pale again, even her hands. She pulled into the cloak.

"The floor's gone black," Joach said, his face full of concern, his eyes on the pale creature in the room's center. "Were we too late?"

Cho turned back to them. *"It is Chi."*

"He's free, isn't he?" Elena asked.

Cho nodded, but her normally stoic expression was wide with fear. *"He's gone to kill your world."*

29

As the others began to gather, Er'ril took Elena in his arms. "What do you mean Chi has gone to kill the world?" he asked the ghostly figure of Cho.

Elena reached a hand to him. He grasped her fingers, snowy white. It was strange to see her without the Rose. She seemed fragile, like porcelain.

Cho scanned the room. Her gaze focused on the pale and skeletal figure half curled on the black floor. One hand scrabbled weakly, all bone and withered flesh. *"Chi has gone to finish this one's dark will."*

Er'ril drew out his sword. "So the Dark Lord still controls him." He stepped from Elena's side, intent to end this now.

"No," Cho warned. *"He is free of this creature's bondage, and is now ruled by madness. He goes blindly, lashing out like a wild beast."* Cho flew up from the floor. *"I must go to him, draw him back."*

Elena stepped after her. "Can you stop him?"

Cho stared back at her for a moment. Then her words repeated softly: *"I must go to him."* With a flume of moonlight, the spirit flew high, then shot like a silver arrow down toward the floor and through its dark surface, vanishing away.

Er'ril returned to Elena's side. "Do you still have the Blood Diary?" she asked.

He patted his own cloak as answer. She nodded and leaned against him.

By now, Joach and others joined them. All had heard the spirit's words. Their faces were grim. Nearby, Tol'chuk crossed toward the feeble figure of his ancestor. He still bore his hammer.

Tyrus spoke, clutching a silver coin in his palm. "I was able to link with

Xin. The black monster guarding Blackhall died. The stronghold has fallen." He turned to Sy-wen, who stood with Kast, and Nee'lahn with Meric. "Hunt and the children made it back to the *Dragonsheart*. They're all fine."

Both Sy-wen and Nee'lahn wore matching expressions of relief.

Tyrus turned back to Er'ril. "And I've sent a scouting party toward the pit to make sure the fighting has ended here, too."

Nodding, Er'ril surveyed the dark chamber. The only light came from the spear of moonlight shining down from the hole in the cavern roof, and even this was fading as the full face of the moon set toward the horizon. Torches began to flare around the room. The wounded and dying were tended. Across the way, he spotted Fardale, in wolf form, mourning the death of Thorn and his brother.

"Did we win?" Joach asked quietly, leaning on his staff.

No one had an answer.

Wennar marched up, his armor stained and bloody. He took off his helmet and ran a hand over his bald pate. "The tunnel to Blackhall is gone." He waved a hand to the far wall. Some of the other passage mouths remained, but the one through which the d'warf army had entered was now solid granite.

"The dark magick linking the caverns has ended," Er'ril mumbled. "Whether due to the setting moon or the breaking of the Dark Lord, it's over."

Meric stood with Nee'lahn. "Our magick, too. At least on this black lake, our powers are severed."

Er'ril frowned. "Maybe we should—"

The ground trembled, silencing his words. The tremor shook rock dust from the roof.

"Maybe we should *leave*," Harlequin suggested, his eyes searching the stone overhead.

The shaking calmed, but not the expressions of worry.

Er'ril nodded. "I think Harlequin is right."

The small man lifted one eyebrow. "Now that's something you don't hear every day, the plainsman actually agreeing with me. Maybe it *is* the end of the world."

Er'ril sighed, realizing he owed the master spy many apologies. But such matters could wait until later. "For now, we should help the wounded and be ready to depart as soon as possible."

Nods answered him. Kast, Wennar, and Tyrus went to see to the injured and gather up their remaining forces.

Er'ril turned to Elena. "I can't go," she said softly, her gaze intent on the black floor. "Not until Cho returns."

Another slight tremble shivered through the cavern. He pulled her into his arms and felt the same shiver in her.

"Cho will rein her brother in," he assured her.

"And if she doesn't?" Elena whispered.

Er'ril sighed. "We will face whatever comes together."

He thought his words would comfort her, but instead, she seemed to withdraw. His heart ached. "Elena, what's wrong?" he whispered.

She simply stared across the dark floor, silent and alone.

As the ground trembled, Tol'chuk stood over the gaunt, pale creature, unsure why he came. It surely deserved no pity, no mercy, no final kindness. It was hard to tell that what lay here was even once an og're. Its spine was twisted, its legs no more than feeble twigs. The very bones of its skull shone through the translucent skin.

Still, he dropped to his knees and set aside his hammer. Eyes, large in the starved face, followed him as he sank to the floor.

They stared at one another, the beginning and end of a bloodline.

Again Tol'chuk wondered why he was here. He was satisfied that though they shared the same blood, his heart was his own. He stared. The rage had dimmed in the other's eyes. Ly'chuk was scant heartbeats from death. Even the strongest corruption could find nothing to grasp in such tenuous life.

A clawed hand moved in his direction, but it was too weak to reach him.

Though there was no pleading in the other's eyes, Tol'chuk reached and took the hand into his own. Again . . . *why*? A single word. What did he need here?

But fingers tightened on his own, one flesh touching another, recognizing life in its last moment.

Tol'chuk shifted closer. He had not been able to comfort his own father in death, slain in one of the senseless og're wars. He remembered back to his own childhood, seeing his father's prone body dragged past, speared through the chest. But they had been no closer in life than in death. His father, embittered by the loss of his mate and burdened with a half-breed son, had left Tol'chuk long before he was dragged bloody past their hearth.

Tol'chuk sighed. He now understood what drew him here. He needed this final act of forgiveness, not to ease Ly'chuk's passing, but to free his own heart.

Fingers tightened again on his own. The weak figure must have sensed the pain in his heart. Words whispered from thin lips. Tol'chuk had not known Ly'chuk had the strength to speak.

"I . . . I never saw my son," he gasped weakly.

Tol'chuk recalled the og're's earlier tale. Ly'chuk had fathered a son, but it was on the day of his son's birth that he had been punished by the Land.

Fingers clasped to his with all the last strength in the feeble body. "See yours . . ."

Between their fingers, a jolt passed into Tol'chuk, shooting up his arm and into the core of his being. It was a burn both icy and searing. It settled low into his belly, then dissolved into a warmth that spread through his loins.

Tol'chuk felt the healing deep in his being.

He stared down at Ly'chuk, unmoving now, eyes gone glassy in death. He held the hand a moment longer, knowing with certainty what had been done. A final gift. Ly'chuk had passed whatever magick had healed his own loins into Tol'chuk.

See yours . . .

Tol'chuk understood the act, sensed for a flickering moment the heart behind it. This last gift was not Ly'chuk's attempt to extend his bloodline, but to give Tol'chuk a chance to start a new one, a bloodline started from an act of kindness and forgiveness. He lowered the thin hand to the other's chest.

"Be at peace."

ELENA STARED ACROSS THE BLACK FLOOR. WITH THE TREMBLING OF THE ground, she knew all was not over. From deep in her heart, the warning of Sisa'kofa rose to haunt her again. She remembered the shadow of the wit'ch floating before the Spirit Stone: *You will face a choice, a cusp of prophecy. Your choosing will either damn or save all.*

"What's wrong?" Er'ril asked again.

She shook her head, sworn to secrecy. This fate was hers alone.

"Tell me, please."

She turned to him, drawn by the pain in his voice. In the storm of those gray eyes, she saw his love, his willingness to sacrifice all to hold her safe. Could she do any less?

"Please . . ." His voice was a strangled whisper. He stepped closer to her. A hand rose to cup her cheek.

She closed her eyes, but it did no good. His touch burned. She could hear him breathing, heavy with his own fear. Her heart ached. Somewhere deep inside her something broke. What was the need for secrets any longer? She opened her eyes and let her fear shine more fully. "Er'ril—"

A violent quake cut off her words. A section of roof cracked. They both leaped back as a slab of rock crashed to the floor. Men and d'warves scattered. No one was injured.

"What's happening?" Joach asked, his staff ready.

This time the ground did not quiet. It continued to shake in fits and jolts. New cracks skittered over the arch of the roof and along the floors.

"We have to leave," Er'ril said, grabbing Elena's arm. "Now!"

Kast came running up as a horn sounded. He had to yell to be heard above the rumblings. "Wennar sounds the rally! We're ready to go!"

Er'ril waved him back. "Then go! Get everyone out of here! We'll follow!" As Kast swung off, Er'ril turned back to Elena. He clearly read her indecision. His grip tightened on her arm. "Cho can reach us on the surface as easily as here."

Joach stood nearby, shifting from foot to foot. "He's right, El."

She glanced between the two of them, then nodded.

But before they could take a single step, the ground bucked under them, throwing them to their hands and knees. Rocks crashed all around. Were they too late?

Then a silvery swirl shook up from the ground, as if expelled by the shaking. Elena sat back on her heels, gazing up as the figure coalesced into a familiar shape. "Cho?"

"No . . . it's Fila." The figure crouched. Her face was lined with concern, her eyes shadowed with fear. Under them, the ground calmed, but a deep rumbling persisted, thunder in the depths of the world. "Cho still attempts to sway her brother."

"What's happening?" Er'ril asked.

Aunt Fila shook her head. "It's certain doom. Chi recognizes his sister, but he raves. I touched his mind—it is chaos and madness."

"Why?" Joach asked. "What's happened to him?"

Moonstone lips grew hard. "These spirits are not like us. They were meant to roam the Void between stars. But Chi has spent over five centuries trapped in those cursed gates, corrupted. What is left is less than animal, a deep rage that intends to burn through all."

"What can be done to stop him?" Elena asked, eyes wide.

Aunt Fila's eyes settled on her own. "There is one way."

Elena felt an icy knot form in her chest.

"What is it?" Er'ril asked.

"Cho can merge with Chi."

Joach leaned closer. "Will she be able to control him?"

The two men looked on hopefully, but Aunt Fila's gaze never left Elena. She answered her brother's question. "Cho intends to destroy her brother ... and herself." Elena remembered those times when her raw magick touched pure Chyric energy. The result was instantaneous and explosive.

Aunt Fila elaborated. "Their two energies are opposite in all ways. They cannot exist in the same space. To merge will create a magickal blast that will consume them both."

"There must be another way," Elena mumbled.

Her aunt sighed, and her voice dropped lower. "Chi is in pain beyond imagining, and his agony is now Cho's. She knows there is no way to ease or undo what's been done. She's tried. Chi is not just twisted ... he's broken in all ways. He will ravage our world, turn our garden into a desert, then move on to others. Cho knows there is only one path to peace for her brother."

"Then let her do it," Er'ril said, "before it's too late."

His urgency was confirmed by another violent shake and shattering rockfalls.

Kast called from across the room. "Er'ril!" The Bloodrider stood near the tunnel to the pit, flanked by Tol'chuk and Wennar. Almost all had cleared out. D'warves fled at a determined run, many with shields slung between them, carrying the wounded.

"Go!" Er'ril ordered. "Get to the pit!"

Kast clearly hesitated, but then nodded and waved Wennar ahead of him.

During this exchange, Aunt Fila's eyes never left hers. "I would speak a moment with Elena."

Er'ril bunched his shoulders, ready to refuse, but Elena touched his arm. "Go. The longer we argue, the shorter our time."

Er'ril stared at her hard, his jawline iron. But she held steadfast. *Go,* her heart cried, *go before I no longer have the strength.*

He finally snapped away, stalking back several steps, cloak swirling. Joach went with him.

Swallowing hard, she turned back to her aunt. "Tell me," Elena whispered, ready for the worst—but what her aunt said next shocked her to the marrow.

"The Spirit Stone. It's already been destroyed."

Elena paled. "What?"

"It happened so fast," Fila said, her eyes suddenly lost. "The brightness blew out of the crystal heart of the world, snuffed like a candle in a windstorm."

"So the world is doomed."

"Not doomed. The living heart pumped elemental energy throughout the lands. Like a body whose heart has ceased to beat, the blood still remains. Elemental energies will continue for now, but their potency will fade over the next several decades, perhaps as long as centuries, until eventually all magick will be gone."

Elena found it hard to breathe. "So the Dark Lord has won after all?"

"Don't think that way. If he had vanquished the Land, he would have created the world in his twisted image. He would have done to the lands what he did to Chi." The apparition shuddered. "I would rather the world were destroyed instead."

Elena fought back her despair. "Then what can we do? What will happen after Cho and Chi merge?"

Again Aunt Fila sighed. "The magickal blast will be cataclysmic. It will be a force a thousandfold stronger than either spirit alone. Something must be done with that magick."

"What?" Her voice was a squeak.

"Remember you are blood-tied to Cho. As the magick explodes outward, the energy will flow through the bridge back to you, Elena. For a brief moment, you will have control over this vast well of power."

Elena sat frozen. "No . . ."

"Yes. And you will face two choices."

Unbidden, her head began shaking. It was Sisa'kofa's prophecy fulfilled.

Aunt Fila continued to speak. "The energy will need a vessel. One choice is to keep the magick for yourself."

Elena recalled her hard struggle with her own wild magick, to balance the wit'ch inside her. *To have the wit'ch a thousandfold stronger* . . . "I couldn't . . . I can't . . ."

Aunt Fila nodded. "It is a hard choice. It would burn away your body. You would become like Chi or Cho, living spiritual energy."

Elena could not fathom such an existence.

"The other choice lies under your own feet. The empty Spirit Stone."

Hope flared. "I could revive the Land with this magick?"

"Yes, but it is too small a cup. The amount of energy far surpasses what the Spirit Stone once held. It would be like a man being hit by lightning. Such a jolt would reshape the world. Our world would end. A new one would begin, as vital as this one, but vastly changed."

"So I either become a god, or I start our world anew." She stared over to Er'ril. He watched from a distance, his gaze hard upon her. No matter what her choice, down either path, she would lose this man who held her heart so tenderly. How could she choose?

And then there was the warning from Sisa'kofa to consider, a prophecy handed down through the centuries: *I have come to tell you that your choice—either way—will doom all.*

Aunt Fila spoke. "But there may be another path, a way to avoid all of this."

Elena turned from Er'ril back to the moonstone spirit. Her eyes pleaded for some way to escape this fate.

"The Blood Diary," her aunt said. "It is Cho's link to you, to this world. Without it, she exists only in the Void."

"I don't understand."

"The book is necessary to hold Cho here so she can merge with Chi, but once this is done, you can sever the link. By breaking the connection to this world, the energies will be released into the Void rather than through you."

"So I wouldn't have to make a choice!"

"Exactly. If you destroy the Blood Diary at the precise moment Cho and Chi fuse, then the energies will have no connection here and will dissipate into the vast emptiness beyond."

Elena's heart surged. Sisa'kofa had said there would be another choice! Here it was! Her voice sharpened. "What must I do?"

"I will help you. I will let you know when to destroy the Blood Diary, but you must not hesitate. It must be done perfectly."

She nodded. "How do I destroy the book?"

"That's the easy part. You've held that power all along." She motioned for Elena to lift her hands. Aunt Fila covered Elena's right hand between her two ghostly palms. "In this hand is wit'ch fire." Her right hand went ruby with a fresh Rose, ignited by the spiritual energy. "And in this hand is coldfire," her aunt said, quickening her left.

Once done, Aunt Fila put her moonstone palms together, opening them like a book between Elena's two hands.

"And between them lies stormfire," Elena finished. "I can destroy the book by unleashing both magicks simultaneously."

A nod of satisfaction. "You must be bloodied, readied, and standing in the center of the confluence. Then act immediately upon my signal. Can you do that?"

Elena considered the alternative. "I won't fail."

Aunt Fila smiled and sighed. "Then prepare yourself. Cho already calls Chi to her." The figure faded back into the black floor, trailing a whisper, full of love. "Your mother would've been proud." Then she was gone.

Er'ril was instantly at her side with Joach. He eyed her ruby hands. "What's happening?"

It was too much to explain in too short a time. She held out a red palm and spoke hurriedly. "I need the Blood Diary."

He caught the edge of her urgency and pulled open his cloak, tugging the tome from a pocket. The gilt rose still shone brightly, though dimmer as the moon set in the skies far above. He held the book out to her.

"What are you going to do with it?" Joach asked.

She slipped out her wit'ch dagger and sliced a deep gash in her palms. She was not taking any chances in the flows of her magick. "The book must be destroyed," she told them.

Joach opened his mouth. Elena met his eyes. He shook his head and closed his mouth, taking a step back. But his eyes remained wounded.

She knew what hopes he held between the covers of this book. After this was over, she'd find a way to help him. She took the book. "Get every-one far back," she warned. She didn't want anyone caught in the magickal backwash as she unleashed her stormfire. Across the room, only a handful of others still remained. She spotted Meric and Nee'lahn, Kast and Sy-wen, Tol'chuk and Tyrus.

Er'ril waved them all back, but he stayed a moment longer. "Elena?"

She met his gaze. "I must do this alone." She walked backward toward the room's center. The ground shook again, vibrating through her legs.

"I love you," he whispered.

"And I you." It was too hard to see him. Her heart ached when it needed to be at its strongest. He seemed to sense this and took a step away, retreating with Joach.

In his face now, she didn't see a knight or guardian or liegeman, simply a man who loved her, and feared for her. His eyes bored into her, as if willing her safe. But he knew he could not walk this next path with her.

Tears welling, she turned away. She could look no longer. She hurried to the center of the dark confluence and stepped into the column of moon-shine. She clutched the book tighter and held her breath. The ground shook again, showering rock dust from the roof.

I'm ready, she whispered.

As if hearing her, the floor under her suddenly grew darker. It started in the center and welled outward. Gasps arose.

Elena stared down between her toes. A glassy well had opened under her, a darkness veined with streaks of crimson. She had seen such a view before, through the Spirit Gate. It was the center of the world. But the crystalline heart no longer shone. Illuminated by two bright wisps that swirled around it, the stone was dark, empty of whatever had once given it life.

Words reached her from the depths of this well. *Elena . . . the time comes . . .*

She lifted the Diary, reaching to her magick, blooming it bright in her hands. She felt the mix of fire and ice.

Down below, the dance of wisps grew wilder. Spinning and whirling, the blend of light became a cloud, shining with a clarity that spoke of life beyond existence.

Elena did not breathe. Tears flowed down her cheeks.

Such beauty could not exist. It did not belong in this plane of reality.

Then a flash of brilliance destroyed all. The concussion lit the entire well. Elena's cloak and hair billowed as something passed through her from below.

Now! The single note rang through her being.

With a gasp, Elena unleashed all her magick into the book between her palms. Wit'ch fire and coldfire fused into a violence as brilliant as below. Magicks ripped into the binding, the ancient spell, the pages. But, tied to her magick, she knew her mistake.

She stared into her hands with horror. Sand fell from between her palms. *Sand . . .* It had not been the Blood Diary, but mere illusion.

Her eyes lifted as she spun around. "Joach!"

Across the way, her brother fell to his knees. Their eyes met for a fraction of a heartbeat—then the blast wave of magicks struck her, carrying her away.

ER'RIL LUNGED FORWARD WITH ELENA'S SCREAM. BUT UP FROM BELOW, A VAST shaft of light blazed forth, encompassing the entire floor. A force came with it. He was lifted off his feet and thrown against the wall, pinned in place. For this moment, the confluence again turned silver before him, blinding all in its brilliance. An immense pressure crushed outward. It threatened to tear the spirit from his body. He felt his moorings stretched and strained.

Such a force could not be contained, not even by this vast room.

He felt something give—not in himself, but in the world.

The pressure popped, and he slid down the wall, crumpling to the stone floor along with the others. All around, their faces were masks of fear.

Tol'chuk was the first to regain his feet. He gaped upward. Others followed the direction of his gaze. The roof of the cavern was gone—not crashed down, simply gone, vanished. Far above, a cloud-streaked night sky shone upon them. Stars glowed. The silver face of the full moon had fallen halfway down the sky.

Meric spoke into the stunned quiet. His words sounded muffled, as if heard through water. "Where's Elena?"

Er'ril had no answer. The floor had gone black again. Elena was gone, vanished as surely as the roof overhead. He fell upon Joach. "What did you do?" He had meant his words to be fierce, but they came out a scream of rage. *What did you do?*

JOACH FACED THE PLAINSMAN'S WRATH. HE HAD NO CHOICE—HE COULD NOT get his legs to move. He knelt where he had fallen, head hanging. He barely saw the others. His mind's eye was still full of Elena's face as she had swung toward him. Then . . . then she was gone. He had seen the blast of magick eat her away, consuming her in a heartbeat from below.

He covered his face. He had killed her. His grief was beyond tears.

"What did you do?" Er'ril grabbed him by the shoulders and hauled him to his feet. He was thrown against the wall again, not by magickal forces, but by simple fury.

Joach fumbled into his cloak and pulled out the Blood Diary. "I couldn't . . ." Words died.

Er'ril snatched the book, releasing him. Joach slumped to the ground.

"For this?" Er'ril yelled. "You sacrificed your sister for this!"

He kept his head hung. It was too heavy. His heart was a boulder in his chest, squeezing his breath, dragging him to the ground.

"Look at it!" Er'ril tore open the covers and waved it before his face. "You slew her for no reason."

Joach didn't understand. Then he saw the pages inside. They were covered with lines and lines of pigeon-scratched ink. The Void was gone.

"It's my brother's diary, returned again." This last was spoken as a sob. Er'ril sank to his knees before Joach. The fury had burned away, leaving only grief. He flung the book away. "The magick is gone. Whatever you sought is gone."

Both men knew what this meant. Elena was truly dead.

Er'ril stared at him, his eyes moist. "Why?"

Joach shook his head. There was no answer to the plainsman's question. He could not explain it himself. Something dark lurked in his heart. It had started as love, but grief and pain and power and pride had blackened it, soured it. It had led him to betray those who truly loved him, while he chased after phantoms.

He stared at Er'ril, but he no longer saw him. He saw Elena. Beyond the anguish and despair in her eyes in that last moment, he had seen something else, something that pained him even more: *understanding and love.*

Joach closed his eyes . . . and his heart.

His sister was gone.

CASCADES OF LIGHT ROLLED LIKE STORM SEAS, SURGING THROUGH THE VAST NOTHINGNESS . . . Stars spun in a dance that defied time but also defined it . . .

She rolled amid the chaos and symmetry. She was too large, too vast. None could see her.

. . . small sparks zipped in furious clouds around a tiny heart . . . Fundamental forces played within the core, blurring where energy ended and substance began . . . One iota bonded to another and another, forming a single bit of granite.

She sailed amid simplicity and complexity. She was a mote in the substrata of life. None knew she was there, not even herself.

As she stretched between the vast and the insignificant, a small corner of consciousness remained.

I am, she thought.

Power sailed through her, expanding her farther outward and more inward. Would she ever stop flowing? Was there no end to existence? As she grew smaller, form turned to energy. As she grew larger, energy took form. She named this stretch of nothingness: *Void.* She filled this Void, fueled by energy that silvered over her and scintillated through her.

From nothingness, she was born and now had returned.

All else was mere *Substance.*

As she pondered her new perspective, a voice reached her. *Elena.*

She named this other in turn, knowing it as she knew herself. *Cho.*

A swirl of moonlight answered her. *The time is at hand, Elena. I am at an end, already ended. You must choose the world or yourself.*

Identity filled in the corners of her consciousness. And with it came memory. *I must not,* she answered. *I must not choose.*

The other faded. *Then the choice will be made for you. You will continue to swell through the Void, becoming the harmony that is nothingness. You must choose.*

Elena felt a flicker of fear at these words. Ancient warnings rang in her ears. And a cautionary retort:

> *Look to your heart.*
> *Look to the friends you love.*
> *Find your own path out of the darkness—*
> *A path that none but you will see.*

These thoughts echoed through her, and her desire became reality. Elena stood in a chamber open to the sky. Others gathered near. None saw her. She was wrapped in raging gales of ghostfire, flaming over her form. She floated a span above a black floor.

She watched two men fight, then both collapse to knees.

Look to your heart.

Elena named these men, for they were in her heart. *Joach . . . and Er'ril.*

Look to the friends you love.

She turned to the others. She knew them, too. She saw them at all the levels of existence, from solid substance down to nothingness. But between those two states, there existed a silvery energy, their lifeforces. Some flared brighter, more elemental to this basic energy. Others less so. Still, one and all, they shone with such beauty.

But one of them drew her attention back.

Er'ril.

He filled her heart and sight. He had saved her once before, drawn her back with his touch and love. But the power here was too great. He could not save her this time.

Find your own path out of the darkness.

Here she must indeed go alone. She stared at all of them again, frozen in a place without time. She saw the traceries of lifeforce, winding among them and outward. She reached a filament of her own energy and touched a vibrating thread.

Then she was away and everywhere at once. That which was consciousness spread in all directions along a silvery web of energy. Before, when in her body, she had been too weak and confined. She had barely brushed the immensity of what lay beyond. But no longer. As with the Void, she expanded out from this single thread and into the web that composed life. She swelled into its myriad shapes and forms, its senses and textures. Voices filled her head. Lives ended and were born again, while new buds of lifeforce grew along the web, stretching out. She raced throughout this complexity, appreciating its simplicity. She stared down at its looming vastness and up through the faceted eyes of a single ant.

She knew what she was seeing, the antithesis to the Void, but the same. A vastness untapped. She knew her answer then. She knew her path.

She sailed from the web, from the room, from the world. But all the while, she trailed a cord of her own energy, a shining wake of ghostfire that led back to this living web.

From a place near the moon, Elena hovered. Energy continued to flow into her. There was no escaping it, only releasing it. She was a font of incalculable magick. The choice was to keep it herself and ascend into the vastness of the Void, or send it down into the hollow heart of the world, giving the energy to that which was Substance, starting a new world.

But she now saw a third choice. *A path none but you will see.*

She took all the blasted energy of two spirits into herself, tying it in the skies over the world while still maintaining a cord to the lifeweb below. She spent an indeterminate amount of time in the boundary between both Void and Substance, balancing the tidal waves of power, matching the ebbs and flows.

She acted and responded with instinct. But a part of her understood.

The energy tied here would flow its magicks equally along the web. Once the Land finished its slow death, there would be no elementals versus ordinary folk. There would be no mages, wit'ches, or Dark Lords. Rather than the few surpassing the many, each and every living thing would be granted its own magick, its own unique talent. Maybe each gift wouldn't be as strong as before, distributed and diluted throughout all life, but maybe it was as Ly'chuk had dreamed, time to end magick's rule of their world and destiny. Maybe it was time for them to forge their own path.

Elena finished her work, then glided down the silvery trail. She was spent, falling, and empty. Without the rage of magick inside her, her identity sharpened and focused back to herself. She stared up at the well of magick above her, glowing in the skies, feeding a constant flow of magick into the web of life below. She was amazed at her handiwork, but her knowledge of its creation was already fading. Her consciousness now was too small to encompass the vast enlightenment necessary to have birthed this new star.

She sank back to the world, back to the web, back to the roofless cavern. She continued to study the twinkle of the star. As long as it shone, as

long as its well of energy lasted, the magicks of the land would be balanced in all things, making each person equal to another. Though such
talents would be smaller—such as the gift of sculpting clay, or an aptitude
for baking, or an ability to understand another's heart—each life would
have its own unique and special gift, free to be recognized and nurtured
or simply ignored.

From this night onward, all would be equal.

Elena stared around the room. There would be only one exception. As
she touched the floor, a magick that she had prearranged ignited. With no
conscious awareness of how it was done, she unfolded herself from the
stream of energy, drawing her consciousness fully back to herself. She
stepped out of nothingness and crossed back into the world, no longer a
god, no longer even a wit'ch, simply a woman.

Senses of the world overwhelmed her: the heat on her skin, the smell of
brimstone and rain, the voices raised in surprise, the swirl of colors and
lights. The world was too bright. She gasped and swooned, surprised at
the intensity of sensations.

Then he was there, holding her, filling all her senses. "Er'ril . . . ," she
whispered. She stared at him: the storm-gray of his eyes, the planes of his
face, the single tear rolling down a stubbled cheek. He filled her.

"Elena!" He sobbed her name, pulling her tight.

She closed her eyes and sank into him. She sheltered in his arms, giving
herself time to settle. She was like a basin of water, shaken and rocked.
She needed a moment for her spirit to calm and reseat itself in her body.

He held her.

When she felt ready to face the new world, she pulled up and opened
her eyes. Others gathered around: Tol'chuk and Harlequin, Meric and
Nee'lahn, Kast and Sy-wen, Tyrus and Wennar, even Fardale in his wolf
form.

The world was still too bright. The first rays of sunlight shone down
into the chamber.

"The star . . . ?" Meric asked, dropping to a knee. "Was that your doing?"

Elena nodded. *So it hadn't been a dream.* She searched the skies, but
dawn had come and bathed the stars away. Still, she felt its glow beyond
the horizon. She knew it would shine again this night. A new star.

"A Wit'ch Star," Meric said. This name echoed among the others, some
with amusement, some with awe.

"What does it signify?" Nee'lahn asked.

Elena sighed, not ready to talk about that yet. She still had one last
duty. She kissed Er'ril, a brief brush that promised a lifetime more, and

stood. She crossed to the lone figure in the shadows by the wall. She stood in sunlight while he hid in darkness. He would not meet her face.

"Joach," she whispered. "It's all right." Deep in her heart, she touched a magick still locked there. The Wit'ch Star would eventually balance and level the magick of the world and make each person equal to another. But there would be one exception. She opened her heart and sailed this gift into her brother. She sensed he would need it—maybe not the way he had originally intended, but a necessity nonetheless.

She passed the gift of immortality into him. His body jerked with the touch. His face lifted, with both surprise and horror. She tied the magick to his silvery lifeforce. As the connection was made, their two energies mixed, spreading to the web beyond. For a scintillating moment, they were connected to all in the room. Each one's story, thoughts, feelings swelled into them.

Joach gasped, crawling back, covering his face.

Then it was over. The gift had been passed.

Joach lowered his hands and stared up at her from his dark corner. "Wh-what have you done?"

What had to be . . . , she thought silently, then whispered softly, "Whether curse or blessing, do with it what you want. But when the marching of years weighs too heavy, tell my story—tell my story *true*—and you will find your end."

He stared at her with horror and disbelief. A pained laugh escaped his throat. He turned from her.

Elena stared down at him. How she longed to reach to him, but she didn't. Instead she did the harder thing; she stepped back. A moment ago, she had been forced to find her own path out of darkness, a path that none but she could see. Now it was Joach's turn. None could walk his path but himself.

She turned and faced the new world. She lifted her pale hands into the sunlight. They remained pure and white, a woman's hands.

She found Er'ril staring at her. She smiled back at him.

Here was magick enough for anyone.

AND SO THE STORY ENDS . . .

From that moment, everything changed. We all left the heights of Winter's Eyrie and entered a new world, one forged within a ruby fist. But what became of us all? I can't truly say. I can only tell my own tale.

Shame drove me west, past the mountains, past the Western Reaches, out to the lands beyond the setting sun. On this road, Elena's last gift to me, her immortality, proved to be true. I didn't age. I lived countless lifetimes, but only the first ever mattered to me. And though I had enough life energy to revive Kesla, I found I didn't have the will. I didn't even try. I was not worthy of her love. She was better off wherever she now slept— whether in the sands of her desert home or in the Mother's gentle arms.

Still, over time, even this choice was taken from me. My dreaming abilities faded, like all the strong magicks of the world. It took several generations, but slowly the world became a simpler and perhaps duller place. Under the glow of the Wit'ch Star, the og'res withdrew into their mountains, the mer'ai into their seas, and the elv'in clans were scattered, never to be found again.

Perhaps someday when the Wit'ch Star dies, magick will return again, surging into peaks and valleys, but for now, it is an age of mankind in all its glory and misery. I've seen golden times and dark pass me by, and still I walked the roads, seeking answers that were always inside me.

Now as I look back at the words I wrote at the beginning of this long tale, I see the anger in my heart. Elena had not cursed me, only given me the opportunity to walk down the dark path that I had started myself. It was a road too long to survive in the span of a single life. There were entire lifetimes of guilt, bitterness, and even madness to survive.

And I did survive, coming at last to the Isles of Kell off the Western Coast. It was as close to Alasea as I could ever bring myself. I had not the heart to walk its lands again, but I could not be far from it, either. So I lived these last centuries in Kell, a drifter among the islands, nameless so none would note my lack of aging.

I stare now at my wrinkled hands that move the quill, the weak scratching at the parchment, the gray hairs that fall like late winter's snow upon the drying ink. Elena's last promise to me has been fulfilled. In that last moment of communion with her, when I touched that silver web, all the stories of the others flowed into me. I packed them away in trunks and cupboards. I did not want to face them in that dark time.

Only after all these centuries did I dare open those secret places in my heart and face those memories, those many lives. I see now why Elena set this task before me, for in these pages, in these stories, I found myself. I saw my journey, not only through the bitter lens of my own heart, but through so many other eyes. And in that moment of clarity, as I finish this story, I finally can do what had escaped me for so many centuries.

I can forgive myself.

Among these stories, I finally see that I was no better nor worse than my companions. We all had secrets, moments of ignominy and honor, cowardice and bravery—even Elena herself.

It is this knowledge that has finally broken the immortal spell. Elena had tied the magick to my heart's guilt. And once this was absolved, the spell fell away.

At last I am free to pass to the Mother, as all good beings are allowed.

Even now, I sense a presence around me. Not the Mother, but something more intimate. Though there is no swirl of spirit nor dance of moonstone, I know someone stands with me. I can almost feel her breath on my cheek.

"Elena," I whisper to the empty room.

And no words come, but I still sense some acknowledgment, a warmth in my heart. At the beginning of this tale, I told how I had described the wit'ch in countless ways: a buffoon, a prophet, a clown, a savior, a hero, and a villain. But in all the centuries, I never described her the way my heart knew her best—as my sister.

"What became of you and Er'ril?" I ask . . . because I never had before. "Did you live a long and happy life?"

Then came the barest whisper from across the ages, sad and joyful at the same time. *We lived . . . That is all one can ask.*

I cannot stand it any longer. I cry. Tears fall upon the parchment. My heart breaks and re-forms into something new, unstained and full of love.

And though not even a shadow moves, I sense a hand held out toward me. I can wait no longer. This is the end of all, my life, my tale, my place in the world and ways of Alasea.

So let me set aside my pen. I have a hand to take.

The Final Question of Scholarship
Why are the Kelvish Scrolls banned?

—Answer this thesis below in ink and seal with a palm print.
—Do not break the seal on the next pages until you have shown your answer to your assigned proctor.

Afterword

by
Jir'rob Sordun, D.F.S., M.A.,
Director of University Studies (U.D.B.)

Welcome, new scholars of the Commonwealth!

It is with great pleasure that I congratulate those who now read these pages. You have passed the final test and have been granted the crimson sash of graduation. As you are well aware, not all of your fellow students stand beside you. Many have walked the long road only to stumble at the very end. They have failed to answer the final question correctly.

Why have the texts been banned?

Of course, by the sashes you wear, you know with certainty the truth of your own answers, but it is just as important to know what others had written. There is a final lesson yet to be learned from those who were sent to the gallows of Au'tree.

For you see, the most common misconception of your failed brethren is to place too much power in the author of the Scrolls, the purported brother of Elena Morin'stal. They answered the final question by supposing that his words were indeed valid at the end, that magick would again return to the world with the dying of the Wit'ch Star. That is plainly absurd, a sure sign of a weak scholarly mind. They have clearly been duped and swayed by the insidious poison of the author.

No, of course, that is not the answer. The true danger of the text is found in Elena's last supposed act: taking the magick and seeding it as special gifts throughout all lands, all peoples. As she says, *"making each person equal."*

Here is the final and seductive treachery of the author.

Plainly, it is cruel to plant such delusions in some commoner working the fields or shoveling manure, to make him think he is equal to the oligarchs of the Commonwealth. And what of the slaves from the lands of Ee'when? Can you imagine if they thought themselves their masters' equals? Such thoughts must be ground down, crushed under the heel of scholarship. Such seeds would lead to unrest, conflict, and disorder.

That must not happen. The Commonwealth is a beacon to all the peoples of the lands. At all costs, our caste systems must be maintained, and the hierarchy of our nobility perpetuated. Nothing must upset the beauty and structure that is our Oligarchy.

Order and rule will thrive.

Thus, you new guardians of the Commonwealth, scholars of antiquity and justice, have an especially important role in the decades that are to come. Celebrate tonight; then fold and box your sashes. There is much to be done. You are born in a time darker than my own. You will bear a greater burden of responsibility for the Commonwealth's well-being.

For there is a reason your fellow students were hanged for their false and misconstrued answers. It stems from a bit of knowledge that our scholars of aetherology have discerned with their many lenses and scopes, a discovery kept hidden for two generations. I will write it here as an end to your lessons and as a final warning. Ponder it deeply and know the importance of your scholarship and diligence in the dark days to come.

Here is what you must know and keep secret.

Even as you read these words . . . the Wit'ch Star fades.